KT-408-556

READER'S DIGEST
BOOKS

With the exception of actual personages identified as such, the characters and incidents in the fictional selections in this volume are entirely the product of the authors' imaginations and have no relation to any person or event in real life.

www.readersdigest.co.uk

The Reader's Digest Association Limited 11 Westferry Circus Canary Wharf London E14 4HE

Printed in France
ISBN 0 276 42867 6

READER'S DIGEST BOOKS

Selected and condensed by Reader's Digest

THE READER'S DIGEST ASSOCIATION LIMITED, LONDON

CONTENTS

When Robert Langdon, a Harvard professor, and Sophie Neveu, a young French cryptographer, are asked to investigate a strange murder at the Louvre, the case sets them on an intriguing quest that soon has the French police on their heels. At stake is a long-buried secret, cataclysmic in its implications. This gripping novel, set in Paris, London and Scotland, broke all sales records in America and is now taking the UK by storm.

PUBLISHED BY BANTAM PRESS

This new collection of reminiscences from Yorkshireman Gervase Phinn is packed with delights. Old friends from previous books are back, together with a host of new and quite unforgettable characters who unintentionally scupper the school inspector's best-laid plans. Phinn offers an escape into an idyllic world in which laughter, a good education and plenty of fresh air are considered every child's natural birthright.

PUBLISHED BY MICHAEL JOSEPH

THE RETURN OF THE DANCING MASTER

page 281

Henning Mankell

Stefan Lindman is intrigued when he learns that Herbert Molin, a retired police officer, has been found murdered at his remote house in northern Sweden. He used to work with Molin at the Borås police department and cannot imagine who would want to kill the old man in such a merciless fashion. As he works alongside the local police, he gradually uncovers a network of evil emanating from a dark secret in Sweden's wartime history.

PUBLISHED BY HARVILL

A GATHERING LIGHT

page 425

Jennifer Donnelly

It's the summer of 1906 and sixteen-year-old Mattie Gokey is working at the Glenmore Hotel in the Adirondack Mountains. When a female guest asks her to burn some letters for her, Mattie reluctantly agrees. But the next day the young woman is found drowned in nearby Big Moose Lake and Mattie has to think hard about her promise. A powerful story, partly based on fact, about a young girl's struggle to make a life for herself.

PUBLISHED BY BLOOMSBURY

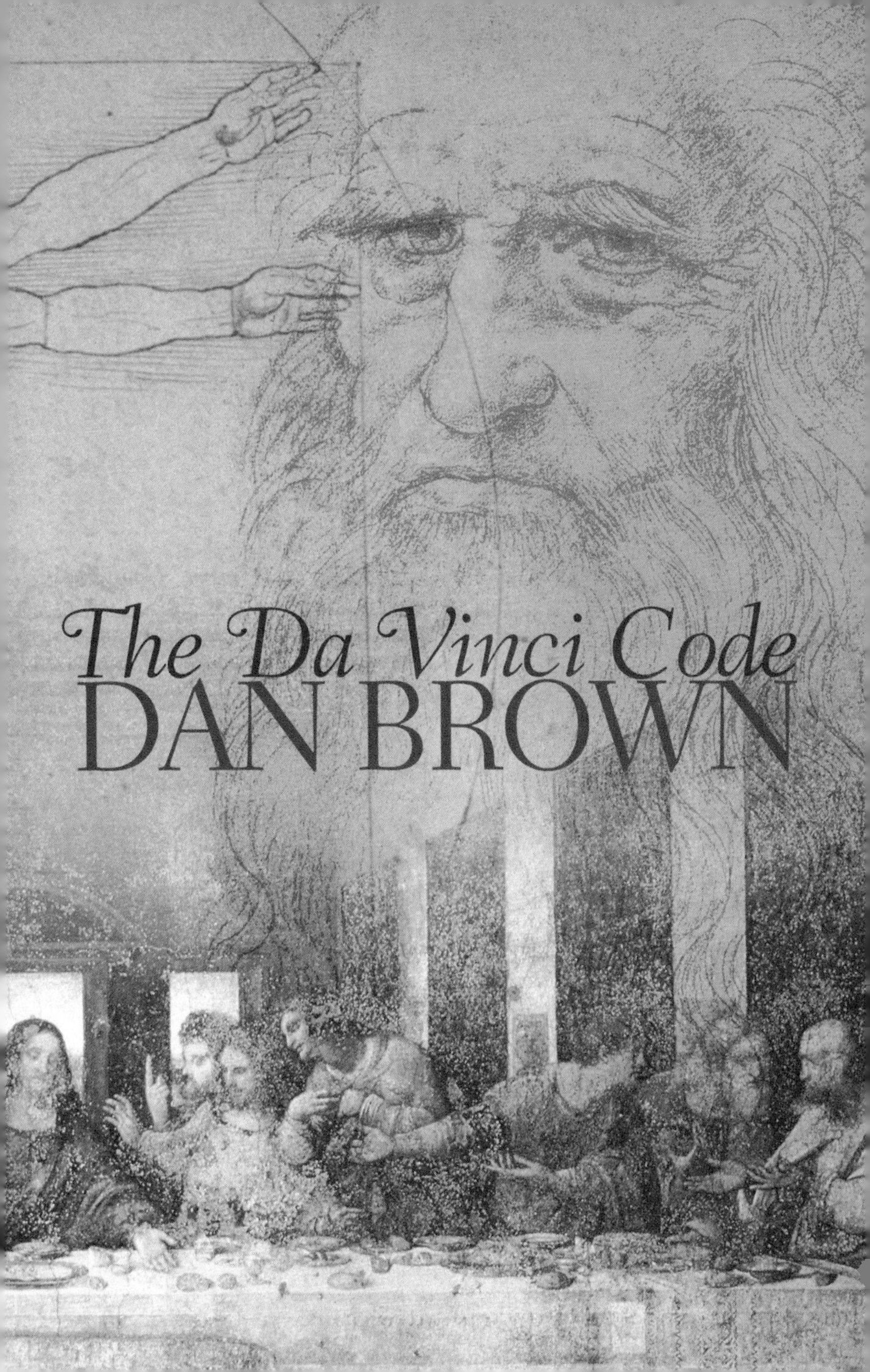
The Da Vinci Code
DAN BROWN

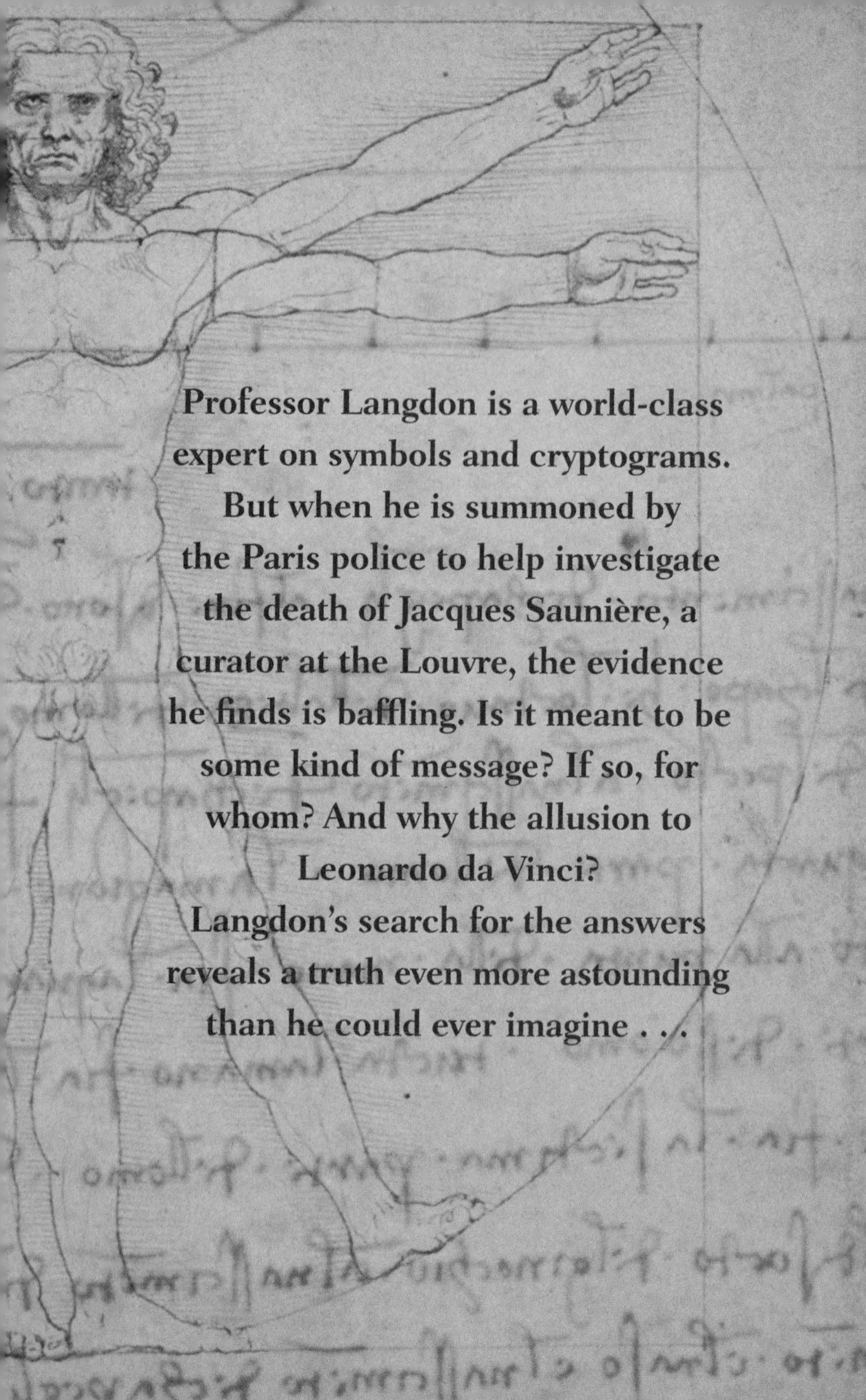

Professor Langdon is a world-class expert on symbols and cryptograms. But when he is summoned by the Paris police to help investigate the death of Jacques Saunière, a curator at the Louvre, the evidence he finds is baffling. Is it meant to be some kind of message? If so, for whom? And why the allusion to Leonardo da Vinci? Langdon's search for the answers reveals a truth even more astounding than he could ever imagine . . .

Prologue

Louvre Museum, Paris, 10.46 p.m.

Renowned curator Jacques Saunière staggered through the museum's Grand Gallery and lunged for the nearest painting he could see, a Caravaggio. Grabbing the gilded frame, the seventy-six-year-old heaved the masterpiece towards himself until it tore from the wall, then collapsed backwards beneath it.

As he had anticipated, a thundering iron gate fell nearby, barricading the entrance to the gallery. Far off, an alarm began to ring.

The curator lay a moment, gasping for breath, taking stock. I am still alive, he thought. He crawled out from under the canvas and scanned the cavernous space for somewhere to hide.

A voice spoke, chillingly close. 'Do not move.'

On his hands and knees, the curator froze, turning his head slowly.

Only fifteen feet away, beyond the sealed gate with its irons bars, his attacker was visible. He was broad and tall, with ghost-pale skin and long white hair. His irises were pink, with dark red pupils.

The albino drew a pistol from his coat and aimed it through the bars, at the curator. 'You should not have run. Now tell me where it is.'

'I told you already,' the curator stammered, kneeling defenceless on the gallery floor. 'I have no idea what you are talking about!'

'You are lying.' The man stared at him, a glint in his ghostly eyes. 'You and your brethren possess something that is not yours. Tell me where it is hidden, and you will live.'

Saunière could not breathe. He held up his hands in defence. 'Wait,' he said slowly. 'I will tell you what you need to know.' He spoke his next words carefully. The lie was one he had rehearsed many times.

When the curator had finished speaking, his assailant smiled. 'Yes. This is exactly what the others told me. All three confirmed what you have just said.'

Saunière recoiled. The curator's true identity, along with the identities of his three *sénéchaux,* was almost as sacred as the ancient secret they protected. He now realised that the *sénéchaux* had told the same lie before their own deaths. It was part of the protocol.

The attacker aimed his gun again. 'When you are gone, I will be the only one who knows the truth.'

The truth. In an instant, the curator grasped the true horror of the situation. If I die, he thought, the truth will be lost for ever. Instinctively, he tried to scramble for cover.

The gun roared and the curator felt a searing heat as the bullet lodged in his stomach. He fell forwards, struggling against the pain. Slowly, he rolled over and stared back through the bars at his attacker, his thoughts a swirling tempest of fear and regret.

'My work here is done,' his attacker said. Then he was gone.

The curator looked down and saw the bullet hole in his white linen shirt, a few inches below his breastbone. He turned his gaze again to the iron gate. He was trapped, and the doors could not be reopened for at least twenty minutes. By the time anyone got to him, he would be dead.

Staggering to his feet, he thought of the generations who had come before him . . . of the mission with which they had all been entrusted.

Suddenly, despite all the precautions, Jacques Saunière was the only guardian of one of the most powerful secrets ever kept. There existed only one person on earth to whom he could pass the torch.

He gazed up at the walls of his opulent prison and its collection of the world's most famous paintings. Wincing in pain, he summoned all of his strength for the desperate task before him.

CHAPTER 1

A telephone was ringing in the darkness. Robert Langdon awoke slowly, fumbled for the bedside lamp and turned it on. Squinting at his surroundings, he saw a plush bedroom with Louis XVI furniture, frescoed walls and a colossal four-poster bed.

His first thought was, Where the hell am I?

The bathrobe hanging on his bedpost bore the monogram: HOTEL RITZ PARIS. Slowly the fog began to lift.

Langdon picked up the receiver. 'Hello?'

'Monsieur Langdon?' a man's voice said. Dazed, Langdon looked at the bedside clock. It was 12.32 a.m. He had been asleep for only an hour, but he felt like the dead. 'This is the concierge, monsieur. I hope I have not woken you. I apologise for this intrusion, but you have a visitor. He insisted it was urgent.'

Langdon still felt fuzzy. *A visitor?* His eyes focused now on a crumpled flyer on his bedside table.

THE AMERICAN UNIVERSITY OF PARIS
PROUDLY PRESENTS AN EVENING WITH ROBERT LANGDON
PROFESSOR OF RELIGIOUS SYMBOLOGY, HARVARD UNIVERSITY

Langdon groaned. Tonight's lecture—a slide show about the pagan symbolism hidden in the stones of Chartres Cathedral—had probably ruffled conservative feathers in the audience. Most likely, some religious scholar had trailed him home to pick a fight. Langdon's books on religious paintings and cult symbology had made him a reluctant celebrity in the art world. Only last month *Boston Magazine* had dubbed the forty-year-old academic 'Harrison Ford in Harris Tweed'.

'I'm sorry,' Langdon said, 'but I'm very tired and—'

'*Mais, monsieur*,' the concierge pressed. 'I apologise, monsieur, but I could not presume the authority to stop him. My apologies. Your guest is now en route to your room.'

Langdon was wide awake now. 'You sent someone to my *room*?'

But the concierge was gone. Almost immediately, a heavy fist pounded on Langdon's door.

Langdon slid off the bed, feeling his toes sink deep into the carpet. He donned the hotel bathrobe and moved towards the door. 'Who is it?'

'Mr Langdon? I need to speak with you.' The man's English was accented—a sharp, authoritative bark. 'My name is Lieutenant Jérôme Collet. *Direction Centrale de la Police Judiciaire.*'

Langdon paused. The Judicial Police? The DCPJ was the rough equivalent of America's FBI. Leaving the security chain in place, he opened the door a few inches.

The man was tall and lean, and dressed in an official-looking blue uniform. 'May I come in?' the agent asked.

Langdon hesitated. 'What is this all about?'

'My *capitaine* requires your expertise in a private matter.'

'Now?' Langdon managed. 'It's after midnight.'

'Am I correct that you were to meet with the curator of the Louvre this evening?'

Langdon felt a surge of unease. He had been scheduled to meet Jacques Saunière for drinks after the lecture, but Saunière had never shown up. 'Yes. How did you know that?'

'We found your name in his daily planner.'

'I trust nothing is wrong?'

The agent gave a sigh and slid a Polaroid snapshot through the narrow opening in the door. 'This photo was taken less than an hour ago. Inside the Louvre.'

As Langdon stared at the bizarre image, revulsion and shock gave way to anger. 'Who would do this?'

'We hope that, with your knowledge of symbology, you might help us answer that very question.'

Langdon stared at the picture, his horror now laced with fear. 'The way his body is so oddly . . . '

'Positioned?' the agent offered.

Langdon nodded, feeling a chill as he looked up. 'I can't imagine who would do this to someone.'

The agent looked grim. 'Monsieur Saunière did that to himself.'

ONE MILE AWAY, the albino named Silas limped through the front gate of a residence on Rue La Bruyère. The spiked cilice belt that he wore around his thigh cut into his flesh, and yet his soul sang with the satisfaction of service to the Lord. Pain is good, he told himself.

His red eyes scanned the lobby as he entered the residence. Empty. He climbed the stairs quietly, entered his room and closed the door behind him.

The room was spartan—hardwood floor, a canvas mat in the corner that served as his bed. He was a visitor here this week, and for many years he had been blessed with a similar sanctuary in New York City. The Lord had provided him shelter and purpose in his life.

Tonight, at last, Silas felt he had begun to repay his debt. He picked up his cellphone and placed a call.

'Yes?' a male voice answered.

'Teacher, I have returned. All four are gone. The three *sénéchaux* . . . and the Grand Master himself.'

There was a pause. 'Then I assume you have the information?'

'All four confirmed the existence of the *clef de voûte* . . . the legendary keystone.'

He heard the Teacher's quick intake of breath over the phone.

'Excellent. I had feared that the brotherhood's reputation for secrecy might prevail. The *keystone*. Exactly as we suspected.'

'It is here in Paris, Teacher.'

'Paris? Incredible. It is almost too easy.'

Silas relayed the earlier events of the evening . . . how all four of his victims, moments before death, had desperately tried to buy back their lives by telling their secret. Each had told Silas the exact same thing—that the keystone was ingeniously hidden in one of Paris's ancient churches—the Eglise de Saint-Sulpice.

'Inside a house of the Lord,' the Teacher exclaimed. 'How they mock us!' He fell silent, as if savouring the triumph of this moment. Finally, he spoke. 'You have done a great service to God. Now you must retrieve the stone. Immediately. You understand the stakes.'

Silas knew the stakes were incalculable, and yet what the Teacher was now commanding seemed impossible. 'But the church, it is a fortress. Especially at night. How will I enter?'

With the confident tone of a man of enormous influence, the Teacher explained what was to be done.

THE CRISP APRIL AIR whipped through the open window of the Citroën ZX as it navigated the chaos of the Place Vendôme, its two-tone siren parting the traffic like a knife. In the passenger seat, Robert Langdon saw the city tear past him as he tried to clear his thoughts. But the image of Jacques Saunière's body remained locked in his mind.

'*Le capitaine* was pleased to discover you were still in Paris tonight,' the agent said. 'A fortunate coincidence.'

Langdon was feeling anything but fortunate, and coincidence was a concept he did not entirely trust. 'I assume,' he said, 'that the American University of Paris told you where I was staying?'

The driver shook his head. 'Interpol.'

Interpol, Langdon thought. Of course. He had forgotten that the seemingly innocuous request of all European hotels to see a passport at check-in was more than a quaint formality. Finding Langdon at the Ritz had probably taken all of five seconds.

As the Citroën accelerated southwards across the city, the illuminated profile of the Eiffel Tower appeared in the distance. When they reached the intersection at Rue de Rivoli, the agent gunned the sedan through a red light and sped into the Tuileries gardens.

As they entered the park, the agent turned off the blaring siren. Langdon exhaled, savouring the sudden quiet as the Citroën angled east down the park's central boulevard, towards the giant stone archway of the Arc du Carrousel. Ahead, Langdon could now see the monolithic Renaissance palace that had become the most famous art museum in the world. The Musée du Louvre.

Across a staggeringly expansive plaza, its imposing façade rose like a citadel against the Paris sky. Shaped like an enormous horseshoe, the museum was the longest building in Europe, stretching farther than three Eiffel Towers laid end to end, and housing 65,300 pieces of art.

The driver pulled out a handheld walkie-talkie and spoke in rapid-fire French. '*Monsieur Langdon est arrivé. Deux minutes*.'

An indecipherable confirmation came crackling back.

The agent stowed the device and turned to Langdon. 'You will meet the *capitaine* at the main entrance.'

The driver ignored the signs prohibiting traffic on the plaza, revved the engine and gunned the Citroën up over the kerb.

The new entrance to the Louvre, La Pyramide, had become almost as famous as the museum itself. The controversial, neomodern glass edifice, designed by Chinese-born American architect I. M. Pei and commissioned by the late François Mitterrand, still evoked scorn from traditionalists who felt it destroyed the dignity of the Renaissance courtyard. Progressive admirers, though, hailed Pei's seventy-one-foot-tall transparent pyramid as a dazzling synergy of ancient structure and modern method—a symbolic link between the old and new.

'Do you like our pyramid?' the agent asked.

Langdon frowned. The French, it seemed, loved to ask Americans this. It was a loaded question, of course. Admitting you liked the pyramid made you a tasteless American, and expressing dislike was an insult to the French. 'Mitterrand was a bold man,' he replied tactfully.

The agent pulled the car to a stop and pointed to a large door in the side of the pyramid. 'There is the entrance. My orders are to leave you here. Good luck, monsieur.'

Langdon climbed out, and the agent sped off. As he watched the departing rear lights, Langdon realised that he could easily exit the courtyard, grab a taxi and head home to bed. But something told him it was probably a lousy idea.

He strode through the mist created by the seven fountains circling the pyramid and approached the main entrance—an enormous revolving door. Do I knock, he wondered. He raised his hand to bang on the glass but then saw a figure appear out of the darkness of the pyramid, striding up the curving staircase. The man was stocky and dark, dressed in a dark double-breasted suit that strained to cover his wide shoulders. He motioned for Langdon to enter.

'I am Bezu Fache,' he announced in a guttural rumble as Langdon pushed through the revolving door. 'Captain of the Central Directorate Judicial Police.'

Langdon held out his hand. 'Robert Langdon.'

Fache's huge palm wrapped Langdon's with crushing force, then he led the professor down the famous marble staircase into the sunken atrium beneath the glass pyramid. The captain carried himself like an angry ox, his wide shoulders thrown back, his chin tucked into his chest. His dark hair was slicked back with oil, accentuating a widow's peak. Langdon fought a rising trepidation as they passed between two police guards with machine guns. Fache's presence was anything but welcoming, and the Louvre itself had an almost sepulchral aura at this hour.

'Do you approve?' Fache asked, nodding upwards with his chin.

Langdon sighed. 'Yes, your pyramid is magnificent.'

Fache grunted. 'A scar on the face of Paris.'

Strike one. Langdon sensed his host was a hard man to please.

They emerged into the subterranean foyer, which was usually vibrant with sunlight and tourists. Tonight, though, it was barren and dark.

'And the museum's regular security staff?' Langdon asked.

'All Louvre night wardens are in the Sully Wing being questioned. My own agents have taken over museum security for the evening.'

Langdon nodded, moving quickly to keep pace with Fache.

'How well did you know Jacques Saunière?' the captain asked.

'Actually, not at all. Our first meeting was to be tonight at the reception following my lecture. He never showed up.'

Fache looked surprised. He scribbled some notes in a little book. As they walked, Langdon caught a glimpse of the Louvre's lesser-known pyramid—*La Pyramide Inversée*, a huge skylight that hung from the ceiling like a stalactite in an adjoining section of the entrance hall.

Fache guided Langdon up a short set of stairs to the mouth of an arched tunnel, over which a sign read: DENON. The Denon Wing was the most famous of the Louvre's three main sections.

'Who requested tonight's meeting?' Fache asked. 'You or he?'

'Mr Saunière did,' Langdon replied. 'His secretary emailed me a few weeks ago. She said the curator wanted to discuss something with me while I was in Paris. Art, I imagine. We had similar interests.'

Fache looked sceptical. 'You have no idea what your meeting was about? It would be helpful if you could at least *guess* what our victim might have wanted to discuss with you on the night he was killed.'

'I really can't imagine. I'm an admirer of Mr Saunière's work and felt honoured to have been contacted at all, so I didn't ask.'

Fache made note of that fact in his book. The two men were now halfway up the Denon Wing's entry tunnel.

'So you shared interests with him?' Fache asked.

'Yes. In fact, I've spent much of the last year writing the draft of a book that deals with Mr Saunière's primary area of expertise. I was looking forward to picking his brain.'

Fache glanced up. 'I see. And what is the topic?'

Langdon hesitated, uncertain how to put it. 'Essentially, the manuscript is about the iconography of goddess worship—the concept of female sanctity and the art and symbols associated with it.'

'And Saunière was knowledgeable about this?'

'Nobody more so.'

Fache ran a meaty hand across his hair. 'I see.'

Langdon sensed Fache did not see at all. Not only did Jacques Saunière have a passion for relics relating to goddess cults and the sacred feminine, but during his twenty-year tenure as curator he had helped the Louvre to amass the world's largest collection of goddess art.

'Perhaps Saunière knew of your manuscript,' Fache suggested as they stopped in front of a service lift. 'And he called the meeting to offer his help on your book.'

Langdon shook his head. 'Actually, nobody yet knows about my manuscript. I haven't shown it to anyone except my editor.'

The lift doors opened. Langdon did not add that the reason he hadn't yet shown the manuscript to anyone else was that it proposed some very controversial interpretations of established religious iconography.

'You and Mr Saunière,' Fache said as the lift began to move, 'you never spoke at all? Never corresponded?'

Langdon shook his head. 'No. Never.'

As they ascended, he noticed in the reflection of the shiny lift door, the captain's tie clip—a silver crucifix with thirteen embedded pieces of black onyx. The symbol—a cross bearing thirteen gems—represented, in Christian symbology, Christ and his twelve apostles.

'It's a *crux gemmata*,' Fache said suddenly.

Startled, Langdon glanced up to find Fache's eyes on him in the reflection. The lift jolted to a stop, and the doors opened.

Langdon stepped out into the hallway, eager for the wide-open space afforded by the famous high ceilings of the Louvre galleries. But the world into which he stepped was startlingly dark. Instead of the customary flat-white light flowing down from above, a muted, oppressive red glow seemed to emanate up from the skirting boards.

As he gazed down the murky corridor, Langdon realised that he should have anticipated this. Virtually all major galleries employed red service lighting at night to slow the fading effects of overexposure to light on the paintings.

'This way,' Fache said, turning sharply right and setting out through a series of interconnected galleries.

Langdon followed, his vision slowly adjusting. Large oil paintings began to materialise all around him like photos developing in an enormous darkroom. Mounted high on the walls, the security cameras sent a clear message to visitors: We see you. Do not touch anything.

'Any of them real?' Langdon asked, motioning to the cameras.

Fache shook his head. 'Of course not.'

Langdon was not surprised. Video surveillance in museums this size was cost-prohibitive and ineffective. Most large museums now used 'containment security'. If an intruder removed a piece of artwork, compartmentalised exits would seal the gallery, putting the thief behind bars even before the police arrived.

Voices echoed towards them down the marble corridor. They seemed to be coming from a large recessed alcove that lay ahead, on the right. A bright light spilled out into the hallway.

'Office of the curator,' the captain said.

As they reached the alcove, Langdon peered down a short hallway into Saunière's luxurious study—warm wood, Old Master paintings and an enormous antique desk on which stood a two-foot-tall model of a knight in full armour. A handful of police agents bustled about the room, talking on phones and taking notes. One was seated at Saunière's desk, typing into a laptop. Apparently, the curator's office had become DCPJ's makeshift command post for the evening.

'*Messieurs*,' Fache called out, and the men turned. '*Ne nous dérangez pas sous aucun prétexte. Entendu?*'

Everyone inside the office nodded. Fache and Langdon were not to be disturbed under any circumstances.

Fache led Langdon further down the main hallway to the Louvre's most popular section—*la Grande Galerie*. Langdon had already discerned that this was where Saunière's body lay; the Grand Gallery's famous parquet floor had been unmistakable in the Polaroid.

As they approached, Langdon saw that the entrance was blocked by an enormous steel grate.

'Containment security,' Fache said, as they neared it. 'This area is still off limits to Louvre security,' he continued. 'My team has just finished its investigation.' He motioned to the two-foot opening at the base of the barricade. 'After you, Mr Langdon.'

Langdon stared at the narrow crawl space at his feet and then up at the massive iron grille. The barricade looked like a guillotine waiting to crush intruders.

Fache grumbled something in French and checked his watch. Then he dropped to his knees and slithered underneath the grille.

Langdon sighed. Placing his palms flat on the polished parquet, he lay on his stomach and followed the policeman through. He was beginning to suspect it was going to be a very long night.

Chapter 2

Murray Hill Place—the new Opus Dei World Headquarters—is located at 243 Lexington Avenue in New York City. With a price tag of just over $47 million, the 133,000-square-foot tower contains over a hundred bedrooms and numerous dining rooms, chapels, libraries, living rooms, meeting rooms and offices. Men enter the building through the main doors on Lexington Avenue. Women enter through a side street and are separated from the men at all times.

Earlier that evening, within the sanctuary of his penthouse apartment, Bishop Manuel Aringarosa had packed a small travel bag and descended to the lobby, where his driver was waiting to take him to the airport. Now, sitting aboard an airliner bound for Rome, he gazed out of the window at the dark Atlantic. Tonight the battle will be won, he thought, amazed that only months ago he had felt powerless against the hands that threatened to destroy his empire.

As president-general of Opus Dei, Bishop Aringarosa had spent the past decade spreading the message of 'God's Work'—literally, *Opus Dei*. The congregation, founded in 1928 by the Spanish priest Josemaría Escrivá, promoted a return to conservative Catholic values and encouraged its members to make sweeping sacrifices in their own lives in order to do the Work of God. Now Opus Dei's traditionalist philosophy was the fastest-growing and most financially secure Catholic organisation in the world. Unfortunately, its escalating wealth and power were a magnet for suspicion, particularly among the media. And five months ago, Opus Dei had found itself threatened by an infinitely more powerful force than the media . . . a foe from whom Aringarosa could not possibly hide. He was still reeling from the blow.

The cellphone in his black cassock began to vibrate. Despite airline regulations prohibiting the use of cellphones during flights, he knew this was a call he could not miss. Only one man possessed this number: the man who had mailed him the phone.

Excited, the bishop answered quietly. 'Yes?'

'Silas has located the keystone,' the caller said. 'It is in Paris. Within the Church of Saint-Sulpice.'

Bishop Aringarosa smiled. 'Then we are close.'

'We can obtain it immediately. But we need your influence.'

'Of course. Tell me what to do.'

When he switched off the phone, his heart was pounding. He gazed into the void of night, feeling dwarfed by the events he had put into motion. If all went as planned, he would soon be in possession of something that would make him the most powerful man in Christendom.

ROBERT LANGDON STOOD just inside the entrance to the Grand Gallery, staring into the mouth of a long, deep canyon. On either side, stark walls rose thirty feet, evaporating into the darkness above. The reddish glow of the service lighting cast an unnatural hue across a staggering collection of da Vincis, Titians and Caravaggios that hung suspended from ceiling cables.

As Langdon's gaze roamed the cavernous space, his eyes fell on an object lying just a few yards to his left, surrounded by police tape. He spun towards Fache. 'Is that . . . a *Caravaggio* on the floor?'

Fache nodded, clearly unmoved. 'The curator was apparently attacked in his office, fled into the Grand Gallery, and activated the security gate by pulling that painting from the wall.'

Langdon felt confused. 'So the curator actually captured his attacker inside the Grand Gallery?'

Fache shook his head. 'The security gate *separated* Saunière from his attacker. The killer was locked out there in the hallway and shot Saunière through the gate.' Fache pointed towards an orange tag on one of the bars. 'The team from the *Police Technique et Scientifique* found flashback residue from a gun.'

'So where is Saunière's body?'

Fache straightened his cruciform tie clip and began to walk. 'As you probably know, the Grand Gallery is quite long.'

They walked briskly for some time, yet Langdon still saw no corpse. 'He went this *far?*'

'Mr Saunière suffered a bullet wound to his stomach. He died slowly. Perhaps over fifteen minutes. He was obviously a man of great strength.'

Langdon was appalled. 'Security took fifteen minutes to get here?'

'Of course not. Louvre security responded immediately to the alarm and found the Grand Gallery sealed. Through the gate, they could hear someone moving around at the far end of the corridor and, assuming it was a criminal, followed protocol and called in the Judicial Police. We arrived fifteen minutes later, raised the barricade enough to slip underneath, and I sent a dozen armed agents inside. They found no one here. Except . . . ' He pointed further down the hall. 'Him.'

Langdon's gaze followed Fache's outstretched finger. Thirty yards down the hall, a single spotlight on a portable stand created a stark island of white light. In the centre, like an insect under a microscope, was the corpse of the curator.

Langdon felt a deep chill as they approached the body.

The pallid corpse lay on the parquet floor exactly as it had appeared in the photograph. Saunière had apparently stripped off every shred of clothing, placed it neatly on the floor, and laid down on his back, aligned with the long axis of the room. His arms and legs were spread-eagled and below his breastbone a bloody smear marked the spot where the bullet had pierced his flesh.

Saunière's left index finger was also bloody, apparently having been dipped into the wound to create the most unsettling aspect of the macabre scene. Using his own blood as ink, and employing his own naked abdomen as a canvas, Saunière had drawn on his flesh five straight lines that formed a five-pointed star.

'Mr Langdon?' Fache's dark eyes settled on him again.

'It's a pentacle,' Langdon offered, his voice feeling hollow. 'One of the oldest symbols on earth. Primarily a pagan religious symbol, used over four thousand years before Christ.'

Fache nodded. 'Devil worship.'

'No,' Langdon corrected the common misconception. Nowadays the term 'pagan' was almost synonymous with devil worship—a gross misconception. The word's roots actually reached back to the Latin *paganus*, meaning country-dwellers. 'Pagans' were literally unindoctrinated country-folk who clung to the old, rural religions of Nature worship. In fact, so strong was the Church's fear of those who lived in the rural *villes*, that the once innocuous word for 'villager', *villain*, came to mean a wicked soul. 'The pentacle,' Langdon clarified, 'is a pre-Christian symbol that relates to Nature worship. The ancients envisioned their world as two halves—masculine and feminine. Yin and yang. When male and female were balanced, there was harmony in the world. When they were unbalanced, there was chaos.' Langdon motioned to Saunière's stomach. 'This pentacle is representative of the *female* half of all things—a concept religious historians call the "sacred feminine" or the "divine goddess". In its most specific interpretation, the pentacle symbolises Venus, the goddess of female sexual love and beauty.'

Fache eyed the naked man, and grunted as if he somehow preferred the idea of devil worship. 'Mr Langdon,' he said abruptly. 'Obviously, the pentacle must *also* relate to the devil. Your American horror films make that point clearly.'

Langdon frowned. The five-pointed star, usually scrawled on a wall of some Satanist's apartment, was now a cliché in many films about the supernatural. 'I assure you,' he said, 'despite what you see in the movies, the pentacle's demonic interpretation is inaccurate. The symbolism of the pentacle has been distorted over the millennia as part of the Catholic Church's campaign to eradicate pagan religions and convert the masses to Christianity. The Church recast the divine symbols of the pagan gods and goddesses as evil.'

'Go on.'

'In the battle between the pagan and Christian symbols, the pagans lost; Poseidon's trident became the devil's pitchfork, the wise crone's pointed hat became the symbol of a witch, and Venus' pentacle became a sign of the devil.' Langdon paused. 'Unfortunately, the United States military has also perverted the pentacle. It now paints it on all its fighter jets and hangs it on the shoulders of all its generals.'

'Interesting.' Fache nodded towards the spread-eagled corpse. 'And the positioning of the body? What do you make of that?'

Langdon shrugged. 'Saunière positioned himself in the shape of a five-pointed star to reinforce the reference to the pentacle.'

Fache's eyes followed the five points of Saunière's arms, legs, and head as he ran a hand across his slick hair. 'Interesting analysis.'

'Mr Fache, I can't tell you why he drew that symbol on himself or placed himself in this way, but I *can* tell you that a man like Jacques Saunière would know that the pentacle symbolises the female deity.'

'Fine. And the use of his own blood as ink?'

'He had nothing else to write with.'

'Actually, I believe he used blood so that the police would follow certain forensic procedures. Look at his left hand.'

Langdon circled the corpse and crouched down. He noted with surprise that the curator was clutching a felt-tipped marker.

'Saunière was holding it when we found him,' Fache said, moving over to a portable table covered with PTS investigation tools, cables and assorted electronic gear. 'Are you familiar with this kind of pen?'

Langdon knelt down to look at the pen's label. STYLO DE LUMIERE NOIRE. He glanced up in surprise. The black-light pen or watermark stylus was a specialised felt-tipped marker that left invisible marks on valuable items. The stylus wrote in a noncorrosive fluorescent ink that was visible only under black light.

As Langdon stood up, Fache walked over to the spotlight and turned it off. The gallery was plunged into darkness, momentarily blinding them both. Then Fache's silhouette appeared, shrouded in a violet haze created by a portable light that he was carrying.

'As you may know,' Fache said, 'police use black-light illumination to search crime scenes for blood and other forensic evidence. So you can imagine our surprise . . . ' He pointed the light down at the corpse.

Langdon's heart pounded as he took in the bizarre sight before him. Scrawled in luminescent handwriting, the curator's final words glowed purple beside his corpse.

ON THE SECOND FLOOR of the Church of Saint-Sulpice, to the left of the choir balcony, were two stone-floored rooms with minimal furnishings, which had been home to Sister Sandrine Bieil for over a decade. She was responsible for overseeing all nonreligious aspects of church operations—general maintenance, hiring guides, securing the building after hours and ordering supplies.

Tonight she awoke to the shrill of her bedside telephone. Tiredly, she lifted the receiver. '*Soeur Sandrine. Eglise Saint-Sulpice.*'

'Hello, Sister,' the man said in French.

Sister Sandrine sat up. Although she recognised her boss's voice, in fifteen years she had never been woken by him.

'I apologise if I have woken you, Sister,' the *abbé* said. 'I have a favour to ask of you. I just received a call from Bishop Manuel Aringarosa. Perhaps you know him?'

'The head of Opus Dei?' Of course she knew of him. Aringarosa's prelature had grown ever more powerful since it had unexpectedly been elevated to a 'personal prelature of the Pope' in 1982, the same year the wealthy sect allegedly transferred almost $1 billion into the Vatican Bank. With their adherence to the arcane ritual of corporal mortification and their medieval views on women, Opus Dei had always made her uneasy. She felt that their good standing in Rome was suspect, but one did not argue with the Holy See.

'Bishop Aringarosa called to ask me a favour,' the *abbé* told her, sounding on edge. 'One of his numeraries is in Paris tonight and has always dreamed of seeing Saint-Sulpice.'

'But the church is far more interesting by day.'

'Sister, I agree, but his plane leaves very early in the morning. I would consider it a personal favour if you could let him in tonight. He can be there in twenty minutes at . . . say, one o'clock?'

Sister Sandrine frowned. 'Of course. It would be my pleasure.'

The *abbé* thanked her and hung up.

Puzzled, Sister Sandrine swung her legs off the bed and stood, chilled by the cold stone beneath her bare feet. As the chill rose through her sixty-year-old body, she felt an unexpected apprehension.

A follower of God, Sister Sandrine had learned to find peace in the calm voice of her own soul. Tonight, however, that voice was as silent as the empty church around her.

LANGDON COULDN'T TEAR his eyes from the glowing purple text scrawled across the parquet floor. Jacques Saunière's final message read:

13-3-2-21-1-1-8-5
O, Draconian devil!
Oh, lame saint!

Although Langdon had no idea what it meant, he now understood Fache's instinct that it had something to do with devil worship.

'Part of it looks like a numeric cipher,' he said, sensing it would take him hours to extract any meaning from the digits. Certainly they did not appear to fit his earlier scenario of goddess worship.

'Yes,' Fache said. 'Our cryptographers are working on it. To your eye, beyond the numbers, what about this message is most strange?'

Most strange? A dying man had barricaded himself in the gallery, drawn a pentacle on himself and scrawled a mysterious accusation on the floor. What about the scenario *wasn't* strange?

'Saunière was a Frenchman,' Fache prompted. 'He lived in Paris. And yet he chose to write this message . . . '

'In English,' Langdon said, realising the captain's meaning.

Fache nodded. '*Précisément*. Any idea why?'

Langdon shook his head. 'I'm sorry I can't be of more help.'

'Perhaps this will clarify.' Fache backed away from the body and raised the black light, letting the beam spread out. 'And now?'

To Langdon's amazement, a circle glowed round the curator's body. Saunière had apparently swung the pen round himself in several long arcs, essentially inscribing himself inside a circle. In a flash, the meaning became clear. '*The Vitruvian Man*,' Langdon gasped. Saunière had stripped off and arranged his body as a life-sized replica of Leonardo da Vinci's most famous sketch. But *why*?

'Mr Langdon,' Fache said, 'certainly a man like yourself is aware that Leonardo da Vinci had a tendency towards the darker arts.'

Langdon was surprised by Fache's knowledge of da Vinci, who had always been an awkward subject for historians. Despite his genius, he was a flamboyant homosexual and worshipper of Nature's divine order, both of which placed him in a perpetual state of sin. Moreover, some of the artist's eccentricities projected an admittedly demonic aura: da Vinci exhumed corpses to study human anatomy; he kept mysterious journals in illegible reverse handwriting; he believed he possessed the alchemic power to cheat God by creating an elixir to postpone death. And he incorporated into many of his Christian paintings hidden symbolism that was anything but Christian—tributes to his own beliefs and a subtle thumbing of his nose at the church.

'I understand your concerns,' Langdon said, 'but da Vinci never really practised any dark arts. He was an exceptionally spiritual man, albeit one in frequent conflict with the Church.' As Langdon said this, a thought popped into his mind. He glanced down at the message again.

'Yes?' Fache said.

'I was just thinking that Saunière shared a lot of interests with da Vinci, including a concern over the Church's elimination of the sacred feminine from modern religion. Maybe, by imitating a famous da Vinci drawing, in which a feminine symbol of protection—a circle—surrounds a nude male, Saunière was simply echoing some of their shared frustrations with the modern Church.'

Fache's eyes hardened. 'Mr Langdon, I have seen a lot of deaths in my work, and let me tell you something. When a man is murdered, I do not believe his final thoughts are of writing an obscure spiritual statement. No, I believe he is thinking of one thing only.' Fache's voice sliced the air. '*La vengeance*. I believe Saunière wrote this note to tell us who killed him.'

Langdon stared. 'But that makes no sense. You told me Saunière was attacked in his office by someone he had apparently invited in. So it seems reasonable to conclude that he knew his attacker.'

Fache nodded. 'Go on.'

'So if Saunière knew the person who killed him, why the numeric code? Lame saints? Draconian devils? It's all too cryptic. If Saunière wanted to tell us who killed him, I would assume he would write down somebody's *name*.'

As Langdon spoke those words, a smug smile crossed Fache's lips for the first time. '*Précisément*,' Fache said. '*Précisément*.'

I AM WITNESSING the work of a master, mused Lieutenant Collet, as he sat huddled over an audio console on the curator's enormous desk, listening to Fache's voice coming through the headphones. The agent knew it was moments like these that had lifted Bezu Fache to the pinnacle of French law enforcement.

Fache's briefing of his agents an hour ago had been unusually succinct and assured. 'I know who murdered Jacques Saunière,' Fache had said. 'You know what to do. No mistakes tonight.'

Collet was not yet privy to the evidence that had cemented Fache's certainty of their suspect's guilt, but he knew better than to question his boss's instincts. Fache's intuition seemed almost supernatural at times. 'God whispers in his ear,' one agent had insisted after a particularly impressive display of Fache's sixth sense.

Turning now to his laptop computer, Collet attended to his main responsibility here tonight—the GPS tracking system. The image on screen revealed a detailed floor plan of the Denon Wing. Deep in the heart of the maze of galleries and hallways, in the Grand Gallery a tiny red dot blinked.

Fache was keeping his prey on a very tight leash tonight. Wisely so. Robert Langdon had proven himself to be one cool customer.

'*CAPITAINE?*' Bezu Fache's cellphone crackled like a walkie-talkie.

Fache clenched his teeth in rage. Contrary to his orders, the two-way radio feature was being used by one of his agents to page him.

He gave Langdon a calm look of apology. 'One moment please.' He pulled the phone from his belt. '*Oui?*'

'*Capitaine, un agent du Département de Cryptographie est arrivé.*'

Fache's anger stalled momentarily. This was probably good news. If a code breaker had arrived, it most likely meant that someone who was working on deciphering Saunière's message had decrypted it.

'I'm busy at the moment,' Fache radioed back. 'Ask the cryptographer to wait at the command post. I'll speak to him when I'm done.'

'Her,' the voice corrected. 'It's Agent Neveu.'

Fache was becoming less amused with this call with every passing moment. Sophie Neveu was a young *déchiffreuse*, or cryptographer, who had been foisted on him two years earlier as part of the ministry's attempt to incorporate more women into the police force. Their foray into political correctness, Fache argued, was weakening the department. Women not only lacked the physicality necessary for police work, but their presence posed a dangerous distraction to the men in the field. As Fache had feared, the thirty-two-year-old Neveu was proving to be a far more distracting woman than most.

The man on the radio said, 'Agent Neveu insisted on speaking to you immediately, Captain. I tried to stop her but she's on her way into the gallery.'

Fache recoiled in disbelief. 'Unacceptable! I made it very clear—'

For a moment, Robert Langdon thought Bezu Fache was suffering a stroke. The captain was mid-sentence when his jaw dropped and his blistering gaze fixed on something over Langdon's shoulder. Before Langdon could turn to see what it was, he heard a woman's voice chime out behind him.

'*Excusez-moi, messieurs*.'

Langdon turned to see an attractive young woman moving down the corridor towards them with long, fluid strides. She was dressed casually in a knee-length, cream-coloured sweater over black leggings, and her thick burgundy hair fell unstyled to her shoulders, framing the warmth of her face.

To Langdon's surprise, the woman walked directly up to him and extended a polite hand.

'Monsieur Langdon, I am Agent Neveu from DCPJ's Cryptology Department.' Her words curled richly around a muted Anglo-French accent. 'It is a pleasure to meet you.'

Langdon took her palm in his and was momentarily fixed in her strong gaze. Her eyes were olive-green—incisive and clear.

Fache drew a seething inhalation, clearly preparing to launch into a reprimand.

'Captain,' she said, turning quickly to Fache, 'please excuse the interruption.'

'*Ce n'est pas le moment!*' Fache spluttered.

'I tried to phone you,' Sophie continued in English, as if out of courtesy to Langdon. 'But your cellphone was turned off.'

'I turned it off for a reason. I am speaking to Mr Langdon.'

'I've deciphered the numeric code,' she said flatly, 'but before I explain, I have an urgent message for Mr Langdon.'

Fache's expression turned to one of deep concern. 'For Mr Langdon?'

She nodded, and turned to the American. 'You need to contact the US Embassy, Mr Langdon. They have a message for you from the States.'

A message from the States? Langdon tried to imagine who could be trying to reach him. Only a few of his colleagues knew he was in Paris.

Fache's jaw tightened. 'How would the US Embassy know to find Mr Langdon here?' he demanded.

Sophie shrugged. 'Apparently they called his hotel, and the concierge told them he had been collected by a DCPJ agent. When I tried to contact you through the DCPJ switchboard, they asked me to pass on the message for Mr Langdon if I got through to you.'

Fache's brow furrowed in apparent confusion. He opened his mouth to speak, but Sophie had already turned back to Langdon.

'Mr Langdon,' she declared, pulling a slip of paper from her pocket. 'This is the number for your embassy's messaging service. They asked that you phone in as soon as possible.' She handed him the paper with an intent gaze. 'While I explain the code to Captain Fache, you need to make this call.'

Langdon studied the slip. It had a Paris phone number and extension on it. 'Thank you,' he said. 'Where do I find a phone?'

Sophie began to pull a cellphone from her sweater pocket, but Fache, looking like Mount Vesuvius about to erupt, waved her off and held out his own. 'This line is secure, Mr Langdon. You may use it.'

Feeling uneasy, Langdon accepted the captain's phone while Fache marched Sophie several steps away and began chastising her in hushed tones. Langdon dialled the number on the slip of paper Sophie had given him.

The line began to ring. After three rings the call connected.

And Langdon found himself listening to an answering machine.

'*Bonjour, vous êtes bien chez Sophie Neveu,*' the woman's voice said. '*Je suis absente pour le moment, mais . . .* '

Confused, he turned back towards Sophie. 'I'm sorry, Ms Neveu? I think you may have given me—'

'No, that's the right number,' Sophie interjected quickly, as if anticipating Langdon's confusion. 'The embassy has an automated message system. You have to dial an access code to pick up your messages. It's the three-digit code on the paper I gave you.'

Langdon opened his mouth to explain the bizarre error, but Sophie flashed him a silencing glare. Her green eyes sent a clear message: Don't ask questions. Just do it.

Bewildered, Langdon punched in the extension number: 454.

Sophie's outgoing message immediately cut off, and Langdon heard an electronic voice announce in French: 'You have *one* new message.' Apparently, 454 was Sophie's remote access code for picking up her messages while away from home.

Langdon heard the machine engage. 'Mr Langdon,' the message began in a fearful whisper. 'Do *not* react to this message. Just listen calmly. You are in danger right now. Follow my directions closely.'

Chapter 3

Twenty thousand feet above the Mediterranean, Alitalia flight 1618 bounced in turbulence, causing passengers to shift nervously. Bishop Aringarosa barely noticed. His thoughts were on the future of Opus Dei. Eager to know how plans in Paris were progressing, he wished he could phone Silas. But he could not. The Teacher had seen to that.

'It is for your own safety,' the Teacher had explained. 'Electronic communications can be intercepted. That could be disastrous for you.'

Aringarosa knew he was right. The Teacher had not revealed his identity, and yet he had proved himself a man worth obeying. After all, he had somehow obtained very secret information: the names of the brotherhood's four top members. This had been one of the coups that convinced the bishop that the Teacher was truly capable of delivering the astonishing prize he claimed he could unearth.

'Bishop,' the Teacher had told him, 'for my plan to succeed, you must allow Silas to answer *only* to me for several days. I will communicate with him through secure channels.'

'You will treat him with respect?' The Bishop had protected Silas ever since the day the young man had saved his life. Aringarosa had been a young priest then, and Silas, starving and homeless, had chased away the thief who was beating him in an effort to get the offertory money. Silas had stayed with him ever since.

'A man of faith deserves the highest,' the Teacher had replied.

'Excellent. Then Silas and I shall not speak until this is over.'

'I do this to protect your identity and my investment.'

'Your investment?' Aringarosa had queried.

'Bishop, if your own eagerness to keep abreast of progress puts you in jail, then you will be unable to pay me my fee.'

The bishop smiled. 'A fine point. We are in accord. Godspeed.'

Twenty million euros, the bishop thought now, gazing out of the plane's window. A pittance for something so powerful.

'A NUMERIC JOKE?' Bezu Fache was glaring at Sophie Neveu in disbelief. 'That is your professional assessment of Saunière's code?'

Fache was in utter incomprehension of this woman's gall. Not only had she just barged in without permission, but she was now trying to convince him that Saunière, in his final moments of life, had been inspired to leave a mathematical gag?

'This code,' Sophie explained in rapid French, 'is simplistic to the point of absurdity. Jacques Saunière must have known we would see through it immediately.' She pulled a scrap of paper from her sweater pocket and handed it to Fache. 'Here is the decryption.'

Fache looked at the paper.

1-1-2-3-5-8-13-21

'All you did was put the numbers in increasing order!' he snapped.

'Captain,' Sophie said, her tone defiant, 'the sequence of numbers you have in your hand happens to be the most famous mathematical progressions in history: the Fibonacci sequence. In it, each term is equal to the sum of the two preceding terms.'

Fache studied the numbers. She was right, and yet he could not imagine what the relevance was to the curator's death. 'Would you like to tell me *why* Jacques Saunière chose to do this. What is he saying?'

She shrugged. 'Absolutely nothing. That's the point. It's a simplistic cryptographic joke. Like taking the words of a famous poem and shuffling them at random to see if anyone recognises what all the words have in common.'

Fache took a menacing step forward. 'I certainly hope you have a much more satisfying explanation than *that*.'

Sophie's soft features grew stern. 'Captain, considering what you have at stake here tonight, I thought you might appreciate knowing that Jacques Saunière might be playing games with you. Apparently not. I'll inform the director of Cryptography you no longer need our services.' And with that, she turned on her heel, and marched off the way she had come.

Stunned, Fache watched her disappear. Was she out of her mind? Sophie Neveu had just redefined professional suicide.

He turned to Langdon, who was still on the phone, looking more concerned than before, listening intently to his phone message. *The US Embassy*. Bezu Fache despised many things . . . but few more than the US Embassy. He and the ambassador locked horns regularly—their most common battleground being law enforcement for visiting Americans. Almost daily, DCPJ arrested American exchange students in possession of drugs, US businessmen for soliciting underage prostitutes, American tourists for shoplifting. Legally, the US Embassy could intervene and extradite guilty citizens back to the United States, where they received nothing more than a slap on the wrist. And invariably the embassy did just that.

Not tonight, Fache told himself. There is far too much at stake.

By the time Robert Langdon hung up the phone, he looked ill.

'Is everything all right?' Fache asked, as he took back his cellphone.

Weakly, Langdon shook his head. 'An accident,' he stammered, looking at Fache with a strange expression. 'A friend . . .' He hesitated. 'I'll need to fly home first thing in the morning.'

Fache had no doubt the shock on Langdon's face was genuine, and yet he sensed another emotion there too. 'Would you like to sit down?' He motioned towards one of the viewing benches in the gallery.

Langdon nodded absently and took a few steps towards the bench. He paused, looking more confused with every moment. 'Actually, I think I'd like to use the toilet.'

Fache frowned at the delay. 'The toilet. Of course. Let's take a break for a few minutes.' He motioned towards a pair of doors at the far end of the long hallway. 'Shall I accompany you?'

Langdon shook his head. 'I think I'd like a few minutes alone.'

Fache was not wild about the idea, but he took comfort in knowing that the Grand Gallery was a dead end. Its only exits were the gate under which they had entered and several emergency stairwells, which had been sealed automatically when Saunière tripped the security system. Though the system had now been reset, unlocking the stairwells, the external doors were alarmed, with DCPJ agents guarding all exits. Langdon could not possibly leave without Fache knowing about it.

'I need to return to Mr Saunière's office for a moment,' Fache said. 'Please come and find me directly. There is more we need to discuss.'

Langdon gave a quiet wave as he disappeared into the darkness.

Turning, Fache marched angrily in the opposite direction. Arriving at the gate, he slid under it, exited the Grand Gallery, marched down the hall and stormed into Saunière's office.

'Who gave the approval to let Neveu into this building?' he bellowed.

Collet was the first to answer. 'She told the guards outside she'd broken the code. She's not with you?'

'She left.' Fache glanced out at the darkened hallway. Apparently Sophie had been in no mood to stop by and chat with the other officers on her way out.

For a moment, Fache considered radioing the guards in the lobby and telling them to stop Sophie and drag her back up here before she could leave the premises. He thought better of it. Deal with Agent Neveu later, he told himself, already looking forward to firing her. He turned back to Collet. 'Do you have him?'

Collet gave a curt nod and spun the laptop towards Fache. The red dot was clearly visible on the floor plan, blinking methodically in a room marked TOILETTES PUBLIQUES.

'Good,' Fache said, lighting a cigarette. 'I've got a phone call to make. Be damned sure the toilet is the only place Langdon goes.'

ILLUMINATED SIGNS bearing the international stick-figure symbols for toilets had guided Robert Langdon through a maze-like series of room dividers and into the empty men's room.

He walked to the sink and splashed cold water on his face. As he towelled off, the door creaked open behind him. He spun.

Sophie Neveu entered, her green eyes flashing with fear. 'Thank God you came. We don't have much time.'

Langdon stared at her in bewilderment. Only minutes ago, he had listened to her phone message, thinking she must be insane. And yet the more he listened, the more he sensed Sophie Neveu was speaking in earnest. *You are in danger right now. Follow my directions closely.*

She stood before him now, still catching her breath after doubling back to the toilets. 'You are under observation, Mr Langdon,' she said.

"But . . . why?' Langdon demanded.

'Because,' she said, stepping towards him, 'Fache's primary suspect in this murder is *you*.'

Langdon was braced for the words, but they still sounded ridiculous. According to Sophie, Langdon had been called to the Louvre tonight not as a symbologist but as a *suspect*, and was currently the unwitting target of one of DCPJ's favourite interrogation methods—*surveillance cachée*—a deft deception in which the police calmly invited a suspect to a crime scene and interviewed him in hopes he would mistakenly incriminate himself.

'Look in the left pocket of your jacket,' she said. 'You'll find proof they are watching you.'

Bewildered, Langdon reached his hand into his jacket's left pocket and felt around inside until his fingers brushed something small and hard. Langdon pulled out the tiny object and stared in astonishment. It was a metallic disk, about the size of a watch battery. 'What the . . . ?'

'GPS tracking dot,' Sophie said. 'Continuously transmits its location to a Global Positioning System satellite that DCPJ can monitor. The agent who picked you up at the hotel slipped it inside your pocket before you left your room. They tagged you with GPS because they thought you might run.'

'Why would I run?' Langdon demanded. 'I'm innocent!'

'Fache feels otherwise.'

Angrily, Langdon stalked towards the trash receptacle to dispose of the tracking dot.

'No!' Sophie grabbed his arm and stopped him. 'If you throw it out, the signal will stop moving, and they'll know you found the dot. Leave it in your pocket. At least for the moment.'

'How could Fache actually believe I killed Jacques Saunière!'

'He has some fairly persuasive reasons to suspect you. Do you recall the three lines of text that Saunière wrote on the floor?'

Langdon nodded. They were imprinted on his mind.

Sophie produced a computer print-out from her sweater pocket and unfolded it. 'Fache sent images of the crime scene to Cryptology earlier tonight. This is a photo of the complete message.' She handed the page to Langdon. 'There was a *fourth* line, which Fache photographed and then wiped clean before you arrived.'

Bewildered, Langdon looked at the image. The close-up photograph revealed the glowing message on the parquet floor:

13-3-2-21-1-1-8-5
O, Draconian devil!
Oh, lame saint!
P.S. Find Robert Langdon

Langdon stared at the photograph in amazement. He could not fathom why Saunière had left a postscript with his name in it.

'Now do you understand?' Sophie asked urgently.

The only thing Langdon understood was why Fache had looked so smug when Langdon suggested Saunière would have accused his killer by name. *Find Robert Langdon.*

'Why would Saunière write this?' Langdon demanded, his confusion giving way to anger. 'Why would I want to kill him?'

'Fache has yet to uncover a motive, but he has been recording his entire conversation with you tonight in hopes you might reveal one.'

'This is insanity! Fache has no evidence!'

Sophie's eyes widened as if to say: *No evidence*? 'Mr Langdon, your name is written on the floor beside the body, and Saunière's diary says you were with him at approximately the time of the murder. Fache has more than enough evidence to take you into custody for questioning.'

'I didn't do this,' Langdon stammered. 'And I have an alibi. I went directly back to my hotel after my lecture. You can ask the hotel desk.'

'Fache already did. His report shows you retrieving your room key from the concierge at about ten thirty. Unfortunately, the time of the murder was closer to eleven. You easily could have left your hotel room unseen.' Sophie sighed. 'Jacques Saunière was a prominent and well-loved figure in Paris, and his murder will be big news in the morning. Fache will be under pressure to make a statement, and will look a lot better if he has a suspect in custody. Whether or not you are guilty, you most certainly will be held by DCPJ until they can figure out what really happened.'

'Why are you telling me all this?'

'Because, Mr Langdon, I believe you are innocent.' Sophie looked into his eyes. 'And also because it is partially *my* fault that you're in trouble. That message on the floor was meant for me.'

Langdon needed a minute to process that one. 'I beg your pardon?'

'He wrote that message for me. I think he had to do everything in such a hurry that he didn't realise how it would look to the police. The number code was to make sure the investigation included cryptographers, so that *I* would know as soon as possible what had happened.'

Langdon felt himself losing touch fast. 'But why do you think his message was for you?'

'*The Vitruvian Man*,' she said flatly. 'That sketch has always been my favourite da Vinci work. He used it to catch my attention.'

'Hold on. You're saying the curator knew your favourite piece of art?'

She nodded. 'I'm sorry. This is all coming out of order. Jacques Saunière and I . . . ' Sophie's voice caught, and Langdon heard a sudden melancholy in it, pain simmering just below the surface. 'We had a falling-out ten years ago. We've barely spoken since. Tonight, when Crypto got the call that he had been murdered, and I saw the images of his body and text on the floor, I realised he was trying to send me a message.'

'Because of *The Vitruvian Man*?'

'Yes. And the letters P.S.'

'*Post Script?*'

She shook her head. 'P.S. is the nickname he called me when I lived with him.' She blushed. 'It stood for *Princesse Sophie*. Silly, I know, but it was years ago. When I was a little girl.'

'You knew him when you were a little *girl?*'

'Quite well,' she said, her eyes welling now with emotion. 'Jacques Saunière was my grandfather.'

IT WAS TIME.

Silas felt strong as he stepped from the black Audi, the night breeze rustling his loose-fitting monk's robe. Knowing the task before him would require more finesse than force, he had left his gun in the car.

The plaza before the church was deserted, except for two teenage hookers showing their wares to the late-night traffic. Their nubile bodies sent a familiar longing to Silas's loins. He flexed his thigh instinctively, causing the leather cilice belt with its sharp metal barbs to cut painfully into the flesh.

The lust evaporated instantly. For ten years now, Silas had denied himself all sexual indulgence. But considering the poverty from which he had come and the violence he had suffered at the hands of his father, the vows of celibacy and relinquishment of all personal assets hardly seemed a sacrifice.

The measure of your faith is the measure of the pain you can endure, the Teacher had told him. Silas was no stranger to pain and felt eager to prove himself to the Teacher, the one who had assured him his actions were ordained by a higher power.

Pausing in the shadow of the massive doorway of the church, he took a deep breath. Then, as he raised his ghost-white fist and banged three times on the door, he thought about what awaited him inside.

The keystone. It will lead us to our final goal.

SEEING THAT LANGDON was overwhelmed, Sophie questioned whether she had done the right thing by cornering him here in the men's room. But what else was I supposed to do? she wondered.

Sophie made her living extracting meaning from seemingly senseless data. Tonight, her best guess was that Robert Langdon, whether he knew it or not, possessed information that she desperately needed. She needed more time with him. Time to sort out this mystery together.

She pictured her grandfather's body, naked and spread-eagled on the floor. Once he had meant the world to her, yet tonight she felt almost no sadness for the man. Their relationship had evaporated one night ten years ago, when Sophie had come home a few days early from university and witnessed her grandfather engaged in something she was obviously not supposed to see.

Too ashamed and stunned to endure her grandfather's pained attempts to explain, Sophie immediately moved out on her own, taking money she had saved and getting a small flat with some roommates. Her grandfather tried desperately to reach her, sending cards and letters begging Sophie to meet him so he could explain, but she forbade him ever to call her or try to meet her in public.

Incredibly, Saunière had never given up on her, but to his credit, had never once disobeyed her request. *Until this afternoon.*

'Sophie?' His voice had sounded startlingly old on her answering machine. She felt a chill at hearing him again after all these years. 'I have abided by your wishes for so long, but now I must speak to you. Something terrible has happened. Princess, I know I've kept things from you, and I know it has cost me your love. But it was for your own safety. Now you must know the truth about your family.'

My family? Sophie's parents had died in a car accident when she was only four. Their car went off a bridge into fast-moving water. Her grandmother and brother had also been in the vehicle.

'Sophie . . . ' her grandfather said on the machine. 'Call me at the Louvre. As soon as you get this. I'll wait here all night. I fear we both may be in danger. There's so much you need to know.'

She had not called him. Nor had she planned to, believing he had used her family as a ploy to get her to visit him. Now, however, her scepticism had been deeply challenged. Her grandfather lay murdered. And he had written a code. A code for her. Of this, she was certain.

Sophie's passion for cryptography was a product of growing up with Jacques Saunière—he himself was a fanatic for codes, word games and puzzles, and many Sundays they'd spent the entire day doing cryptograms and crosswords.

Tonight, the cryptographer in Sophie was forced to respect the efficiency with which her grandfather had used a simple code to unite her with Robert Langdon. The question was why.

Unfortunately, from the bewildered look in Langdon's eyes, Sophie could see that the American had no more idea than she did.

She took a deep breath. 'My grandfather called me this afternoon and told me he and I were in grave danger. Does that mean anything to you?'

Langdon's blue eyes clouded with concern. 'No, but considering what just happened . . . '

Sophie nodded. Considering tonight's events, she would be a fool not to be frightened. Feeling drained, she walked to the small plate-glass window at the far end of the bathroom and gazed out, through the mesh of alarm tape embedded in the glass, at Paris's dazzling landscape. They were high up—forty feet at least. On her left, across the Seine, the illuminated Eiffel Tower. Straight ahead, the Arc de Triomphe. And to the right, high atop the sloping rise of Montmartre, the glowing white dome of Sacré-Coeur.

Here at the westernmost tip of the Denon Wing, the north–south edge of Place du Carrousel was almost flush with the building, with only a narrow pavement separating it from the Louvre's outer wall. Far below, the usual caravan of the city's night-time delivery trucks sat idling, waiting for the traffic lights to change.

'I don't know what to say,' Langdon said, coming up behind her. 'Your grandfather is obviously trying to tell us something. I'm sorry I'm so little help.'

Sophie sensed a sincere regret in Langdon's deep voice. The teacher in him, she thought, having read DCPJ's report on their suspect. She turned from the window. 'Bezu Fache will be taking you into custody at any minute. I can get you out of this museum. But we need to act now.'

Langdon's eyes went wide. 'You want me to run?'

'It's the smartest thing you could do. If you let Fache take you into custody, you'll spend weeks in a French jail while DCPJ and the US Embassy fight over which courts try your case. But if we can get you to your embassy, then your government will protect your rights while you and I prove you had nothing to do with this murder.'

'But Fache has armed guards on every single exit! Even if we escape without being shot, running away only makes me look guilty. You need to tell Fache that the message on the floor was for you, and that my name is not there as an accusation.'

'First, Mr Langdon,' she said hurriedly, 'I need to ask you one last question. Can you think of any other reason, other than the writing on the floor, why Fache might be convinced you're guilty?'

Langdon was silent for several seconds. 'None whatsoever.'

Sophie sighed. *Which means Fache is lying*. Why, Sophie could not begin to imagine, but she needed Langdon for herself, and it was this that left her only one logical conclusion: Robert Langdon was about to escape the Louvre, whether he wanted to or not.

'WHAT DO YOU MEAN she's not answering?' Fache looked incredulous.

'Maybe her batteries are dead. Or her ringer's off,' Collet replied.

Fache had looked distressed since talking to Sophie's boss, the director of Cryptography, on the phone. After hanging up, he had marched over to Collet and demanded he get Agent Neveu on the line. Now Collet had failed, and Fache was pacing like a caged lion.

'Why did Crypto call?' Collet now ventured.

Fache turned. 'To tell us they had just identified the numerics as Fibonacci numbers.'

Collet was confused. 'But they'd sent Agent Neveu to tell us that.'

Fache shook his head. 'They didn't send Neveu.'

'What?'

'According to the director, Agent Neveu took one look at the photos I'd wired them of Saunière, and left the office without a word. The director said he didn't question her behaviour because she was understandably upset by the photos. It seems that Sophie Neveu is Jacques Saunière's granddaughter.'

Collet was speechless. He could barely conceive of the unfortunate coincidence that brought a young woman to decipher a code written by a dead family member. No wonder she was upset. Still, why would she leave the office without telling anyone she had recognised the numbers as a Fibonacci sequence?

Before Collet could ponder it any further, the silence of the deserted museum was shattered by an alarm.

'*Alarme*,' one of the agents yelled, eyeing his feed from the Louvre security centre. '*Grande Galerie! Toilettes Messieurs!*'

Fache wheeled round to face Collet. 'Where's Langdon?'

'Still in the men's room.' Collet pointed to the blinking red dot on his laptop screen. 'He must have broken the window!' Collet knew the American wouldn't get far. Exiting a Louvre second-storey window without the help of a ladder would be suicide. 'My God,' he exclaimed. 'He's moving to the window ledge!'

But Fache was already in motion. Yanking his revolver from his shoulder holster, the captain dashed out of the office.

Collet watched the screen in bewilderment as the blinking dot moved farther outside the perimeter of the building. Fumbling with the controls, Collet called up a Paris street map and recalibrated the GPS. Zooming in, he could now see the exact location of the signal. It lay at a dead stop in the middle of the Place du Carrousel.

Langdon had jumped.

FACHE SPRINTED down the Grand Gallery as Collet's radio blared over the distant sound of the alarm. 'He jumped!' Collet was yelling. 'And he's not moving at all. I think he's just committed suicide.'

Fache heard the words, but kept running, setting his sights on the toilets at the end of the hallway.

'Wait!' Collet's voice blared again over the radio. 'He's moving! My God, he's alive. He's running. Wait . . . he's picking up speed. He's moving too fast! He must be in a car! I think he's in a car! I can't—'

Collet's words were swallowed by the alarm as Fache finally burst into the men's room with his gun drawn.

The stalls were empty. The toilets deserted. Fache's eyes moved immediately to the shattered window at the far end of the room. He ran to the opening and looked over the edge. Certainly if Langdon had dropped that far, he would be badly injured.

The alarm cut off finally, and Collet's voice became audible again over the walkie-talkie. '. . . crossing the Seine on Pont du Carrousel!'

Fache looked to his left. The only vehicle on Pont du Carrousel was an enormous twin-bed delivery truck moving south away from the Louvre. The truck's open-air bed was covered with a vinyl tarpaulin, roughly resembling a giant hammock. Fache felt a shiver of apprehension. An insane risk, he told himself. Langdon had no way of knowing what the truck was carrying beneath that tarp. What if it were steel? Or concrete? A forty-foot leap? It was madness.

It was over, Fache knew. His men would have the truck surrounded within minutes. Langdon was not going anywhere.

Stowing his weapon, Fache exited the toilets and radioed Collet. 'Bring my car round. I want to be there when we make the arrest.'

CHAPTER 4

Only fifteen yards from the toilets, Langdon and Sophie stood in the darkness of the Grand Gallery.

The last sixty seconds had been a blur. Langdon had been standing inside the men's room refusing to run from a crime he didn't commit, when Sophie began examining the plate-glass window and the alarm mesh running through it. Then she peered down into the street. 'With a little aim, you can get out of here,' she said.

'Sophie, there's no way I'm jump—'

'Take out the tracking dot.'

Langdon fumbled in his pocket until he found the tiny metallic disk. Sophie took it from him and strode to the sink. She grabbed a thick bar of soap, placed the tracking dot on top of it, and used her thumb to firmly embed the device in the bar. Handing the soap to Langdon, she retrieved a heavy cylindrical rubbish bin from under the sinks and drove the bottom of the bin into the centre of the window, shattering the glass. Alarms erupted overhead at earsplitting decibel levels.

'Give me the soap!' Sophie yelled, barely audible over the alarm.

Langdon thrust the bar into her hand.

She peered out of the shattered window at the tarpaulin-covered eighteen-wheeler lorry idling below. It was less than ten feet from the side of the building. As the traffic lights prepared to change, Sophie took a deep breath and lobbed the bar of soap out into the night. It plummeted down, landing on the tarp.

'Congratulations,' Sophie said, dragging him towards the door. 'You just escaped from the Louvre.' Fleeing the men's room, they moved into the shadows just as Fache rushed past, gun drawn.

Langdon decided not to say another word all evening. Sophie Neveu was clearly a hell of a lot smarter than he was.

THE CHURCH OF SAINT-SULPICE, it is said, has the most eccentric history of any building in Paris. Built over the ruins of an ancient temple to the Egyptian goddess Isis, the church has played host to the baptisms of the Marquis de Sade and Baudelaire, as well as the marriage of Victor Hugo. And the attached seminary was once the clandestine meeting hall for numerous secret societies.

Tonight, the cavernous nave was as silent as a tomb. Silas sensed an unease in Sister Sandrine's demeanour as she led him inside, but he was accustomed to people being uncomfortable with his appearance.

'You're an American,' she said.

'French by birth,' Silas responded as he followed her down the main aisle. 'I now study in the United States.'

Sister Sandrine nodded. 'And you have never seen Saint-Sulpice?'

'I realise this is almost a sin in itself.'

'She is more beautiful by day.'

'I am certain. Nonetheless, I am grateful that you have provided me this opportunity to see the church tonight. I apologise, Sister, for the fact that you were awoken on my behalf.'

'Not at all. You are in Paris a short time. You should not miss Saint-Sulpice. Where would you like to begin your tour?'

Silas's eyes focused on the altar. 'A tour is unnecessary. You have been more than kind. I can show myself around.'

'It is no trouble,' she said.

Silas stopped walking at the front pew. He turned his massive body towards the small woman, and he could see her recoil as she gazed up into his red eyes. 'Sister, I feel guilty already for having awoken you. Please, you should return to bed. I can let myself out.'

Sister Sandrine looked uneasy, but she muttered, 'As you wish,' and headed for the stairs.

'Sleep well, Sister. May the peace of the Lord be with you.'

EMERGING from the shadows, Langdon and Sophie moved stealthily up the deserted Grand Gallery towards the emergency exit.

'Is there a possibility that the numbers in your grandfather's message hold the key to understanding the other lines?' Langdon asked.

'I've been thinking about the numbers all night, but I don't see anything. Mathematically, they're arranged at random.'

'And yet they're all part of the Fibonacci sequence.'

She nodded. 'It was my grandfather's way of catching my attention—like writing the message in English, and arranging himself like my favourite piece of art, and drawing a pentacle on himself.'

'The pentacle has meaning to you?'

'Yes. It was a special symbol for my grandfather and me when I was growing up. We used to play Tarot cards for fun, and my indicator card *always* turned out to be from the suit of pentacles. I'm sure he stacked the deck, but pentacles got to be our little joke.'

They arrived at the emergency stairwell, and Sophie carefully pulled open the door. No alarm sounded—only the doors to the outside were wired. Sophie led Langdon down towards the ground level.

'When your grandfather told you about the pentacle,' Langdon said, hurrying behind her, 'did he mention that pentacles is the Tarot suit for feminine divinity? Did he mention goddess worship?'

Sophie shook her head. 'I was more interested in the mathematics of the pentacle—Fibonacci sequences, Phi, that sort of thing . . .'

Langdon was surprised. 'Your grandfather taught you about Phi?'

'Of course. The Divine Proportion.' Her expression turned sheepish. 'In fact, he used to joke that I was half divine . . . you know, because of the letters in my name.'

Langdon considered it a moment and then groaned. *S-o-phi-e*. He was starting to realise that Saunière's clues were even more consistent than he had first imagined. *Da Vinci . . . Fibonacci numbers . . . the pentacle*. Incredibly, all of these things were connected by a single concept fundamental to art history: Phi.

He felt himself suddenly reeling back to Harvard, standing in front of his 'Symbolism in Art' class, writing his favourite number on the chalkboard: 1.6180339887 . . .

He turned to his students. 'Who can tell me what this number is?'

A long-legged maths major at the back raised his hand. 'That's the number Phi.' He pronounced it *fee*.

'Nice job, Stettner,' Langdon said. 'Everyone, meet Phi. This number is very important in art. It's derived from the Fibonacci sequence—a progression famous not only because the sum of adjacent terms equal the next term but because the *quotients* of adjacent terms approach the number 1.6180339887 . . . Phi!'

Despite Phi's seemingly mystical mathematical origins, Langdon explained, the truly mind-boggling aspect of it was its role as a fundamental building block in nature. Plants, animals and even human beings all possessed dimensional properties that adhered with eerie exactitude, to the ratio of Phi to 1.

'Phi's ubiquity in nature,' Langdon said, 'exceeds coincidence. Early scientists heralded one-point-six-one-eight as the Divine Proportion.'

'Hold on,' said a young woman in the front row. 'I'm a bio major and I've never seen this Divine Proportion in nature.'

'No?' Langdon grinned. 'Ever study the relationship between females and males in a honeybee community?'

'Sure. The female bees always outnumber the male bees.'

'Correct. And did you know that if you divide the number of female bees by the number of male bees in any beehive in the world, you always get the same number?'

'You do?'

'Yup. Phi.'

The girl gaped.

Langdon smiled as he projected a close-up of a sunflower's seed head. 'Sunflower seeds grow in opposing spirals. Can you guess the ratio of each rotation's diameter to the next?'

'Phi?' everyone said.

'Bingo.' Langdon began racing through slides now—spiralled pine-cone petals, leaf arrangement on plant stalks, insect segmentation—all displaying astonishing obedience to the Divine Proportion.

'This is amazing!' someone cried out.

'Yeah,' someone else said, 'but what does it have to do with art?'

'Aha!' Langdon said. 'Glad you asked.' He pulled up a slide displaying Leonardo da Vinci's famous male nude—*The Vitruvian Man*—named for Marcus Vitruvius Pollio, the brilliant Roman architect who praised the Divine Proportion in his text *De Architectura*.

'Nobody understood better than da Vinci the divine structure of the human body. Da Vinci actually exhumed corpses to measure the exact proportions of the human bone structure. He was the first to show that the human body is made of building blocks whose proportional ratios always equal Phi. Try it. Measure the distance from the tip of your head to the floor. Divide that by the distance from your belly button to the floor. Guess what number you get?'

'Not Phi,' one of the students blurted out in disbelief.

'Yes, Phi, Langdon explained. 'One-point-six-one-eight.' He could see they were all astounded. 'As you can see, the chaos of the world has an underlying order. When the ancients discovered Phi, they were certain they had stumbled across God's building block for the world.'

Over the next half hour, he showed them slides of artwork by Michelangelo, Albrecht Dürer, Leonardo da Vinci and many others, demonstrating each artist's rigorous adherence to the Divine Proportion in his compositions. Langdon unveiled Phi in the architectural dimensions of the Greek Parthenon, the pyramids of Egypt, and even the United Nations Building in New York. Phi appeared in the organisational structures of Mozart's sonatas, Beethoven's Fifth Symphony, as well as the works of Bartók, Debussy and Schubert.

'In closing,' Langdon said, walking to the chalkboard, 'we return to symbols.' He drew five intersecting lines that formed a five-pointed star. 'This symbol, the pentacle, is considered both divine and magical by many cultures. Can anyone tell me why?'

Stettner, the maths major, raised his hand. 'Because if you draw a pentacle, the lines automatically divide themselves into segments according to the Divine Proportion.'

Langdon gave a nod. 'Yes, the ratios of line segments in a pentacle all equal Phi, making this symbol the ultimate expression of the Divine Proportion. For this reason, the five-pointed star has always been the symbol for beauty and perfection associated with the goddess and the sacred feminine.'

'COME ON,' Sophie whispered. 'What's wrong? We're almost there!'

Langdon glanced up, returning from his faraway thoughts. He realised he was standing at a dead stop on the stairs, paralysed by sudden revelation. It can't be that simple, he thought. But he knew that it was. He had deciphered Saunière's code.

'O, Draconian devil!' he said. 'Oh, lame saint! It's simple! The scrambled Fibonacci sequence is simply a hint as to how to decipher the rest of the message. O, Draconian devil? Oh, lame saint? Those lines mean nothing. They are simply letters written out of order.'

Sophie needed only an instant to take in the implication. It seemed laughably simple. 'You think this message is an anagram?'

Without another word, Langdon pulled the print-out and a pen from his jacket pocket and rearranged the letters in each line.

O, Draconian devil!
Oh, lame saint!

was a perfect anagram of . . .

Leonardo da Vinci!
The Mona Lisa!

For an instant, Sophie forgot all about trying to leave the Louvre. She was embarrassed at not having deciphered the message herself. Her expertise in complex cryptanalysis had caused her to overlook simplistic word games, and yet she knew she should have seen it. After all, she was no stranger to anagrams in English. When she was young, her grandfather often used anagram games to hone her English spelling. But why his final words to her referred to a famous painting, Sophie had no idea. Though perhaps they were not his final words. Was she supposed to visit the Mona Lisa? Had her grandfather left her a message there? The idea seemed plausible. After all, the painting hung in the Salle des Etats—a chamber only some twenty yards from where he had been found dead.

Sophie gazed back up the emergency stairwell and felt torn. She knew she should usher Langdon from the museum immediately, and yet instinct urged her to do the contrary. As she recalled her first, childhood visit to the Denon Wing, she realised that if her grandfather needed to convey a secret, few places were more apt than the vicinity of da Vinci's *Mona Lisa*.

'SHE'S JUST a little bit farther,' her grandfather had whispered, clutching Sophie's tiny hand as he led her through the museum.

Sophie was six years old. It was after hours and the empty museum frightened her, though she was not about to let her grandfather know that.

'*C'est ennuyeux*,' she grumbled.

'Boring,' he corrected. 'French at school. English at home.'

'*Le Louvre, ce n'est pas chez moi!*' she challenged.

He laughed. 'Right you are. Then let's speak English just for fun.'

Sophie pouted and kept walking. As they entered the Salle des Etats, her eyes settled on the centre of the right-hand wall, where a lone portrait hung behind protective Plexiglas. Arriving in front of the portrait, Sophie held her breath. She was not sure what she had expected to feel, but it most certainly was not this. There was no jolt of amazement, no instant of wonder. She stood in silence.

'What do you think?' her grandfather whispered. 'Beautiful, yes?'

Sophie shook her head. 'She's even worse than in the books. Her face is . . . *brumeux*.'

'Foggy,' her grandfather tutored.

'Foggy,' Sophie repeated.

'That's called the *sfumato* style of painting,' he told her, 'and it's very hard to do. Leonardo da Vinci was better at it than anyone.'

Sophie still didn't like the painting. 'She looks like she knows something . . . like when kids at school have a secret.'

Her grandfather laughed. 'That's part of why she is so famous. People like to guess why she is smiling.'

'Do *you* know why she's smiling?'

'Maybe.' He winked. 'Someday I'll tell you all about it.'

Sophie stamped her foot. 'I don't like secrets!'

'Princess,' he smiled. 'Life is filled with secrets. You can't learn them all at once.'

'I'M GOING BACK UP,' Sophie declared now to Langdon, her voice hollow in the stairwell. 'I think my grandfather may have left me a message at the *Mona Lisa*—some kind of clue as to who killed him. Or why I'm in danger. I have to go and see.'

'But if he wanted to tell you why you were in danger, why wouldn't he simply write it on the floor where he died?'

'Whatever my grandfather was trying to tell me, I don't think he wanted anyone else to see it.'

'I'll come with you.'

'No! You must go to the embassy. Now.'

Langdon seemed hesitant, as if his curiosity were threatening to override sound judgment.

'Go. Now, Mr Langdon. I'll see you at the embassy.' She handed over a set of car keys. 'Mine is the red SmartCar in the employee lot directly outside. Do you know how to get to the embassy?'

Langdon nodded. 'I'll meet you there on one condition.'

She paused, startled. 'What's that?'

'That you stop calling me *Mr* Langdon.'

Sophie noticed the faint hint of a lopsided grin growing across Langdon's face, and felt herself smile back. 'Good luck, Robert.'

LANGDON REACHED the bottom of the stairs. Ahead, an illuminated SORTIE/EXIT sign pointed down a long corridor. As he walked along it, he couldn't help wondering what Sophie would find at the *Mona Lisa*. And why was it Saunière's dying wish that his estranged granddaughter find Langdon? What was it that Saunière thought he knew? After all, it had been Sophie who had spotted the Fibonacci sequence, and, no doubt, given a little more time, she would have deciphered the message with no help from Langdon.

With an unexpected jolt, Langdon stopped. Eyes wide, he dug in his pocket and yanked out the computer print-out. He stared at the last line of Saunière's message. *P.S. Find Robert Langdon.*

P.S.

Saunière's puzzling mix of symbolism suddenly fell into stark focus. Everything the curator had done tonight suddenly made perfect sense. Langdon wheeled round and broke into a sprint, back towards the stairs.

KNEELING IN THE FRONT PEW, Silas pretended to pray as he scanned the layout of Saint-Sulpice. Like most churches of its period, it had been built in the shape of a giant Roman cross. The intersection of the nave and the transept occurred directly beneath the main cupola, the heart of the church, her most sacred and mystical point. But Saint-Sulpice hides her secrets elsewhere, Silas thought, remembering the information that he'd extracted from his victims.

He turned his head to the right. There it was. A thin strip of polished copper, embedded in the grey granite floor of the south transept. The line bore graduated markings, like a ruler, and was part of a kind of astronomical clock, or sundial. The sun's rays, shining through the round window, or oculus, on the south wall, moved farther down the line every day, indicating the passage of time, from solstice to solstice. Tourists, scientists and historians from around the world came to Saint-Sulpice to gaze upon this famous line. The Rose Line.

Slowly, Silas traced the copper strip across the floor. Slicing across the ground on which the main altar stood, it cleaved the communion rail in two and then crossed the entire width of the church, finally arriving at the base of a colossal marble obelisk. Here, the Rose Line took a ninety-degree vertical turn and continued directly up the face of the obelisk to its very apex.

The keystone is hidden beneath the Rose Line. At the base of the Sulpice obelisk. All the brothers had concurred.

For centuries, the symbol of the rose had been used on maps. The compass rose indicated north, east, south and west, the northern direction marked by an arrowhead . . . or, more commonly, a fleur-de-lis.

On a globe, a Rose Line—also called a meridian or line of longitude—was any imaginary line drawn from the North to the South Pole. There were, of course, an infinite number of Rose Lines connecting the poles. The question for early navigators was *which* of these lines should be called *the* Rose Line—zero longitude—the line from which all other longitudes would be measured.

Today that line was in Greenwich, England. But it had not always been so. Long before the establishment of Greenwich as the prime meridian, the line of zero longitude had passed directly through Paris—through the Church of Saint-Sulpice. Although Greenwich had stripped Paris of the honour in 1888, the original Rose Line was still visible today, following a perfect north–south axis within the church.

Silas knelt at the base of the obelisk and ran his hands across the floor. He saw no cracks or markings to indicate a movable tile, so he began rapping softly with his knuckles on the stone surface. Finally, one of the tiles echoed strangely.

Silas smiled. There was a hollow area beneath the floor! His victims had spoken the truth. The keystone lay beneath the sign of the rose.

HIGH ABOVE SILAS, crouching in the shadows of the choir balcony above the altar, Sister Sandrine knew her darkest fears had just been confirmed. The mysterious Opus Dei monk had come to Saint-Sulpice not for sightseeing but for another purpose, a secret purpose.

You are not the only one with secrets, she thought. Sister Sandrine was more than the keeper of this church. She was its sentry. And tonight, the arrival of this stranger meant danger for the brotherhood.

CHAPTER 5

Sophie arrived, breathless, outside the Salle des Etats, reached for the huge wooden doors and pushed. She stood on the threshold a moment, scanning the rectangular chamber, which was bathed in soft red light. The Salle des Etats was one of the museum's rare culs-de-sac, and the only room off the middle of the Grand Gallery.

Even before Sophie entered, she knew she was missing something. If her grandfather had written anything in here, he would have written it with the watermark stylus. She needed a black light.

Taking a deep breath, she hurried out to the Grand Gallery and rushed along it to the well-lit crime scene. Unable to look at her grandfather's body, she focused solely on the PTS tools. Finding a small ultraviolet penlight, she slipped it in the pocket of her sweater and hurried back to the Salle des Etats.

As she turned the corner, the unexpected sound of muffled footsteps came racing towards her. A ghostly figure emerged suddenly from out of the reddish haze and Sophie jumped back.

'There you are!' Langdon's hoarse whisper cut the air.

Her relief was only momentary. 'Robert, if Fache finds you here—'

'Where were you?'

'I had to get the black light. If my grandfather left a message—'

'Sophie, listen.' Langdon's blue eyes held hers firmly. 'The letters P.S. . . . do they mean anything other than your grandfather's pet name for you? Anything at all?'

Afraid their voices might echo down the hall, Sophie pulled him into the Salle des Etats and closed the enormous twin doors silently.

She had indeed seen the initials P.S. once before. It was on the day before her ninth birthday. She had been secretly searching the drawers and cupboards in her grandfather's bedroom for hidden birthday presents, while he was asleep downstairs on the couch. She tiptoed across the creaky wooden floor to his bureau and opened the top drawer. Pulling aside some clothes, she caught a glimpse of a gold chain. Her heart raced. It must be a necklace for me! she thought.

Sophie carefully pulled the chain from the drawer. To her surprise, on the end was a very unusual gold key. Spellbound, she held it up. The shaft was a triangular column with little pockmarks all over it. The large golden head was in the shape of a cross, and embossed in the middle of it were two letters intertwined in a flowery design.

'P.S.,' she whispered as she read them. Whatever could this be?

'Sophie?' her grandfather spoke from the doorway.

Startled, she spun round. 'I . . . was looking for my present,' she said, knowing she had betrayed his trust.

For what seemed like an eternity, her grandfather was silent. Finally, he let out a long breath. 'Sophie, you need to respect other people's privacy.' Gently, he walked over and knelt down beside her. 'This key is very special. If you had lost it . . .'

'I'm sorry, *Grand-père.* I really am.' Sophie paused. 'I thought it was a necklace for my birthday.'

He gazed at her. 'I know, sweetie. You're forgiven. Grandfathers and granddaughters always forgive each other.'

Sophie couldn't help asking, 'What does it open?'

Her grandfather seemed uncertain how to answer. 'It opens a box,' he finally said. 'Where I keep many secrets, important secrets. And someday, if you can keep my key a secret, and never talk about it ever again, to anybody, then someday I will give it to you.'

Sophie couldn't believe her ears. 'You will?'

'I promise. One day the key will be yours. It has your name on it.'

Sophie scowled. 'No it doesn't. It says P.S. My name isn't P.S.!'

'P.S. is a code, Sophie. Your secret initials.'

Her eyes went wide. 'I have secret initials?'

'Of course. Granddaughters *always* have secret initials that only their grandfathers know. And yours stand for *Princesse Sophie.'*

She giggled. 'I'm not a princess!'

'You are to me.'

INSIDE THE SALLE DES ETATS, Sophie endured a sharp pang of loss and remorse. Her grandfather had reached out to her so many times over the past ten years, yet Sophie had remained immovable—leaving his letters unopened in a drawer. Now he was dead, talking to her from the grave.

'The initials,' Langdon whispered. 'Have you seen them?'

Sophie sensed her grandfather's voice whispering in the corridors of the museum. *Never speak of this key, Sophie. To anyone.* But then she remembered: *P.S. Find Robert Langdon.* Her grandfather *wanted* Langdon to help. She nodded. 'Yes, I saw the initials P.S. once. When I was very young.' She hesitated. 'On something very important to him.'

Langdon locked eyes with her. 'Sophie, this is crucial. Can you tell me if the initials appeared with a symbol? A fleur-de-lis?'

Sophie was amazed. 'But . . . how could you possibly know that!'

Langdon lowered his voice. 'I'm fairly certain your grandfather was a member of a secret society. The fleur-de-lis, combined with the initials P.S., is the brotherhood's official emblem.'

'How do you know this?'

'Researching the symbols of secret societies is a specialty of mine. Your grandfather's group call themselves the *Prieuré de Sion*—the Priory of Sion. They're based here in France and some of history's most cultured individuals have been members: men like Botticelli, Sir Isaac Newton, Victor Hugo—and Leonardo da Vinci.'

Sophie stared. 'Da Vinci was in a secret society?'

'Da Vinci was the brotherhood's Grand Master between 1510 and 1519. He and your grandfather share a fraternal bond. And it all fits perfectly with their fascination for feminine deities. But more important, they are the guardians of an ancient secret. One that made them immeasurably powerful.'

Sophie's reaction was one of stark disbelief. And yet—her mind reeled back ten years—to a night when she had witnessed her grandfather in a role she still could not accept. Could that explain—?

'The identities of living Priory members are kept extremely secret,' Langdon continued, 'but the P.S. and fleur-de-lis that you saw as a child are proof. It could *only* have been related to the Priory.'

Sophie realised now that Langdon obviously had much to share with her, but this was not the place. 'There's a lot we need to discuss, but I can't afford to let them catch you, Robert. You need to go!'

A FEW MILES AWAY, on the riverbank beyond Les Invalides, a bewildered lorry driver stood at gunpoint and watched as Bezu Fache let out a roar of rage and threw a bar of soap out into the Seine.

The captain of the police felt dumbstruck as he paced the banks of the river. Who the hell had Langdon rung from the Louvre, he wondered, who might have tipped him off about the GPS dot? He knew Agent Neveu had told him the US Embassy had a message for him from America. And she had given him a code to retrieve the message . . .

It was at that moment, as he eyed his cellular phone, that Fache realised the answer was in the palm of his hand.

Using the cellphone's menu, Fache pulled up a list of recently dialled numbers and found the call Langdon had placed. It had been to a Paris number, followed by the three-digit code 454.

Fache redialled the number and waited as the line began ringing.

Finally a woman's voice answered. '*Bonjour, vous êtes bien chez Sophie Neveu,*' the recording announced. '*Je suis absente pour le moment, mais . . .* '

Fache's blood was boiling as he typed the numbers 4 . . . 5 . . . 4.

DESPITE HER monumental reputation, the *Mona Lisa* was a mere thirty-one by twenty-one inches. Painted on a poplar wood panel, she hung on the northwest wall of the Salle des Etats behind a two-inch-thick pane of protective Plexiglas.

The portrait was still twenty yards ahead when Sophie turned on the black light, and the purplish crescent of its illumination fanned out on the floor in front of them. She swung the beam back and forth across the floor, searching for any hint of luminescent ink.

Langdon, who had made it clear that he had no intention of leaving for the embassy just yet, walked beside her, feeling a tingle of anticipation. The *Mona Lisa*'s status as the most famous piece of art in the world had nothing to do with her enigmatic smile, he knew. She was famous quite simply because Leonardo da Vinci claimed she was his finest accomplishment. He carried the painting with him whenever he travelled and, if asked why, would reply that he found it hard to part with his most sublime expression of female beauty.

Many art historians, however, suspected that da Vinci's reverence for the *Mona Lisa* stemmed from something far deeper, that there was a message hidden in the layers of paint. The public at large still considered the *Mona Lisa*'s smile a great mystery, and yet, to Langdon, there was no mystery.

Recently Langdon had shared the *Mona Lisa*'s secret with a group of students. Standing at an overhead projector, he had told them, 'You may notice that the background behind her face is uneven.' He walked up to the projected image of the painting, and motioned to the glaring discrepancy. 'Da Vinci painted the horizon line on the left significantly lower than the right. It's a trick he played, to make Mona Lisa look larger from the left side than from the right side. A little da Vinci inside joke. Historically, the concepts of male and female have assigned sides—left is female, and right is male. Because da Vinci was a big fan of feminine principles, he made Mona Lisa look more majestic from the left than the right.'

'Why was he into that whole feminine thing?' someone asked.

'Actually, da Vinci was in tune with the *balance* between male and female. He believed that a human soul could not be enlightened unless it had both male and female elements. His Mona Lisa carries a subtle message of androgyny. It is a fusing of male and female. Has anyone here ever heard of an Egyptian god named Amon?'

'Hell yes!' another student said. 'God of masculine fertility!'

'Well done. Amon is indeed represented as a man with a ram's head, and his promiscuity and curved horns are related to our modern sexual slang "horny". And do you know who Amon's counterpart was? The Egyptian goddess of fertility?'

The question met with several seconds of silence.

'It was Isis,' Langdon told them, grabbing a marker pen. 'So we have the male god, Amon.' He wrote it down. 'And the female goddess, Isis, whose ancient pictogram was once called L'ISA.'

Langdon finished writing and stepped back from the projector.

AMON L'ISA

'Mona Lisa,' somebody gasped.

Langdon nodded. 'Not only does the face of Mona Lisa look androgynous, but her name is an anagram of the divine union of male and female. And that, my friends, is da Vinci's little secret, and the reason for Mona Lisa's knowing smile.'

SOPHIE SUDDENLY DROPPED to her knees. 'My grandfather was here,' she said, pointing the black light to a spot on the parquet floor, only ten feet from the *Mona Lisa*.

As Langdon knelt beside her, he saw a tiny drop of dried liquid that was luminescing. Suddenly he recalled what black lights were actually used for. Blood. His senses tingled. Sophie was right. Jacques Saunière had indeed paid a visit to the *Mona Lisa* before he died.

'He must have left a message,' she said. Striding over to the painting she waved the light back and forth across the parquet in front of it. 'There's nothing here!'

But at that moment, Langdon saw a faint purple glimmer on the protective glass. Reaching down, he took Sophie's wrist and slowly moved the light up to the painting itself.

They both froze.

On the glass, six words glowed in purple, scrawled across Mona Lisa's face.

SEATED AT SAUNIÈRE'S DESK, Lieutenant Collet pressed the phone to his ear in disbelief. 'A bar of soap? But how could Langdon have known about the GPS dot?'

'Sophie Neveu told him,' Fache replied. 'I just heard a recording that confirms she tipped him off.'

Collet was speechless. Neveu was not only going to be fired; she was going to jail.

'Have any fire alarms gone off there?' Fache demanded.

'No, sir.'

'And no one has come out under the Grand Gallery gate?'

'No. We've got a security officer on it, as you requested.'

'OK, Langdon must still be inside the Grand Gallery. Send an armed guard to the gate. I don't want Langdon breaking for an exit.' Fache paused. 'And you'd better tell the guard that Agent Neveu is probably in there with him.'

'Agent Neveu left, I thought.'

'Nobody on the perimeter saw her leave. They only saw her go in.'

Collet was flabbergasted by Sophie Neveu's bravado.

'Handle it,' Fache ordered. 'I want Langdon and Neveu at gunpoint by the time I get back.'

LANGDON STARED in astonishment at the six words glowing on the Plexiglas. The text seemed to hover in space, casting a jagged shadow across Mona Lisa's mysterious smile.

SO DARK THE CON OF MAN

'The Priory,' Langdon whispered. 'This proves your grandfather was a member!'

Sophie looked at him in confusion. 'You *understand* this?'

'It's a proclamation of one of the Priory's most fundamental beliefs,' Langdon said, nodding. 'They believe that powerful men in the early

Christian Church "conned" the world—that Constantine and his successors converted the world from matriarchal paganism to patriarchal Christianity by waging a propaganda war that demonised the sacred feminine and obliterated the goddess from modern religion.'

Sophie's expression remained uncertain. 'My grandfather must have been trying to tell me more than *that*.'

Whether a hidden meaning existed in the phrase or not, Langdon could not say. He was still grappling with the bold clarity of the outward message. So dark the con of man, he thought. So dark indeed.

Nobody could deny the enormous good the modern Church did in today's troubled world, and yet the Church had a deceitful and violent history. It was the Catholic Inquisition that published what arguably could be called the most blood-soaked publication ever: *Malleus Maleficarum*—or *The Witches' Hammer*—indoctrinated the world in 'the dangers of freethinking women' and instructed the clergy how to locate, torture and destroy them. Those deemed 'witches' by the Church included all female scholars, priestesses, gypsies, mystics, herb gatherers and any women 'suspiciously attuned to the natural world'. During three hundred years of witch hunts, the Church burned at the stake an astounding five million women.

Women, once celebrated as an essential half of spiritual enlightenment, had been banished from the temples of the world. There were still no female Orthodox rabbis, Catholic priests or Islamic clerics. The once hallowed act of *hieros gamos*—the natural sexual union between man and woman through which each became spiritually whole—had been recast as a shameful act.

Not even the feminine association with the left-hand side could escape the Church's defamation. In France and Italy, the words for 'left'—*gauche and sinistra*—came to have deeply negative overtones, while their right-hand counterparts rang of righteousness, dexterity and correctness.

The Priory of Sion believed that the obliteration of the sacred feminine in modern life had caused an unstable situation marked by testosterone-fuelled wars, a plethora of misogynistic societies and a growing disrespect for Mother Earth.

'Robert!' Sophie's whisper yanked him back. 'Someone's coming!'

He heard the approaching footsteps out in the hallway as Sophie extinguished the black light.

'Over here!' she called.

For an instant Langdon felt totally blind. *Over where?* As his vision cleared he saw Sophie's silhouette ducking out of sight behind the octagonal viewing bench in the centre of the room. He was about to dash after her when a voice stopped him cold.

'*Arrêtez!*' The Louvre security agent advanced, his pistol aimed at Langdon's chest. '*Couchez-vous!*' the guard commanded. 'Lie down!'

INSIDE SAINT-SULPICE, Silas carried the heavy iron votive candle holder from the altar back towards the obelisk. He examined the grey marble panel that covered the apparent hollow in the floor and realised he could not shatter it without making considerable noise.

Silas wrapped the altar's linen mantle over the end of the iron rod, then drove it into the centre of the floor tile. A muffled thud. He drove the pole into the tile again. Again a dull thud, but this time accompanied by a crack. On the third swing, the tile shattered, and fragments fell into a hollow beneath the floor.

Quickly pulling the remaining pieces from the opening, Silas reached inside. At first he felt nothing. Then, reaching deeper, he touched something! A thick stone tablet. He gripped it and gently lifted it clear. As he read the words engraved on it, he felt surprise. He had expected the keystone to be a map, or a complex series of directions. Instead, it bore the simplest of inscriptions: Job 38:11.

Silas was barely able to contain his excitement. The Book of Job told the story of a man whose faith in God survived repeated tests.

Smiling, he went to get the enormous leather-bound Bible that sat on the main altar, propped open on a gilded book stand.

UP IN THE BALCONY, Sister Sandrine was shaking. She could not imagine how he knew of the keystone, and she knew she did not have time to think. Trembling, she raced down the hall to her quarters where she reached beneath her wooden bed frame and retrieved the sealed envelope she had hidden there years ago.

Tearing it open, she found four Paris phone numbers.

SILAS FLIPPED through the Old Testament until he found the Book of Job. He located chapter thirty-eight and ran his finger down the column of text, anticipating the words he was about to read.

They will lead the way!

Finding verse number eleven, Silas read the text. Seven words. Confused, he read them again, sensing something had gone terribly wrong. The verse simply read:

HITHERTO SHALT THOU COME, BUT NO FURTHER

SECURITY GUARD Claude Grouard simmered with rage as he stood over his prostrate captive in front of the *Mona Lisa*. This bastard killed Jacques Saunière, he thought. The curator had been like a father to Grouard and his team.

Grouard yanked his walkie-talkie off his belt and attempted to radio for back-up. All he heard was static. The additional electronic security in this chamber was playing havoc with the signal. Still aiming his weapon at Langdon, Grouard backed slowly towards the entrance. On his third step he spied something that made him stop short.

An inexplicable mirage was materialising near the centre of the room. A silhouette. Someone else was in the room. A woman was moving through the darkness, swinging a purplish beam of light back and forth across the floor in front of her.

'*Qui est là?*' Grouard demanded.

'PTS,' the woman replied, still scanning the floor with her light.

Grouard was sweating now. Why would they be looking for evidence in here?

'*Votre nom!*' Grouard yelled, sure something was amiss.

'*C'est moi*,' the voice responded in calm French. '*Sophie Neveu.*'

The name registered in Grouard's mind. Sophie Neveu? Wasn't she Saunière's granddaughter? She used to come in here as a little kid. But that was hardly a reason to trust her; Grouard had heard the rumours of the falling-out between Saunière and his granddaughter.

'You know me,' the woman called. 'And Robert Langdon did not kill my grandfather. Believe me.'

Grouard was not about to take *that* on faith. He needed back-up. Trying his walkie-talkie again, he got only static. The entrance was still a good twenty yards behind him, and he began backing up slowly, his gun still trained on the man on the floor. He could see the woman raising her UV light and scrutinising a large painting that hung on the far side of the Salle, opposite the *Mona Lisa*.

Grouard gasped. What in the name of God is she doing?

ACROSS THE ROOM, Sophie Neveu felt a cold sweat breaking across her forehead. She was scanning the area round another da Vinci masterpiece. But the UV light revealed nothing out of the ordinary. Not on the floor, on the walls, or even on the canvas itself.

There must be something here! she thought.

Sophie pictured the message her grandfather had scrawled on the protective glass of the *Mona Lisa. So dark the con of man.* The painting before her had no protective glass, and Sophie knew her grandfather would never have written on the painting itself.

At least, not on the front. Grabbing the bottom of the frame, which was suspended by cables from the ceiling, she pulled it towards her, away from the wall. She slipped her head and shoulders in behind the painting and raised the black light to inspect the back. Had her instinct been wrong? There was no text on the back of the painting, only the backside of ageing canvas and—

Wait. Sophie's eyes locked on a glint of lustrous metal lodged near the bottom edge of the frame. A shimmering gold chain dangled off it.

To Sophie's amazement, the chain was affixed to the familiar gold key, the key she had not seen since she was nine years old. In that instant, she realised the entire purpose of tonight's word game. Not wanting it to fall into the hands of the police, her grandfather had devised an ingenious treasure hunt to ensure only Sophie would find it.

'*Au secours!*' the guard yelled.

Sophie snatched the key from behind the painting and slipped it deep in her pocket, along with the black-light pen. She could see the guard was still trying desperately to raise someone on the walkie-talkie. He was backing quickly towards the entrance now, and Sophie knew she had to act immediately, before he found a signal.

Gazing up at the large painting, Sophie realised that Leonardo da Vinci, for the second time tonight, was there to help.

ANOTHER FEW STEPS, Grouard told himself, his gun still levelled.

'*Arrêtez! Ou je la détruis!*' the woman's voice echoed across the room.

Grouard glanced over and stopped in his tracks. The woman had lifted the painting off its cables and propped it on the floor in front of her. His first thought was to wonder why the painting's trip wires hadn't set off alarms, then he realised the sensors hadn't yet been reset.

'Set down your gun and radio,' the woman said calmly in French, 'or I'll destroy this painting.' The canvas started to bulge in the middle. She was pushing her knee into it from behind.

'Please . . . no,' Grouard pleaded, realising that he couldn't put a bullet through a da Vinci. He dropped his gun and radio, raising his hands over his head.

'Thank you,' the woman said. 'Now do exactly as I tell you, and everything will work out fine.'

MOMENTS LATER, Langdon was running beside Sophie down the emergency stairwell towards the ground level. Neither of them had said a word since leaving the trembling Louvre guard lying in the Salle des

Etats. His pistol was now clutched tightly in Langdon's hands.

'You chose a valuable hostage,' he said as they ran.

'*Madonna of the Rocks*,' she replied. 'But I didn't choose it; my grandfather did. He left me a little something behind the painting.'

Langdon shot her a startled look. 'How did you know which painting?'

'So dark the con of man.' She flashed a triumphant smile. 'I missed the first two anagrams, Robert. I wasn't about to miss the third.'

CHAPTER 6

'They're dead!' Sister Sandrine stammered into the telephone. 'Please pick up! They're all dead!'

The first three phone numbers on the list had produced terrifying results—a hysterical widow, a detective working late at a murder scene and a sombre priest consoling a bereaved family. All three had told her that her contacts were dead. And now, having called the fourth and final number, she had got an answering machine.

Sister Sandrine did not know the identities of the four men she protected, but the private phone numbers stashed beneath her bed were for use on one condition only. *If that floor panel is ever broken,* she had been told, *it means one of us has been mortally threatened and been forced to tell a desperate lie. Call the numbers. Warn the others.*

'Please answer,' she whispered in fear.

'Hang up the phone,' a deep voice said from the doorway.

Turning in terror, she saw the monk, clutching a heavy iron candle stand. Shaking, she set the phone back in the cradle.

'They are dead,' he said. 'All four of them. And they have played me for a fool. Tell me where the keystone is.'

'I don't know!' Sister Sandrine said truthfully.

The man advanced, his white fists gripping the candle stand. 'You are a sister of the Church, and yet you serve *them*?' A sudden rage erupted behind the monk's eyes. He lunged, using the iron stand like a club.

As Sister Sandrine fell, her last thought was: The precious truth is lost for ever.

THE SECURITY ALARM on the west end of the Denon Wing sent the pigeons in the nearby Tuileries gardens scattering as Langdon and Sophie dashed out into the Paris night. As they ran to Sophie's car,

Langdon could hear police sirens wailing in the distance.

'That's it there,' Sophie called, pointing to a red SmartCar.

The vehicle was easily the smallest car Langdon had ever seen. He had barely thrown himself into the passenger seat before Sophie gunned the little two-seater up and over a kerb onto a gravel island. He gripped the dashboard as the car shot out across a pavement, circled the Carrousel du Louvre and exited towards Rue de Rivoli.

The police sirens blared louder behind them. Langdon looked out of the rear window. The police did not seem to be chasing them. The sea of blue lights was assembling at the museum. His heartbeat finally slowing, he turned back round. 'The painting. What was behind it?'

Her eyes remained on the road. She was now turning into the Champs-Elysées. 'I'll show you once we're safely inside the embassy.'

Langdon was surprised. 'He left you a physical object?'

Sophie nodded. 'Embossed with a fleur-de-lis and the initials P.S.'

Langdon couldn't believe his ears.

WE'RE GOING to make it, Sophie thought as she cut sharply past the luxurious Hôtel de Crillon into Paris's tree-lined diplomatic neighbourhood. The embassy was less than a mile away.

Even as she drove, Sophie's mind remained locked on the key in her pocket. Her work in the intelligence community taught her plenty about security, and she knew that the key's peculiar shaft was a laser-tooled, varying matrix, impossible to duplicate. Rather than teeth that moved tumblers, the complex series of hexagonal pockmarks were designed to be examined by an electric eye.

Sophie could not begin to imagine what a key like this opened, but the cruciform top implied the key belonged to some kind of Christian organisation. Yet Sophie knew her grandfather was no Christian . . .

She'd had proof of that one Saturday ten years ago. Returning from university in Britain for spring break a few days early, she had been disappointed not to find her grandfather at their Paris home. His car was gone from the garage. Jacques Saunière despised city driving, and kept a car for one destination only: his house in Normandy, where he went at weekends. Sophie decided to leave immediately and surprise him. Borrowing a friend's car, she drove west.

She turned into the long private driveway to her grandfather's retreat at just after ten o'clock at night. Having half expected to find him asleep at this hour, she was excited to see lights twinkling at the windows. Her delight turned to surprise, however, when she found the driveway filled with cars—Mercedeses, BMWs and a Rolls-Royce.

She hurried to the front door, but found it locked. She knocked. Nobody answered. Puzzled, she walked round and tried the back door. It too was locked. She hurried to the side of the house, clambered up on a woodpile and pressed her face to the living-room window. The entire ground floor looked deserted.

Heart racing, Sophie ran to fetch the spare key her grandfather kept hidden under a kindling box. She let herself in through the front door and stepped into the deserted foyer.

She stood a moment in the silence, wondering what could possibly be happening. And then she heard it. Muffled voices, coming from underneath her. Crouching, she put her ear to the floor. Yes, the sound was definitely coming from below. The voices seemed to be singing, or . . . *chanting*? She was frightened. Almost more eerie than the sound itself was the realisation that this house did not even have a basement. At least, none she'd ever seen.

Scanning the living room, Sophie's eyes fell on the only object that seemed out of place—an Aubusson tapestry that usually hung on the east wall beside the fireplace. Tonight it had been pulled aside on its brass rod, exposing the panelled wall behind it.

As she walked towards the wall, the chanting seemed to get louder. Sophie leaned her ear against the wood. The voices were clearer now, intoning words she could not discern. She felt around the edge of the panels, and to her surprise found a recessed fingerhold. Heart pounding, she placed her finger in it and pulled. With noiseless precision, the heavy wall slid sideways. Voices echoed up from the darkness beyond.

Sophie slipped through and found herself on a rough-hewn stone staircase that spiralled downwards. Holding her breath, she descended. What she saw when she rounded the last step took her several seconds to process.

The room was a coarse chamber, lit only by flaming torches on the walls. Thirty or so people stood in a circle, all wearing masks. The women were dressed in white gossamer gowns and golden shoes. Their masks were white, and in their hands they carried golden orbs. The men wore long black tunics, and their masks were black. Everyone in the circle rocked back and forth, chanting in reverence to something on the floor before them . . . something Sophie could not see.

The chanting grew louder, faster. The participants took a step inward and knelt. In that instant, Sophie could finally see what they were witnessing. Even as she staggered back in horror, the image seared itself into her memory for ever. She clambered up the stairs and fled the house.

That night, with her life shattered by disillusionment, she drove back to Paris, packed her belongings and left her home. On the dining-room table, she left a note for her grandfather: *I was there. Don't try to find me*.

'Sophie!' Langdon's voice intruded. 'Stop! Stop!'

Emerging from her reverie, Sophie slammed on the brakes, skidding to a halt. 'What? What happened?!'

Langdon pointed down the long street before them.

Sophie's blood went cold. A hundred yards ahead, the intersection was blocked by a couple of DCPJ police cars. They had sealed off Avenue Gabriel.

Putting the car in reverse, she performed a composed three-point turn. As she drove away, she heard the sound of squealing tyres behind them. Sirens blared to life.

Cursing, Sophie slammed down the accelerator.

LANGDON SAT white-knuckled in the passenger seat as Sophie tore through the diplomatic quarter, and finally emerged back onto the Champs-Elysées. Behind the wheel, Sophie was fishing in her sweater pocket. She removed a small metal object and held it out for him.

'Robert, you'd better have a look at this,' she said. 'This is what my grandfather left me behind *Madonna of the Rocks*.'

Feeling a shiver of anticipation, Langdon took the object and examined it. It was heavy and shaped like a cross, and its triangular shaft was pockmarked with hundreds of tiny hexagons.

'It's a laser-cut key,' Sophie told him, changing lanes. 'Those hexagons are read by an electric eye. Look at the other side.'

When Langdon turned the key over, his jaw dropped. There, intricately embossed on the centre of the cross, was a stylised fleur-de-lis with the initials P.S. 'Sophie,' he said, 'this is the seal I told you about! The official emblem of the Priory of Sion.'

She nodded. 'As I told you, I saw the key a long time ago. My grandfather told me it opened a box where he kept many secrets, and that I should never speak of it again.'

Langdon tried to imagine what kind of secrets a man like Jacques Saunière might keep. What was an ancient brotherhood doing with a futuristic key? 'Do you know what it opens?' he asked.

Sophie looked disappointed. 'I was hoping *you* knew.'

Langdon frowned. 'I haven't a clue. All I can tell you is that equal-armed crosses like this one predate Christianity by fifteen hundred years and are considered peaceful crosses. Their balanced vertical and horizontal arms convey a natural union of male and female, making them symbolically consistent with Priory philosophy.'

'OK, we have to get off the road.' Sophie checked her rearview mirror. 'We need a safe place to figure out what that key opens.'

Langdon thought longingly of his comfortable room at the Ritz, then said, 'Let's call the embassy. I can explain the situation and have them send someone to meet us somewhere.'

'Meet us?' Sophie turned and stared at him as if he were crazy. 'Robert, your embassy has no jurisdiction except on their own property. Sending someone to retrieve us would be considered aiding a fugitive of the French government. It won't happen. How much cash do you have?'

'A few hundred dollars. A few euros. Why?'

'Credit cards?"

'Of course."

She accelerated towards the Arc de Triomphe, and Langdon sensed she was formulating a plan. Her eyes were on the rearview mirror as they approached the immense nine-lane roundabout encircling the arch.

'We lost them for the time being,' she said, 'but we won't last another five minutes if we stay in this car.'

'What are you going to do?'Langdon asked.

'Trust me.'

Langdon made no response. Trust had not got him far this evening.

Now they were heading away from the rich, tree-lined streets, plunging into a darker, industrial neighbourhood. Sophie took a quick left, and a moment later, Langdon realised where they were.

The Gare Saint-Lazare.

Even at this hour, a half-dozen taxis idled near the main entrance to the glass-roofed train terminal. Sophie pulled in behind them and, before Langdon could ask what was going on, she was out of the car and speaking to one of the drivers.

As Langdon got out of the SmartCar, he saw Sophie hand the taxi driver a wad of cash. The driver nodded and then, to Langdon's bewilderment, sped off without them.

'What happened?' Langdon demanded, joining Sophie on the kerb as the taxi disappeared.

Sophie was already heading for the train station entrance. 'Come on. We're buying two tickets on the next train out of Paris.'

Langdon hurried along beside her. What had begun as a one-mile dash to the US Embassy had now become a fully fledged evacuation from Paris. Langdon was liking the idea less and less.

THE DRIVER who collected Bishop Aringarosa from Leonardo da Vinci International Airport pulled up in an unimpressive black Fiat sedan. Gone were the days when all Vatican transports were luxury cars sporting flags emblazoned with the seal of the Holy See.

Bundling his black cassock around himself, Aringarosa climbed into the back seat and settled in for the long drive to Castel Gandolfo. It would be the same ride as the one he'd taken five months ago.

The longest night of my life, he thought, and sighed.

Five months ago, the Vatican had phoned to request Aringarosa's immediate presence in Rome, and he had had no choice but to accept the invitation, albeit reluctantly. Like most conservative clergy, he was not a fan of the current papal administration and had watched with grave concern as the new Pope settled into his first year in office. The Holy Father had wasted no time in flexing all the muscle associated with the highest office in Christendom. Drawing on a tide of liberal support within the College of Cardinals, he was declaring his papal mission to be 'the updating of Catholicism for the third millennium'.

Aringarosa had been using all of his political sway—substantial considering the size of the Opus Dei constituency and its bankroll—to try to persuade the Pope and his advisers that softening the Church's laws was political suicide. He reminded them that previous tempering of Church law—the Vatican II fiasco—had left a devastating legacy: Church attendance was now lower than ever, donations were drying up, and there were not even enough Catholic priests to preside over their churches. People needed structure and direction from the Church, Aringarosa insisted, not coddling and indulgence!

On that night, Aringarosa had been taken to the Pope's summer residence, an impressive sixteenth-century citadel in a dramatic cliffside setting in the Alban hills.

As he followed the young Jesuit priest who greeted him up the wide marble staircase that rose from the foyer of Castel Gandolfo, Bishop Aringarosa could not have imagined the shocking news he was about to receive, or the deadly chain of events it would put into motion.

Now, seated in the Fiat, the bishop tried to ease his nerves, fingering his fourteen-carat gold bishop's ring with its purple amethyst and large diamonds. He reminded himself that this ring was symbolic of a power far less than that which he would soon attain.

THE INSIDE OF GARE Saint-Lazare looked like every other train station in Europe, a gaping cavern dotted with the usual suspects—homeless men holding cardboard signs, collections of bleary-eyed college kids sleeping on backpacks, and clusters of blue-clad station staff.

Sophie raised her eyes to the enormous departure board overhead. The first listing read: LILLE—RAPIDE—03.06.

'I wish it left sooner,' Sophie said, 'but Lille will have to do.'

Sooner? Langdon checked his watch: 2.59 a.m. The train left in seven minutes and they didn't even have tickets yet.

Sophie guided Langdon to the ticket window and told him, 'Buy us two tickets with your credit card.'

'I thought credit card usage could be traced by—'

'Exactly.'

Langdon decided to stop trying to keep ahead of Sophie Neveu. Using his Visa card, he purchased two tickets to Lille, then Sophie guided him out towards the platforms. Tones chimed overhead and a PA announcer gave the final boarding call to passengers for Lille. At platform three, the train to Lille was belching and wheezing in preparation for departure, but Sophie had her arm through Langdon's and was guiding him in the opposite direction. They hurried through a side door and out onto a quiet street on the side of the station.

A lone taxi sat idling by the doorway. The driver saw Sophie and flicked his lights. She jumped in the back seat. Langdon got in after her.

As the taxi pulled away from the station, Sophie took out their newly purchased train tickets and tore them up.

Langdon sighed. Seventy dollars well spent.

As soon as they had settled into a monotonous northbound hum on Rue de Clichy, Langdon examined the cruciform key again. In the intermittent glow of passing streetlights, he saw no markings on it that might have indicated where the key had been made.

'It doesn't make sense,' he said. 'Are you sure your grandfather didn't write anything else on the back of the painting?'

'I searched the whole area. This key is all there was.'

Langdon frowned, peering at the blunt end of the triangular shaft. Nothing. He brought the key close to his eyes and examined the rim of the head. Nothing there either. 'I think this key was cleaned recently. It smells of rubbing alcohol.' He held the key to his nose and sniffed. 'Yes, it's like it's been buffed with a cleaner or—' Langdon stopped, angled the key to the light and looked at the smooth surface of one of the arms of the cross. It seemed to shimmer in places . . . like it was wet. 'Do you still have the black light?' he asked.

Sophie reached in her pocket and produced the penlight. Langdon took it and switched it on, shining the beam on the key.

Instantly, a line of luminesced writing appeared: *24 RUE HAXO*.

OUTSIDE THE SALLE des Etats, Bezu Fache was fuming as Grouard explained how Sophie and Langdon had disarmed him.

'Captain?' Lieutenant Collet loped towards them from the direction of the command post. 'They've located Agent Neveu's car.'

'Did she make the embassy?'

'No. Train station. Bought two tickets. Train just left.'

Fache waved off warden Grouard and led Collet to a nearby alcove, addressing him in hushed tones. 'What was the destination?'

'Lille.'

'Probably a decoy.' Fache exhaled, formulating a plan. 'OK, alert the next station, have the train stopped and searched, just in case. Leave her car where it is and put plainclothes on watch in case they try to come back to it. Send men to search the streets around the station in case they fled on foot. Are buses running from the station?'

'Not at this hour, sir. Only the taxi queue.'

'Good. Question the drivers. See if they saw anything. Then contact the taxi company with descriptions. I'm calling Interpol.'

Collet looked surprised. 'You're putting this on the *wire*?'

Fache regretted the potential embarrassment, but he saw no choice. He had to close the net fast, and close it tight. The first hour was critical. Fugitives were predictable during the first hour after escape. They always needed the same thing. Travel. Lodging. Cash. By broadcast-faxing photos of Langdon and Sophie to Paris travel authorities, hotels and banks, Interpol would leave them no options—no way to leave the city, no place to hide, and no way to withdraw cash without being recognised. Usually, fugitives panicked and did something stupid. Stole a car. Robbed a store. Whatever mistake they committed, they quickly made their whereabouts known.

A female cryptologist and a professor? They wouldn't last till dawn.

'TELL ME EVERYTHING you know about the Priory of Sion,' Sophie said, as the taxi sped through the Bois de Boulogne towards Rue Haxo.

Langdon wondered where to begin. The brotherhood's astonishing history spanned more than a millennium. 'The Priory of Sion,' he began, 'was founded in Jerusalem in 1099 by a French king named Godefroi de Bouillon, immediately after he had conquered the city. King Godefroi was allegedly the possessor of a powerful secret that had been in his family since the time of Christ. Fearing it might be lost when he died, he founded a secret brotherhood—the Priory of Sion—and charged them with protecting his secret by passing it on from generation to generation. Then, after Godefroi's death, the Priory learned of documents buried beneath the ruins of Herod's temple, which had been built on top of the earlier ruins of Solomon's temple. These documents, they believed, corroborated Godefroi's secret and were so explosive in nature that the Church would stop at nothing to get them.'

Sophie's eyes were riveted on him.

'The Priory vowed that no matter how long it took, these documents must be recovered and protected for ever, so that the truth would never die. In order to retrieve the documents from the ruins, the Priory created a military arm—a group of nine knights called the Order of the Poor Knights of Christ and the Temple of Solomon.' Langdon paused. 'More commonly known as the Knights Templar.'

Sophie looked surprised. 'I thought the Knights Templar were founded to protect the Holy Land.'

'A common misconception. Protection of pilgrims was the *guise* under which the Templars sought to retrieve the documents from beneath the temple. They were allowed to take up residence inside the shrine and for almost a decade they excavated secretly through solid rock.'

'And did they find anything?'

Langdon grinned. 'Nobody knows for sure, but the one thing on which all academics agree is this: the Knights eventually discovered *something* down there in the ruins that made them wealthy and powerful beyond anyone's wildest imagination. They took the treasure from the temple and travelled to Europe, where their influence seemed to grow overnight. Nobody was certain whether the Knights had blackmailed the Vatican or whether the Church simply tried to buy the Knights' silence, but Pope Innocent II immediately issued an unprecedented papal bull that afforded the Knights Templar limitless power and declared them "a law unto themselves".

'With their new carte blanche from the Vatican, the Knights Templar expanded at a staggering rate, amassing vast estates in over a dozen countries. They began extending credit to bankrupt royals and charging interest in return, thereby establishing modern banking and broadening their wealth and influence still further. By the 1300s, Pope Clement V decided that something had to be done to diminish the Knights' influence, so he devised an ingenious operation to quash the Templars and seize their treasure. On Friday, October the 13th, 1307, in a military manoeuvre worthy of the CIA, he issued secret sealed orders to be opened simultaneously by his soldiers all across Europe.

'Clement's orders pronounced that God had visited him in a vision and warned him that the Knights Templar were heretics, guilty of devil worship, sodomy, defiling the cross and other blasphemous behaviour.

He said he'd been asked by God to cleanse the earth by rounding up all the Knights and getting them to confess their crimes. The operation went off with clockwork precision. On that day, countless Knights were captured, tortured and burned at the stake as heretics. To this day, Friday the 13th is considered unlucky.'

Sophie looked confused. 'The Knights Templar were obliterated? I thought fraternities of Templars still existed today?'

'They do, under a variety of names. Despite Clement's best efforts, some of the Knights managed to escape the Vatican purges, and the Templars' potent treasure trove of documents, which had apparently been Clement's true objective, slipped through his fingers.'

'Where did the documents go?'

Langdon shrugged. 'The answer to that is probably known only to the Priory of Sion, but current speculation places the documents somewhere in the United Kingdom.'

Sophie looked uneasy.

'For a thousand years,' Langdon continued, 'legends about this secret have been passed on, and the secret has become known by a single name—Sangreal. Few mysteries have inspired as much interest among historians as the Sangreal.'

'The Sangreal? Does the word have anything to do with the French word *sang* or Spanish *sangre*—meaning "blood"?'

Langdon nodded. 'The legend is complicated, but the important thing to remember is that the Priory guards the proof, and is purportedly awaiting the right moment in history to reveal the truth.'

'What truth? What secret could possibly be that powerful?'

Langdon took a deep breath. 'Sophie, the word *Sangreal* is an ancient word that has evolved over the years into another term . . . a more modern name.' He paused. 'When I tell you it, you'll realise you already know a lot about it.'

Sophie looked sceptical.

Langdon smiled. 'The phrase derives from the French *Sangraal*, which evolved into Sangreal, and was eventually split into two words, *San Greal*. You're used to hearing it called by the name "Holy Grail".'

Sophie was clearly surprised. 'But I thought the Holy Grail was a *cup*, the cup that Jesus drank from at the Last Supper and with which Joseph of Arimathea later caught his blood at the crucifixion.'

Langdon leaned towards her. 'According to the Priory of Sion,' he said softly, 'the Sangreal documents are buried with the Grail itself, and reveal its true meaning. That's why they gave the Knights Templar so much power. The Priory also claim that the Grail legend of a chalice is actually an allegory, that the chalice is a metaphor for something far more powerful.' He paused. 'Something that fits perfectly with all your grandfather's symbologic references to the sacred feminine.'

'But if the Holy Grail is not a cup, what is it?'

Langdon had known this question was coming, and yet he still felt uncertain exactly how to present the answer.

'This manuscript claims *what*?' his editor had said a few months earlier, after Langdon handed him a draft of the manuscript he was working on. 'You can't be serious.'

With a quiet smile, Langdon had replied, 'Serious enough to have spent a year researching it.'

Now Langdon's thoughts were shattered as Sophie's shouts cut the air inside the taxi. '*Laissez-le!*'

She was leaning forwards and yelling at the taxi driver, who was clutching his radio mouthpiece and speaking into it.

Before Langdon knew what had happened, Sophie had turned and plunged her hand into the pocket of his tweed jacket, yanking out the security guard's pistol and pressing it to the back of the driver's head. The man instantly dropped his radio.

'Sophie!' Langdon choked. 'What the hell—?'

'*Arrêtez!*' Sophie commanded the driver.

Trembling, the driver obeyed, stopping the car.

It was then that Langdon heard the metallic voice of the taxi company's dispatcher. '. . . *qui s'appelle Agent Sophie Neveu* . . .' the radio crackled. '*Et un Américain, Robert Langdon* . . .'

Langdon's muscles turned rigid.

'*Descendez,*' Sophie demanded.

The bewildered driver raised his arms over his head as he got out of his taxi and took several steps backwards.

Sophie had rolled down her window and now aimed the gun outside at the cabbie. 'Robert,' she said quietly, 'take the wheel.'

Langdon was not about to argue with a woman wielding a gun. He climbed out of the car and jumped in the driver's seat. He looked down at the controls and hesitated. 'Sophie? Maybe you—'

'Go!' she yelled. 'Drive us out of here.'

Langdon groped for the car's controls. The tyres howled as the taxi leapt forward, fishtailing wildly.

'*Doucement!*' Sophie said, as the car lurched down the road. 'What are you doing?'

'I tried to warn you,' he shouted over the sound of gnashing gears. 'I drive an automatic!'

SILAS DOUBTED that anything could match the anguish now gripping his pale body. He had been deceived. The brothers had lied, choosing death instead of revealing their true secret. Not only had he killed the only four people who knew where the keystone was hidden, he had killed a nun in Saint-Sulpice. Her death complicated matters, and endangered Bishop Aringarosa, who had placed the phone call that got Silas into Saint-Sulpice.

Silas gazed blankly at the floor of his room at the Opus Dei residence in Rue de la Bruyère, and pondered taking his own life. After all, it had been Aringarosa who gave Silas life in the first place: educating him, giving him purpose. Before that, Silas had lived a life of homelessness and violence on the streets of Marseilles, an outcast even among other runaways because of his strange appearance.

'My friend,' Aringarosa had told him, 'you were born an albino. Do you not understand how special this makes you? You are destined for great things, Silas. The Lord needs your help to do His work.'

Kneeling now on the wooden floor, Silas prayed for forgiveness. Then, stripping off his robe, he reached for the Discipline—the heavy knotted rope with which he would whip himself.

STRUGGLING with the gear shift, Langdon managed to get the hijacked taxi to the far side of the Bois de Boulogne, stalling only twice. Unfortunately, the taxi dispatcher repeatedly hailed their cab over the radio. '*Voiture cinq-six-trois. Où êtes-vous? Répondez!*'

When Langdon reached the edge of the park, he jammed on the brakes. 'You'd better drive.'

Sophie looked relieved as she jumped behind the wheel.

'Which way is Rue Haxo?' Langdon asked.

'It's near the Roland Garros tennis stadium. I know the area.'

Langdon pulled the heavy key from his pocket again, feeling its weight in his palm. He sensed it was an object of enormous consequence. Quite possibly the key to his own freedom.

Earlier, while telling Sophie about the Knights Templar, Langdon had realised that this key, in addition to having the Priory seal embossed on it, possessed a more subtle tie to the Priory of Sion. In paintings, Knights Templar were depicted wearing white tunics emblazoned with red crosses like the square cross on the key, except that the arms of the Templar cross were slightly flared at the ends.

Langdon felt his imagination starting to run wild as he fantasised about what they might now find. *The Holy Grail*. He almost laughed out loud at the absurdity of it. The Grail was believed to be somewhere in England, buried in a hidden chamber beneath one of the many Templar churches, where it had been hidden since at least 1500.

To keep their powerful secret safe, the Priory had been forced to move the documents many times. Historians now reckoned there had been six Grail relocations. The last Grail 'sighting' had been in 1447, when numerous eyewitnesses described a fire that had broken out and almost engulfed the documents before they were carried to safety in four huge chests. After that, nobody had claimed to have seen the Grail ever again. All that remained were rumours that it was in Britain, in the land of King Arthur and the Knights of the Round Table.

Wherever it was, two important facts remained: Leonardo, as a Grand Master of the Priory, knew where the Grail resided during his lifetime. And that hiding place had probably not changed to this day.

For this reason, Grail enthusiasts still pored over da Vinci's art and diaries in hopes of unearthing a clue to the Grail's current location. Some claimed the mountainous backdrop in *Madonna of the Rocks* matched the topography of a series of cave-riddled hills in Scotland. Others insisted that the suspicious placement of disciples in *The Last Supper* was some kind of code.

Sophie interrupted Langdon's thoughts. 'Is it possible that the key you're holding unlocks the hiding place of the Holy Grail?'

Langdon's laugh sounded forced, even to him. 'I really can't imagine. Besides, the Grail is believed to be hidden in the United Kingdom somewhere, not France. Sophie, the location of the Holy Grail is one of the best-kept secrets in history. Priory members must prove themselves trustworthy over decades before being elevated to the highest echelons of the fraternity. Although the Priory brotherhood is large, only *four* members at any given time know where the Grail is hidden—the Grand Master and his three *sénéchaux*. The probability of your grandfather being one of those four top people is very slim.'

Sophie said nothing. Her eyes remained focused on the road. Sirens howled somewhere in the distance.

'There!' Langdon said, excited at seeing the huge complex of the Roland Garros tennis stadium looming ahead.

Soon they were turning into Rue Haxo.

We need number twenty-four, Langdon told himself, realising he was secretly scanning the rooftops for the spire of a church. Don't be ridiculous. A forgotten Templar church in this neighbourhood?

'There it is,' Sophie exclaimed, pointing.

Ahead of them was a squat, modern building with a giant, neon equal-armed cross emblazoned atop its façade. Beneath the cross were the words: DEPOSITORY BANK OF ZÜRICH.

Langdon was thankful he had not shared his Templar church hopes with Sophie. He had entirely forgotten that the equal-armed cross had been adopted as the symbol for the flag of neutral Switzerland.

He was holding the key to a Swiss bank deposit box.

OUTSIDE CASTEL GANDOLFO, the mountain air sent a chill through Bishop Aringarosa as he stepped from the Fiat.

The priest who greeted him at the door was the same one who had greeted him five months ago. Tonight he did so with much less hospitality. 'We were worried about you, Bishop,' he said, checking his watch and looking more perturbed than worried.

'My apologies. Airlines are so unreliable these days.'

'They are waiting in the library. I will escort you up.'

The library was a vast square room with dark wood from floor to ceiling. On all sides, towering bookcases groaned under the weight of volumes. The floor was amber marble, edged with black basalt.

'Welcome, Bishop,' a voice said from across the room.

Aringarosa tried to see who had spoken, but the lights were ridiculously low. He could just about see the shapes of three men at a long table on the far side of the room. The silhouette of the man in the middle was immediately recognisable—the obese Secretarius Vaticana, overlord of all legal matters within Vatican City. The other two were high-ranking Italian cardinals.

Aringarosa crossed the library towards them. 'My humble apologies for the hour. We're on different time zones. You must be tired.'

'Not at all,' the secretarius said. 'We are grateful you have come so far. And we are very pleased with your expediency. You have acted more quickly than we imagined. The least we can do is be awake to meet you. Can we offer you some refreshment?'

'I'd prefer we don't pretend this is a social visit. I have another plane to catch. Shall we get to business?'

'Of course,' the secretarius said.

Aringarosa's eyes travelled the length of the long table to a large black briefcase. 'The funds are exactly as I requested?'

'They are.' The secretarius sounded uneasy. 'Although I admit we are concerned. Are you certain we cannot wire them to you somewhere?'

'I have no concerns for my own safety. God is with me.' Aringarosa walked to the end of the table and opened the briefcase. Inside were two thick stacks of bonds, each embossed with the Vatican seal and the title PORTATORE, making the bonds redeemable anywhere in the world by whoever possessed them.

The secretarius looked tense. 'I must say, Bishop, all of us would feel less apprehensive if these funds were in cash. These bonds are traceable directly to the Vatican Bank.'

Aringarosa smiled inwardly. That was precisely the reason the Teacher had suggested that Aringarosa get the money in Vatican Bank bonds. It served as insurance. 'This is a perfectly legal transaction,' he said. 'Opus Dei is a personal prelature of the Vatican City, and His Holiness can disperse monies however he sees fit. No law has been broken.'

'True, and yet . . . ' The secretarius leaned forwards and his chair creaked under the burden. 'We have no knowledge of what you intend to do with these funds, and if it is in any way illegal . . .'

'Considering what you are asking of me,' Aringarosa countered, 'what I do with this money is not your concern. Now, I imagine you have something for me to sign?'

A paper was pushed towards him, as if they wished he would simply leave. The sheet bore the papal seal. Aringarosa was surprised at how little emotion he felt as he signed the document.

'Thank you, Bishop,' the secretarius said. 'Your service to the Church will never be forgotten.'

Aringarosa picked up the briefcase and walked out of the door.

THE DEPOSITORY BANK of Zürich offered a full array of anonymous banking services. The bread and butter of its operation, however, was its oldest and simplest offering—the anonymous safe-deposit box. Switzerland's reputation for secrecy in banking had made the industry's services one of the country's most lucrative exports.

Sophie stopped the taxi at an imposing gate that blocked the bank's driveway—a concrete ramp that descended beneath the building and was monitored by a video camera. She rolled down the window and surveyed the electronic pass machine on the driver's side. An LCD screen provided directions in seven languages. Topping the list was English: INSERT KEY. And below the screen was a triangular hole.

'Something tells me it will fit,' said Langdon.

Sophie took the gold laser-cut key from him and slid it in until the entire shaft had disappeared. Instantly, the gate swung open. She coasted down to a second gate and machine, also bearing a direction to INSERT KEY. Behind them, the first gate closed.

When Sophie inserted the key, the second gate opened. Moments later they were winding down the ramp into a small dim garage with room for about a dozen cars. Sophie pulled the taxi into a space near the entrance to the building and killed the engine.

'You'd better leave the gun here,' she said.

With pleasure, Langdon thought, sliding the pistol under the seat.

They got out and walked towards a huge steel door. It had no handle, but on the wall beside it was another triangular keyhole. No directions were posted this time.

'Keeps out the slow learners,' Langdon said.

Sophie laughed nervously. 'Here we go.' She stuck the key in the hole. The door swung inwards with a low hum. Exchanging glances, Sophie and Langdon entered. The door shut with a thud behind them.

The foyer of the Depository Bank of Zürich was wall-to-wall metal. The floor, walls, counters, doors, even chairs appeared to be fashioned of moulded steel. The message was clear: You are walking into a vault.

A large, muscular man behind the counter glanced up as they entered. He turned off the small television he was watching and greeted them with a smile. 'How may I help you?' he asked.

Sophie simply laid the gold key on the counter in front of the man, who glanced down and immediately stood straighter.

'Of course. Your lift is at the end of the hall. I will alert someone that you are on your way.'

Sophie took her key back. 'Which floor?'

The man gave her an odd look. 'Your key instructs the lift which floor.'

She smiled. 'Ah, yes.'

THE GUARD WATCHED as the two newcomers disappeared into the lift. As soon as the door had closed, he grabbed the phone and called the bank's night manager. As the line rang, the guard switched the television back on and stared at the two faces on the screen.

The manager answered. '*Oui?*'

'We have a situation down here. The French police are tracking two fugitives tonight, and they just walked into our bank.'

The manager cursed. 'OK. I'll contact Monsieur Vernet.'

The guard hung up and placed a second call. To Interpol.

LANGDON HAD NO IDEA how many floors they descended beneath the Depository Bank of Zürich before the door finally opened.

Displaying impressive alacrity, a host was already standing there to greet them. He was elderly, wearing a neatly pressed flannel suit—an old-world banker in a high-tech world. He greeted them, then said,

'Would you be so kind as to follow me, *s'il vous plaît*?'

Langdon and Sophie followed him down a series of corridors, past several large rooms filled with blinking mainframe computers.

'*Voici*,' their host said, arriving at a steel door and opening it for them. 'Here you are.'

Langdon and Sophie stepped into what looked like a lavish sitting room at a fine hotel. Gone were the metal and rivets; instead they saw oriental carpets, dark oak furniture and leather chairs.

The man smiled. 'I sense this is your first visit?'

Sophie hesitated and then nodded.

'Understood. Keys are often passed on as inheritance, and our first-time users are invariably uncertain of the protocol.' He motioned to a table bearing two crystal glasses, a bottle of Perrier, a pot of coffee and two cups. 'This room is yours for as long as you care to use it.'

'You say keys are sometimes inherited?' Sophie asked.

'Indeed. Such accounts are often willed through generations. On our gold accounts, the shortest safety-deposit box lease is fifty years. Now shall I run through the process of accessing your box?'

Sophie nodded. 'Please.'

He walked them to the far wall, where a wide conveyor belt entered the room in a graceful curve, vaguely resembling a baggage claim carousel. 'You insert your key there . . .' He pointed to a triangular hole beside a keypad, which was similar to that of a bank ATM terminal. 'Once the computer confirms the markings on your key, you enter your account number, and your safe-deposit box will be retrieved robotically from the vault below and arrive here for your inspection. When you are finished with your box, you place it back on the conveyor belt, insert your key again, and the process is reversed. If you need anything at all, simply press the call button on the table.'

Sophie seemed to be about to ask a question when a telephone rang.

The man looked puzzled. 'Excuse me, please.' He walked over to the phone, which was sitting on the drinks table. '*Oui?*' he answered. His brow furrowed as he listened to the caller. '*Oui . . . oui . . . d'accord.*' He hung up, and gave them an uneasy smile. 'I'm sorry, I must leave you now. Make yourselves at home.'

'Excuse me,' Sophie called, as he moved towards the door. 'You mentioned that we enter an account number?'

The man paused at the door, looking pale. 'But of course. Our safe-deposit boxes are identified by a number, not a name. Your key is only half of your identification. Your personal account number is the other half. Otherwise, if you lost your key, anyone could use it.'

'And if my benefactor gave me no account number?'

The banker paused, then smiled reassuringly. 'I will ask someone to come and help you.'

Leaving, he closed the door behind him. Langdon and Sophie heard the sound of a heavy lock twisting, sealing them inside.

ACROSS TOWN, Collet was standing in the Gare Saint-Lazare when his phone rang.

It was Fache. 'Interpol got a tip,' he said. 'Forget the train. Langdon and Neveu just walked into the Paris branch of the Depository Bank of Zürich, 24 Rue Haxo. I want your men over there right away.'

'Any leads yet on what Saunière was trying to tell Agent Neveu and Robert Langdon?'

Fache's tone was cold. 'If you arrest them, Lieutenant Collet, then I can ask them personally.'

Collet took the hint. 'Rue Haxo. Right away, Captain.'

ANDRÉ VERNET—president of the Paris branch of the Depository Bank of Zürich—lived in a lavish flat above the bank. He had been awake only six and a half minutes, yet as he hurried through the bank's underground corridors he looked as if his personal tailor and hairdresser had polished him to a fine sheen. Impeccably dressed in a silk suit, he tightened his tie as he walked. The arrival of a gold key client always required an extra flurry of attention, but the arrival of a gold key client who was wanted by the police would be an extremely delicate matter. The bank had enough battles with the law over the privacy rights of their clients without two of them turning out to be criminals.

Five minutes, Vernet told himself, as he stopped at the doorway. I need these people out of my bank before the police arrive.

Taking a deep breath and forcing a smile, he unlocked the door and swirled into the room like a warm breeze. 'Good evening,' he said. 'I am André Vernet. How can I be of serv—?' The rest of the sentence lodged somewhere beneath his Adam's apple. The woman before him was as unexpected a visitor as Vernet had ever had.

'I'm sorry, do we know each other?' Sophie asked. She did not recognise the banker, but for a moment he looked as if he'd seen a ghost.

'No . . .' the bank president fumbled. 'I don't . . . believe so.' He exhaled. 'My colleague tells me you have a gold key but no account number? Might I ask how you came by this key?'

'My grandfather gave it to me,' Sophie replied.

'Really? But he failed to give you the account number?'

'I don't think he had time,' Sophie said. 'He was murdered tonight.'

Her words sent the man staggering backwards. 'Jacques Saunière is dead?' His eyes filled with horror. 'But . . . how?'

Now it was Sophie who reeled. 'You *knew* my grandfather?'

Banker André Vernet calmed himself. 'Jacques and I were dear friends. When did this happen?'

'Earlier this evening. Inside the Louvre.'

Vernet sank into a deep leather chair. 'I need to ask you both a very important question.' He glanced up at Langdon and then at Sophie. 'Did you have anything to do with his death?'

'No!' Sophie declared. 'Absolutely not.'

Vernet's face was grim. 'Your pictures are being circulated by Interpol. You're wanted for a murder.'

Fache ran an Interpol broadcast already? Sophie thought. Quickly she told Vernet what had happened in the Louvre that night.

Vernet looked amazed. 'And your grandfather left you only the key? Nothing else? No slip of paper?'

'No. Just the key.'

Vernet gave a helpless sigh. 'I'm afraid every key is electronically paired with a ten-digit account number that functions as a password. Clients select their own numbers, which are known only to the client and the computer. Without that number, your key is worthless.'

Ten digits. Sophie calculated the odds. Ten billion possible choices. 'Monsieur Vernet,' she said, 'our time tonight is short. I am going to be very direct if I may.' She laid the gold key on the coffee table in front of the banker, with the Priory of Sion seal face up. 'Does the symbol on this key mean anything to you?'

Vernet glanced down at the fleur-de-lis seal and shook his head. 'Many of our clients emboss corporate logos onto their keys.'

Sophie watched him carefully. 'This seal is the symbol of a secret society known as the Priory of Sion.'

'I know nothing of this. Your grandfather was a friend, but we spoke mostly of business.' Vernet adjusted his tie, looking nervous now.

'Monsieur Vernet,' Sophie insisted, her tone firm. 'My grandfather called me tonight and told me he and I were in grave danger. He said he had to give me something. It turned out to be a key to your bank. Now he is dead. Anything you can tell us would be helpful.'

Vernet broke a sweat. 'We need to get out of here. I'm afraid my watchman felt obliged to call Interpol.'

Sophie had feared as much. She gave it one last shot. 'My grandfather said he needed to tell me the truth about my family. Does that mean anything to you?'

'Mademoiselle, your family died in a car accident when you were young. I'm sorry. I know your grandfather loved you very much, and that it pained him that you had fallen out of touch.'

As Sophie wondered how to respond, Vernet's cellphone rang, and he snatched it off his belt.

'*Oui?*' He listened a moment. '*La police? Si rapidement?*' He cursed, gave some quick directions in French, and said he would be up to the lobby in a minute. Hanging up the phone, he turned back to Sophie. 'Jacques was a friend, and my bank does not need this kind of press, so for those two reasons I have no intention of allowing this arrest to be made on my premises. Give me a minute and I will help you to leave the bank undetected. Beyond that, I cannot get involved.' He stood up and hurried to the door. 'Stay here. I'll be right back.'

'But the safe-deposit box,' Sophie declared. 'We can't just leave.'

'There's nothing I can do,' Vernet said, hurrying out. 'I'm sorry.'

Sophie stared after him, wondering if the account number was buried in one of the countless letters her grandfather had sent her over the years, which she had left unopened. Then she noticed an unexpected glimmer of contentment in Langdon's eyes.

'Robert? You're smiling.'

'Your grandfather was a genius.' Langdon fumbled in his pocket, and produced the print-out of the crime scene photo.

When he spread it out, Sophie needed only to glimpse the first line to know he was correct: 13-3-2-21-1-1-8-5. Her grandfather had written his account number on the Louvre floor!

When Sophie had first seen the scrambled Fibonacci sequence on the parquet, she had assumed its sole purpose was to encourage DCPJ to call in their cryptographers and get Sophie involved. Now she saw that the numbers had a more important meaning. She hurried to the conveyor belt and inserted her key into the hole beside the keypad.

The screen refreshed instantly: ACCOUNT NUMBER . . . The cursor blinked. Waiting.

Ten digits. Sophie read the numbers off the print-out, and Langdon typed them in: 1332211185.

A message in several languages now appeared. In English it said:

> CAUTION: Before you strike the enter key, please check the accuracy of your account number. If the computer does not recognise the number, this system will automatically shut down.

Sophie frowned. 'Looks like we only get one try.' She extended her index finger towards the ENTER key, but hesitated as a thought hit her.

'Go ahead,' Langdon urged. 'Vernet will be back soon.'

'No.' She pulled her hand away. 'This isn't the right number.' She deleted everything she had just typed in. 'He wouldn't have chosen this *random* account number.' Sophie tapped in a different sequence. 'He'd have chosen something he could easily remember.' She gave a sly smile. 'Something that appeared random . . . but was not.'

Langdon looked at the screen: ACCOUNT NUMBER: 1123581321.

It took him an instant, but when he spotted it, he knew she was right. It was the Fibonacci sequence. 1-1-2-3-5-8-13-21.

She pressed the ENTER key. For a moment nothing happened.

Then, after what seemed an age, the conveyor belt began to move. Above the narrow slit where it entered the room, a metal door slid up, and a black plastic crate emerged.

The crate coasted to a stop directly in front of them. Wasting no time, Sophie unhooked the two clasps facing her. Then she glanced at Langdon and, together, they raised the heavy lid and peered inside.

At first glance, Sophie thought the crate was empty. Then she saw something sitting at the bottom. It was a polished wooden box about the size of a shoe box, with an inlaid design of a rose on the lid. Sophie leaned in and lifted the box out. The wood was a lustrous deep purple with a strong grain. Rosewood, she realised. She carried it gingerly to a large receiving table.

As she set it down, Langdon stared at the lid's inlay. 'The five-petal rose,' he whispered, 'is a Priory symbol for the Holy Grail.'

Sophie turned to him. She knew what he was thinking. 'It's a perfect size,' she whispered, 'to hold . . . a chalice.'

Reaching forwards, she unhooked the clasp and raised the lid.

The object inside was unlike anything Sophie had ever seen. One thing was immediately clear to both of them, however. This was definitely not the Cup of Christ.

'THE POLICE are blocking the street,' André Vernet said, walking back into the viewing chamber. 'Getting you out will be difficult.' As he closed the door behind him, Vernet saw the black crate and halted in his tracks. My God! he thought. They accessed Saunière's account?

Sophie and Langdon were huddled over what looked to be a wooden jewellery box. Sophie immediately closed the lid and looked up. 'We had the account number after all,' she said.

Vernet was speechless. This changed everything. He had to get them out of the bank. But with the police already having set up a roadblock, he could imagine only one way to do that. 'Mademoiselle Neveu, if you wish to take the item with you, I suggest that you wrap it in Mr Langdon's jacket.'

As Langdon shed his jacket, Vernet hurried over to the conveyor belt, closed the empty crate and typed a series of commands. The belt began moving again, carrying the container back down to the vault. He pulled out the key and handed it to Sophie. 'This way please. Hurry.'

When they reached the loading dock at the rear of the building, Vernet motioned to one of the bank's armoured trucks. 'Get in the cargo hold,' he said, heaving open the massive door.

Sophie and Langdon climbed in and sat down on the floor of the glistening steel compartment, Langdon cradling the treasure in his tweed jacket. Swinging the heavy doors closed, Vernet locked them inside. Then he went to the dock overseer's office, collected the keys for the truck, and found a driver's uniform jacket and cap. Shedding his own suit coat and tie, he donned a shoulder holster and put on the driver's jacket. On his way out, he grabbed a driver's pistol from the rack, put in a clip and stuffed it in the holster.

He got in behind the steering wheel and revved the engine. As the truck powered up the ramp, the interior gate swung inwards to let him pass. Vernet advanced and waited while the gate closed behind him before pulling forwards and tripping the next sensor. The second gate opened, and the exit beckoned.

Except for the police car blocking the top of the ramp.

Vernet dabbed his brow. A lanky officer stepped out and waved him to a stop beside four patrol cars.

Vernet stopped and opened his window. Pulling his driver's cap down further, he effected as rough a façade as his cultured upbringing would allow. '*Qu'est-ce qui se passe?*' he asked.

'*Je suis Lieutenant Collet,*' the agent said. '*Police Judiciaire.*' He motioned to the cargo hold. '*Qu'est-ce qu'il y a là dedans?*'

'Hell if I know,' Vernet replied in crude French. 'I'm only a driver.'

Collet looked unimpressed. He held up a passport picture of Robert Langdon. 'Was this man in your bank tonight?'

Vernet shrugged. 'No idea. They don't let us anywhere near the clients. You need to go in and ask the front desk.'

'Your bank is demanding a search warrant before we can enter.'

Vernet gave a disgusted look. 'Administrators. Don't get me started.'

'Open your truck, please.' Collet motioned towards the cargo hold.

Vernet forced a laugh. 'You think they trust us with keys for the cargo area? These trucks get sealed by overseers on the loading dock. Then the truck sits in dock while someone drives the cargo keys to the drop-off. Once we get the call that the cargo keys are with the recipient, then I get the OK to drive.'

'When was *this* truck sealed?'

'Must have been hours ago. I'm driving all the way up to St Thurial tonight. Cargo keys are already up there.'

The agent made no response, his eyes probing Vernet's.

A drop of sweat was preparing to slide down Vernet's nose. 'Do you mind?' he said, motioning to the police car blocking his way. 'I'm on a tight schedule.'

Collet pointed to Vernet's wrist. 'Do all the drivers wear Rolexes?'

Vernet glanced down and saw the glistening band of his absurdly expensive watch peeking out from beneath the sleeve of his jacket. 'This piece of shit? Bought it for twenty euro from a street vendor in St Germain des Prés. I'll sell it to you for forty.'

The agent stepped aside. 'No thanks. Have a safe trip.'

Vernet did not breathe again until the truck was a good fifty yards down the street. Now he had another problem. Where to take his cargo.

SILAS FELL TO HIS KNEES on the canvas mat in his room. Tonight's session with the Discipline had left him weak. I have failed the Church, he told himself. Far worse, I have failed the bishop.

Tonight was supposed to have been Bishop Aringarosa's salvation. Divine intervention he had called it. 'Silas,' he had whispered, all those months ago, 'God has bestowed upon us an opportunity to protect The Way. Will you join the battle and be a soldier of God?'

Bishop Aringarosa had then put Silas in contact with the proposer of the plan—a man who called himself the Teacher. Although the Teacher and Silas never met face to face, each time they spoke by phone Silas was awed, both by the profundity of the Teacher's faith and by the scope of his power. The Teacher seemed to be a man who knew all, a man with eyes and ears in all places.

Aringarosa had placed enormous trust in the Teacher, and he had instructed Silas to do the same. 'Do as he commands you,' the bishop told him. 'And we will be victorious.'

Victorious. Silas gazed at the bare floor and feared victory had eluded them. The Teacher had been tricked. The keystone was a devious dead end. And with the deception, all hope of protecting The Way had vanished. He crawled to his feet and went to find his cellphone. Hanging his head in shame, he dialled.

'Teacher,' he whispered, 'all is lost.' Silas truthfully told the man how he had been tricked.

'You lose your faith too quickly,' the Teacher replied. 'I have just received news. Most unexpected and welcome. Jacques Saunière transferred information about the secret before he died. I will call you soon. Our work is not yet done.'

'I THINK WE'RE on the highway now,' Sophie whispered.

After an unnerving pause atop the bank ramp, the armoured truck had moved on, snaking left and right for a minute or two, and was now accelerating to what felt like top speed.

Langdon didn't reply. He had unwrapped his jacket from the rosewood box, and was holding the box in front of him.

Sophie shifted her position so that they were sitting side by side. 'Go ahead,' she said. 'Open it.'

Langdon took a deep breath. He stole one more admiring glance at the intricate woodwork, then unhooked the clasp and opened the lid, revealing the object within. It was a polished white marble cylinder, about the size of a tennis ball can, and it appeared to have been assembled from five disks of marble that had been affixed to one another within a delicate brass framework. Each of the disks bore the entire alphabet engraved round its circumference. As Langdon tilted the box towards him, gurgling sounds came from the cylinder.

'Amazing, isn't it?' Sophie whispered.

Langdon glanced up. 'What the hell is it?'

'It's called a cryptex, and the blueprint for it came from one of Leonardo da Vinci's secret diaries.'

'What is it for?'

'It's for storing secret information,' Sophie said, and then explained that one of her grandfather's best-loved hobbies was creating models of da Vinci's inventions—timepieces, water pumps, and even a fully articulated model of a medieval knight, which now stood proudly on the desk in his office. 'He made me a cryptex when I was little, but I've never seen one so ornate and large.'

'I've never heard of a cryptex.'

Sophie was not surprised. Most of Leonardo's unbuilt inventions had never been studied or even named. And the term 'cryptex' was possibly her grandfather's creation. But he'd told her that the cylinder had been da Vinci's way of sending secure messages over long distances. In an era without telephones or email, anyone wanting to convey private information to someone far away had no option but to trust a messenger to carry the letter, which was risky. Sealed inside the cryptex, however, the information was accessible only to the individual with the proper password.

'So, we require a password,' Sophie concluded, pointing out the lettered dials. 'A cryptex works much like a combination lock. If you align the dials in the proper position, the lock slides open. Then you have access to a hollow central compartment.'

Langdon eyed the device again, still looking sceptical. 'But why not just pry it apart? Or smash it? Marble is a soft rock.'

Sophie smiled, and carefully lifted the cylinder out of the box. 'Da Vinci was too smart for that. He designed the cryptex so that if you try to force it open the information self-destructs. It was always written on a thin papyrus scroll, and before it was inserted into the cryptex's compartment, it was rolled round a delicate glass vial.' She tipped the cryptex, and the liquid inside gurgled. 'A vial of vinegar.'

Langdon nodded. 'Brilliant. If someone attempted to force open the cryptex, the glass vial would break, and the vinegar would dissolve the papyrus. By the time anyone extracted the secret message, it would be a glob of meaningless pulp. What do you think is inside?'

'Whatever it is, my grandfather obviously wanted very badly to keep it secret.' She paused, eyeing the five-petal rose inlaid on the lid. Something was bothering her. 'Did you say earlier that the rose is a symbol for the Grail?'

'Yes. In Priory symbolism, the rose and the Grail are synonymous.'

'My grandfather always told me that the rose meant secrecy. Something to do with an ancient Roman custom.'

'*Sub rosa*,' Langdon said. 'The Romans hung a rose over confidential meetings. Attendees understood that whatever was said under the rose—or *sub rosa*—had to remain a secret.' He quickly explained that the rose's overtone of secrecy was not the only reason the Priory used it as a symbol for the Grail. *Rosa rugosa,* one of the oldest species of rose, had five petals and pentagonal symmetry, just like the guiding star of Venus, giving the rose strong iconographic ties to womanhood. In addition, the rose signified 'true direction'; hence the compass rose, which helped travellers to navigate.

As Langdon finished, his expression seemed to tighten suddenly.

'Robert? Are you OK?'

His eyes were riveted on the box. '*Sub . . . rosa*. It can't be.'

'What?'

Langdon slowly raised his eyes. 'Under the sign of the rose,' he whispered. 'This cryptex . . . I think I know what it is.'

Chapter 7

Langdon could scarcely believe his own conclusion: I am holding the Priory keystone.

'Robert?' Sophie was watching him. 'What's going on?'

Langdon gathered his thoughts. 'Every stone archway requires a central wedge-shaped stone at the top that locks the pieces together and carries all the weight. This stone is, in architectural parlance, the key to the vault, or *la clef de voûte*. In English we call it a *keystone*.'

Sophie glanced down at the cryptex. 'And you think this is it?'

Langdon spoke carefully, not sure where to begin. 'Sophie, according to Priory lore, the keystone is an encoded map . . . a map that reveals the hiding place of the Holy Grail.'

Even to Langdon it sounded unbelievable. Yet it was the only logical conclusion he could muster. An encrypted stone hidden beneath the sign of the rose. Grail seekers, familiar with the Priory's history of cryptic double-talk, had concluded that *la clef de voûte* was a literal keystone—a wedge-shaped stone inserted into an archway in a church. In architecture there was no shortage of roses: rose windows, rosette reliefs and cinquefoils, the five-petalled decorative flowers often found at the top of archways. It had seemed simple. The map to the Holy Grail was incorporated high in an archway of some forgotten church.

'But this can't be the keystone,' Sophie argued. 'It's not old enough. I'm certain my grandfather made it.'

'Actually,' Langdon replied, 'the keystone is believed to have been created by the Priory some time in the past couple of decades.' He then explained that for centuries the Priory's biggest secret—the location of the Grail—was never written down. It was verbally transferred to each new rising *sénéchal* at a clandestine ceremony. However, at some point in the last century, perhaps on account of new electronic eavesdropping capabilities, rumours surfaced that the Priory had vowed never again even to speak the location of the sacred hiding place.

'But then how could they pass on the secret?' Sophie asked.

'That's where the keystone comes in,' Langdon explained. 'When one of the top four members died, the remaining three *sénéchaux* would choose a new candidate to join them. But rather than *telling* him where the Grail was hidden, they gave him a test through which he could prove he was worthy.'

'So if a rising Priory *sénéchal* can open the keystone,' Sophie said, 'he proves himself worthy of the information it holds.'

Langdon nodded. 'Sophie, you realise that if this is indeed the keystone, your grandfather's access to it implies he was exceptionally powerful within the Priory of Sion.'

Sophie sighed. 'He was powerful in a secret society. I'm certain of it. I can only assume it was the Priory.'

Langdon did a double take. 'You *knew* he was in a secret society?'

'I saw some things I wasn't supposed to see ten years ago. We haven't spoken since.' She paused. 'My grandfather was not only a ranking top member . . . I believe he was *the* top member.'

'Grand Master? But . . . there's no way you could know that!'

'I'd rather not talk about it.' Sophie looked away.

Langdon sat in stunned silence. He had the eerie sensation that it made perfect sense. After all, previous Priory Grand Masters had also been distinguished public figures with artistic leanings. Proof had been uncovered years ago in Paris's Bibliothèque Nationale in papers that became known as *Les Dossiers Secrets*. They confirmed what Grail buffs had long suspected: Priory Grand Masters included Leonardo da Vinci, Botticelli, Sir Isaac Newton, Victor Hugo and, more recently, the artist Jean Cocteau. So why not Jacques Saunière?

Langdon suddenly realised that he had been due to meet Saunière that night. The Priory Grand Master called a meeting with me, Langdon thought. Why? A piece of this puzzle is missing.

The answers were going to have to wait. The sound of the slowing engine caused them both to look up. Gravel crunched beneath the tyres. Why was Vernet pulling over already? He had told them he would take them well outside the city to safety.

The truck came to a stop, but the engine remained idling as the doors swung open. Langdon saw they were parked in a wooded area off the road, then Vernet stepped into view, holding a pistol.

'I'm sorry about this,' he said. 'I really have no choice. I have a duty to protect your grandfather's assets. Set the box down.'

Sophie clutched the box to her chest. 'My grandfather entrusted this to me!' she declared.

Vernet's visage turned ice-cold. 'Mademoiselle Neveu, I don't know how you got that key and account number, but it seems obvious that foul play was involved. Had I known the extent of your crimes, I would never have helped you leave the bank.'

'We had nothing to do with my grandfather's death!' Sophie said.

Vernet looked at Langdon. 'Yet the radio claims you are wanted not only for his murder but for three others as well?'

'What!' Langdon was thunderstruck. The number hit him harder than the fact that he was the prime suspect. It must be more than a coincidence. The three *sénéchaux*? His eyes dropped to the rosewood box. If the three *sénéchaux* had been murdered, Saunière had to transfer the keystone to someone else—his granddaughter.

'The police can sort that out when I turn you in,' Vernet said. 'I have got my bank involved too far already.'

Sophie glared at Vernet. 'You obviously have no intention of turning us in. You would have driven us back to the bank. And instead you bring us out here and hold us at gunpoint?'

'Whatever the box contains, I have no intention of letting it become evidence in a police investigation. Mr Langdon, bring me the box.'

Sophie shook her head. 'Don't do it.'

A gunshot roared, and a bullet tore into the wall above them.

Langdon froze.

'Mr Langdon, bring the box to me.' Vernet was standing on the ground near the rear bumper, his gun pointing into the cargo hold.

Box in hand, Langdon moved towards the open door.

I've got to do something! he thought. I'm about to hand over the Priory keystone! As he neared the doorway, he began to wonder if he could use his higher position to his advantage. Vernet's gun was at Langdon's knee level. A well-placed kick perhaps? Unfortunately, as Langdon neared, Vernet took several steps back, well out of reach.

'Place the box beside the door,' he commanded.

Langdon knelt down and did so.

'Now stand up and return to the back wall.'

Langdon began to stand up but paused, spying the small, spent pistol shell on the cargo-hold floor. Discreetly brushing the shell onto the narrow ledge that was the door's lower sill, he straightened up and stepped backwards.

'Return to the back wall and turn around.'

Langdon obeyed.

VERNET COULD FEEL his heart pounding. Aiming the gun with his right hand, he reached for the box with his left, and set it on the ground. Neither of his prisoners, who had their backs to him, had moved.

Now all that remained was to close and lock the door. Leaving the box on the ground for the moment, he heaved the metal door closed with a thud. Then he grabbed the single bolt that needed to be slid into place, pulling it to the left. It slid a few inches and crunched to an unexpected halt. Vernet pulled again, but the bolt wouldn't lock. The door wasn't fully closed. Something was blocking it. He turned to throw his full shoulder into the door, but as he did so it exploded outwards, striking him in the face and sending him reeling backwards onto the ground. The gun flew out of his hand as he reached for his face and felt warm blood running from his nose.

Robert Langdon hit the ground somewhere nearby. Vernet tried to get up, but his vision was blurred and he fell backwards. Sophie Neveu was shouting. Moments later, Vernet heard the crunching of tyres on gravel and felt a cloud of dirt and exhaust billowing over him. He sat up just in time to see the armoured truck speed away.

'ARE YOU OK?' Langdon asked Sophie. She was sitting in the passenger seat of the armoured truck, staring out at the woods beside the highway. She looked shaken.

'Do you believe him?' she asked.

'About the three additional murders? Absolutely. It answers a lot of questions—why your grandfather was desperate to pass on the keystone, as well as why Fache is hunting me with such intensity.'

'No, I meant about Vernet trying to protect his bank.'

Langdon glanced over. 'As opposed to?'

'Taking the keystone for himself.'

Langdon had not even considered it. 'How would he even know what this box contains?'

'His bank stored it. He knew my grandfather. Maybe he knew things. He might have decided he wanted the Grail for himself.'

Langdon shook his head. 'In my experience, there are only two reasons people seek the Grail. Either they believe they are searching for the long-lost Cup of Christ . . .'

'Or?'

'Or they know the truth and are threatened by it. Many groups throughout history have sought to destroy the Grail.'

A silence fell between them, and Langdon felt the ponderous weight of a new responsibility. He and Sophie might actually be holding an encrypted set of directions to one of the most enduring mysteries of all time. He wondered where they should go next. They had no idea how to open the cryptex, or why Saunière had given it to them. Yet their survival seemed to depend on getting answers to those very questions.

We need help, Langdon decided. Professional help. That meant a visit to the man who knew more about the Holy Grail and the Priory of Sion than anyone on earth, outside the brotherhood itself.

THE SPRAWLING 185-acre estate of Château Villette, designed by François Mansart in 1668 for the Count of Aufflay, was twenty-five minutes southwest of Paris, near Versailles. The castle's present owner was Sir Leigh Teabing, a former British Royal Historian whom Langdon had first met when they had worked together on a BBC documentary about the history of the Holy Grail. Langdon hoped the historian would be able to help them figure out the mystery.

Langdon brought the armoured truck to a stop at the foot of the long driveway. Beyond the security gate, Sir Leigh Teabing's residence rose imposingly in the distance. The sign on the gate was in English: PRIVATE PROPERTY. NO TRESPASSING.

As if to proclaim his home a British colony, Teabing had also installed an intercom system on the *right-hand* side of the truck—the passenger's side everywhere except in Britain.

Sophie gave the misplaced intercom an odd look and rolled down her window. 'Robert, you'd better do the talking.'

Langdon leaned across Sophie to press the button. He waited there, awkwardly prone, while a telephone began to ring over the small speaker.

Finally, the intercom crackled and an irritated voice with a French accent spoke. 'Château Villette. Who is this?'

'Robert Langdon,' he called out, sprawled across Sophie's lap. 'I'm a friend of Sir Leigh Teabing. I need his help.'

'My master is sleeping. What is your business with him?'

'It is a private matter. One of great interest to him.'

'Then I'm sure he will be pleased to receive you in the morning.'

'It's very important. Please let him know that I have uncovered new information about the Grail.'

There was a long pause.

Langdon and Sophie waited, the truck idling loudly.

Finally, someone spoke. 'My good man, I dare say you are still on Harvard Standard Time! My manservant tells me not only that you are in Paris but that you speak of the Grail.'

'I thought that might get you out of bed.'

'And so it has.'

'Any chance you'd open the gate for an old friend?'

'Those who seek the truth are more than friends. They are brothers. You may pass.'

Well accustomed to Teabing's predilection for drama, Langdon rolled his eyes at Sophie. The gate clicked open and he accelerated along the winding, poplar-lined driveway.

'MONSIEUR VERNET!' The night manager of the Depository Bank of Zürich felt relieved to hear the bank president's voice on the phone. 'Where did you go, sir? The police are waiting for you!'

'I have a little problem,' the president said, sounding distressed.

You have more than a little problem, the manager thought. The police had entirely surrounded the bank and the DCPJ captain himself was threatening to show up with a warrant.

'Armoured truck number three. I need to find it.'

Puzzled, the manager checked his delivery schedule. 'It's here. Downstairs at the loading dock.'

'Actually, no. The truck was stolen by the two individuals the police are tracking. I can't go into the specifics on the phone, but we have a situation here that could be extremely unfortunate for the bank. I want you to activate the truck's emergency transponder, and inform me of its exact location the instant you have it.'

The night manager's eyes moved to the control box across the room. 'Right away, sir.'

CHÂTEAU VILLETTE came into view, three storeys tall and a hundred and ninety feet long, its grey stone façade illuminated by spotlights.

Rather than driving up to the front door, Langdon pulled into a parking area hidden in the evergreens, unaware that somewhere in the truck's undercarriage a tiny transponder had now blinked into life.

'No reason to have Leigh wondering why we arrived in a armoured truck,' he said, wrapping his jacket round the cryptex in its rosewood box a second time.

A cobblestone pathway led to a carved oak door. Before Sophie could grasp the huge brass knocker, the door swung open. A prim and elegant butler stood before them, his austere expression leaving little doubt that he was unamused by their presence.

'Sir Leigh will be down presently,' he declared in a thick French accent. 'May I take your coat?' He scowled at the bunched-up tweed in Langdon's arms.

'Thank you, I'm fine.'

'Of course you are. This way, please.'

The butler guided them through a lush marble foyer into an exquisitely adorned drawing room, softly lit by tassel-draped Victorian lamps. Set in the far wall, flanked between two glistening suits of armour, was a rough-hewn fireplace large enough to roast an ox in. The butler knelt and touched a match to a pile of oak logs and kindling, and a fire quickly crackled to life.

The man stood, straightening his jacket. 'Sir Leigh requests that you make yourselves at home.' With that, he departed.

As soon as they were alone, Langdon walked to the velvet divan beside the fire, unwrapped the wooden box and slid it underneath the divan, well out of sight. He put his jacket back on and sat down directly over the stashed treasure. Sophie took a seat beside him.

'Robert!' a voice bellowed somewhere behind them. 'I see you travel with a maiden.'

The voice had come from the top of a staircase that snaked up to the shadows of the first floor. At the top, a silhouette was just visible.

Langdon stood up. 'Good evening,' he called. 'Sir Leigh, may I present Sophie Neveu.'

'An honour.' Teabing moved into the light.

'Thank you for having us,' Sophie said, now seeing the man wore metal leg braces and used crutches. 'I realise it's quite late.'

Teabing was coming down the stairs one at a time. 'It is so late, my dear, it's early.' He laughed. '*Vous n'êtes pas Américaine?*'

Sophie shook her head. '*Parisienne.*'

'Your English is superb,' he said, arriving at the bottom of the stairs.

'Thank you. I studied at Royal Holloway.'

'So then, that explains it.' Portly and ruby-faced, Sir Leigh Teabing had bushy red hair and jovial hazel eyes that twinkled as he spoke. He extended a hand to Langdon. 'Robert, you've lost weight.'

Langdon grinned. 'And you've found some.'

Teabing laughed heartily, patting a rotund belly that was covered by a silk shirt and paisley waistcoat. 'Touché. My only pleasures these days seem to be culinary.' Turning now to Sophie, he gently took her hand, bowing his head slightly. 'M'lady.'

Sophie glanced at Langdon, uncertain whether she'd stepped back in time or into a nuthouse.

The butler who had answered the door now entered carrying a tea service, which he arranged on a table in front of the fireplace.

'This is Rémy Legaludec,' Teabing said, 'my manservant.'

The slender butler gave a stiff nod and disappeared yet again.

'Rémy is *Lyonnais*,' Teabing whispered, 'but he does good sauces.'

Langdon looked amused. 'I'd have thought you'd import English staff.'

'Goodness, no! I wouldn't wish an English chef on anyone except the French tax collectors who steal my money.' He glanced at Sophie then looked back at Langdon. 'What's happened? You seem shaken.'

Langdon nodded. 'We've had an interesting night, Leigh.'

'No doubt. You arrive on my doorstep unannounced speaking of the

Grail. Tell me, what is this new information, Robert?'

'We're not quite sure. We might have a better idea if we could get some information from you first.'

Teabing wagged his finger. 'A game of quid pro quo. Very well. I am at your service. What is it I can tell you?'

Langdon sighed. 'I was hoping you'd be kind enough to explain to Ms Neveu the true nature of the Holy Grail.'

Teabing looked stunned. 'She doesn't *know*?'

Langdon shook his head.

Teabing turned eagerly to Sophie, a smile growing on his face.

SOPHIE DRANK HER TEA and ate a scone, feeling the welcome effects of caffeine and food. Sir Leigh Teabing was awkwardly pacing before the open fire, his leg braces clicking on the stone hearth.

'The Holy Grail,' he said, his voice sermonic. 'Most people ask me only *where* it is, a question I fear I may never answer. The far more relevant question is this: *What* is the Holy Grail?'

Sophie waited in silence.

'To fully understand the Grail,' Teabing continued, 'we must first speak of the Bible, and the thing you need to know about it is that it did not arrive by fax from heaven.'

'I beg your pardon?'

'The Bible is a product of *man,* my dear. Not of God. Man created it as a historical record of tumultuous times, and it has evolved through countless translations, additions and revisions.'

'OK.'

'Jesus Christ was a historical figure of staggering influence, perhaps the most enigmatic and inspirational leader the world has ever seen. As the prophesied Messiah, he toppled kings, inspired millions and founded new philosophies. As a descendant of the lines of King Solomon and King David, he possessed a rightful claim to the throne of the King of the Jews. Understandably, his life was recorded by thousands of followers across the land in more than *eighty* gospels. Yet only a few were chosen for inclusion in the New Testament.'

'Who chose which gospels to include?' Sophie asked.

'Aha!' Teabing exclaimed with enthusiasm. 'The fundamental irony of Christianity! The Bible, as we know it today, was collated by the pagan Roman emperor, Constantine the Great.'

'I thought Constantine was a Christian,' Sophie said.

'Hardly,' Teabing scoffed. 'He was a lifelong pagan who was baptised on his deathbed, too weak to protest. In Constantine's day,

Rome's official religion was Sun worship and Constantine was its head priest. Unfortunately for him, a growing religious turmoil was gripping Rome, and the conflict between Christians and pagans grew to such proportions that it threatened to rend Rome in two. Constantine decided something had to be done. In AD 325, he decided to unify Rome under a single religion—Christianity.'

Sophie was surprised. 'Why would a pagan emperor choose Christianity as the official religion?'

Teabing chuckled. 'Constantine could see that Christianity was on the rise, and he simply backed the winning horse. Historians still marvel at the brilliance with which he fused pagan symbols, dates and rituals with the growing Christian tradition, creating a kind of hybrid that was acceptable to both sides.'

'Transmogrification,' Langdon said. 'The vestiges of pagan religion in Christian symbology are undeniable: Egyptian sun disks became the halos of Catholic saints, and virtually all the elements of Catholic ritual—the mitre, the altar, the doxology and communion, the act of "God-eating"—were taken directly from earlier pagan religions.'

Teabing groaned. 'Don't get a symbologist started on Christian icons. Nothing in Christianity is original. The pre-Christian God Mithras was born on December 25, died, was buried in a rock tomb, and then resurrected after three days. By the way, December 25 is also the birthday of Osiris, Adonis and Dionysus.'

Sophie's head was spinning. 'And all of this relates to the Grail?'

'Indeed,' Teabing said. 'Stay with me. During this fusion of religions, Constantine needed to strengthen the new Christian tradition by establishing the *divinity* of Jesus.'

'I don't follow. His divinity?'

'My dear,' Teabing declared, 'until that moment in history, Jesus was viewed by his followers as a mortal prophet . . . a great and powerful man, but a *man* nonetheless. By officially endorsing Jesus as the Son of God, Constantine turned Jesus into a deity, an individual whose power was unchallengeable. This not only precluded further pagan challenges to Christianity, but now the followers of Christ were obliged to redeem themselves via the established sacred channel—the Roman Catholic Church.'

Sophie glanced at Langdon, who gave her a soft nod of concurrence.

'Constantine's political manoeuvres don't diminish the majesty of Christ's life,' Teabing continued. 'Jesus inspired millions to better lives. All we are saying is that Constantine took advantage of Christ's influence and, in doing so, shaped Christianity as we know it today.

The twist is this. When Jesus' status was upgraded almost four centuries after his death, thousands of documents already existed chronicling his life as a *mortal* man. So Constantine commissioned a new Bible, one that omitted the gospels that spoke of Christ's human traits and embellished those that made him godlike. The earlier gospels were outlawed, gathered up and burned. But some survived—the Dead Sea Scrolls, found hidden in a cave near Qumran in the 1950s, and the Coptic Scrolls found in 1945 at Nag Hammadi. In addition to telling the true Grail story, these documents speak of Jesus in very human terms. Of course the Vatican tried hard to suppress them. And why wouldn't they? The scrolls highlight glaring historical discrepancies and confirm that the modern Bible was compiled by men who promoted Christ's divinity to solidify their own power base.'

'And yet,' Langdon countered, 'it's important to remember that the modern Church's desire to suppress these documents comes from a sincere belief in an established view of Christ. The Vatican is made up of deeply pious men who truly believe that these contrary documents are false testimony.'

Teabing chuckled as he eased himself into a chair opposite Sophie. 'As you can see, our professor has a far softer heart for Rome than I have. Nevertheless, he is correct.' He picked up a book from a table in front of him and opened it. 'I assume you recognise this fresco?'

Sophie found herself staring at the most famous fresco of all time—*The Last Supper*—da Vinci's portrayal of Jesus and his disciples at the moment Jesus announced that one of them would betray him. 'I know the fresco, yes.'

'Then perhaps you would indulge me this little game? Close your eyes if you would.'

Sophie closed her eyes.

'Can you tell me what Jesus and his disciples are drinking?'

'Wine. They drank wine.'

'Great. And how many wineglasses are on the table?'

Sophie paused, realising it was a trick question. *And after dinner, Jesus took the cup of wine, sharing it with his disciples*. 'One cup,' she said. *The Holy Grail*. 'Jesus passed a single chalice of wine.'

Teabing sighed. 'Open your eyes.'

Sophie looked down at the painting, seeing to her astonishment that *everyone* at the table had a cup of wine, including Christ. Thirteen cups, tiny, stemless and made of glass. No single chalice.

Teabing's eyes twinkled. 'A bit strange, considering that both the Bible and Grail legend celebrate this moment as marking the arrival of the Holy Grail, don't you think? Oddly, da Vinci appears to have forgotten to paint the Cup of Christ. This fresco, in fact, is the entire key to the Holy Grail mystery.'

'Does it tell us *what* the Grail really is?' Sophie asked eagerly.

'Not what it is,' Teabing whispered. 'But rather who it is.'

Sophie stared at Teabing a long time, then turned to Langdon. 'The Holy Grail is a person?'

Langdon nodded. 'A woman, in fact.' Seeing the blank look on her face, he pulled a pen and a notebook from his pocket. 'Sophie, are you familiar with these icons?' He drew the common male symbol ♂ and female symbol ♀.

'Of course,' she said.

'These symbols,' he said quietly, 'originated as astronomical symbols for Mars and Venus. The more ancient symbols for male and female are far simpler.' Langdon drew an inverted V on the paper. 'This is the original symbol for male,' he told her. 'A rudimentary phallus. It is formally known as the *blade*, and it represents aggression and manhood. In fact, it is still used today on modern military uniforms to denote rank. The female symbol, as you might imagine, is the exact opposite.' He drew another symbol on the page: an upright V shape, and could see Sophie had made the connection. 'This is called the *chalice*. It resembles a cup or vessel, and, more important, it resembles the shape of a woman's womb. This symbol implies womanhood and fertility.' Langdon looked directly at her. 'Sophie, legend tells us the Holy Grail is a chalice—a cup. But that's actually a metaphor for something more important.'

'A woman,' Sophie said.

'Exactly.' Langdon smiled. 'The Grail is literally the ancient symbol for womanhood, and the *Holy* Grail represents the sacred feminine, the female deities, which of course have now been lost, virtually eliminated by the Church. The power of the female and her ability to produce life was once very sacred, but it posed a threat to the rise of the predominantly male Church and so was pronounced unclean.'

'I should add,' Teabing chimed in, 'that this concept of woman as life-bringer was the foundation of ancient religion. Sadly, Christian philosophy decided to make *man* the Creator. Genesis tells us that Eve was created from Adam's rib. Woman was an offshoot of man, and a sinful one at that. Genesis was the beginning of the end for the goddess.'

'Legends of chivalric quests for the lost Grail were in fact stories of forbidden quests to find the lost sacred feminine,' Langdon continued. 'Knights who claimed to be "searching for the chalice" were speaking in code as a way to protect themselves from a Church that had subjugated women, banished the goddess and forbidden the pagan reverence for the feminine.'

Sophie shook her head. 'I'm sorry, when you said the Holy Grail was a person, I thought you meant it was an actual person.'

'It is,' Langdon said.

'And not just *any* person,' Teabing agreed. 'If we adjourn to the study, it would be my honour to show you da Vinci's painting of her.'

IN THE KITCHEN, Teabing's manservant stood in silence before a television. The news station was broadcasting photos of a man and woman—the same two individuals to whom he had just served tea . . .

STANDING AT THE ROADBLOCK outside the Depository Bank of Zürich, Lieutenant Collet wondered why Fache was taking so long to come up with the search warrant. His cellular phone rang—it was the command post at the Louvre. 'Do we have a warrant yet?' Collet demanded.

'Forget about the bank,' the agent told him. 'We just got a tip. We have the location where Langdon and Neveu are hiding. An address somewhere near Versailles.'

'Does Captain Fache know?'

'Not yet. He's busy on an important call.'

'Have him call as soon as he's free.' Collet took down the address and jumped in his car. Here was a chance to redeem himself, to make the most high-profile arrest of his career.

TWENTY-FIVE MILES AWAY, a black Audi pulled off a rural road and parked on the edge of a field. Silas got out and peered through the wrought-iron fence that encircled the vast grounds before him. He gazed at the château in the distance. I will not leave this house without the keystone, he vowed. I will not fail the bishop and the Teacher.

Checking the thirteen-round clip in his Heckler Koch, he pushed it through the bars and let it fall onto the mossy ground inside the château grounds. Then, gripping the top of the fence, he heaved himself up and over, dropping silently on the other side.

TEABING'S 'STUDY' was like no study Sophie had ever seen. Lit by three overhead chandeliers, the enormous tiled floor was dotted with worktables buried beneath books, artefacts and a surprising amount of electronic gear—computers, projectors, scanners.

'I converted the ballroom,' Teabing said, looking sheepish as he led them into the room. 'I have little occasion to dance.'

Sophie felt as if the entire night had become some kind of twilight zone where nothing was as she expected. 'This is all for your work?'

'Learning the truth has become my life's love,' Teabing said. 'And the Sangreal is my favourite mistress.'

The Holy Grail is a woman, Sophie thought, her mind buzzing with interrelated ideas that seemed to make no sense. 'You said you have a picture of this woman who you claim is the Holy Grail.'

'Yes, but it is not I who claim she is the Grail. Christ himself made that claim.' Teabing pointed to the far wall on which hung an eight-foot-long print of *The Last Supper*, the same image Sophie had just been looking at. 'There she is!'

Sophie turned to Langdon for help. 'I'm lost. *The Last Supper* is a painting of thirteen men.'

'Is it?' Teabing arched his eyebrows. 'Take a closer look.'

Sophie made her way closer to the painting, scanning the thirteen figures—Jesus Christ in the middle, six disciples on his left, and six on his right. 'They're all men,' she confirmed.

'How about the one seated in the place of honour, at the right hand of the Lord?'

Sophie examined the figure to Jesus' immediate right and a wave of astonishment rose within her. The figure had flowing red hair, delicate folded hands, a demure face and the hint of a bosom. It was, without a doubt, female. 'That's a woman!' Sophie exclaimed, moving closer. She had seen this image many times, and never noticed. 'Who is she?'

'That, my dear,' Teabing replied, 'is Mary Magdalene.'

Sophie turned. 'The prostitute?'

Teabing drew a short breath, as if the word had injured him personally. 'Magdalene was no such thing. That misconception is the legacy of a smear campaign launched by the early Church to cover up her role as the Holy Grail.'

'Her *role*?'

'As I mentioned,' Teabing clarified, 'the early Church needed to convince the world that Jesus was a divine being. Therefore, any gospels that described *earthly* aspects of his life, like his marriage to Mary Magdalene, had to be omitted from the Bible. And da Vinci was certainly aware of that fact. Yet *The Last Supper* practically shouts at the viewer that Jesus and Magdalene were a pair. Note that they appear to be joined at the hip and are leaning away from one another. If you view the two figures as compositional elements rather than as people, you will see a letter of the alphabet leap out at you.'

Sophie saw it at once. In the centre of the painting was the unquestionable outline of an M. She was amazed. 'Why is it there?'

Teabing shrugged. 'Conspiracy theorists will tell you it stands for Mary Magdalene, but to be honest, nobody is certain. The only certainty is that the hidden M is no mistake. Countless Grail-related works contain the hidden letter M.'

Sophie weighed the information. 'I assume nobody is claiming that this is proof of Jesus' marriage to Magdalene.'

'No, no,' Teabing said, going to a nearby table. 'As I said earlier, the marriage of Jesus and Mary Magdalene is part of the historical record.' He located a huge leather-bound book and pulled it towards him. The cover read: *The Gnostic Gospels*. Teabing heaved it open, and Sophie could see it contained photographs of tattered papyrus covered with handwritten text. She did not recognise the ancient language, but the facing pages bore typed translations.

'These are photocopies of the Nag Hammadi and Dead Sea scrolls, which I mentioned earlier,' Teabing said. He flipped to a passage in the middle of the book. 'The Gospel of Philip is always a good place to start.'

Sophie read the passage:

> And the companion of the Saviour is Mary Magdalene. Christ loved her more than all the disciples and used to kiss her often on her mouth. The rest of the disciples were offended by it and they said to him, 'Why do you love her more than all of us?'

'It says nothing of marriage.' Sophie said.

'*Au contraire*.' Teabing smiled, pointing to the first line. 'As any Aramaic scholar will tell you, the word companion, in those days, literally meant spouse.' He pointed out several other passages that, to Sophie's surprise, clearly suggested Magdalene and Jesus had had a romantic relationship.

Sophie was starting to feel overwhelmed. 'I'm sorry, I still don't understand how all of this makes Mary Magdalene the Holy Grail.'

'Aha!' Teabing exclaimed again. 'Therein lies the rub!' He turned to another table and pulled out a large chart. It was an elaborate genealogy. 'Few people realise that Mary Magdalene, in addition to being Christ's right hand, was of royal descent.'

Sophie could now see the title of Mary Magdalene's family tree: THE TRIBE OF BENJAMIN.

'But I was under the impression she was poor,' Sophie said.

Teabing shook his head. 'Magdalene was recast as a whore in order to erase evidence of her powerful family ties.'

'But why would the early Church *care* if Magdalene had royal blood?'

'As you know, the Gospel of Matthew tells us that Jesus was of the House of David. By marrying into the powerful House of Benjamin, Jesus fused two royal bloodlines, creating a potent political union. Potentially he could make a legitimate claim to the throne and restore the line of kings descended from Solomon.'

Sophie sensed he was at last coming to his point.

Teabing looked excited now. 'The legend of the Holy Grail is a legend about royal blood. When Grail legend speaks of "the chalice that held the blood of Christ", it speaks, in fact, of Mary Magdalene—the female womb that carried Jesus' royal bloodline.'

The words seemed to echo across the ballroom and back before they registered in Sophie's mind. 'But how could Christ have a bloodline unless . . .?' She paused and looked at Langdon.

Langdon smiled softly. 'Unless they had a child.'

Sophie stood transfixed.

'Behold,' Teabing proclaimed, 'the greatest cover-up in human history. Not only was Jesus Christ married, but he was a father. My dear, Mary Magdalene was the chalice that bore the royal bloodline of Jesus Christ, the womb from which the sacred fruit sprang forth!'

Sophie felt the hairs stand up on her arms. 'And the Sangreal documents contain proof that Jesus had a royal bloodline?'

'They do.'

'So the entire Holy Grail legend is all about royal blood?'

'Quite literally,' Teabing said. 'The word Sangreal derives from *San Greal*—or Holy Grail. But in its most ancient form, the word *Sangreal* was split differently.' Teabing wrote on a piece of scrap paper and handed it to Sophie.

She read what he had written: *SANG REAL*. Which literally meant 'royal blood'.

CHAPTER 8

'Have I had any messages?' Bishop Aringarosa demanded anxiously.

'Yes, sir,' replied the receptionist at the Opus Dei headquarters in New York. 'I'm very glad you called in. You had an urgent phone message about half an hour ago.'

'Did the caller leave a name?'

'No, sir, just a number.' The operator relayed the number.

'Prefix thirty-three? That's France, am I right?'

'Yes, sir. The caller said it was critical you contact him immediately.'

'Thank you. I have been waiting for that call.' Aringarosa quickly severed the connection.

My cellular phone must not have been receiving because of the hills around Gandolfo, Aringarosa thought as the Fiat approached the exit for Rome's Ciampino Airport. The Teacher was trying to reach me. Despite his concern at having missed the call, he felt encouraged that the Teacher had been confident enough to call Opus Dei headquarters directly. Things must have gone well in Paris tonight.

As Aringarosa began dialling the number, he felt excited to think he would soon be flying to Paris on a specially chartered turboprop.

The line began to ring.

A female voice answered. '*Direction Centrale Police Judiciaire.*'

Aringarosa felt himself hesitate. The French Judicial Police? This was unexpected. 'Ah, yes . . . I was asked to call this number?'

'*Qui êtes-vous?*' the woman said. 'Your name?'

'Bishop Manuel Aringarosa.'

'*Un moment.*' There was a click.

After a long wait, a man came on the line, his tone gruff. 'Bishop, I am glad I finally reached you. We have much to discuss.'

SANGREAL . . . Sang Real . . . San Greal . . . Royal Blood . . . Holy Grail. Sophie felt disorientated as she stood in the silence of the ballroom and stared at Robert Langdon. The more pieces that he and Teabing revealed, the more unpredictable this puzzle became.

'As you will realise, my dear,' Teabing said, 'the threat Mary Magdalene posed to the men of the early Church was potentially ruinous. She was proof that the Church's newly proclaimed deity had spawned a mortal bloodline. In order to defend itself against that threat, the Church perpetuated an image of her as a whore and buried evidence of Christ's marriage to her.'

Langdon nodded. 'Sophie, the historical evidence supporting this is substantial. Mary Magdalene became secretly known by many pseudonyms—the Chalice, the Holy Grail, the Rose.' He paused. 'The Priory of Sion, to this day, still worships her as the Divine Mother.'

'According to the Priory,' Teabing continued, 'Mary Magdalene was pregnant at the time of the crucifixion. For the safety of Christ's unborn child, she had to flee the Holy Land. With the help of Jesus' trusted uncle, Joseph of Arimathea, she secretly travelled to France, then known as Gaul. There she found safe refuge in the Jewish community and she gave birth to a daughter. Her name was Sarah.'

Sophie glanced up. 'They actually know the child's name?'

'Far more than that. Magdalene's and Sarah's lives were scrupulously chronicled by their Jewish protectors. Remember that they revered her as the progenitor of the royal line of David and Solomon.'

Sophie was startled. 'There exists a family tree of Jesus Christ?'

'Indeed. And the genealogy is purportedly one of the key Sangreal documents. Another, rumoured to be part of the Sangreal treasure, is the legendary Q Document—a book of Jesus' teachings, possibly written in his own hand.'

'Writings by Christ himself?'

'Of course,' Teabing said. 'Why wouldn't Jesus have kept a chronicle of His ministry? Most people did in those days.'

Sophie was silent for a long moment. 'And these documents were what the Knights Templar found under Solomon's Temple?'

'Exactly. The documents that have been the object of countless Grail quests throughout history.'

'But if people are searching for documents, why call it a search for the Holy Grail?'

Teabing's expression softened. 'Because the hiding place of the Holy Grail includes a sarcophagus.' He spoke quietly now. 'The quest for the Holy Grail is the quest to kneel before the bones of Mary Magdalene, the wronged Queen, entombed with proof of her family's rightful claim to power.'

'So members of the Priory,' Sophie said, 'are charged with protecting the Sangreal documents and the tomb?'

'Yes, but the brotherhood had another, more important duty as well—to protect the bloodline itself, which survived quietly under cover in France before boldly intermarrying with French royal blood in the fifth century, creating a lineage known as the Merovingian bloodline.'

This news surprised Sophie. Merovingian was a term learned by every student in France. 'The Merovingians founded Paris.'

'Yes. That's one of the reasons the Grail legend is so rich in France.' Teabing gave a ponderous sigh. 'The modern Priory of Sion has a momentous duty. They must nurture and protect the bloodline of Christ—those few surviving members of the royal Merovingian line.'

His words hung in the air, and Sophie felt an odd vibration, as if her bones were reverberating with some new kind of truth. Her grandfather's voice was again whispering in her ear. *Princess, I must tell you the truth about your family.*

A chill raked her flesh. *Princess Sophie.*

'Sir Leigh?' The manservant's voice crackled through the intercom.

Teabing scowled at the ill-timed intrusion. He went over to the intercom and pressed the button. 'Rémy, as you know, I am busy with my guests. Can it not wait?'

'No, sir. Could you join me in the kitchen? My question won't take a minute.'

Teabing rolled his eyes. 'I'll be right there.'

AS SHE LISTENED to the clicking of Teabing's crutches fading down the hallway, Sophie turned and faced Langdon in the deserted ballroom.

He was already shaking his head as if reading her mind. 'No, Sophie,' he whispered, his eyes reassuring. 'The same thought crossed my mind as soon as you told me your grandfather wanted to tell you a secret about your family. But it's impossible. Saunière is not a Merovingian name.'

Sophie wasn't sure whether to feel relieved or disappointed. 'And Chauvel?' she asked. Chauvel was her mother's maiden name.

Again he shook his head. 'Only two direct lines of Merovingians remain. Their family names are Plantard and Saint-Clair. Both families live in hiding, protected by the Priory.'

Sophie felt suddenly weary. She realised she was no closer than she had been at the Louvre to understanding what truth her grandfather had wanted to reveal to her. She wished he had never mentioned her family. He had torn open old wounds. *They are dead, Sophie. They are not coming back.*

'Robert?' she said softly. 'I know Leigh said the Grail story is all around us, but tonight is the first time I've ever heard any of this.'

'You've heard her story before, Sophie,' Langdon said. 'Everyone has. We just don't realise it. The Grail story is everywhere, but hidden.' He motioned to *The Last Supper*. 'A perfect example. Some of today's most enduring art, literature and music secretly tell the history of Mary Magdalene and Jesus.' Langdon quickly told her about legends like Sir Gawain and the Green Knight, King Arthur and the Sleeping Beauty, all of which were Grail allegories. Victor Hugo's *Hunchback of Notre Dame* and Mozart's *Magic Flute* were filled with Masonic symbolism and Grail secrets. Walt Disney loved retelling tales like Cinderella, the Sleeping Beauty and Snow White, which all dealt with the incarceration of the sacred feminine. Snow White—a princess who fell from grace after partaking of a poisoned apple—was a clear allusion to the downfall of Eve in the Garden of Eden.

The clicking of Teabing's crutches approached in the hallway, his pace unusually brisk. When their host entered the study, his expression was stern.

'You'd better explain yourself, Robert,' he said coldly. 'You have not been honest with me.'

'I'M BEING FRAMED, Leigh,' Langdon said, trying to stay calm. 'You know me. I wouldn't kill anyone.'

Teabing's tone did not soften. 'Robert, you have abused my trust. I'm astonished you would put me at risk by coming here and asking me to ramble on about the Grail so you could hide out in my home.'

'I didn't kill anyone.'

'Jacques Saunière is dead, and the police say you did it.' Teabing looked saddened. 'Such a contributor to the arts . . . '

'Sir?' The manservant had appeared now, standing behind Teabing in the study doorway. 'Shall I show them out?'

'Allow me.' Teabing hobbled across the study, unlocked a set of glass doors, and swung them open onto a side lawn. 'Please leave.'

Sophie did not move. 'We have information about the *clef de voûte*. The Priory keystone. That's why we came to you tonight.'

Teabing stared at her for several seconds and scoffed derisively. 'A desperate ploy. Robert knows how I've sought it.'

'She's telling the truth, Leigh,' Langdon said. 'We know where it is.'

Rémy now marched stiffly across the room. 'Leave at once! Or I will call the authorities.'

'Rémy!' Teabing snapped. 'Excuse us for a moment.'

The servant's jaw dropped. 'Sir? These people are—'

'I'll handle this.' Teabing pointed to the hallway.

After a moment of stunned silence, Rémy skulked out.

Teabing turned to Sophie and Langdon. 'This had better be good.'

IN THE THICK BUSHES outside Teabing's study, Silas clutched his pistol and gazed in through the open glass doors. Moments ago, he had seen Langdon and the woman talking in the large study. Before he could move in, a man on crutches entered, yelled at his guests and demanded they leave. Then the woman mentioned the keystone, and everything changed. The glass doors were quickly closed.

Silas was eager to hear what was being said. The keystone was somewhere inside the house. He could feel it. He would give them five minutes. If they did not reveal where they had placed the keystone, he would have to enter and persuade them with force.

INSIDE THE STUDY, Langdon could sense their host's bewilderment.

'Grand Master?' Teabing choked. 'Jacques Saunière?'

Sophie nodded. 'He was my grandfather.'

Teabing staggered back on his crutches, shooting a glance at Langdon, who nodded. 'Miss Neveu, if this is true, then I am truly sorry for your loss. But it still makes no sense. Even if your grandfather were the Priory Grand Master and created the keystone himself, he would never tell you how to find it. Granddaughter or not, you are not eligible to receive such knowledge.'

'Mr Saunière was dying when he passed on the information,' Langdon said. 'He had limited options.'

'He didn't need options,' Teabing argued. 'His three *sénéchaux* also know the secret. That is the beauty of their system.'

'I presume you didn't see the entire news broadcast,' Sophie said. 'In addition to my grandfather, three other prominent Parisians were murdered today. All in similar ways. All had been interrogated.'

Teabing's jaw fell. 'And you think they were . . .?'

'The *sénéchaux*,' Langdon said. 'It's possible someone hoped they would reveal the location of the keystone.'

Teabing looked unconvinced. 'But the brothers would never talk. They are sworn to secrecy. Even in the face of death.'

'And if they never divulged the secret, and they were killed . . .'

Teabing gasped. 'Then the location of the keystone would be lost for ever!'

'And with it,' Langdon said, 'the location of the Holy Grail.'

Teabing flopped in a chair and stared out of the window.

Sophie walked over, her voice soft. 'Considering my grandfather's predicament, it seems possible that in total desperation he tried to pass the secret on to someone outside the brotherhood. Someone he could trust. Someone in his family.'

Teabing was pale. 'But someone capable of such an attack . . .' He paused, stunned by a new fear. 'It could only be one force. The Priory's oldest enemy.'

Langdon glanced up. 'The Church.'

'Who else? It would not be the first time in history that the Church has killed to protect itself. If the Holy Grail documents got out, the Vatican would face a crisis of faith unprecedented in its history.' He heaved an ominous sigh and glanced at Langdon. 'Robert, I assume you are familiar with the Priory's final charge?'

'I am.'

'Miss Neveu,' Teabing said, 'part of the Priory history has always included a plan to unveil the secret on a specific date in history. If that date is approaching and the Church knows it, it would certainly provide the motivation for an all-out attack to find the documents.'

Langdon had the uneasy feeling that Teabing was making good sense. 'Do you think the Church would actually be capable of uncovering hard evidence of the Priory's date?'

'Why not—if the Church was able to uncover the identities of the Priory members, then certainly they could have learned of their plans. And even if they don't have the exact date, their superstitions may be getting the better of them.'

'Superstitions?' Sophie asked.

'We are currently in an epoch of enormous change,' Teabing said. 'The second millennium has recently passed, and with it has ended the two-thousand-year-long astrological Age of Pisces—the fish, which is also the sign of Jesus. As any astrological symbologist will tell you, the Piscean worldview holds that man must be *told* what to do by higher powers because he is incapable of thinking for himself. Hence it has been a time of religious fervour. Now, however, we are entering the Age of Aquarius—the water bearer—and the Aquarian view is that man will learn the truth and be able to think for himself. The ideological shift is enormous, and the Church calls this transitional period the End of Days.'

Sophie looked sceptical. 'As in the end of the world? The Apocalypse?'

'No.' Langdon replied. 'It refers not to the end of the world, but rather to the end of the Age of Pisces.'

'Many Grail historians,' Teabing added, 'believe that if the Priory is indeed planning to release this truth, this point in history would be a symbolically apt time. Which explains why the Church might be motivated to launch a pre-emptive attack against the Priory.' Teabing frowned. 'And believe me, if the Church finds the Holy Grail, they will destroy it.' His eyes grew heavy. 'Then, my dear, the Church will have won their age-old war to rewrite history.'

Sophie pulled the cruciform key from her sweater pocket and held it out to Teabing. 'My grandfather gave me this before he died.'

Teabing ran his fingers across it. 'A key to a church?'

She drew a deep breath. 'This key provides access to the keystone.'

Teabing's head snapped up, his face wild with disbelief. 'Impossible! I've searched every church in France!'

'It's not in a church,' Sophie said. 'It's in a Swiss depository bank.'

'A *bank*?' Teabing shook his head violently. 'That's impossible. The keystone is supposed to be hidden beneath the sign of the Rose.'

'It is,' Langdon said. 'It was stored in a safe-deposit box, in a wooden box inlaid with a five-petal Rose.'

Teabing looked thunderstruck. 'You've seen the keystone? My friends, we must do something. If the keystone is in danger, we have a duty to protect it. If the Church gains access to the bank—'

'Then they will be too late,' Sophie said. 'We removed it.'

'What!'

'Don't worry,' Langdon said. 'The keystone is well hidden.'

'*Extremely* well hidden, I hope!'

Langdon was unable to hide his grin. 'That depends on how often you dust under your couch.'

THE WIND OUTSIDE Château Villette had picked up, and Silas's robe danced in the breeze as he crouched near the window. Although he had been unable to hear much of the conversation, the word 'keystone' had sifted through the glass.

The Teacher's words were fresh in his mind. *Enter Château Villette. Take the keystone. Hurt no one.*

Now, Langdon and the others had adjourned to another room, extinguishing the study lights as they went. Like a panther stalking its prey, Silas crept to the glass doors and slipped inside.

LIEUTENANT COLLET STOOD at the foot of Leigh Teabing's driveway and watched his agents silently spreading out along the length of the fence. They could be over it and have the house surrounded in minutes. He was about to call Fache himself when at last his phone rang.

Fache sounded not nearly as pleased with developments as Collet would have imagined. 'Why didn't someone tell me we had a lead on Langdon?'

'You were on a phone call and—'

'I'm coming out there now,' Fache said. 'Don't make a move. I'll handle this personally.'

Collet's jaw dropped. 'But Captain, you're twenty minutes away! We should act immediately. I have him staked out. I'm with eight men. Four of us have field rifles and the others have sidearms.'

'Wait for me. That is an order.' Fache hung up.

Stunned, Lieutenant Collet switched off his phone. Why the hell was Fache asking him to wait? He knew the answer. Fache was notorious for his pride. He wanted credit for the arrest.

'Lieutenant?' One of the agents came running over. 'We found a car.'

Collet followed the agent about fifty yards past the driveway. There, parked almost out of sight, was a black Audi. It had rental plates. Collet felt the hood. Still warm. Hot even.

'That must be how Langdon got here,' Collet said. 'Call the rental company. Find out if it's stolen.'

Another agent waved Collet back over in the direction of the fence. 'Lieutenant, have a look at this.' He handed Collet a pair of night vision binoculars. 'The grove of trees near the top of the driveway.'

Collet aimed the binoculars up the hill and adjusted the image intensifier dials. Slowly, the greenish shapes came into focus. There, shrouded in the greenery, was an armoured truck identical to the one permitted to leave the Depository Bank of Zürich earlier tonight.

If Langdon and Neveu had arrived in the armoured truck, then who had driven the Audi?

TEABING SAT on the divan, cradling the wooden box on his lap and admiring the lid's intricate inlaid rose. Having spent over a decade searching for this keystone, he wanted to savour this moment.

'Lift the lid,' Sophie whispered, standing over him.

'The Rose,' he murmured. *The Rose is Magdalene, is the Holy Grail. The Rose is the compass that guides the way.*

Slowly he unlatched the lid and raised it. As his eyes gazed upon the contents, he knew in an instant it could only be the keystone. He was staring at a stone cylinder, crafted of interconnecting, lettered dials.

'Designed from da Vinci's diaries,' Sophie said. 'My grandfather made them as a hobby.'

Of course, Teabing realised. He had seen the sketches. The key to finding the Holy Grail lies inside this stone. He lifted the heavy cylinder from the box, holding it gently. He sensed his own destiny lay inside. The ancient words, the foundation of the Grail legend, ran through his mind: *Vous ne trouvez pas le Saint-Graal, c'est le Saint-Graal qui vous trouve.* You do not find the Grail, the Grail finds you.

And that night, incredibly, the key to finding the Holy Grail had walked right through his front door.

WHILE SOPHIE and Teabing sat talking about what the password might be, Langdon carried the rosewood box across the room to a well-lit table to get a better look. He ran his finger over the inlaid rose, wondering if he could prise it out, but the craftsmanship was perfect.

Opening the box, he examined the inside of the lid. As he shifted position the light caught what appeared to be a small hole on the underside, positioned exactly in the centre. Langdon closed the lid and examined the inlay from the top. No hole.

Setting the box on the table, he looked around the room and spied a stack of papers with a paper clip on it. Borrowing the clip, he returned to the box, opened it, and studied the hole again. Carefully, he unbent the paper clip, inserted one end into the hole and gave a gentle push. Something clattered quietly onto the table. It was a small piece of wood, like a puzzle piece. The wooden rose.

Speechless, Langdon stared at the bare spot on the lid where the rose had been. There, engraved in the wood, written in an immaculate hand, were four lines of text in a language he had never seen. The characters looked vaguely Semitic, he thought to himself.

Then, out of nowhere, a crushing blow to the head knocked Langdon to his knees. Everything went black.

SOPHIE NEVEU, despite working in law enforcement, had never found herself at gunpoint until tonight. Almost inconceivably, the gun into which she was now staring was clutched in the pale hand of an enormous albino monk with long white hair.

He looked at her with red eyes. 'You know what I have come for,' he said, his voice hollow.

Sophie and Teabing were seated on the divan, arms raised as commanded. Langdon lay groaning on the floor. The monk's eyes fell immediately to the keystone in Teabing's lap.

Teabing's tone was defiant. 'You will not be able to open it.'

'My Teacher is very wise,' the monk replied, inching closer, the gun shifting between Teabing and Sophie.

'Who is your teacher?' Teabing asked. 'Perhaps we can make a financial arrangement.'

'The Grail is priceless.' The monk moved closer. 'Stand up and give it to me.'

'You know of the keystone?' Teabing asked.

'Never mind what I know. Give it to me.'

Teabing slipped his right hand through one of his crutches and grasped the keystone in his left. Lurching to his feet, he stood erect, leaning unsteadily on his right crutch.

The monk closed to within a few feet, keeping the gun aimed directly at Teabing's head. Sophie watched, feeling helpless as the monk reached out to take the cylinder.

'You will not succeed,' Teabing said. 'Only the worthy can unlock this stone.'

GOD ALONE JUDGES the worthy, Silas thought.

'It's quite heavy,' the man on crutches said, his arm wavering now. 'If you don't take it soon, I shall drop it!' He swayed perilously.

Silas stepped forwards to take the stone, and, as he did, the man on crutches lost his balance. The crutch slid out from under him, and he began to topple sideways to his right. Silas lunged to save the stone, lowering his weapon in the process. As the man fell, his hand swung backwards, and the cylinder fell onto the couch. At the same instant, the crutch seemed to accelerate through the air towards Silas's leg.

Splinters of pain tore up Silas's body as the crutch made contact with his cilice, crushing the barbs into his already raw flesh. As Silas crumpled to his knees, the pistol discharged with a deafening roar and the bullet buried itself harmlessly in the floorboards. Before he could raise the gun and fire again, the woman's foot caught him squarely beneath the jaw.

IN THE DISTANT RECESSES of his groggy mind, Robert Langdon had heard a gunshot and a scream of pain. A jackhammer was boring a hole into the back of his cranium and somewhere nearby, people were talking.

'Where the devil were you?' Teabing was yelling.

The manservant hurried in. 'What happened? Oh my God! Who is that? I'll call the police!'

'Bloody hell! Don't call the police. Make yourself useful and get us something with which to restrain this monster.'

'And some ice!' Sophie called after him.

Langdon drifted out again. More voices. Movement. Now he was seated on the divan and, as his vision began to clear, he found himself staring at the massive body of an albino monk lying on the floor, the robe over his right thigh soaked with blood.

He turned to Sophie. 'Who is that? What . . . happened?'

Teabing hobbled over. 'You were rescued by a knight brandishing an Excalibur made by Acme Orthopaedic.'

Huh? Langdon tried to sit up.

Sophie's touch was tender. 'Just give yourself a minute, Robert.'

'He was wearing a cilice,' Teabing explained, pointing to a bloody strip of barbed leather that lay on the floor. 'A discipline belt. He wore it on his thigh. I took careful aim.'

Langdon rubbed his head. 'But how . . . did you know?'

Teabing grinned. 'Christianity is my field of study, Robert, and there are certain sects who wear their hearts on their sleeves.' He pointed at the blood soaking through the monk's cloak. 'As it were.'

'Opus Dei,' Langdon whispered, recalling recent media coverage of the Catholic sect and the stringent discipline of its 'numerary' members.

'Robert,' Sophie said, walking to the wooden box. 'What's this?' She was holding the small rose inlay he had removed from the lid.

Langdon considered it groggily. 'It covered an engraving on the box. I think the text might tell us how to open the keystone.'

Before Sophie and Teabing could respond, a sea of blue police lights and sirens appeared snaking up the driveway.

Teabing frowned. 'My friends, it seems we have a decision to make. And we'd better make it fast.'

GUNS DRAWN, Collet and his agents burst through the front door. Fanning out, they began searching the rooms on the ground level. They found a bullet hole in the drawing-room floor, signs of a struggle, a small amount of blood, a strange, barbed leather belt. But the entire floor seemed deserted. Just as Collet was about to send his men to search the grounds behind the house, he heard voices on the level above them. 'They're upstairs!'

Rushing up the wide staircase, Collet and his men moved through the huge home, securing darkened bedrooms and hallways as they closed in on the sounds of voices. As they neared the final bedroom, the voices stopped suddenly, only to be replaced by an odd rumbling, like an engine.

Sidearm raised, Collet gave the signal. Charging into the room with men pouring in after him, he aimed his weapon at . . . nothing.

An empty guest bedroom.

The rumbling sounds of a car engine poured from a black electronic panel on the wall beside the bed.

They had been lured upstairs with the intercom! Collet was downstairs in seconds, running towards the back door, grabbing one of his agents on the way. The two men crossed the rear lawn and arrived breathless at a grey barn. Even before they entered, Collet could hear the fading sounds of a car engine.

He ran through the barn, past a black Ferrari and an Aston Martin Coupé, to the rear door, which was open to a dark slope of muddy fields. All he could make out was the faint shadow of a forest in the distance. No headlights. This valley was probably crisscrossed by dozens of unmapped hunting trails, but Collet was confident his quarry would never make the woods. 'These fancy sports cars can't handle rough terrain.'

'Um, sir?' The agent pointed to several sets of keys hanging on a pegboard. The labels bore familiar names: FERRARI . . . ROLLS-ROYCE . . . ASTON MARTIN . . .

But the last peg was empty. When Collet read the label above it, he knew he was in trouble.

THE RANGE ROVER was a Java Black Pearl, four-wheel drive, standard transmission, with high-strength polypropylene lamps, rear light cluster fittings and the steering wheel on the right. Langdon was pleased he was not driving.

Teabing's manservant, Rémy, was doing an impressive job of manoeuvring the vehicle across the moonlit fields behind Château Villette, with no headlights.

Cradling the keystone, Langdon turned in the passenger seat and eyed Teabing and Sophie in the back.

'How's your head, Robert?' Sophie asked, sounding concerned.

Langdon forced a pained smile. 'Better, thanks.' It was killing him.

Beside her, Teabing glanced over his shoulder at the bound and gagged monk lying in the cramped luggage area behind the back seat. Teabing had the monk's gun on his lap.

'So glad you popped in this evening, Robert,' Teabing said, grinning as if he were having fun for the first time in years. He tapped Rémy on the shoulder from behind. 'I want to get into the woods a bit. No reason to risk them seeing us from the house.'

Rémy coasted to a crawl and guided the Range Rover through a gap in the trees. He pressed a button and the muted yellow glow of fog lights fanned out across the path in front of them.

'Where are we going?' Sophie asked.

'This trail continues into the forest,' Teabing said. 'Cutting across the estate and then heading north. We shall emerge unscathed on the shoulder of highway five.'

Unscathed. Langdon's head begged to differ. He turned his eyes down to his lap, where the keystone was safely stored in its wooden box. The inlaid rose on the lid was back in place and, although his head felt muddled, he was eager to remove the inlay again, to examine the engraving beneath. He unlatched the lid and began to raise it when Teabing laid a hand on his shoulder from behind.

'Patience, Robert,' he said. 'It's bumpy and dark. Let's focus on getting away in one piece, shall we? There will be time for that soon.'

The monk in the back was moaning now.

'Are you sure we should have brought him?' Langdon asked.

'Bloody well positive!' Teabing exclaimed. 'You're wanted for murder, Robert. This scoundrel is your ticket to freedom. The police apparently want you badly enough to have tailed you to my home.'

'My fault,' Sophie said. 'The truck probably had a transmitter.'

'Not the point,' Teabing said. 'I'm not surprised the police found you, but I *am* surprised that this Opus Dei character found you. From all you've told me, I can't imagine how this man could have tailed you to my home unless he had a contact either within the Judicial Police or within the Zürich Depository Bank. He is not working alone, Robert, and until you learn who is behind all this, you both are in danger. Now, could you be so kind as to hand me that phone?' Teabing pointed to the car phone on the dashboard.

Langdon handed it into the back, and Teabing dialled a number.

'Richard? Did I wake you? . . . Silly question. I'm sorry. I have a small problem. I'm feeling a bit off and Rémy and I need to pop up to England for my treatments. Can you have Elizabeth ready in twenty minutes? . . . I know, do the best you can. See you shortly.' He hung up.

'Elizabeth?' Langdon said.

'My plane. She cost me a Queen's ransom.'

Langdon turned round and looked at him.

'What?' Teabing demanded. 'You two can't expect to stay in France with the entire Judicial Police after you. London will be much safer.'

'You're running a big risk by helping us,' Sophie said. 'You won't make any friends with the French police.'

Teabing gave a wave of disgust. 'I am finished with France. I moved here to find the keystone. That work is now done. I shan't care if I never again see Château Villette. Furthermore, the Grail is now believed to be in Great Britain.'

Sophie was uncertain. 'How will we get through airport security?'

Teabing chuckled. 'I fly from Le Bourget every fortnight to take my treatments in England. I pay for certain special privileges at both ends. Once we're airborne, you can make a decision as to whether or not you'd like someone from the US Embassy to meet us.'

Langdon suddenly didn't want anything to do with the embassy. All he could think of was the keystone, the inscription and whether it would all lead to the Grail.

'Sir?' Rémy said. 'Are you truly thinking of returning to England for good?'

'Rémy, you needn't worry,' Teabing assured him. 'Just because I am returning to the Queen's realm does not mean I intend to subject my palate to bangers and mash for the rest of my days. And I expect you to join me there permanently. An adventure, Rémy. An adventure!'

Langdon had to smile. He glanced back at Sophie and saw that she too seemed caught up in the man's infectious enthusiasm. Despite his troubles, Langdon was thankful to have landed in such good company, and as he sat back, he began to relax.

After several minutes, an incredible notion occurred to him out of nowhere. He turned to Sophie, his heart racing. 'I need to use your cellphone, Sophie. I need to make a call to the States.'

Sophie looked wary. 'You'll have to reverse the charges. My service doesn't cover transatlantic.'

Langdon nodded, then dialled zero, hoping that this next conversation might answer a question that had been puzzling him all night.

CHAPTER 9

New York-based editor Jonas Faukman had just climbed into bed for the night when the telephone rang. Grumbling, he picked up the receiver.

An operator's voice asked, 'Will you accept charges for a collect call from Robert Langdon?'

Puzzled, Jonas turned on the light. 'Uh . . . sure, OK.'

The line clicked. 'Jonas?'

'Robert? You wake me up *and* you charge me for it?'

'Jonas, forgive me,' Langdon said. 'I'll keep this very short. I really need to know. The manuscript I gave you. Did you send any copies out without telling me?'

Faukman hesitated. Langdon's newest manuscript—an exploration of the history of goddess worship—was going to raise eyebrows. Faukman had no intention of printing advance reading copies of the book without at least a few endorsements from serious historians. He had indeed chosen ten big names in the art world and sent them all sections of the manuscript, along with a polite letter asking if they would be willing to write a short endorsement for the dust jacket.

'Jonas?' Langdon pressed. 'Did you send my manuscript to the curator of the Paris Louvre?'

'What do you think? Saunière's books are in your bibliography, and the guy has serious clout for foreign sales.'

A pause. 'When did you send it?'

'About a month ago. I also mentioned you would be in Paris soon and suggested you two chat. Hold on, aren't you supposed to *be* in Paris this week?' Faukman said, rubbing his eyes.

'I *am* in Paris.'

Faukman sat upright. 'You called me collect from *Paris*?'

'Take it out of my royalties. I've got to run Jonas. Thanks.'

INSIDE THE RANGE ROVER, Leigh Teabing let out a guffaw. 'Robert, you're saying you wrote a manuscript that delves into a secret society, and your editor sent a copy to that secret society?'

Langdon slumped. 'Evidently.'

'Here's the million-dollar question,' Teabing said, still chuckling. 'Was your position on the Priory favourable or unfavourable?'

Langdon shrugged. 'I took no position. I simply provided history on the brotherhood and described them as a modern goddess worship society, keepers of the Grail and guardians of ancient documents.'

Sophie looked at him. 'Did you mention the keystone?'

Langdon winced and nodded. He had. Numerous times.

'I guess that explains *P.S. Find Robert Langdon*,' she said.

Langdon sensed it was actually something else in the manuscript that had piqued Saunière's interest, but that topic was something he would discuss with Sophie when they were alone.

WHEN THE RANGE ROVER arrived at Le Bourget Airfield, Rémy drove to a small hangar at the far end of the airstrip. As they approached, a man in wrinkled khakis hurried from the hangar.

Langdon stared at the sleek white jet within. 'That's Elizabeth?'

Teabing grinned. 'Beats the bloody Chunnel.'

'Almost ready, sir,' the man in khakis called in a British accent. 'Apologies for the delay, but you took me by surprise and—' He stopped short as he watched the group unload. 'Sir, my humble apologies, but my diplomatic flight allowance provides only for you and your manservant. I cannot take your guests.'

Teabing took the pistol out of the vehicle. 'Richard,' he said, smiling warmly, 'two thousand pounds sterling and this loaded gun say you *can* take my guests.' He motioned to the Range Rover. 'And the unfortunate fellow in the back.'

STANDING IN THE DRAWING room of Château Villette, Lieutenant Collet listened despondently as Captain Fache yelled into the phone, coordinating the failed attempt to locate the missing Range Rover.

It could be anywhere by now, Collet thought. Having disobeyed

Fache's direct orders and lost Langdon for a second time, he was grateful that PTS had located a bullet hole in the floor, which at least corroborated his claims that a shot had been fired. Unfortunately, none of the clues they were turning up here seemed to shed light on what was going on or who was involved. The black Audi outside had been rented on a false credit card, and the prints inside it matched nothing in the Interpol data base.

Another agent hurried into the living room heading for Fache, who had just come off the phone. 'Sir, Central just heard from André Vernet at the Depository Bank of Zürich. He wants to talk to you privately. Apparently now he's admitting that Langdon and Neveu spent time inside his bank tonight.'

'We figured that out,' Fache said. 'Why did Vernet lie about it?'

'He said he'll talk only to you, but he's agreed to cooperate fully in exchange for our keeping his bank's name out of the news.'

From the kitchen, another agent yelled to Fache. 'Captain? I'm going through Mr Teabing's speed dial numbers, and I'm on the phone with Le Bourget Airfield. I've got some bad news.'

As the Hawker levelled off, Langdon carefully lifted the rosewood box from his lap. Using the tip of a pen, he removed the inlaid Rose on top and revealed the text beneath it:

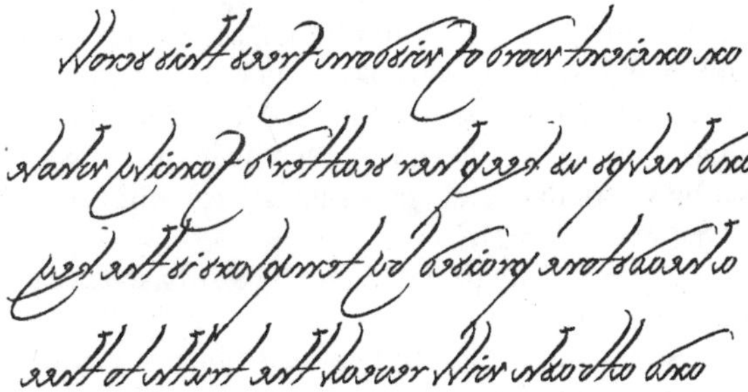

After several seconds, Langdon sighed with frustration. 'I just can't seem to place it. My first guess was a Semitic, but now I'm not so sure. It does look familiar somehow.'

'Perhaps if I just . . . ' Reaching over, Teabing pulled the box away from Langdon. Taking a deep breath, he examined the engraving. He said nothing for a very long time. Then at last he admitted, 'This looks like nothing I've ever seen!'

'Might I see it?' Sophie asked.

'Of course, dear,' Teabing said, pushing it over to her.

'Aah,' Sophie said. 'I should have guessed.'

'Guessed what?' Teabing demanded.

'That this would be the language my grandfather would have used.'

'You're saying you can *read* this text?' Teabing exclaimed.

'Quite easily,' Sophie was enjoying herself now. 'My grandfather taught me this language when I was only six years old. I'm fluent.' She fixed Teabing with an admonishing glare. 'And frankly, sir, I'm a little surprised you didn't recognise it.' She smiled. 'I can read the first few words. It's English.'

'Of course,' Langdon said at last. 'Reverse text. Da Vinci used it in his notebooks to keep people from stealing his ideas. We need a mirror.'

'No we don't,' Sophie said. 'I bet this veneer is thin enough to view the text through.' She lifted the rosewood box up to a light on the wall and examined the underside of the lid.

The script was instantly legible.

Sophie quickly found some paper and copied the text down longhand. When she was done, Langdon read the text aloud slowly.

'An ancient word of wisdom frees this scroll . . . and helps us keep her scatter'd family whole . . . a headstone praised by templars is the key . . . and atbash will reveal the truth to thee.'

'The password,' Sophie said, 'appears to have something to do with the Templars—"A headstone praised by Templars is the key."'

'Leigh,' Langdon said, 'you're the Templar specialist. Any ideas?'

Teabing sighed. 'Well, it's possible the poem is referencing a gravestone the Templars praised at the tomb of Magdalene, but that doesn't help us much because we have no idea where her tomb is.'

'The last line,' Sophie said, 'says that *atbash* will reveal the truth. I've heard that word. Atbash.'

'I'm not surprised,' Langdon replied. 'The Atbash Cipher is one of the oldest codes known to man.'

Of course! Sophie thought. The famous Hebrew encoding system.

The Atbash Cipher had been part of Sophie's early cryptology training. A common form of Jewish cryptogram, dating back to 500 BC, it was a simple substitution code based on the twenty-two-letter Hebrew alphabet. In Atbash, the first letter was substituted by the last letter, the second letter by the next to last letter, and so on.

'Atbash is sublimely appropriate,' Teabing said. 'Text encrypted using its code is found throughout the Kabbala, the Dead Sea Scrolls and even the Old Testament. The Priory would certainly include the Atbash Cipher as part of their teachings.'

'The only problem,' Langdon said, 'is that we don't have anything on which to apply the cipher.'

Teabing sighed. 'There must be a code word on the headstone. We must find this headstone praised by Templars.'

Sophie had grown up solving her grandfather's riddles, and sensed that this poem contained more information, ingeniously hidden. But she knew that the cryptex would not give up its secrets easily.

BOURGET AIRFIELD'S air-traffic controller had been dozing before a blank radar screen in his small tower when the captain of the Judicial Police practically broke down his door.

'Teabing's jet,' Bezu Fache blared, marching into the small tower. 'Where did it go?'

The controller's initial response was a babbling, lame attempt to protect the privacy of one of their most respected customers.

'OK,' Fache said, 'I am placing you under arrest for permitting a private plane to take off without registering a flight plan.' He motioned to another officer, who approached with handcuffs.

'Wait!' the controller whimpered. 'Sir Leigh Teabing makes frequent trips to London for medical treatments. He has a hangar at Biggin Hill Executive Airport in Kent.'

'Did he have others on board?'

'I swear, sir, there is no way for me to know that. Our clients can drive directly to their hangars, and load as they please.'

Fache checked his watch. 'If they're going to Biggin Hill, how long until they land?'

'It's a short flight. His plane could be on the ground by . . . around six thirty. Fifteen minutes from now.'

Fache turned to one of his men. 'Get a transport up here. I'm going to London. And get me the Kent Police. Tell them I want Teabing's plane to be permitted to land, then surrounded on the tarmac. Nobody deplanes until I get there.'

'YOU'RE QUIET,' Langdon said, gazing across the cabin at Sophie.

'Just tired,' she replied. 'And the poem . . . I don't know.'

Langdon nodded. He was feeling the same way. Teabing had gone to the back of the plane to get a snack, and so he decided to take advantage of a moment alone with Sophie to tell her something that had been on his mind. 'I think I know part of the reason why your grandfather conspired to put us together. I think there's something he wanted me to explain to you. Maybe he was hoping I could somehow heal the rift between you by explaining what drove you apart.'

'I haven't told you what drove us apart.'

Langdon eyed her carefully. 'Sophie, you told me you witnessed something that convinced you your grandfather was in a secret society. And whatever you saw upset you enough that you haven't spoken to him since. I know a fair amount about secret societies, so I can guess what you saw. Was it in the spring?' he asked. 'Sometime around the equinox? Mid-March?'

Sophie's eyes began to well with emotion. 'I was on spring break from university. I came home a few days early.'

'Were the people present dressed in white and black?'

She wiped her eyes and then nodded. 'The women were in white gossamer gowns . . . with golden shoes. They held golden orbs. The men wore black tunics and black shoes. Everyone wore masks.'

'It's called *hieros gamos*,' he said softly. 'Egyptian priests and priestesses performed it regularly to celebrate the reproductive power of the female. *Hieros gamos* means "sacred marriage".'

'The ritual I saw was no marriage.'

'Marriage as in *union*, Sophie.'

'You mean as in sex.'

'No.'

'No?' she said, her olive eyes testing him.

Langdon back-pedalled. 'Well . . . yes, in a manner of speaking, but *hieros gamos* is a spiritual act. The ancients believed that the male was spiritually incomplete until he had carnal knowledge of the sacred feminine. In a climactic state, he could see God. It's important to remember that the ancients' view of sex was entirely different from ours today. Sex produced new life—the ultimate miracle—and miracles could be performed only by a god. The ability of the woman to produce life from her womb made her sacred. *Hieros gamos* is a deeply sacred ceremony, some two thousand years old.

'But for the early Church,' Langdon continued in a soft voice, 'mankind's use of sex to commune directly with God posed a serious threat to the Catholic power base. It left the Church out of the loop, undermining their self-proclaimed status as the sole conduit to God. For obvious reasons, they worked hard to demonise sex and recast it as a disgusting and sinful act. Other major religions did the same.'

His words seemed to strike a nerve. Sophie had been remarkably poised all evening, but now, for the first time, Langdon saw her composure beginning to crack.

SOPHIE STARED BLANKLY out of the plane's window, trying to process what Langdon had just told her. A new regret welled inside her as she pictured the stacks of unopened letters her grandfather had sent her. Without turning from the window, she began to speak quietly.

As she recounted what had happened that night in the basement of her grandfather's house in Normandy, she felt herself drifting back. She saw the shadows of her hiding place on the staircase, as she watched the strangers swaying and chanting by flickering candlelight.

The women's white gossamer gowns billowed as they raised golden orbs and called out in unison, '*I was with you in the beginning, in the dawn of all that is holy, I bore you from the womb before the start of day.*' The women lowered the orbs, and everyone rocked back and forth as if in a trance, watching something in the centre of the circle. The voices grew louder, faster. The participants stepped inwards and knelt, and in that instant Sophie saw what they were all watching.

On a low altar in the centre of the circle lay a naked man whom Sophie instantly recognised. She almost cried out. *Grand-père!* This image alone would have shocked her, and yet there was more—a naked woman wearing a white mask, her luxuriant silver hair flowing out behind it. She was making love to Sophie's grandfather.

IN THE CHARTERED turboprop, Bishop Aringarosa hung up on Fache for the second time. The captain's newest update seemed unfathomable, and yet almost nothing tonight made sense any more. What have I got Silas into? What have I got myself into? He walked to the cockpit.

'I need to change destinations. I have to go to London immediately.'

The pilot glanced over his shoulder and laughed. 'You're joking, right? This is a charter flight, not a taxi, Father.'

'I will pay you extra, of course. How much?'

'It's not a question of money, Father, there are other issues.'

'Ten thousand euros. Right now.'

The pilot turned, his eyes wide with shock. 'How much?'

Aringarosa walked back to his black briefcase and removed one of the bearer bonds. He handed it to the pilot. 'It's a bearer bond drawn on the Vatican Bank. It's the same as cash.'

'Only cash is cash,' the pilot said, handing the bond back.

Aringarosa steadied himself against the cockpit door. 'This is a matter of life or death. I need to get to London.'

The pilot eyed the bishop's gold ring. 'Real diamonds?'

Aringarosa looked at the ring. 'I could not possibly part with this.'

The pilot shrugged, and turned back to the controls.

Aringarosa felt a deepening sadness. He looked at the ring. Everything it represented was about to be lost anyway. He slid it from his finger and placed it on the instrument panel.

Fifteen seconds later, back in his seat, he felt the plane banking a few more degrees to the north.

'VICTUALS, MY DEARS?' Teabing reappeared with a flourish, placing several cans of Coke and a box of biscuits on the table. 'Our friend the monk isn't talking yet, but give him time.' He eyed the poem, then looked at Sophie. 'So, any headway? What is your grandfather trying to tell us? Where is this headstone praised by Templars?'

Sophie shook her head and remained silent. Langdon could see she was still shaken from recounting her experience of *hieros gamos*.

While Teabing contemplated the verse, Langdon popped a Coke and turned to the window. *A headstone praised by Templars is the key.* The veil of night was dissolving quickly now, and he saw a shimmering sea beneath them. It wouldn't be long now. Langdon willed the light of day to bring with it another kind of illumination, but the lighter it became outside, the further he felt from the truth.

The plane was over land again when it struck him. He set down his can of Coke. 'The Templar headstone—I figured it out,' he said.

Teabing's eyes turned to saucers. 'You know where it is?'

Langdon smiled. 'Not *where* it is. *What* it is.'

Sophie leaned in to hear.

'During the Inquisition,' Langdon began, 'the Church accused the Knights Templar of all kinds of heresies, right?'

'Correct,' said Teabing. 'They fabricated all kinds of charges. Sodomy, devil worship, quite a list.'

'And on that list was the worship of *false idols*, right? The Church accused the Templars of secretly performing rituals in which they prayed to a carved stone head . . . the pagan god—'

'Baphomet!' Teabing blurted. 'My heavens, Robert, you're right! A headstone praised by Templars!'

Langdon explained to Sophie that Baphomet was a pagan fertility god often represented as a ram or goat. The Templars honoured him by encircling a stone replica of his head and chanting prayers.

'Yes, yes, Baphomet must be what the poem is referring to,' Teabing said excitedly. 'The ceremony honoured the creative magic of sexual union, but Pope Clement convinced everyone that Baphomet's head was that of the devil. The Pope used the head of Baphomet as the linchpin in his case against the Templars.'

Langdon concurred. The modern belief in a horned devil known as Satan could be traced back to Baphomet.

'OK,' Sophie said, 'but if Baphomet is the headstone praised by Templars, then we have a new dilemma.' She pointed to the dials on the cryptex. 'Baphomet has eight letters. We only have room for five.'

Teabing grinned broadly. 'This, my dear, is where the Atbash Cipher comes into play.'

LANGDON WAS IMPRESSED. Teabing had just finished writing out the entire twenty-two-letter Hebrew alphabet—*alef-beit*—using Roman letters instead of Hebrew characters, and was now reading through them with flawless pronunciation.

'*Alef, Beit, Gimel, Dalet, Hei, Vav, Zayin, Chet, Tet, Yud, Kaf, Lamed, Mem, Nun, Samech, Ayin, Pei, Tzadik, Kuf, Reish, Shin* and *Tav*.' He mopped his brow. 'In formal Hebrew spelling, the vowel sounds are not written. So when we write the word Baphomet using the Hebrew alphabet, it will lose its three vowels in translation, leaving us—'

'Five letters,' Sophie blurted.

Teabing nodded and began writing again. 'OK, here is the proper spelling of Baphomet in Hebrew letters. I'll sketch in the missing vowels for clarity's sake.'

B a P V o M e Th

'Next, we create our substitution scheme by rewriting the entire alphabet in reverse order beneath the original alphabet. Like this.'

A	B	G	D	H	V	Z	Ch	T	Y	K
Th	Sh	R	Q	Tz	P	O	S	N	M	L

Looking at Teabing's substitution matrix, Langdon could not control his excitement. 'We're getting close,' he whispered.

'Within inches, Robert,' Teabing said. He glanced over at Sophie and smiled. 'You ready?'

She nodded.

'OK. B is Sh . . . P is V . . .' Teabing was grinning like a schoolboy at Christmas. 'And the Atbash Cipher reveals . . . ' He stopped short. 'Good God!'

Langdon's head snapped up.

'What's wrong?' Sophie demanded.

'This is . . . ingenious,' he whispered. 'Utterly ingenious!' Teabing wrote again on the paper. 'Drumroll, please. Here is your password.' He showed them what he had written.

Sh-V-P-Y-A

Sophie scowled. 'What is it?'

Teabing was laughing. 'An ancient word of wisdom. Quite literally!'

Langdon read the letters again. *An ancient word of wisdom frees this scroll.* An instant later he got it.

Sophie looked at the word and then at the dial. 'Hold on! This can't be the password,' she argued. 'The cryptex doesn't have an Sh on the dial. It uses a traditional Roman alphabet.'

'*Read* the word,' Langdon urged. 'Keep in mind two things. In Hebrew, the symbol for the sound Sh can also be pronounced as S, just as the letter P can be pronounced F. And the letter Vav is often used to signify for the vowel sound O!'

Sophie again looked at the letters, attempting to sound them out. '*S . . . o . . . f . . . y . . . a.*'

Langdon was nodding enthusiastically. 'Yes! *Sophia* literally means *wisdom* in Greek.'

Sophie turned her gaze to the five lettered dials on the cryptex. 'But wait . . . the word Sophia has *six* letters.'

Teabing's smile never faded. 'Look at the poem again. Your grandfather wrote, 'An *ancient* word of wisdom."'

'Yes?'

Teabing winked. 'In ancient Greek, wisdom is spelled S-O-F-I-A.'

SOPHIE FELT a wild excitement as she cradled the cryptex and began dialling in the letters: S . . . O . . . F . . . I . . . A.

She aligned the final dial. 'OK,' she whispered, glancing up at the others. 'I'm going to pull it apart.'

Gripping the stone tube, Sophie slowly pulled and the stone slid apart like a well-crafted telescope. She set the heavy end piece on the table and tipped the cylinder to peer inside.

A scroll!

Sophie could see that it had been wrapped round a cylindrical object—the vial of vinegar, she assumed. Strangely, though, the paper was not the customary delicate papyrus, but vellum. That's odd, she thought, vinegar can't dissolve vellum. She looked again and realised that the object in the centre was not a vial of vinegar after all.

'What's wrong?' Teabing asked. 'Pull out the scroll.'

Frowning, Sophie grabbed the rolled vellum and the object round which it was wrapped, pulling them both out of the container. She unrolled the scroll and revealed what was wrapped inside.

'God help us,' Teabing said, slumping.

LANGDON STARED in amazement. I see that Saunière has no intention of making this easy, he thought.

On the table sat a second cryptex. Smaller, made of black onyx, it had been nested within the first. Saunière's passion for dualism. Two cryptexes. Everything in pairs. Male within female. Black within white.

Langdon reached over and lifted the black cryptex, which was half the size of the first. He heard the familiar gurgle. Apparently, the vinegar they had heard earlier was inside this smaller cryptex.

'Well, Robert,' Teabing said, sliding the page of vellum over to him. 'You'll be pleased to hear that we're flying in the right direction.'

Written in ornate penmanship on the thick vellum sheet was another four-line verse. Langdon read the first line:

In London lies a knight a Pope interred

He looked excitedly at Teabing. 'Do you have any idea what knight this poem is referring to?'

Teabing grinned. 'Not the foggiest. But I know precisely where we should look.'

'SEAT BELTS, PLEASE,' the pilot announced as the Hawker 731 descended into a gloomy morning drizzle. 'We'll be landing in five minutes.'

Teabing felt a joyous sense of homecoming when he saw the misty hills of Kent beneath the descending plane. My time in France is over, he thought. I am returning to England victorious. The keystone has been found. He was already tasting the glory.

As Langdon and Sophie looked on, Teabing went over to a wall safe. He dialled in the combination, opened the safe and extracted two passports. 'Documentation for Rémy and myself.' He then removed a thick stack of fifty-pound notes. 'And documentation for you two.'

Sophie looked sceptical. 'A bribe?'

'Creative diplomacy. A British customs official will greet us at my hangar and ask to board the plane. Rather than permitting him to come on, I'll say I'm travelling with a French celebrity who prefers that nobody knows she is in England—press considerations, you know—and I'll offer this generous tip as gratitude for his discretion. These people know me. I'm not an arms dealer, for heaven's sake. I was knighted.' Teabing smiled. 'Membership has its privileges.'

Rémy approached up the aisle, the Heckler Koch pistol cradled in his hand. 'Sir, my agenda?'

Teabing glanced at his servant. 'You will stay on board with our guest until we return. We can't drag him all over London with us.'

'Leigh, what happens if the French police find your plane before we return?' Sophie asked warily. 'You transported a bound hostage across international borders. This is serious.'

'So are my lawyers.' He scowled towards the monk in the rear of the plane. 'That animal broke into my home and almost killed me.'

'Sir?' the pilot called back. 'The tower just radioed. They've got some kind of maintenance problem out near your hangar, and they're asking me to bring the plane directly to the terminal instead.'

Teabing had been flying to Biggin Hill for over a decade, and this was a first. 'Did they mention what the problem is?'

'Something about a petrol leak at the pumping station. They asked me to park in front of the terminal and keep everyone on board until further notice. Safety precaution.'

Teabing was sceptical. Must be one hell of a petrol leak, he thought. The pumping station was a good half-mile from his hangar. He turned to Sophie and Langdon. 'My friends, I have an unpleasant suspicion that we are about to be met by a welcoming committee.'

Langdon sighed. 'I guess Fache still thinks I'm his man. Maybe I should turn myself in and sort this out legally. Leave you all out of it.'

'Oh, heavens, Robert!' Teabing waved it off. 'Do you really think they would let the rest of us go? No, we're all in this together.'

He hobbled towards the cockpit. Bold action was necessary if they were to have any chance of finding their prize.

'What are you doing?' Langdon asked.

'Sales meeting,' Teabing said, wondering how much it would cost him to persuade his pilot to perform one highly irregular manoeuvre.

CHAPTER 10

Simon Edwards, Executive Services Officer at Biggin Hill Airport, paced the control tower, squinting nervously at the runway. He had been woken early on a Saturday morning and called in to oversee the arrest of one of his most lucrative clients. Although he had not yet been told what the charges were, they were obviously serious.

Eight policemen with handguns stood inside the terminal building, awaiting the moment when the plane's engines powered down. A runway attendant would then place safety wedges under the tyres so the plane could no longer move. Kent Police officers would step into view and detain the occupants until the French police arrived.

The Hawker was low in the sky now, skimming the treetops. Simon Edwards went downstairs to watch the landing from tarmac level. Out on the runway, the Hawker's tyres touched down in a puff of smoke. But rather than braking and turning into the terminal, the jet coasted calmly on towards Teabing's hangar.

The chief inspector spun and stared at Edwards. 'I thought you said the pilot agreed to come to the terminal!'

Edwards was bewildered. 'He *did*!'

Seconds later, Edwards found himself wedged in a police car, racing across the tarmac towards the distant hangar into which Teabing's Hawker had just disappeared. When the cars arrived and skidded to a stop outside the gaping hangar door, the Hawker's engines were still roaring, and the jet was just finishing its usual rotation.

As the pilot brought the plane to a final stop, the police streamed in, guns drawn, and took up positions round the jet. Edwards joined the chief inspector, who moved warily towards the fuselage door. After several minutes it popped open.

Leigh Teabing appeared as the plane's electronic stairs smoothly dropped down. As he gazed out at the sea of weapons aimed at him, he scratched his head and said, 'Simon, did I win the policemen's lottery while I was away?'

Simon Edwards stepped forwards, swallowing the frog in his throat. 'Good morning, sir. I apologise for the confusion. We've had a petrol leak and your pilot said he was coming to the terminal. I need to ask you to stay on board for another half an hour or so.'

'Yes, well, I told my pilot to come here instead.' He hobbled down the stairs. 'I'm late for a medical appointment. I cannot afford to miss it.'

The chief inspector blocked Teabing's progress away from the plane. 'The French Judicial Police claim you are transporting fugitives.'

Teabing stared at the policeman a long moment, then burst out laughing. 'Is this one of those hidden camera programmes? Jolly good!'

The chief inspector never flinched. 'This is serious, sir. The French police claim you also may have a hostage on board.'

Teabing's manservant Rémy appeared in the doorway at the top of the stairs. 'Sometimes I *feel* like a hostage working for Sir Leigh, but he assures me that I am free to go.' He checked his watch. 'Master, we really are running late.' Rémy nodded towards the custom-built Jaguar stretch limousine that Teabing kept fully tanked in the corner of the hangar. 'I'll bring the car.' He started down the stairs.

'I'm afraid we cannot let you leave,' the chief inspector said. 'Please return to your aircraft. Both of you. Representatives from the French police will be landing shortly.'

Teabing looked now towards Simon Edwards. 'Simon, for heaven's sake, this is ridiculous! We don't have anyone else on board. Go and have a look, and verify that the plane is empty.'

Edwards knew he was trapped. 'Yes, sir. I will have a look.'

'The devil you will!' the chief inspector declared, apparently suspecting that Edwards might lie about the plane's occupants in an effort to secure Teabing's future business. 'I will look myself.'

Teabing shook his head. 'No you won't, Inspector. Not until you have a search warrant. I am offering you a reasonable option here. Mr Edwards can perform the inspection.'

'No deal.'

Teabing's demeanour turned frosty. 'Inspector, I'm afraid I don't have time to indulge in your games. I'm late, and I'm leaving. If it is that important to you to stop me, you'll just have to shoot me.' With that, Teabing and Rémy walked to the limousine.

THE CHIEF INSPECTOR was unimpressed. Technically, Teabing was correct and the police needed a warrant, but because the powerful Bezu Fache had given his authority, the policeman felt his career would be far better served by finding out what it was on this plane that Teabing seemed so intent on hiding.

'Stop them,' he ordered. 'I'm searching the plane.'

His men raced over, guns levelled, and physically blocked Teabing and his servant from reaching the limousine.

Gripping his sidearm the chief inspector marched up the plane's gangway and into the cabin.

With the exception of the frightened-looking pilot in the cockpit, the aircraft was empty. Quickly checking the seats, the bathroom and the luggage areas, the chief inspector found no traces of anyone. It seemed Leigh Teabing had been telling the truth. His face flushed, he stepped back onto the gangway and gazed across the hangar at Leigh Teabing and his servant, who were still being held at gunpoint. 'Let them go,' he ordered. 'We received a bad tip.'

Teabing's eyes were menacing even from across the hangar. 'You can expect a call from my lawyers.'

With that, Teabing's manservant opened the door at the rear of the stretch limousine and helped his crippled master into the back seat. Then he climbed in behind the wheel, and gunned the engine. Policemen scattered as the limo sped out of the hangar.

'WELL PLAYED, my good man,' Teabing proclaimed from the rear seat as the limousine accelerated out of the airport. 'Everyone comfy?'

Langdon gave a weak nod. He and Sophie were still crouched on the floor beside the bound and gagged albino.

Moments earlier, as the plane had jolted to a stop halfway through its turn, Rémy had popped open the hatch. With the police closing in fast, Langdon and Sophie had dragged the monk down the gangway to ground level and hidden inside the limousine. Then the jet engines had roared again, the plane completing its turn as the police cars came skidding outside the hangar.

Now, as the limousine raced towards London, they clambered onto the rear seat of the limo's long interior, leaving the monk on the floor.

The Englishman gave them both a roguish smile and said, 'So then, about this knight's tomb . . .'

Sophie fished in her pocket, pulled out the black cryptex, unwrapped the vellum from it and handed the sheet to Langdon. He read the poem again, hoping that a clearer meaning would be revealed.

In London lies a knight a Pope interred
His labour's fruit a Holy wrath incurred
You seek the orb that ought be on his tomb
It speaks of Rosy flesh and seeded womb

It seemed simple enough. There was a knight buried in London who had laboured at something that had angered the Church. A knight whose tomb was missing an orb. The poem's final reference—*Rosy flesh and seeded womb*—alluded to Mary Magdalene.

'No thoughts?' Teabing clucked in disappointment, although Langdon sensed that the historian was enjoying being one up. 'Langdon?'

He shook his head.

'What would you two do without me?' Teabing said. 'Very well, I shall walk you through it. It's quite simple really. "In London lies a knight a Pope interred." What does that mean to you?'

Langdon shrugged. 'A knight buried by a Pope? A knight whose funeral was presided over by a Pope?'

Teabing laughed. 'Look at the second line, Robert. This knight obviously did something that incurred the holy wrath of the Church.'

'A knight a Pope *killed*?' Sophie asked.

Teabing smiled and patted her knee. 'Well done, my dear.'

Langdon thought of the Pope Clement's notorious Templar round-up in October 1307, unlucky Friday the 13th. 'But there must be endless graves of knights killed by Popes,' he said.

'Aha, not so!' Teabing said. 'Many were tossed unceremoniously into the Tiber. And there are very few buried in London.' He paused, eyeing Langdon as if waiting for light to dawn. Finally he huffed. 'Robert, for heaven's sake! In London there is a church built by the Priory's military arm—the Knights Templar themselves!'

'The Temple Church?' Langdon drew a startled breath.

'Its crypt holds ten of the most frightening tombs you'll ever see.'

Langdon had never actually visited the Temple Church, although he'd come across numerous references in his Priory research.

'It's an eerie old place,' Teabing said. 'Hidden away on Inner Temple Lane, just off Fleet Street. And the architecture is pagan to the core. The Templars built a perfectly circular church in honour of the sun.' His eyebrows did a devilish dance. 'They might as well have resurrected Stonehenge in central London.'

Sophie eyed Teabing. 'What about the rest of the poem?'

The historian's mirthful air faded. 'I'm not sure. With luck, one of the ten tombs will have a conspicuously absent orb.'

The poem was like some kind of primordial crossword puzzle, Langdon thought. A five-letter word that speaks of the Grail? They had already tried all the obvious passwords—GRAIL, GRAAL, GREAL, JESUS, MARIA, SARAH—but the small black cylinder had not budged. Apparently there existed some other five-letter reference to the Rose's seeded womb. The fact that it eluded a specialist like Leigh Teabing signified that it was no ordinary Grail reference.

'Sir Leigh?' Rémy called over his shoulder, through the open divider. 'You said Fleet Street is near Blackfriars Bridge?'

'Yes, take Victoria Embankment.'

'I'm sorry. I'm not sure where that is.'

Teabing rolled his eyes at Langdon and Sophie. 'I swear, sometimes it's like baby-sitting a child. One moment, please.' He left them, clambering towards the open divider to talk to Rémy.

Sophie turned to Langdon now, her voice quiet. 'Robert, nobody knows that you and I are in England.'

Langdon realised she was right. The Kent Police would tell Fache the plane was empty, and he would assume they were still in France. Leigh's little stunt had bought them a lot of time.

'But Fache will not give up easily,' Sophie went on. 'He has too much riding on this arrest now.'

Langdon nodded. He had been trying not to think about Fache.

'Robert, I'm sorry you're so deeply involved,' Sophie said, placing her hand on his knee. 'My grandfather asked me to trust you and I'm glad I listened to him for once. I'm very glad you're here.'

The comment sounded more pragmatic than romantic, and yet Langdon felt an unexpected flicker of attraction between them. He gave her a tired smile. 'I'm a lot more fun when I've slept.'

Sophie was silent for several seconds. 'What do you think we should do with the Sangreal documents, if we ever find them?'

'What I think is immaterial,' he said. 'Your grandfather gave the cryptex to you. You should do with it what your instinct tells you to.'

'And yet you're writing a book about it, so you obviously feel the information should be shared.'

'There's an enormous difference between hypothetically discussing an alternative history of Christ and . . .' he paused. 'And presenting to the world ancient documents as scientific evidence that the New Testament is false testimony.'

'But you told me the New Testament is based on fabrication.'

Langdon smiled. 'Sophie, every faith in the world is based on fabrication. That is the definition of faith—acceptance of that which we imagine to be true, which we cannot prove.'

'So you are in favour of the documents staying buried for ever?'

'I'm a historian. I'm opposed to the destruction of documents and I would love to see religious scholars have more information to ponder regarding the exceptional life of Christ.'

'You're arguing both sides of my question.'

'Am I? The Bible represents a guidepost for millions of people, in much the same way that the Koran and the Torah do. Those who truly understand their faiths, understand that the stories are metaphorical. Religious allegory has become part of the fabric of reality. Living in that reality helps millions of people to cope and be better people.'

'But it appears their reality is false.'

Langdon chuckled. 'No more false than that of a mathematical cryptographer who believes in the imaginary number "i" because it helps her break codes.'

IT WAS ALMOST seven thirty when the threesome emerged from the limousine onto Inner Temple Lane and wound through a maze of buildings to a small courtyard outside the Temple Church.

Constructed entirely of rough-hewn Caen stone, the dramatic circular edifice with its central turret and a nave protruding off one side looked more like a military stronghold than a place of worship. Consecrated in 1185, it had survived eight centuries of political turmoil, the Great Fire of London and the First World War, only to be heavily damaged by the Luftwaffe in 1940. After the war, it was restored to its original, stark grandeur.

'It's early on a Saturday,' Teabing said, hobbling towards the entrance, 'so I'm assuming we won't have services to deal with.'

The church's entryway was a large wooden door inside a stone recess. To the left of the door hung a bulletin board.

Teabing frowned as he read the service schedule. 'They don't open to sightseers for another couple of hours.' He moved to the door and tried it, but it didn't budge. Putting his ear to the wood, he listened. After a moment, he pulled back, a scheming look on his face.

INSIDE THE CHURCH, an altar boy had almost finished vacuuming the communion kneelers when he heard a knocking on the sanctuary door. He ignored it. The Reverend Harvey Knowles had his own keys and, anyway, was not due for another couple of hours.

Suddenly, the knocking turned to a forceful banging. The young man switched off the vacuum cleaner and marched angrily to the door. Unlatching it from within, he swung it open. Three people stood in the entryway. Tourists. 'We open at nine thirty,' he grumbled.

The heavyset man stepped forwards using metal crutches. 'I am Sir Leigh Teabing,' he said. 'As you are no doubt aware, I am escorting Mr and Mrs Christopher Wren the Fourth.' He waved his arm at the attractive couple behind him.

The altar boy had no idea how to respond. Sir Christopher Wren was the Temple Church's most famous benefactor. He had made possible all the restorations following damage caused by the Great Fire. He had also been dead since the early eighteenth century. 'Um . . . an honour to meet you?'

The man on crutches frowned. 'Good thing you're not in sales; you're not very convincing. Where is the Reverend Knowles?'

'It's Saturday. He's not due in until later.'

The crippled man's scowl deepened. 'He assured us he would be here, but it looks like we'll do it without him. It won't take long.'

The altar boy blocked the doorway. 'I'm sorry, *what* won't take long?'

The visitor leaned forwards whispering as if to save everyone some embarrassment. 'Young man, apparently you are new here. Every year, Sir Christopher Wren's descendants bring a pinch of the old man's ashes to scatter in the Temple sanctuary. It is part of his last will and testament. Nobody is particularly happy about making the trip, but what can we do?'

The altar boy hesitated. He was well acquainted with Mr Knowles' deep observance of church tradition . . . and his foul temper when anything cast this time-honoured shrine in anything but favourable light. He had clearly forgotten these family members were coming. What harm could it do to let them in?

He stepped aside to let them pass.

LANGDON SMILED as the threesome moved deeper into the church. 'Leigh,' he whispered, 'you lie entirely too well.'

Teabing's eyes twinkled. 'Oxford Theatre Club. They still talk of my Julius Caesar.'

As they moved through the rectangular annexe towards the archway leading into the main church, Langdon was surprised by its barren austerity. 'Bleak,' he whispered.

Teabing chuckled. 'Church of England. Anglicans drink their religion straight. Nothing to distract from their misery.'

Sophie motioned through the vast opening that gave way to the circular section of the church. 'It looks like a fortress,' she said.

'The Knights Templar were warriors,' Teabing reminded her. 'Their churches were their strongholds and their banks.'

'Banks?' Sophie asked, glancing at Leigh.

'Heavens, yes. The Templars *invented* the concept of modern banking. For European nobility, travelling with gold was perilous, so the Templars allowed nobles to deposit gold in their nearest Temple Church and then draw it from any other Temple Church across Europe. All they needed was proper documentation.' He winked. 'And a small commission. They were the original ATMs.'

As they arrived within the circular chamber, Langdon took in the carved gargoyles, demons, monsters and pained human faces, all staring inwards from the perimeter. And then he saw them.

The ten stone knights. Lying supine on the floor, the life-sized figures in full armour rested in peaceful poses.

In London lies a knight a Pope interred. This had to be the place.

IN AN ALLEY close to Temple Church, Rémy Legaludec pulled the limousine to a stop behind a row of industrial waste bins. Killing the engine, he got out of the car, walked towards the rear and climbed back into the limousine's main cabin.

Sensing Rémy's presence, the monk emerged from a prayer-like trance, his red eyes looking more curious than fearful. All morning Rémy had been impressed with the man's ability to stay calm, as if he had given over his fate to a higher power.

Rémy unbuttoned his high, starched, wing-tipped collar, went to the limousine's bar and poured himself a large vodka, which he drank in a single swallow. Soon I will be a man of leisure, he thought.

He found a standard service wine-bottle opener and flicked open the sharp blade designed to slice the foil from fine bottles of wine. Then he turned and faced Silas, holding up the glimmering knife.

Now those red eyes flashed fear. Rémy smiled, and moved towards the back of the limousine. The monk struggled against his bonds.

SILAS COULD NOT BELIEVE that God had forsaken him. He cried out, unable to believe he was going to die here, unable to defend himself.

He felt a slash of pain spreading across his back and shoulders, and clenched his eyes tighter, determined that the final image of his life would not be of his killer. Instead he pictured a younger Bishop Aringarosa, standing before the small church that he and Silas had built with their own hands.

'Take a drink,' a voice whispered.

Silas's eyes flew open in surprise. The tuxedoed man was leaning over him, offering a glass of liquid. A mound of shredded duct tape lay on the floor beside the bloodless knife.

'Drink this,' the man repeated. 'The pain you feel is the blood rushing into your muscles. This will help with your circulation.'

The vodka tasted terrible, but Silas drank it, feeling grateful.

'I wanted to free you earlier,' the servant apologised, 'but it was impossible. With the police arriving at Château Villette, and then at Biggin Hill, this was the first possible moment. You understand, don't you, Silas?'

Silas sat up now, rubbing his stiff muscles. 'How do you know my name?' he asked. 'Are you . . . the Teacher?'

Rémy shook his head, laughing at the proposition. 'No, I am not the Teacher. Like you, I serve him. My name is Rémy.'

Silas was amazed. 'I don't understand. If you work for the Teacher, why did Langdon bring the keystone to your home?'

'Not *my* home. The home of the world's foremost Grail historian, Sir Leigh Teabing.'

'But you live there. The odds . . . '

Rémy smiled, seeming to have no trouble with the apparent coincidence. 'Robert Langdon was in possession of the keystone, and he needed help. What more logical place to run than to the home of Leigh Teabing? That I happen to live there is why the Teacher approached me in the first place.' He paused. 'How do you think the Teacher knows so much about the Grail?'

Now it dawned, and Silas was stunned at the Teacher's brilliance. He had recruited a servant who had access to Leigh Teabing's research.

'There is much I have to tell you,' Rémy said, handing Silas the loaded Heckler Koch pistol. 'But first, you and I have a job to do.'

CAPTAIN FACHE descended from his transport plane at Biggin Hill and listened in disbelief to the Kent Police chief inspector's account of what had happened in Teabing's hangar.

'Did you interrogate the pilot?' he asked.

'Of course not. He is French, and our jurisdiction requires—'

'Take me to the plane.'

Arriving at the hangar, Fache needed only sixty seconds to locate a smear of blood on the ground where the limousine had been parked. He walked up to the plane and rapped loudly on the fuselage. 'This is the captain of the French Judicial Police. Open the door!'

The terrified pilot opened the hatch and lowered the stairs.

Fache ascended. Three minutes later, he had a full confession, including a description of the bound albino monk. In addition, he learned that the pilot saw Langdon and Sophie leave something behind in Teabing's safe, a wooden box of some sort, which had been the focus of attention during the flight.

'Open the safe,' Fache demanded.

The pilot looked terrified. 'I don't know the combination!'

'Too bad. I was going to offer to let you keep your pilot's licence.'

The pilot wrung his hands. 'I know some men in maintenance here. Maybe they could drill it?'

'You have half an hour.'

Fache's phone rang. '*Allo?*'

'I'm en route to Heathrow.' It was Bishop Aringarosa. 'I'll be arriving in an hour. Do you have Silas?'

'No. His captors eluded the local police before I landed.'

'You assured me you would stop that plane!'

Fache lowered his voice. 'Bishop, considering your situation, I recommend you do not test my patience today. I will find Silas and the others as soon as possible. Now, tell your pilot to divert to Biggin Hill

Airport in Kent. I'll get clearance. If I'm not here when you land, I'll have a car waiting for you.'

'Thank you.'

'And you would do well to remember, Bishop, that you are not the only man on the verge of losing everything.'

You seek the orb that ought be on his tomb.

Each of the carved knights within the Temple Church lay on his back with his head resting on a rectangular stone pillow. Sophie felt a chill as she advanced with Langdon and Teabing towards the group of five knights on the left. The poem's reference to an 'orb' conjured images of the night in her grandfather's basement, and briefly she wondered if the *hieros gamos* ritual had ever been performed in this very sanctuary. The circular room seemed custom-built for such a rite.

Scrutinising the tombs, she could see no hint anywhere of a conspicuously absent orb. Feeling the weight of the cryptex in her sweater pocket, she glanced back at Langdon and Teabing. The men were moving slowly, still only at the third knight, apparently having no luck either. In no mood to wait, she crossed over to the second group of knights. Like the first group they all lay, wearing armour and swords.

All, that was, except the tenth and final tomb.

Hurrying over to it, she stared down.

No pillow. No armour. No tunic. No sword.

'Robert? Leigh?' she called, her voice echoing around the chamber. 'There's something missing over here.'

'An orb?' Teabing called excitedly. His crutches clicked out a rapid staccato as he hurried across the room. 'Are we missing an orb?'

'Not exactly,' Sophie said, frowning.

Arriving beside her, Leigh and Langdon gazed down in confusion at the tenth tomb, which was simply a sealed stone coffin.

'Why is this knight in a coffin rather than in the open?' Sophie asked.

Teabing shrugged. 'One of this church's mysteries.'

'Hello?' the altar boy said, arriving with a perturbed look on his face. 'Forgive me if this seems rude, but you told me you wanted to spread ashes, and yet you seem to be sightseeing.'

Teabing turned to Langdon. 'Mr Wren, apparently your family's philanthropy does not buy you the time it used to, so perhaps we should take out the ashes and get on with scattering them among the tombs.'

The altar boy's expression grew sceptical. 'These are not tombs.'

'Of course they are tombs,' Teabing declared.

The altar boy shook his head. 'Tombs contain bodies. These are effigies. There are no bodies beneath these figures.'

'This is a crypt!' Teabing said.

'Only in outdated history books. It was revealed as nothing of the sort during the 1950 renovation.' He turned to Langdon. 'And Mr Wren should *know* that, as it was his family that uncovered that fact.'

An uneasy silence fell, broken by the sound of a door slamming out in the annexe.

'That must be Mr Knowles,' Teabing said. 'Should you go and see?'

The altar boy looked doubtful but departed, leaving Langdon, Sophie and Teabing to eye one another gloomily.

'No bodies?' Langdon whispered. 'What is he talking about?'

Teabing looked distraught. 'I don't know. I always thought . . . It makes no sense. We must be missing something!'

ENTERING THE ANNEXE, the altar boy was surprised to find it deserted. 'Mr Knowles?'

A thin man in a tuxedo stood near the doorway, scratching his head and looking lost. Realising that he had forgotten to relock the door when he let the others in, the altar boy called out. 'I'm sorry, we're closed.'

A flurry of cloth ruffled behind him, and before the altar boy could turn, his head snapped backwards, a powerful hand clamping hard over his mouth from behind.

The prim man in the tuxedo calmly produced a very small revolver, which he aimed at the boy's forehead. 'Listen carefully,' he whispered. 'You will exit this church silently, and you will run. You will not stop. Is that clear?'

The boy nodded as best he could with the hand over his mouth.

LIKE A GHOST, Silas drifted silently behind his target. Sophie Neveu sensed him too late. Before she could turn, Silas pressed the gun barrel into her spine and wrapped a powerful arm across her chest, pulling her back against his huge body. She yelled in surprise.

Teabing and Langdon both turned, their expressions fearful.

'What . . . ?' Teabing choked out. 'What did you do to Rémy!'

'Your only concern,' Silas said calmly, 'is that I leave here with the keystone.' This recovery mission, as Rémy had described it, was simple: *Take the keystone and walk out; no killing, no struggle.*

Holding Sophie firm, Silas dropped his hand down to her waist, slipping it inside her deep sweater pockets, searching. 'Where is it?' he whispered. He knew that the keystone was in her sweater pocket earlier. So where was it now?

'It's over here,' Langdon's voice resonated from across the room.

Silas turned to see Langdon holding the black cryptex before him, waving it back and forth.

'Set it down,' Silas demanded.

'Let Sophie and Leigh leave the church,' Langdon replied. 'You and I can settle this.'

Silas pushed Sophie away from him and aimed the gun at Langdon, moving towards him. 'You are in no position to make demands.'

'I disagree.' Langdon raised the cryptex high over his head. 'I will not hesitate to smash this on the floor and break the vial inside.'

Silas felt a flash of fear. Keeping his voice as steady as his hand, he said, 'You would never break the keystone. You want to find the Grail as much as I do.'

'You're wrong. You want it much more. You've proved that you're willing to kill for it.'

FORTY FEET AWAY, peering out from the annexe pews near the archway, Rémy Legaludec felt a rising alarm. The manoeuvre had not gone as planned, and he could see that Silas was uncertain how to handle the situation. And to complicate matters, he knew the Teacher had strictly forbidden him to show his face. On that he had been resolute: 'Silas served us well with the four Priory members. He will recover the keystone. *You* must remain anonymous. Do not reveal your face.'

My face can be changed, Rémy thought now. With what you've promised to pay me, I will become an entirely new man.

'For your own knowledge, Rémy,' the Teacher had told him, 'the tomb in question is not in the Temple Church. So have no fear. They are looking in the wrong place.'

'And you know where the tomb is?' Rémy had asked the Teacher less than half an hour ago, when he got the order to steal the keystone.

'Of course. Later, I will tell you. For now, you must act quickly. If the others figure out the true location of the tomb and leave the church before you take the cryptex, we could lose the Grail for ever.'

Rémy didn't give a damn about the Grail, except that the Teacher refused to pay him until it was found. With Langdon threatening to break the keystone, Rémy's entire future was at risk. He decided to take bold action.

Stepping from the shadows, he marched into the circular chamber and aimed his small-calibre gun directly at Teabing's head. 'Old man, I've been waiting a long time to do this.'

SIR LEIGH TEABING'S heart stalled when he saw Rémy aiming a gun at him. 'Rémy?' he spluttered in shock. 'What is going on?'

Langdon and Sophie looked equally dumbstruck.

Rémy circled behind Teabing and rammed the pistol barrel into his back, high and on the left, directly behind his heart. 'I'll make it simple,' he snapped, watching Langdon over Teabing's shoulder. 'Set down the keystone, or I pull the trigger.'

Langdon seemed momentarily paralysed. 'The keystone is worthless to you,' he stammered. 'You cannot possibly open it.'

'Arrogant fools,' Rémy sneered. 'Have you not noticed that I have been listening tonight as you discussed these poems? Everything I heard, I have shared with others. Others who know more than you. You are not even looking in the right place. The tomb you seek is in an other location entirely'

Teabing felt panicked. What was he saying?

'Silas, take the keystone from Mr Langdon,' Rémy called.

As the monk advanced, Langdon stepped back, raising the keystone high, looking fully prepared to hurl it at the floor. 'I would rather break it,' Langdon said, 'than see it in the wrong hands.'

Teabing now felt a wave of horror. He could see his life's work evaporating before his eyes—all his dreams about to be shattered.

'Robert, no!' he exclaimed. 'Don't! Rémy would *never* shoot me. We've known each other for ten—'

Rémy aimed at the ceiling and fired. The gunshot echoed like thunder inside the stone chamber and everyone froze.

'I am not playing games,' Rémy said. 'The next one is in his back. Hand the keystone to Silas.'

Langdon reluctantly held out the cryptex. Silas stepped forward and took it. Slipping the keystone into the pocket of his robe, the monk backed off, still holding Langdon and Sophie at gunpoint.

Teabing felt Rémy's arm clamp hard round his neck as the servant also began backing out of the building, dragging Teabing with him.

'We're taking Mr Teabing for a drive,' Rémy said. 'If you call the police, he will die. Is that clear?'

'Who are you working for?' Sophie demanded.

The question brought a smirk to the departing Rémy's face. 'You would be surprised, Mademoiselle Neveu.'

Chapter 11

The fireplace in Château Villette's drawing room was cold, but Collet paced before it nonetheless as he read the faxes from Interpol.

Not at all what he expected.

André Vernet, according to official records, was a model citizen. No police record—not even a parking ticket. Educated at the Sorbonne, he had apparently helped to design the ultramodern security system in the Depository Bank of Zürich.

Collet sighed. Zero. The only red flag was a set of fingerprints that belonged to Teabing's servant, Rémy Legaludec.

'Wanted for petty crime,' said the chief PTS examiner, who was seated in a comfortable chair across the room. 'Nothing serious. Breaking and entering. Theft from a hospital where he'd just had an emergency tracheotomy.' He glanced up, chuckling. 'Peanut allergy.'

Collet sighed. 'All right, you'd better forward this to Captain Fache.'

The examiner headed off just as another PTS agent burst into the living room. 'Lieutenant! We found something in the barn.'

'A body?'

'No, sir. An advanced surveillance system. Hidden in the hay loft.'

Collet followed the agent out of the room. 'Do you have any idea what target is being bugged?'

'Well, Lieutenant,' the agent said. 'It's the strangest thing . . .'

LANGDON FELT UTTERLY SPENT as he and Sophie dashed into the ticket hall of Temple tube station. Guilt ripped through him. He had involved Leigh, and now Leigh was in enormous danger.

Rémy's involvement had been a shock, and yet it made sense. Whoever was pursuing the Grail had recruited someone on the inside. They went to Teabing's for the same reason that Langdon did. The fact that Teabing had been a target all along should have made Langdon feel less guilty about involving him. It did not.

Sophie hurried to a payphone to call the police, despite Rémy's warning to the contrary. Langdon stood nearby feeling remorseful.

'The best way to help Leigh,' Sophie reiterated as she dialled, 'is to involve the London authorities immediately. Trust me.'

Sophie's logic was beginning to make sense. Teabing was safe at the moment. Even if Rémy and the others knew where the knight's tomb was located, they would probably need Teabing's help in deciphering the orb reference. What worried Langdon was what would happen after the Grail map had been found. If Langdon were to have any chance of helping Leigh, or of ever seeing the keystone again, it was essential that he find the tomb first.

Slowing Rémy down had become Sophie's task. Finding the right tomb had become Langdon's.

Sophie would make Rémy and Silas fugitives of the London police. Langdon's plan was less certain, but first he would take the tube to nearby King's College, renowned for its theological data base. He wondered what the data base might say about 'a knight a Pope interred'.

SOPHIE'S CALL finally connected to the London police. 'I'm reporting a kidnapping,' she said.

'Name please?' the dispatcher asked.

'Agent Sophie Neveu of the French Judicial Police.'

'Right away, ma'am. Let me get a detective on the line for you.'

As the call went through, Sophie began to wonder if the police would even believe her description of Teabing's captors. A man in a tuxedo partnered with an albino monk. Impossible to miss. Moreover, they had a hostage on crutches.

Finally a man came on the line. 'Agent Neveu?'

Stunned, Sophie registered the gruff tone immediately.

'Where the hell are you?' Bezu Fache demanded.

Sophie was speechless. Captain Fache had apparently requested that the London police dispatcher alert him if Sophie called in.

'Listen,' Fache said, speaking to her in terse French. 'I made a terrible mistake tonight. Robert Langdon is innocent. All charges against him have been dropped. I fully intend to overlook your insubordination on account of the emotional stress you must be under in the light of your grandfather's death. At the moment, however, you and Langdon are in danger and need to go to the nearest London police headquarters for refuge.'

He knows I'm in London. What else does he know? Sophie heard an odd clicking on the line. 'Are you tracing this call, Captain?'

Fache's voice was firm now. 'You and I need to cooperate, Agent Neveu. We both have a lot to lose here. I made errors in judgment last night, and if those errors result in the deaths of an American professor and a DCPJ cryptologist, my career will be over. I've been trying to pull you back into safety for the last several hours.'

'The man you want is Rémy Legaludec,' Sophie said. 'Teabing's servant. He kidnapped Teabing in the Temple Church and—'

'Agent Neveu!' Fache bellowed. 'This is not something to discuss on an open line. You and Langdon will come in now. For your own well-being! That is a direct order!'

Sophie hung up and dashed, with Langdon, towards the trains.

THE CABIN of Teabing's Hawker was now covered with steel shavings and smelt of propane. Bezu Fache had sent everyone away and sat alone with the wooden box found in the safe, pondering his brief conversation with Sophie, as well as the information he'd received from PTS in Château Villette.

The sound of his phone shook him from his daydream. It was the DCPJ switchboard. The dispatcher was apologetic. The president of the Depository Bank of Zürich was insistent. He wanted to speak to the Captain. Begrudgingly Fache told the operator to forward the call.

Vernet told Fache how Langdon and Sophie had extracted a small wooden box from the bank and then persuaded Vernet to help them escape. 'Then when I heard on the radio that they were criminals, I pulled over and demanded the box back, but they attacked me and stole the truck.'

'You are concerned for a wooden box,' Fache said, gently opening the ornate lid to reveal the white cylinder in its padded resting place. 'Can you tell me what was in the box?'

'The contents are immaterial,' Vernet fired back. 'I am concerned with the reputation of my bank. We have never had a robbery. *Ever*. It will ruin us if I cannot recover this property on behalf of my client.'

'You said Agent Neveu and Robert Langdon had a password and a key. What makes you say they stole the box?'

'They murdered people tonight. Including Sophie Neveu's grandfather. The key and password were obviously ill-gotten.'

'Mr Vernet, I give you my word as commanding officer of the *Police Judiciaire* that your box is in the safest of hands.'

UP IN THE HAY LOFT, Collet stared at the computer monitor. 'This system is eavesdropping on *all* these people?' He read the list again.

Colbert Sostaque—Chairman of the Conseil Constitutionnel
Jean Chaffée—Curator, Musée du Jeu de Paume
Edouard Desrochers—Senior Archivist, Mitterrand Library
Jacques Saunière—Curator, Musée du Louvre
Michel Breton—Head of DAS (French Intelligence)

'Yes,' the agent said, pointing to the screen. 'Number four is of obvious relevance.'

Collet nodded. 'Have you sent anyone in to sweep for the bug?'

'No need. I know exactly where it is.' The agent went to a pile of blueprints on a worktable. He selected a page and handed it to Collet. 'Look familiar?'

Collet was amazed. He was holding a photocopy of an ancient schematic diagram, which depicted a fully articulated medieval knight. It was the knight sitting on Saunière's desk!

Scribbled in the margins in red felt-tipped marker were instructions in French on how best to insert a listening device into the knight.

SILAS SAT in the passenger seat of the parked limousine, waiting for Rémy to finish tying and gagging Teabing in the back. Finally, Rémy slid back into the driver's seat beside him. 'Secure?' Silas asked.

Rémy chuckled. 'He's not going anywhere.'

Reaching to a control panel on the elaborate dashboard, he pressed a button and an opaque partition rose, sealing off the back compartment.

Minutes later, as the stretch limo powered through the streets, Silas's cellphone rang. The Teacher. He answered excitedly. 'Hello?'

'Silas,' the Teacher said, 'I am relieved to hear your voice. This means you are safe.'

Silas was equally comforted to hear the Teacher. At last the operation seemed to be back on track. 'I have the keystone.'

'This is superb news,' the Teacher told him. 'Is Rémy with you?'

Silas was surprised to hear the Teacher use Rémy's name. 'Yes. Rémy freed me.'

'As I ordered him to do. I am only sorry you had to endure captivity for so long. But now I need Rémy to bring the keystone to me.'

Silas was crestfallen. The Teacher favoured Rémy?

'I sense your disappointment,' the Teacher said, 'which tells me you do not understand my meaning.' He lowered his voice to a whisper. 'Rémy must be dealt with. He disobeyed my orders and made a grave mistake that has put our entire mission at risk.'

Silas glanced at Rémy. Kidnapping Teabing had not been part of the plan, and deciding what to do with him posed a problem, but Silas was surprised the Teacher was not more understanding. After all, Rémy had saved the keystone. 'I understand,' Silas managed.

'Good. For your own safety, you need to get off the street immediately. The police will be looking for the limousine soon, and I do not want you caught. Opus Dei has a residence in London, as you know.

Go there now. I will call you the moment I am in possession of the keystone and have attended to my current problem.'

'Yes, sir.'

The Teacher heaved a sigh, as if what he now had to do was profoundly regrettable. 'It's time I speak to Rémy.'

Silas handed Rémy the phone.

'Listen carefully,' the Teacher said. 'Take Silas to the Opus Dei residence hall then drive to St James's Park. Park the limousine on Horse Guards Parade. We'll talk there.' With that, the connection went dead.

LANGDON STILL FELT shaky as he and Sophie came in from the rain and entered the library of King's College Department of Theology and Religious Studies. On the far side of the room, a reference librarian was pouring a mug of tea and settling in for the day's work.

'Lovely morning,' she said cheerfully. 'May I help you?'

'Thank you, yes,' Langdon replied. 'My name is—'

'Robert Langdon.' She smiled pleasantly. 'I know who you are.'

For an instant, he feared Fache had put him on English television, but the librarian's smile suggested otherwise. Langdon still had not got used to these moments of unexpected celebrity.

'Pamela Gettum,' the librarian said, offering her hand.

'A pleasure,' Langdon said. 'This is my friend Sophie Neveu. If it's not too much trouble, we could use your help finding some information.'

Gettum shifted, looking uncertain. 'Normally our services are by appointment only, unless you're a guest of someone at the college.'

'I'm afraid we've come unannounced, but a friend of mine speaks very highly of you. Sir Leigh Teabing?'

Gettum brightened now. 'Heavens, yes. What a character. Fanatical! Every time he comes in, it's always the same search strings. Grail. Grail. Grail. I swear that man will die before he gives up on that quest.'

'Is there any chance you can help us?' Sophie asked. 'We're trying to find a knight's tomb.' She produced a slip of paper on which she had written out the poem. 'This is what we know.'

Gettum sensed an urgency in the eyes of this famed American scholar and the woman accompanying him. Puzzled, she examined the paper:

In London lies a knight a Pope interred.
You seek the orb that ought be on his tomb.
It speaks of Rosy flesh and seeded womb.
His labour's fruit a Holy wrath incurred.

Gettum smiled, noting the references to the Rose and her seeded womb. *The Grail*. 'You are friends with Leigh Teabing, you are in England, and you are looking for a knight.' She folded her hands. 'Can I assume you are on a Grail quest?'

Langdon and Sophie exchanged startled looks.

Gettum laughed. 'My friends, this library is a base camp for Grail seekers, Leigh Teabing among them. I wish I had a shilling for every time I'd run searches for the Rose, Mary Magdalene, Sangreal, Merovingian, Priory of Sion, et cetera, et cetera. Might I ask where this verse came from?' she asked, looking up from the slip of paper.

'You might ask,' Langdon said, with a friendly smile, 'but it's a long story and we have very little time.'

'Sounds like a polite way of saying "mind your own business" but, very well, I'll play along anyway.' Sitting down at a workstation, Gettum looked at the slip of paper and began typing. 'We'll search for the keywords KNIGHT, LONDON, POPE and TOMB. If this is a Grail-related issue, we should cross-reference against the Grail keywords GRAIL, ROSE, SANGREAL and CHALICE.

'How long will this take?' Sophie asked.

'A few hundred terabytes with multiple cross-referencing fields?' Gettum clicked the SEARCH key. 'A mere fifteen minutes.'

Langdon and Sophie said nothing, but Gettum sensed this sounded like an eternity to them.

'Tea?' she asked. 'Leigh always loves my tea.'

LONDON'S OPUS DEI CENTRE is a modest brick building at 5 Orme Court, overlooking Kensington Gardens. Silas felt a sense of relief as he approached it.

At Rémy's suggestion, he had wiped down his gun and disposed of it through a sewer grate. He was glad to get rid of it. He felt lighter.

'What will you do with Teabing?' he had asked, just before Rémy had dropped him off.

Rémy had shrugged. 'That is a decision for the Teacher.'

Now, as Silas approached the Opus Dei building, the rain fell harder. It was cleansing. He was ready now to leave behind the sins of the last twenty-four hours and purge his soul. His work was done.

Silas was not surprised to find the door unlocked. He opened it and stepped into the foyer. An electronic chime sounded upstairs as Silas stepped onto the carpet. The bell was a common feature in these halls, where the residents spent most of the day in their rooms in prayer.

A man in a cloak came downstairs. 'May I help you?' He had kind eyes that seemed not even to register Silas's startling appearance.

'Thank you. My name is Silas. I am an Opus Dei numerary and I am in town only for the day. Might I rest here?'

'You need not even ask. There are two empty rooms on the third floor. Shall I bring you some tea and bread?'

'Thank you.' Silas was famished.

He went upstairs to a modest room with a window, where he knelt down to pray. Later, after he had eaten his food, he lay down to sleep.

THREE STOREYS BELOW, a phone was ringing. The Opus Dei numerary who had welcomed Silas answered it.

'This is the Metropolitan police,' the caller said. 'We are trying to find an albino monk and we've had a tip-off that he might be there. Have you seen him?'

'Yes, he is upstairs praying. Is something wrong?'

'Leave him precisely where he is,' the officer commanded. 'Don't say a word to anyone. I'm sending officers over right away.'

CHAPTER 12

St James's Park is a sea of green in the middle of London, a royal park bordering the palaces of Westminster, Buckingham and St James's. From the park, the Teacher could see the spires of the building that housed the knight's tomb—the real reason he had told Rémy to come to this spot.

As the Teacher approached the front passenger door of the parked limousine, he paused to take a pull from the flask of cognac he was carrying. Then he opened the door and slid in beside Rémy.

Rémy held up the keystone like a trophy. 'It was almost lost.'

'You have done well,' the Teacher said, taking the keystone in his eager hands. He admired it a long moment, smiling. 'And the gun? You wiped it down?'

'Back in the glove box where I found it.'

'Excellent.' The Teacher took another drink of cognac and handed the flask to Rémy. 'Let's toast our success. The end is near.'

RÉMY ACCEPTED THE BOTTLE gratefully. The cognac tasted salty, but he didn't care. He and the Teacher were truly partners now. He could feel himself ascending to a higher station in life.

Taking another swig from the flask, Rémy could feel the cognac warming his blood. The warmth in Rémy's throat, however, mutated quickly to an uncomfortable heat. Loosening his bow tie, Rémy tasted an unpleasant grittiness and handed the flask back to the Teacher. 'I've probably had enough,' he managed, weakly.

Taking the flask, the Teacher said, 'Rémy, as you are aware, you are the only one who knows my face. I placed enormous trust in you.'

'Yes,' he said, feeling feverish as he loosened his tie further. 'And your identity shall go with me to the grave.'

The Teacher was silent a long moment. 'I believe you.' Pocketing the flask and the keystone, the Teacher reached for the glove box and pulled out the tiny revolver. For an instant, Rémy felt a surge of fear, but the Teacher simply slipped it in his trousers pocket.

What was he doing? Rémy felt himself sweating suddenly.

'I know I promised you freedom,' the Teacher said, his voice now sounding regretful. 'But when you brazenly showed yourself in the Temple Church you sealed your own fate.'

The swelling in Rémy's throat came on like an earthquake, and he lurched against the steering column, tasting vomit in his narrowing trachea. As his world slowly went black he let out a muted scream, not even loud enough to be heard outside the car.

MINUTES LATER, the Teacher was crossing St James's Park. Only two people now remained. Langdon and Neveu. They were complicated. But manageable. At the moment, however, the Teacher had the cryptex to attend to. Gazing triumphantly across the park, he could see his destination. *In London lies a knight a Pope interred.* As soon as the Teacher had heard the poem, he had known the answer. Having listened to Saunière's conversations for months now, the Teacher had heard the Grand Master mention this famous knight on occasion, expressing an esteem almost matching that which he held for da Vinci. Yet how the tomb would reveal the final password was still a mystery.

Within minutes, he was stepping into the quiet sanctuary of London's grandest 900-year-old building.

JUST AS THE TEACHER was stepping out of the rain, Bishop Aringarosa was stepping into it, on the tarmac at Biggin Hill Airport.

A young British police officer approached with an umbrella. 'Bishop Aringarosa? Captain Fache had to leave. He asked me to look after you. He suggested I take you to Scotland Yard. He thought it would be safest.'

Safest? Aringarosa looked down at his heavy briefcase. He had almost forgotten the bonds. 'Yes, thank you.'

Aringarosa climbed into the police car, wondering where Silas could be. Minutes later, the police scanner crackled with the answer: 5 Orme Court. Aringarosa recognised the address immediately. The Opus Dei Centre in London.

He spun to the driver. 'Take me there at once!'

LANGDON'S EYES had not left the computer screen since the search began. Five minutes. Only two hits. Both irrelevant.

Finally, the computer pinged happily.

'Sounds like you got another,' Gettum called from the next room, where she was preparing hot drinks. 'What's the title?'

Langdon eyed the screen.

Grail Allegory in Medieval Literature: A Treatise on Sir Gawain and the Green Knight.

'Allegory of the Green Knight,' he called back.

'No good,' Gettum said. 'Not many mythological green giants buried in London.'

Langdon and Sophie sat patiently in front of the screen and waited through two more searches. When the computer pinged again, though, the offering was unexpected.

The Gravity of Genius: Biography of a Modern Knight.

'Gravity of Genius?' Langdon called out to Gettum. 'Bio of a modern knight?'

Gettum stuck her head around the corner. 'How modern?

Let's have a look.' Langdon summoned up the hypertext keywords.

. . . honourable **knight**, Sir Isaac Newton . . .
. . . in **London** in 1727 and . . .
. . . his **tomb** in Westminster Abbey . . .
. . . Alexander **Pope**, friend and colleague . . .

'I suppose 'modern' is a relative term,' Sophie said to Gettum. 'It's an old book. About Sir Isaac Newton.'

Gettum shook her head. 'No good. Newton was buried in Westminster Abbey, the seat of English Protestantism. There's no way a Catholic Pope was present. Milk and sugar?'

Sophie nodded.

Gettum waited. 'Robert?'

Langdon's heart was hammering. He pulled his eyes from the screen and stood up. 'Sir Isaac Newton is our knight. He is buried in London, his scientific labours incurred the wrath of the Church. And he was a Grand Master of the Priory of Sion. What more could we want?'

'What more?' Sophie pointed to the poem. 'How about a knight a Pope interred? Newton was not buried by a Catholic Pope.'

Langdon reached for the mouse. 'Who said anything about a *Catholic* Pope?' He clicked on the 'Pope' hyperlink, and the complete sentence appeared:

> Sir Isaac Newton's burial, attended by kings and nobles, was presided over by Alexander Pope, friend and colleague.

Langdon looked at Sophie, who stood up, looking stunned. Jacques Saunière, the master of double-entendres, had proven his cleverness once again.

SILAS AWOKE with a start. He had no idea what had woken him or how long he had been asleep. Sitting up on his straw mat, he listened to the quiet breathing of the Opus Dei residence hall, the stillness textured only by the murmurs of someone praying aloud in a room below him. These were sounds that should have comforted him.

And yet he felt a sudden and unexpected wariness. Standing, wearing only his undergarments, he walked to the window. Was I followed? he wondered. Peering out, he now saw the faint outline of a flashing police light through the hedge. A floorboard creaked in the hallway. A door latch moved.

Silas reacted on instinct, surging across the room and sliding behind the door as it crashed open. The first police officer stormed through, swinging his gun left then right at what appeared to be an empty room. Before he realised where Silas was, Silas had thrown his shoulder into the door, crushing a second officer as he came through. As the first officer wheeled to shoot, Silas dived for his legs. The gun went off, the bullet sailing above Silas's head, as he connected with the officer's shins, driving his legs out from under him. The second officer staggered to his feet but Silas drove a knee into his groin, then clambered over the writhing body into the hall.

Almost naked, Silas hurled his pale body down the staircase. He knew he had been betrayed, but by whom? When he reached the foyer, more officers were surging through the front door. Silas turned the other way and dashed deeper into the residence hall. The women's entrance. Every Opus Dei building has one. Winding down narrow hallways, Silas snaked through a kitchen, past terrified workers, until he saw an exit light gleaming at the end of a dark hallway.

Running full speed through the door, Silas did not see the officer coming the other way until it was too late. The two collided, Silas's broad, naked shoulder driving the officer backwards onto the pavement, landing hard on top of him. The officer's gun clattered away. Silas could hear men running down the hall shouting. Rolling, he grabbed the loose gun just as two officers emerged. A shot rang out, and Silas felt a searing pain below his ribs. Filled with rage, he opened fire at the three officers.

A dark shadow came out of nowhere. The angry hands that grabbed at his shoulders felt as if they were infused with the power of the devil himself. The man roared in his ear, *SILAS, NO!*

Silas spun and fired. Their eyes met. Silas was already screaming in horror as Bishop Aringarosa fell.

CHAPTER 13

More than 3,000 people are entombed or enshrined within Westminster Abbey. The colossal stone interior burgeons with the remains of kings, statesmen, scientists, poets and musicians. Their tombs are packed into every last niche and alcove. Robert Langdon felt no interest in any of them, save one—Sir Isaac Newton.

Hurrying through the grand portico on the north transept, Langdon and Sophie were ushered politely through a large walk-through metal detector before continuing to the abbey entrance. Stepping across the threshold, Langdon felt the outside world evaporate. There was a sudden hush. No rumble of traffic. No hiss of rain. Just a deafening silence that seemed to reverberate through the shadows.

Before them the wide alley of the north transept stretched out like a deep canyon, flanked by sheer cliffs of stained glass. On sunny days the abbey floor was a prismatic patchwork of light. Today, the rain and darkness gave this massive space a wraithlike aura . . . more like that of the crypt it truly was.

'We passed through metal detectors,' Sophie reminded him, apparently sensing his apprehension. 'If anyone is in here, they can't be armed.'

Langdon nodded but still felt anxious. As they moved into a side aisle behind a row of pilasters, he couldn't shake the image of Leigh

Teabing being held captive, probably tied up in the back of his own limousine. Whoever had ordered the top Priory members killed would not hesitate to eliminate others who stood in the way.

'Which way is it?' Sophie asked, looking around.

Langdon had no idea. 'We should find a guide and ask.' He knew better than to wander aimlessly in here. The abbey was laid out in the shape of a crucifix, but it had a series of sprawling cloisters attached. One false step through the wrong archway, and a visitor was lost in a labyrinth of outdoor passageways surrounded by high walls.

AT THAT MOMENT, a hundred yards down the nave, behind the choir screen, the tomb of Sir Isaac Newton had a lone visitor. The Teacher had been scrutinising the monument for ten minutes now.

Newton's tomb consisted of a massive black-marble sarcophagus on which reclined the sculpted form of the scientist, leaning proudly against a stack of his own books. Behind Newton's recumbent body rose an austere pyramid, and what intrigued the Teacher most was the giant shape mounted halfway up the pyramid.

An orb.

The Teacher pondered Saunière's riddle. *You seek the orb that ought be on his tomb.* The massive orb protruding from the face of the pyramid depicted constellations, comets, stars and planets—a complicated map of the heavens. Was there a missing planet? Had some astronomical orb been omitted from a constellation? He had no idea. Even so, the Teacher suspected that the solution would be ingeniously simple.

He stepped closer to the tomb, scanning it from bottom to top. What orb ought to be here . . . and yet is missing?

Pacing now near the corner of the choir screen, he glanced up the long nave towards the main altar and his gaze was caught by an abbey guide, who was being waved over by two familiar individuals.

Langdon and Neveu.

Calmly, the Teacher moved back behind the choir screen. He had anticipated that they would eventually decipher the poem's meaning and come to Newton's tomb, but this was sooner than he had imagined. Taking a deep breath, he considered his options.

Reaching down to his pocket, he touched the cryptex and the second object that gave him confidence: the revolver. As expected, the abbey's metal detectors had blared as the Teacher passed through with the concealed gun. Also as expected, the guards had backed off when the Teacher glared indignantly and flashed his identification card. Official rank always commanded the proper respect.

Although the Teacher had hoped to solve the cryptex alone, he now sensed that the arrival of Langdon and Neveu was a welcome development. He might be able to use their expertise to divine the password. Then it would be just a matter of applying the right pressure . . .

Not here, of course. The Teacher recalled a sign he had seen on his way into the abbey. Immediately he knew the perfect place to lure them. The only question now . . . what to use as bait?

LANGDON AND SOPHIE moved down the north aisle, keeping to the shadows. The tomb they were seeking was obscured from this angle.

'At least there's nobody over there,' Sophie whispered.

Langdon nodded, relieved. 'I'll go over,' he whispered. 'You stay hidden in case someone—'

But Sophie was already headed across the open floor towards the elaborate sepulchre.

As they approached, Langdon felt a slow sinking sensation. Newton's tomb was covered with orbs—stars, comets, planets. *You seek the orb that ought be on his tomb?* It could turn out to be like trying to find a missing blade of grass on a golf course.

'Astronomical bodies,' Sophie said. 'And a lot of them.'

Langdon frowned as Sophie tilted her head and read the titles of the books on which Newton was leaning. '*Divinity, Chronology. Opticks. Philosophiae Naturalis Principia Mathematica*?' She turned to him. 'Ring any bells?'

Langdon stepped closer. '*Principia Mathematica*, as I remember, has something to do with the gravitation pull of planets . . . which admittedly are orbs, but it seems a little far-fetched.'

'Look!' Sophie gasped, grabbing his arm. She was staring aghast at the top of the sarcophagus. 'Someone was here,' she whispered, pointing to Newton's right foot.

Langdon did not understand her concern. A careless tourist had left a grave-rubbing pencil on the sarcophagus lid near Newton's foot. Langdon reached out to pick it up, but as he did so, the light shifted on the polished black-marble and Langdon froze.

Scrawled on the sarcophagus lid was a barely visible message:

I have Teabing. Go through Chapter House,
out south exit, to public garden.

Langdon's heart was pounding wildly. Despite the trepidation that settled over him upon seeing the words, he told himself this was good news. Leigh must be still alive. There was another implication here, too. 'They don't know the password either,' he whispered. 'Otherwise why make their presence known?'

'Or it's a trap.'

Langdon shook his head. 'I don't think so. The garden is outside the abbey walls. A very public place.' Langdon had once visited the abbey's famous College Garden where monks once grew natural pharmacological remedies. Boasting the oldest living fruit trees in Britain, it was a popular spot for tourists. 'I think sending us outside is a show of faith. So we feel safe.'

Sophie was dubious. 'You mean where there are no metal detectors?'

Langdon scowled. She had a point.

'The note says to go through the Chapter House to the south exit,' Sophie said. 'Maybe from the exit we would have a view of the garden. That way we could assess the situation before we walked out there and exposed ourselves to any danger.'

The idea was a good one. It had been years since he had visited the Chapter House, but he remembered it being out through the cloisters somewhere. Stepping back from the tomb, Langdon peered round the choir screen to the opposite side of the nave, where a large sign directed visitors to the Chapter House and Cloisters.

Langdon and Sophie moved too quickly to notice the small announcement apologising that certain areas were closed for renovations.

They emerged immediately into a high-walled courtyard, then entered the narrow, low-hanging walkways that bordered it and followed the signs for the Chapter House.

Forty yards down the deserted cloister, an archway materialised on their left, giving way to another hallway. Although this was the entrance they were looking for, it was cordoned off by an official-looking sign: CLOSED FOR RENOVATION.

The corridor beyond was littered with scaffolding and dust sheets, but at the far end of the long hallway, the heavy wooden door to the Chapter House was wide open.

'We just left the east cloister,' Langdon said, 'so the south exit to the garden must be through there and to the right.'

Sophie was already stepping over the cordon. 'It looks huge,' she whispered as they approached the large octagonal interior.

Crossing the threshold, they found themselves having to squint. After the gloomy cloisters, the Chapter House with its enormous windows and octagonal vaulted ceiling, felt like a solarium. They were a good ten feet into the room before they realised there was no south exit.

They were standing in an enormous dead end.

The heavy door closed with a resounding thud behind them. The lone man who had been standing behind the door looked calm as he aimed a small revolver at them.

For a moment Langdon thought he must be dreaming.

It was Leigh Teabing.

SIR LEIGH TEABING felt rueful as he gazed at their shocked faces. 'My friends,' he said, 'since you walked into my home last night, I have done everything in my power to keep you out of harm's way. But you have put me in a difficult position.'

'Leigh?' Langdon finally managed. 'We thought you were in trouble. We came here to help you!'

'As I trusted you would,' he said. 'We have much to discuss.'

Langdon and Sophie seemed unable to tear their stunned gazes from the revolver aimed at them.

'It is simply to ensure your full attention,' Teabing said. 'If I had wanted to harm you, you would be dead by now. I have risked everything to spare your lives. I had vowed to myself only to sacrifice those who had betrayed the Sangreal.'

'What are you talking about?' Langdon said. 'Betrayed the Sangreal?'

'I discovered a terrible truth,' Teabing said, sighing. 'I learned *why* the Sangreal documents were never revealed to the world, why the millennium passed without any revelation. The Priory was charged with releasing the Sangreal documents when the End of Days arrived. And yet, at the ultimate moment of truth, Jacques Saunière eschewed his duty. He decided the time was not right.' Teabing turned to Sophie. 'He failed the Grail. He failed the Priory. And he failed the memory of all the generations that had worked to make that moment possible.'

'You?' Sophie declared, her green eyes boring into him with rage. '*You* are the one responsible for my grandfather's murder?'

Teabing scoffed. 'Your grandfather and his *sénéchaux* were traitors to the Grail. Your grandfather sold out to the Church. It is obvious they pressured him to keep the truth quiet.'

Sophie felt a fury rising from deep within. She shook her head. 'The Church had no influence on my grandfather!'

Teabing laughed coldly. 'My dear, the Church has two thousand years of experience of pressuring those who threaten to unveil its lies.' He took a deep breath. 'The deaths of your mother, father, grandmother and brother were, I fear, *not* accidental.'

The words sent Sophie's emotions reeling.

Langdon shook his head. 'What are you saying?'

'Robert, it explains everything. With the End of Days imminent, killing the Grand Master's loved ones was an effective way of sending him a clear message. Be quiet, or you and Sophie are next.'

'It was a car accident,' Sophie stammered, feeling her childhood pain welling inside her. 'An *accident*!'

'Leigh,' Langdon argued, visibly riled, 'you have no proof that the Church had anything to do with those deaths, or that it influenced the Priory's decision to remain silent.'

'Proof?' Teabing fired back. 'The new millennium has arrived, and yet the world remains ignorant! Is that not proof enough?'

In Teabing's words, Sophie heard another voice echoing. *Sophie, I must tell you the truth about your family.* Could this be that truth her grandfather had wanted to tell her? That her family had been murdered? What did she know about the crash that took her family? Only sketchy details. Even the stories in the newspaper had been vague.

'You suspected he was being manipulated,' Langdon said, glaring with disbelief at Teabing. 'So you murdered him?'

'Something had to be done. Should the world be ignorant for ever? Should the Church be allowed to cement its lies into our history books for all eternity? No, something needed to be done! And now we are poised to carry out Saunière's legacy and right a terrible wrong.' He paused. 'The three of us. Together.'

Sophie felt only incredulity. 'How could you possibly believe that we would help you?'

'Because, my dear, *you* are the reason the Priory failed to release the documents. Your grandfather's love for you prevented him from challenging the Church. His fear of reprisal against his only remaining family crippled him. Now you owe the world the truth.'

DESPITE THE TORRENT of questions running through his mind, Langdon knew that only one thing mattered now: getting Sophie out of here alive. He glanced over at her. She looked shaken. The Church murdered her family to silence the Priory? There had to be another explanation.

'Let Sophie leave,' he declared. 'You and I should discuss this alone.'

Teabing gave an unnatural laugh. 'I'm afraid that is one show of faith I cannot afford. I can, however, offer you this.' He propped himself fully on his crutches, gracelessly keeping the gun aimed at Sophie, and removed the keystone from his pocket. He swayed a bit as he held it out for Langdon. 'A token of trust, Robert.'

Robert didn't move.

'Take it,' Teabing said, thrusting it awkwardly towards Langdon.

'We must work together. Mankind deserves to know the truth.'

Despite Teabing's pleas for cooperation and trust, his gun remained trained on Sophie as Langdon stepped forwards and accepted the black onyx cylinder. He glanced down at the cryptex. The dials were still in random order, and the cryptex remained locked. 'I cannot help you, Leigh,' he said. 'I have no idea how to open this. And even if I knew the password . . . ' Langdon paused, realising he had said too much.

'You would not tell me?' Teabing sighed. 'I am disappointed and surprised, Robert, that you do not appreciate the extent to which you are in my debt. My task would have been far simpler had Rémy and I eliminated you both when you walked into Château Villette. Instead I risked everything to take the nobler course.'

'This is noble?' Langdon demanded, eyeing the gun.

'Saunière's fault,' Teabing said. 'He and his *sénéchaux* lied to Silas. How was I to imagine the Grand Master would go to such ends to deceive me and bequeath the keystone to an estranged granddaughter?' Teabing looked at Sophie with disdain. 'Someone so unqualified to hold this knowledge that she required a symbologist baby sitter.' Teabing glanced back at Langdon. 'Fortunately, Robert, your involvement turned out to be my saving grace. You extracted the keystone from the depository bank and walked into my home.'

Langdon glared. 'And if we had not?'

'I was formulating a plan to extend you a helping hand. One way or another, the keystone was coming to Château Villette. The fact that you delivered to me only serves as proof that my cause is just.'

'What!' Langdon was appalled.

'Silas was supposed to break in and steal the keystone from you in Château Villette—thus removing you from the equation without hurting you, and exonerating me from any suspicion. However, when I saw the intricacy of Saunière's codes, I decided to include you both in my quest a bit longer. Silas could steal the keystone later.'

'The Temple Church,' Sophie said, her tone awash with contempt.

LIGHT BEGINS TO DAWN, Teabing thought. The Temple Church was the perfect location. Rémy's orders had been clear—stay out of sight while Silas recovers the keystone. But Langdon's threat to smash the keystone had caused Rémy to panic. If only he had not revealed himself, Teabing thought ruefully, recalling his own mock kidnapping. He was the sole link to me, and he showed his face. Fortunately, Silas remained unaware of Teabing's true identity and was easily fooled into compliance. An anonymous tip to the police was all it needed to remove him from the picture once he was at the Opus Dei centre.

The other loose end was harder. Teabing struggled with the decision, but Rémy had proved a liability. The cleanest solution had been staring Teabing in the face from the limousine's bar—a flask, some cognac and a packet of peanuts. The powder at the bottom of the packet was enough to trigger Rémy's deadly allergy. When Rémy parked the limo on Horse Guards Parade, Teabing had climbed out of the back, walked to the passenger door and sat in the front next to Rémy. Minutes later, he had got out, climbed into the rear again and cleaned up the evidence. Westminster Abbey had been a short walk, and when Teabing's leg braces, crutches and gun had set off the metal detector, the guards hadn't known what to do. His embossed card identifying him as a Knight of the Realm had presented the guards with an easy solution. They had practically tripped over one another ushering him in.

Now, looking at the bewildered Langdon and Neveu, Teabing resisted the urge to reveal how he had brilliantly implicated Opus Dei in the plot that would soon bring about the demise of the entire Church. That would have to wait. Right now there was work to do.

'I implore you both to recognise this opportunity,' he said. 'Help me break the final code and open the cryptex.' Teabing paused, his eyes alight. 'We hold the key to two thousand years of history—the lost key to the Sangreal. Can't you feel the souls of all the knights burned at the stake to protect her secret? Would you have them die in vain? We need to swear an oath together, to uncover the truth and make it known.'

Sophie spoke in a steely tone. 'I will never swear an oath with my grandfather's murderer. Except an oath that I will see you go to prison.'

Teabing turned grave, then resolute. 'I am sorry you feel that way, mademoiselle.' He aimed the gun at Langdon. 'And you, Robert? Are you with me, or against me?'

BISHOP MANUEL ARINGAROSA opened his eyes and saw that the man cradling him was Silas. The albino was carrying him along a misty pavement, shouting for a hospital, his voice a wail of agony.

'My son,' Aringarosa whispered. 'You're hurt.'

Silas glanced down, his visage contorted in anguish. 'I am so very sorry, Father.' He seemed almost too pained to speak.

'No, Silas,' Aringarosa replied. 'It is I who am sorry. This is my fault. I was too eager. Too fearful. You and I were deceived.'

Aringarosa recalled, in vivid detail, the meeting inside Castel Gandolfo five months ago that had changed his life . . . the news that had set this entire calamity into motion. He had entered Gandolfo's

Astronomy Library with his head held high, fully expecting to be lauded for his superior work representing Catholicism in America. But as soon as he entered the room he sensed something was wrong.

'I am not skilled in small talk, Bishop,' the rotund secretarius, overseer of the vatican's legal affairs, said, 'so allow me to be direct about the reason for your visit.'

'Please. Speak openly.' Aringarosa glanced at the two other men present, both Italian cardinals.

'His Holiness and others in Rome have been concerned by the political fallout from Opus Dei's more controversial practices.'

Aringarosa bristled. He had already been through this on numerous occasions with the new pontiff, who had turned out to be a distressingly fervent voice for liberal change in the Church.

'Two days ago, the Secretariat Council voted unanimously to revoke the Vatican's sanction of Opus Dei. Six months from today, it will no longer be considered a prelature of the Vatican. You will be a church unto yourself. We are already drawing up the legal papers.'

'But . . . that is impossible!'

'On the contrary, it is quite possible. And necessary. Your practices of corporal mortification, and your policies regarding women, quite frankly make Opus Dei a liability and an embarrassment.'

Bishop Aringarosa was stupefied. 'An embarrassment? But Opus Dei is the only Catholic organisation whose numbers are growing!'

'True. A troubling issue for us all.'

Aringarosa shot to his feet. 'Ask His Holiness if Opus Dei was an embarrassment in 1982 when we helped the Vatican Bank!'

'The Vatican will always be grateful for that,' the secretarius said, his tone appeasing, 'and yet there are those who believe your financial munificence in 1982 is the only reason you were granted prelature status in the first place.'

'That is not true!'

'Whatever the case, we plan to act in good faith. We are drawing up severance terms that will include a reimbursement of those monies.'

Aringarosa stood up. 'His Holiness would not *dare* abolish a personal prelature established by a previous Pope!'

'I'm sorry.' The secretarius's eyes did not flinch. 'The Lord giveth and the Lord taketh away.'

Aringarosa had staggered from that meeting in bewilderment and panic. Several weeks later, he received the phone call that changed everything. The caller said he knew of the Vatican's plans to pull support from Opus Dei. How could he know? Aringarosa had wondered.

As if reading his mind, the man who called himself the Teacher said, 'I have ears everywhere, Bishop. With your help, I can uncover the hiding place of a sacred relic that will bring you enormous power . . . Enough power to make the Vatican bow before you, to save the Faith. Not just for Opus Dei. But for all of us.'

Aringarosa had felt a glorious ray of hope. 'Tell me your plan.'

NOW, ARINGAROSA'S EYES flickered, and he gazed at Silas. 'My child . . .'

Silas's soul thundered with remorse and rage. 'Father, if it takes my lifetime, I will find the one who deceived us, and I will kill him.'

The bishop shook his head. 'Silas . . . if you have learned nothing from me, please . . . learn this.' He took Silas's hand and gave it a firm squeeze. 'Forgiveness is God's greatest gift.'

'But father . . .'

Aringarosa closed his eyes. 'Silas, you must pray.'

ROBERT LANGDON stood beneath the lofty cupola of the deserted Chapter House and stared into the barrel of Leigh Teabing's gun.

He feared that discovering the cryptex's elusive password would be his only remaining hope of bartering for Sophie's release. Forcing his mind to this critical task, he moved slowly towards the far windows, searching for any inspiration in their stained-glass mosaics . . .

You seek the orb that ought be on his tomb
It speaks of Rosy flesh and seeded womb

Place yourself in Saunière's mind, he urged himself, gazing outwards now into College Garden. What would he believe is the orb that ought be on Newton's tomb? Images of stars, comets and planets twinkled in the falling rain, but Langdon ignored them. Saunière was not a man of science. He was a man of humanity, of art, of history.

Legend had always portrayed the Grail as a cruel mistress, luring you one more step and then evaporating. Langdon sensed her playful presence now, dancing in the rain, peeking out from behind the bud-filled branches of Britain's oldest apple tree, as if to remind him that the fruit of knowledge was growing just beyond his reach.

ACROSS THE ROOM, behind him, Teabing glanced now at Langdon.

'He won't open it for you,' Sophie said coldly. 'Even if he can.'

The historian was fairly certain now that he was going to have to use the weapon. I have given her every opportunity to do the right thing, he told himself. The Grail is bigger than any one of us.

At that moment, Langdon turned. 'The tomb . . . ' he said suddenly. 'I know where to look on Newton's tomb.'

Teabing's heart soared. 'Where, Robert? Tell me!'

Sophie sounded horrified. 'Robert, no! You're not going to help him, are you?'

'No,' he said. 'Not until he lets you go.'

Teabing's optimism darkened. 'We are so close, Robert. Don't you dare start playing games with me!'

'No games,' Langdon said. 'Let her go. Then I'll take you to Newton's tomb. We'll open the cryptex together.'

'I'm not going anywhere,' Sophie declared. 'That cryptex was given to me by my grandfather. It is not yours to open.'

Langdon looked fearful. 'Sophie, please! I'm trying to help you!'

'Truly, Robert? You know where on the tomb to look?' Teabing asked.

'I do.'

The hesitation in Langdon's eyes was fleeting but Leigh caught it. There was a lie there. A desperate, pathetic ploy to save Sophie. Your poker face needs work, my friend. I can see that you are lying. You have no idea where on Newton's tomb the answer lies. I am a lone knight, surrounded by unworthy souls. And I will have to decipher the keystone on my own.

As painful as the solution was going to be, Teabing knew he could carry it out with a clean conscience. The only challenge would be to persuade Langdon to set down the keystone so the charade could safely end without damage to the contents.

'A show of faith,' Teabing said, lowering the gun. 'Set down the keystone, and we'll talk.'

LANGDON HAD ALREADY made his decision several minutes ago, while overlooking College Garden. He had experienced a clarity unlike any he had ever felt. The Truth is right before your eyes, Robert.

Now, bowing down several yards in front of Teabing, he lowered the cryptex to within inches of the stone floor.

'Set it down, Robert,' Teabing whispered, aiming the gun at him.

Crouching lower, Langdon muttered. 'I'm sorry, Leigh.' Then in one fluid motion, he leapt up, swinging his arm skywards, launching the cryptex towards the dome above.

LEIGH TEABING did not feel his finger pull the trigger, but the gun discharged with a thundering crash, and a bullet exploded in the floor near Langdon's feet.

Time seemed to freeze as Teabing watched the keystone rise to the apex of its climb, hover for a moment in the void, and then tumble down, end over end, back towards the stone floor. All his hopes and dreams were plummeting towards earth, and his body reacted on instinct. He released the gun and heaved himself forwards, dropping his crutches as he reached out and snatched the keystone in midair.

With the keystone victoriously clutched in his hand, Teabing suddenly realised he was falling. His outstretched arms hit first, and the cryptex collided with the floor. There was a crunch of glass within.

For a full second, Teabing did not breathe. Lying there outstretched on the cold floor, he implored the glass vial inside to hold. Then the acrid tang of vinegar cut the air and he felt himself sobbing uncontrollably. *The Grail is gone!* Shuddering in disbelief, he tried to force the cylinder apart, longing to catch a fleeting glimpse of history before the papyrus dissolved for ever.

To his shock, the cylinder separated. He peered inside. It was empty except for shards of wet glass. No dissolving papyrus. Teabing rolled over and looked up at Langdon. Sophie stood beside him, aiming the gun down at Teabing.

Bewildered, Teabing looked back at the keystone. The dials were no longer at random. They spelled a five-letter word: APPLE.

'The orb from which Eve partook,' Langdon said coolly, 'incurring the Holy wrath of God. Original sin. The symbol of the fall of the sacred feminine.'

Teabing felt the truth come crashing down on him. The orb that ought be on Newton's tomb could be none other than the apple that fell from heaven, struck Newton on the head, and inspired his life's work. *The Rosy flesh with a seeded womb!*

'Robert,' Teabing stammered. 'Where . . . is the map?'

Without blinking, Langdon reached into the breast pocket of his tweed jacket and carefully extracted a delicate rolled papyrus. Only a few yards from where Teabing lay, he unrolled the scroll and looked at it. A smile crossed his face.

'Tell me!' Teabing demanded. 'Oh God, please! It's not too late!'

As the sound of heavy footsteps thundered down the hall towards the Chapter House, Langdon quietly rolled the papyrus and slipped it back in his pocket.

'No!' Teabing cried out, trying in vain to stand.

When the doors burst open, Bezu Fache entered like a bull into a ring, his feral eyes scanning, finding his target—Leigh Teabing—helpless on the floor. In relief he holstered his sidearm and turned to

Sophie. 'Agent Neveu, I am relieved you and Mr Langdon are safe. You should have come in when I asked.'

The British police entered on Fache's heels, seizing the anguished prisoner and placing him in handcuffs.

Sophie seemed stunned to see Fache. 'How did you find us?'

Fache pointed to Teabing. 'He made the mistake of showing his ID when he entered the abbey. The guards had heard a police broadcast about our search for him.'

Teabing was screaming like a madman, as the police officers led him away. 'Robert! Tell me where it's hidden!'

As Teabing passed him Langdon looked him in the eye. 'Only the worthy find the Grail, Leigh. You taught me that.'

THE MIST HAD SETTLED low on Kensington Gardens as Silas limped into a quiet hollow, out of sight. Kneeling on the wet grass, he could feel the blood flowing from the bullet wound below his ribs, but with every cell in his broken body, he prayed. He prayed for forgiveness. He prayed for mercy. And, above all, he prayed for his mentor, Bishop Aringarosa, that the Lord would not take him before his time.

Closing his eyes, he said a final prayer, and from somewhere in the mist, the voice of Manuel Aringarosa whispered to him, *Our Lord is a good and merciful God.*

Silas's pain at last began to fade, and he knew the bishop was right.

IT WAS LATE AFTERNOON when Bezu Fache emerged from the interrogation room. Sir Leigh Teabing had vociferously proclaimed his innocence, and yet from his incoherent rantings about the Holy Grail, secret documents and mysterious brotherhoods, Fache suspected he was setting the stage for his lawyers to plead an insanity defence.

Yet Teabing had displayed ingenuity in formulating a plan that protected his innocence at every turn. He had exploited both the Vatican and Opus Dei, two groups that had turned out to be completely innocent, and his dirty work had been carried out unknowingly by a fanatical monk and a desperate bishop. More cleverly still, Teabing had situated his electronic listening post in the one place a man with polio could not possibly reach. The actual surveillance had been carried out by his manservant, Rémy—the only person privy to Teabing's true identity—now conveniently dead of an allergic reaction.

Hardly the handiwork of someone lacking mental faculties.

Now, sitting in the back of a cab, Fache closed his eyes. He had one more thing to attend to before he returned to Paris.

The St Mary's Hospital recovery room was sunny.

'You've impressed us all,' the nurse said cheerfully. 'Nothing short of miraculous.'

Bishop Aringarosa smiled weakly. 'I have always been blessed.'

The nurse left the bishop alone, and he thought again of Silas, whose body had been found in the park. *Please forgive me, my son.*

Aringarosa had longed for Silas to be part of his glorious plan. Last night, however, the bishop had received a call from Bezu Fache, questioning him about a nun who had been murdered in Saint-Sulpice. News of the four other murders transformed his horror to anguish. *Silas, what have you done!* Unable to reach the Teacher, the bishop knew he had been cut loose. Used. The only way to stop the horrific chain of events he had helped to put in motion was to cooperate fully with Fache.

Aringarosa closed his eyes and listened to the television coverage of the arrest of a prominent historian, Sir Leigh Teabing. The Teacher laid bare for all to see. Teabing had caught wind of the Vatican's plans to disassociate itself from Opus Dei. He had chosen Aringarosa as the perfect pawn in his plan. After all, who more likely to leap blindly after the Holy Grail than a man with everything to lose? Leigh Teabing had protected his identity shrewdly—feigning a French accent and a pious heart, and demanding as payment the one thing he did not need—money. And Aringarosa had been far too eager. The price tag of 20 million euros had seemed paltry when compared with the prize of obtaining the Grail, and with the Vatican's separation payment to Opus Dei, the finances had worked nicely. Teabing's ultimate insult, of course, had been to demand payment in Vatican bonds, so that if anything went wrong, the trail would lead to Rome.

'I am glad to see you're well, My Lord.'

Aringarosa recognised the gruff voice in the doorway, but the face was unexpected—stern, powerful features, slicked-back hair and a broad neck that strained against his dark suit. 'Captain Fache?'

The captain approached the bed and hoisted a familiar, heavy black briefcase onto a chair. 'I believe this belongs to you.'

Aringarosa looked away in shame. 'Yes . . . thank you.' He paused, then said. 'Captain, would you be kind enough to divide the contents of this briefcase among the . . . the families of the deceased.'

Fache's dark eyes studied him a long moment. 'A virtuous gesture, My Lord. I will see to it your wishes are carried out.' Fache ran his hand over his forehead. 'My Lord, there is one final matter I'd like to discuss—your impromptu flight to London. In bribing your pilot to change course, you broke a number of international laws.'

Aringarosa slumped. 'I was desperate.'

'Yes. As was the pilot when my men interrogated him.' Fache reached in his pocket and produced a familiar amethyst ring.

Aringarosa felt tears welling as he slipped the ring back on his finger. 'You've been so kind. Thank you.'

Fache waved off the gesture, walking to the window and gazing thoughtfully out at the city. When he turned, there was an uncertainty about him. 'My Lord, where do you go from here?'

Aringarosa had been asked that question as he had left Gandolfo the night before. 'I suspect my path is as uncertain as yours.'

'Yes.' Fache paused. 'I suspect I will be retiring early.'

Aringarosa smiled. 'A little faith can do wonders, Captain.'

Chapter 14

Built by the Knights Templar in 1446, Rosslyn Chapel stands seven miles south of Edinburgh, on the same north–south meridian that runs through Glastonbury. This longitudinal Rose Line is the traditional marker of King Arthur's Isle of Avalon and is considered the axis of Britain's sacred geometry. It is from this hallowed Rose Line that Rosslyn, originally spelled Roslin, takes its name.

Rosslyn's rugged spires were casting long evening shadows as Robert Langdon and Sophie Neveu pulled their rental car into the grassy parking area near the chapel. Gazing up at the stark edifice framed against a cloud-swept sky, Langdon felt like Alice falling headlong into the rabbit hole. *This must be a dream*. And yet he knew the text of Saunière's final message could not have been more specific:

The Holy Grail 'neath ancient Roslin waits

The Priory's final secret had been unveiled to them through another of Saunière's simple verses. Four lines that pointed without a doubt to this very spot, which now seemed obvious. For centuries, Rosslyn Chapel had echoed with whispers of the Holy Grail's presence. In recent decades, when ground-penetrating radar had revealed the presence of an astonishing chamber *beneath* the chapel, the whispers had turned to shouts. Not only did the deep vault dwarf the chapel atop it, but it appeared to have no entrance or exit. Rosslyn had thus become a pilgrimage site for Grail seekers, eager to absorb its mystery.

'Robert?' Sophie was standing outside the car, looking back at him. 'Are you coming?' She was holding the rosewood box, which Captain Fache had returned to them, complete with cryptexes, before they took the flight to Edinburgh.

Making their way up the long gravel path, they passed the oddly protruding west wall of the chapel, a section that seemed not to have been finished. The Knights Templar had designed Rosslyn as an exact architectural blueprint of Solomon's Temple in Jerusalem, complete with west wall and subterranean vault like the Holy of Holies in which the original knights had unearthed their treasure.

Entering the chapel through arches covered with carved cinquefoils, Langdon took in its arrestingly intricate stonework.

Every surface had been carved with symbols—Christian cruciforms, Jewish stars, Masonic seals, Templar crosses, cornucopias, pyramids, astrological signs, pentacles and roses. The Knights Templar had been master stonemasons, and Rosslyn was considered their most sublime labour of love and veneration. Symbology heaven, one of Langdon's colleagues had called it. It was a shrine to all faiths, all traditions—and, above all, to Nature and the goddess.

The sanctuary was empty except for a handful of visitors listening to a young man giving the day's last tour. He was leading his party along a well-known route linking six key architectural points within the sanctuary. This hexagram had once been the secret symbol of stargazing priests and was later adopted by the Israelite kings—David and Solomon—becoming known variously as the Star of David, or Solomon's Seal.

Sophie suddenly stood riveted, a puzzled look on her face.

'What is it?' Langdon asked.

She stared at the chapel. 'I think . . . I've been here. My grandfather must have brought me when I was very young. It feels familiar.' As her eyes scanned the room, she nodded with more certainty. 'Yes.' She pointed. 'Those two pillars . . . I've seen them.'

Langdon looked at the two intricately sculpted columns, positioned where the altar would normally stand. They were an oddly matched pair; the pillar on the left was carved with simple, vertical lines, while the one on the right was embellished with an ornate spiral of flowers.

'I don't doubt you've seen them,' Langdon said, 'but it wasn't necessarily here. These two pillars are the most duplicated architectural structures in history. Replicas exist in every Masonic temple in the world. They are exact replicas of the two pillars that stood at the head of Solomon's Temple. That's called Boaz, or the Mason's Pillar. The other, on the right, is Jachin, or the Apprentice's Pillar.'

Langdon had already explained to her the Templars' historic link to the Masons.

'I've never been in a Masonic temple,' Sophie said, still eyeing the pillars. 'But I am positive I saw these here.' She looked for something else to jog her memory.

The visitors were now leaving, and the young guide made his way across the chapel to them with a pleasant smile. He was a handsome young man with a Scottish brogue and strawberry-blond hair. 'I'm about to close up for the day. May I help you find anything?'

How about the Holy Grail? Langdon wanted to say.

'The code,' Sophie blurted suddenly. 'There's a code here!'

The man looked pleased by her enthusiasm. 'Yes, there is,' he said.

'It's on the ceiling,' she said, turning to the right-hand wall. 'Somewhere over . . . there.'

He smiled. 'Not your first visit to Rosslyn, I see.'

The code, Langdon thought. He had forgotten that little bit of lore. Among Rosslyn's numerous mysteries was a vaulted archway from which hundreds of stone blocks protruded, each one carved with a symbol. Some people believed it was a cipher, a code that revealed the entrance to the underground vault. The Rosslyn Trust offered a generous reward to anyone who could unveil the secret meaning, but to this day the code remains a mystery.

'I'd be happy to show you . . . '

THE GUIDE'S VOICE trailed off.

My first code, Sophie thought, moving towards the encoded archway, and recalling her first visit here.

She had been a little girl . . . it was a year or so after her family's death. Her grandfather had brought her to Scotland on a short vacation and they had come to see Rosslyn Chapel before going back to Paris. It was late evening.

'Can we go home, *Grand-père*?' Sophie had begged, feeling tired.

'Soon, dear, very soon.' His voice was melancholy. 'I have one last thing I need to do. How about if you wait in the car?'

'Can I do the archway code again? That was fun.'

'You won't be frightened in here alone? I have to step outside.'

'Of course not!' she said in a huff. 'It's not even dark yet!'

He smiled. 'Very well then.' He led her back to the elaborate archway, then exited into the soft evening light, leaving the door open.

Sophie gazed up at the code, for what seemed an age. '*Grand-père?*' she called eventually.

There was no answer, so she walked outside and could see her grandfather standing on the porch of a stone house directly behind the church. He was talking quietly to a person barely visible in the doorway.

'*Grand-père?*' she called.

Her grandfather turned and waved, motioning for her to wait a moment. Then, he appeared to say some final words to the person inside and blew a kiss towards them.

He came to Sophie with tearful eyes.

'Why are you crying, *Grand-père*?'

He picked her up and held her close. 'Oh, Sophie, I have just said good-bye to someone whom I love very much,' he replied, his voice heavy with emotion. 'I will not see her again for a very long time.'

STANDING WITH THE GUIDE, Langdon watched as Sophie wandered off to look at the code. He was thinking about Saunière's poem:

The Holy Grail 'neath ancient Roslin waits
The blade and chalice guarding o'er Her gates

'I hate to pry,' the guide said, eyeing the rosewood box in Langdon's hands. 'But this box . . . might I ask where you got it?'

Langdon gave a weary laugh. 'That's an exceptionally long story.'

The young man hesitated. 'It's the strangest thing. My grandmother has a box *exactly* like that—same inlaid rose.'

Langdon knew the young man must be mistaken. If ever a box had been one of a kind, it was *this* one. 'They may be similar but—'

The side door closed loudly, drawing both of their gazes. Sophie had exited without a word. Langdon stared after her. Where was she going? He turned to the guide. 'There's a house out there. Do you know whose it is?'

The guide nodded, also looking puzzled at the idea that Sophie might be going there. 'The chapel curator lives there. She also happens to be the head of the Rosslyn Trust.' He paused. 'And my grandmother.'

'Your grandmother heads the Rosslyn Trust?'

The young man nodded. 'My grandmother brought me up in that house. Now I help maintain the chapel and give tours.'

Concerned for Sophie, Langdon moved towards the chapel door to call out to her. He was only halfway there when he stopped short. *Impossible*. Slowly, Langdon turned back to the young man. 'You said your grandmother has a box like this one—Where did she get it?'

'My grandfather made it for her. He died when I was a baby.'

Langdon sensed an unimaginable web of connections emerging. 'You said your grandmother brought you up. Do you mind my asking what happened to your parents?'

The young man looked surprised. 'They died when I was young.'

Langdon's heart pounded. 'In a car accident?'

The guide recoiled, a look of bewilderment in his olive-green eyes. 'Yes. My entire family died that day. I lost my grandfather, my parents, and . . . ' He hesitated, glancing down at the floor.

'And your sister,' Langdon said.

THE STONE HOUSE was exactly as Sophie remembered it. Night was falling now, and the house exuded a warm and inviting aura. As Sophie approached the front door, which stood open, she could hear the quiet sounds of sobbing from within.

An elderly woman with long, luxuriant silver hair was standing in the hallway, her back to the door. Feeling herself drawn closer, Sophie stepped closer. The woman was clutching a framed photograph of a man, touching her fingertips to his face. The woman turned, revealing the picture as she did so. It was a face Sophie knew well. *Grand-père.*

The woman had obviously heard the sad news of his death.

The woman heard Sophie's footsteps and turned slowly, her sad eyes finding Sophie's. An eternity seemed to pass as the two women stared at one another. Then, the woman's look transformed from one of uncertainty . . . to disbelief . . . to hope . . . and finally, to joy.

'Sophie,' she sobbed, rushing forwards and kissing her.

Sophie's words were a choked whisper. 'But *Grand-père* said you were . . . '

'I know.' The woman placed her hands tenderly on Sophie's shoulders and gazed at her with familiar eyes. 'Your grandfather and I did what we thought was right. It was for your own safety, princess.'

When Sophie heard that last word, she knew for certain.

The woman threw her arms around Sophie, the tears flowing faster. 'Your grandfather wanted so badly to tell you everything. But things were difficult between you two. There's so much to explain.' She kissed Sophie's forehead, then whispered in her ear. 'No more secrets, princess. It's time you learn the truth about our family.'

NIGHT HAD FALLEN over Rosslyn. Robert Langdon stood alone on the porch of the stone house, enjoying the sounds of laughter drifting through the door behind him.

'You slipped out quietly,' a voice behind him said.

He turned. Sophie's grandmother emerged, her silver hair shimmering in the night. 'I thought I'd give them some time together.' Through the window, he could see Sophie talking with the guide, her brother.

Marie Chauvel came over and stood beside him. 'Mr Langdon, when I first heard of Jacques's murder, I was terrified for Sophie's safety. Seeing her tonight was the greatest relief of my life. I cannot thank you enough.'

Earlier Langdon had listened in mute astonishment as she told them the story of Sophie's late parents. Incredibly, both had been from Merovingian families—direct descendants of Mary Magdalene and Jesus Christ. For protection, their family names had been changed from Plantard and Saint-Clair, but when they were killed in a mysterious car accident, the Priory feared the identity of the royal line had been discovered.

'Your grandfather and I,' Marie had explained in a voice choked with pain, 'had to make a grave decision the instant we received the phone call. Your parents' car had just been found in the river. All six of us were supposed to have been travelling together that night, but we changed our plans at the last moment, and your parents were alone. Hearing of the accident, Jacques and I knew we had to protect our grandchildren, and we did what we thought was best. Jacques reported to the police that your brother and I had been in the car . . . our two bodies apparently washed away in the current. Then your brother and I went underground with the Priory. Jacques, being a man of prominence, did not have the luxury of disappearing. It made sense that Sophie, being the eldest, would stay in Paris to be raised by him, close to the heart and protection of the Priory.'

Her voice fell to a whisper. 'Separating the family was the hardest thing we ever had to do. Jacques and I saw each other only very infrequently, and always in secret . . . There are certain ceremonies to which the brotherhood always stays faithful.'

Now, gazing up at the spires of Rosslyn, Langdon's thoughts flashed to the three *sénéchaux* who had also been killed. 'And the Priory? What happens now?'

'The wheels are already in motion, Mr Langdon. The brotherhood will endure. There are always those waiting to move up and rebuild.'

'Was the Church pressuring your husband not to release the Sangreal documents at the End of Days?' he asked.

'Heavens no. The End of Days is a legend of paranoid minds. There is nothing in the Priory doctrine that identifies a date at which the Grail should be unveiled. In fact the Priory has always maintained that the Grail should *never* be unveiled.'

'Never?' Langdon was stunned.

'The beauty of the Grail lies in its ethereal nature.' Marie Chauvel gazed up at Rosslyn's spires. 'For some, the Grail is a chalice that will bring them everlasting life. For others, it is the quest for lost documents and secret history. And for most, I suspect the Holy Grail is simply a grand idea . . . a glorious unattainable treasure that somehow, even in today's world of chaos, inspires us.'

'But if the Sangreal documents remain hidden, the story of Mary Magdalene will be lost for ever,' Langdon said.

'Will it? Look around you. Her story is being told in art, music and books every day. And we are beginning to sense the need to restore the sacred feminine, to sense the dangers of our destructive paths.' She paused. 'You are writing a manuscript about the symbols of the sacred feminine, are you not?'

'I am.'

She smiled. 'Finish it, Mr Langdon. Sing her song. The world needs modern troubadours.'

Langdon fell silent. Turning his eyes again towards Rosslyn, he felt a boyish craving to know her secrets, and could no longer stop himself asking the question. 'Is the Grail here?'

She laughed in mock exasperation. 'Why is it that men simply *cannot* let the Grail rest? Why do you think it's here?'

'Well, your husband's poem speaks specifically of Rosslyn, except it also mentions a blade and chalice watching over the Grail. I didn't see any symbols of the blade and chalice there.'

'The blade and chalice?' Marie asked, playfully. 'Let me see. The blade represents all that is masculine, and is drawn like this, no?' Using her index finger, she traced a shape on her palm.

'Yes,' Langdon said. Marie had drawn the 'closed' form of the blade, although Langdon had seen the symbol portrayed both ways.

'And the inverse,' she said, drawing again on her palm, 'is the chalice, which represents the feminine.'

'Correct,' Langdon said.

'And you are saying that these two shapes appear nowhere in Rosslyn Chapel?

'I didn't see them.'

'If I show them to you, will you get some sleep?'

Before Langdon could answer, Marie Chauvel had headed towards the chapel. He hurried after her.

Entering the ancient building, Marie turned on the lights and pointed to the centre of the sanctuary floor. 'There you are, Mr Langdon. The blade and chalice.'

Langdon stared. The scuffed stone floor was blank. 'There's nothing here . . .'

Marie sighed and began to walk along the famous path worn into the chapel floor, the same path Langdon had seen the visitors following earlier this evening.

'But that's the Star of Dav—' Langdon stopped short, mute with amazement. The blade and chalice. Fused as one.

The Star of David . . . the perfect union of male and female . . . Solomon's Seal . . . marking the Holy of Holies, where the male and female deities—Yahweh and Shekinah—were thought to dwell.

'So the Holy Grail is in the vault beneath us?'

She laughed. 'Only in spirit. Jacques's charge when he became Grand Master was to return the Grail to France and build her a resting place fit for a queen.'

'And he succeeded?'

'All I can tell you for certain is that the Grail is no longer here.'

'But your husband's poem points to Rosslyn as the place where the Holy Grail is hidden.' He recited it aloud to her.

The Holy Grail 'neath ancient Roslin waits
The blade and chalice guarding o'er Her gates
Adorned in masters' loving art, She lies
She rests at last beneath the starry skies

Marie was still for several seconds, until a knowing smile crossed her lips. 'Aah, Jacques.'

Langdon watched her expectantly. 'You *understand* this?'

'Mr Langdon, I will make a confession to you. I have never officially been privy to the present location of the Grail. But my woman's intuition is strong. I am sorry that, after all your hard work, you will be leaving Rosslyn without any real answers. And yet something tells me you will eventually find what you seek.' She smiled. 'And when you do, I trust that you, of all people, can keep a secret.'

'Both of you disappeared,' Sophie said, arriving in the doorway.

'I was just going back to the house,' her grandmother replied, walking over to Sophie. 'Good night, princess.' She kissed Sophie's forehead. 'Don't keep Mr Langdon out too late.'

Langdon and Sophie watched Marie Chauvel leave. When Sophie turned to Robert, her eyes were awash with deep emotion. 'Not exactly the ending I expected.'

That makes two of us, he thought. Langdon could see she was overwhelmed. The news she had received had changed everything in her life. 'Are you OK? It's a lot to take in.'

She smiled quietly. 'I have a family. I have a home. Who we are and where we came from will take some time.'

Langdon remained silent.

'Will you stay with us for a few days?' Sophie asked

Langdon sighed, wanting nothing more. 'You need some time here with your family, Sophie. I'm going back to Paris in the morning.'

Sophie looked disappointed but seemed to know it was the right thing to do. She reached over and, taking his hand, led him out of the chapel. They walked to a small rise from which the Scottish countryside was visible before them, suffused in pale moonlight. They stood in silence, holding hands, both of them fighting a shroud of exhaustion.

Langdon looked at Sophie, and felt an unexpected sadness that he would be returning to Paris without her. 'I may be gone before you wake up.' He paused, a knot growing in his throat. 'I'm sorry, I'm not very good at—'

Sophie placed her hand on the side of his face, and kissed him tenderly on the cheek. 'When can I see you again?'

Langdon reeled, lost in her eyes. He paused, curious to know if she had any idea how much he had been wondering the same thing. 'Well, next month I'm lecturing at a conference in Florence. They're giving me a room at the Brunelleschi.'

Sophie smiled playfully. 'You presume a lot, Mr Langdon.'

He cringed at how it had sounded. 'What I meant—'

'I would love nothing more than to meet you in Florence, Robert. But on *one* condition. No museums, no churches, no tombs, no relics.'

'In Florence? For a week? There's nothing else to do.'

Sophie kissed him again, this time on the lips. Their bodies came together, softly at first, and then completely. When she pulled away, her eyes were full of promise.

'Right,' Langdon managed. 'It's a date.'

Epilogue

Robert Langdon awoke with a start. He had been dreaming. The bathrobe beside his bed bore the monogram HOTEL RITZ PARIS and he saw a dim light filtering through the blinds. Was it dusk or dawn?

His body felt warm and deeply contented. He had slept the better part of the last two days. Sitting up slowly in bed, he now realised what had awoken him . . . the strangest thought. Could it be?

Twenty minutes later, he stepped out of the Hotel Ritz into Place Vendôme. Night was falling. Walking east on Rue des Petits Champs, Langdon felt a growing excitement. He turned south onto Rue Richelieu and walked until he saw what he was looking for—the famous royal arcade—a glistening expanse of polished black marble. Langdon scanned the surface beneath his feet. Within seconds, he found what he knew was there—several bronze medallions embedded in the ground in a straight line, each one embossed with the letters N and S.

Nord. Sud.

The streets of Paris, Langdon had learned years ago, were adorned with 135 of these bronze markers, embedded in sidewalks, courtyards and streets, on a north–south axis across the city. The earth's original prime meridian. Paris's ancient Rose Line.

Langdon broke into a jog, crossing Rue de Rivoli and entering the long tunnel of Passage Richelieu. The hairs on his neck began to bristle with anticipation. He knew that at the end of this tunnel stood the most mysterious of Parisian monuments—conceived and commissioned in the 1980s by François Mitterrand, a man rumoured to move in secret circles, a man whose final legacy to Paris was a structure Langdon had visited only days before. The Louvre Pyramid.

Tracing the invisible path of the ancient Rose Line, Langdon crossed the Carrousel du Louvre, the enormous circle of grass surrounded by a perimeter of neatly trimmed hedges. There in the centre, plunging into the earth like a crystal chasm, gaped the giant inverted pyramid of glass that he had seen a few nights ago when he entered the Louvre's subterranean entresol. *La Pyramide Inversée.*

Langdon walked to the edge and peered down into the Louvre's sprawling underground complex, aglow with amber light. On the floor of the chamber below stood the tiniest of structures . . . a structure Langdon had mentioned in his manuscript.

Thrilled by the unthinkable possibility, Langdon raised his eyes, sensing the huge wings of the Louvre enveloping him . . . hallways that burgeoned with the world's finest art. Da Vinci . . . Botticelli . . .

Adorned in masters' loving art, She lies

He hurried back towards the towering pyramid entrance. The day's last visitors were trickling out of the museum.

Pushing through the revolving door, Langdon descended the curved staircase, then headed for the long tunnel that stretched beneath the Louvre's courtyard, back towards *La Pyramide Inversée*.

As he emerged into a large chamber it hung directly before him. A breathtaking gleaming V-shaped contour of glass.

The Chalice.

Langdon's eyes traced its narrowing form down to its tip, suspended only six feet above the floor. There, directly beneath it, was a miniature pyramid, three feet tall.

'The miniature structure itself protrudes up through the floor as though it were the tip of an iceberg,' Langdon had written in his manuscript, 'the apex of an enormous, pyramidal vault, submerged below like a hidden chamber.'

Illuminated in the soft lights of the deserted entresol, the two pyramids pointed at one another, their tips almost touching. The Chalice above. The Blade below.

The blade and chalice guarding o'er Her gates

Now at last, he understood the true meaning of the Grand Master's verse. Raising his eyes to heaven, he gazed upwards through the glass to a glorious, star-filled night.

She rests at last beneath the starry skies

Like the murmurs of spirits in the darkness, forgotten words echoed. *The quest for the Holy Grail is the quest to kneel before the bones of Mary Magdalene, the wronged Queen.*

With a sudden upwelling of reverence, Robert Langdon fell to his knees. For a moment, he thought he heard a woman's voice . . . the wisdom of the ages . . . whispering up from the chasms of the earth.

DAN BROWN

The Da Vinci Code, which shattered all records in America by selling almost four million copies in eight months, has made publishing history. So what explains the book's huge success? Brown's own theory is that everyone loves a puzzle—and the book is chock full of them. Also, almost everyone knows of Leonardo da Vinci's paintings of the *Mona Lisa* and *The Last Supper*, both of which feature in the tantalising trail of clues that leads Professor Robert Langdon to a centuries-old secret.

How much of Dan Brown's extraordinary story is true? He says: 'All of the locations, the paintings, the ancient history, the secret documents, the rituals, all of this is factual. The people who ask me how much is true need to realise that this theory about Mary Magdalene has been around for centuries. It's not my theory. This has been presented, really, over the last two thousand years and it has persisted.'

Brown made several trips to Paris during the two years he spent writing the book, visiting the Louvre where the action begins and where Leonardo da Vinci's famous portrait, the *Mona Lisa*, hangs. 'There are many codes in da Vinci's works. I first learned about them while I was studying art history at the University of Seville. Later, I married an art historian who happens to be a da Vinci fanatic. And from there, there was no escape. Da Vinci was centuries head of his time. He was fascinated by secrets . . . and devised many ways to keep information secret and portray it in ways that most people, when you look at a painting, don't really see. That's really what the book is about. When you look at paintings like the *Mona Lisa* there is really more there than meets the eye.'

The son of an award-winning maths professor and a professional 'sacred musician', Dan Brown grew up surrounded by books and discussions about both science and religion—and also by puzzles. 'On Christmas morning,' he remembers, 'my siblings and I might find a treasure map with codes that we would follow from room to room, eventually finding our presents hidden somewhere else in the house. So for me, codes have always been fun.'

UP AND DOWN IN THE DALES

GERVASE PHINN

Gervase Phinn considers himself a lucky man. He's got a beautiful wife, a picture-postcard cottage in the Dales and a deeply rewarding job. It's hard to imagine that anyone, or anything, could possibly put a spanner in the works.

But then a school inspector's life is about as predictable as the Yorkshire weather . . .

ONE

I stared with disbelief at the object in the display cabinet. It took pride of place amidst the shells, pebbles, bits of driftwood and other detritus collected from the beach.

'What do you think?' asked the nun, with a smile.

'It's . . . er . . . interesting,' was all I could manage to splutter.

I was at Our Lady of Lourdes Roman Catholic Primary School in the second week of the new school term, to inspect the English teaching. I had been a school inspector now in the great county of Yorkshire for three years and each week brought something new and unexpected.

'You see,' explained Sister Marie-Thérèse, the headteacher, 'I like to mount a colourful display in the first week, to make the entrance hall that little bit brighter and more cheerful. This year, I have decided it should be about the seashore. At the end of last term we took the junior children on a school trip to Whitby. We had some lovely long walks along the beach and I asked them to pick up any interesting items that might have been washed up. No old bottles, though, I had to put my foot down about bottles.'

'I see,' I said, still staring incredulously.

'You'd be surprised what gets washed up on a beach.'

No, I wouldn't, I thought to myself.

'Mrs McPhee even found some pieces of jet on the beach. It's fossilised monkey-puzzle tree, you know. Quite rare, I'm told. It was all the rage in Victorian times. Of course, it's not so popular today. Oh, and one child found some fossils and another a dried starfish . . . Such intriguing bits and bobs. So we have a nice little collection to stimulate the children's discussion.'

'Sister,' I said, 'about the . . . er . . . bits and bobs.'

'Yes, Mr Phinn?' She looked directly at me, with a wide and innocent expression.

'Well, Sister, there is . . .' I opened my mouth to continue but lost courage. 'Oh, nothing.' Someone was going to have to tell her, but it certainly wasn't going to be me.

'Last week,' she babbled on, 'the older children wrote some delightful little poems, which I've mounted on the wall around the display. I want the school to look really nice for when the bishop visits on Monday.'

'The bishop's coming on Monday?' I asked in a doom-laden voice.

'Yes, he's coming to talk to the children about their first Holy Communion. Last year he brought his crosier to show them. One child wrote to him afterwards: "Thank you for coming to see us, Bishop Michael. I now know just what a real crook looks like."'

Just then a small boy approached the headteacher and tugged on her cloak. The nun bent down to hear what the child wanted to tell her and I grabbed my chance to get help. 'Sister,' I said quickly, 'I've forgotten to sign in. I'll just do it now.'

I shot across the hall and into the school office, making the school secretary jump with surprise. 'Quick!' I hissed. 'Can you come with me? It's urgent!'

'I'm in the middle of checking the dinner money,' she told me. 'It's extremely inconvenient.'

'Please,' I begged. 'It really is *very* important.'

'Oh, very well, but I don't know what can be so urgent.'

'You'll see,' I said, and popped my head out of the office to see where Sister Marie-Thérèse was. Fortunately, she had moved down the corridor with the small boy.

'Look,' I whispered, pointing to the display cabinet.

There was a sharp intake of breath. 'Oh dear,' groaned the secretary, raising her hand to her neck and wincing visibly.

'Do you see what I mean?'

'I do,' she mumbled. 'However did *that* get in there?'

'I suppose Sister must have put it in, without realising what it is. Perhaps you ought to tell her.'

'Tell her?' she hissed. 'Why me? You're the English inspector, you're the one who's supposed to be good with words.'

'It would be much better coming from you.'

'Mr Phinn,' she said, looking me straight in the eyes, 'I am prepared to do most things as a school secretary, but explaining to a nun what a condom is, is not one of them.'

'And what are you two talking about?' came a cheerful voice from behind us. We swung round to find Sister Marie-Thérèse.

'We were just looking at your lovely display, Sister,' I replied.

'I'm very pleased with it,' trilled the nun.

'It's very nice, Sister,' said the school secretary, giving a watery smile. There was a nervous red rash creeping up her neck. Then she turned and gave me a conspiratorial look. 'I'll see to it,' she whispered. 'Just keep her occupied.'

'Perhaps we should make a start, Sister,' I said pleasantly.

'Yes, yes, of course, Mr Phinn,' said the nun. 'The children are all very excited about meeting you.'

I followed the headteacher as she headed for the infant department. When I glanced back, I saw the school secretary still staring at the display cabinet like a hungry cat watching a tank full of goldfish.

The junior classroom was warm and welcoming. The children, aged between nine and eleven, looked up eagerly as we entered.

'Good morning, children,' said the headteacher.

'Good morning, Sister Marie-Thérèse,' chorused the children.

'Have they been good, Mrs McPhee?' the nun asked the teacher.

'Need you ask, Sister?' replied her colleague.

Mrs McPhee was a plump woman with a thick fuzz of white hair and the pale eyes of a piranha. She wore a tight-fitting, wheat-coloured turtleneck sweater, a heavy brown tweed pleated skirt, thick woollen stockings the colour of mud, and substantial brogues. I could tell she was the 'I-stand-no-nonsense' sort of teacher.

'This is my indispensable deputy headteacher, Mr Phinn,' said the nun. 'She's worth her weight in gold.'

'Oh, Sister, really!' said Mrs McPhee, laughing in a horsy way.

'Now, children, said the headteacher, 'I told you that we would be having a very special visitor this morning and here he is. Mr Phinn is a school inspector, here to look at all the lovely work you have been doing.' The nun turned in my direction, rested a hand on my arm and said, in a lower voice, 'There's quite a range of age and ability in this group, Mr Phinn, as you will see. Would you like to listen to some of the children read, and examine the work they have been doing?'

'There's not much written work in their books,' interrupted Mrs McPhee in one of those loud voices possessed by market traders.

'But you will not be expecting to see a lot, will you, Mr Phinn, this being the start of term?' She gave me a look which said: 'Disagree with me, if you dare!'

'No,' I assured her. 'I shall not be expecting to see a lot.'

'I'll leave you to it then,' said Sister Marie-Thérèse. 'I have paperwork to attend to.'

As she headed for the door, the headteacher stopped in her tracks and peered out of the window. I followed her gaze to see the school secretary creeping past in the direction of the dustbins. She was wearing bright yellow rubber gloves and was carrying something, at arm's length, on a shovel.

'Whatever is Mrs Sanders up to?' said the nun to Mrs McPhee. 'Perhaps the school cat has . . .' and she mouthed 'mouse' to her colleague before leaving the room.

The first pupil I approached was very keen to tell me about the books he liked to read. He was a small boy with shiny blond hair, clear blue eyes and a face full of freckles. His name was Alexander.

'I expect all your pals call you Alex,' I said to him.

'No they don't, actually,' he told me seriously. 'They call me Alexander. I don't like my name shortened.'

'No,' I said smiling, 'neither do I.' Connie, the caretaker at the Staff Development Centre sometimes referred to me as 'Gerv'. It sounded like a brand of cheap petrol. 'And what is your reading book about, Alexander?'

'Dinosaurs. I'm really into dinosaurs,' the boy explained solemnly. 'Do you know much about dinosaurs, Mr Phinn?'

'No, not a lot.'

'Do you know which was the longest?' asked the boy.

'I'm not entirely sure,' I said and I wasn't. 'Is it the brontosaurus?'

'No. It's the diplodocus. As long as two double-decker buses, end to end. Do you know which was the biggest?'

'Was *that* the brontosaurus?'

'Wrong again. It was the brachiosaurus. It was taller than two giraffes and as heavy as eight full-grown elephants. Mind-blowing, isn't it? They weighed about thirty tonnes. You'll not know which was the fastest, then?'

'No, I'm afraid not.'

'Gallimimus,' said the boy. 'It was a bit like an ostrich and could run over thirty miles an hour.'

'Really. I do know which was the fiercest,' I said. 'The tyrannosaurus rex.'

The boy smiled and shook his head. 'Wrong again, I'm afraid. It was the deinonychus. It had huge slashing claws on each back foot and a set of killer teeth. Its name means "terrible claw". A lot of people think the tyrannosaurus rex was the fiercest,' he said leaning back in his chair, 'but they're wrong.'

'Which was the last dinosaur to live on earth?' I asked him, genuinely interested.

'Now that's a tricky one, Mr Phinn.' He sucked in his breath. 'Most people would say it was the triceratops, but we can't be sure. Shall I read you a bit from my book?'

'Yes, I think that's a very good idea.'

So the boy read with gusto from a thick tome, stopping at intervals to tell me additional fascinating facts.

'You're a very good reader, Alexander,' I told him.

'Yes, I know,' he said in a matter-of-fact voice. 'And you're a very good listener.'

I smiled. I have met many a precocious child in my time but Alexander took the biscuit. 'And when you leave school, I expect you want to work in the Natural History Museum in London, don't you, and be the world expert on dinosaurs?'

'Oh, no, Mr Phinn, I want to be a solicitor, like my father. There's not much of a future in dinosaurs.'

The next child was a large girl with saucer eyes and thick black hair tied in great bunches. While I was listening to her read, I heard Mrs McPhee's threatening voice again. I looked up with interest.

'No, Alexander, I said a prayer.'

'But, miss, I want to write about my holidays,' appealed the child.

'Well, you are not going to,' said the teacher sharply. 'You are to write a prayer for Bishop Michael's visit, like everyone else, and that is that.'

'But, Mrs McPhee,' persisted the child, 'I don't want to write a prayer.'

'Alexander,' snapped the teacher, 'we have looked at prayers, listened to prayers and read prayers. I have spent a full lesson telling you how to write a prayer. When the bishop comes on Monday and we are in assembly reading out our prayers starting "Thank you, God", it would sound rather strange your reading out "Last summer we went to Blackpool", wouldn't it?'

'We didn't go to Blackpool, miss. We went to a *gîte* in France.'

'I'm not in the slightest bit interested where you went, Alexander. Now get on with your prayer. Chop! Chop!'

But the child wouldn't let it lie. 'You see, Mrs McPhee, I don't know whether I believe in God.'

'Not believe in God!' exclaimed the teacher, ample bosom heaving.

'I think I believe in the big bang theory like my father,' said the child, quite undaunted by the teacher's outrage.

'Alexander Maxwell-Smith,' said Mrs McPhee, in a hushed and slightly sinister voice, 'if you do not start your prayer "Thank you, God" in the next few seconds, there *will* be a big bang!'

I turned round to look at Alexander. The boy, shoulders drooping and with a weary expression on his small face, slouched in his chair, sighed and took up his pen.

A little while later, having heard more children read, I arrived back at Alexander's desk. His prayer was written in large, neat handwriting. 'Thank you, God,' it started. 'Thank you for my holidays. This year we stayed in a *gîte* in Vence and had a most enjoyable time.' An account of his holiday, which sounded anything but 'most enjoyable', followed. His mother, he wrote, had got sunburnt and looked like a cooked lobster, his father had been ill for three days with his head down the lav, and his little sister had got lost and they had all ended up at the police station. I left before the big bang that would surely occur when his teacher read Alexander's prayer, and headed for the next room on my list.

In the next class, I discovered Miss Reece, a young woman with sandy-coloured hair tied in a ponytail, wearing a bright yellow jumper and pale cream slacks. She sat with the children clustered around her and was reading them a story from a large picture book. I crept to the back of the classroom, perched on a small melamine chair and listened.

When the story was over and the children were busy writing, I listened to a series of very competent little readers who had a great deal to say for themselves. One little girl, with apple-red cheeks, was particularly chatty.

'Are you a good speller, Mr Phinn?'

'I am a very, very good speller,' I teased. 'I can spell any word.'

'Any word?' she gasped.

'Any word at all. I'm the world's best speller. Would you like to tell me a word and I will spell it for you?'

'Yes, but you're a grown-up,' she said, folding her small arms across her chest. 'Grown-ups can spell words.' She thought for a moment. 'Can you spell my name?'

'Of course I can,' I replied, but knew that this might prove tricky. I have met children with a range of unusual, not to say bizarre names. There was Curston, Mykell, Kaylee, Heyleigh, Barby, Blasé (pronounced Blaze), Gooey (spelt Guy) and a child called Portia but spelt Porsche. Then there were the brother and sister, Sam and Ella which, when said at a speed, sounded like food poisoning.

'My name is Roisin,' said the little girl bringing me back to the present. 'It's Irish. It means "little rose".'

How very apt, I thought, looking at the rosy cheeks. I spelt it correctly and pulled a smug expression.

'My sisters are called Siobhaun and Nuala.'

I got those right, as well. I was obviously now impressing my little interrogator.

'And there's my brother, Rory and remember, Mr Phinn, he has eight letters in his name. And my cousin, Orlah, has nine in hers.'

I buried my head in my hands in mock helplessness and heard the child giggle uncontrollably. Then Roisin spelt the names for me, speaking loudly and slowly as if I was hard of hearing. 'R-u-a-r-a-i-d-h and O-r-f-h-l-a-i-t-h,' she told me. 'Easy-peasy!'

I STOOD with Sister Marie-Thérèse in the entrance hall at the end of the morning.

'Well, thank you, Sister,' I said. 'I shall send in my report in a few days' time, but everything appears to be fine. The children read extremely well, the writing is above average, and the teaching very good.' I looked in the direction of the display cabinet. 'And the display . . . is wonderful.'

'"How beautiful upon the mountains are the feet of him who bringeth good tidings",' said the nun.

My attention, however, was caught by the school secretary standing in her doorway and giving me a vigorous thumbs-up sign.

'I'm sorry, what did you say, Sister?'

'Isaiah, Mr Phinn, from the Bible,' said the nun.

'Yes, of course, Sister.'

'Now, that's most odd,' she said, resting a small hand on my arm. 'I think I am either going mad or we have a ghost. I'm sure I put a little coloured balloon which one of the children found on the beach in Whitby in my display and it's disappeared into thin air.'

'A balloon?'

'Don't you recall seeing a pink balloon in my display this morning?'

'No, Sister,' I said firmly, 'there was no balloon in your display. I would have remembered. No, no, there was definitely no balloon.'

I WAS STILL SMILING later that afternoon as I began to draft the report on Our Lady of Lourdes Primary School. The inspectors' office was unusually peaceful, because my three colleagues, with whom I shared the cramped and cluttered room, had not yet returned from their school visits. I was grateful for a bit of peace and quiet; there would be precious little of it when Sidney and David arrived.

Sydney Clamp, the larger-than-life inspector for creative and visual arts, and David Pritchard, the mathematics, PE and games inspector who could talk for Wales, were witty, warm, clever and generous people who had worked together for many years and were good friends. However, when they started bouncing insults off each other and regaling anyone within earshot with anecdotes and opinions, it was quite impossible to concentrate.

The final member of our team, who put us to shame with her razor-sharp intelligence and superhuman efficiency and tidiness, was Dr Geraldine Mullarkey, in charge of science and technology. Gerry liked to keep herself to herself. She was a single parent with a young child and tended to hide herself away at the Staff Development Centre at lunchtimes to catch up with paperwork. Down the corridor was our team leader, Dr Harold Yeats, the senior inspector, and next to his room was the small office where Julie, our secretary, presided.

She tottered in at that moment cradling a large mug of coffee, which she set down in front of me before perching on the end of my desk. She looked as if she was off to a disco in her bright red top, incredibly short black skirt, dangling metallic earrings and the ridiculously high-heeled shoes she was so fond of wearing. With her bubbly blonde hair, cheerful good humour and incessant chatter, she was guaranteed to brighten up the dullest of days. Harold had taken her on a couple of years before I had come to County Hall. The inspectors' secretary at the time, I had been told, was the rather serious and nervous Miss 'a martyr to my joints' Pruitt. She was due to retire (and not before time from what my colleagues said) and Harold had chosen Julie to replace her.

I told her the saga of the nun and the condom and she looked at me quizzically. 'You would have thought, in this day and age, she'd have known what a condom was.'

'Julie, she's a *nun*, for goodness' sake!' I exclaimed. 'When would a nun come across a condom?'

'I thought everybody knew what one was. You can't get away from them. I mean, my little nephew, Kenny, is only nine and he knows. I suppose it's all this sex education at school. We were never told anything.' She stood up and straightened her skirt. 'We were very naive.' That, I thought to myself, was a trifle difficult to believe.

'I once went as a nun to a fancy-dress party,' she went on. 'But that long habit got in the way of my dancing. I had to take it off in the end.'

'Well, I suppose Sister Marie-Thérèse has got used to it by now,' I said. 'And I shouldn't imagine she will be doing much dancing.'

'I couldn't be a nun,' said Julie, examining her long nails.

'No,' I replied, 'you couldn't. Well, not in that outfit anyway.'

'What's wrong with this outfit?'

'Oh nothing. It looks . . . er . . . very becoming.'

'It's my power-dressing combination, if you must know. I've just read this magazine article all about it. The clothes you wear say a lot about you and different colours give off different messages. Red warns of potential danger. Black means strength. It says to people: "Don't you mess with me, mate, or you'll get a smack in the face." If you want to appear really nice, you wear pastel colours; light greens and pale yellows. I've not got any outfits like that.'

'So, why do you want to be power-dressed this afternoon?' I asked. 'Is there something special on?'

'Yes, there is, as a matter of fact. I need to be assertive when I meet Lady Macbeth later today.'

'Mrs Savage,' I sighed.

Mrs Brenda Savage, personal assistant to Dr Gore, the chief education officer, was the bane of Julie's, the inspectors' and most other people's lives. She was a strikingly elegant-looking woman of indeterminate age but could be extremely prickly and had her long-nailed fingers in every pie around. She had a fearsome reputation, an acerbic manner and could curdle milk with one of her sour stares. We all felt she had been promoted way beyond her capabilities.

'We've got a meeting on "Health and Safety in the Workplace",' Julie continued, 'and she's been put in charge. Goodness knows why. She's a danger to everyone's health, the stress she causes. Anyway, she's produced this set of wretched guidelines and all the ancillary staff are going to have to listen to one of her lectures. She's only been on a one-day course; now she thinks she knows everything there is to know about health and safety. She sounds like Mussolini in knickers when she gets started, sticking out her chin, stabbing the air with those sharp witch's nails and laying down the law. Anyway, I must be off. When you've finished that report, pop it on my desk and I'll get on with it tomorrow. See you.' With that Julie tottered out.

I returned to the report. 'The school is enhanced by interesting and colourful displays . . .' I re-read but got no further. The sound of argumentative voices wafted up the stairs, signalling the imminent arrival of two of my colleagues.

A moment later Sidney breezed in followed by David. You would be hard-pressed to find two people so different in appearance: the one a burly, bearded figure with a thick head of woolly hair, rather like a friendly old lion; the other small, dark-complexioned with a close-shaven face and black eyebrows that seemed to fly outwards like wings. As usual, they were in animated discussion.

'I might have predicted that you would take a contrary view,' Sidney was saying irritably. He dropped his briefcase on the nearest desk and flopped into a chair. 'Good afternoon, Gervase. David is being perverse again.'

'Good afternoon,' I said.

'Good afternoon, Gervase,' said David, hanging up his coat. 'I am not taking a contrary view, Sidney. I am merely attempting to put things into some sort of perspective.'

'What things?' I asked.

'Art, what else,' sighed David, settling behind his desk. 'He's miffed because the headteacher of West Challerton High School has reduced the amount of curriculum time for creative and visual arts.'

'I hardly think "miffed" is the most appropriate description,' said Sidney angrily. '"Irate", "incensed", "enraged", might be more fitting.' He swivelled round in his chair to face me. 'That insufferable new headteacher, Mr double-barrelled Smith, was outrageously rude and dismissive. He kept me waiting for half an hour and then said he could only spare a few minutes. I then discover that he has castrated the visual arts to give more time to mathematics and science. It is quite frankly scandalous.'

'He's a great one for changes is Mr Pennington-Smith,' I said. His predecessor, Mr Blunt ('Blunt by name and blunt by nature') had not been one for anything fancy but he ran a very good school. A great many changes took place at West Challerton when Mr Pennington-Smith arrived last year and few had been for the better.

'The man is a Philistine and a poltroon,' said Sidney, his voice now squeaky and petulant, like a child forbidden an ice-cream.

'I take it you had a run-in with Mr Pennington-Smith?' I observed.

'Something of an understatement, Gervase,' Sidney told me angrily. 'Pennington-Smith says he has "realigned his priorities", as he put it. I felt like realigning *his* priorities, I can tell you! No consultation with the head of department or myself. He just made "an executive decision". When I demanded to see him at the end of the afternoon, he had the brass neck to tell me that, in his opinion, art decorated the margins of the more serious business of study and that it had very little relevance in the modern world. I'm just bereft of words. Speechless.'

'Well, there's a first!' remarked David, removing his spectacles and polishing them with the end of his tie.

'Don't you think you are rather overreacting, Sidney?' I said. 'You make it sound as if Armageddon is on us.'

Sidney slammed his fist on his desk. 'No, I am *not* overreacting. How would you feel if English were described as "decorating the margins of the more serious business of study"?'

'But English is a core subject,' I said. 'There is a difference.'

'Well, I can see I'm to get precious little support from my colleagues,' blustered Sidney, rising from his chair. 'We will see what Harold has to say about it.'

'Leave the poor man alone,' said David. 'You know how busy he is.'

'Not at all!' said Sidney, heading for the door. 'I shall have a few well-chosen words to say to him, I can tell you.'

'And what will they be?' I asked.

'I don't know. I haven't chosen them yet,' replied Sidney, making a grand exit.

With Sidney's departure, peace descended. When the clock on the County Hall tower struck six o'clock, I surveyed my empty desk with great satisfaction.

'You appear remarkably pleased with yourself,' said David, staring over the top of his spectacles.

'Well, I *am* pretty pleased with myself, if truth be told,' I replied. 'This term has started off really well.'

'Long may it continue,' said David, 'but be warned. In my experience, there is always something or somebody who manages to spoil one's equilibrium when things seem to be going really well. You are cycling along a country lane without a care in the world. The birds are singing, the sun is shining, the wind blowing through your hair, when suddenly somebody pushes a thundering great stick through your spokes and you're over the handlebars.'

'Ah, well, I think it is highly remote that anyone will push a stick through my spokes at the moment. Only one more school visit this week, and then a conference on Friday.'

'And where are you tomorrow?' asked David.

'King Henry's College,' I replied. 'It's just a routine visit.'

'Ah, your first introduction to the Admiral.'

'Who?'

'Mr Nelson, the headteacher. Known as the Admiral. You know, Horatio Nelson.'

'Do I detect a certain ominous tone to your voice?' I asked.

'Not at all,' said David. 'The headteacher of King Henry's is an amiable enough sort of chap, but try to get him to make a decision, give an opinion or take a stand on anything, and you will wait until the proverbial cows come home. He's all for a quiet life and, like his namesake, a great one for turning a blind eye.'

'Well, I can't say he was over-keen on my visiting, that's for sure,' I said. 'He tried his hardest to put me off. I can't think why because the English department's examination results are good.'

'So they should be,' interrupted David. 'It's a highly selective school. You have to have a PhD to pass the entrance examination at King Henry's. If the teachers cannot get good results from that calibre of student, they might as well pack their bags and go home. And speaking of going home, it's about time we made tracks. If I don't see you tomorrow, Gervase, enjoy your weekend with that lovely wife of yours. How is Christine?'

'She's fine,' I told him.

'You are a very lucky man,' said David, rising from his chair and stretching.

'Yes, I know,' I replied.

As I drove home, I pondered David's words. I was indeed a very lucky man. The Easter before, on a bright, cloudless spring morning, I had married the most beautiful, talented and gentle woman in the world, Miss Christine Bentley, headteacher of Winnery Nook Nursery and Infant School. I had met her a few weeks after starting in my post as county English inspector and, for me, it had been love at first sight. We had honeymooned in the Lake District and had returned to our dreamy Peewit Cottage in the village of Hawksrill in the Dales. The dream cottage, in fact, had woodworm, dry rot, rising damp, cracked walls and broken guttering, but we had fallen in love with the magnificent views and were now spending most of our spare time renovating and refurbishing.

At the end of the previous summer term Christine had told me the most wonderful news: that I was to be a father the following spring. So everything in the world seemed right: home, family, friends and job. I was cycling along that country lane of David's on a bright summer's day without a care in the world. The birds were singing, the sun was shining, and nothing and nobody could possibly spoil the sense of elation I felt.

Little did I know that there was someone lurking in the bushes ready to push the thundering great stick through my spokes.

TWO

The frosted glass at the reception desk at King Henry's College slid back sharply and I was confronted by a tall, hawk-faced school secretary with small, cold, blue eyes behind unfashionable horn-rimmed spectacles. She gave me a stony stare. 'Would you mind not tapping on the glass,' she told me in a superior voice. 'There is a buzzer, you know.'

'Where?' I enquired innocently, giving her an exaggerated smile.

She poked her head through the hatch like a tortoise emerging from its shell, and tutted noisily. 'The buzzer is under those registers, which should not have been left there,' she announced, giving me an accusative glare as though I were the culprit. She snatched up the registers and pulled them through the window and into the office. There was a great in-drawing of breath. 'The number of times I tell the students not to leave them there,' she said to no one in particular. 'I might just as well talk to myself for all the notice they take.'

I continued to smile and await the apology, but it soon became apparent that none would be forthcoming.

'Now,' she said, 'may I help you?' Her face remained tight-lipped and stern, her voice retained its tone of weary condescension.

'I hope so. I have an appointment with the headteacher at a quarter to nine.'

She flicked through a large black book, then glanced up at the clock on the office wall. 'You're rather early.'

'I often am.'

She continued to turn the pages. 'And you are?'

I passed through the brown envelope that I had received from the school the week before. It was addressed to: 'Mr Gervase R. Phiss, Inspector of Schools.' Had my welcome been warmer, I would have pointed out that the name was Phinn and not Phiss, but after the reception I had just received, I felt like saying nothing.

'Oh, yes, the school inspector.' The secretary allowed herself a small, thin-lipped smile. 'I'm so sorry, I thought you were a parent or a book salesman. Do please take a seat in the waiting room, Mr Phiss. I shall inform Mr Nelson that you have arrived.'

As I sat patiently in the small room, I thought to myself that the reception I had received did not bode well for the coming inspection. At some schools I was welcomed like a long-lost relative, all smiles and handshakes; at others it was as if the Gestapo had turned up. It was rare, however, to be addressed with such polar hostility as I had been that morning.

The woman reappeared before me. 'Mr Phiss,' she said. 'The headteacher will see you, if you would care to follow me.'

The secretary strode ahead of me, her heels clicking on the hard floor. In the air was a smell that I recalled from my school days: a mixture of stale cabbage, disinfectant and floor polish. I remembered the long, cold corridor, too; the wood, block floor; the high ceilings; the heavy oak doors to the classrooms. It was like going back in time.

At the school secretary's approach, the hubbub of noise in the corridors subsided and the pupils parted ranks to allow her through.

'I can't say I've ever heard the name Phiss before,' she said over her shoulder.

'It's French Huguenot,' I told her, keeping a straight face. 'My ancestors came over with the weavers in the seventeenth century after severe persecution at the hands of Henry of Navarre. My mother's still not quite got over it.'

'Oh, I am sorry,' she said, in a matter-of-fact voice.

'Actually, it's not pronounced Phiss,' I said mischievously, 'it has a silent "aitch".'

We arrived at the headteacher's study and Mr Nelson rose from his desk to greet me.

'Headteacher,' said the school secretary, her face as solemn as ever. 'This is the inspector of schools, Mr . . . er . . . Pice.'

Mr Nelson was a gaunt man with grizzled grey hair and a pained expression. A black academic gown enveloped his lean frame, giving him the appearance of a giant spider. He surveyed me critically through small, rimless spectacles, before extending a long, cold hand. 'Mr . . . er . . .'

'Phinn,' I said. 'There was a misspelling on your letter.'

'You might have said!' snapped the secretary, her face white with displeasure.

'Thank you, Mrs Winterton,' said Mr Nelson. But she was already heading for the door, tut-tutting as she went.

When she had gone the headteacher indicated an uncomfortable-looking, ladder-back chair placed to the front of his desk. 'Well, Mr Phinn, do take a seat. So, you are to spend a day in the school inspecting the English department?'

'Yes, that's right,' I replied.

The headteacher sat down, rubbed his chin and sighed. 'Not the best time, I have to say, the beginning of term, for a school inspection. I did point this out in my reply to you when you informed me of this proposed visitation. No, not the best time at all. Teachers are just becoming acquainted with their classes, sorting out their rooms, et cetera. I have an exceptionally busy day ahead of me and this morning I have to see several parents, including one who is contesting our decision not to accept his son at the school. All very trying. Your visit has come at a most inconvenient time.'

'I should imagine there is never a convenient time for a school inspection, Mr Nelson. As I explained in my letter, I do have a very busy programme of visits this term and I must start somewhere. King Henry's is high on my list.'

'High on your list,' repeated the headteacher, twisting his mouth to one side. 'My goodness! That does sound ominous.'

'Not at all,' I assured him, 'it's just a short day's visit to look at the English teaching in the school. I have been working for the Education Department for three years now, and I thought it was high time that I paid you a visit.' He looked at me sceptically. 'It is quite routine and I am sure everything will be fine.'

Mr Nelson took a slow, deep breath. 'I did say in my letter to you, Mr Phinn, that I would have preferred a more suitable time.' He sat drumming his long fingers on the desk top, awaiting a response. Perhaps he expected me to agree with him and depart forthwith. When I remained silent, his voice hardened a fraction. 'Well, if you *are* to join us for the day, I am sure that you will find things in order. As you will have surmised, our examination results are outstanding. Mr Frobisher, the head of the English Faculty, is not entirely enthusiastic about the visit. You will find him a somewhat formal and traditional teacher, one of the "old school" and he does have his share of—' There was a sharp knock on the door. 'Ah, that must be him now. I asked him to join us. Come!'

Mr Frobisher bore an unnerving resemblance to the headteacher. He was also a lean, sallow-complexioned man with heavy-lidded eyes and a pained expression. The only difference was the hair. Whereas Mr Nelson's was grizzled, Mr Frobisher's hair was straight and black and carefully parted down one side. He too wore rimless spectacles and a capacious black gown.

'Good morning,' he intoned, giving me a calculating stare.

Oh dear, oh dear, I thought to myself; another chilly reception. I took a deep breath, stood up and smiled. 'Good morning.'

'This is Mr Phinn,' the headteacher told him. 'The school inspector.'

'I thought it was Mr Fish.'

'There was a misprint on the letter,' explained the headteacher, 'Mrs Winterton again, I'm afraid.'

'Oh,' said the head of English. 'Well, I have to say, today is a very inopportune time for your visit, Mr Phinn.'

'The headteacher *has* pointed this out to me, Mr Frobisher,' I explained, 'but I do have a heavy schedule over the next few weeks.' Before he could answer I looked theatrically at my watch. 'I see lessons are about to begin. Perhaps we should make a start?'

'Very well,' said Mr Frobisher loftily, glancing in the direction of the headteacher, as if to enlist his support, before turning his attention back to me. 'I hope the programme I have devised for you to follow is acceptable. I think you are to start with Mr Poppleton, the second-in-charge of the department, and his fifth year form.'

'Mr Frobisher,' I replied amicably, 'I have planned my own programme for the day. I do prefer to work from one of my own.'

'One of your own?' he repeated, bristling like an angry cat.

'Yes, that is the usual practice. I try to visit all the teachers and see as wide a range of lessons as possible.'

'Well, it seems quite irregular to me. Do you mean the teachers will not know when you are going to visit their lessons?'

'I generally start with the head of department,' I said. 'I noticed you did not include yourself on the programme you sent me, Mr Frobisher.'

The headteacher sighed wearily. 'I really must ask you gentlemen to excuse me. I have a waiting room full of expectant parents who are here to see me. Mr Frobisher, if you wouldn't mind showing our visitor where the English rooms are . . . I look forward to seeing you at the end of the day, Mr Phinn. And, now, if you wouldn't mind . . .'

MR FROBISHER'S CLASSROOM was spacious and warm, with long, elegant sash windows and a high ceiling with ornamental coving. At the front, on a dais, was a sturdy teacher's desk made of pine and a high-backed chair. The students' desks were of the small, lidded variety with holes for inkwells, entirely unsuitable for large adolescent boys.

Save for a few dog-eared and faded posters, the walls were bare.

The class of thirty or so fourth-year students, most in smart blazers, stood up when we entered.

'Sit down,' ordered Mr Frobisher, sweeping to his desk, gown a-flutter. He surveyed the class before him and his eyes settled on two gangly boys at the back. 'I was not aware, Lister, that I had given permission for the removal of blazers.'

'It's really hot in here, sir,' replied the boy.

'Neither did I request a weather forecast. You know the school rules as well as I. Put on your blazer, and that goes for you, too, Wilsdon.'

'Can I open a window then, sir?' persisted the boy.

'You *can* indeed open a window, Lister, but whether or not you *may* is an entirely different matter.'

'What, sir?'

'I said you *can* open a window. Obviously my lesson on the auxiliary verb last term has had very little impact.' He picked up a stick of chalk and wrote the word CAN in capitals on the board. 'The word "can" is an auxiliary verb expressing an ability or knowledge of how to do something as in the sentence, "I can throw this chalk."' He twirled the chalk round between finger and thumb and smiled at his own witticism. 'The verb "may" is also an auxiliary verb expressing the possibility or the permission to do something as in the sentence, "You may open the window . . ."'

'So, can I open it then, sir?' asked the boy, looking puzzled.

'No, you *may* not!' snapped the teacher. 'Now, it will not have escaped your notice that we have a visitor with us today. Mr Phinn is from the Education Office.' He gestured to an empty chair at the side of the room.

'Good morning,' I said cheerfully, as I headed for the chair.

'Good morning, sir,' chorused the boys.

'I was not impressed, not impressed at all with your homework this week,' said Mr Frobisher, reaching for the neat pile of exercise books on his desk. 'There was a great deal of slipshod writing. And in some books we seem to have had an epidemic of the greengrocer's disease. Apostrophes everywhere. I do not know how many times I have told you that, in general, in the singular, the apostrophe appears before the letter *s*, and in the plural after the letter *s* when the plural does not end in the letter *s*. It is quite simple.'

The pupils were staring at him, entirely perplexed.

'Rutter here,'—Mr Frobisher held up an exercise book—'scatters apostrophes across the page like peppercorns. I don't know about you, Mr Phinn,' said the teacher, turning his attention to me, 'but I find it so irritating to see flagrant misuse of the English language wherever I go. One passes the local fruiterer who sells "banana's" and "potatoe's", or the supermarket promising "hundreds of product's" at half price, all with redundant apostrophes before the *s*.' As he spoke, Mr Frobisher wrote the erroneous words on the board.

The teacher now picked up a red chalk from his desk and with flamboyant strokes crossed out the offending apostrophes.

'Some people think that every time there is a letter *s* at the end of a word there needs to be an apostrophe.' He faced the students. 'As you have heard me say on countless occasions, the only use of the apostrophe is to denote possession or omission. Now—'

'Excuse me, sir.' The speaker was a thin boy with lanky brown hair. 'What about in this sentence: "The word 'Mississippi' contains four *i*'s and four *s*'s but only two *p*'s." Surely apostrophes are needed, otherwise the reader will be left very confused.'

Mr Frobisher removed his glasses and stared heavenwards. 'Yes, indeed, Smith,' he replied. 'Whether the apostrophe should be used to denote the plural of a word that does not ordinarily make a plural depends on whether the plural is easily recognisable as such. Unless the reader needs assistance in understanding, which is the case with your example, one should not use the apostrophe. Now—'

'But didn't you just say, sir, that the apostrophe is only used to denote possession or omission?' enquired the boy politely.

The teacher sighed. 'Yes, I did, but this is an exception. It is clearly justifiable, as it is in this sentence: "Well-behaved and attentive students watch their *p*'s and *q*'s." Does that clarify the matter for you?' He fixed the boy with a rattlesnake look.

'Oh yes, sir,' replied the boy, smiling. 'Thank you, sir.'

'Now—' began the teacher again, replacing his spectacles.

'Excuse me, sir.'

'Yes, Smith, what is it now?'

'What about the pronoun "one" sir,' said the boy. 'Surely an apostrophe is needed in the sentence: "One is taking one's time in explaining oneself."'

The teacher eyed the boy momentarily, wondering if he was being impertinent. 'That is the one exception,' he finally replied.

'It is all very confusing, sir,' sighed the boy, leaning back on his chair. 'There seem so many exceptions to the rule.'

'It is quite simple, Smith, if you listen and learn.'

'Do you not think, sir, that the apostrophe has had its day? And that the greengrocer perhaps deliberately misuses the apostrophe to draw attention to his fruit and vegetables?'

'No, I do not! It is just plain ignorance.'

'I don't suppose that in the great scheme of things, it's that important,' said the boy, turning to address the class as a whole. 'I don't imagine that people buy less of the greengrocer's produce because he decides to insert an apostrophe here and there. I should think it's the quality of his fruit and vegetables and the prices that count.'

'It is important to me, Smith!' snapped the teacher. 'And it is also important to those who mark your examination papers.'

This remarkable exchange, the likes of which I had rarely observed in a classroom before, was like a battle of wits between a clever barrister and a defendant. Mr Frobisher was clearly disconcerted and his earlier self-assurance seemed to be disappearing fast. He turned and vigorously cleared the board of the list of criminal apostrophes.

'Excuse me, sir,' began the boy again. Some of his classmates sniggered quietly.

'Smith,' said the teacher, attempting to control his displeasure, 'you are becoming wearisome in the extreme. Enough is enough. I think a quiet word with you is in order. See me at lunchtime. Now, I shall write on the board some sentences in which the apostrophes have been omitted. I would like you to copy out the sentences.'

While the class completed the exercise, I took the opportunity to walk round the desks and look at some of the work. In due course, I reached the young man who had challenged the teacher.

'May I look at your book?' I asked pleasantly.

'Who exactly are you?' he said, looking me straight in the eyes.

'A school inspector.'

'Really? And what is it that you do exactly?'

'Watch lessons, examine books, talk to pupils, study examination results,' I explained.

'Bit of a cushy number that, isn't it? How long are you here for?'

'Just the day.'

'You'll not see much in a day.'

'You'd be surprised.'

'And what will be in your report of this lesson?' he asked bluntly.

Now it was my turn to be in the witness box and face the tricky questions. 'I haven't quite decided yet.'

'But you must have formed some impression.'

'It is usually me who asks the questions, you know.'

The boy was not going to let me off the hook so lightly. 'But surely in a good school,' he said, 'the pupils are encouraged to ask questions, are they not?'

'They are,' I replied, 'but with some questions it would be inappropriate for me to answer.'

'Sounds a bit of a cop-out to me.'

I changed the subject. 'Do you like English?'

'I like the language. I can't say that I like the lessons. I'm afraid I can't get too excited about where to put the apostrophe, can you? It seems to me to be a very outdated concept and so deeply uninteresting. When Shakespeare or Dickens put pen to paper, I am sure the last thing on their minds was where to stick their apostrophes.'

'Your book, please,' I said.

He slid his open book casually across the desk for me to examine. It contained work of quite exceptional quality.

'I am sure you do not need me to tell you that this work is excellent,' I told him.

'No, I don't really.' I could see that dealing with this young man was no easy matter. He smiled. 'But it is always nice to be told.'

I closed his book and passed it back to him. It was then that I saw the name on the cover: Hugo Maxwell-Smith. 'Do you have any brothers or sisters?' I asked.

'Yes, a younger brother and sister. My brother isn't at this school yet.'

'Ah, so that would be Alexander, a pupil at Our Lady of Lourdes?'

That did surprise the young man, but he didn't have a chance to question me because the bell rang shrilly.

'When you have handed your books in,' said Mr Frobisher, 'you can go.'

'You may go,' murmured Hugo Maxwell-Smith, rising from his seat and giving me the fullest and most charming of smiles.

FOR THE SECOND PERIOD of the day, I joined a gentle-mannered if somewhat nervous young teacher called Mr Adams. The lesson had been well planned, the teaching was competent and the work interesting. It was a vast improvement on the previous class.

When the bell signalled morning break, I went in search of Mr Poppleton who, I was informed, taught in a temporary classroom.

Behind the main school building, I discovered an ugly shed balanced on six raised concrete blocks. The exterior of the structure resembled a prisoner-of-war hut: wooden walls the colour of a stagnant pond, grey asphalt roof, small square windows and dirty brown steps leading up to a plywood door. It was a far cry from Mr Frobisher's elegant room. As I headed for the hut, the door opened and a small, spherical individual appeared, like an actor stepping onto the stage.

Mr Poppleton could have walked straight out of the pages of a Dickens' novel. His cheeks were as wrinkled as an overripe russet apple and his claret-coloured nose was as round as a turnip. Bright gingery-red hair sprouted from around his ears, and he was dressed in a loud checked suit (a size too small), a rust-coloured waistcoat and an enormous, spotted bow tie.

'Mr Poppleton?' I enquired, approaching the rotund little figure.

'Indeed, it is I,' he said, beaming. 'Vernon Poppleton at your service. And you must be the expected Inspector Fish.'

'Phinn,' I said. 'It was a misprint.'

'You were a misprint? How very unfortunate.'

'On the letter.'

'Ah.' Mr Poppleton raised a ginger eyebrow. 'The inimitable Mrs Winterton,' he said knowingly. 'I recall once she sent a letter out to parents from "The Deadteacher".' He added in an undertone, 'Not entirely inappropriate, if you have met our esteemed leader. I mustn't be unkind, but dear Mr Nelson does have the touch of death about him. He's a physicist, you know.'

Mr Poppleton produced a small, silver, heart-shaped box from a waistcoat pocket, flipped open the top and took a generous pinch of snuff, which he sniffed up his nostril with a flourish.

I climbed up the steps and, when he had returned the silver snuffbox to his pocket and had sneezed tumultuously, I shook the soft, fleshy hand he extended. 'Once,' I told him, 'when I had to type a letter to a school, I wrote, "Dear Headamster". Fortunately, the person in question had a sense of humour and replied, "Dear Gerbil".'

'Ho, ho,' he chuckled, 'very droll! Would that our esteemed leader had been endowed with a sense of humour. He seems to carry the troubles of the world on his shoulders. Mr Nelson is most industrious and well meaning, but he is a man of very sombre disposition. I suppose one has to be like that to ascend to the dizzy heights of headship. I don't suppose I should be telling a school inspector such things, but I do think a sense of humour is an attribute of considerable importance in teaching, don't you think? Humour, in my opinion, adds inestimably to our quality of life. But I apologise for pontificating on the steps like a preacher of old. Do come along in, Mr Phinn. My little kingdom is not the most tasteful, architecturally speaking, but it is home and I can make as much noise as I like without disturbing others. Of course, it heats up like the Gobi Desert in summer and cools down like the polar icecap in winter, so I sincerely hope you are going to be warm enough. I am thermally insulated and, as you may observe, I get my suits from Fritters of Fettlesham.'

I had a suit, not dissimilar, from that ancient emporium, bought in the January sales at an incredibly knock-down price. It was a sort of mustardy-brown with a dogtooth check in dark red, and it had unfashionably wide lapels and large leather buttons. Once, in a hot classroom, the heavy suit had stuck to my body and I had nearly fainted with the heat. I had vowed never to wear the wretched garment again. In fact, I didn't have the chance, since Christine had given the jacket to a local farmer for his sheepdog to lie on, and had cut up the trousers for polishing cloths.

As I followed him into the room, Mr Poppleton remarked, 'I was under the impression that you were to join me for the first lesson.'

'Yes, but as I explained to Mr Frobisher, I prefer to work to my own programme. I joined the head of department for the first period.'

'Ho, ho!' chortled Mr Poppleton, smiling broadly. 'He would not have been best pleased with that little ploy.'

'No, I don't think he was,' I said.

'However, you are now here to watch me and it is my turn to feel the frenzied flutter of fright. The first period, which I was told you would be observing, was rigorously planned, carefully prepared and though I say so myself, quite a *tour de force*. This next lesson will, I fear, be rather lacklustre by comparison.'

'I'm not really interested, Mr Poppleton,' I told him, 'in rehearsed performances. The reason I don't tell teachers when I am visiting their classrooms is to try to ensure that nothing special is prepared. I just want to see a typical lesson.'

'You certainly won't find my lessons typical, Mr Phinn,' he replied with mock horror. 'Every lesson of mine is a unique experience. Now, this morning, my "little ones"—the first-year pupils—are completing a poem. I do hope you like poetry.'

'Yes, I do,' I replied. 'It's an essential component of the English curriculum.'

'I fear that Mr Nelson would take issue with you on that one. He has a much more utilitarian view of language. But I believe poetry defines the world, it deals with the deepest emotions, it is language at its most precise, creative and vivid. Well, do feel free to look around.'

Mr Poppleton's room was as colourful and unusual as the man himself. Every conceivable wall space was covered with prints, portraits, photographs, articles, letters, and pupils' work. From the ceiling dangled multicoloured mobiles; the windowsills were crammed with plants, clay figures, animal skulls, and all manner of strange artefacts. Dominating the room was an ancient oak desk entirely covered with folders and files, exercise books, thick dictionaries and numerous books. Facing it were rows of tables and hard-backed chairs.

I made my way to a shabby but comfortable-looking armchair in one corner of the room and lowered myself charily into its sagging seat, creating a small cloud of dust in the process.

Presently the pupils entered, went quietly to their desks and stood facing the front.

'Good morning, boys!' trumpeted Mr Poppleton, with a theatrical wave of his hand.

'Good morning, sir,' they replied.

'Do sit down, please. Now, boys, the gentleman in the corner is Mr Phinn, a school inspector, here to see how well we are doing. I hope he leaves us with a good impression. Do you think he will?'

'Yes, sir,' they replied.

'Right, boys,' continued Mr Poppleton. 'Today I would like you to continue with the poems you started last lesson. Mr Phinn is an *aficionado* of poetry, as I am, and might care to tour the classroom, talk with you and read some of your poems.'

I levered myself out of the armchair to look at the pupils' books. The boys were keen to talk about their work.

'When we arrived,' said one, 'we had to write a short autobiography so "Poppo"—I mean, Mr Poppleton—could learn a bit about us.' He opened his book to reveal a neat and informative account of his short life, together with illustrations and photographs. The work had been carefully and constructively marked in pencil. At the bottom was a long, useful comment from the teacher, with ideas for improvement.

'And how do you like English?' I asked.

'It's great. At prep school, I didn't enjoy it much. We did lots of boring exercises and copying. But here it's really good. Mr Poppleton's a bit out of the ordinary but he's a really good teacher.'

'So what is your poem about?'

'We've been asked to write about somebody who is very special in our lives. I chose my gran. Grandparents are different from parents, aren't they? They're more fun, they don't tell you off as much as parents and they give you money.'

Beneath the poem, appropriately, was a small sketch in black ink of a smiling old lady with sparkling eyes and curly hair.

Next, I made my way to the back corner desk where a boy was putting the final touches to a poem about his father.

'May I look?' I asked.

He passed across his book, carefully backed in shiny brown paper, with his name, 'Russell Davis, Class 1A', written in large, neat letters on the front. I read the first few pages—a potted autobiography. It was immensely poignant. He informed the reader in a matter-of-fact way that he was an only child and lived with his father in a 'pretty ordinary' terraced house close to the town centre. There was not a great deal of money and they rarely went on holiday. His mother, he wrote, had left when he was small and he saw her infrequently. He saw nothing of his maternal grandparents. He felt sad about this and found it difficult to understand. However, he said he was happy living with a father who was as much a friend as a parent. The poem that followed was about a father who he described as 'ordinary-looking, a bit bald and overweight, the kind of man who wears shiny trousers, baggy cardigans and old slippers', but it went on to tell how special he was and how much Russell loved him.

'Your autobiography is a very honest account, Russell,' I told him. 'Do you not mind sharing such personal details with other people?'

'Why should I, sir?' he replied. 'It's the truth. I'm not ashamed of it. My father says it is always best to be honest.'

'He sounds a remarkable man, your father.'

'He is, sir. He works hard, he takes me to the cinema and football matches and once we went to the theatre. We like to go for long walks and we talk about things a lot. He's just . . . well, special, you know.'

'And what quality do you admire most in this very special father of yours?'

The boy thought for a moment, biting his bottom lip. Then he looked into my eyes. 'When *he* makes a mistake, my father says he's sorry. Grown-ups don't tend to do that. If my father gets its wrong, he says so. He says it's not being weak to admit you don't always get things right or that you don't know something.'

I remembered a strident newspaper article I'd read recently, which had had little good to say about the younger generation. The writer ought to meet this polite, mature-for-his-age, young student. There are many, many children who come from loving homes and are in the hands of hard-working and dedicated teachers but they are not the ones who appear on the front pages of newspapers. Boys like Russell do not make news.

'Sir?' The boy's voice broke into my thoughts.

'Oh, I'm sorry!' I exclaimed. 'I was miles away. I was just thinking about what you said. Well, Russell, I hope that if I have a son, he will speak about me in the same way as you speak about your father.'

'That's really up to you, isn't it, sir?' replied the boy, smiling.

'Yes, I suppose it is,' I said.

When the bell sounded, the boys packed their bags, stood behind their desks and waited to be dismissed.

'For homework,' the teacher told the class, 'learn the spellings I gave you yesterday and, remember, half an hour's reading every night. I tell them frequently, Mr Phinn, that they cannot become great writers unless they are great readers, for on the back of reading is writing.'

'Yes, indeed,' I said.

'Good morning, boys,' trumpeted Mr Poppleton.

'Good morning, sir, good morning, Mr Phinn,' they answered and filed out of the room.

'You have some talented pupils, Mr Poppleton,' I told him as we headed across the school yard.

'Yes, they are very good, but you would expect no less in a selective school. Pupils of this calibre are sometimes a little daunting, I have to say, but I have always been of the opinion that teachers should show children the ropes and not be at all surprised if they manage to climb higher than they. I'm sure somebody famous said that. Now, Mr Phinn, would you care to partake of a pre-prandial cup of tea prior to braving the school dining room and a plate of Mrs Payne's chicken nuggets and chips? Had Napoleon used Mrs Payne's chicken nuggets in his cannons at Waterloo instead of balls, the unfortunate emperor would, without a doubt, have won the day.'

'That's kind, Mr Poppleton, but I want to look in at the library to see the extent and range of the stock.'

'Ho, ho,' he chuckled. 'I shall await your observations with interest.'

We had now arrived at the bicycle sheds, where a knot of boys were in loud and intense discussion about a particularly impressive-looking machine with a shiny black frame and silver handlebars.

'What have we here?' asked Mr Poppleton. 'A little *conversazione*?'

'Oh, no, sir,' said one of the boys, patting the bicycle they were discussing. 'It's a Raleigh Mustang.'

With a resounding laugh, the amazing Mr Poppleton scurried off in the direction of the school dining room for his chicken nuggets.

THE SCHOOL LIBRARY was a cold, gloomy room with wall-to-wall shelving in dark oak. There was not a student in sight, which was hardly surprising given the temperature and the inhospitable atmosphere. I scanned the dull green and grey covers of the books on the shelves, and knew immediately that they had not been updated for many years. I found *Scouts in Bondage* by Henry Prout, *The Walking Stick Method of Self Defence* by an Officer of the Indian Army, *Leadership Secrets of Attila the Hun* by Wess Roberts, PhD and, perhaps most bizarre of all, *Flashes from the Welsh Pulpit* by the Reverend G. Davies. These were for the collector of the weird and wonderful but not of any interest to teenagers. I looked in vain for bright, glossy paperbacks and sports magazines.

I sat down at a square table and began writing up some comments about the lessons I had seen that morning, but my mind kept wandering back to the conversation with young Russell. What would my sons or daughters say of me when they were teenagers, I thought. Would I be so loved and respected? I pushed the notes away and began to scribble a poem of my own, dedicated to my unborn child.

Always believe in yourself.
Promise always to be compassionate.
Appreciate that you make mistakes,
Recognise that I do, too.
Entrust me with . . .

I suddenly sensed a presence and, looking up, found Master Hugo Maxwell-Smith peering over my shoulder.

'Writing up your report?' he asked.

I quickly covered the poem. 'Yes. I am.'

'Should make interesting reading.'

I changed the subject. 'Is the library well used?' I asked inanely, looking round the empty room.

'No, sir,' replied the boy. 'As you can see, there's nobody here except you and me. I hope your report will include some mention of the library. It needs a complete overhaul.'

'Yes, it will. So why are *you* here?' I asked.

'Doing a little research on the apostrophe, actually,' he replied.

'Really? I gathered it wasn't one of your favourite topics.'

'It isn't, but I have been checking up on the rules.'

No doubt to challenge poor Mr Frobisher again, I thought.

'It is interesting that the great writers didn't think much of the apostrophe,' the boy continued. 'This for example is what George

Bernard Shaw wrote back in 1902. "There is not the faintest reason for persisting in the ugly and silly trick of peppering pages with these uncouth bacilli." I couldn't have put it better myself,' he said, before shutting his notepad with satisfaction.

THE LAST LESSON of the day was with the sixth form and a newly qualified teacher. I arrived at the rather noisy classroom to find twenty or so students, all of whom, I noted, were in shirtsleeves, sitting round tables in animated discussion.

'Is there a teacher here?' I asked one young man sitting near the door, raising my voice above the hubbub.

'I'm the teacher,' he replied, smiling. 'Simon Purdey.'

'Oh, I'm sorry, Mr Purdey,' I said. 'I thought you were one of the students.'

'Well, there's only a few years between us and I have been told that I look young for my age. You must be Mr Fish, the inspector.'

'Phinn,' I corrected. 'What are the students doing this afternoon?'

'We're studying *Hamlet* as our A-level text and I've asked the students to read through Act 1 and rewrite it in a different genre: as a modern radio play, the opening chapter of a detective novel, a thriller or a documentary drama, that sort of thing. Each group has a different genre to consider.'

'Sounds interesting,' I said.

'Well, I thought it would get them into the play and also be a bit of fun. I think it's a better way than wading drearily through Shakespeare as I did at school. Do you know, we were made to write out passages as a punishment? Would you credit that? The greatest words in the English language and they were set as a punishment! Anyway,' continued Mr Purdey, 'would you like to see how far the students have got?'

As I watched the series of highly original openings being acted out in front of the rest of the class, I recalled my sixth-form years when I was taught by a Miss Wainwright, a softly spoken woman who invariably wore a white blouse buttoned up at the neck, a large cameo brooch and a long dark skirt. Her eyes shone with intensity, especially when she was discussing Shakespeare. She had taken us to see a production of *King Lear* at the Rotherham Civic Theatre. I realise now that the acting had been wooden and the costumes bizarre, but the beauty and poignancy of the language had come through, and I often thanked God for the good fortune of having been taught by Miss Mary Wainwright. She brought Shakespeare to life, and developed in me a love of literature for which I shall be forever grateful.

My thoughts were interrupted when I heard my name mentioned by the teacher. 'The last version is one that Mr Phinn, as a Yorkshireman, will appreciate. It's the Yorkshire version of *Hamlet*.'

Two boys ambled towards each other at the front of the room, hands thrust deep in their pockets.

'Hey up, 'Amlet.'

'Hey up, 'Oratio, what's tha doin' 'ere?'

'Nowt much. 'Ow abaat thee then, 'Amlet? I ant seen thee for a bit.'

'Nay, I'm not that champion, 'Oratio, if t'truth be towld.'

'Whay, 'Amlet, what's oop?'

'Mi dad's deead, mi mam's married mi uncle and mi girlfriend does nowt but nag, nag, nag. I tell thee, 'Oratio, I'm weary wi' it.'

'Aye, tha's not far wrong theer, 'Amlet, she's gor a reight gob on 'er, that Hophilia. Teks after 'er owld man.'

'Anyroad, 'Oratio, what's tha doin' 'ere in Helsinor?'

'I've come for thee dad's funeral.'

'More like mi mam's wedding.'

'Aye, she dint let t'grass grow under 'er feet, did she?'

'I don't know what mi owld man 'ud mek of it, 'Oratio, I really don't.'

'Well, tha can ask 'im theeself, 'Amlet. 'E's been walkin' on t'battlements every neet this week, a-mooanin' and a-grooanin' and purrin' t'wind up iverybody. We're sick to deeath on it, 'Amlet.'

'I wonder wor 'e wants?'

'Well, tha can ask 'im thaself, 'cos 'ere 'e comes now . . .'

As I watched and laughed along with the teacher and students, I thought of Mr Poppleton's words. He was right: humour adds inestimably to our quality of life. There are few things more pleasurable to hear than young people laughing unselfconsciously.

Following the performance, there was loud and spontaneous applause that died suddenly when the door opened and there stood Mr Frobisher, like the Ghost of Christmas Past.

'There is a great deal of noise coming from this room,' he said.

'We're studying *Hamlet*,' explained Mr Purdey.

'Really? I wasn't aware, Mr Purdey, that *Hamlet* was quite so amusing.' Mr Frobisher then caught sight of me and gave a watery smile. 'Ah, Mr Phinn, I didn't see you sitting there. I was wondering where you had got to. I will join you and Mr Nelson at about half past four, if that is convenient.'

'Yes, that's fine,' I said.

He peered round the room. 'And you boys will be aware of the school rules on the wearing of blazers. Well, do carry on, Mr Purdey.'

AT THE END of the school day, I sat before the headteacher on the uncomfortable ladder-back chair, thinking that a cup of tea would be welcome. Clearly one was not forthcoming and, anyway, if it had been, the school secretary might well have added more than milk to it.

'Mr Frobisher will not be long,' said Mr Nelson.

'Actually, Mr Nelson,' I replied, deciding to get the difficult bit over with as quickly as possible, 'I would prefer to have a private word with you before Mr Frobisher arrives.'

The headteacher's brow furrowed. 'Do I take it you are not entirely satisfied with what you have seen today?'

'Not entirely,' I told him. 'On the whole, the lessons I observed were very good, but there is one exception, I am afraid to say.'

'Ah,' sighed the headteacher, 'Mr Poppleton. It has to be said, he is rather eccentric and individualistic, but the boys do so enjoy—'

'It's not Mr Poppleton,' I interrupted.

'Is it Mr Purdey? Mr Adams? I am sure you're aware that they have just started their teaching careers and it is to be expected that—'

'No, their lessons were fine.'

The headteacher began rubbing his temples. 'Then, by a process of elimination, it must be the head of department.'

'It is Mr Frobisher,' I said. 'I am aware that I have observed only the one class, but I did judge it to be less than satisfactory. It was an extremely dreary lesson on the use of the apostrophe.'

'I was under the impression, Mr Phinn,' said Mr Nelson, 'that the apostrophe *is* a dreary subject.'

'More importantly,' I said, 'Mr Frobisher has not the best relationship with the students, and the work that I saw was extremely narrow in range.'

Mr Nelson thought for a moment. 'Mr Frobisher, it has to be admitted, is not the most dynamic of teachers, but he is very loyal to the school and has not had a day's absence.'

'But as a teacher?' I enquired.

'He is, how does one put this, not as good as he was. He finds the students these days rather more outspoken and less attentive, and he harks back to a golden age, I'm afraid, when pupils did what they were told without question. I realise Mr Frobisher is not the best teacher in the world, but he is sound enough, don't you think?

Certainly his classrooms are quiet and he marks his books thoroughly. And he has only a couple more years to go.' This monologue sounded to me as if the headteacher was trying to convince himself.

'As I said, I have only observed one lesson,' I replied, 'and it would be unreasonable to judge on the evidence of that alone, but I am sufficiently concerned to make a return visit and to spend more time observing him.'

'I don't think that will be very well received,' sighed the headteacher. 'Your predecessor, Mrs Young, spent time a few years ago doing just that but with little effect. I am sure her report will be filed at the Education Office. Did you not read through it prior to your visit?'

'No, I didn't,' I replied, feeling rather guilty.

'Well, Mrs Young felt very much the same way as you do. Following her visit, Mr Frobisher agreed to relinquish the sixth form teaching that he was finding the most irksome. He also attended one or two courses on communication skills, but it is very difficult to change the habits of a lifetime.'

'So, there have been reservations expressed about his competence before?' I asked.

'Well, yes, but I never considered them serious enough to institute any kind of disciplinary proceedings. I've seen far worse teachers than Mr Frobisher in my career and so I have, it's fair to say,' said Mr Nelson staring out of the window like the great admiral himself, 'tended to turn a bit of a blind eye. As I intimated, Mr Frobisher is near the end of his career. Is it really worth all the time and trouble, quite apart from the effect it will have upon the man himself, to pursue this further?'

'Children deserve the best, Mr Nelson,' I said.

At that very moment there was a rap on the door and the man himself entered.

THREE

That evening I arrived home to find a note from Christine. She had a governors' meeting after school, followed by a parents' meeting in the evening, so would not be in until late. I was pleased in a way, because I could settle down without any disturbance and try to put together the report on King Henry's.

It was after ten o'clock when I finally put down my pen and placed the completed report in my briefcase, just at the very moment when Christine walked in.

'Hello,' she said brightly, coming over and pecking me on the cheek.

'How did it go?' I asked.

'Fine. The evening went like a dream. It's so good to have supportive colleagues and parents. It makes such a difference. Did you have a good day?'

'How long have you got?'

'Oh dear,' she said, 'that bad? Do you want to talk about it?' She slipped her arm through mine. 'We could have glass of wine, snuggle up in front of the fire.'

'Not now, love,' I replied. 'I've had a really tiring day. I'm sorry I'm such a misery. I'll snap out of it this weekend, I promise.'

The next day, on my way to a conference in York, I dropped the report off at the office for Julie to type. I spent the morning in lectures, the content of which, I fear, passed clean over my head. I sat there in brooding silence, my mind full of the events of the previous day at King Henry's College.

I arrived back at the office at the end of the afternoon to find Julie had typed out the report, placed a copy on my desk and sent another to Dr Gore's office. This would be despatched to the school. I read through what I had written. In the cold light of day, it sounded extremely critical.

At that moment Sidney and David breezed in. 'Thank God it's Friday!' exclaimed Sidney.

'Hello,' I replied wearily.

'Oh dear,' said Sidney, flopping into his chair. 'Our young colleague looks down in the dumps. Whatever's the matter?'

'I've got things on my mind,' I told him peevishly.

'We've all got things our minds,' said Sidney unsympathetically.

'Well, you don't look as if you have,' I retorted. 'I've never seen you so cheerful.'

'That is because,' said David, 'Harold has laid down the law to the headteacher of West Challerton High School and Sidney is to make his triumphant return next week.'

'Yes, indeed,' chortled Sidney. 'Harold was quite superb. It was a bravura performance on the phone. I heard it all. He's going in with me next week to see Mr Pennington-Smith.'

'I'm glad somebody's happy,' I said.

'Gervase,' said David, peering over the top of his spectacles, 'if I had pulled an expression like that when I was a lad, my old Welsh grandmother would have told me I had a face like a smacked bottom.'

'Yes, for goodness' sake, cheer up,' said Sidney, throwing a ball of screwed-up paper in my direction. 'You are about as much fun as an incontinent trapeze artist. There's the weekend ahead of you. No more school visits and, above all, a blessed rest from David's old Welsh grandmother who, if I could get hold of her, I would cheerfully throttle. What, pray, could a healthy young man like you, with a beautiful wife, a youngster on the way, a picture-postcard cottage in the Dales and a rewarding profession, have to worry about? As Connie would say, "A trouble shared is trouble doubled." Do tell.'

Connie, the caretaker of the Staff Development Centre, was a mistress of malapropisms.

So I told them about my visit to King Henry's College.

'And how did the head of department react,' asked Sidney, sitting up, 'when you informed him that he was useless?'

'Sidney!' I snapped. 'I did not say he was useless. I said that his lesson was less than satisfactory.'

'It's much the same thing. You're just couching it in euphemistic language.'

'Look, Sidney,' interrupted David, holding up a restraining hand, 'let the poor man finish. Now, Gervase, what happened?'

I related the whole dreadful episode: how Mr Frobisher had turned a ghastly white, shot bolt upright in his chair and begun to tremble with anger; how he had told me that he had never in all his forty years of teaching had his professional competence challenged and how he intended to take matters further.

'And what was old Horatio doing while all this was going on?' asked David.

'Turning a blind eye,' I said glumly. 'He never opened his mouth.'

'Typical,' said David. 'Anything for a quiet life. It's a case, at KHC, of the admiral having lost control of the fleet.'

'Well, to be frank,' said Sidney, 'I think you could have employed greater tact and diplomacy. Had it been me, I would have told the headteacher that I would be submitting a report of my visit and that I would make another appointment with the head of English. I should then have left the school before the arrival of the head of department. I really think it was neither the time nor place to give critical feedback to the man, particularly in front of the headteacher. I would have written the report, shown it to Harold and sought his advice.'

'He wasn't the sort of man to readily accept any advice and support,' I said glumly. 'Anyway, it's easy with hindsight. It's too late to do any of that now. I've already sent the report in.'

'My goodness, how expeditious!' exclaimed Sidney.

'There are some people in life who like to get things done quickly,' David told him, staring at the pile of papers on Sidney's desk. 'Of course, there are others who do not.' He turned back to me. 'Have you got a copy to hand?'

I reached over to my out-tray and passed the document across the desk. David read it without comment then passed it to Sidney, who grimaced his way through it.

'You don't mince your words,' Sidney said. 'Talk about "going for the juggler", as Connie would say.'

'Well, I was irritated by the man,' I said defensively. 'He was quite offhand with me and his lesson was unsatisfactory. Furthermore, one of the English staff told me he was difficult to work with.'

'Well, if I received a report like that,' said Sidney, 'I would contemplate throwing myself head first down a pothole.'

I felt considerably worse now. Perhaps the report was, after all, too critical. 'Does it sound that bad?' I asked.

'I'm afraid it does,' said David. 'But all is not lost. The county mail into schools doesn't go out until next Tuesday. If you retrieve the report, moderate the tone a little, let Harold have a glance through it and get his advice on the matter, all is not lost. Of course, it will have to be Monday morning. Harold will have left by this time.'

'An excellent idea,' said Sidney, just as the clock on the County Hall struck six. 'And that's home time, I think. Oh, and Julie said there was a loud man on the phone asking to speak to you. I hope it isn't another problem, old boy.'

CHRISTINE HAD TAKEN considerable trouble to prepare my favourite fillet steak with garlic butter that evening, but I just did not feel like eating. I poked the food around the plate.

'What's wrong?' she asked, sliding a hand across the table and taking mine. 'You were upset about something last night.'

'I think I really mishandled a situation in a school yesterday,' I told her gloomily. 'There was a head of department who I criticised in front of the headteacher and he stormed out. I feel bad about it now.'

'I'm sure you're overreacting,' said Christine. 'Did you have a word with Harold about it?'

'No, but I should have done.'

'Do you think the pupils were enjoying his lessons?'

'No, I don't think that they were.'

'Look, Gervase, you are always going on about children deserving the best that teachers can give, how they only have the one chance at education, that they need to be taught by enthusiastic, committed, good-humoured and hard-working people.'

'Yes, I know,' I said.

'Be honest, would you want this man teaching our child?'

'No, I wouldn't.'

'Was he committed, good-humoured and hard-working?'

'Not when I saw him, he wasn't.'

'Then you had to say so. Your job is not to go round schools telling poor teachers that they are fine, that everything in the garden is rosy. It's to tell the truth as you see it, which sometimes means being critical.'

'Yes, I know you're right,' I said. 'It's just that it was pretty unpleasant. Anyway, once I've got the report back and made it less trenchant, I'm sure I'll feel better.'

'You're changing the report?' she asked. 'I think you have to stick to what you believe, grasp the nettle and face the consequences.'

'Christine!' I snapped irritably. 'I wish I had never brought the wretched matter up. I'm feeling even worse about it now.'

'OK! OK! You do what you think best,' she said, beginning to clear the plates away.

I lapsed into a moody silence. When Christine began washing the dishes, I crept up behind her and put my arms round her waist. 'I'm sorry I was sharp with you,' I said. 'It's just that I was really looking forward to a break from work. This thing is like a black cloud. Anyway, I'm not going to think about it any more. Let's enjoy the weekend.'

Christine turned and kissed me on the cheek. 'It will be a taboo subject,' she said.

ON THE FOLLOWING Monday morning I made my way across the well-tended lawns in front of County Hall to retrieve my report.

The interior of the building was daunting: cold, echoey corridors, high ceilings, huge marble statues, endless oil paintings of stern-looking dignitaries and sepia photographs of former mayors and aldermen. It was like a mausoleum.

Mrs Savage's office was in the annexe, a modern block which clung to the older building like some pale brown parasite. Emablazoned on her door in large black letters, was: MRS BRENDA SAVAGE, PERSONAL ASSISTANT TO THE CHIEF EDUCATION OFFICER. Since my last visit, a small box had been fastened to the frame of the door, encasing what appeared to be a set of miniature traffic lights: red, amber and green. Above were instructions to press the buzzer beneath and then wait.

I pressed the buzzer and, much to my amusement, every light lit up. I knocked and entered.

Mrs Savage stood beside her desk, a clutch of papers in her hand. She was, as usual, immaculately dressed. That morning she wore a calf-length, pleated blue suit with diamante buttons, a cashmere jumper and some impressively pointed black shoes.

She glanced at me imperiously as I entered. 'I did ask you to wait, Mr Phinn,' she said irritably. 'I've not quite finished reading through this Health and Safety document for Dr Gore yet.'

'All your lights lit up, Mrs Savage,' I told her.

'I beg your pardon?' she asked witheringly.

'On your door. All your little lights, they lit up at the same time.'

'Well, that is most strange,' she said. She looked down at her desk and scrutinised a small box with buttons on the top. 'I hope you were not heavy-handed with my buzzer,' she said. When I just smiled, she sat down and continued, 'I shall ask the janitor to take a look at it. Now then, Mr Phinn, you will have to wait a moment while I finish reading this report. You may sit there,' she said, indicating the chair that was placed strategically in front of her desk.

I did as I was bid, and gazed around me. Her office was plush and equipped with comfortable furniture. Through the windows was a fine view of the moors and distant purple peaks beyond.

Mrs Savage put aside the report, and said briskly, 'Now, Mr Phinn, is there something you want?'

What a stupid question to ask, I thought. 'Yes, there is,' I replied. The chair on which I was sitting was lower than her huge swivel chair, so I found myself staring up into her eyes. 'I would like to have back a report that I sent over on Friday, please.'

'Like it back!' she exclaimed, as if I had made some sort of improper suggestion. 'That is out of the question.'

'I don't see why,' I said. 'It hasn't been sent out to the school yet.'

'Mr Phinn,' she said, carefully folding her hands before her on the desk and presenting me with the all-too-familiar unpleasant smile. 'Once I have received reports they cannot be returned.'

'Why?'

'Because they can't!' she snapped, defiance blazing in her eyes.

'But I can't see why there should be a problem. I need to amend my report and make certain important additions.'

'Mr Phinn,' she said in an exaggeratedly patient tone of voice, 'once a report is received in this office, it is duplicated. One copy goes in Dr Gore's in-tray and is then placed on file and the top copy is despatched to the school. There is no procedure for the return of reports. If inspectors started demanding their reports back once they had completed them, we would descend into chaos in no time.'

'In the three years I have been working as an inspector, Mrs Savage,' I told her, trying to keep calm, 'I have never requested the return of a single report. However, it is extremely important that I have this particular one back.'

She gave me a look of flat finality. 'I am sorry, Mr Phinn, but there is not the slightest possibility of my surrendering that report.'

I drew a deep and exasperated breath. 'Is Dr Gore in?' I asked.

'I don't see why that is pertinent,' she said.

'I would like to ask him if he would authorise the return of the report.'

'Dr Gore is extremely busy, particularly on Mondays.'

'Tomorrow morning first thing?'

Mrs Savage's eyes narrowed in triumph. 'He is in London at a conference tomorrow morning.'

'Mrs Savage,' I said gripping the edge of her desk, 'are you going to let me have that report back?'

'No, Mr Phinn, I am not. Procedures must be followed and—'

Without waiting to hear her out, I jumped to my feet and strode for the door. 'Dreadful woman!' I muttered, as I marched down the corridor.

Once in the inspectors' office, I immediately telephoned King Henry's College. I had decided to have a word with Mr Frobisher prior to his reading the damning report, and was planning to suggest that I call in at the school to discuss it with him later that week.

'Good morning, King Henry's College,' came a formal voice down the line. 'Mrs Winterton, school secretary speaking.'

'Oh, good morning,' I replied, with a sinking feeling in my stomach. 'This is Gervase Phinn from the school inspectors' division at County Hall. May I speak to Mr Frobisher, please?'

'I am afraid not. Mr Frobisher is away today.'

'What's wrong?' I asked. 'Is he ill?'

'I believe he felt unwell after your visit last Friday.'

'Oh, I see.' My heart sank into my shoes. 'Perhaps when he does return, you would ask him to contact me at the education office.'

'I shall pass on your message.'

'Thank you,' I said, placing the telephone down with a sigh. Now what was I going to do?

THE WEEK AHEAD was so busy I did not have time to dwell on the fate of Mr Frobisher. Tuesday found me bright and early at Butterthwaite, a small rural school set in the most magnificent countryside. Sheltered by sycamores and ancient oaks, the two-room schoolhouse stood square and solid at the head of the dale. From the classroom window, pale green pastures, dotted with sheep and crisscrossed by grey stone walls, rolled upwards to the distant hills.

The school had no major problems and I was able to give the headteacher a positive evaluation. At the end of the day I joined a sturdy-looking little boy with a healthy complexion, who was standing at the window surveying the panorama that stretched out before him. He was about six or seven years old.

'Just waiting for mi mam to come,' he told me. 'She's often a bit late. She 'as a lot to do on t'farm.'

'Well, I'm sure she'll not be long,' I said. 'Beautiful view, isn't it?'

'It's not bad, int it?' He dug his hands into his pockets. 'Autumn's comin' on,' observed the child like a little old man. 'Not be long afoor t'leaves start to fall and t'bracken turns gowld. Looks like it's gunna be a bad winter an' all. Mi dad can't be doin' wi' snow.'

'I'm not overkeen,' I said. 'And what's your name?'

'Andrew.'

'Well, Andrew,' I said. 'You're a lucky boy to live up here.'

'Aye, it's all reight. Better in t'summer than winter though.'

'And what do you like best at school?' I asked.

'I likes to read and I likes number work. I'm good at sums.'

'Are you?' I thought I'd test him on his arithmetic. 'How many sheep can you see in that field?' I asked him.

'Eh?'

'Can you tell me how many sheep you can see in the field?'

'Aye, I can see all on 'em,' he replied.

I chuckled. 'No, I meant could you count them for me.'

'Aye, I suppose I could. There's five Swaledales and six Texels, three hybrids and four hoggits.' He paused for a moment. 'That makes eighteen in total, dunt it? And don't ask me to count t'rabbits because they waint stay still long enough for me to tot 'em up.' A large, rusty Land Rover pulled up outside the school gate. 'Hey up, mi mam's 'ere.' With a wave he scurried off. 'Tarra!'

I saw him clamber up beside his mother, who was a large, cheerful-looking woman with ruddy cheeks. She gave him a great hug, strapped him in his seat and drove off.

Driving back to the office that afternoon, I thought of the children I had met during the last couple of weeks. All of them, I guessed, came from homes where there was justice and honesty, compassion and love. And then, too, there had to be others who were not so lucky. I thought about our own unborn child, and promised myself that I would make him or her as happy as possible. If it was a boy, we thought we might call him Matthew. The name means Gift of God.

I ARRIVED AT THE OFFICE one lunchtime a week later in a sombre mood. The whole sorry business at King Henry's was still preying on my mind. The last thing I wanted to hear was Julie's resounding laughter coming down the stairs.

'Someone's in a good mood,' I said gloomily as I entered the room.

'And someone's obviously not,' came back Julie's quick riposte. She was perched on the end of a desk, sharing something very amusing with Geraldine. 'Why aren't you at West Challerton?' she asked. 'You're running a course there this afternoon, aren't you?'

'Not until four o'clock,' I told her, heading for my desk. 'It's an after-school session. Language and learning,' I told her, pulling a face, 'and I am not looking forward to it at all. Mr Pennington-Smith is not my favourite headteacher.'

'I sympathise,' said Geraldine. 'I never feel comfortable in Mr Pennington-Smith's company. He's forever blowing his own trumpet and criticising the former headteacher. You should be flattered he's asked you to run a course for him, Gervase. He doesn't strike me as the sort of man to listen to advice.'

'Tell Sidney about it,' I said, recalling his differences with the headteacher over the place of art and design in the curriculum.

'Well, I'd better get on with this little lot.' I picked up the heap of papers in my in-tray. 'Oh, by the way, Julie, I was hoping to have a word with Harold, if he's in.'

'He's been in since seven this morning, but he's not to be disturbed for at least another hour. He's had Dr Gore, Councillor Peterson, Lord Marrick, various governors, everyone bar the Queen, on his phone all day. Something's going on at County Hall by the sound of it. There's been comings and goings all week. All very hush-hush.'

'Sounds intriguing. I guess we'll hear soon enough,' I sighed, starting to sort through the papers. 'What's this?'

I had come upon a bright yellow sheet of paper with URGENT printed in large black block capitals at the top.

'That's what we were laughing at,' said Geraldine. 'It's Mrs Savage's latest memorandum. You know she's been named as the Health and Safety contact in the Education Office? Well, she seems to be taking her new role very seriously.'

'She'll be in combat outfit next,' added Julie, 'going on courses for bomb disposal.'

'Listen to this.' Geraldine took the piece of paper, cleared her throat and read out: "Urgent! Health and Safety Circular Number One: Suspicious Packages. Should you discover a package, parcel, box, bundle, envelope, container or any other suspect receptacle with protruding wires and/or stains and/or powdery substances and/or residues which might be emitting unusual noises and/or has a strange odour, do not attempt to touch, loosen, open, move, shake or interfere with it, and under no circumstances must it be immersed in water. This constitutes a suspicious package."'

'You don't say,' said Julie sarcastically. 'She must think our brains are made of porridge. I mean, who in their right mind is going to pick up a ticking box that smells and start shaking it?'

Geraldine read on. '"The County now has its own nuclear fall-out shelter at Collington. The facility, for use by senior county council members"—that presumably doesn't include us—"in the case of nuclear holocaust or national emergency, is situated to the rear of Roper's Salesroom, Furnival's Funeral Parlour and Kwik Cutz Hairdressing Salon. The official opening by Councillor George Peterson has been postponed for the time being due to vandals damaging the shelter." It could survive a nuclear attack,' chuckled Gerry, 'but not the activities of the Collington vandals.'

'I remember once,' said Julie laughing, 'when Mrs Savage sent a staffing bulletin round County Hall with an advert in it for a children's crossing patrol warden, and she had added that application forms were also available in Braille.' She looked pointedly in my direction. 'And speaking of staffing bulletins, I notice that Dr Yeats's job is in the Staff Vacancy Bulletin this week.'

'So I believe,' I said casually.

The previous academic year Harold had informed the team of his intention to retire early. He had had enough. The pressures of the job and the increasing workload were getting him down. Spurred by my colleagues, but not by Christine, who thought I had quite enough on my plate, I had applied. I had not even been short-listed, never mind interviewed, but had been reassured by Harold and Dr Gore that they would look favourably on an application from me at some time in the future when I had had more experience. A new senior inspector, one Simon Carter, had been appointed but had not lasted long. A know-all, he had managed to alienate everyone at County Hall, and we were greatly relieved when he left. Harold had been prevailed upon to remain in post until his replacement was appointed, which would be at the end of this term. A new senior inspector would then be in post after the Easter holidays.

'You are going to apply, aren't you?' asked Julie, breaking into my thoughts.

'I've not decided yet,' I replied. 'Part of me says, "Yes, it will be a tremendous challenge" and another part says, "Don't touch it with a barge pole."'

'You ought to,' said Gerry. 'I reckon you'd have a really good chance this time round.'

'We'll see,' I told her, starting to open my letters.

'My, you are in a glum mood this afternoon, aren't you,' observed Julie, sliding off the desk. 'Well, I'm going to the canteen for my lunch and will try to find out what's going on from Doris. She hears everything from behind that serving hatch.' Julie straightened her meagre skirt and headed for the door. 'By the way, will you please, please ring that man with the loud voice. He keeps on calling and he's nearly sent me demented bellowing down the line. I never got a word in, so I don't know what his name was or what it was about. His telephone number is on your pad.' With that she departed.

Gerry and I both got on quietly with our work for the next hour or so, which was, thankfully, clear of interruptions.

AT THREE O'CLOCK I decided to see if Harold was free.

'Come in!' he exclaimed when I knocked and poked my head round his door. 'I wanted to speak to you. Pull up a chair.'

Harold's office was large but cluttered. A row of ugly olive-green metal filing cabinets stretched along one wall and a set of heavy book-cases, crammed with box files, and thick reports from the Ministry of Education, filled the other. Harold's ancient oak desk, buried beneath a mountain of paper, faced a sash window through which he had an uninspiring view of the rear of County Hall. It was a world away from the plush office of Mrs Savage.

'You look busy,' I said, nodding in the direction of his desk.

'Always am, dear boy. Every Thursday I set the afternoon aside to try to deal with all the problems and complaints that dear Dr Gore, in his wisdom, sends my way. He has an uncanny habit of passing the most awkward things on to me to deal with.' Harold gestured to a bright red folder before him. 'There's a letter from an irate parent claiming compensation. Apparently his child's teacher simulated a volcanic eruption in class and the boy arrived home like the Gingerbread Man, a bright golden colour from head to foot. Then I've received several letters about bullying, which, of course, have to be taken very seriously, and a letter from Sister Clare of the Sacred Heart Convent, complaining, in no uncertain terms, about the opening of a sex shop opposite the school.'

'I never realised you had all this to do.'

He gave a great toothy smile. 'But not for much longer. I shall pass on all such matters, with a light heart, to my successor. Now, I'm pleased you popped in, Gervase, because my biggest and most urgent problem this week concerns Hawksrill Primary School.'

'Hawksrill's a splendid school,' I said. 'What's the problem?'

'Well, the fact of the matter is, it's closing.'

'Closing!' I exclaimed.

'I'm afraid so. There was an acrimonious Education Subcommittee meeting earlier this week, at the end of which it was decided that five small schools, including Hawksrill, will be closed.'

'Why, for heaven's sake?'

'Well, I'm sure you are aware that there have to be big cuts in the educational budget and small schools like Hawksrill are not really viable. It's much more cost-effective to have larger schools and close the ones in some of the very small villages. Hawksrill's building needs quite a deal of work on it. The roof's leaking, the toilets require refurbishing and the perimeter fence needs repairing. The headteacher, Mrs Beighton, and her assistant, Mrs Brown, have both indicated that they are looking to retire in the near future so there would be no redundancies. All in all, it's quite fortuitous.'

'It's not fortuitous for the children at the school,' I protested.

'Perhaps not,' said Harold, 'but they can be bussed the few miles to the neighbouring school. You see, Hawksrill only has about thirty children and the village has an ageing and declining population.'

'Hang on, I live in Hawksrill,' I reminded him.

'Yes, yes, I know, and that is why I wanted to have a quiet word with you prior to the news getting out.'

'I don't like the idea of this at all, Harold,' I said. 'I'm not at all keen on any child of mine being bussed in and out of the village every day, particularly in winter along those twisting, narrow roads. One of the reasons Christine and I decided to live in Hawksrill was its lovely school.'

'Yes, I quite understand that, but there is really no alternative. It's just not economic. I'm sorry, but there it is. Parents will be informed by letter next Friday. Then, no doubt, there will be a meeting with the governors, followed by the appeals procedures and possibly a tribunal.' Harold smiled. 'Your child might very well be at secondary school by the time Hawksrill actually closes.' I didn't smile. I was feeling shell-shocked. 'Anyway, Gervase, I just wanted you to know before it hits the papers. Now, was there something you wanted to have a word with me about?'

'No, nothing,' I said getting up. 'Nothing at all.'

I RETURNED to the office even more depressed than before. Geraldine had gone but Julie was there, placing my typed letters on my desk along with a mug of coffee.

'Have you rung that man with the loud voice yet?' she asked.

I sighed heavily. 'No, but I'll do it now.' I stared at the notepad on my desk. It's amazing, I thought to myself, how life can suddenly change. First Mr Frobisher, now Hawksrill school closing.

I dialled the number on the pad. 'Hello, my name is Gervase Phinn,' I said wearily when I heard the phone being picked up at the other end. 'I believe someone on this number wishes to speak to me.'

''Ello! 'Ello! Is that Mester Phinn?' came a thunderous voice down the line.

'It is,' I said, before holding the receiver at arm's length.

'Jacob Bannister, 'ere. Tha' might 'ave 'eard of us. "JBB's Quality Animal Feeds". We're very big in these parts!' he shouted.

'Well, I don't have much call for animal feeds in my line of work,' I told him.

'Eh?' he bellowed.

'I said, I don't have—what can I do for you, Mr Bannister?'

'Tha're like t'Scarlet bloody Pimpernel. "They seek 'im 'ere, they seek 'im theer." Tha're never in.'

'No, I spend most of my time in schools, Mr Bannister,' I replied, rather piqued. 'That's what I do for a living. Now, what can I do for you?'

'I 'ear you do talks.'

I should have guessed. Shortly after becoming a school inspector I had been dragooned into speaking at a charity event. I had been delighted, and not a little surprised, to discover that my talk had been warmly received. Some weeks later, I had received an invitation from the very formidable the Honourable Mrs Cleaver-Canning to speak at her golf club ladies' night dinner. Things had then snowballed and I was soon receiving invitations from all manner of clubs, guilds and societies.

'After-dinner talks like t'one my brother's wife's 'eard you at, at t'Countrywomen's Association Dinner in Ribsdyke a couple o' months back? She said tha were a funny man.'

I was not feeling particularly 'funny' that afternoon. 'I've been called many things, Mr Bannister, but—'

'Eh?'

'I am rather busy at the moment,' I told him.

'I don't want tha to speak this very minute, Mester Phinn,' he said.

I sighed. 'So would you like me to speak at a function?' I asked.

'Eh?'

'I said, would you like me to speak at a dinner?' I was raising my voice an octave higher.

'Aye, that's t'idea. At Fettlesham Farmers' Club Dinner, December the first. We're raisin' money for t'Children's Society.'

'Yes, I know The Children's Society,' I said. 'It's a very worthy charity.'

'Well,' shouted the speaker down the line, 'I know it's a fair bit off but I wants to get things soarted. To tell you t'truth, we was let down by t'speaker we booked, cricketer for Yorkshire in t'dim and distant past. Never 'eard of 'im mi'sen. I'm a Rugby Union man. Anyroad, how're tha fixed?'

'I should explain, Mr Bannister—'

'Jacob!'

'I should explain, Jacob, that I am not a comedian. I don't tell blue jokes or anything like that.'

'We don't want owt like that. We want sommat funny wi'out being mucky. My brother's wife said tha'd fit t'bill a treat.'

'It's December the first, you say.' I flicked through my diary. I was free but felt like saying no, such was the mood I was in. Then I thought of all the disadvantaged children the Children's Society helped.

'I'll do it,' I told him.

'Champion!' he roared, nearly bursting my eardrum. 'We meet at

T'Marrick Arms in Chapelwatersthwaite at seven prompt. Now, it's nowt fancy. Tha dunt need no "penguin suit" or owt o' that sooart. Ee, I'm reight glad tha can do it, Mester Phinn. My brother's wife said tha were a real barrel of laughs.'

'Really,' I sighed.

FOUR

'I am not happy, Mr Clamp,' complained Connie. 'I'm *not* happy at all, having harems of naked women cavorting about the place.'

'Connie,' replied Sidney, his beard bristling and his eyes flashing wildly, 'there will be no harems. There will be one woman, and she will be doing no cavorting, I can assure you of that.'

'I don't care how many,' retorted the caretaker, 'I just do not like that sort of thing going on on my premises.'

Connie, with her florid face, bright, copper-coloured perm, brilliant pink nylon overall and large multicoloured feather duster, which she invariably wielded like a field marshal's baton, was a blunt, hard-working, down-to-earth Yorkshirewoman. She kept the premises spotless but ruled with a rod of iron. Like many Yorkshire folk, she had strong and unwavering views that she was not afraid to express. She was, as they say in Yorkshire, 'not backwards in coming forwards'. She had no conception of rank or status and treated everyone who entered her empire exactly the same.

It was a warm Friday afternoon towards the end of September and I had arrived at the Staff Development Centre just after lunch to find Connie and Sidney in heated discussion in the entrance hall.

'Look here, Connie,' said Sidney forcing a smile, 'there will be nothing going on here. The person is not a striptease *artiste*, she is a professional model, one who poses tastefully for artists.'

'But she'll have nothing on,' persisted Connie.

'Of course she'll have nothing on,' said Sidney, trying to contain his anger. 'She is a nude. Nude models pose nude so artists can draw them. The whole point is for the artist to see them *au naturel*.'

'See them what?' asked Connie.

'In the natural form, unencumbered.'

'With nothing on,' persisted Connie. 'I don't like it, Mr Clamp. Well, I think it's disgusting, grown men ogling a young woman and calling it artificated. I'm as broad-minded as the next person and I like nice pictures but they have to leave something to the imagination. Nobody can accuse me of being a Pharisee.'

'Philistine,' murmured Sidney. 'It's Philistine, not Pharisee.'

'What is?'

'Oh, never mind,' sighed Sidney.

'As I was saying,' said Connie, 'I'm not one of these Pharisees, but I draw the line at naked women.'

'You make it sound like Sodom and Gomorrah,' mumbled Sidney.

'There's no call for that sort of language, Mr Clamp, thank you very much!'

Sidney appealed to me. 'Gervase, I have an art course coming up next week and I have a female model coming for the figure-drawing workshop. Can you impress upon Connie here that I am not opening a Soho strip joint?'

'Connie,' I said, coming to Sidney's defence, 'all the great artists painted and drew the naked female form: Picasso, Matisse, Goya, Leonardo da Vinci, Michelangelo—'

'All foreigners,' Connie interrupted. 'Well, of course, that doesn't surprise me one jot. But what I am surprised at, Mr Phinn, is you, a newly married man with a baby on the way, liking that sort of thing.'

'What I'm trying to say,' I persevered, 'is that there's really nothing disgusting about it.'

'Well, you would say that,' replied Connie, in no way mollified. 'You're a man. You're all the same when it comes to naked women. I've seen my Ted at it. You can call it tasteful if you like, Mr Clamp, and try to talk me round until the cows come home. I think a young girl taking off her clothes for men to have a good gander at is disgusting.'

'She is not a girl,' groaned Sidney. 'Miriam is getting on for sixty, for goodness' sake.'

'Getting on for sixty!' Connie gasped. 'Well, she ought to be ashamed of herself. She ought to be going ballroom dancing or flower arranging at her time of life, not taking her clothes off for men. I've warned Mrs Osbaldiston already.'

'Who's Mrs Osbaldiston?' I asked.

'Didn't I say? She's my neighbour, and I've asked her to hold the fort while I'm off next week, for three days.'

'So you'll not be here for Mr Clamp's course?' I asked.

'No, I won't and I'm glad I won't as well.'

I changed the subject. 'Are you going on holiday?'

'Not at this time of year, I'm not,' she told me. 'I'm taking my father's ashes to Dunkirk. It's something I promised him I would do, but I've just not got around to doing it.' Connie's father had died the previous year. 'He lived in a cellar for a week at Dunkirk, you know, with nothing but a pound of sugar and rain water until he managed to get out on one of those little boats. He always said he wanted to rest with those pals of his who never made the journey home.' Connie sniffed. 'Oh, look at me now, I'm getting all weepy.'

'He was a brave man, Connie,' I said.

'He was the best father you could hope for, was Dad. Never raised a hand to me, never used a bad word. He was always there for me. When you're growing up you spend most of your time trying to get away from your parents, don't you? You always think you know better.' She blinked quickly and sighed. 'You never really appreciate them when you're young. Oh, I nearly forgot, you have a message from Mrs Savage. She said to phone her immediately. She's got a tongue as sharp as a butcher's knife, that one, and a look as cold as a cemetery. I've had confrontations with her before now, parking that fancy red sports car so it blocks my entrance, flouting Health and Safety regulations.'

'She's been put in charge of Health and Safety at County Hall,' I told Connie.

'Well, she's the last one to tell people about Health and Safety. Mind you, it doesn't surprise me. People without much substance always rise to the top like froth on the top of coffee. Anyway, I wouldn't bother phoning now. Let her wait until Monday.'

What an end to the week! Ignoring Connie's advice, I headed for the office, with a sinking heart, to telephone Mrs Savage.

'You wanted to speak to me, Mrs Savage?' I said rather formally when I finally got through.

'Yes, I did,' she replied icily. 'Dr Gore wishes to see you at once.'

'I see.' I resisted the urge to ask what about but I had a shrewd idea it concerned the report on King Henry's. 'I'll be there presently.'

'I will inform Dr Gore that you are on your way.' With that she thumped down the phone.

'She gets worse,' I murmured to myself.

DR GORE, chief education officer for the county of Yorkshire, peered over the top of his gold-framed spectacles and smiled like a contented cat. 'And how are you, Gervase?' he purred, steepling his long fingers on the large mahogany desk in front of him.

'I'm very well, Dr Gore, thank you.'

'Good, good,' the CEO murmured. 'And how is that lovely wife of yours? Is she keeping well?'

'Very well, thank you, Dr Gore.'

'And when is the baby due?'

'The end of March.'

'"Whan that Aprill with his shoures soote, The droghte of March hath perced to the root."'

'Er, yes.'

'Chaucer.'

'Yes,' I replied, wishing he would get on with it and put me out of my misery.

'Well,' he said, 'I'm sure you are wondering why I sent for you.'

'Yes, I *was* wondering,' I replied, getting more and more tense.

'I was speaking to Mr Nelson last week,' he said casually. Here we go, I thought. 'He's in the same Rotary Club as I am, you know. Anyway, he mentioned you had paid a visit to King Henry's recently. Took a look at the English department, I believe.'

'I did, yes.'

'I gather you were not impressed with one particular teacher?'

'About the report, Dr Gore—' I started to say.

'Ah, yes, the report,' said the CEO, peering at me. 'Mr Nelson said that he had never read a report quite like it. I must say that when I read it, I found it, how shall we put it, rather direct and to the point. You certainly didn't pull any punches.' He leaned back in his chair. 'But, of course, that's as it should be.'

I stared at him. 'It is?'

'Why, yes. I want my school inspectors to give clear, honest and objective assessments of what they see. I thought your report on King Henry's was excellent. Well done.'

'Mr Nelson thought it was excellent?' I asked, dumbfounded.

'Yes, indeed. He mentioned it was extremely well written and to the point. Just wanted to put in a good word on your behalf. I must say you certainly have got to the nub of the problem in the English department. From what I gather, the head of department, Mr Frobisher I believe his name is, has become rather tired and a little cynical over the past few years. Not incompetent but, to use common parlance, past his sell-by-date. He can, I believe, be quite difficult at times. When Mr Frobisher returned to school last week after having been away ill for the first time in living memory, the headteacher asked to see him and it was not a very good-humoured meeting, by all accounts. Mr Frobisher decided, in the end, to take early retirement.'

'I see,' I mumbled, hardly able to take in what I was hearing.

'So, your report was extremely effective.' Dr Gore paused and stared again over his glasses. 'You know, Gervase, when you applied for the senior inspector's post last year, one reservation I did have about you was that you might not have the mettle to be quite as critical as it is sometimes necessary to be. Sometimes one has to say the unpalatable and I think you have proved that you can.'

'Thank you, Dr Gore,' I said. I suppose I should have felt happy and relieved but for some reason I felt even more depressed. My report had been the means to end a teacher's career.

'Anyhow,' continued the CEO amiably, 'it wasn't about King Henry's that I wanted to see you. I have a little job for you.'

'Oh,' was all I could muster. I was well acquainted with Dr Gore's 'little jobs', having been given quite a number of them in my time with the Education Department and they were never 'little'.

'You are, no doubt, aware that I sit on several major national committees. One is the European Intermediary Education Initiative—the EIEI.'

'Oh,' I said, again.

'The EIEI enables teachers and inspectors to visit other European countries to study and compare the education systems there.'

This didn't sound too bad, I thought to myself. A week in Sweden, Spain or France sounded a 'little job' I could very much enjoy.

'Next term,' continued Dr Gore, 'there will be a small group of inspectors from various European countries visiting the county to look at the education we provide. It's all funded by the EIEI.'

'Oh,' I said, once more. It was beginning to sound like the chorus to 'Old Macdonald had a Farm'.

'I would like you to arrange for our foreign colleagues to visit a number of different schools. In addition, you could perhaps set up a couple of meetings at the Staff Development Centre with headteachers and governors to talk about our education system and maybe organise an informal evening reception. That sort of thing. Mrs Savage will be on hand to deal with all the administration—and the European inspectors will only be with us for a few days, so it's not a massive undertaking. Does that sound reasonable?'

'Fine,' I replied, thinking of all the extra work it would involve just when Christine would need all the support I could give her in the months running up to the birth of the baby.

'Good, good,' murmured Dr Gore. 'Well, thank you for coming to see me.'

I SPENT A FAIRLY uncomfortable weekend hiding the knowledge that Hawksrill School might be closing, having decided I was not in a position to pass on news that Harold had given me in confidence. Christine and the village would know soon enough.

On the following Tuesday, I set off early for the Staff Development Centre. I had received a memorandum from Mrs Savage asking me to meet her to discuss the EIEI initiative. 'It is imperative,' she had written, 'that we put our heads together asap so that wheels can be put in motion.' Such was the tone of sharp command in the memo that I was minded to ignore it or reply that I was far too busy, but then I thought that it would be better to get the meeting over and done with. There was a lot to do.

It was a particularly cold morning with what they call in Yorkshire 'a cheeky wind' as I drove along the twisting road from Hawksrill to Fettlesham. The views in the Dales are stunning and never cease to fill me with awe. I love travelling in this vast county with its soft green valleys, soaring fells, dark pine forests, and empty moors flooded with bright purple heather in autumn. Every journey is different and every scene has a unique beauty. What a place to work, I thought.

The Staff Development Centre was eerily quiet that morning.

I discovered Mrs Osbaldiston in the kitchen, scrutinising a wadge of papers and shaking her had thoughtfully. She was a lean, elderly woman with tightly curled, silver-white hair, a thin-lipped mouth and an amazingly wrinkled face. An apron, depicting some large and gaudy flowers, enveloped her small frame. As I approached I detected a curiously pervasive smell of mothballs.

'Good morning.' I said cheerfully. 'You must be Mrs Osbaldiston.'

She looked up from the papers and maintained a blank expression. 'Are you Mr Camp?'

'No, I'm Gervase Phinn, the English inspector,' I replied.

'Oh, I was expecting Mr Camp, the art man.'

'It's Clamp, not Camp. He'll be along later.'

'Well,' she said, 'there's been telephone calls for you this morning. I arrived well before eight o'clock and that phone has never stopped. I thought I was here to clean, not answer calls. I've made a note of them on a pad in the office.'

'Right, I'll go and return the calls and leave you to it. Have you everything you need?' I should not have asked.

'Ee, what I need, young man, is a cup of strong sweet tea and a long sit-down, that's what I need.' The poor woman looked as if the troubles of the world had been heaped on her small rounded shoulders.

'There's nothing on this list what Connie left me about answering telephone calls or about any English courses here today. She never said you was to be in this morning, just that Mr Camp. I don't think I could cope with anything else, I really don't.'

'No, there isn't an English course on today,' I reassured her. 'I'm here to meet someone.'

'Connie's left this list of instructions as long as my arm,' Mrs Osbaldiston went on, with the expression of one suffering from chronic constipation. 'I just don't know where to begin, I really don't. I mean, I only said I'd do a bit of dusting and wiping and keep things tidy to help out, but my goodness just look what she's left me.' She prodded the papers. 'It'd take an army of cleaners to do this little lot. There's no question of my bending what with the legs, and I can't overexert myself what with my angina. Connie knows I'm allergic to bleach, and floor polish brings me out in a rash.'

'I really wouldn't worry, Mrs Osbaldiston,' I told her, 'Connie's a perfectionist.'

'Tell me about it,' she said. 'I lives next door to her. Inside her house is like Buckingham Palace and you should see her garden! The lawn's like a billiard table. There's not a flower out of place and she uses scissors on the Virginia creeper.' Mrs Osbaldiston looked distressed. 'Then there's this Mr Camp. Connie's warned me about him and his goings on. She said he wants watching.'

'Oh, he's not that bad.' I smiled and patted her arm. 'Don't worry, Mrs Osbaldiston. You make yourself that nice strong cup of tea.'

This proposal resulted in a remarkable transformation, as I had guessed it would. The old lady visibly mellowed and a small smile came to her thin lips. It is a known fact that in Yorkshire, whatever the problem, the prospect of a cup of tea seems to have a remarkably calming effect.

'By the way, have you put the water urn on yet?' I asked.

'No, I haven't.' She glanced at the papers in her hand. 'Oh dear, here it is, look, at the top of Connie's "to do" list. First thing she asks me to do and I gets it wrong.'

'Well, you put out the cups and saucers in the lounge area and I'll see to the water. Don't worry, Mrs Osbaldiston, everything will be fine.'

She left the kitchen, mumbling to herself, while I filled the huge metal urn with water, switched it on and headed for the office. On the desk was an indecipherable list of scrawled numbers: no name, no message, just the numbers. Come back, Connie, I said to myself. I was about to ring the first number, when the telltale click-clack of high heels on the hard corridor floor outside heralded the arrival of an unwelcome visitor.

'Good morning,' I heard Mrs Savage say, beyond the office door.

Then I heard the morose tones of Mrs Osbaldiston reply, 'Mornin'. You're early, aren't you?'

I was tempted to show myself at this point but resisted the temptation, deciding instead to eavesdrop. This was going to be interesting.

'I beg your pardon,' replied Mrs Savage curtly.

'I said you're early,' said Mrs O.

'No, I am not,' came the curt replay. 'In fact, I am prompt. I am always prompt. I said I would be here at eight fifteen and if I am not mistaken that is the exact time.'

'Well, I was told you'd be here at nine. I've got it on my list.'

'And who are you, may I ask?'

'Mrs Osbaldiston.'

'And what is your function here?'

'My function?'

'What exactly do you do?'

'What do I do?'

'Am I in an echo chamber?' asked Mrs Savage.

'For your information,' Mrs Osbaldiston informed her. 'I'm filling in for Connie, the caretaker. She's in France scattering her father's ashes at Dunkirk, and I'm holding the fort, so to speak. Doing a bit of cleaning and that.'

'I see.'

'Anyway, now you're here, do you want to see where you'll be? You're in the end room where it's warmer and more private. I've pulled the curtains as well. I'm sure you don't want people gawping at you through the window. I'll put a cushion on your chair before you start posing. Being sat on a hard chair for any length of time must be uncomfortable on the nether regions, specially if you have no clothes on.'

'No clothes on!' snapped Mrs Savage. 'What are you talking about?'

I nearly betrayed my presence with a burst of laughter, but smacked a hand over my mouth.

'Well, I was told you'd be taking your clothes off for Mr Camp,' continued Mrs Osbaldiston blithely.

'Taking my clothes off for Mr Camp!' repeated Mrs Savage. 'What *are* you talking about? Have I entered bedlam?'

'No, this is the Staff Development Centre,' replied Mrs Osbaldiston calmly.

'Do you know who I am?' asked Mrs Savage.

'The nude model, aren't you?'

'The *what?*' spluttered Mrs Savage. 'I am Mrs Savage, personal assistant to Dr Gore, the chief education officer.'

'Can't say I've heard of him,' replied the old lady.

At this point I emerged from the office, attempting to keep a straight face. 'Good morning, Mrs Savage,' I said seriously.

She was attired in a scarlet jacket with silver buttons, tight-fitting black skirt and high-heeled patent-leather shoes. I tried not to smirk.

'Mr Phinn,' said Mrs Savage, 'This . . . this person here, was under the misapprehension that I was some sort of . . . of model.'

'Really?' I said innocently.

'I told her it was the Staff Development Centre,' said Mrs Osbaldiston. 'I don't know where she wants to be. Anyway, you'll have to deal with her, Mr Flynn. I've got lots to do.' With that she waddled off, mumbling to herself.

The meeting with Mrs Savage was short but not very sweet. I agreed to nominate certain schools for the foreign inspectors to visit, prepare some briefing papers and devise a programme. Mrs Savage announced that she would organise the travel and accommodation.

'And do keep me up to speed, Mr Phinn,' she said in a hectoring tone, as she rose to leave. 'I will arrange a further mutually convenient meeting to tie up any loose ends just prior to their visit. And I shall be having a word with Dr Gore about nude models at the Staff Development Centre. I assume it is Mr Clamp who has organised this. The man gets worse.' I did not reply. 'I am afraid that particular colleague of yours sails very close to the wind at times. By the way, I sincerely hope that that Connie woman has cleared having time off. She can't just take leave when she wants to and it is up to the office to arrange replacements, not her. Personnel will be informed of this as soon as I get back to County Hall.' She stroked out the creases in her skirt. 'Now, I must return to the office,' she continued, as if I were deliberately detaining her. 'Dr Gore is finalising arrangements for the appointment of Dr Yeats's successor this morning.'

When Mrs Savage had departed, I bade my farewell to a harassed-looking Mrs O, and headed for the door. In the car park I discovered a woman climbing from an extremely old and rusty car. She could have been Mrs Osbaldiston's twin sister: tightly curled greying hair, small down-turned mouth and an amazingly wrinkled face.

'Excuse me,' she said, 'is this the Staff Department Centre? I'm here to see Mr Clamp. I'm the artists' model.'

St Helen's Church of England Primary School served the two villages of Kirby Crighton and Kirby Ruston and a few children from the nearby United States Air Force Base at Ribbon Bank. I had visited the school during my first year on just such a nippy day as this when the trees were beginning to turn golden.

Mrs Smith, the headteacher, greeted me at the door and ushered me into a small but welcoming entrance area. 'It's very nice to see you again, Mr Phinn. You'll find we've grown a bit since your last visit.'

I had given the school a very good report on the last occasion and this visit was to see if standards in English had remained high.

'A victim of your own success, eh, Mrs Smith?' I suggested.

'One would like to think so,' said the headteacher, clearly pleased with the flattering observation, 'but it is rather the result of more American children attending from the base.'

In the infant classroom, the headteacher introduced me to Imogen. She looked like a china doll: golden curls, huge blue eyes and a flawless complexion. The child was casually turning the pages of an early reader. Each page displayed an object: house, bus, man, dog, car and so on, beneath which was the word in large black letters. 'Will you read it to me, please?' she asked.

'Of course,' I replied.

When I had finished reading the book, I wrote the word 'car' on a piece of paper. 'Now,' I said, 'can you read this word for me?'

'No, I can't,' she replied.

'It begins with a curly "c". Would you like to have a guess?'

'No, I can't read it.'

'Let me give you a clue,' I said. 'Your daddy or mummy might drive you to school in it in the morning.'

'Oh yes!' she cried. 'You mean Wolls Woyce.'

The older children were in the middle of a discussion when I joined them after morning break. Their teacher, a round, jolly woman, in an orange skirt, white blouse and green cardigan, greeted me warmly and ushered me to a chair at the front of the classroom.

'Now, this is Mr Phinn,' she told the children. 'Some of you might remember him because he visited us before, didn't you, Mr Phinn.'

'Yes, I did,' I said.

'And Mr Phinn is very interested in children's reading and writing, aren't you, Mr Phinn.'

'Yes, I am,' I said.

'And today, Mr Phinn, we are writing a cautionary tale. We've been reading a story about children who did not do as they were told and as a result they all came to a sticky end.'

'Oh dear,' I said.

'There's the disobedient boy who did not listen to his father's warnings, played with fire, and ended up burnt to a crisp. It's not as gruesome as it sounds,' she said to me in an undertone. 'Nothing gratuitous.' She turned back to the class. 'And the girl who ignored her mother's cautions and played near the river bank. She came to a watery end. Then there was the boy who went near the railway line, ignoring all the signs that warned him of danger. That had a very unfortunate outcome. Now, before they write their own cautionary tales, Mr Phinn, the children are describing an accident they have had because they did not take sufficient care. Let me see. Katy, would you like to tell our important visitor what you are going to be writing about?'

'Miss,' said the girl enthusiastically, 'when I was little we went to a pizza parlour and I sniffed some pepper up my nose.'

There was a ripple of laughter. 'It's not funny, children,' said the teacher seriously. 'The pepper might have gone right down into Katy's lungs. It could have been very serious, couldn't it, Mr Phinn?'

'It could,' I agreed, wishing that the teacher would not constantly keep referring to me for an opinion.

'And I couldn't stop sneezing and coughing,' continued the child. 'My mum went bananas—'

'I think a better phrase to use would be "became very angry", Katy,' interrupted the teacher.

'She became very angry and said what a stupid thing to do. We had to go home and my dad said I would not do that in a hurry again.'

'I think your father was right, Katy,' said the teacher. 'One more, before we get on with our writing,' she said, turning to a large, friendly-looking boy with cropped hair and large ears. 'Scott's from America, Mr Phinn. All the way from Tennessee. Come along then, Scott, what was your accident?'

'Well, I guess the worst was when I was riding my bike along the sidewalk—'

'We call it "pavement" over here, Scott,' interrupted the teacher.

'Oh, yeah, pavement, and I came to this slope. I was pedalling so fast I could not stop. I put on my brakes but I carried on skidding until I hit one of those great white things in the middle of the road—'

'Bollards,' said the teacher.

'Straight up, miss,' said the boy. 'I really did.'

FIVE

One of the great joys of being a school inspector is the opportunity to meet so many interesting, unusual and sometimes truly bizarre people. And Maurice Hinderwell was certainly out of the ordinary.

I arrived at Scarthorpe Primary School one bright October morning to undertake a half-day's follow-up inspection. The small school was a squat, dark, stone building, tucked away behind an ancient Norman church and partially hidden by a towering oak tree. As I approached, I recalled the first occasion when I had driven up the same twisting ribbon of road. In the valley bottom, the rolling green pasture had been dotted with ewes and their lambs contentedly cropping the lush grass. Before me an ocean of bright green bracken had swept upwards to a belt of dark pines. Above, the sky had been a vast canopy of pale blue. It had taken my breath away. The scene was equally magnificent now in its autumnal beauty.

I had been driving behind a tractor for some time, and so arrived a little later than expected. The bell had just gone for the start of the school day so, not wishing to interrupt assembly, I headed for the staff room. There I discovered a small man in an incredibly creased grey suit, loud, spotted bow tie and shiny boots. He was balancing a cup of steaming coffee on the arm of his chair with one hand and holding a chocolate biscuit in the other.

'Nice morning,' he said jovially as I entered.

'Yes, indeed,' I replied. 'It's beautiful.'

To my amazement, the little man posted the whole of the chocolate biscuit into his mouth and crunched noisily. Clearly he was not a member of staff or he would have been at assembly. I decided he was a book representative or, more likely, here to see about the plumbing or electrics.

'I'm here to inspect the school,' I told him. 'I'm a school inspector.'

'Oh, yes?' he said, spitting bits of biscuit in my direction. I sat in the chair the furthest away from him. He made no effort to introduce himself. 'I wouldn't like that job myself,' he told me, poking a bit of biscuit from his teeth. 'Too much like hard work. And I don't suppose you're very popular either. Having you in must be like a visit from the KGB.' He took a great gulp of coffee and smacked his lips noisily. 'No, it can't be the most rewarding line of work, school inspecting.' Before I could enlighten him, he continued, 'Most important thing for me is job satisfaction, not money or fancy perks. It's knowing that you're doing something worth while. I love my work. I get up every morning raring to go.'

I just had to ask: 'And what exactly do you do?'

'I'm the county pest control officer.'

'Indeed. I see.'

'I deal with pests. Cockroaches, bed bugs, rabbits, moles, bats, wasps, ants, beetles, fleas, every pest imaginable. You name it, I kill it. You'll be pleased to hear we don't include human pests like VAT officers, traffic wardens, tax investigators and'—he paused for effect—'school inspectors are not on the list either.' He chuckled.

'So the school has a problem with pests, has it?' I asked.

'Rats. They've got rats. Quite a colony, by all accounts. Got a call last week from Mrs Fox, the headteacher. Now there's a name to conjure with. I do foxes as well, you know. Anyway, she'd got her knickers in a real twist. Teachers were in a panic, dinner ladies hysterical, caretaker a nervous wreck and parents up in arms. Rats have this effect on people, you know. Kiddies weren't worried, to be honest. Quite took to the rats they did, watching their antics. They were running up and down the climbing frame and burrowing behind the bicycle sheds. The rats, I mean, not the kiddies.'

'It sounds frightful,' I said. I must have looked horrified.

'No, no, as I said to Mrs Fox, I'll soon have the little buggers, pardon my French. Mind you, some of them aren't so little. They can grow to the size of small rabbits, you know. But I'll get them, oh yes, I'll get them.' He took another gulp of coffee before adding philosophically. 'I always do.'

'Well, good luck,' I said.

'It's not a matter of luck,' my sharp-faced companion informed me. 'It's more a matter of skill, intuition and know-how. You have to appreciate how rats think, you see.' He licked his lips. With his dark, inquisitive eyes, small pointed nose, protuberant white teeth and glossy black hair bristling on his scalp, he did not look so dissimilar to the creatures he had come to exterminate. 'I think of all the pests I have to deal with, the rat is my favourite. He's a much greater challenge than you're average cockroach or bed bug.'

'Really?'

'Aye, it's a fact. Intelligent creatures are rats, but they're walking death traps too. One in ten rats carries *Leptospira,* which can lead to a whole host of very unpleasant diseases, you know. One of the varieties of leptospirosis is called Weil's disease. Very unpleasant that. Very unpleasant indeed. It's contracted through rats' urine, often found in contaminated water, and is fatal more often than not. They urinate eighty times a day, do rats. Did you know that?'

'No, I didn't,' I replied weakly.

'And one in ten rats carries *Listeria* and *Cryptosporidium*, both of which can cause very nasty gastroenteritis. Of course, humans are very susceptible and rats' urine and faeces get everywhere. They like to live near kitchens where there's lots of cooked food and waste. I don't eat out much myself. I say, is there another chocolate digestive going?'

I was beginning to feel quite ill.

'One in twenty-five rats has the Hantavirus antibody,' continued my companion blithely, 'which can lead to haemorrhagic fever. That's a killer. Once you've got that, mate, you're dancing with death.'

I quickly picked up the packet of biscuits that lay on the table and passed it to him. 'It's fortunate then,' I said, 'that there aren't so many rats about.'

'Not so many about!' he squeaked derisively. 'Not so many about! There's seventy million in this country alone, that's how many. There are more rats than humans on this planet, over six billion of the buggers, pardon my French. Rats have sex twenty times a day and can give birth every four weeks. One in twenty domestic premises are infested with rats and that's a conservative estimate, so I'm kept pretty busy, I can tell you. You think there aren't so many because you don't see them. But they're there all right. Watching, waiting, breeding. You're never more than fifteen feet away from a rat. You see, your rat is very clever, quick-witted and adaptable. Rats' teeth are harder than aluminium or copper. They can gnaw through cables, climb brickwork, get into cavity walls and swim up toilet U-bends. You could be sitting there, reading your paper, minding your own business, if you'll excuse the pun, and up he pops.'

I shifted uncomfortably in my chair. 'How will you dispose of the rats?'

'Traps and poison, simple but effective. You know, I have a certain respect for *Rattus*. He's quite amazing. Body like a coiled spring, calibrated senses, razor-sharp incisors, superb night vision, fast mover, brilliant swimmer and agile climber. I almost admire him in a funny sort of way.'

Thankfully, the bell for the end of assembly sounded. My companion rose to his feet, brushing the crumbs from his trousers. 'Well,

I shall have to make a start, I suppose. Nice meeting you, and if ever you do need anything disposing of and I don't include your mother-in-law in that list, then phone Maurice Hinderwell at the County Pest Control Unit in Crompton. Service with a smile, that's me.'

THE MRS FOX I REMEMBERED from my last visit was a large, cheerful woman with a foghorn voice. On this morning, however, she was very different. She appeared so careworn and subdued that I suggested to her that I cancel my visit and return at a later date when the problem with the rats had been resolved.

She readily agreed to my suggestion. 'Oh, yes, that would suit very well, Mr Phinn,' she said. 'Was it not Hamlet who said that "troubles come not in single spies, but in battalions"?' I knew exactly how she felt. 'First we had the blocked drains, then the leaking roof, then an outbreak of scabies. And then'—she took a deep breath—'the rats arrived. Parents are beginning to think this school is cursed. A school inspection would just about finish us off.'

'I'm very happy to fix another date, Mrs Fox,' I told her. 'I have plenty of paperwork to catch up with back at the office.'

'It's ironic, really,' she sighed. 'We were about to start rehearsals for the Christmas play next week. Well, that will have to be cancelled. There's no way I'm staging that particular piece of drama.'

'What was it to have been?' I asked.

'*The Pied Piper*,' she replied, giving me a weak smile.

I ARRIVED HOME later that evening, after a particularly tiresome governors' meeting, tired, hungry and not in the best of moods. I found Christine sitting at the kitchen table.

Before I could even say hello she flourished a copy of the *Fettlesham Gazette* and asked, 'Have you seen this?'

'No,' I replied taking off my coat and throwing my briefcase on the table. 'I need a whisky.'

'They're closing the village school.'

I took a deep breath, poured myself a generous measure of whisky, took a gulp and replied, 'Yes, I know.'

'You know?' she gasped.

'Yes.'

'How long have you known?'

'About a week,' I told her, taking a sip from the glass.

'Why didn't you say anything?'

'You know I can't discuss office matters at home.'

'Even when it affects us so personally?'

'Look, Chris,' I sighed, 'I didn't say anything because, well, it was said to me in confidence and, anyway, I knew how you would react. I felt exactly the same when Harold dropped the bombshell but, as he explained, there have got to be savings in the education budget next year and Hawksrill is one of the county's most uneconomic schools and—'

'I don't believe I'm hearing such claptrap!' I had never seen her quite so angry. 'Hell's teeth! All you government people can think of are your costs. Saving redundancy here, killing off jobs there. What about the children? How can you just sit back and let them close the school? The school *our* child would go to?'

'If I could wave a magic wand and keep the school open, I would,' I said, draining the glass, 'but the decision has been made.'

'That's a defeatist attitude if ever I heard one,' Christine said angrily. 'Well, I do not intend to let a bunch of miserable councillors and petty officials at County Hall close the school without a fight.' She thumped the kitchen table so hard my glass fell over. 'There are such things as protests, demonstrations, sit-ins and pressure groups.'

'I can't be part of any pressure group,' I told her, 'because I'm an officer of the County.'

'Even if your child's future is at stake?'

'That's not very fair, Christine. If there was anything I could do—'

'Well, there's no point in discussing it any further. There's the remains of a cottage pie in the oven. I'm going to bed.'

'Christine,' I sighed, 'can't we talk about this?'

'There's nothing to talk about. By the way, Harry Cotton called earlier.' Harry was our nearest neighbour and could be a real pain in the neck. 'He says we've got rats at the back of the house. He's seen them running along the fence. Good night.'

THE FOLLOWING SATURDAY morning found me at the Staff Development Centre where I could hear Connie clunking and clanking behind the hatch in the kitchen. The volume was such that I knew she was not in the best of tempers. I took a deep breath, popped my head charily around the door and said, 'Good morning, Connie.'

'Oh, it's you,' she replied, looking up glumly. 'Why are *you* here today? It's Saturday. I thought I had the place to myself for once.'

'I wanted to sort out the room for next week's course,' I told her, 'while the place is quiet. Anyway, you're a one to talk. What are you doing here? You should be in your caravan at Mablethorpe.'

'You're right. You wouldn't get me in here on a weekend normally but you should have seen the state of this building when I came in yesterday. Three days away and it's like a tip. These cups and saucers couldn't have seen a drop of hot water. And the state of my floors and toilets! She was less than useless, Mrs Osbaldiston. I should never have asked her to fill in for me.'

I quickly changed the subject. 'How was France?'

She glared at me. 'Don't ask.'

'Oh dear,' I said. 'Not too good then.'

'Not too good?' she repeated. 'It was a nightmare from beginning to end.' She withdrew her hands from the soapsuds and wiped them vigorously on a towel. 'We got on the ferry at Dover and the sea started to heave. Up and down, up and down, like a roller coaster. I thought I was going to die. When we finally arrived in Calais, you would not believe what happened. I was intercepted, that's what. Intercepted by this little French customs official. Ignoranus he was. Out of all the people going through, he picks on me. I mean, I ask you, do I look like a terrorist? Rootles through my bag, he does, probing and prying, laying everything out without a by-your-leave. All my personal accoutrements exposed to the world. "And what's this?" he asks me, holding up the urn. "That is my father," I told him. ''Course he didn't understand, did he? Well, they don't these foreigners. He takes the lid off, pokes his big nose in and starts to sniff. "Kindly stop," I tells him, "he's not that pope puree stuff." "I shall have to take a sample," he says. "Over my dead body," I tells him. At this point a nice old priest comes to my assistance and starts jabbering on in the lingo to the horrible little man in the uniform. "He thinks it might be an illegal substance," he tells me at last. "That's no illegal substance," I says, "it's my father and kindly ask him to stop interfering with him." "He wants to take a specimen," says the priest, and I says, "Tell him that if he so much as lays a finger on my father, I'll be across that counter. And tell him if it wasn't for the likes of men like my father defending *his* country from the Nazis, Adolf's lot would be goose-stepping up and down Calais, instead of him."'

'Oh dear,' I sighed.

'I don't think the priest told him that though.'

'I guess not,' I murmured. 'So what happened?' I asked.

'He just sort of smiled, did the priest. Anyroad, he gets my father off of the Frenchman. They're very persuasive are clerics, aren't they? He blesses my father, which was very nice of him, and me and Ted go on our way and not before time.'

'So you managed to scatter your father's ashes after all,' I said.

'No, I didn't. I was so hot and flushed after that run-in with the customs man, and so loaded down with duty free and I don't know what else, I only dropped the urn, didn't I?'

'Oh, no, Connie!' I gasped.

'Just slipped clean out of my hands on the seafront, smashed to smithereens before my eyes and Dad was blown out to sea.'

'Well, if it's any consolation,' I told her, 'there are many people who ask for their ashes to be scattered on the sea, carried forever in the currents of time.'

'Well, it *isn't* any consolation. I didn't want Dad flushed out to sea on the currents of time. He hated water, couldn't swim and was sick on the boating lake at Scarborough. And what do I come back to? Scuffs on my floor, chips out of my plates, dust on my shelves. I could have wept. She was about as much use as a chocolate teapot, Mrs Osbaldiston.'

'Well, she is getting on a bit, Connie,' I told her, 'and she does have a lot of ailments.'

'The only ailment Mrs Osbaldiston has is a dose of idleitis.'

'Well, you can have a rest tomorrow,' I replied.

THAT AFTERNOON I decided to tackle the garden at the back of the cottage. Harry Cotton had already been across to offer his usual unsolicited advice, this time on the pruning that needed to be done, how I might improve the weed-infested lawn, and other horticultural suggestions. The subject of rats, of course, had arisen in the course of our conversation.

'Must have been about four or five of 'em runnin' along that fence o' yourn as large as life. Big as babby badgers they were,' he had told me, almost gleefully. 'There's nowt I don't know abaat rats. Tha wants a dog or a couple o' cats. They'll sort your problem out. Take my Buster, for example. Border terrier she is, and as tough as owld boots. I was only talkin' to George Hemmings a week back and 'e says 'is Patterdale bitch is ready to whelp. I could get you one o' those pups, if tha likes. Can't beat a terrier. My Buster's a rare little ratter.'

Harry had banged his stick on the ground as though knocking a rat on the head. He was an old man with a shock of white hair and a wide-boned face the colour and texture of an unscrubbed potato.

'Well, I don't think Christine would be all that keen, Harry, but I'll think about it,' I had told him. 'Mr Hinderwell, the pest control officer, is coming out to have a look. I'll see what he says.'

'Suit yourself,' Harry had said. 'But I'll tell thee this. He can put all t'traps and poison down in t'world but they'll be back. Mark my words, they'll be back. Tha wants a dog or a couple of cats, tha's what tha wants. Well, I'll get on,' he said and ambled off to give someone else the benefit of his uncalled-for advice and words of wisdom.

Maurice Hinderwell, when he came, was very helpful but agreed with Harry that the rats would return, without a shadow of doubt.

You have to destroy their habitat,' he had advised, nodding sagely. 'Take that derelict building you've got at the bottom of your garden. That's where they'll likely be, out of sight, breeding and spreading disease. There'll be nests of them in there, where it's dry and dark. My advice to you is knock it down and lawn it over. Then your rats will move somewhere else. That old building takes up half your garden anyway and it's an eyesore.'

So, the next Saturday afternoon I made a start on demolishing the old building. One wall had completely collapsed, the exposed beams were rotten and little remained of the grey slate roof. Soon all that remained of it was a pile of rubble. I was surveying my handiwork when Christine appeared with a mug of tea.

'For the worker,' she said. 'My goodness, it's all gone. The garden looks a lot bigger, doesn't it?'

'I have an idea,' I told her. 'I thought we might have a wall across the back. Remember last year when those two sheep got through the fence and into the garden? You certainly weren't too pleased with what they did to your plants. Well, I thought a dry-stone wall with flowering shrubs and creepers against it would be ideal there.'

'Good idea,' she said. 'Now, I'm off to the school action group meeting. I'll see you later.'

We had been assiduously avoiding the subject of the school closure thus far, but she had spent most of the morning on the telephone so I wasn't surprised about the meeting.

It was that evening that my knee began to hurt. One of the rotten beams from the old building had suddenly fallen and, in an attempt to avoid it crashing down on top me, I had leapt smartly to the side and fallen heavily, cracking my knee in the process. Later that evening the knee had swollen to the size of a pomegranate.

Examining it when she got home, Christine said, 'It looks dreadful. You had better see the doctor about that.'

'I had worse bangs than that when I played rugby. It's not nearly as bad as it looks.'

Would that that had been the case.

BY THE FOLLOWING SUNDAY, the small garden at the back of Peewit Cottage was transformed. Tom Fields, the local dry-stone waller, had built a magnificent new wall. Straight and solid, it looked as if it had been there for centuries. I had pruned the trees and shrubs, dug up the weeds and turned over the soil where the derelict building had been. I would sew grass seed there next year.

I heard the garden gate click and a moment later Harry Cotton appeared, accompanied by his bristly little dog.

'Hello, Harry,' I said. 'Have you had a nice time away?'

Harry had told me he was going to spend a few days at his sister's and had asked me to keep a neighbourly eye on his cottage.

'Aye. It were reight enough wi' our Bertha, but it's allus better in yer own 'ome, in't it? She dunt shurrup, that's 'er trouble and there's nowt she dunt know abaat.' Two peas in a pod, I thought to myself, smiling. 'She 'as a view on everything, our Bertha and it's all nowt abaat owt. It's like 'avin a conversation wi' a bloody Gatling gun.' Harry poked into some shrubs with his gnarled walking stick. 'Got rid o' your rats then, 'ave you?' he asked, regarding me balefully.

'Yes, I think so,' I replied. 'Maurice Hinderwell caught about six in his traps and has put some poison down, so keep Buster well away. I should think that that will be the last of them. He reckoned that they were breeding underneath the old outbuilding.'

'Oh, aye,' said Harry, approaching my new dry-stone wall which he patted as he might a pet animal. 'Nice bit of work this. Very nice.' His terrier nosed along the base of the wall. 'I reckon she can smell a rat. Got a nose for 'em.'

'I doubt it very much, Harry,' I said.

'Aye, well, we'll see,' he said, as ever the prophet of doom. 'Who did t'wall for thee?' he asked.

'Tom Fields.'

'Oh, well, 'is family's been building dry-stone walls since time o' Vikings. I thought it were one of 'is.'

'He's made a splendid job of it.'

Harry remained staring at the wall for a good long time before saying, 'I'm surprised they let you pull that owld chapel down, tha knaas.'

'What old chapel?' I asked.

'That what were int'corner o' your plot.'

'You mean the old outhouse?'

'Nay, it were no outhouse. It were t'owld Wesleyan chapel. Built seventeen 'undred and summat. One o'oldest chapels in t'country.

Did nob'dy tell thee?' Harry said, rubbing the whiskers on his chin.

'No, they didn't,' I said in a shocked whisper. 'This is terrible.'

'Aye, it is,' agreed Harry. 'Probably got some sort of preservation order on it. Could 'ave been a listed building, tha knaas.'

'I don't believe it. I just don't believe it. It was derelict,' I said feebly.

'Old Mrs Olleranshaw, who 'ad cottage afoor thee, was very big in t'chapel and asked minister to come out and conduct a special service. They do say that Wesley himself preached 'ere and that—'

'Please, Harry,' I pleaded, 'don't go on.'

'I reckon you'll be having a visit from George Hemmings. He's on t'Parish Council, tha knaas, and is very keen on preservation. Then I expect 'istorical people from York will be up to see thee. I shouldn't be at all surprised if tha were prosecuted and fined.'

'Harry!' I snapped.

'I won't say another word,' he said, 'but I reckon tha'll be even more unpopular in t'village when they 'ears abaat this. They'll be thinking that tha wants t'school closed so tha can knock it down to use t'bricks for an extension to t'cottage.'

SIX

The first visit of the following week was to Manston Church of England Parochial School, a quaint, two-storey stone building which nestled in a small village on the extensive estate of Lord Marrick, Valentine Courtnay-Cunninghame, 9th Earl Marrick, a delightfully cheerful, bombastic and somewhat eccentric peer who loved the Dales as passionately as any farmer.

As I sat in the corner of the classroom, making a few preliminary notes on the display of work, I became conscious of a small boy, aged about seven or eight, observing me. I could feel his eyes taking in every detail of my appearance. Eventually he approached me.

'May I ask you what you are doing?' he enquired.

'I'm writing about your school,' I replied, looking up and smiling. 'I'm a school inspector.'

'Yes, I know. Our teacher told us you would be visiting us today and that you would be looking at our books and listening to us read. I'm Benedict,' he went on, holding out a small hand, which I shook.

'Well, Benedict, shouldn't you be getting on with your work?'

'I've done it. When we've finished our writing, we're allowed to select a book from the reading corner. I was on my way there when I thought I'd stop and say hello.'

His manner was amusingly old-fashioned for one so young.

'Well, that's very nice of you, Benedict,' I said.

'Mrs McGuire, she's our teacher, but you probably know that already, well, Mrs McGuire says there are much better words to use in our stories than "nice".'

'I'm sure she's right,' I said, chuckling. 'I'll try to remember in future.'

'Do you like stories, Mr Phinn?'

'I do,' I replied.

'Would you like to see some of mine?'

'Perhaps later,' I told him. 'I'm a little busy at the moment.'

'Righto, I'll get along then and choose a book.' He thought for a moment and then said, 'Do you know, Mr Phinn, we've had a very interesting conversation, haven't we?'

'We have, Benedict,' I replied, 'indeed we have.'

He patted me gently on the arm. 'We must do lunch sometime.'

WHEN I GOT BACK to the office that afternoon I went in search of old Perkins, or Jasper Perkins, to be correct, in the architects' department. David had told me he was 'big on ruins', a Fellow of the Royal Historical Society, and could put my mind at rest about the chapel. I found him poring over a large map in an office tucked away at the rear of County Hall, explained about the chapel and waited in trepidation for his considered opinion.

He chuckled. 'I think you've got friends with very vivid imaginations, or ones that enjoy a little ruse, Mr Phinn. Speaking as a lay preacher of some thirty years, I know of no Methodist chapel on your property. As for the Reverend Jessop, the minister, conducting some sort of service up where you live, I think it extremely unlikely. Now, speaking as an architect, you would have been made fully aware when you purchased the property if there was a listed building or a site of particular historical interest. I think you can rest assured that you won't be locked up for the desecration of a church.'

'Thank you so much, Mr Perkins,' I said, shaking his hand vigorously. 'You don't know what a weight you have lifted off my shoulders.'

There would have been a veritable spring in my step as I made my way down the top corridor of County Hall that afternoon had it not been for the swollen knee which was still extraordinarily painful. I determined to make an appointment with the doctor just as soon as I got back to the office.

I stopped in my tracks, however, when I turned a corner to find a group of councillors huddled round a loud gesticulating individual in a baggy tweed suit. Although he had his back to me, I recognised the bull neck, the mop of jet-black hair and the bombastic voice instantly. It was Councillor George Peterson, who always managed to make my hackles rise with his clever comments and tasteless observations. In a determined effort to avoid him I continued down the corridor, limping and looking down as if I were preoccupied. I sailed past the cabal and thought that I had not been seen, but as I reached the top of a long curved staircase, a voice echoed down the corridor. 'Hey! Hey! Mr Phinn. Not tryin' to avoid me, are you?'

I turned round and gave a watery smile. 'Councillor Peterson.'

'You were goin' at a fair lick. I'll walk across to t'inspectors' office wi' you. I've got a meetin' with Dr Yeats.' He said farewell to his fellow councillors, before striding towards me. 'This is a right carry-on about these school closures, in't it?' he said as we descended the stairs together. 'We've just 'ad an hextrahordinary meeting of the subcommittee about them. It's a right can of worms and no mistake.' He puffed out his cheeks and grimaced theatrically.

'Feelings are running very high,' I remarked.

'Too right, they are, and I'll tell you which school is t'fly in t'ointment. It's Hawksrill. Everybody bar the cat and its mother is gettin' in its two-pennyworth and it's turning very nasty. We've 'ad letters of protest, pictures in t'paper of people wi' placards. That chairman of governors, Reverend Braybrook, has put it on t'agenda of t'full Education Committee and when *'e* gets started there's no stoppin' 'im. We've 'ad t'local member of Parliament writin' me notes and Lord Marrick grumbling at me down t'phone, and next week, blow me, if one of these HMIs isn't comin' up from London to see me about it—woman with a funny name and a very sharp manner.'

'Miss de la Mare?'

'Aye, that's 'er. Anyroad, I don't suppose I should be tellin' you all this.' We stopped at the bottom of the stairs. 'Because it might get back to t'opposition. Meanin' that wife of yours and 'er protest group.'

My hackles began to rise but I kept calm and looked him in the eye. 'I can assure you, Councillor Peterson, I have not discussed the situation with my wife or anyone else, for that matter. Like you, I keep County Council business to myself.'

'That's as may be, but that wife of yours gave me a real grillin' at t'public meetin' and you don't even 'ave kiddies at t'school. What your wife and these protestors don't seem to realise is that we 'ave to cut costs. I don't want to close a school any more than you do, but we 'ave to save money somehow and that's t'top and bottom of it. You should per'aps 'ave a quiet word with your wife and tell 'er to go easy.'

'Councillor, gone are the days when a husband tells his wife what to do.'

'I am sure you realise, Mr Phinn, that should she keep up this pressure, it could make it tricky for you. If you were to get Dr Yeats's job, you'll be t'one that 'as to deal wi' t'closures. 'As that crossed your mind?'

'Yes, it has,' I replied.

'I mean, you can't be on t'side of the angels and drink wi' t'devil and it's not goin' to do much for marital harmony, is it?'

'That situation will not arise,' I assured him. 'You see, I don't intend applying for Dr Yeats's job. Good afternoon, Councillor.'

With that I limped off towards the car park.

'WELL, I THINK it's very strange, very strange indeed,' said Sidney, twisting a large paper clip out of shape, 'I cannot recall any other occasion when this has happened.'

It was Friday afternoon and Harold had called a meeting for all the team at the Staff Development Centre to consider a new initiative from the Ministry of Education. Discussion, however, centred on the appointment of the new senior inspector.

'I must admit,' agreed David, 'I think it is highly unusual for an appointment to be made and for us not to be told who it is.'

'The appointment has *not* been made,' said Harold. 'The position has been *offered* but the person involved has asked for time to think about it and to consult their present employer.'

'Well, he shouldn't have applied for the post in the first place, if he wasn't sure that he wanted it,' said Sidney, leaning back on his chair.

'It's far more complicated than that,' said Harold. 'There are one or two things to be clarified and certain conditions to be agreed by the Education Committee before the person in question is prepared to take up the post.'

'You aren't the mystery candidate are you, Geraldine?' asked David, peering over the top of his spectacles.

Gerry threw her head back and laughed. 'No! I think I have quite enough to do at the moment without taking on Harold's job.'

'And don't start looking at me,' I said. 'I've told you, I didn't apply.'

'Well, I sincerely hope they make a better job of it than the last time,' said David. 'That Simon Carter was a complete disaster.'

'Hear, hear,' said Sidney.

'Look!' said Harold, consulting his watch. 'We really must press on. You will know who it is after Christmas. Now, can we address the task in hand? The new initiative is called "Spirituality in the Curriculum".'

'Oh, glory be,' sighed Sidney, tilting the chair back even further. 'Where do they dream these things up from? I'm sure there are better things to occupy our time than this, Harold.'

'Like it or not, Sidney,' Harold replied, 'we are obliged to consider this new directive when we inspect schools as from the first of January. It is statutory. And it has a relevance to all aspects of the curriculum, including art and design. So, if you would bear with me?'

'And when is *she* coming?' asked Sidney, who had now taken to twisting an elastic band around his fingers.

'I have asked Miss de la Mare'—Harold glanced at his watch again—'to join our discussions when she has finished a meeting with Councillor Peterson at County Hall.'

'That will be about Hawksrill,' said Sidney.

'Well, if she's closeted with George "Gasbag" Peterson we could be here all night,' moaned David.

There was an impatient intake of breath from the senior inspector. 'All the more reason to make a start,' he said. 'So, before her arrival, colleagues, I really would like to get to grips with the document, which I hope everyone has read. Miss de la Mare will then clarify anything we are unsure about.'

My first encounter with the formidable Winifred de la Mare, Her Majesty's principal divisional inspector of schools, had been a few months after I had first been appointed as a school inspector. Dr Gore had asked me to coordinate the visit of the Minister of Education to the county and liaise with the HMI responsible, Miss de la Mare. Prior to meeting her, I had imagined a strapping great woman in heavy tweeds, with savagely cropped, steel-grey hair and glittery eyes. She would be entirely humourless and exceptionally critical; the sort of person to put the fear of God into anyone. In the event, Miss de la Mare turned out to be the very opposite.

'I'm sorry, Harold,' said Sidney now, 'but I really do feel I have quite enough on my plate without taking on yet another cock-eyed project from London, involving another mountain of paperwork.'

'Look,' said Harold impatiently, 'I am not an apologist for this initiative. I did not devise it and I, like all of you, have quite enough on my own plate without yet more work. But we shall be implementing it, and that is an end to the matter.'

The Ministry of Education had asked inspectors to consider, on their visits, each school's strengths and weaknesses in its provision of spiritual development in different subjects; to evaluate how each subject area provided children with an understanding of moral values and developed their spiritual awareness.

'It says here,' Harold said, 'that, "Effective spiritual development enables young people to appreciate, through their own thoughts and emotions, something of their own life and that of others. It enables them to cope with their anxieties and fear, encourages them to appreciate a diversity of cultures, religions and beliefs, and to know the difference between right and wrong."'

'But surely this is the province of religious education,' said Sidney. 'I can't see it has any relevance to art and design or, for that matter, to mathematics, science, music or English?'

'Would you not say, Sidney,' said Geraldine who, up to this point, had been characteristically silent, 'that there is more to art and design than just getting children to draw, paint and construct? Doesn't art also involve reflection, imagination, feeling, creativity, sensitivity? Don't you want young people to *appreciate* painting and sculpture and architecture on a spiritual level?'

'Well,' conceded Sidney, 'I suppose there is some art that touches the soul, moves one to a sort of awe and wonder, and I would hope that youngsters come to understand and appreciate this.'

'Well, it's the same in science,' continued Gerry. 'A scientist uses his or her brain to see cause and effect, follow a series of logical steps, reason and infer and then reach a conclusion. There is no moral question in that, no right or wrong. It is merely a scientific process. But there is an ethical responsibility. To what use do we put all these advances in science? Do we use our knowledge of fertility to help a desperate couple have a baby or to produce clones? That is where spirituality comes in. It helps us to decide. It has more to do with the heart than the brain. It's about right and wrong, about feelings, and that is why it is important to foster it in education.'

'My, my,' said Sidney, clapping his hands together silently. 'I'm impressed, Geraldine. That was a bravura performance.'

'May I join you?' We all swivelled round in our chairs to see a plump, cheerful-looking woman with neatly bobbed silver hair. She was dressed in a coat as red as a pillar-box, which was edged with a black fur collar and cuffs, and she sported a bright yellow scarf.

The remainder of the afternoon was spent in lively discussion with the HMI, who clearly and eloquently explained the new initiative.

'Education,' she said, 'is not about filling heads with a few arid facts. And while it's certainly about encouraging young people to have lively, enquiring minds and the ability to question and argue, it is also about fostering their sensitivity and emotions.'

And with that point we could not disagree.

'YOU'VE CERTAINLY changed your tune, Sidney,' I remarked over my cup of tea and one of Connie's garibaldi biscuits. Sidney, David and I were having a break in the staff room; Harold and Gerry were still in deep conversation with Miss de la Mare.

'Well,' replied my colleague, stirring his tea vigorously, 'I'm nothing if not open-minded.'

'Huh,' responded David. 'The danger of being open-minded, Sidney, is that your brains might fall out.'

'I am, at heart, a very flexible thinker,' continued Sidney, undaunted. 'If an argument is put simply, effectively and convincingly, as I feel it was this morning, I will willingly consider it. And I do have to concede that there may very well be something in this spirituality thing. It's just all the paperwork that I do so abhor. I must say,' he went on, pausing to take a great gulp of tea, 'our pale Irish beauty continues to be a bit of a dark horse, doesn't she? She sits there for ages without a word, but when she gets started there's no stopping her. I've never seen her so animated.'

'She was very impressive,' I agreed.

'Do you think she was *trying* to impress?' asked David.

'I just wonder whether she did put in for Harold's job,' said Sidney.

'You may very well be right,' said David. 'She didn't sound all that convincing to me when she denied that she had applied. And why is she with Harold and that HMI now? Why are they closeted together and what are they talking about? I think she may very well be our next senior inspector. Everything is pointing to it.'

'You might be sorry you did not put in for Harold's job, old chap,' said Sydney. 'I agree. I think Geraldine might well be our new boss.'

'She's welcome to it,' I said.

'Geraldine wouldn't be all that bad,' said David.

'No,' agreed Sidney. 'I could live with it.'

'My, my,' I said, 'this must be a record. You two agreeing for more than an hour.'

Further discussion was curtailed by Connie entering in her pink overall and holding a clipboard like a game-show host. 'Good afternoon,' she said, casting a critical glance round the room to make sure everything was as it should be.

'Good afternoon, Connie,' we chorused.

'I've been doing my monthly stock check and things have gone missing.' She consulted her clipboard. 'Have any of you seen my pair of steps, the small wooden ones which I keep in the store room? They've gone walkabout again.'

'No, Connie,' we chorused.

'Well, somebody's got them. They haven't got legs. I need them next week when they're coming from the Parks Department to cut back that ivy what's creeping all over the place. Are you sure you haven't had them, Mr Clamp, for when you do your mounting?'

Sidney arched an eyebrow. 'I have not, Connie, and if I had borrowed your steps, I should have made sure they were put back. Have you asked Dr Mullarkey?' asked Sidney.

'She wouldn't have them,' said Connie. 'She's the only one of you who puts everything back and leaves the room as she finds it.'

'Another fan,' murmured Sidney.

'It's a mystery to me where they've gone,' moaned Connie. 'Well, if they're not back next week, steps will be taken.'

'I thought that they already had been, Connie,' remarked Sidney, keeping a deadpan expression.

'What?' she snapped. 'It's no laughing matter, Mr Clamp. You'll soon be complaining if the top surfaces are dirty because I can't reach to do my dusting.'

And with that she departed, clipboard under her arm.

SEVEN

The North Yorkshire scenery was at its best on the bright December morning when I visited St Margaret's Church of England Primary School in the picturesque village of Hutton-with-Branston. I was a little early, so I drove at a leisurely rate along twisting narrow roads bordered by black hawthorn hedges or walls of stone, marvelling at the views that stretched around me.

The discrete, grey-stone building with its red-tiled roof stood adjacent to the old church and faced the village green. The chairman of governors, the Reverend Featherstone, who I had arranged to interview, was a dour-looking individual with grey wispy hair and heavy-lidded eyes.

'I'm afraid we live in a secular society, Mr Phinn,' he told me, 'a world of fast food, television and fancy holidays. There's precious little spirituality these days. My Sunday School teacher read the story of David and Goliath last week and asked the children who beat the Philistines. One child replied that he didn't know because he didn't follow the minor leagues.' The cleric shook his head wearily. 'I've had children tell me about Moses going up Mount Cyanide to receive the Ten Commandments, and Solomon with his three hundred wives and seven hundred porcupines. Do you find this lack of biblical awareness on your travels, Mr Phinn?'

'I'm afraid so,' I told him. 'Scripture isn't taught a great deal in schools these days, unless of course it's a church school.'

'Well, this is church school,' he reminded me. 'Yet I cannot say that the children here are any more acquainted with the Bible than in any other school. I've come across children being christened Jezebel and Salome and Delilah,' bemoaned the vicar. 'It's very difficult trying to explain to the parents who these women were and what their line of work was.' He chuckled. 'But then one child very nearly went through life with the exotic name of Onacardie. I asked the parents at the christening: "What do you name this child?" The mother replied loudly, "Onacardie." I had just begun sprinkling the water over the baby's head and intoning: "I christen this child Onacardie," when I was interrupted by the irate mother. "No, no, vicar!" she hissed. "On 'er cardy. The name's written on 'er cardigan. We want her to be called Siobhan."'

I was reminded all too forcefully of the discussion about children's lack of biblical knowledge when I visited Holmdale Junior and Infant School, later that week. It was situated deep in a secluded dale in the heart of the North York Moors, and was surrounded on all sides by rugged moorland. When I arrived, the local Baptist minister, an evangelical young man wearing a T-shirt, was retelling the parable of The Lost Sheep. He started well. The great majority of his audience came from farming families so at the mention of sheep all ears pricked up.

'When Jesus was alive,' he told them, 'sheep were very important.'

'They still are,' said one rosy-cheeked girl, sitting at the front.

'Yes, indeed,' continued the minister. 'And in those days, sheep provided meat, milk and cheese. But pasture was poor on the hills—'

'Not too good up here, either,' said the girl.

'No,' agreed the minister. 'So the shepherd had to move his flock from place to place to find grass for his sheep. Unlike today, the shepherd of Jesus' day did not drive his flock in front of him but led it, and he knew each of his sheep personally and they answered to his call.'

There were several sceptical looks at this point. 'How many would he have in his flock, then?' asked a boy with a shock of red hair.

'Well, in the parable I'm going to tell you in a minute, the shepherd has a hundred sheep,' replied the minister.

'He's not likely to know an 'undred sheep personally,' observed the boy. 'Cows, mebbe, but not sheep.'

'Well, I . . . he probably would have known his sheep very well.'

'But not an 'undred!'

'Let's make a start on the story and then we can talk about it afterwards, shall we?' said the minister, looking a little uneasy. 'Now, if any of those sheep strayed, the shepherd would search for them until he found them.'

'He wanted a good collie,' said the red-haired boy. 'Save a lot o' time and trouble.'

'Aye,' nodded a few of his companions.

The minister speeded up his delivery, hoping by doing so to discourage any further interruptions. 'The shepherd protected his sheep from wild animals and thieves by using a catapult—'

'Shotgun would 'ave been better,' remarked a child.

'And at night,' continued the minister, ignoring the observation, 'the shepherd kept his flock in a stone-walled sheepfold topped with thorns and he would block the entrance by lying across in.'

'I can't see my dad doing that,' said the girl at the front, laughing.

'Now this parable is called The Lost Sheep and it was told by Jesus nearly two thousand years ago.' The minister took a deep breath, rubbed his hands and began to tell the story.

'So, the shepherd left the ninety-nine and went in search of the one lost sheep,' he concluded eventually.

'What breed o' sheep were they, then?' asked the girl.

'Well, does it make a difference?' he asked.

'It makes an 'ell of a lot o' difference. Some sheep are docile, others are reight frisky. If you're talking 'erdwicks, they never shift, they'll stop where they are till t'cows come home. We've got 'erdwicks. They may be small but they're a tough breed and eat owt that's going—grass, heather, couch grass—owt. Now, if t'shepherd left a flock of 'erdwicks, he'd still find 'em theer when he got back.'

'I see,' said the minister lamely and wrinkling his forehead into a frown. 'Well, I shouldn't imagine that the sheep were Herdwicks.'

'But if you're talking Leicesters,' continued the girl, 'they'll be leaping all ovver t'show. They'd be off as soon as shepherd's turned 'is back. So what breed were they?' asked the girl.

'Well,' said the minister, having a sudden flash of inspiration, 'these were Palestine Blues, a very lively breed.'

'Never 'eard of them,' commented the girl sulkily. 'What do they look like?'

'Oh, big and woolly and white.' He pressed on quickly to prevent any further interruptions and awkward questions. 'What joy the shepherd felt when he found his lost sheep. He put it on his shoulders and hurried back to tell everyone his good news and to invite his friends to share his happiness.'

'And were his other sheep still there?' asked the boy with red hair.

'Indeed they were, and the shepherd was very happy. Now, in the same way, there is great rejoicing in heaven over one sinner who turns back to God than over ninety-nine people who see no reason to repent. Remember, children, none of us is a lost sheep in the eyes of God. Did you enjoy that story?' he asked the sea of little faces.

There was a long pause. Then the little boy with the red hair gave a great heaving sigh. 'It were rubbish,' he said simply. 'Nowt 'appened. I like a story wi' a bit o' action.'

THE LAST SCHOOL on my programme that day was St Bartholomew's School. The headteacher, Sister Brendan, was most intrigued by the spirituality initiative and quizzed me unmercifully about it. 'And how does one go about assessing something as intangible as spirituality?' she asked, fixing me with her small, dark eyes. 'Surely, love of poetry or appreciation of music is impossible to evaluate.'

'Well, it is difficult, Sister, but—' I started. I endeavoured to explain but felt on very shaky ground. Eventually, I extricated myself from her room, having prevailed upon her to let me sit in on the rehearsal for the school play about the life of St John the Baptist.

Sister Brendan's assistant teacher, Mrs Webb, was in full flow when I entered the hall. On stage, a large, shaven-headed boy holding a paper crown and a large plastic sword was staring impassively at her.

'Now, Herod,' said Mrs Webb, 'when Salome brings on John the Baptist's head, you look very sad. You really didn't want to have him killed but had to keep your promise to Salome that she could have anything she wanted.' The teacher caught sight of a small boy at the side of the hall, holding a large papier-mâché plate. 'John,' she said irritably, 'where is John the Baptist's head? It should be on the platter.'

'I haven't got it, miss,' replied the child. 'No one has given it to me.'

'Peter,' the teacher instructed another child, 'go to the staff room and fetch the bleeding head.'

The boy returned moments later with Sister Brendan.

'Did you wish to see me, Mrs Webb?' asked the nun.

THAT EVENING I was to speak at a local Farmers' Club Christmas dinner. All spruced up, I was limping for the car when I caught sight of Harry Cotton taking his terrier for her constitutional. There was an icy wind blowing in my face but I just could not wait to tell him about the chapel.

'Good evening, Harry,' I called out. 'You know the Methodist chapel you were telling me about? It wasn't a Methodist chapel, after all.'

'Aye, I know,' he said to my surprise. 'I was goin' to pop up and tell thee. I got it wrong. I was talkin' to Albert Tattersall last week in t'Golden Ball and 'e put me right.'

'Well, we all make mistakes,' I said. I felt pretty smug.

'No, it weren't a Methodist chapel at all. It were Quaker. Built in seventeen 'undred and summat, according to Harry. Very pacific people are your Quakers, can't be doin' wi' violence and the like. I remember in t'war they were conscientious objectors. It's just as well for you that they're a peaceful lot because they'll not be dead chuffed to see what thy's gone and done to their meeting 'ouse. Even rarer than a Methodist chapel, so Albert Tattersall were telling me.'

I was lost for words.

'I 'eard from yer missis that you 'ad a bit of an accident when you were demolishin' it. Still limpin', I see.'

'Yes,' I sighed, 'still limping.'

'Could be divine providence that,' said Harry, ambling off.

MY FAVOURITE TIME in the school year is Christmas, when classrooms are ablaze with colour, fir trees twinkle in entrance halls and corridors are festooned with bright decorations.

Of all the activities that take place at Christmas, it is the infant Nativity play I most look forward to. To see Mary, aged six, draped in pale blue and tightly clutching Baby Jesus (usually a large plastic doll) to her chest, never fails to bring a tear to the eye.

Every infant headteacher has a story to tell about the Christmas

Nativity play. There was the time the Archangel Gabriel had informed Mary that he 'had tidings of great joy to bring' but had completely forgotten what they were; the memorable moment when the large cardboard star that had been suspended above the stage had fallen onto Joseph, who, very much out of character, had rubbed his head and exclaimed, 'Bloody 'ell!'

Infant Nativities are rarely without incident and the one I attended that year at Tupton Road Primary School was no exception. The play opened in the traditional fashion with Mary and Joseph setting off for Bethlehem. Joseph, a confident little boy in large glasses, spoke his lines clearly and loudly and led Mary gently across the makeshift stage. Things didn't go so well when the Innkeeper appeared. He was a sturdily built child with spiky ginger hair and his two front teeth missing. Before Joseph could even enquire whether there might be room at the inn, the little bruiser, arms folded tightly over his chest and chin jutting out like a miniature Mussolini, announced: 'There's no room!'

'But we have travelled far and—' began Joseph.

'There's no room,' repeated the innkeeper even louder. 'Did you not hear me? You can go round the back in the barn. Take it or leave it.'

At this point the little ginger-haired boy caught sight of an elderly woman in the front row, obviously his granny. He grinned and tinkled the air with his fingers. The old lady, rather unhelpfully, smiled and waved back. This continued for what felt like an age.

'Shane!' came the teacher's disembodied voice from offstage. 'Shane! Come off!'

The innkeeper continued to wave. The voice from the wings grew more insistent. 'Shane Merryweather, get off the stage right now!'

The child was finally prevailed upon to exit stage left, and things then went smoothly until the arrival of the Three Wise Men.

'I bring you gold,' said the first child, laying a small golden box at Mary's feet and bowing low.

'I bring you myrrh,' said the second, laying a coloured jar at Mary's feet and bowing low.

'And I bring you frankincense,' said the third, laying down his gift.

'Bow!' came the disembodied voice from the wings. 'Bow!'

The third king looked perplexed. He stared around him like a rabbit caught in a headlight's glare.

'Jason!' came the voice again. 'Bow! Bow!'

The little boy looked first at the audience and then at Mary. 'Woof!' he said. 'Woof! Woof!'

ONE EVENING, just after the schools had broken up for Christmas, Christine and I were snuggled up on the sofa in front of a blazing fire.

'I can't remember when we last did this,' she said. 'I hope I shall see more of you when the baby arrives. When our child starts to talk, I don't want him or her asking who that strange man is who disappears early in the morning and arrives home late at night with his big black bag.'

'You make me sound like Dr Crippen,' I said.

'Well, we'll want to see more of you.'

'You will,' I said. 'I'm determined to have more nights in and try to get home earlier. I want to snuggle up with my little girl and read to her every night.'

'And what about the baby?' asked Christine mischievously.

'I'll read to her as well.'

'You are certain it's going to be a girl, aren't you?' asked Christine.

'Of course, I am,' I said. 'The eldest child in every Phinn family has always been a girl and it's been the same with the Bentleys on your side. Little Lizzie will be blonde, blue-eyed and beautiful, just like her mother. And she'll be clever, too. Elizabeth Gaskell, Elizabeth Barrett Browning, Elizabeth Phinn—it's the name of a great writer. And if it's a boy he'll be called Fred and play cricket for Yorkshire.'

'I thought we had decided on Matthew,' said Christine.

'I think Matthew for son number two. A first-born son should have his father's names.'

'Certainly not!' exclaimed Christine. 'One Gervase in the family is more than enough.'

'Anyway, this is all academic, Christine,' I said, 'because it will be a girl—little Lizzie Phinn.'

We sat in silence for a while, watching the flickering flames and feeling the warmth of the open fire. I was well and truly in the Christmas spirit. My decision not to apply for Harold's job had lifted a weight from my shoulders. And the nightmare scenario of my standing at the gate of Peewit Cottage facing a coachload of American Quakers who had come to see the famous historic building had faded like the bad dream that it was. Harry had not mentioned the subject on any of his frequent visits, nor had anyone else in the village.

There was reason to feel a little optimistic about the proposed closure of Hawksrill School as well. Christine's informants at County Hall had told her that, largely due to the fuss the Action Group had caused, the plans for closure had been delayed. Then there was the gammy knee, which was feeling a whole lot better. Christine was not enamoured of the flesh-coloured elastic stocking that I wore permanently, but it had certainly relieved the pain. Dr Sadler had arranged for me to see a specialist at Fettlesham Royal Infirmary and now I was on a waiting list for an operation that was fairly routine.

'What are you thinking about?' Christine asked.

'Oh, just how lucky I am.'

We sat there just enjoying the warmth and closeness of each other.

'You know what this room needs?' she said suddenly. 'The ticking of a clock. A grandfather clock.'

'I don't think we can afford a grandfather clock at the moment, darling,' I told her. 'Maybe in a couple of years.'

'Yes,' she sighed. 'It was just a thought.'

It was a thought, however, which firmly planted itself in my head. Though I wasn't going to admit it to Christine.

THE FOLLOWING SATURDAY I set off for Roper's Salesroom in Collington to look for a grandfather clock. I always enjoyed browsing around auction houses, breathing in the smell of beeswax and watching the bargain hunters rootling through the boxes of bric-a-brac.

I had a special reason to be rather sentimental about Roper's Salesroom. It was where, three years earlier, I had caught sight of the person I would come to love: the stunning young woman with soft blonde hair and dazzling blue eyes who was now my wife.

On this particular day, the salesroom was full of prospective buyers. Perhaps someone had the wall space for one of the huge, dark landscapes in ornate gold frames: some were as big as the end wall in our sitting room. There were sculptured bronzes, shimmering crystal and delicate porcelain, but none of that interested me this time. My eye was caught by a grandfather clock that looked as though it had come straight out of the palace at Versailles. I read the catalogue description.

'It's a beautiful piece, isn't it?' said a distinguished-looking man standing next to me. He wore an expensive woollen overcoat and, beneath, I could see an equally expensive black-striped suit and red and white silk bow tie. 'What age do you think it is?'

'I'm afraid I've no idea,' I replied. 'I'm no expert on clocks.'

The man, who was obviously interested in the piece himself, had clearly thought that I was intending to make a bid for the clock. He realised now that I posed no threat. 'I should say *circa* 1775,' he informed me. 'More late Georgian than early. I'm looking for a companion for my flame mahogany long-case.'

'How much do you think this clock will fetch?' I asked him.

He sucked in his breath. 'Oh, anything between two and three.'

'Hundred?'

He chortled. 'You're a tease. Thousands, of course,' he replied.

'It's way beyond my pocket,' I told him. 'I just want a plain, ordinary grandfather clock.'

'They're called long-case clocks, to be correct, and I think you will find there are very few that are plain and ordinary. Each one is unique. However, you might try the new shop that's just opened in Station Parade in Brindcliffe. I bought a very attractive oak-cased bracket clock from there only last week. Very reasonable prices. And I did notice the chap has a long-case—it might be the thing you're looking for.'

'Thank you very much,' I said, 'I'll pop along there now.'

JUST CLOCKS was sandwiched between a health-food shop and a dry cleaners. Its newly painted dark green façade with gold lettering above the door stood out from the rest of the shops in the parade.

The bell tinkled discreetly as I entered, and then a voice came from the back. 'I'll be with you in one moment.' I stopped in my tracks. I had heard that voice before. It was deep, resonant, authoritative. Before I could escape, the familiar, lean, sallow-complexioned figure with black carefully-parted hair emerged from behind the red velvet curtain that separated the showroom from the back of the shop.

'Mr Frobisher!' I gasped.

'Mr Phinn,' he said calmly.

We were saved further embarrassment by the bell as another customer entered, a small woman in a bright headscarf and large furry boots. 'I'm looking for a clock—' she said.

'I'll just have a look round,' I said to Mr Frobisher, relieved by the interruption. 'Please go ahead and deal with this customer.' The thought entered my head that I could wander casually to the door and exit quietly, but that would be cowardly, so I crossed the room to peer at the fine selection of timepieces on display. There were bronze mantel clocks, portico clocks under glass domes, mahogany-cased clocks, clocks of every size and shape and colour. Despite my genuine interest, my mind was buzzing with wondering what I would say to the man who I had driven out of teaching.

After a few moments, Mr Frobisher finished helping his other customer. 'Now then,' he said, looking me straight in the eye.

'How are you?' I asked. It sounded so feeble.

'Well, as you see, I'm pretty well.'

'It's a lovely shop.'

'Yes, it is.'

I coughed nervously. This was a nightmare. 'I did ring the school a couple of times to have a word with you, but you were not available. I meant to say—'

'Please, please, Mr Phinn, don't look so abashed. You really don't need to say anything. Your visit to King Henry's College was quite possibly one of the best things that could have happened to me.'

'Really?'

'In a strange and rather unexpected sort of way, that is,' he added. 'No teacher likes to be told he is not up to scratch. I have to admit at first I was very hurt by your report and by what I considered to be some quite unfounded comments. Then I became angry, particularly when Mr Nelson seemed to accept without question what you had said. You really come to know who your friends are in situations like that. I know I was not the best teacher in the world, Mr Phinn, and, I have to admit, that over the past few years I have been ground down by the incessant paperwork, by the interference of so-called experts, negative media reports and the deteriorating behaviour of the pupils. However, I always thought I did a decent enough job. But that's water under the bridge, so to speak. When I was offered early retirement with a lump sum, I got to thinking that perhaps all this was for the best. For some time, I had toyed with the idea of opening a shop. My father was a great collector of timepieces and I, too, am fascinated by them.' He paused for a moment and took a long, deep breath. 'My wife is not a well woman, and retiring early meant I could spend more time with her. The bank manager was most helpful, the premises came up for rent and, as you see, here I am and I have never felt more contented.'

'Well, I'm very pleased it has worked out for you, Mr Frobisher,' I said, and meant it.

'And here you are,' he said. 'Not here to inspect me again, I hope.'

'No, no,' I said hastily. 'I'm looking for a clock and I think I've seen just the one.' I turned to the grandfather clock in the corner.

'Ah, the long-case clock. Not very old. Nineteenth century. Quite plain but no less attractive for all that. Unusual painted dial, eight-day movement and signed Percy Farrington of Fettlesham. Now, I expect you wish to know the price. Let me see.' Mr Frobisher turned, picked up a ledger and ran a long finger down the page. 'Five hundred and fifty pounds. If you purchase it, I would, of course, deliver the clock and ensure that it works well in its new home. Long-case clocks are a trifle temperamental, you know. Rather like people.' He stroked the side gently as he might a treasured pet. 'They have to be looked after. If they are cared for, they will go on and on.'

The man had become animated. His eyes shone. He smiled. Had he only shown the same enthusiasm with his pupils that he showed for his clocks, I thought sadly, he would still be teaching.

EIGHT

A few days later I was due at the Royal Infirmary. It was a square, featureless, redbrick building on the outskirts of Fettlesham. After the consultation with the specialist, I had expected to wait for quite some time for the operation, but a cancellation meant I was called into hospital at short notice, which suited me fine.

From the reception desk, I was directed to Men's Surgical. There were four tubular metal beds in Ward 6, three of which were occupied. By the window, an extremely large and heavily tattooed man with a bald head and a neck as thick as a pitbull terrier's, sat propped up, reading a newspaper. He nodded in my direction as I entered. Across from him lay an emaciated individual with a deathly pallor, pained expression and closed eyes. In the third bed was a round-faced man with cheeks so red and shiny they looked as if they had just been scrubbed. I had never seen anyone look quite as healthy. He watched me critically as I made my way to the bed opposite and started to put my various personal items in the small bedside cabinet.

'How do,' he said.

'Oh, hello,' I replied.

'Another for the butcher's knife then?'

'Yes.'

'What you in for?'

'An operation on my knee,' I told him.

'Very tricky things are knees. I've heard it's a bit of a hit and miss with knees. My cousin, Stan, had an operation on his knee and limped for the rest of his life. Had to give up his ballroom dancing. Never climbed a ladder again. Like hips are knees. Tricky.'

'Really.'

'I'm in with haemorrhoids myself. By the heck, you know what pain is with haemorrhoids. Fifty per cent of the population have had haemorrhoids by the age of fifty. It's a fact. Do you know why they're called piles?'

'I have no idea,' I said, 'but I expect you're going to tell me.'

'Because the Latin word *pila* means ball,' he explained. 'I like to go into my medical condition in some detail before I comes into hospital. They pays more attention to you if they think you're in the know, you know.'

'Fascinating,' I said.

'I've tried everything for my haemorrhoids but they are unusually stubborn, as my doctor said. In fact, in all his years of practising medicine he's never seen anything like them. Have you had 'em?'

'No, I haven't,' I said.

'When you go to the toilet it's like passing glass.'

'Why don't you put a bleeding sock in it!' said the bullet-headed individual. 'You've been going on and on about your haemorrhoids all morning. You're like a bleeding gramophone record.'

'Who rattled your cage then?' asked the haemorrhoids.

'I'll come and rattle your bleeding haemorrhoids in a minute. And as for pain, you don't know what pain is. You have an 'ernia, mate, then you'll know what pain is.'

I climbed into bed. The visit to Fettlesham Royal Infirmary was going to be an experience and no mistake.

At this point the emaciated individual with the pained expression opened his eyes and yawned widely.

'The Sleeping Beauty awakes,' remarked the haemorrhoids, 'we thought you'd popped off!'

'Did I miss the tea trolley?'

'You look as if you need an undertaker's trolley, state you're in, squire.'

'Do you know,' said the hernia slowly and with malice, 'you really are a pain in the arse.'

'You never did say what you was in for,' said the haemorrhoids, addressing the prone figure next to him.

'I'd rather not say,' replied the man in a mournful tone of voice.

'Vasectomy?'

'No.'

'Circumcision?'

'No, nothing like that.'

'For God's sake just tell him,' snapped the hernia, 'and shut the bugger up.'

'I've got an anal ulcer,' announced the man without any gloss.

The haemorrhoids sucked in his breath noisily. 'Oooooh,' he groaned. 'Nasty.' He didn't open his mouth again for the next ten minutes. During the welcome period of quiet, I managed to get on with some work.

I had arrived at the hospital with a large red folder with the words STRICTLY CONFIDENTIAL and THE INSPECTORS' DIVISION written in bold black letters on the cover—some reports that Harold had, rather tentatively, asked me to read before the operation. I soon sensed that I was being watched and, looking up, found the haemorrhoids staring intently at me.

'You're an inspector then,' he remarked. 'Police?'

'No.'

'Tax?'

'No.'

'Public health?'

'No.'

'It's not a bloody quiz show. What sort of inspector are you?'

'All right,' I said in a hushed voice, 'I'll tell you, but you must promise me not to breath a word to anyone in the hospital. And I can't shout it across the ward,' I said. 'It's strictly confidential.'

The haemorrhoids clambered out of bed and, considering his medical condition, moved with remarkable speed to my side.

'Well—' I began. At this point the tea trolley arrived. 'I'll tell you later,' I whispered.

The tea trolley had barely left the room when the haemorrhoids was at my side again, leaning over the bed, his ear in my face. 'Come on, then,' he said, 'spill the beans.'

'You really have to keep it to yourself,' I told him. 'It's very hush-hush.' Then I whispered conspiratorially in the haemorrhoids' ear, 'I'm a hospital inspector, but I wish to remain incognito, sort of undercover.'

'But you're here for an operation, aren't you?'

'That's right,' I said. 'Strictly speaking, I'm off duty. I do need this operation, of course, and it's only a minor one, but it will give me the opportunity of gaining an inside picture of how the hospital is performing. But I am sure you understand that I would rather no one knows my identity so could we keep things to ourselves.'

'Get on,' snorted the haemorrhoids, shuffling back to his bed. 'You must think my brains are made of porridge. Hospital inspector. Huh.'

'Well you did ask,' I said, returning to the reports.

'YOU'RE CAUSING quite a stir,' said the nurse later that morning when she came to take my blood pressure.

'Really?' I replied innocently.

'Telling them you're a hospital inspector, indeed.'

'People will believe anything, nurse,' I said, smiling.

She caught sight of the red folder on my bedside cabinet. 'So, what sort of inspector are you, then?' she asked casually.

'I'm afraid I'm not at liberty to say, nurse,' I replied. 'It's strictly confidential.' As she leaned over to attach the flap of black material to my arm to take my blood pressure, I scrutinised the badge pinned to her bosom. 'Staff Nurse R. Leach,' I said.

'That's right.'

'A rather appropriate name for someone taking blood pressure.'

'Pardon?'

'Leach, although your name is spelt with an *a*, isn't it?'

She began to pump the machine. 'That's right.'

'Is that Rowena?'

'Robin.'

'Lovely name. And how long have you worked at Fettlesham Royal Infirmary, Nurse Leach?'

She stopped pumping. 'You do ask a lot of questions.'

'It's the nature of my job.'

'So what sort of inspector are you?' she asked again.

'I'm afraid it's strictly confidential,' I replied.

JUST BEFORE LUNCH, Mr Todd, the surgeon, arrived, accompanied by the ward sister in a smart blue uniform complete with black belt and silver buckle, and a group of medical students in white coats with the obligatory stethoscopes draped round their necks.

'And how are we, today, Mr Siddall?' Mr Todd asked the hernia.

'We're not too bad, thank you, Mr Todd,' replied the hernia.

'Excellent.' The surgeon turned to the students who were watching his every move. 'Hernia,' he remarked dismissively, 'very straightforward case, no complications,' and he swiftly moved on. 'And how are you, Mr Prout?' he asked the haemorrhoids.

'Mustn't grumble,' replied the rosy-cheeked chatterer.

'Chance'd be a fine thing,' commented the hernia under his breath.

'But now you ask, Mr Todd—' began the haemorrhoids, sitting upright quickly and becoming very animated.

'Haemorrhoids,' interrupted the surgeon, turning to his young colleagues. 'I will save you the ordeal of an examination. Again, simple case, no complications. Have you back on your bicycle in no time, Mr Prout.'

Mr Todd was now at the bottom of the anal ulcer's bed. The patient was sleeping peacefully. 'Little point in disturbing Mr Quayle. Anal ulcer.' He then turned on his heel, looked me full in the face and smiled rather disconcertingly. 'And that brings us to Mr Phinn.' All eyes settled on me. 'Mr Phinn, who has a most interesting, not to say intriguing, condition, the result of a rugby accident when he was a youth. Screens please, Sister,' he said. 'I would like these would-be medics to give me their considered opinions of Mr Phinn's condition.' The screens were hastily pulled round my bed and all the white coats gathered round like dogs with a bone. 'It is the ankle, isn't it, Mr Phinn?' observed the surgeon mischievously.

'No, no,' I spluttered, 'the knee. It's the left knee.'

'Quite so. Now, what is all this I have been hearing from Nurse Leach about you being a hospital inspector?'

'I'm a school inspector,' I told him, smiling pathetically like a naughty child caught out by a teacher. 'Your wife will vouch for me. I believe I inspected her earlier this year.'

'Did you, by God?' he exclaimed, laughing loudly.

'Professionally speaking,' I said. Then I added deferentially, 'I know nothing about hospitals, but I must say that I'm getting five-star treatment.'

'I am so glad to hear it,' said Mr Todd, smiling like Dracula about to sink his teeth into a victim. 'We aim to please. Now, let us look at this troublesome knee of yours.'

AT VISITING TIME, Christine arrived with an immense bunch of purple grapes, which she placed in a bowl on thc bedside cabinet.

'Sidney phoned earlier this evening to wish you well for tomorrow,' she said. 'He said word is out that the Education Committee is at last going to announce the person to replace Harold.'

'It's about time,' I said. 'It's dragged on for months. Anyway, how are you feeling?'

'Mother and baby doing fine. No swollen ankles, no mad cravings. But I'll be glad when you're home.'

'You've got the clock to keep you company,' I said.

Christine had been over the moon when she saw the long-case clock on Christmas Day in pride of place in the sitting room. I had had the devil's own job keeping it a surprise—collecting it from Mr Frobisher, hiding it in Harry Cotton's outbuilding, creeping out late on Christmas Eve after Christine had gone to bed to collect it, then trying to put it together and set the pendulum going without waking her. Of course, I had forgotten about the chiming. Christine saw her Christmas present fifteen seconds after midnight, when the clock had struck the hour. She loved it on the spot.

'Any other news?' I asked now.

'Indeed there is!' replied Christine, beaming. 'I heard just before coming out to see you that they're definitely deferring the closure of the school. We'll go on campaigning and maybe we'll overturn the decision officially.'

'You've done a magnificent job,' I told her.

'Well, I don't know about that,' she said. 'Anyway, I must be off, darling. I've got so much to do before I leave Winnery Nook. Good luck tomorrow. I'll be saying a prayer and I'll be thinking of you.' She gave me a great big hug and a kiss and left.

'Nice-looking young woman, your daughter,' observed the haemorrhoids as he watched Christine leave the ward. 'Is she expecting?'

'She's my wife actually and, yes, she is.'

It was five minutes after visiting time had finished when Harold breezed in, looking very distinguished in a charcoal-grey suit.

'However did you manage to get past the ward sister?' I asked, when he reached my bed. 'I'm told she's a stickler for people keeping to the visiting hours.'

'Charm, dear boy, charm,' said Harold, 'and a little help from this.' He tapped a badge on his chest that said in bold black lettering: DR HAROLD J. YEATS. 'I think the good sister assumed I was one of the medical fraternity and I didn't disabuse her. Anyway, I've spent the day with Dr Gore and the person who will take over from me in April, and I now have the go-ahead to release the name of the new senior inspector. I wanted you to know as soon as possible.'

'Who is he? What's he like?'

'She,' replied Harold. 'It's a she.' He smiled widely.

'It's not Geraldine, is it?'

'No, no, not Geraldine,' replied Harold. 'She hasn't quite got the experience yet. And she told me back in the autumn that she wasn't planning to apply because she puts young Jamie before her job and quite right too.'

'Who is it, then, Harold?' I urged.

'Miss de la Mare.'

'*What?!*' I cried. 'But she's an HMI,' I spluttered. 'Why on earth would she want the job?'

'She's become wearied with the hectic life in London,' Harold told me. 'All the travelling on the Tube every morning and evening has taken its toll. She's ready for a different sort of challenge. Of course, Dr Gore was very keen to appoint her. However, as you know, she's a forceful character and, before accepting the position, there were certain conditions she wanted the Education Committee to agree to, including that it would support certain innovations she would wish to put in place. I think she'll be excellent.'

'That's wonderful,' I said. 'Wonderful! And Christine tells me they're holding fire with the Hawksrill School closure.'

'That's right,' said Harold, 'and I have a feeling nothing will happen in that direction for quite some time now. Councillor Peterson has just about thrown in the towel, by all accounts. Now, I must let you get some rest. I promised the ward sister five minutes and no more. Oh, did you manage to finish reading through the reports?'

'Yes, they're here,' I said, reaching into my bedside cabinet.

'Splendid. I'll take them with me. Well, good luck for tomorrow. And don't think of coming back to work until you are fully fit.'

'Thanks for calling in, Harold.'

As Harold made for the door he was verbally waylaid by the haemorrhoids. 'If I could have a word, Doctor,' he said.

'Well, I am in a bit of a hurry,' Harold told him pleasantly.

'I thought you might want a quick look at my haemorrhoids.'

'No, no!' spluttered Harold. 'Thank you kindly for the offer but I really must decline.' With that he shot out of the door.

'Well, what about that!' cried the haemorrhoids, addressing no one in particular. 'Not so much as a glance in my condition.'

I held up the big bunch of purple grapes and smiled sweetly. 'Would you care for a grape?'

NINE

'I'm looking for a man!'

I recognised immediately the aristocratic tones of the Honourable Mrs Cleaver-Canning at the end of the line. The previous year I had received a telephone call from the honourable lady inviting me to speak at the Totterdale and Clearwell Golf Club Christmas ladies' night dinner. Much to my relief, the audience, no doubt buoyed up by good food and wine, had been extremely warm and receptive and I had left with a generous cheque to swell Sister Brendan's charity appeal. Now, here was Mrs Cleaver-Canning on the telephone again, no doubt wanting me to do a repeat performance.

'Good morning, Mrs Cleaver-Canning,' I said brightly. 'And how are you?'

'I'm extremely well, thank you, Mr Phinn,' she replied, 'but I am desperate for a man. And you fit the bill.'

'I am certainly flattered, but what about Winco?' I said, referring to her long-suffering husband, a former RAF officer with an extravagant handlebar moustache.

'Oh, you are a one,' she chortled down the line. 'No, no, I want a man for our musical drama. Next month the Fettlesham Literary Players will be staging *The Sound of Music* at the Civic Theatre in town. Unfortunately, one of the cast, Mr Dutton of "Dutton's Carpets of Distinction" has dropped out. So, how about it? We only have six weeks to go and, as I said, I'm desperate.'

'I fear not,' I said hastily. 'I'm so very busy at the moment, Mrs Cleaver-Canning, and I've not long been out of hospital. I really couldn't commit myself to—'

'Hospital? Oh dear, I trust it wasn't serious?'

'No, no, a minor operation on the knee.'

'I'm very pleased to hear it. Well, the exercise will do it good. It's only a small walk-on part. You would come on stage in the last act, say a couple of lines and walk off. You would only need to attend a few rehearsals.'

'Yes, I appreciate that, but—'

'As I mentioned, I don't think you have got above two or three lines. It's the part of the SS lieutenant who is pursuing Captain von Trapp. He only appears at the very end when the family are making their escape across the mountains. It wouldn't be at all onerous.'

'I am flattered to be asked, Mrs Cleaver-Canning,' I began, 'but—'

'We are really desperate,' she continued. 'It's so hard to get men these days. All I ask is that you glance through the libretto before you give a definite thumbs down. Will you do that?'

'Well—'

'Excellent! Winco will pop it in the post today.'

'WHY DO YOU let yourself be dragged into things?' Christine asked when we were sitting having a coffee after dinner that evening. 'Why didn't you just say no and put the phone down. I should have thought you've got enough amateur dramatics at the inspectors' office with Sidney and David without looking for any more.'

'She's a very persuasive woman,' I began. 'She just wouldn't let me get a word in. Anyway, it's only a few lines, not a major role.'

'You really are infuriating at times, Gervase,' she said good-humouredly. 'You take all these things on without a thought for the commitment. Have you forgotten what's happening next month?'

'Well, if little Lizzie does arrive early, I'll just have to goose-step it down to the hospital. The Civic Theatre isn't that far. I could be there in ten minutes. Look, Christine, if you are dead set against it, I'll tell her I won't do it. I really don't want to argue with you about it.'

Christine leaned over, smiled and gave me a peck on the cheek. 'Neither do I. Actually, you might look rather dishy in the uniform.'

ON THE NEXT TUESDAY, I made my way through the main entrance of Castlesnelling High School for the first rehearsal. I was greeted (hardly the right word) by the caretaker, an extremely thin man with a baleful countenance who was attired in grey overalls, and accompanied by a fat, vicious-looking dog. As I approached, he jangled an enormous set of keys noisily. 'They're in the hall,' he said in a voice as dry as sawdust. 'And watch the floor, I've just buffed it.'

In the hall, a group of people was standing just below the stage, one small man waving his hands around and talking excitedly. When I reached the gathering, I coughed quietly.

The small man, who was wearing a pair of extremely tight jeans and a T-shirt, spun round. 'Ah, and you must be Gervase Phinn! Welcome, welcome!' he cried, grasping my hand and shaking it vigorously. 'I'm Raymond, but everyone calls me Ray. I'm your original drop of golden sun.'

'I'm sorry?' I said.

'You know,' he replied, breaking into song: '"Doe a deer, a female deer. Ray a drop of golden sun."'

'Ah, indeed.' I smiled weakly.

'Oh, ye-es!' said Ray, scrutinising me as an art expert might an old master. 'I can just see you in black boots. You're ideal.' He swung back to the group of people waiting patiently. 'This is our little troupe of thespians. As per usual, we have a surfeit of nuns and an abundance of children, but we are, like all amateur dramatic productions these days, bereft of young men.' He smiled and took my arm. 'You'll get to know us all in the course of the evening, Gervase, so I will dispense with introductions. Just take a pew and I'll let you know when I want you on stage. Now, let us make a start, so a bit of hush everyone. I want to go through the scene with Liesl and Rolf again.'

I watched Liesl and Rolf going through their paces with a sinking feeling. Why on earth had I let myself be press-ganged into this? I recognised the woman playing the part of Liesl, Captain von Trapp's eldest child. She was the head of food technology at the school in whose hall we were rehearsing—an extremely thin and intense-looking woman with long straggly hair. As we watched she launched into song with: '"I am sixteen going on seventeen, innocent as a rose."'

'More like thirty going on forty, if you ask me,' commented Mr Furnival of Furnival's Funeral Parlour. He was playing the part of Herr Zeller, the Gauleiter who comes to arrest Captain von Trapp, and was tailor-made for the part, with his despondent face, cold eyes as grey as the autumn sky, and a vulpine mouth. 'Mind you, with a bit of stage make-up, a long blonde wig and subdued stage lights, she should be all right. It's amazing what make-up can do. I do a lot of embalming, you know. It's quite an art form.'

It soon came to what Ray described as 'Gervase's little spot'.

'Now,' said the producer, 'this is the dramatic climax of the drama. We are in the garden of Nonnberg Abbey. A gaggle of nuns is standing anxiously by the door. Could we look anxious, please, nuns? You're not waiting for a number nine bus. The von Trapps enter nervously, clutching their cases. They hear a noise and hide in the shadows. Do try to look as if you're frightened, von Trapps. Cluster, don't queue. Rolf enters. Gone are his lederhosen and Tyrolean hat. He is now dressed in SS uniform. The light from his torch picks out Maria. She gasps. Then it lights up the captain. He scowls, and walks towards Rolf. Rolf flashes. Flash, please, Rolf. Now, draw your pistol. Just use your fingers for the time being, please, Fraser. He calls: "Lieutenant!" Then he sees Liesl. She looks appealingly at him. We hear the lieutenant's footsteps approaching. Rolf clicks off the light. The footsteps draw nearer and nearer. The lieutenant struts onto the stage. This is you, Gervase.' I limped onto the stage. 'He looks around arrogantly,' continued the producer. 'He should have with him two or three stormtroopers, but we haven't got enough men and, anyway, we can't afford to hire all those uniforms, so it'll just have to be you, Gervase.' His voice became suddenly dramatic again. 'Then Rolf changes his mind and decides not to betray the von Trapps after all. He calls: "No one out here, sir!" "All right!" snarls the lieutenant. "Come along."'

We tried the scene a couple of times and Ray seemed well satisfied.

'However, Gervase, I was wanting more of a *braggadocio*.'

'Braga-what-o?' I asked, quite perplexed.

'A strut. Can you strut or swagger, onto the stage?'

'Difficult, really. I've just had a knee operation,' I told him.

'Oh, well, we'll have to keep the limp in then.'

'But I have a limp!' called Mr Furnival, who had been watching proceedings intently. 'There can't be two of us with limps.'

'No, you are quite right, George,' said Ray. 'Dispense with yours.'

At nine o'clock prompt the caretaker arrived.

'Let's call it a day. Next Tuesday, please, for those in the ball scene.'

'HOW DID IT GO?' asked Christine when I limped through the door of Peewit Cottage later that evening.

'Fine. I only need to attend a couple more times and the dress rehearsal, of course.' I flopped into the nearest chair.

'I'll put the kettle on,' Christine said. 'I'm sure you could do with a cup of tea after all that goose-stepping. By the way, you've had a phone call from Harold. He had just come out of one of his late meetings about the school closures and he rang here straight away. He wanted us to be the first to know. They've reversed the decision to close Hawskrill School. Isn't it fantastic? Evidently the Ministry of Education has blocked it.' She put her arms round me. 'So you see, all our efforts on the Action Committee have paid off.'

I didn't say anything to Christine, but I thought to myself that there was far more here than a pressure group's efforts. I just wondered if our senior inspector designate had a hand in the decision. Miss de la Mare had been the HMI sent from London to look into the matter and report back. Did she delay her acceptance of the post until she had seen this through? I wondered.

TEN

Mrs Savage sat stiffly behind her impressive desk, enthroned in her large swivel chair, looking haughtier than ever. She was dressed in an elegant chartreuse-coloured suit and plain cream silk blouse and adorned in her usual assortment of heavy jewellery. As Sidney often remarked, Mrs Savage was never knowingly under-dressed and that morning she had really gone to town. She had adopted the Eva Peron style, with hair scraped back and gathered immaculately behind her head. I had to admit she looked magnificent.

'Good morning, Mr Phinn,' she said, looking up from the papers before her. 'Do take a seat.'

'Good morning, Mrs Savage,' I replied, sitting on the hard wooden chair in front of her and placing my briefcase on the floor beside me. 'Shall we make a start?' she went on. 'I have a briefing with Dr Gore later this morning, so we do need to knock on. The CEO wants to touch base and go through a few items with me regarding the new senior inspector. I have to prepare a detailed dossier for Miss de la Mare to acquaint her with the workings of the department.'

'You have such a big remit, Mrs Savage,' I remarked, taking some papers from my briefcase.

'I beg your pardon, Mr Phinn?' she said sourly.

'I was observing that you seem to have more and more responsibilities thrust upon your shoulders these days. Personnel issues, secretarial duties, the Health and Safety initiative, the EIEI. It's a wonder you have the time to fit everything in.'

'Oh,' she said, oblivious of the sarcasm. 'I see what you mean. Yes, I am indeed kept extremely busy and that is why we need to expedite the business of the EIEI.'

She flicked open a file on her desk and tapped the document inside. 'I have received from you the names of some suitable schools for the foreign inspectors to visit, but these need to be ratified by Dr Gore. He wishes you to set up a meeting at the Staff Development Centre with invited headteachers and governors to talk about the education system over here. He, of course, will address them. If I might suggest—'

'That has all been taken care of, Mrs Savage,' I assured her.

'Oh, then we can move on. Now, if two of your colleagues and yourself,' she suggested, 'accompany one of these foreign inspectors each for the two days and look after him or her, it would mean that they would see a range of different subjects in a variety of schools.'

'I have taken care of that, too, Mrs Savage,' I told her, gritting my teeth. 'Mr Clamp and Mr Pritchard are happy to be involved.'

There was a long silence before she said, 'Do you think that those two colleagues are the most suitable for this endeavour?'

'Eminently.'

'I see,' she said curtly. 'Well, that, of course, is your decision. But it is imperative, Mr Phinn,' she announced, snapping shut the file in front of her and giving me an icy glare, 'that you liaise with me at all times. I need to be kept fully informed.'

'Of course,' I replied, wishing that this totally unnecessary meeting would end. 'Surely that is the point of this meeting?'

'There is one other thing I would like you to do as a matter of some urgency. I would appreciate it if you would have a word with that janitor at the Staff Development Centre.'

'Connie,' I reminded her.

'I have to say that I find her quite abrasive and difficult. Sometimes I don't think she knows what position I hold at County Hall. She has a most offhand manner.'

'So what's this matter of some urgency that you wish me to deal with?' I asked irritably.

'The matter of the catering,' she replied. 'As we agreed, there will be a reception for our foreign visitors at the SDC. There will be nibbles and drinks, that sort of thing.' She cleared her throat. 'I can see problems with . . . with that woman. If she is unable to provide tea and biscuits, how will she cope with a buffet? I really do not feel inclined to liaise with her over the provision of the food and drink. As I said, she can be very difficult.'

That's ripe coming from you, I thought.

'Well, this really is part of *your* remit,' I said.

'Not necessarily,' she replied. There was a softer tone to her voice now. 'You spend far more time at the SDC. It occurred to me that you might like to deal with that side of things.' Mrs Savage twisted a ring round on her long finger. 'Mr Phinn,' she said, 'I would be very grateful if you could see fit to arrange the catering. I would find it very helpful.' There was another long pause, then, 'Please.'

'I don't recall your being particularly helpful, Mrs Savage,' I told her, 'when I wanted that report back.'

'That was an entirely different matter,' she told me. 'It was—'

'More than your job was worth? Yes, I recall you telling me.' I then added, 'Very well, Mrs Savage, I will arrange the catering.'

'Thank you,' she said simply.

SEÑOR CARLOS ITTURIAGA was a small, plump, jolly man with dark Spanish eyes, a friendly face and black lustrous hair slicked back in rippling waves. Wearing a crumpled linen suit and clutching a giant multicoloured umbrella, he was waiting in the hotel lobby with Signor Toria, a very tall and thin inspector from Florence, and a stunning Brigitte Bardot lookalike from Tours called Simone.

The foreign inspectors had arrived late the previous evening and gone straight to the hotel where they were staying. Sidney, David and

I arrived early the next morning to collect them and take them round the selected schools. Of course, it was Sidney who made a bee-line for the divine Simone and whisked her off before we could discuss who was accompanying whom. David Pritchard ended up taking tall, thin Signor Toria, and I took the plump, little Spaniard.

Carlos Itturiaga talked all the way to the car, chattering, commenting, laughing and asking questions, all the while gesticulating, rolling his eyes and waving his plump-fingered hands. By the time we arrived at the first school on our itinerary I had learned all about Vigo, the city where he lived, his family, his interests, and I was pretty well conversant with the whole of the Spanish education system.

From Fettlesham, I took the scenic route to the first school and wound my way, in low gear, up a track that twisted and turned like a coiled spring. I had travelled this narrow road many times before and knew what an amazing panorama we would see when we reached the brow of the very steepest hill. Presently, I pulled over into a small lay-by so my companion could view the scene that lay below.

Señor Itturiaga immediately ceased his constant chatter and stared out of the car window. 'It ees very beautiful,' he said. 'Not at all as I expected. I was told England ees very green, very flat.'

'You are in Yorkshire, Carlos,' I told him. 'There is nothing quite like Yorkshire. It's called God's own country.'

'And it ees cold,' he observed. 'Very cold for me at thees time of the year.'

'Now, in Yorkshire we would say you were "nesh". Rather sensitive to the cold.'

'Nesh,' he repeated. 'Nesh. Very interesting.'

Below us stretched a vast canvas of empty grey moorland, scattered with great jags of rock. It was a rugged and primitive landscape, naked save for a few hardy sheep foraging for food, and a small copse of skeletal trees clawing for the sky. In the far distance, pale purple hills shrouded in mist rose majestically to a pale blue sky.

Returning to the car, we dropped down into the village huddled round the old church in the bottom of the valley.

Loxley Chase was typical of a Dales village school: a square and solid stone building enclosed by low limestone walls.

Following a tour of the school with the headteacher, Mr Leatherboy, Carlos and I joined a junior class—a group of twenty or so seven- to eleven-year-olds. It was one of the healthiest groups of youngsters I had ever seen: sturdy bodies, rosy-red cheeks, bright eyes and clear complexions. The children obviously came from good farming stock and spent a great deal of the time out of doors.

'Why do the sheep on the hills have a red colour on their backs?' asked Carlos of a stocky boy.

'Tha knaas.'

'Pardon?' asked Carlos.

'I said tha knaas.'

'Tha knaas?' repeated my colleague appearing flummoxed. He looked appealingly in my direction. 'Translate, plees.'

'He is sure you already know,' I replied. 'I'm afraid my friend doesn't know,' I told the boy, 'and, for that matter, I don't either.'

'Gerron wi' thee! Tha does,' chuckled the boy.

'Really,' I laughed. 'I don't know. Is it to tell which shepherd they belong to?'

The boy looked at me with a wry smile on his face and a twinkle in his brown eyes. He glanced out of the window at the sheep lazily cropping the grass on the hillside beyond. 'Nay,' said the lad. 'They all belong to t'same shepherd. They're ruddled.'

'Ruddled?' I repeated.

'Aye, in some dales they say "raddled" but up 'ere we says "ruddled".'

Carlos looked at me and repeated slowly, 'Ruddled. Interesting.'

I shrugged and turned back to the boy. 'I'm still in the dark,' I told him.

'Well, tha sees,' began the boy, 'on yer fells yonder is a goodly number of "yows"—them's ewes, female sheep—and one or two "tups", which are rams, male sheep. Are tha wi' me so far?'

'I am.'

'Reight then. Tha dunt need many tups. Does tha know why?'

'Yes, I'm still with you. Go on.'

'Reight then, t'shepherd puts an 'arness under yer tup's belly, sooart o' leather strap affair wi' a sooart of big red wax crayon in it. It 'angs down under 'im. Are tha still wi' me?'

The scales were falling from my eyes. 'Yes, I've got the picture now, thank you very much. I think I can work the rest out for myself. Shall we have a look at your writing book?'

'Naa then.' The boy carried on regardless. 'When 'e's served a yow . . . Does tha—'

'Yes, I know what that means,' I interrupted.

'Well, when 'e's served a yow, t'tup leaves 'is mark on 'er back, which means she's been ruddled. Does tha follow mi drift? Cooarse, if there's no colour on 'er back at all, then tha knaas t'tup's not been doin' what Nature's intended 'im to do, and 'e needs a bit o' encouragin' like. T'shepherd knaas, tha sees, that she's not been seen to.'

'What language ees thees boy speaking?' asked Carlos, looking completely dumbfounded. 'I thought my Engleesh was quite good, but I have not understood a seengle word.'

'It's "Yorkshire", a variation of English,' I told him. 'Dialect.'

'Thees "seen to",' he asked, still with a puzzled expression on his round face. 'Could you explain thees "seen to" for me, plees?'

'It's rather complicated,' I told him. 'I'll explain it later.'

I WAS DISMAYED to learn from the headteacher later that morning that Mrs Savage was to make an appearance. No doubt she wanted to check up on things and make her presence felt.

'There's a very nice little pub in the village,' Mr Leatherboy told Carlos and me. 'I expect the three of you will want to go out for something to eat so you can discuss things.'

Under no circumstances was I having lunch with Mrs Savage. 'Oh, no,' I said. 'I always eat with the children when I visit schools. It's an excellent opportunity to meet them informally and I always find they are far more relaxed and talkative over the dinner table. We'll have school lunch here, if that is all right.'

'Of course,' replied the headteacher, 'it's fish fingers today.'

Mrs Savage, resplendent in her early spring ensemble—a pale cream suit and matching accessories—was all smiles and jangling jewellery when she sailed through the headteacher's door. '*Buenos días*,' she said, holding out a manicured hand to the Spanish inspector.

'*Ah, buenos días, senora*,' replied Carlos.

'I do so love Spain,' said Mrs Savage, giving him the most charming of smiles. 'The sunshine, the colours, the people, the wine. I am Brenda Savage, personal assistant to Dr Gore, the chief education officer, by the way. You'll be meeting him tomorrow evening, Señor Itturiaga, at our little reception.'

'Carlos, plees.'

'Carlos,' she said somewhat breathlessly.

It was as if the headteacher and I were invisible.

'This is Mr Leatherboy, the headteacher,' I said stiffly. 'This is Mrs Savage.'

'Good morning,' said the headteacher. I could see he was rather put out by this woman swanning into his office without a word to him.

'I've just popped in to see how things are going,' said Mrs Savage, as if she were in complete charge.

'Things are going very well,' I said. 'You needn't have troubled yourself.'

'Oh, it's really no trouble.' She looked at me. 'And have you lunched?' she asked.

'We were just about to eat,' I said, 'if you would care to join us.'

'Very much,' she trilled. 'There's a very quaint and typically English country inn in the village, The Marquis of Granby—'

'We're eating with the children, Mrs Savage,' I said. 'We always do when we visit schools. I'm sure you have no objection.'

'Oh,' she replied, making a face. 'That would be very nice,' she lied.

'And, as it so happens, it's a seafood delicacy today,' I told her, giving the headteacher a sideways glance.

'Really?'

'Yes, fish fingers.'

I very much enjoyed watching Mrs Savage's discomfiture as she sat on a long wooden bench designed for small children, sandwiched between two rather messy little infant eaters who chattered without pausing, liberally spitting out food. Mrs Savage managed to force down half a fish finger before placing her knife and fork together.

'Are you 'avin' them fish fingers?' asked the little girl on her right.

'No, dear, I'm not,' replied Mrs Savage.

'Can I have 'em?'

'Please do.'

'Are you 'avin' yer chips?'

'No, dear.'

'Can I 'ave them, an' all?'

'Yes, you may.'

'Are you 'avin' yer yoghurt?' asked the child on her left.

'No.'

'Can I 'ave it?'

'Please do.' The fish fingers, chips and the yoghurt were quickly commandeered. 'Well,' said Mrs Savage, 'if you will excuse me, I need to freshen up.' She turned to the child who had just scooped out a great spoonful of pink yoghurt. 'Could you tell me, dear, where the staff toilets are?'

'Over theer,' replied the child, waving the spoon in front of her and, in the process, spattering Mrs Savage with strawberry yoghurt.

Mrs Savage rose from the bench with surprising equanimity, stared for a moment at the thin pink line which ran across her pale cream suit with matching accessories, and took a deep breath. 'Thank you, dear,' she said, with a sour smile. 'Thank you so very much.'

CARLOS AND I visited four schools during the two days and my colleague seemed immensely impressed with the high standard of work, the excellent teaching, the rich and challenging environments and the friendly children.

'The small schools are quite *excepciónal*,' he told me on the way back to Fettlesham. 'I am very much in favour of the small schools. They are like families.'

I thought at once of Hawksrill. 'You might share your observations with Dr Gore at the reception this evening,' I said. 'I am sure he would be very interested to hear your views on small rural schools.'

The Staff Development Centre was at its burnished best on the evening of the reception for the foreign inspectors. Connie had surpassed herself and the whole place sparkled. For the guests' arrival, she had abandoned the pink overall in favour of a bright floral dress and lemon-coloured cardigan, enhanced by a rope of large orange beads and an extremely colourful brooch in the shape of a parrot.

'I didn't recognise you, Connie,' remarked Sidney as he walked with David and me into the entrance where she was standing sentinel.

'To what are you alluring?' asked Connie.

'I was merely observing how very nice you look,' burbled Sidney.

'That's as may be. Anyway, there's that Semen woman looking for you,' she told him.

'I *beg* your pardon?'

'The French inspector, Semen.'

'Her name, Connie, is Simone,' Sidney informed her.

'Semen, Simone, whatever. I don't know why these foreigners have such funny names.' She huffed and turned to me. 'I've put the food in the lounge area, as per instructed, but there's no frogs' legs, snails, smelly French cheeses and the like, and there's no fancy bagatelles, just plain Yorkshire baps. It's good simple English food.'

'Good plain English fare? Spotted Dick? Jam roly-poly? Yorkshire pudding? Tripe and onions? Fish and chips?' enquired David.

'It's a buffet,' Connie told him, pronouncing it 'buff-it', 'not a five-course meal.'

'Ignore them, Connie,' I said. 'It sounds splendid.'

The evening was a success. Dr Gore's address went down well and Connie's plain English food was consumed with gusto.

'Splendid evening,' enthused Dr Gore as he made ready to depart. 'Many thanks, Gervase, for all your hard work and for your sterling efforts, too, Brenda. You make a formidable team.' I kept a deliberately straight face. Mrs Savage raised an eyebrow.

At this point, Connie materialised.

'Many thanks, Connie, for your help,' said Dr Gore. 'As efficient as ever.'

As Connie blushed prettily and preened a little, I could see out of the corner of my eye that Mrs Savage was looking thunderous.

'WELL, THE EIEI visit seemed to go very well,' said Sidney. It was Saturday morning and we were sitting in the lounge at the Staff Development Centre having said our farewells to the three inspectors.

'Signor Toria was delightful,' said David, who looked a whole lot happier than he had done for weeks. 'He's invited me over to Italy, you know, to see the schools there. Florence. *Firenze!*' he said expansively, waving his arms in the air. 'He said the standard of numeracy was higher in our country schools than in Italy. I must say I felt quite vindicated. Yes, he was absolutely delightful and he felt very much at home, did Mario. I took him to Willingforth Primary and he thought he had arrived at an Italian school. There was a child shouting out at the gate: "*Mama mia! Mama mia!*" I had some difficulty in explaining to him that the boy was not, in fact, speaking Italian but trying to get his mother's attention. "Mum, I'm 'ere! Mum, I'm 'ere!" We did laugh,' chuckled David.

'And how was Simone?' I asked Sidney. 'She seemed very amiable.'

'Amiable? Amiable?' scoffed Sidney. 'Hardly the most appropriate adjective to describe a woman of such outstanding beauty and composure. Simone was exquisite.'

'And how did she cope with the Yorkshire dialect?' I asked.

'I had to translate a great deal of what the teachers said to her, let alone what the children said,' Sidney told us, leaning back on his chair. 'She just stood and shrugged in that Gallic way they have. Actually, we got on great guns, though I have to admit she did have a few difficulties appreciating my sense of humour.'

'Does anyone appreciate your sense of humour, Sidney?' asked David.

IT WAS THE FIRST NIGHT of *The Sound of Music*. Christine was intending to come with me but had been feeling rather tired and the thought of two and a half hours in the same position on a small seat, in a stuffy theatre, listening to nuns climbing mountains, was not that appealing to her. She had told me, patting her very large stomach, that she had her very own mountain, without climbing any others.

'I'll be fine. Really,' she said. 'But I'll be happier staying at home.'

'I don't suppose anybody would notice if I don't make an appearance,' I said. 'After all, I only have a couple of lines. Are you sure you don't want me to stay?'

'No!' she said firmly. 'I'm going to have a hot bath and go to bed with a cup of cocoa and a romantic novel.'

'If you're sure.'

'Do you want me to throw something at you?' she said. 'I'll be fine.'

As it turned out, how wrong she was. The evening of the first performance of *The Sound of Music* would become part of Phinn folklore.

DESPITE THE FACT that all the cast had arrived on time, the orchestra had its full complement and the Civic Theatre was beginning to fill up, Ray was in a panic, buzzing around like a jam-crazed wasp.

The rather spotty young man playing Rolf approached him, waddling slowly and carefully as if he had a ferret down his trousers. 'Ray, do I *have* to wear these leather shorts?' he asked, sucking in his breath. 'They're cutting off my circulation.'

The producer looked heavenwards and sighed heavily. 'Yes, you have to wear the shorts, Fraser.'

'They are incredibly tight. I can hardly move.'

'They're lederhosen. They're supposed to be tight.'

'It's like having two tourniquets round my legs. They really are very constricting and as for going to the toilet—'

'They'll give,' replied Ray. 'They're made of leather. Just move about a bit and—' He stopped mid-sentence as Mrs Cleaver-Canning sailed past the door in her capacious black Mother Abbess costume, hung with a huge silver cross. She was like a galleon in full sail. Ray smacked his hand to his forehead dramatically and looked as if he was about to swoon. 'Margot, darling, could I have a small word?'

Mrs Cleaver-Canning retraced her steps. 'Yes, Raymond?' she asked. 'What is it?'

'Don't you feel you've gone just a teensy-weensy bit overboard with the greasepaint?'

'Not at all.'

'You cannot go on stage with that face, Margot,' moaned Ray. 'Don't you feel, just a smidgen, that scarlet Cupid-bow lips, bright blue eye shadow and crimson rouge are a touch out of character for a nun? You're supposed to be the Mother Abbess, not a woman of ill-repute looking for sailors on the dockside.'

'I deeply resent that analogy, Raymond. This, for your information, is my normal make-up, slightly exaggerated for dramatic purposes, and I have not the slightest intention of removing it. And another thing, there is no possibility, no possibility at all, of Winco trimming his moustache. It may look somewhat out of character, I have to admit, for a German admiral, but he has had that handlebar since he was a pilot officer in the RAF and I don't—'

'Of course, you don't! Why should you?' snapped Ray petulantly. 'Why should anyone listen to me? I'm just the producer after all. My opinion counts for nothing.' He then pushed past her and strutted off.

'He'll be fine, once the curtain rises,' Mrs Cleaver-Canning told me calmly, adjusting her wimple in the mirror. 'Opening-night nerves, that's all. He was the same last year when we did *Carousel*. Nearly fainted with the stress. It's always the case with these creative people. They're terribly temperamental. Now, come along, Mr Phinn. You must see Winco in his German admiral's uniform. He looks quite dashing.'

ALTHOUGH I SAY IT myself, the Fettlesham Literary Players put on the performance of their lives. Of course, it was Mrs Cleaver-Canning who stole the show, filling the hall with her deep, resonant contralto voice. Following the first rendering of 'Climb Every Mountain', the wholly enthusiastic audience demanded a reprise to which she graciously acceded.

When the curtain fell, Ray danced onto the stage, ecstatic. 'Wonderful! Marvellous! Magnificent! Superlative! Margot, you were a tour de force!' he cried, embracing Mrs Cleaver-Canning—not that his little arms reached round more than half her considerable size. 'Oh, my dears, I think I'm going to cry. You were all so good.'

All the players were milling around on the stage, reliving the performance, when the theatre manager appeared from the wings. 'Is there a Mr Pin here?' he called loudly.

'There's a Mr Phinn?' I said. 'That's me.'

'There's been a phone call. From your wife. She's gone to the hospital.'

'What? When?' My stomach was doing kangaroos jumps.

Everyone on the stage was hushed, listening to the little drama.

'When was this phone call?' asked Mrs Cleaver-Canning, pushing her way through people to where I was standing with the theatre manager.

'About half an hour ago,' he told her casually.

'What!' she hissed.'You silly man!' snapped Mrs Cleaver-Canning. 'His wife's having a baby.'

'I must go at once,' I said, feeling all hot and flustered.

Mrs Cleaver-Canning, resting a chubby hand on my arm, said calmly. 'Now, *calma*, Gervase, deep breaths, deep breaths. Women have had babies before. Your wife will be fine. Winco will take you to the hospital in the Mercedes. Winco!' she bellowed. Her husband appeared from behind a piece of mountain scenery.

'Here!' he shouted back.

'Bring the car round. We are taking Mr Phinn to the hospital.'

WE HAD HARDLY crawled out of the theatre car park, held up by people going home after the performance, when Mrs Cleaver-Canning prodded Winco. 'Put your foot down. Chop chop!'

'Righto,' he replied, slamming his foot down on the accelerator and screeching away in a cloud of exhaust smoke.

Anyone who caught sight of the occupants of the Mercedes that evening, as it sped through the centre of Fettlesham in the direction of the Royal Infirmary, would have thought they were hallucinating: an ageing German admiral with a handlebar moustache was at the wheel, a heavily be-medalled SS officer was in the passenger seat, and an overweight nun with crimson lips and sky-blue eye shadow was sitting in the back gesticulating.

THE MATERNITY WING of Fettlesham Royal Infirmary appeared particularly busy when we arrived. It seemed that the whole county was giving birth that night.

Mrs Cleaver-Canning swept through the doors and headed for the reception desk, with me following and Winco bringing up the rear. All conversation ceased when the majestic figure in a nun's habit strode to the front of a small queue and asked the startled man behind the reception desk, 'Could you tell us where Mrs Phinn is, please? She was brought in earlier this evening in labour.'

The receptionist ran his finger down a list of names. 'Yes, here we are. First name Christine. Christine Patricia Phinn.She's in Ward Six.'

'Has the baby arrived yet?' I asked, my heart in my mouth.

The man stared at the uniform.

'This is the worried father,' Mrs Cleaver-Canning informed him.

'I can't say,' the receptionist told me, still eyeing the uniform. 'You'd better go straight down there now. Ward Six.'

'You've been marvellous,' I told Mrs Cleaver-Canning and Winco. 'Thank you so much. You really don't need to hang around.'

'Nonsense!' said Mrs Cleaver-Canning. 'We would like to have a progress report. You hurry off to see your wife. Winco and I will wait.'

I WAS JUST IN TIME. Christine was being wheeled to the delivery room when I rushed down the corridor in search of Ward 6.

'Thank God!' I said, bending down and giving her a hug. 'Are you all right, darling?'

'She's fine,' said the nurse who was by the side of the trolley. 'This is the husband, I presume?'

'This is the husband,' Christine said.

My panic fled as I looked down at the smiling mother-to-be. She was calm and serene. Her blue eyes shone and she looked rose-cheeked and so beautiful.

I squeezed her hand. 'Are you ready?'

'As ready as I'll ever be,' she replied softly.

'I suppose you want to be in at the birth,' the nurse said to me.

'Of course,' I said.

'Well, if you faint, nobody will bother with you. I've got a far more important person to deal with.'

'I won't faint,' I said confidently.

'Aye, bigger men than you have said that.' She caught sight of the uniform. 'Didn't anyone tell you the war is over? What on earth are you wearing? Cover yourself up or you'll frighten the nurses.'

'Yes, nurse,' I said meekly.

At ten thirty, Richard Leslie Phinn was born, weighing in at seven pounds, one ounce. As I cradled him in my arm and stroked his little head, my eyes began to fill. He was so tiny and delicate, red as a radish, with a small round face, soft wisps of golden hair and great blue eyes. He was his mother's son all right.

'Richard Leslie?' said the nurse. 'Is that what you're calling him?'

'That's right,' I told her. 'Richard after my father and Leslie after my wife's.'

'Oh,' she said, 'I thought you would call him Adolf.'

BECAUSE LITTLE RICHARD Leslie had arrived prematurely, Christine stayed in hospital for the next few days. I visited her and my son every day that week, usually in the early evening before I went down to the theatre for the evening performance. On the Friday, we sat together with our child between us, marvelling at his tiny fingers and toes, his head of soft, silky blond hair and his great blue eyes.

Christine looked radiant. We were both so happy.

'Motherhood suits you,' I told her. 'I'd like another five, please.'

'We'll talk about that when we get home,' she said. The baby stirred. 'He's a little tinker, this one,' she said, stroking his cheek. 'He cries for his milk and then takes ages getting started. It's hard work.'

'I'll have a strong word with him,' I said. 'We should start as we mean to go on.' I stroked the baby's head gently. 'Are you listening to me, young man,' I said. 'You must drink plenty of milk.' The baby screwed up his little face and gave a great burp.

'There's your answer,' laughed Christine.

As I looked down at our baby, snuggling up to his mother, I thought of the sad, fragile children who I had come across on my travels as a school inspector; children who were neglected, disparaged, damaged and sometimes abused, children who would never know the warmth, encouragement and love of a good home.

'Penny for them,' said Christine.

'I'm thinking how very lucky I am,' I said, and kissed her tenderly.

'The doctor's been and everything is fine,' said the ward sister coming in at that moment. She examined the chart at the foot of the bed then turned to me. 'You can take them home when you're ready.'

As Christine was packing the few things she had in her bedside cabinet, I picked the clipboard off the bottom of the bed. The sheet of paper attached to it read: FETTLESHAM ROYAL INFIRMARY/MATERNITY UNIT. Below was BABY: RICHARD LESLIE PHINN. WEIGHT: 7LBS 1oz. Then, at the bottom was space for DOCTOR'S COMMENT. I was removing the sheet of paper when the ward sister came into the room again and caught me red-handed.

'What are you up to?'

'May I have this, please?'

'No, you may not. It's hospital property.'

'Oh, please,' I begged.

'Why do you want it, anyway?'

'I want to keep it until my son is twenty-one,' I told her seriously, 'and on that birthday I want to present it to him in a gilt frame, saying: "When I am dead and gone, Richard, perhaps you might sometimes look upon that scrap of paper in the golden frame and remember this very special day, and I hope you might remember a father and a mother who were so very proud of you and loved you more than any other parents loved a son. You see, it's the first thing anybody wrote about you," I shall tell him.'

'Oh,' said the nurse, who had listened open-mouthed to my commentary. 'How lovely. And what does the doctor say?'

Smiling, I passed over the piece of paper so she could read what the doctor had written: *Poor sucker*.

GERVASE PHINN

It was television personality Esther Rantzen who first set Gervase Phinn's career as a writer in motion. She saw him give a talk at the Leeds branch of Childline, the children's charity she founded, and was impressed by his optimistic and positive view of young people. She invited him to appear as a guest on her show, *Esther*, and after the programme he was contacted by no less than five publishers, all offering him deals. His first book of fictionalised memoirs, *Over Hill and Dale*, became an overnight best seller and gave him the confidence to relinquish his job in education in order to become an author.

'At the time, I was becoming more and more critical of various things going on nationally,' he explains. 'I was saying things that weren't politically correct for someone who was a principal inspector of schools.' These days, however, he feels far more optimistic, and believes that inspection is moving in the right direction. As a champion of poetry, art, music and drama, he is delighted that the words 'creativity' and 'enjoyment' are back on the education agenda. And his own passion for drama is evident in *Up and Down in the Dales*, in which he is seen taking part in an amateur production of *The Sound of Music*. As a young man, in fact, Gervase Phinn wanted to be an actor, but his father persuaded him that a degree in English would be of more use than a drama course.

After graduating, Phinn spent thirty years in education and says, unequivocally, that it was all because of 'a diminutive woman in tweeds who introduced me to the glories of literature. When Miss Wainwright taught Shakespeare, she never went through it in pleasure-destroying detail, she brought it to life. She was everything a teacher should be—hardworking, dedicated and respectful of children. All my life, I have been repaying a debt to her by trying to make a difference to other children's lives.'

Henning
Mankell
The Return
of the Dancing
Master

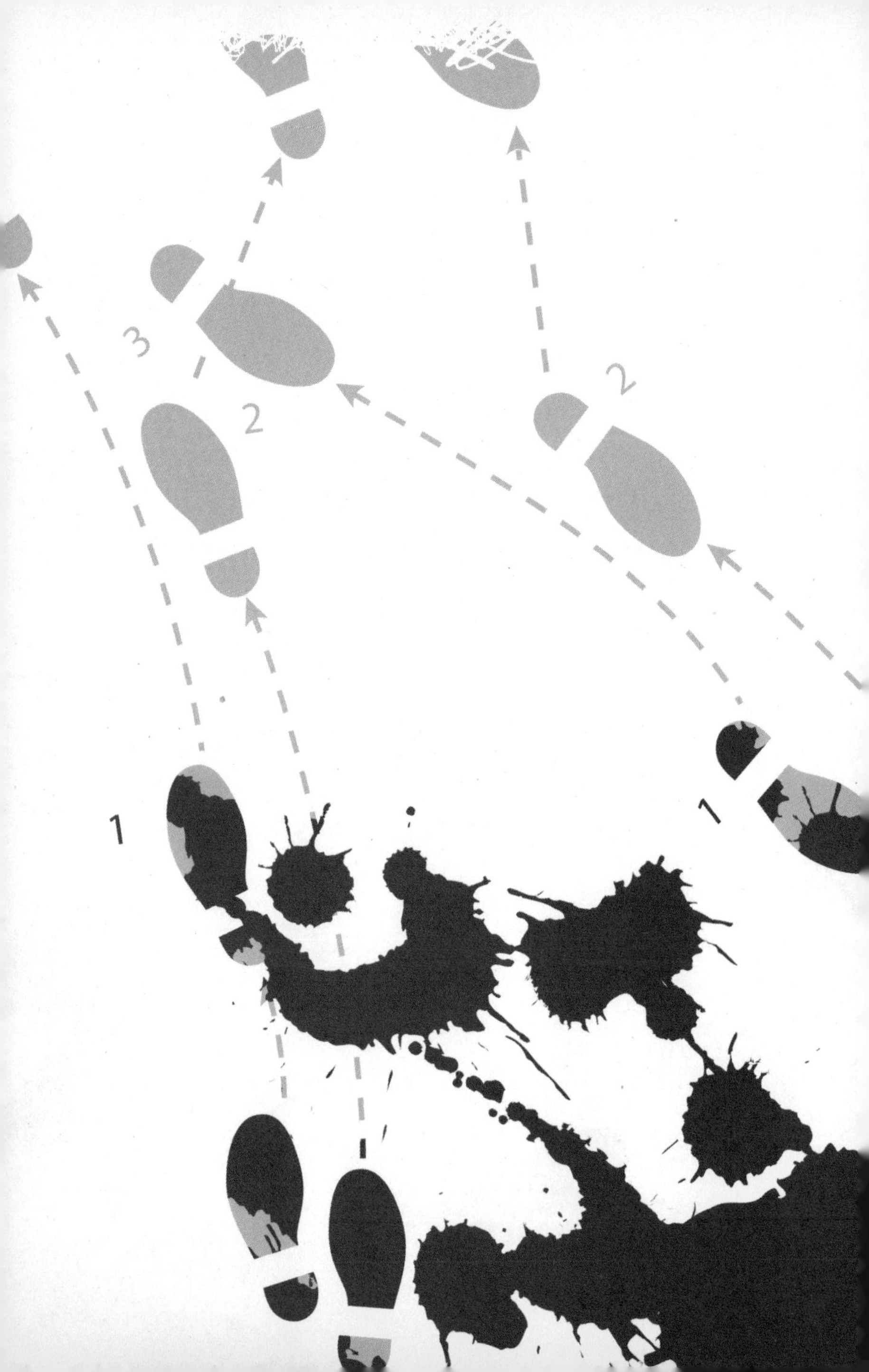

3
2
2
1
1

In the dense forests of Härjedalen, in northern Sweden, an old man lives alone. He bothers no one, barely even talks to his nearest neighbours. Why, then, should someone come to kill him? What secrets does he keep?

Prologue

The plane took off from the aerodrome near London shortly after 2 p.m. It was December 12, 1945. It was drizzling and chilly. Occasional gusts set the windsock fluttering, then all was calm again. The aircraft was a four-engined Lancaster bomber that had made countless sorties over German airspace. Now it was used for transport jobs, taking essential supplies to British troops stationed in defeated and devastated Germany.

Flight Lieutenant Mike Garbett had been told that he would fly a passenger to somewhere called Bückeburg, near the city of Hamelin. The passenger would be picked up and flown back to England the following evening. Who he was and why he was going to Germany, Squadron Leader Perkins, Garbett's commanding officer, did not tell him, nor did he ask. Even though the war was over, secret missions were not unusual.

Shortly before 2 p.m. a car had driven in through the gate. Peter Foster, the first officer, and Chris Wiffin, the navigator, were already aboard the big Lancaster. Garbett had been waiting on the cracked concrete apron. The man who emerged from the back seat of the car was wearing civvies. He took a black suitcase from the boot just as Squadron Leader Perkins drove up in his staff car. The man who was to be flown to Germany had his hat pulled down and Garbett could not see his eyes. Something about him made Garbett feel uncomfortable. When Perkins introduced them, the passenger mumbled his name. Garbett didn't catch what he said.

He helped the passenger aboard. There were three metal seats inside the plane, which was otherwise empty. The man sat down and placed his suitcase between his legs.

The landing at Bückeburg airfield went smoothly, despite the fact that it was dark and the lighting dim. Several military vehicles were already standing by. Garbett prepared to help the passenger off the plane, but when he reached for the suitcase the man insisted on taking it himself. He got into one of the cars and the convoy drove off immediately. Wiffin and Foster had clambered to the ground and watched the rear lights fade away. It was cold, and they were shivering.

'Makes you wonder what's going on,' Wiffin said.

'Best not to ask,' Garbett said.

DONALD DAVENPORT left the British prison for German war criminals soon after 11 p.m. He had a room in a hotel that served as a base for British officers stationed in Hamelin. He needed some sleep if he was going to carry out his duties efficiently the following day. He was a little uneasy about Sergeant MacManaman, his nominated assistant. Davenport disliked working with people unused to the job. All manner of things could go wrong, especially when the assignment was as big as the one in store.

He declined the offer of a cup of tea and went straight to his room. He sat at the desk and read the typewritten document he had received from a young major by the name of Stuckford, who was in charge of the operation.

He read the names. Kramer, Lehmann, Heider, Volkenrath, Grese . . . Twelve in all, three women, nine men. He studied the data on their weights and heights, and made a few more notes. It was a slow process. His professional pride required him to be meticulous. It was 1.30 a.m. by the time he had it all sorted. He checked his calculations again, just to be certain. He had overlooked nothing.

WHEN THEY KNOCKED at his door just after 5 a.m., he was already up and dressed. They had a light breakfast and then drove through the dark, drab town to the prison. Sergeant MacManaman was waiting for them. He was deathly pale, and Davenport wondered again whether he would be up to the job.

By 11 a.m. everything was ready. All those required to be present had taken up their positions. Davenport nodded to Stuckford, who signalled to one of the warders, and a cell door opened.

The first to appear was Irma Grese. A fleeting sensation of surprise disturbed Davenport's icy calm. How could this slight, blonde twenty-two-year-old possibly have whipped prisoners to death at the Belsen concentration camp? She looked him in the eye, then glanced up at the gallows. The warders led her up the steps. Davenport adjusted her feet so that they were immediately above the trap door, and placed the noose round her neck while checking to make sure MacManaman made no mistake with the leather strap he was fastening round her legs. Just before Davenport pulled the hood over her head he heard her utter one scarcely audible word: '*Schnell!*'

MacManaman took a step back and Davenport reached for the handle that operated the trap door.

The executions took two hours and seven minutes. Davenport had reckoned on two and a quarter hours. All had gone according to plan. Twelve German war criminals had been put to death. Davenport packed the rope and the leather straps into his suitcase, and said goodbye to Sergeant MacManaman.

'Come and have a glass of brandy. You did a good job.'

'They deserved all that they got,' MacManaman said. 'I don't need any brandy.'

DAVENPORT LEFT THE PRISON with Major Stuckford, who took him to the hotel dining room and ordered lunch. They had a side room to themselves. Davenport approved of Stuckford, not least because he asked no unnecessary questions. There was nothing Davenport disliked more than people asking him questions about what it had been like, hanging this or that notorious criminal. They exchanged pleasantries as they ate, about the weather, and whether there would be extra rations of tea or tobacco for Christmas, not far away now.

Only over a cup of tea, afterwards, did Stuckford refer to what had happened that morning. 'We execute the worst of the criminals,' he said. 'The really monstrous war criminals. But we also know that lots of them are getting away with it. Like Josef Lehmann's brother.'

Lehmann was the last to be hanged that morning. A little man who had met his death placidly, almost nonchalantly.

'Waldemar Lehmann was a brutal, sadistic man,' Stuckford continued. 'It wasn't just that he was ruthless with the prisoners, he also took a devilish delight in teaching his subordinates the art of torture.'

They sat in silence. Outside the window, rain was now falling.

'We should have hanged him, as we did his brother,' Stuckford went on. 'But he made himself invisible. Maybe he's slipped away through one of the Nazis' escape routes. He could be in Argentina or South Africa, and we'll never track him down there.'

DAVENPORT RETURNED to the aerodrome at 5 p.m. He was cold, even though he was wearing his thick winter overcoat. The pilot was standing by the plane, waiting for him. Davenport took his seat in the chilly fuselage and turned up his coat collar.

Garbett settled in the cockpit, the Lancaster gathered speed and flew into the clouds.

Davenport had completed his assignment. He had justified his reputation as England's most accomplished hangman. He dozed off in the uncomfortable seat, while Mike Garbett was still wondering about the identity of his passenger.

Chapter 1

Härjedalen, Sweden, October–November 1999

He woke in the night, besieged by shadows. It had started when he was twenty-two. Fifty-four years of sleepless nights, constant shadows. This night was no exception. The shadows generally turned up a few hours after darkness fell, and stayed by his side, with silent, white faces, until dawn. He would sleep in the end, but usually for only a few hours. He had grown used to their presence over the years, but he knew he couldn't trust them. One of these days they would be bound to break loose. He didn't know what would happen then. Would they attack him, or would they betray him?

He had been tired all of his adult life. Looking back, he could recognise only an endless string of days that he had somehow or other muddled through. The shadows had also taken their revenge on him during his two marriages: his wives had been frustrated by his constant state of unease, and the fact that, when he wasn't working, he was always half asleep. In the end they had left him.

He looked at his watch: 4.15 a.m. He went to the kitchen and made coffee. The thermometer outside the window showed –2°C. He moved the curtain, and the dog started barking out there in the darkness. Shaka, his Norwegian elkhound, was the only security he had.

He took his coffee into the living room, sat at the table and contemplated the jigsaw pieces spread out before him. He made sure he always had a store of puzzles. The one he was working on now was a 3,000-piece puzzle based on Rembrandt's *The Conspiracy of the Batavians under Claudius Civilis*.

He sat holding a piece that obviously belonged in the background of the painting. It took him nearly ten minutes to find where. He checked his watch again: 4.30. Hours to go before dawn, before the shadows would withdraw and he could get some sleep.

On the whole, everything had become much simpler since he had turned sixty-five and retired. He didn't need to be anxious about feeling tired all day. But the shadows ought to have left him in peace ages ago. He had served his time. They had no need now to keep their eye on him. His life had been ruined.

He went to the bookcase where he kept his CD player. He put the disc in the machine back on. It was a tango, a genuine Argentinian tango. He turned up the sound and went to the bedroom. He took his dark suit from the wardrobe, and chose a rust-brown tie to go with his white shirt. Most important of all were the shoes. He had several pairs of Italian dancing shoes, all expensive. For the serious dancer, the shoes had to be perfect.

When he was ready, he studied his appearance in the mirror on the wardrobe door. His hair was grey and cropped short. He was thin. But he looked considerably younger than his seventy-six years.

He knocked at the spare bedroom door. He imagined hearing somebody bidding him enter. He opened the door and switched on the light. His dancing partner was lying in the bed. He was always surprised by how real she looked, even though she was only a doll. He pulled back the duvet and lifted her up. She was wearing a white blouse and a black skirt. He had given her the name of Esmeralda. On the bedside table were some bottles of scent. He sat her down, and selected a discreet Dior, which he sprayed gently onto her neck.

He escorted Esmeralda to the living room, and slid his shoes into the loops attached to the soles of her feet. Then he started dancing. As he twirled the doll round the floor, he felt that he was sweeping all the shadows out of the room. He danced for more than an hour. When finally he carried Esmeralda back to the spare room, he had been sweating. He undressed and took a shower. It would soon be light.

He put on his dressing gown and made some more coffee. Shaka barked briefly out there in the darkness. He thought about the forest surrounding him. This was what he had dreamed of. A remote cottage with no neighbours. A house at the very end of a road.

He sat at the kitchen table with his coffee. Another bark from Shaka. Then all was quiet. It must have been an animal. Probably a hare. He washed up his cup, then went into the bedroom. He took off his dressing gown and snuggled into bed. It was still dark, but he would wait for the first faint signs of light outside the house before he switched off the light and went to sleep.

Shaka barked again. But it was different now. The dog was barking away frantically. That could only mean that there was an elk in the vicinity. Or a bear. He got out of bed and put on his dressing gown. Shaka fell silent. He waited, but nothing.

Something odd was going on. Shaka's last barks hadn't stopped in a natural way; they seemed to have been cut off. He pulled on a pair of trousers and a jumper. He took out the gun he always kept under his bed, a shotgun. He went into the hall and stuck his feet into a pair of boots, listening all the time. Not a sound from Shaka. He unlocked the three locks on the front door and slowly opened it. He picked up a torch and shone it into the darkness. There was no sign of the dog in the pen. He shouted for Shaka and shone the torch along the edge of the woods. Still no reaction. Sweat was pouring off him. He cocked the gun and walked cautiously over to the dog pen, then stopped in his tracks. Shaka was lying on the ground. The animal's eyes were staring and its greyish-white fur bloodstained. He turned on his heel and ran back to the house, slamming the door behind him.

He was shaking. The shadows had fooled him. He had thought that he had got away with it, but he had been wrong.

He resolved not to give up without a fight. He kicked off his boots and put on his trainers. His ears were alert all the time. He wouldn't allow himself to be taken by surprise.

And then the house collapsed. That's what it felt like, at least. At the explosion he flung himself to the floor. His finger had been on the trigger and his gun went off, shattering the mirror on the wardrobe. He crawled to the door and looked into the living room. Somebody had fired a shot or maybe thrown a grenade through the big window facing south. The room was a sea of splintered glass.

He had no time to think any further as the window facing north was demolished by another shot. He pressed himself against the floor and searched desperately for a way out.

Then there was a whistling noise, followed by a thud right next to him. He raised his head and saw it was a tear-gas canister. He turned his head away, but it was too late. The gas was in his eyes and his lungs and the pain was unbearable. He had no choice but to leave the house. He scrambled to the front door. He flung the door open and rushed out, shooting at the same time. Although he couldn't see a thing, he ran as fast as he could to the trees.

Branches made deep wounds in his face, but he knew he must not stop. Whoever it was was somewhere behind him. He stumbled over a rock and fell. He was about to get up when he felt something on the back of his neck. A boot on his head. The game was up. The shadows had defeated him.

It would be nearly two hours before he finally died. First he felt the breath of the person placing the blindfold over his eyes and tying the knot at the back of his head. He tried to say something. But when he opened his mouth, no words came out, just a new attack of coughing. Then somebody pulled off his trousers and jumper. He could feel the cold earth against his skin before the whiplashes hit him and transformed everything into an inferno. He could hear himself screaming, but there was nobody there to help him.

The last thing he felt was being dragged over the ground, into the house, and then being beaten on the soles of his feet. Everything went black. He was dead.

STEFAN LINDMAN was a police officer. Once every year at least he had found himself in a situation where he experienced considerable fear. On one occasion he had been attacked by a psychopath weighing over a hundred kilos. If one of his colleagues hadn't succeeded in stunning the man with a blow to the head, he would certainly have died. Another time he had been shot at while approaching a house to deal with domestic violence. The shot narrowly missed one of his legs. But he had never been as frightened as he felt now, on the morning of October 25, 1999, as he lay in bed staring up at the ceiling.

He had barely slept. During the night he had devised a plan. A plan that was also an invocation. He wouldn't go directly up the hill to the hospital. He would take a roundabout route and search for signs that the news he was going to receive from the doctor would be positive.

Generally, when he wasn't in uniform, he would be in jeans and a T-shirt. Today, though, he felt his best suit was called for. As he knotted his tie he contemplated his face in the bathroom mirror. He was a vain man, and his reflection would generally raise his spirits, but this morning everything was different. It was obvious he hadn't been sleeping or eating properly for weeks. His cheeks were hollow. This morning he didn't at all like what he saw in the mirror.

When he had finished dressing he made coffee. He didn't feel like eating anything. His appointment was for 8.45. It was 7.57. So he had exactly forty-eight minutes for his walk to the hospital.

When he came onto the street it had started drizzling.

Lindman lived on Allégatan, a busy street running through the centre of Borås. His flat was within walking distance of the police station, and he could even walk to the Ryavallen stadium when Elfsborg were playing at home. Football was his biggest interest, apart from his work.

He was thirty-seven and he had worked in Borås ever since leaving police college. It was where he had wanted to be posted. Born in Kinna, he had grown up there, the youngest of three children. His father was a secondhand car salesman and his mother worked in a bakery. His two sisters were seven and nine years older than him.

When Lindman thought back to his childhood, it sometimes seemed strangely uneventful and boring. Life had been secure and routine. His parents disliked travelling. The furthest they could bring themselves to go was Borås or Varberg. His sisters had rebelled against this life and moved away early, one to Stockholm and the other to Helsinki. His parents had taken that as a failure on their part, and Lindman had realised that he was almost bound to stay in Kinna.

As a teenager, he'd had no idea what he wanted to do when he grew up. Then, by chance, he had got to know a young man devoted to motocross. He became this man's assistant, and spent a few years travelling around racetracks in central Sweden. But he tired of that eventually, and returned to his parents. He still didn't know what to do with his life, but then he happened to meet a policeman from Malmö who was visiting some mutual friends in Kinna. And the thought struck Lindman: Maybe I could become a police officer.

To his surprise, he was accepted by police college at his first attempt. The training didn't cause him any problems. He was among the better ones in his year. One day he went back home to Kinna in uniform and announced that he would be working in Borås, just forty kilometres down the road.

For the first few years he commuted from Kinna, but when he fell in love with one of the girls at the police station, he moved into Borås. They lived together for three years. Then one day she told him out of the blue that she had met a man from Trondheim and was moving there. Lindman took the development in his stride. He realised that their relationship was beginning to bore him.

Then his father had a heart attack and died, and a few months later his mother died as well. The day after her funeral he inserted a lonely hearts advert in the local paper. He received four replies. One of the women was a Pole who had lived in Borås for many years. She had two grown-up children, and worked as a dinner lady at the grammar school. She was nearly ten years older than him, but they never really noticed the difference. He couldn't understand at first what there was that had made him fall in love with her. Then it dawned on him: she was completely ordinary. She took life seriously, but didn't fuss about anything. For the first time in his life, Lindman felt something for a woman that was more than lust. Her name was Elena and she lived in Norrby. He spent the night there several times a week.

It was there, one day, that he was in the bathroom and discovered that he had a strange lump on his tongue.

Lindman interrupted his train of thought. He was standing in front of the hospital. It was 8.26 by his watch. He walked past the entrance and quickened his pace. He walked round the hospital twice.

By the time he got to the doctor's door, he was scared stiff. He knocked and went in. It was a woman doctor. He tried to work out from her face what he could expect. She gave him a smile, but that only confused him.

He sat down. She organised some papers on the desk.

'I'm afraid I have to tell you that the lump you have on your tongue is a malignant tumour.'

He swallowed. He had known all along, ever since that morning in Elena's flat. He had cancer.

'We can't see any sign of it spreading. As we've found it in the early stages, we can start treating it. It will be radiotherapy to start with. And then an operation.'

'Will I die of it?' This was not a question he had prepared in advance. It burst out without him being able to stop it.

'Cancer is always serious,' the doctor said, 'but nowadays we can take measures. It's been a long time since diagnosing cancer meant passing a death sentence.'

He sat with the doctor for more than an hour. When he left her office he was soaked in sweat. In the pit of his stomach was a spot as cold as ice. He forced himself to be calm. He would go for a coffee.

He sat down in the cafeteria and, as he drank his coffee, thumbed through one of the previous day's national papers. He had forgotten all about the words and the pictures the moment he turned over a page. The ice-cold knot was still there.

Something caught his attention. A photograph. A headline about a brutal murder. He stared at the photograph and the caption: HERBERT MOLIN, AGED 76, FORMER POLICE OFFICER.

When he had first arrived in Borås as a probationer, he had been introduced to the oldest and most experienced detective on the staff, Herbert Molin. They worked together in the serious crimes division for some years until Molin retired. Lindman had often thought about him afterwards. The way he was always looking for links and clues. A lot of people spoke ill of him behind his back, but he had always been a rich source of learning for Lindman. One of Molin's main theories was that intuition was the most important and most underestimated resource for a true detective. The more experience Lindman accrued, the more he realised that Molin was right.

Molin had been a recluse. Nobody Lindman knew had ever been to Molin's house. Some years after he had retired, Lindman heard that Molin had left town, but nobody could say where he had moved to.

Lindman put the newspaper down.

So Molin had moved to the province of Härjedalen. According to the paper, he had been living in a remote house in the middle of the forest. That was where he had been murdered. There was no discernible motive, nor any clues as to who the killer might have been.

Lindman got to his feet. When he left the hospital it was still drizzling. He started downhill to the town centre. Herbert Molin was dead, and he himself had been assigned to the category of people whose days might be numbered. He paused on the pavement to get his breath back. He wasn't just scared, he also had the feeling that he was somehow being swindled. By something invisible that had smuggled its way into his body and was now busy destroying him.

The doctor had given him an appointment for further tests the next day. She had also extended his sick leave. He would start his course of treatment in three weeks' time.

Lindman went into the library. He collected a speedway magazine before sitting at one of the tables. He used it to hide behind. Stared at a picture of a motorbike while trying to make up his mind what to do.

The doctor had said he wasn't going to die. Not yet, at least. There was a risk that the tumour would grow and the cancer might spread. It would be a head-to-head battle. He would either win or lose; there was no possibility of a draw. If there was anybody he should be able to talk to and who could give him the support he needed, it was Elena. But he couldn't bring himself to phone her. He hadn't even told her about his hospital appointment.

He leafed through the pages of the magazine. Leafed his way to a conclusion.

Half an hour later he knew what he was going to do. He would talk to his boss, Superintendent Olausson, who had just got back from a hunting holiday. He would tell him he had been given a medical certificate without mentioning why. He would just say he had to undergo a thorough examination because of pains he had been having in his throat. He could hand the doctor's certificate in to the staffing office himself. Then he would go home, phone Elena and tell her he was going away for a few days. Maybe to Helsinki to see his sister. He had done that before. It wouldn't arouse her suspicions. Next, he would go to the wine shop and buy a couple of bottles.

LINDMAN LEFT the police station after talking to Olausson. He queued up in the wine shop and took home two bottles of Italian wine. Before he had even taken off his jacket he opened one of the bottles and filled a glass, which he emptied in one go. He kicked off his shoes and threw his jacket over a chair. He took his glass and the bottle of wine with him into the bedroom. He lay down on the bed. After another glass of wine, he rolled onto his side and fell asleep.

IT WAS NEARLY midnight when he woke up. He had slept for almost eleven hours. His shirt was soaked in sweat.

His first thought was that he was going to die.

Then he decided that he would fight it. After the next set of tests he would have three weeks in which to do whatever he liked. He would spend that time finding out all there was to find out about cancer. And he would prepare for the fight he was going to put up.

He got out of bed, took off his shirt and tossed it into the basket in the bathroom. Then he stood in the window overlooking Allégatan. The street was shiny with rain. He thought about Molin. A vague thought had been nagging at him since he read the report in the paper. Now it came back to him.

They had once been chasing an escaped murderer through the woods north of Borås. It was late autumn, like now. Lindman and Molin had somehow become separated among the trees, and when Lindman eventually found him he had approached so quietly that he surprised Molin, who turned to stare at him with terror-stricken eyes.

'I didn't mean to scare you,' Lindman said.

Molin just shrugged. 'I thought it was somebody else,' he said.

That was all. I thought it was somebody else.

It dawned on Lindman that he had known all the time: Molin had been scared stiff all those years they had worked together. His fear had always been there. Molin had usually managed to hide it, but not always. Lindman frowned. Molin had been murdered in the depths of the northern forests, having always been frightened. The question was: of whom?

GIUSEPPE LARSSON was a man who had learned from experience never to take anything for granted. He woke up on October 26 when his back-up alarm clock rang. He looked at his front-line clock on the bedside table and noted that it had stopped at 3.04. So you couldn't even rely on alarm clocks. That was why he always used two. He got out of bed and opened the roller blind with a snap. The television weather forecast the night before had said there would be a light snowfall over the province of Jämtland, but Larsson could see no sign of snow. The sky was dark, but full of stars.

Larsson had a quick breakfast made for him by his wife. Shortly after 7 a.m. he set off for work. He was faced with a drive of a couple of hundred kilometres. This last week he had done it there and back several times, apart from one occasion when he had been so tired that he had felt obliged to book into a hotel in Sveg. Now he had to drive there yet again for the meeting with the forensic unit.

The emergency call had reached the Östersund police station seven days earlier. Larsson had been on the point of leaving when somebody thrust a telephone into his hand. The woman at the other end was very upset. Her name was Hanna Tunberg. Twice a month she used to char for a man called Herbert Molin, who lived some miles outside Sveg. When she arrived that day she had found a dog lying dead in its pen, and had seen that all the windows in the house were broken. She didn't dare stay. She had driven back to Sveg and collected her husband. They had gone back to the house together. Her husband had entered the house but emerged immediately and shouted to his wife, who had stayed in the car, that the place was full of blood. Then he thought he saw something at the edge of the forest. He had gone to investigate, then sprinted to the car and started vomiting into the grass. On their return to Sveg, she had phoned the police and they had passed the call on to Östersund.

Larsson had gone immediately to Nisse Rundström, who was in charge of emergencies, and explained the situation. Twenty minutes later he was on his way to Sveg in a police car with blue lights flashing.

Hanna Tunberg had been waiting for them at the turnoff, along with Inspector Erik Johansson, who was stationed in Sveg. It was already dark by then. They went first to the spot on the edge of the forest that Hanna Tunberg had described. They shone their torches on the dead body. The man on the ground in front of them was worse than anything that Larsson had been obliged to look at before. It wasn't really a man at all, just a bloody bundle. The face had been scraped away, the feet were no more than blood-soaked lumps and his back had been so badly beaten that bones were exposed.

They had then approached the house with guns drawn. When they entered they had found that the floor was covered in bloody footprints and broken glass.

Larsson was now approaching Svenstavik. It was still dark. Several days had passed, but they were no nearer to solving the mystery of the murdered man in the forest.

It had transpired that the dead man was a retired police officer who had moved up to Härjedalen after working for many years as a detective in Borås. Larsson had spent the previous evening reading through documents faxed to him from Borås. He was now familiar with all the basic information that forms an individual's profile. Nevertheless, he had the impression he was staring into a vacuum. There was no motive, no clues, no witnesses. It was as if some mysterious evil force had emerged from the forest to attack Molin with all its might, and then disappeared.

Larsson passed through Svenstavik and continued towards Sveg. It was getting light now, and the wooded ridges surrounding him were acquiring a shade of blue. His mind turned to the preliminary report he had received from the coroner's office in Umeå. The wounds on Molin's back appeared to have been caused by lashes with a whip. It was probable that the injuries to the soles of Molin's feet had been caused by the same instrument. The scrape marks on the face indicated that he had been dragged face down over the ground. The wounds were full of soil. There were bruises on the victim's neck, but he had not been choked to death. Nor did he die from the residue of tear gas found in his eyes, throat and lungs. Molin had died from exhaustion. He had, literally, had the life whipped out of him.

Frenzy, fury, Larsson thought. That's what it's all about. Perhaps this fury is the motive. Fury and a thirst for vengeance. The question was: had Molin simply been murdered? Or was it an execution?

Everything gave the impression of having been carefully planned. The guard dog had had its throat cut. The murderer had been equipped with whips and tear-gas cartridges. The fury had to have been an outburst within the framework of a meticulous plan.

That meant that whoever killed Molin had most probably been to the house before. Somebody ought to have noticed strangers hanging around in the vicinity. Or maybe nobody had noticed anything. Which would mean that the murderer, or murderers, would have been friends of Molin. But Molin didn't have any friends. That was something Fru Tunberg had been very clear about. He had been a recluse.

IT WAS 9.40 by the time Larsson drove up to Molin's house. The scene-of-crime tapes were still in place, but there was no sign of a police vehicle. Larsson got out of his car and looked slowly around. There was quite a wind now. The swishing sound from the forest imposed itself upon the autumn morning.

The phone rang. He gave a start. He retrieved his mobile from his jacket pocket and answered. 'Giuseppe Larsson.'

He had lost count of the number of times he had cursed his mother for giving him his first name after an Italian crooner she had heard at a concert in Östersund's People's Park one summer night. Every time anybody phoned him and he said his name, whoever was at the other end of the line always paused to consider.

'Giuseppe Larsson?'

'Speaking.'

He listened. The man at the other end said his name was Stefan Lindman, and that he was a police officer. He was ringing from Borås. He had worked with Molin and was curious about what had happened. Larsson tried to answer Lindman's questions, but reception wasn't good, and he could see the forensic team arriving.

'I've got your number,' Larsson said. 'And you can get hold of me at this number or at the station in Östersund. Meanwhile, is there anything *you* can tell *me*? Any information could be of value. We really don't have much to go on.'

He listened to the response without comment. The scene-of-crime van drove up to the house and Larsson concluded the call.

The policeman from Borås had said something important. Molin had been scared. He had never explained why he was uneasy, but Lindman had no doubt. Molin had been scared all the time, wherever he had been, whatever he had been doing.

Larsson followed the two forensic officers into the house, and picked his way to the small bedroom off the living room. Lying on the bed was a bloodstained doll, life size. He thought at first it was some kind of sex aid used by lonely Molin, but the doll had no orifices. The loops on its feet suggested that it was used as a dancing partner.

His mobile rang. It was the chief of police in Östersund. Larsson told him the current state of affairs and that they had not yet found anything new at the scene of the crime. Fru Tunberg was in Östersund, talking to Artur Nyman who was a detective sergeant and Larsson's closest colleague. The chief of police was able to inform Larsson that the victim's daughter, who was in Germany, would soon be on her way to Sweden. They'd also been in touch with his son, who worked as a steward on a cruise ship in the Caribbean. Molin's second wife had proved difficult to trace.

Larsson scrutinised the bloody footprints on the floor just inside the house. He frowned. There was something about them that puzzled him. He took out his notebook and made a sketch. There were nineteen prints in all, ten made by a right foot and nine by a left foot.

He went outside. He pressed his feet down into the gravel in front of the house to reproduce the pattern he had sketched. He stepped to one side and studied the result. Then he carefully stepped into the footprints, one after the other, moving slowly. He did it again, faster now, with his knees slightly bent. The penny dropped.

One of the forensic officers came out onto the steps and lit a cigarette. He stared at the footprints in the gravel. 'What are you doing?'

'Testing a theory. Wasn't there a disc in the CD player?'

'That's right,' said the man.

'What kind of music was it?'

The technician went inside. He was back in a flash. 'Argentinian stuff. An orchestra. I can't pronounce the name.'

'What we have here are tango steps. It's a bit like when you were little and went to dancing classes. The teacher used to tape footprints onto the floor, and you had to follow them. The steps are tango steps.'

To prove his theory Larsson started to hum a tango tune. At the same time he followed the footprints in the gravel. The steps fitted.

'Somebody dragged Molin around and placed his blood-soaked feet on the floor as if he had been attending a dancing class. The question,' Larsson said, 'is who? Who invites a dead man to dance with him?'

LINDMAN WAS BEGINNING to feel that his body was being drained of blood. He spent many hours at the hospital every day, having blood taken for testing. He also talked to the doctor on two more occasions. Each time he had lots of questions, but never got round to asking any of them. In fact, there was only one question he really wanted answering: was he going to survive?

The second night he had gone to Elena's. The moment she saw him in the doorway, she knew something was wrong. Lindman had tried to make up his mind whether or not to tell her, but he was unsure right up to the moment he rang the doorbell. He had barely had time to hang up his jacket before she asked him what was wrong.

'I'm ill,' he had said. 'I've got cancer.'

They had sat up far into the night, and she had been sensible enough not to try to console him. What he needed was courage. She brought him a mirror and said look, the man on her sofa was very much alive, not a corpse, that was how he ought to approach the situation. He had stayed the night, lying awake long after she had gone to sleep. He had got up at dawn, quietly, so as not to wake her, and left the building as discreetly as possible.

The doctor had said that they would finish all the tests today. He had asked if he could go away, possibly abroad, before the treatment started, and she said he could do whatever took his fancy. Shortly after ten he went to the travel agent's. He started going through the brochures. He had more or less made up his mind that it would be Majorca when the thought of Herbert Molin came to him. He knew there and then what he was going to do. He wasn't going to fly to Majorca. If he did, all he would do was to wander around a place where he knew no one, worrying about what was going to happen. If he went to Härjedalen, he would be able to devote his attention to something other than himself and his problems. He reckoned it would take him twelve to fifteen hours to drive there.

When he returned home he packed his suitcase. He looked up the weather on teletext and saw that the temperature in Östersund was forecast at between 5° and 10°C. Before he went to bed, it occurred to him that he ought to tell Elena that he was leaving. She would be worried if he simply disappeared. But he put it off. He had his mobile, and she had the number. Perhaps he wanted her to worry. Maybe he wanted to hurt an innocent party to make up for his being the one who was ill.

BY NIGHTFALL the following day, Lindman had driven as far as Orsa. He stopped for an evening meal, a greasy steak in a roadside café, then settled down on the back seat of his car. He was tired out, and fell asleep at once. In his dreams, he was running through an endless succession of dark rooms.

He woke up while it was still dark, feeling stiff and with a splitting headache. He wriggled his way out of the car, and as he was having a pee he noticed that his breath was coming out like steam. The temperature was around or even below zero.

He started the engine. It was another 100 kilometres to Sveg. He reminded himself that he must be on the lookout for elks. It grew gradually lighter. Lindman sifted through what he could remember about Molin, every conversation, all those meetings, times when nothing special happened. But he had difficulty in remembering. The only thing he was sure about was that Molin had been frightened.

The forest came to an end, and after crossing the River Ljusnan Lindman found himself driving into Sveg. The place was so small that he nearly drove out of it the other side before realising that he had reached his destination. He turned left and saw a hotel sign. He had assumed it wouldn't be necessary to book a room, but when he went to reception the girl behind the desk told him that he'd had a stroke of luck. They had one room, thanks to a cancellation.

'Who wants to stay in a hotel in Sveg?' he said, in surprise.

'Test drivers,' the girl told him. 'They book in up here and test new car models. And then there are the computer people. New firms setting up.' She asked him how long he intended staying.

'A week,' he said. 'Maybe longer. Is that possible?'

She checked in the ledger. 'Well, I think so, but I can't promise.'

Lindman left his case in his room, and went downstairs for breakfast. Then he went back to his room, took a shower and crept between the sheets. What am I doing here? he wondered. I could have gone to Majorca. But I'm in Sveg. Instead of walking along a beach and looking at a blue sea, I'm surrounded by endless trees.

WHEN HE AWOKE, he lay in bed and tried to construct some sort of plan. First he would have to see the place where Molin had died. The simplest thing, of course, would be to talk to the detective in charge of the case in Östersund, Giuseppe Larsson, but something told him it would be better to take a look at the scene of the crime without anybody knowing about it. He could talk to Larsson later.

He dressed and went down to reception. The girl who had checked him in was on the phone. Lindman spread out his map and waited.

'Is the room OK?' she asked as she put the receiver down.

'All in order,' Lindman said. 'I have a question, though. I'm here because a friend of mine was murdered not far from here last week.'

Her expression turned serious. 'The bloke who lived out at Linsell?'

'That's the one.' He showed her his police ID, then pointed to his map. 'Can you show me where he lived?'

She turned the map round and took a good look at it. Then she pointed to the spot. She looked at him. 'I'm not really nosy,' she said. 'But we've had some police from Östersund staying here, and I heard them describing how to get there over the telephone.'

When Lindman left the hotel he could see that the weather had changed. There was a clear sky; the morning clouds had dispersed. He breathed in the fresh air.

Suddenly he wondered who would come to his funeral.

He reached Molin's house at around two in the afternoon. He drove into the parking area at the front. The place was deserted. He got out of the car. He stood still and looked around. Molin had moved from Borås to be in this remote spot in the depths of the forest. And somebody had found their way here in order to kill him. Lindman approached the front door and tried it. Locked. Then he walked round the building. Every window was broken. From the rear he could see the water of the lake glittering through the trees.

He walked up to one of the windows. There was a kick-sledge parked next to the house wall. He used it as a stepladder to open the broken window from the inside. Carefully he removed the protruding bits of glass and clambered into the house.

He was in a small bedroom. The bed was made, but it was covered in patches of dried blood. The forensic examination had no doubt been completed, but he preferred not to touch anything. He wanted to see the same things as the forensic officers had seen. But what did he think he was doing? What did he think he might uncover? He told himself he was in Molin's house as a private person. Not as a policeman or a private detective, just a man who had cancer and who wanted to find something other than his illness to think about.

He went into the living room. Furniture had been overturned. There were bloodstains on the walls and on the floor. Only now did he realise how horrific Molin's death must have been. He had clearly been subjected to a violent attack, and it looked as though he had resisted. Lindman walked carefully round the room. Stopped at the CD player, which was standing open. No disc in it, but an empty case beside the player. Argentinian tango.

All the time he was trying hard to imagine Molin walking at his side. A lonely man of about seventy-five. How had he spent his days? Lindman scrutinised the floor. Next to one of the bloody footprints was a piece of a jigsaw puzzle. There were other pieces strewn over the floor. He went over to a cupboard. It was full of jigsaw puzzles. Molin spent a lot of time doing jigsaw puzzles, he thought. Odd.

He looked round the room again, and then at the bloody footprints just inside the front door. They formed a pattern. What surprised him was that they were so clear, suggesting that they had been put there intentionally, and were not the accidental traces of a struggle. He wondered what Giuseppe Larsson had made of that.

Then he walked over to the big broken window in the living room. Stopped in his tracks, and ducked down. There was a man standing outside. Holding a rifle. Motionless, staring straight at the window.

Lindman had no time to be afraid. He crouched by the side of the window. He at once heard a key in the front-door lock.

The door opened. The man paused in the entrance to the living room. He was holding the gun pointing down at his side.

'There's not supposed to be anybody here,' the man said.

'I knew the dead man.'

'I believe you,' the stranger said 'I just wonder who you are.'

'Herbert Molin and I worked together for several years. He was a police officer in Borås, and I still am. Who are you?'

'I live about ten kilometres away, but I was one of Herbert's nearest neighbours even so. My name's Abraham Andersson. But round here they call me Dunkärr, because I live at a farm called Dunkärret.'

'Are you a farmer, then?'

The man laughed. 'No,' he said. 'I play the violin. I was in the symphony orchestra in Helsingborg for twenty years. Then one day I simply felt I'd had enough. And moved up here. I still play sometimes. In fact, that was how I met Herbert.'

'How so?'

'I take my violin into the forest. It sounds different there. After all those years in a concert hall it's as if I've got a new instrument in my hands.' He pointed at the lake that was just visible through the trees. 'I was standing down there, playing away. Mendelssohn's violin concerto, I think it was, the second movement. Then Herbert appeared with his dog. He was upset because I was trespassing on his land. But we became friends after that. Or whatever you'd call it. I don't suppose anybody became a friend of Herbert's.'

'What do you mean?'

'He'd bought this house in order to be in peace. But you can't entirely cut yourself off from other people. After a year or so, he told me that there was a spare key on a hook in the shed. I don't know why.'

'But you used to see a bit of each other socially?'

'No. To tell you the truth, I had never set foot in this house before today. He never came round to me either.'

'Was there anybody else who visited him?'

Lindman noticed the slight hesitation before the man answered. 'Not as far as I know.'

So, he did have visitors, Lindman thought. But he said: 'So you've hidden yourself away in the forest, just like Herbert.'

The man laughed again. 'Not at all,' he said. 'I write a bit for a few dance bands. The occasional song. I use a pseudonym. Siv Nilsson.'

'A woman's name?'

'The name of a girl I was in love with at school.'

Lindman wondered if Andersson was pulling his leg, but decided that he was telling the truth.

'This place was crawling with police until yesterday,' the man said. 'There's been folk roaming around with dogs, police knocking on doors for miles around. But nobody knows a thing. I leave here for one week every month. I go to Helsingborg to see my wife. It's odd that it should happen when I wasn't here.'

'So you think that somebody was keeping watch and made his move when you weren't around?'

'I don't think anything. I'm just saying that it's odd. I'm probably the only one who wanders about around here. Apart from Herbert.'

'What do you think happened?'

'I don't know. I've got to go now.'

Lindman walked him to his car.

'Where did you say you lived?' he said. 'Dunkärret?'

'Just this side of Glöte. About six kilometres. There's a sign pointing to the left: DUNKÄRRET 2.' He got into the car. 'You've got to catch whoever did this,' he said.

Lindman watched the car drive off. Then he went back to the house and along the path that led to the lake. All the time he was chewing over what Andersson had said. Nobody knew Molin but somebody had paid him visits. Andersson hadn't been prepared to say who. And the murder had taken place when Andersson wasn't in the vicinity.

The lake was bigger than he had expected. The water was brown, with only a very few gentle ripples. He squatted down and dipped his hand in. It was cold. He stood up and suddenly saw Borås hospital in his mind's eye. It was several hours since he had last thought about what was in store for him. He sat on a rock and gazed over the lake. I should be preparing myself for what's going to happen, he thought. My doctor has given me a good chance of surviving. I'm still young, and I'm strong, but the bottom line is that nobody can know for sure whether I'm going to make it or not.

He walked along the shore, with no aim in mind, until he came to an opening in the trees, and sat down again, this time on a fallen tree trunk. The ground seemed well trodden. He noticed some cuts on the trunk that could only have been made with a knife. Perhaps Molin used to come here, he thought vaguely. Between jigsaw puzzles.

Then something occurred to him: somebody else could have been sitting here. He started to look around more attentively. The site had been cleared. Somebody had removed the undergrowth and levelled the ground. The levelled area was hardly more than twenty square metres, but it was pretty well shielded from view. Lindman looked hard at the ground. He could just make out a faint shape in the moss. A square. He felt with his fingers in the four corners. There were holes there. He stood up. A tent, he thought. Unless I'm much mistaken, there's been a tent pitched here. It must have been this year, otherwise the snow would have obliterated all the marks.

He looked around again, more slowly. He could find no trace of a fire, but people nowadays used camping gas stoves when they were in the forest. He kept on searching and asked himself what he would have done if he had pitched a tent here. You'd need a shit hole, he thought. It was possible to clamber into the forest past the side of a large rock. He worked his way in, a metre at a time.

He stopped short. Next to the trunk of a pine tree was a pile that had clearly been made by a human. Faeces and paper. His heart started beating faster. He was right. Somebody had camped by the side of the lake. But there was nothing to link the camper with Molin. Lindman went back to where the tent must have been. There had to be a track to the main road, or a place where the camper might have left his car. Or perhaps somebody else had driven him here.

Lindman looked over the lake. There was another possibility, of course. The camper could have come that way. But where's the boat?

Larsson is the man I have to talk to, he thought. There's no reason why I should be playing the private detective here. It's the police in Jämtland and Härjedalen that have to sort this out.

LINDMAN PARKED outside his hotel. He thought about phoning Elena, but decided to eat first. He went to the dining room and chose a window table. He was the only customer. To his surprise he found that the girl in reception had been reincarnated as a waitress. He ordered a steak and a beer, and stared out into the darkness.

After the meal he went to his room and rang Elena's number. She picked up immediately. Lindman had the impression that she had been sitting by the phone, waiting for him to ring.

'Where are you?'

'In Sveg.'

'What's it like there?' she asked hesitantly.

'Cold, and I feel lonely.'

'I don't understand why you've gone there.'

'Nor do I.'

'Come home, then.'

'If I could, I'd start back right away. But I'll be here a few more days.'

He gave her the hotel telephone number, and hung up. Neither of them liked talking on the phone. Their conversations were often short. Even so, Lindman felt that she was close by his side.

He was tired. It had been a long day. He untied his laces. Then, as he was pulling off his shoes, he discovered something stuck to one of the soles, trapped in the pattern of the rubber. A stone from the gravel path, he thought. He reached to winkle it out.

But it wasn't a stone. It was part of a jigsaw puzzle piece, soft and discoloured by soil. He was certain he hadn't stood on any pieces inside the house. It might have been outside the house. Nevertheless, his intuition told him that the jigsaw piece had stuck to his shoe at the place where the tent had been pitched. Whoever killed Herbert Molin had been camping at the lakeside.

Chapter 2

It was 10 p.m. He hesitated, but decided to phone Larsson at home. He looked for the number in the phone book. There were a lot of Larssons, but predictably only one Giuseppe. His wife answered and Lindman explained who he was. Larsson came to the phone.

'Stefan Lindman,' he said. 'From Borås. I hope this isn't too late.'

'Not quite. Where are you?'

'In Sveg.'

'Just down the road, then.' Larsson roared with laughter. 'A couple of hundred kilometres is nothing to us up here.'

'I thought I might visit you in Östersund tomorrow.'

'You're welcome. The police station is behind the National Rural Agency building. It's a small town. You'll have no trouble in finding it. When had you thought of coming?'

'I can fit in with you. Whenever you've got time.'

'How about eleven a.m.?'

LINDMAN WALKED through the front door of Östersund police station at eleven o'clock precisely. He explained who he was to the woman in reception.

'Larsson told us to expect you,' she said, pointing to the nearest corridor. 'His office is down there, the second room on the left.'

Lindman knocked on the door with DETECTIVE INSPECTOR LARSSON on it. The man who opened it was tall and powerfully built.

'You're punctual,' he said, almost hustling him into the room and closing the door behind them.

Lindman sat in the visitor's chair. He recognised the way the office was furnished from the police station in Borås. We don't only wear uniforms, he thought. Our offices are uniform as well.

Larsson sat in his desk chair and crossed his hands over his stomach. 'Have you been up in this part of the world before?' he asked.

'Never. Uppsala's as far north as I've ever been.'

'Uppsala is southern Sweden. Here in Östersund you still have half of Sweden to go as you travel north.'

'How many police officers are there in Härjedalen?' Lindman asked.

Larsson thought for a moment. 'Five, maybe six in Sveg, a couple in Hede. And the odd one more here and there, in Funäsdalen, for instance. Possibly fifteen in all, depending on how many are on duty at a given time.'

They were interrupted by a knock on the door. It opened before Larsson could react. The man in the doorway was the polar opposite of Larsson, short and very thin.

'I thought Nisse should sit in on this,' Larsson said. 'We are both in charge of the investigation.'

Lindman stood up to shake hands. The man who had joined them was reserved and serious. He spoke softly and Lindman had difficulty gathering that his surname was Rundström. Larsson sat up straighter in his chair and his smile disappeared. The mood had changed.

'We thought we ought to have a little chat,' Larsson said, cautiously. 'About this and that.'

Rundström had not sat down, although there was a spare chair. He leaned against the door frame and said, 'We don't like police officers from faraway places poking their noses into our investigations.'

Lindman had broken out into a sweat. 'As I told Larsson,' he said, 'I'd worked with Molin for quite a few years. I'm on holiday, and so I came here. I'm not conducting my own investigation.'

'What exactly do you want to know?' Rundström asked.

'Who killed my colleague.'

'That's what we want to know as well. Needless to say, we've given this investigation top priority. We've had some pretty violent crimes up here over the years. We're not exactly unused to it.'

'It goes without saying that I am not questioning the way you are working.'

'Have you any information you can give us that would be of use to the investigation?'

'No,' Lindman said. He didn't want to tell Rundström about the tent site until he had discussed it with Larsson. 'I didn't know Molin well enough to be able to tell you anything about the life he led in Borås, never mind here. And in any case, I'll be leaving soon.'

Rundström nodded and opened the door. 'Any news from Umeå?'

'Nothing so far,' Larsson said.

Rundström smiled curtly at Lindman and was gone.

Larsson stretched out an arm apologetically. 'Rundström can be a bit abrupt at times. But he means well.'

'He's within his rights to complain about my poking my nose in.'

Larsson eyed him speculatively. 'Is that what you're doing?'

'Sometimes you can't avoid stumbling over things.'

Larsson looked at his watch. 'How long are you thinking of staying in Östersund? Overnight?'

'I haven't decided anything.'

'Stay overnight, then. I'll be working here tonight as well. Come round some time after seven. With a bit of luck everything will be quiet here then. I have to be on call tonight. You can make yourself at home in my office.' Larsson pointed to some files on a shelf behind him. 'You can look through the material we have. Then we can talk.'

'And Rundström?'

'He lives in Brunflo. You can bet your life he won't be here tonight. Nobody will ask any questions.'

Larsson rose from his chair. Lindman understood that the conversation was over.

'The old theatre's been converted into a hotel,' Larsson said. 'A good hotel. And it won't be full in October.'

Lindman buttoned up his jacket. 'Umeå?' he wondered aloud.

'That's where we send our dead bodies.'

Larsson went out into the street with him.

'Herbert Molin must have bought the house from somebody,' said Lindman. 'Privately, or through an estate agent.'

'We've looked into that. Molin bought the house from an independent estate agent. His name's Hans Marklund.'

'What did he have to say?'

'Nothing yet. He's been on holiday in Spain. Got back yesterday. He's on my list for tomorrow.' Larsson thought for a moment. 'I can tell my colleagues that I'll take the responsibility for interviewing him. Which means that there's nothing to prevent you from talking to him. He works from his house in Krokom. Take the road north. In Krokom itself, you'll see a sign saying RURAL PROPERTIES.'

Larsson went back inside. Rundström's attitude had annoyed Lindman, but at the same time it had given him renewed energy. And Larsson wanted to help him by letting him go through the material they had so far accumulated. In doing so Larsson was putting himself at risk, even if there was no real impropriety in allowing a colleague from another force to take part in the investigation.

Lindman found the hotel that Larsson had suggested, and got a room under the eaves. He left his case there and returned to his car. He phoned the hotel in Sveg and spoke to the girl in reception. He explained that he would be back the next day.

It was only twenty kilometres to Krokom, where Lindman found the estate agent's straight away. It was a yellow-painted house with a large garden. A man was walking around the lawn vacuuming up dead leaves. He switched the machine off when he saw Lindman. The man was tanned and about Lindman's age.

'Are you looking for a house?' he asked.

'Not exactly. Are you Hans Marklund?'

'That's me.'

'Giuseppe Larsson told me I'd find you here.'

'The policeman. Are you a police officer as well?'

Lindman hesitated. 'Yes,' he said. 'You once sold a house to a man called Herbert Molin. As you know, he's been murdered.'

'Come inside,' Marklund said.

One of the rooms on the ground floor had been fitted out as an office. There were maps on the walls, and coloured photographs of houses up for sale. Marklund made some coffee and they sat down at a table strewn with files.

'Eleven years ago, or so, you sold the house near Linsell to Herbert Molin,' Lindman said. 'What can you tell me about that sale?'

Marklund disappeared into an adjoining room. He came back with a file in his hand. He soon found what he was looking for.

'March the 18th, 1988,' he said. 'The deal was signed and sealed here in this office. The seller was an old forester. The price was a hundred and ninety-eight thousand kronor. No mortgage. The transaction was paid for by cheque.'

'What do you remember about Molin?'

'Nothing.'

The reply surprised Lindman. 'Nothing?'

'I never met him. Somebody else looked after the matter for him.

A woman by the name of Elsa Berggren. With an address in Sveg.' Marklund passed the file over. 'Here's the authorisation. She had the right to make decisions and sign the deal on Molin's behalf.'

Lindman examined the signature. He remembered it from the Borås days. It was Molin's signature.

Marklund leafed through the file, then pointed. 'Here's her address and telephone number. She's the person you should talk to. Not me.'

'Isn't it a bit unusual? Not meeting the person with whom you were doing business?'

'Not really. I sell holiday cottages in the mountains to German and Dutch clients. They have people who sort out the details for them.'

'So there was nothing unusual about this transaction.'

'Nothing at all.'

Marklund accompanied Lindman as far as the front gate. 'Maybe there was, though,' he said. 'I remember Elsa Berggren saying on one occasion that her client didn't want to use any of the big firms of estate agents. I recall thinking that was a bit odd.'

Lindman turned. 'Why?'

'If you're looking for a house you wouldn't as a rule start off with a small firm.'

'How do you interpret that?'

Hans Marklund smiled. 'I don't interpret it at all. I'm merely telling you what I remember.'

As Lindman drove back towards Östersund, he wondered why the Berggren woman had been asked by Molin to avoid the big estate agents. He could think of only one reason. Molin had wanted to buy his house as discreetly as possible.

The impression that Lindman had had from the start was turning out to be correct. The house in which Molin had spent the last years of his life wasn't really a house at all. It was a hiding place.

THAT EVENING, Lindman wandered through the life of Herbert Molin. Reading between the lines of all the notes, reports, statements and forensic details that had been collected in Larsson's files, Lindman was able to compile a picture of Molin that was new to him. The man he thought he had known turned out to be a complete stranger.

It was midnight when he closed the last of the files. Larsson had occasionally called in during the evening. They had drunk coffee and exchanged a few words. Everything had been quiet at first, but soon after 9 p.m. Larsson had left to sort out a burglary in Häggenås.

Lindman had made notes as the evening progressed. When he had finished the last file he looked through his notebook and summarised what he had discovered.

The most surprising thing was that, according to documents from the tax authorities, Herbert Molin had been born with a different name. On March 10, 1923, he had come into this world at the hospital in Kalmar and had then been baptised August Gustaf Herbert. His parents were the cavalry officer Axel Mattson-Herzén and his wife Marianne. In June 1951 he had been allowed by the Swedish Patent and Registration Office to change his name.

Two questions occurred to Lindman. Why had Mattson-Herzén changed both his surname and his forenames? And why Molin, which must be about as common as Mattson? Most people who changed their surname did so to escape from a common one.

August Mattson-Herzén was twenty-eight years old in 1951. At the time he had been serving in the regular army, a lieutenant of infantry in Boden. Then there was a series of significant changes. In 1951 he changed his name. The following year, in March 1952, he applied for a discharge from the army. He married when he left the army, and had children in 1953 and 1955, first a son christened Herman, and then a daughter Veronica. He and his wife Jeanette moved from Boden in 1952, to an address outside Stockholm. Nowhere could Lindman find any information about what Molin did to earn a living. Five years passed before he appeared again as an employee, in October 1957, in the local authority offices in Alingsås. He was posted from there to Borås, and in the 1960s he became a police officer. In 1981 his wife filed for divorce. The following year he remarried, but wife number two, Kristina Cedergren, divorced him in 1986.

When Larsson returned from the break-in in Häggenås, Lindman was standing by the window, looking at the deserted street below.

Larsson explained that somebody had stolen two power saws from a garage. 'What about you?' he asked. 'What have you found out?'

'It's quite remarkable,' Lindman said. 'I find a man I thought I knew, but he turns out to be somebody else altogether.'

'How so?'

'The change of name. And the gap between 1952 and 1957.'

'I've thought about that,' Larsson said. 'But we haven't really got that far in the investigation as yet.' He yawned. 'I need to get some sleep. I'll come to your hotel tomorrow morning. Perhaps we can have breakfast together. Seven thirty?'

Lindman agreed. They put the files back on a shelf and walked together through the dimly lit reception area.

'It always boils down to motive,' Larsson said. 'Somebody wanted to murder Molin. That's for sure. He was a specifically targeted victim. Somebody saw in him a motive to commit murder.' He yawned again. 'But we can talk about that tomorrow.'

WHEN LINDMAN CAME DOWN to breakfast at precisely 7.30 a.m., Larsson was already waiting for him at a corner table. As they ate, Lindman told him about meeting Abraham Andersson and finding the site where the tent had been. Larsson pushed his half-eaten omelette to one side. Lindman produced the piece of the jigsaw puzzle.

'I can only assume the dogs didn't get that far,' he said.

'There was nothing to go on,' Larsson said. 'We brought in three dogs but they didn't find a single scent.'

He picked up his briefcase from the floor and produced a photocopy of a map of the area around Molin's house. Lindman indicated the spot where the tent had been pitched. Larsson examined the map.

'There's no road that could take a car to that part of the shore. Whoever set up camp there must have walked at least two kilometres over quite difficult ground. Unless he used the track to Molin's house, and that seems unlikely.'

'What about the lake?'

'That's a possibility. There are several forestry roads on the other side. It would obviously be possible to paddle over in a canoe or an inflatable.' Larsson turned his attention to the jigsaw piece. 'I'll take this and get forensic to give it the once-over,' he said. 'Your campsite must also be examined, of course.'

'What's Rundström going to have to say about this?'

Larsson smiled. 'There's nothing to stop me telling him that I was the one who found the place. What did the estate agent have to say?'

Lindman told him. Again, Larsson was all attention.

'You'd better leave Elsa Berggren to me.'

'Of course.'

'You've weighed in with some very useful observations,' Larsson said. 'But Rundström's right when he says that this is something we have to sort out ourselves. I wanted to give you the opportunity of seeing how far we've got, but I can't let you get further involved.'

'I never expected you to.'

Larsson drained his coffee. 'So why did you really come to Sveg?'

'I'm on sick leave. I had nothing else to do. And I knew Molin.'

'Or thought you did.'

Lindman was aware that he didn't know the man sitting opposite him at all. Even so, he had an urge to tell him about his illness. It was as if he could no longer bear the burden alone.

'I came here because I've got cancer,' he said, 'and I'm waiting for the treatment to start. I had to choose between Majorca and Sveg. I chose Sveg because I wanted to know what had happened to Molin.'

They sat in silence for a minute or so.

'People always ask me where I got Giuseppe from,' Larsson said. 'You didn't. Because you had something else on your mind, no doubt. I wondered what it was. Do you want to talk about it?'

'Not really. But I wanted you to know.'

Larsson took a notepad out of his briefcase. He found the page he was looking for and passed the pad over to Lindman. On the page was a sketch of footprints forming a pattern. Lindman saw that it was the pattern of the bloody footprints in Molin's house. He had been reminded of them by the photograph in Larsson's files. It also occurred to him that he hadn't mentioned to Larsson that he'd been inside Molin's house. So he told him exactly what had occurred.

Larsson didn't seem to be surprised, and pointed once more to his notepad. 'This is a depiction of the basic steps for the tango.'

Lindman stared at him in amazement. 'The tango?'

'There's no doubt about it. But this means that somebody carted Molin's corpse around and made those bloody prints. No doubt you read the pathologist's provisional report. His back and the soles of his feet were lacerated by lashes from the skin of some animal. Why?'

'It could be a greeting to the police, of course.'

'Correct. But the question remains: why?' Larsson closed his briefcase. 'Did Molin use to dance the tango while he was in Borås?'

'Not as far as I know.'

'We'll find out sooner or later, no doubt,' Larsson said. 'Maybe you ought to go to Majorca after all. I can keep you posted as the case develops.'

Lindman didn't answer. Larsson was right, of course. There was no reason for him to stay in Härjedalen any longer.

They went out into reception and said their goodbyes in the street. Lindman went up to his room, collected his things, paid his bill, and left Östersund. He would go back to Borås the very next day.

He was driving slowly. Just under sixty kilometres per hour. He was churning things over in his mind. Molin had been afraid, and his fear had driven him to his hideaway in the forest. Someone had traced him to his refuge. But why?

Something must have happened in the early 1950s, Lindman thought. August Mattson-Herzén abandons his military career and hides behind a new name. How does he earn his living, until he turns up in the local council offices in Alingsås in 1957? Could the events of nearly fifty years ago have caught up with him?

That was as far as he got. He ran out of ideas. He stopped in Ytterhogdal and filled up with petrol before driving on to Sveg and parking outside the hotel. There was a man he had never seen before in reception, who gave him a friendly nod and handed over the key. Lindman went up to his room, took off his shoes and stretched out on the bed. He wondered what he should do. He didn't have the energy to organise a trip to Majorca. The idea of going back to his flat in Borås depressed him. He would only sit there, worrying.

It seemed that he was incapable of making the simplest of decisions. He ran his tongue over his teeth. The lump was still there. I'm carrying death in my mouth, he thought. He shook his head at the idea, and decided to find out where Elsa Berggren lived. True, he had promised Larsson that he wouldn't talk to her, but that didn't mean he couldn't find out where she lived.

He went down to reception and scrutinised the wall map of the town. He found the street on the other side of the river, in an area called Ulvkällar. There was another bridge, an old railway bridge: that was the one to use for crossing the river.

As he left the hotel, there was a thick layer of cloud over Sveg. A few hundred metres along Fjällvägen, he came to the bridge. It was arched, and he stopped in the middle and looked down into the brown water. When he got to the other side, he turned left. Elsa Berggren's house was a white-painted wooden house in a well-tended garden. There was a freestanding garage in the grounds. The doors were wide open, but there was no car inside. Lindman kept on walking. A man was standing in the middle of the road, staring at the sky.

'Is it going to snow?' he asked.

'Could be,' Lindman said. 'But it's only just turned November.'

The man shook his head. 'It can snow here in September, June even.' His face was wrinkled and he could have done with a shave. 'Are you looking for somebody?' he asked.

'I'm just visiting. And thought I'd take a walk.' Lindman hadn't promised not to talk *about* Berggren. 'A nice house,' he said, pointing to the house he had just passed.

The man nodded. 'Elsa takes good care of her house. The garden too. Do you know her?'

'No.'

The man looked at him, as if he were waiting for the next step. 'The name's Björn Wigren,' he said eventually.

'I'm Stefan. Stefan Lindman.'

'And you've come out for a walk? I've lived here in my house since 1959,' the man said. 'But I've never known a stranger to take a walk here. Not at this time of year.'

'There's always a first time.'

'I could offer you a coffee,' said Wigren. 'If you'd like one?'

'A coffee would be nice.'

Wigren's house was a bungalow. On a wall in the entrance hall there were several trophies, including a pair of elk antlers. On the kitchen table was a vacuum flask, and a plate covered by a napkin. Wigren produced a second cup, and invited Lindman to sit.

'We don't need to talk,' he said, surprisingly. 'You can drink coffee with a stranger and not say a word.'

They each drank a cup of coffee and ate a cinnamon bun.

Lindman asked, 'If somebody wanted to buy a house around here, like the one we mentioned before, how much would it cost?'

'Elsa's house, you mean? Houses are cheap around here. Two or three hundred thousand, no more. But I don't think Elsa has any intention of selling.'

'Does she live alone?'

'I don't think she's ever been married. She can be a bit stand-offish at times. After my wife died, I thought I might make a move for her, but she wasn't interested.'

'What sort of age is she?'

'Seventy-three, I think.'

So, more or less the same as Molin, Lindman thought.

'Has she always lived here?'

'She was here when we built our house. That was in the late fifties. She must have lived in that house for forty years.'

'What did she do?'

'She said she'd been a teacher before she came here. Something fishy there, don't you think? Who retires in their thirties?'

'She must have had some means of support?'

'She inherited her parents' estate. That's when she moved here. Or so she says.'

Lindman tried to keep up. 'So she wasn't born here?'

'Skåne, I think she came from.'

'So why here? Had she any family in the area?'

Wigren looked hard at him. 'You're talking like a police officer.'

'I'm curious, like everybody else. You have to ask why somebody would move here from southern Sweden unless they were going to get married or had found their dream job,' Lindman said, sensing that he might be making a serious mistake not telling the truth.

'I wondered about that as well. My wife too. But you don't ask questions if you don't have to. Elsa is nice, and helpful. She baby-sat for us when we needed it.' Wigren fell silent. Lindman waited. He had the impression that there was more to come.

'You might think it's a bit odd,' said Wigren. 'I've been living next door to Elsa for a whole generation, but I've never set foot in her house. Nor did my wife while she was alive. Nobody has ever seen anyone set foot inside her house. Let's face it, that's a little strange.'

Lindman agreed. There was something about Berggren's life that was reminiscent of Molin's. Both came from elsewhere, and both led isolated lives. How had they got to know each other? Did they have anything else in common?

Lindman decided it was time to move on. He looked at his watch. 'I'm afraid I've got to go now,' he said. 'But thanks for the coffee.'

They headed for the front door.

'We could be in for some snow tonight,' Wigren said. Then he turned to face Lindman. 'I don't know why you've been asking all these questions about Elsa, but I'm not going to say anything. One of these days though, you'll come and tell me what's going on.'

Lindman nodded. He had been right not to have underestimated the old man.

LINDMAN WALKED BACK the way he had come. There was still no car on Berggren's drive, or in the garage. In the centre of the town he found the public library in the community centre. There was a large stuffed bear in the foyer, staring at him. He had a sudden urge to attack it in a trial of strength. The thought made him burst out laughing. A man carrying a bundle of papers looked up at him in surprise.

Lindman located the shelves for medical literature, but when he sat down with a book containing information on cancer, he couldn't bring himself to open it. It's too soon, he thought. One more day. But not more. Then I will have to come to terms with my situation.

He started marching back to the hotel. On the way, he decided to stop at the wine shop. He bought two bottles of wine. As he emerged onto the street, his phone rang. He put his bag down on the pavement and answered it. It was Elena.

'I was wondering why you hadn't phoned me.' Lindman could hear that she was hurt and disappointed.

'I don't feel too good,' he said guiltily.

'Are you still in Sveg?'

'Where else could I be?'

'Do you want me to come? I could take some time off work.'

He nearly said yes, and yes, he did want her to come. 'No,' he said. 'I think it's better for me to be on my own.'

She didn't ask again. They talked for a while without anything being said. Afterwards, he wondered why he hadn't told her the truth. Why hadn't he told her that he missed her? That he didn't want to be on his own? It was as if he understood less and less about himself.

When he got back to the hotel, he rested for an hour, then went down to the dining room. The girl from reception was in her waitress outfit again. He sat at his usual table. He read the menu and saw to his disappointment that it was the same as before.

He had just begun eating elk steak again when he heard someone come into the dining room behind him. He turned and saw a woman walking towards his table. She stopped. Lindman couldn't help observing that she was strikingly attractive.

'I don't want to disturb you,' she said, 'but a policeman in Östersund told me that one of my father's old colleagues was here.'

Lindman didn't understand at first. Then it dawned on him: the woman was Molin's daughter.

Veronica Molin was one of the most beautiful women Lindman had ever met. He remembered that Molin's daughter had been born in 1955. The woman standing at his table now was therefore forty-four. If he hadn't known, he would have guessed she was his own age. He stood up, introduced himself and expressed his condolences.

'Thank you.' Her voice was flat. It didn't belong with her beauty.

He invited her to join him. As she sat down, he noticed that she was wearing a wedding ring. That depressed him, just for a moment. It was an absurd reaction.

The girl from reception came over to their table.

Veronica Molin consulted the menu. 'Could I have a salad?' she said. 'And an omelette? Nothing else.'

'No problem,' the girl said.

Lindman wondered if she also did the cooking.

'I misunderstood the situation,' Veronica Molin said. 'I thought it was here in Sveg that I was going to meet the police, but it is in Östersund. I'll be going there tomorrow.'

'Where have you come from?'

'Cologne. That's where I was when the news of my father's death reached me.'

'Do you live in Germany, then?'

She shook her head. 'In Barcelona. Or Boston. It depends. But I was in Cologne. It was very strange and frightening. I'd just got back to my hotel room. The church bells started ringing at the same time as the phone rang, and a man told me that my father had been murdered. I flew to Stockholm this morning.' She fell silent.

'I'm really very sorry about what happened,' Lindman said. 'A completely pointless murder.'

'Aren't all murders pointless?'

'Of course. But some have a motive that one can understand.'

'Nobody could have had any reason to kill my father,' she said. 'He had no enemies. He wasn't rich.'

But he was scared, Lindman thought, and perhaps that fear was at the root of what happened. Her food arrived on the table. Lindman had a vague sense that the woman sitting opposite him had the upper hand. She had an assurance that he lacked.

'I gather you and he used to work together,' she said.

'Yes, in Borås. Your father left a big gap when he retired. I wondered why he moved up here to Härjedalen.'

'He wanted to be left in peace. My father was a recluse. So am I.'

There's no answer to that, thought Lindman. She hadn't only given him a reply, she had nipped the conversation in the bud. Why is she sitting at my table if she doesn't want to talk to me?

'Were you often in contact with him?'

'Very seldom. I'm a consultant for a computer firm. I'm nearly always travelling. I used to send him a postcard once or twice every year, maybe phoned him at Christmas. But that was about it.'

He looked hard at her. He still thought she was beautiful, but she radiated coldness and remoteness.

'It doesn't sound as if you had a very good relationship.'

'What kind of relationship I had with my father is hardly anybody else's business. He wanted to be left in peace. I respected that.'

'You have a brother as well, I believe?'

Her response was firm and outspoken. 'We avoid speaking to each other unless it's absolutely necessary. Why that should be is no business of anybody else either.' That was the end of the conversation.

They ordered coffee. She lit a cigarette and blew smoke rings towards the ceiling. Then she looked at him.

'Why did you come here,?' she asked.

Lindman gave her part of the truth. 'I'm on sick leave. I had nothing else to do.'

'The policeman I spoke to in Östersund said you were helping with the investigation.'

'I've just spoken to a few people, that's all.'

'Who?'

'Mainly the police officer you'll be meeting tomorrow, Giuseppe Larsson. And Abraham Andersson, your father's nearest neighbour.'

'Had he anything interesting to say?'

'No. But if anyone was going to notice something, it would have been him.'

She stubbed out her cigarette.

'Your father changed his name,' Lindman said. 'From Mattson-Herzén to Molin. That was a few years before you were born. At about the same time he left the army and moved to Stockholm. When you were two, there was another move, to Alingsås. There's one thing I wonder about. What did he do in Stockholm?'

'He had a music shop.' She could see that he was surprised. 'I don't recall anything about it, of course. But I heard later. He opened a shop in Solna. It went well in the early years. He opened a second one in Sollentuna. But things went rapidly downhill from there.'

'Why did he change his name?'

'I don't know.'

Lindman suddenly had the feeling that he ought to be careful. He was asking questions and she was answering, but at the same time something quite different was going on. Veronica Molin was finding out how much he knew about her father.

'When we worked together I had the impression that your father was scared,' he said. 'What of, I've no idea, but I can remember his fear still, though it's more than ten years since he retired.'

She frowned. 'What should he have been scared of?'

'I don't know. I suppose I'm asking you.'

She shook her head. 'My father wasn't the frightened type. On the contrary, he was brave.'

'In what way?'

'He was never afraid of doing things. Never afraid of refusing to do things.'

Her mobile phone rang. She apologised, and answered. The conversation took place in a foreign language, perhaps Spanish. When it was over she beckoned the girl from reception and asked for her bill.

'Did you go out to see the house?' Lindman said.

Veronica Molin looked at him for a while before answering. 'I have a good memory of my father. We were never close, but I've lived long enough to know what sort of a relationship some children can have with their parents. I don't want to spoil the image of my father by seeing the place where he was killed.'

Lindman understood. Or at least, he thought he did.

The girl from reception came with two bills. Lindman tried to take them both, but she insisted on taking hers.

'I prefer to pay my own way.'

They parted in reception. Her room was on the ground floor.

'Thanks for your company,' she said.

He watched her walk away. Her clothes, her shoes, everything about her looked expensive. Their conversation had restored some of his lost energy. He decided to walk over to Berggren's house again. There was a connection between Berggren and Molin that he wanted to know more about.

THE MAN MOVED very quietly. He had been watching Lindman for some time before deciding that he had seen enough. He came diagonally from behind, keeping all the time in the shadows.

'Hello,' he said. 'I was wondering what you're doing here.'

Lindman was startled. He'd had no idea there was anybody there. 'Who are you, asking me these questions?'

'Erik Johansson. I'm a police officer. I am asking myself just what you are doing here.'

'I'm looking at a house,' said Lindman. 'I'm in a public place, I'm sober, I'm not creating a disturbance. Is it forbidden to stand looking at a pretty house?'

'Not at all. But the lady who lives there was made nervous and telephoned. I thought I'd find out who you were. People are not used to strangers standing in the street staring at them.'

Lindman produced his police ID.

Johansson grinned. 'So it's you,' he said. 'Larsson told me you were here. But he didn't say anything about you spying on Elsa.'

'I'm not spying,' Lindman said. 'I went out for a walk. I don't know why I stopped.' He realised that it was an idiotic answer. He had been standing there for ages.

'We'd better move on,' Johansson said. 'Otherwise Elsa will start wondering.'

Johansson's car was parked in a nearby side street.

'So you went out for a walk,' Johansson said. 'And just happened to land up outside Elsa's house?'

'Yes. She was the one who bought Molin's cottage for him. Do you know her?'

'She's always lived here. Nice and friendly. She runs children's dancing classes in the community centre. Or used to. I don't know if she still does it.'

Lindman nodded, but didn't ask any questions.

'Are you staying at the hotel? I can give you a lift.'

'I'd rather walk,' Lindman said. 'But thanks for the offer. I haven't noticed a police station in Sveg.'

'We're in the community centre.'

'Can I call in tomorrow morning? Just to have a chat.'

'Of course.'

Johansson opened his car door. 'I'd better give Elsa a ring and tell her everything's OK.' He got into the car. Lindman waited until the car was out of sight before walking away towards the bridge.

The link, he thought. It's not just that Berggren and Molin knew each other. There's more to it than that. Maybe Molin had moved to Härjedalen to be close to Berggren.

As he reached the bridge, another thought struck him. Berggren had noticed him in the street, despite the fact that he had avoided the light of the street lamps. That could only mean that she was keeping watch over the street. That she either expected or feared that somebody would come. He was certain of it. She couldn't possibly have seen him by chance. And it seemed to him that the interest Berggren and Molin shared in dance could not have been a coincidence.

The reception was closed by the time he got back to the hotel. He unlocked his door and switched on the light. On the floor, pushed under the door, was a message: *Phone Giuseppe Larsson in Östersund. Urgent.*

It was Larsson himself who answered. 'I couldn't find your mobile number,' he said. 'I must have left it at the office. I thought I'd entertain you with something we heard from Umeå today. Dr Hollander says he's found three old entry wounds.'

'What does he mean by that?'

'That at some time Molin had been shot. Not just one bullet. Three. And Dr Hollander considers that Molin was fantastically lucky to have survived. Two of the bullets hit him in the chest just beneath his heart, and the third in his left arm. On the basis of the scars and other things I don't understand, Hollander concludes that Molin received these wounds when he was a young man. He can't tell whether all three bullets came at the same time, but it seems likely. There's nothing about bullet wounds in the police files.'

'So it must have happened while he was in the army?'

'That's the conclusion I'd come to. But it takes time to get at military archives. And we're going to have to dig deep.' Larsson paused. 'Incidentally, I shall be meeting Molin's daughter tomorrow.'

'She's staying here in the hotel.'

'I thought you might meet her. What's she like?'

'Reserved. But she's a very good-looking woman.'

'I've something to look forward to, then. Have you spoken to her?'

'We had dinner together. She told me something about those missing years in the mid-fifties. She says Molin owned a couple of music shops in the Stockholm area, but he went bankrupt.'

'I'll certainly ask her about that. Have you decided how long you're going to stay?'

'Perhaps tomorrow as well. Then I'm off. But I'll stay in touch.'

'Make sure you do.'

Lindman put the phone down and slumped onto the bed. He felt tired. Without even taking off his shoes, he stretched out and fell asleep.

HE WOKE UP with a start and checked his watch: 4.45. He had been dreaming. Somebody was chasing him. Then he was surrounded by a pack of dogs that were tearing at his clothes and biting him all over his body. His father was there somewhere, and Elena.

In the bathroom he rinsed his face in cold water. It wasn't difficult to interpret the dream. The illness I have, the cells multiplying out of control, they're like a pack of wild dogs careering around inside me. He burrowed into the bedclothes, but couldn't get back to sleep.

It was always in the early morning that he felt most defenceless. He was thirty-seven, a police officer trying to lead a decent life. Now he was having to fight an illness that might overcome him. He might never be able to demonstrate his true worth.

I need a plan, he thought. If I don't have a plan, I won't be able to cope with what's in store for me. At last he made up his mind. He would go back to Borås, repack his bag and hope to find a cheap package holiday to Majorca.

HE PARKED OUTSIDE the community centre and went in. The bear was still glaring at him. He found his way to the police offices and bumped into Johansson, who was on his way out.

'I was going to have a coffee with the library staff,' he said. 'But that can wait. I have news for you.'

They went to his office. Lindman sat in the visitor's chair.

'Elsa Berggren rang this morning,' Johansson said. 'I tried to get hold of you at the hotel.'

'What did she want?'

'She wanted to invite you round for coffee.'

'That sounds odd.'

'She'll be at home now,' Johansson said. 'Go round straight away. She's going shopping later on. By all means come back here and tell me what she said, if it's of any interest. But not this afternoon or this evening. I'm off to Funäsdalen. I have a spot of police business to see to, and then I'm going to play poker with some mates.'

SHE OPENED THE DOOR before he could ring the bell. Lindman didn't know what to expect, but certainly not the elegantly dressed lady in the doorway. She had long black hair, obviously dyed, and she was heavily made up around her eyes.

'I thought you might as well come in,' she said. 'Instead of standing out there in the street.'

Lindman stepped into the hall. He had got further than Wigren had managed in forty years. She led him into the living room, which was at the back of the house, facing the garden. The room was expensively furnished, and there were original oil paintings.

Berggren excused herself and disappeared into the kitchen. Lindman sat down to wait.

She came back in with coffee and biscuits. 'A man appears and stands staring at my house,' she said. 'Naturally, I'm surprised. And worried as well. After what happened to Herbert, things will never be the same again in Sveg.'

'I'll tell you why I was there,' Lindman said. 'I used to work with Herbert Molin. I'm also a police officer.'

'Erik told me that.'

'I'm on sick leave and was kicking my heels. So I came here. I happened to speak to an estate agent in Krokom who told me you had bought Herbert's house on his behalf. I'm trying to understand who he was. I've realised that he was not who I thought he was.'

'In what way?'

'In many ways.'

She stood up and adjusted a curtain in one of the windows. 'I knew Herbert's first wife,' she said. 'We were at school together. So I also got to know Herbert. That was when he lived in Stockholm. Then I lost contact with her after they divorced. But not with Herbert.' She returned to her chair. 'He phoned me before he retired. He asked me to help him buy a house. That's all there is to it. And now he's dead. And I'm sad about that.'

'Did he move here because you were here?'

She looked him straight in the eye. 'That is something that concerned only him and me. And now it concerns only me.'

'Of course.'

Lindman took a sip of coffee. There was something about what she had said that didn't add up. He put down his cup.

'Have you any idea who could have killed him?'

'No. An old man who wanted to live in peace,' she said. 'Who on earth would want to kill him?'

There was only one other question Lindman wanted to ask.

'I find it strange that you haven't spoken to the police in Östersund. The ones who are in charge of the investigation.'

'I was waiting for them to contact me.'

Lindman was certain that Berggren wasn't telling him the whole truth. 'I've been thinking a lot about why Herbert came here,' he said. 'Why would anybody want to live such a lonely life?'

'It's not lonely up here,' Berggren said. 'There's lots you can do if you want to. For instance, I'm going to a concert in the church tonight. There's an organist coming here from Sundsvall.'

'I heard from Erik Johansson that you give dancing lessons.'

'Children should learn how to dance. But I don't know if I've got the strength to go on for much longer.'

Lindman decided not to ask any questions about Molin's interest in dancing. Larsson was the man to ask those questions, nobody else.

A telephone rang somewhere in the house. She excused herself and left the room. Lindman stood up and unfastened the catch on a window, making sure it held tight and didn't open. Then he sat down again. She returned a minute later.

'I won't impose on you any longer,' Lindman said, getting to his feet. 'Thank you for the coffee.'

As he put on his jacket in the hall, he looked around to see if the house had a burglar alarm. He could see no sign of one.

He drove back to the hotel. There was a notice board next to the reception desk. On it was a yellow poster advertising an organ concert in the church that evening, starting at 7.30, of music by Johann Sebastian Bach.

SHORTLY AFTER SEVEN o'clock that evening Lindman went to the church. He took up a position outside the church wall. At 7.25, Berggren arrived and walked into the church.

Lindman hurried back to his car. He drove to the river and parked on the other side of the bridge. Then he approached Berggren's house from the back, along a narrow path. There was a light on in the room where he had had his coffee. He paused at the garden fence and listened. Then he jumped over and ran to the house wall, crouching low. He stood, opened the window carefully and hoisted himself up.

He wiped the soles of his shoes with a handkerchief, and looked around the room. He had no idea what he was looking for. Perhaps some confirmation that Berggren hadn't been telling the truth. He left the living room, glanced into the kitchen, then ran up the stairs. The first room seemed to be a guest room. He walked into Berggren's bedroom. She slept in a large double bed. He looked into the bathroom. Bottles were lined up in neat rows in front of the mirror.

He was about to go downstairs when he had the idea of opening the double doors of the wardrobe. The hangers were tightly packed. He ran his hand over the clothes. They all seemed to be of high quality. At the furthest left of the hangers, something caught his eye. He pulled some dresses to one side to get a closer look.

A uniform. It was several seconds before he realised what it was—a German army uniform. On the shelf above was an army hat. He took it down and saw the skull. Hanging in Elsa Berggren's wardrobe was an SS officer's uniform.

LINDMAN DROVE BACK to the hotel, poured himself a glass of wine and tried to make up his mind whether to phone Larsson right away. He hesitated to do so. He had promised not to contact Berggren. Now he had not only spoken to her, he had broken into her house. This was not the kind of thing to discuss on the telephone, he thought.

He took out his notebook and tried to develop a few plausible theories about the reason for Molin's death. The first, the most obvious one, was that Molin had been the victim of a madman. Where he had come from and why he had been equipped with a tent and some tear gas was impossible to explain, of course.

The second theory involved an unknown connection between the murder and something concealed in Molin's past. As Veronica Molin had pointed out, her father did not possess a fortune. Money could hardly be the motive. But police officers acquired enemies, Lindman thought. It was not uncommon for them to receive death threats.

There was a third possibility, connected with Berggren. Had the uniform in her wardrobe anything to do with Molin? Or was there something in Berggren's past that linked her with Hitler's Germany?

Berggren and Molin were about the same age. Berggren could have been born a year or so later, around 1924 or 1925. So she would have been fifteen when war broke out, and twenty-one when it ended. Lindman shook his head. That didn't fit. But Berggren has a father, and perhaps also an elder brother.

That was as far as he could get. He put down the notebook. He would talk to Larsson the following day, and then return to Borås.

He drank another glass of wine before settling down in bed. I have one more person to see before I talk to Larsson, he thought as he was falling asleep, and then I can put all of this behind me.

HE WOKE UP before dawn with excruciating pain in one of his cheeks. He was also running a temperature. The doctor had warned him that he might suddenly find himself in pain. He lay still in the darkness and tried to wish away the pain by sheer will-power. It didn't work.

After another hour, he couldn't stand it any longer. He looked up the telephone number for the hospital in Borås, and had a stroke of luck. His doctor answered as soon as he was put through. She said she would write him out a prescription and phone it through to the chemist in Sveg. If that didn't ease the pain, he was to phone her again.

At 9 a.m. he got up, dressed and went downstairs. He left his key on the reception desk.

He collected his tablets and took the first dose immediately. Then he went back to the hotel and stayed in bed for the rest of the day. The pain came and went. It was late afternoon before it became clear that the pain was going away rather than just becoming more bearable.

He went back down to reception, left his key and opened the hotel door. He decided to visit Abraham Andersson.

He got into his car and set off in the direction of Linsell. For now, at least, the pain was leaving him in peace.

He passed Dravagen, kept going towards Glöte until he saw the sign: DUNKÄRRET 2. The road was bumpy and narrow. After two kilometres he was there. Andersson had put up a sign with the name DUNKÄRR. The house lights were on. Lindman switched off the engine and got out of the car. A dog started barking. Lindman walked up a slope. He could see the dog now, running back and forth along a line stretched between a tree and the house wall. There was a kennel by the tree. It was a Norwegian elkhound, the same breed as Molin's.

He walked up the steps to the front door and knocked hard. The dog started barking again. Lindman knocked harder, then tried the door. It was unlocked. He opened it and shouted into the house.

He stepped into the hall, feeling that all was not as it should be. He went into the kitchen. There was an empty coffee cup on the table. He shouted again, but there was no answer. He went into the living room. There was a music stand next to the television, and a violin on a sofa. He frowned. Then he went upstairs and looked everywhere, but found no one. Something was definitely wrong.

Lindman went back outside. The dog was still barking, but stopped and wagged its tail as he walked towards it. He stroked it cautiously. Not much of a guard dog, he thought. Then he went back to the car and collected a torch. He shone it around, and shouted again. The dog answered him with a bark.

The dog, he thought. It knows. He went back to the house and took a lead hanging from the wall. The dog stood still while he attached the lead to its collar and released it from the running line. Immediately it began dragging him towards the forest behind the house, heading for a path into the pine trees. I shouldn't be doing this, Lindman thought, not if there's a madman loose in the forest.

The dog turned off the path. It was rough ground, and Lindman kept stumbling in the undergrowth. The dog forged ahead. Then it stopped and sniffed the air. Lindman shone his torch among the trees. The lead was long enough for him to tie it round a tree trunk.

The dog was staring intently at some rocks just visible through a dense clump of pine trees. Lindman walked to the trees and made out a path leading to the rocks.

He stopped. At first he wasn't sure what he had seen. Something white, shining. Then, to his horror, he realised that it was Andersson. He was naked, tied to a tree. His chest was covered in blood. His eyes were open and staring straight at Lindman. The gaze was lifeless.

Chapter 3

When Aron Silberstein woke up he didn't know who he was. There was a belt of fog between dream and reality that he must find his way through to discover if he really was Aron Silberstein, or if at that moment he was Fernando Hereira. In his dreams his two names often switched. Every time he woke up, he experienced a moment of great confusion. This morning was no exception, when he opened his eyes and saw light seeping through the canvas. He slid his arm out of his sleeping-bag and looked at his watch. It was 9.03. He listened. All quiet. The night before he had turned off the main road after passing through a town called Falköping, and found a cart track leading into the forest. There he had been able to pitch his tent.

Soon it would all be over. He would drive to Malmö, return his rented car and spend a night in a hotel. Early the next day he would make his way to Copenhagen and in the afternoon board a plane that would take him home to Buenos Aires.

He settled down in the sleeping-bag and closed his eyes. He didn't need to get up yet. His mouth was dry and he had a headache. I overdid it last night, he thought. I drank too much.

He thought about the dream he had had during the night. In it he was Aron Silberstein again. He was a child and his father Lukas was still with him. His father was a dancing master and he received his pupils at home in their Berlin flat. It was during that last horrific year—he knew because in the dream his father had shaved off his moustache. He had done that a couple of months before the catastrophe. They were sitting in the only room that didn't have broken windows. Just Aron and his father: the rest of the family had disappeared. And they waited. They said nothing, just waited. Even now, it seemed to him that his childhood was one long, drawn-out wait. Waiting and terror.

Everything went as it was destined to go, he told himself. I waited more than fifty years for that moment to come. I had almost given up the hope of finding out what had ruined my life, and how to avenge it. Then, by some incredible coincidence, somebody turned up and enabled me to discover what had happened.

As soon as he got back to Buenos Aires he would go to the cemetery where Höllner was buried and put a flower on his grave. But for him, he would never have been able to carry out his mission.

He had met Höllner by pure chance in La Cabaña, two years ago. Even then Höllner was showing signs of the stomach cancer that would soon kill him. Filip Monteiro, the old waiter with the glass eye, had asked him if he would consider sharing a table with Höllner one night when the restaurant was very full.

They knew immediately that they were both immigrants from Germany—they had similar accents. Silberstein had expected to discover that Höllner was one of the many Germans who had come to Argentina via the well-organised lifelines that helped Nazis flee the ruins of the Third Reich, war criminals who lived in constant fear of being arrested. But Höllner had referred to the war as the catastrophe it was. His father had been a high-ranking Nazi, but Höllner was one of the many German immigrants who had come to Argentina in search of a future they thought they could never find in Europe.

After the meal they had walked home together, as they lived in the same neighbourhood. Silberstein invited Höllner to visit the workshop where he restored old furniture. Höllner accepted the invitation, and then it became the norm for him to visit Silberstein in his workshop in the mornings. They would occasionally go out to the courtyard for a coffee and a smoke.

They had compared their lives, as old people do. And it was then that Höllner asked him if he happened to be related to a certain Herr Jacob Silberstein from Berlin, who had escaped being deported with his fellow Jews in the 1930s, and then avoided persecution during the war because he was the only person who could give Hermann Goering a satisfactory massage to ease his back pains. Feeling that history had caught up with him at a stroke, Silberstein told him that the masseur Jacob Silberstein was his uncle. And that it was thanks to Jacob that his brother Lukas, Silberstein's father, had also evaded deportation. Höllner explained that he himself had met Jacob because his own father had also been massaged by him. Silberstein was so touched that he felt obliged to embrace Höllner.

Now, lying in his tent, he remembered all that as if it had happened yesterday. Silberstein checked his watch: 10.15. He changed identity again in his thoughts. Now he was Fernando Hereira, an Argentinian citizen on holiday in Sweden.

He dressed, broke camp and drove back to the main road. He stopped for lunch outside Varberg. Two more hours and he would be in Malmö, where he had collected the car forty days earlier. Before then he would have to get rid of the tent and the sleeping-bag. He had dumped the camping stove, saucepans, plates and cutlery in a rubbish bin at a lay-by in Dalarna.

A few kilometres north of Helsingborg, behind a petrol station where he stopped to fill up, he found a skip. He buried the tent and the sleeping-bag under cardboard boxes and plastic bottles, shedding the last physical traces of a journey during which he had taken a person's life, and sent a final horrific greeting to the equally horrific past by means of some blood-soaked footprints on a wooden floor.

From now on the only traces would be inside his head.

He returned to his car and sat at the wheel. A question was nagging away at the back of his mind. He had made an unexpected discovery about himself. On the way to Sweden he had spent the whole of the long flight wondering how he would manage to achieve the mission he had set himself. So far in his life he had never been anywhere near close to harming another human being. He hated violence.

As it turned out, it was not at all difficult. That was what he couldn't understand. Why had it been so easy? He had worried that he would be overcome by remorse, but his conscience had remained at peace.

He sat in the car for ages, trying to understand. In the end, when his urge to drink something very strong got the better of him, he started the engine and drove away.

He drove into Malmö and had no difficulty finding the car hire company. He paid the bill in cash. He set off towards the city centre and stopped at a hotel in a side street off the first square he came to. No sooner had he entered his room than he stripped down and took a shower. At last he could wash off all the ingrained dirt.

Afterwards, he wrapped himself in a bath towel and sat down with the last of the bottles in his rucksack. Freedom! He took three large swigs of brandy, and felt the warmth spreading over his body.

What had happened was rapidly becoming a memory. His aim now was to get home to his workshop. His whole life revolved round that. And his family, of course. He loved his wife, Maria, and his children. Nevertheless, it was his workshop that was the mainspring of his life. He would soon be back there. August Mattson-Herzén was dead. Now there was a chance that all the events that had been haunting him since 1945 might leave him in peace.

HE LEFT THE HOTEL at 6.30. The cold wind almost bowled him over. He looked around. Further down the street, a restaurant sign was swaying in the wind. He set off in that direction, but hesitated when he got there. There was a television set high in a corner showing an ice hockey match. Some men were sitting at a table, drinking beer, watching the game. He suspected the food wouldn't be especially good, but he couldn't face more of the cold. He sat at an empty table. At the next table was a man staring in silence at his almost empty beer glass. The waitress came with a menu, and he ordered beef steak with béarnaise sauce and chips. And a bottle of wine.

'I hear that you speak English,' said the man with the beer glass.

Silberstein nodded. He hoped to goodness that the man wouldn't start talking to him. He wanted to be at peace with his thoughts.

'Where do you come from?' the man asked.

'Argentina.'

The man looked at him, his eyes glassy. '*Entonces, debe hablar español*,' he said. His pronunciation was almost perfect.

Silberstein looked at him in surprise.

'I used to be a sailor,' the man said, still speaking Spanish. 'I lived in South America for some years. That was a long time ago, but when you learn a language properly, it stays with you.'

Silberstein agreed.

'I can see you want to be left in peace,' the man said. 'That suits me fine. So do I.' He ordered another beer.

A loud roar filled the premises. Something had happened in the ice hockey match. Players dressed in blue and yellow embraced each other. The food arrived. To Silberstein's surprise, it was good. He drank his wine. He felt calm now. All the tension had faded away.

When he finished eating he glanced at the television screen again. There was evidently a break in the match. A woman was reading the news. He almost dropped his glass when the dead man's face appeared on the screen. He sat motionless, and could feel his heart pounding. For a moment, he half expected his own face to appear there as well. But the face that did appear was not his own, but that of another old man. A face he recognised.

He turned to the man at the next table, who seemed to be lost in thought. 'What are they saying on the news?' he asked.

The man turned to the television and listened. 'Two men have been murdered,' he said. 'Up in Norrland. One was a policeman, the other played the violin. They think they were killed by the same murderer.'

He knew that the first man was Mattson-Herzén, and the second one was the man he had once seen playing his violin in the forest.

Silberstein put down his glass and tried to think straight. *The same murderer*. That wasn't true. He had killed the man who called himself Molin, but not the other man.

He sat quite still. The ice hockey match had started again.

THE NIGHT of November 3, 1999, was one of the longest that Stefan Lindman had ever endured. When dawn finally broke, faint light creeping over the wooded hills, it felt as though he were in a weightless vacuum. Everything happening around him seemed surreal, a nightmare. A nightmare that began when he found Andersson's body.

The body had still been warm—at least, rigor mortis had not yet set in—which meant that whoever killed him could still be in the vicinity. The light from Lindman's torch had shown where the shot blast had hit him, just over his heart. He had almost fainted. It was a big hole. Andersson had been executed from close quarters, with a shotgun.

The dog had started howling as soon as Lindman tied it up. His first thought was that it might have found the scent of the killer. Lindman had raced back to it, scratching his face on tree branches. Somewhere along the way he had also lost his mobile phone. He had taken the dog back to the house, and rung the emergency number.

The first to arrive had been Johansson, with a colleague. Lindman had led them to Andersson's body, and both officers had drawn back in horror. They set up their base in Andersson's house. Johansson had been in constant telephone contact with Östersund and announced that Larsson was on his way. The cars from Jämtland turned up soon after midnight, and were closely followed by the doctor. The forensic team had rigged up a floodlight in the forest, but the investigation had been marking time, waiting for the light of morning.

At 4 a.m. Larsson and Lindman had been alone in the kitchen.

'Rundström will be here as soon as it gets light,' Larsson had said. 'He's bound to wonder what you're doing here.'

Lindman had thought for a while before answering. 'I wanted to know if he'd remembered anything,' he said. 'Concerning Molin.'

Then one of Larsson's colleagues had appeared and reported that the Helsingborg police had informed Andersson's wife. Larsson had gone off to talk to somebody, possibly Fru Andersson, on one of the many mobile phones that seemed to be ringing constantly.

This is no straightforward little murder, Lindman thought several times as the night progressed. Andersson had been executed. There has to have been a link between Molin and Andersson. They form the base of a triangle. At its missing tip is somebody who turns up under cover of night, not once but twice, and kills two old men who, on the face of it, have nothing in common.

Now, morning had come at last. A helicopter landed on the patch of grass behind the house. Out jumped Rundström and three dog handlers with German shepherds tugging eagerly at their leads.

In the morning light, all the activities that had gone so slowly during the hours of darkness changed character. The officers who had been working nonstop since they arrived on site were tired and their faces as grey as the sky, but now their tempo increased. Larsson and the dog handlers gathered round a map of the area and divided the search between the three of them.

The first dog found Lindman's mobile straight away. Somebody had stepped on it during the night and the battery wasn't functioning.

After an hour or so of silent and steady work, Rundström summoned all the police officers to the house to go through the case so far. Rundström asked Lindman to join in.

Rundström opened the meeting by talking about roadblocks. They had been set up on all the major access roads. Before the police had arrived in Särna, there had been a report of a car driving at high speed, south towards Idre. This was an important sighting. Rundström asked Johansson to talk to colleagues in Dalarna.

Then he turned to Lindman. 'We have a colleague from Borås here, who used to work with Herbert Molin,' he said. 'I think it will be best if you explain the circumstances in which you came to discover Abraham Andersson's body.'

Lindman described what had happened. Rundström asked him a few questions. The meeting was short. The forensic team was keen to get back to work. Lindman went outside with Larsson.

'There's something that doesn't fit,' Larsson said. 'You suggested that the reason for Molin's death may well be found in his past. That sounded reasonable to me. But where do we stand now? Andersson has never been a police officer. He and Molin didn't know each other until they happened to settle in the same remote spot. That sinks your theory, I'd have thought.'

'It must be looked into, though, surely. Molin and Andersson may have had something in common that we don't yet know about.'

Larsson frowned. 'Of course we'll look into it. But I don't buy it.'

Johansson interrupted them. 'We can forget about the car at Särna. It was a man in a hurry to get his wife to the maternity hospital.'

They went back towards the house. The clouds scuttling across the sky were getting darker.

'How long are you thinking of staying?' Larsson asked.

'I'd intended leaving today. Now I suppose it'll have to be tomorrow.'

'I'll get in touch with you later today.'

'Call me at the hotel. My mobile's not working.'

Lindman drove off. After a few kilometres he felt sleepy. He turned onto a forestry track, switched off the engine and reclined the seat.

WHEN HE WOKE UP, he was enclosed by silent white walls. It had started snowing while he was asleep, and the car windows were already covered. He sat and held his breath. Could this be what death is like? A white room with pale light filtering through the walls? He readjusted his seat and looked at his watch: 11.15. He had been asleep for more than two hours. He opened the door and got out for a pee. The ground was white, but it had stopped snowing already. There was no movement in the trees. No wind.

He drove back to the main road. He would return to Sveg, have something to eat, then wait for Larsson to phone. He would tell him about his visit to Berggren. He wasn't going to leave until he had passed on everything that might help Larsson in his investigation.

He came to the turning to Molin's house, and stamped so hard on the brakes that he skidded on the slippery surface. One last visit, he thought. He drove up to the house and got out.

Lindman looked hard at the house. It seemed different, now that the ground was white. He turned his attention to a shed at the back of the house. He opened the door. It was one room with a concrete floor. He switched on the light. There was a stack of firewood along one wall. On the opposite wall was a bench and shelves full of tools.

In a corner was a pair of skis with poles. Lindman took one of the skis to the doorway. The binding was worn. So, Molin had used them. Maybe he had skied over the lake when it was covered in ice and the weather was good. He put the ski back. What was this? Another pair of skis, shorter, possibly ladies' skis. Now he could envisage two people gliding over the frozen lake, in glitteringly clear winter weather. Molin and Berggren. He continued his search. In another corner was a broken sledge and some roof tiles.

Something caught his eye. It took him almost a minute to realise what it was. The tiles were lying haphazardly. Here was something that didn't fit into the pattern. Molin stacked firewood with a feeling for symmetry and order. The tools were all neatly arranged. But not the tiles. He bent down and removed them, one by one.

Underneath was a sheet of metal sunk into the concrete floor. A lid, locked. Lindman stood up and fetched a crowbar from among the tools. He forced it into the crack between the floor and the edge of the lid, and used all his strength to lever it open. It gave way suddenly, and Lindman fell over.

Then he looked into the hole in the floor. There was a package inside. When he lifted it, he could see it was something wrapped in an old black raincoat and tied with thick string. Lindman put the package on the bench. He untied the knots and removed the raincoat.

There were three objects: a black notebook, some letters tied with red ribbon, and an envelope.

He started by opening the envelope. It contained three black and white photographs. He was not surprised by what he saw. Deep down, he had known, ever since that visit to Berggren's, and here was the confirmation. The first was of four young men with their arms round one another's shoulders. One of the four was Herbert Molin, at that time August Mattson-Herzén. The second photograph was of Molin alone, taken in a studio.

The third photograph was also of Molin as a young man. He was standing beside a motorcycle and sidecar, holding a rifle. Lindman laid the photographs side by side. They also had this in common: Molin's uniform. It was the same as the one in Berggren's wardrobe.

THERE WAS A STORY about Scotland.

It was in the middle of the diary, slotted like an unexpected parenthesis into the account Molin had written of his life. Lindman decided to start with that.

In May 1972, Molin had a fortnight's holiday. He took a ferry from Göteborg to the east coast of England, then a train to Glasgow. He arrived late in the afternoon of May 11 and booked into Smith's Hotel. The next day he rented a car and continued his journey northwards. In the afternoon he reached the town of Dornoch, situated on a peninsula east of the Highlands. He booked into the Rosedale Hotel near the harbour. So far he had made no mention of why he was there. Just that he would meet 'M'. And he did in fact meet 'M' that same evening. 'Long walk through the town with M,' he wrote. He made the same note for each of the next seven days. Nothing more. It was not clear who 'M' was, nor what they talked about. A few days later he drove back the same way as he came. He returned to Göteborg and then Borås. By May 26 he was back at work.

The passage about Scotland was a mysterious insertion in the middle of a diary that had large time gaps. Sometimes several years passed without Molin applying pen to paper. The trip to Dornoch was an exception. On one occasion, Wednesday, May 17, Molin made one of the very few personal comments in the diary. 'Woke up this morning fully rested. Realised I ought to have made this journey ages ago.'

It was afternoon by the time Lindman had read this far. When he found the package, his first thought had been to take the diary to his hotel. Then he had changed his mind, and for the second time entered Molin's house by climbing in through the window. He had set out the three photographs beside the diary on the living-room table. Before opening it, he untied the red ribbon round the letters. There were nine of them, from Molin to his parents in Kalmar, dated between October 1942 and April 1945. All of them were written in Germany. Lindman decided to work his way through the diary first.

It started with notes from Oslo on June 3, 1942. Molin recorded the fact that he had bought the diary in Stortingsgatan, Oslo, with the intention of 'noting down significant events in my life'. He had crossed the border into Norway on a road passing through Flötningen. The road had been recommended by a certain 'Lieutenant W from Stockholm, whose job it is to ensure that those who wish to join the German army can find the way there through the mountains'.

Lindman paused. It was 1942, and Molin was nineteen. His name at that time was August Mattson-Herzén. He had left Kalmar to fight for Hitler. What were his motives? Was he fighting Bolshevism? Or was he just a mercenary bent on adventure? It was not clear.

Lindman read on. On June 28, Mattson-Herzén noted in capital letters that he had 'BEEN ENLISTED'. His notes exuded triumph. He had been accepted by the German army!

The next note was hard to decipher. After a while Lindman realised why. Mattson-Herzén was on a train, on his way to Germany. He was travelling with another Swede who had joined the Waffen-SS, Anders Nilsson from Lycksele. They were accompanied by some Norwegians, but he didn't record their names.

His next note was from Klagenfurt, Austria. It was October by now. 'I've almost finished basic training for the Waffen-SS. In other words, I'm about to become one of Hitler's elite soldiers. Wrote a letter that Erngren will take back to Sweden: he's been taken ill, and has been discharged.'

Lindman turned to the pile of letters. The first one was dated October 11, from Klagenfurt.

Dear Mother and Father!

I realise you may have been worried because I haven't written before now. It's not always easy to find time and a place to sit down with pen and paper. I just want to assure you that I am well. I came from Norway via Germany to France, where the basic training took place. And now I'm in Austria for weapons training. Discipline is strict, and not everybody can cope with it. I've kept my nose clean so far. We're all waiting impatiently for the moment when we can get out there and start doing some good. I don't know when I'll be able to get leave and come to Sweden. I'm longing to see you again, but I grit my teeth and do my duty. And that is the great task of fighting for the new Europe and the defeat of Bolshevism.

Love from your son August.

Lindman held the paper up to the light. The watermark, the German eagle, was as clear as August Mattson-Herzén's motive. He was no mercenary; he joined the German war effort to contribute to the emergence of a new Europe, which required the elimination of Bolshevism. At nineteen, the boy was already a convinced Nazi.

Lindman returned to the diary. By the beginning of January 1943, Mattson-Herzén found himself deep in Russia, on the Eastern Front. The optimism changed to doubt, then despair, and finally fear. Lindman was struck by an extract from the winter:

> *March 14. Location unknown. Russia. Freezing cold as ever. Scared stiff every night of losing a body part. Strömberg killed by shrapnel yesterday. We are dug in and expecting a counter-attack. I'm frightened. The only thing that keeps me going is the thought of getting to Berlin and taking some dancing lessons. I wonder if I'll ever make it.*

He's dancing, Lindman thought. He survives by dreaming about how he might be gliding around a dance floor.

It was starting to grow dark. The chill seeped in through the broken windows. Lindman took the book into the kitchen, and covered the windows with a blanket from the bedroom. Molin's life can be split in two, he thought. There's a decisive watershed, before the fear and with the fear. It creeps up on him in the winter of 1943 when he tries to survive on the Eastern Front. It could be the same fear that I detected in the forest near Borås, more than forty years later.

He carried on reading. In April 1943, Mattson-Herzén wrote that the soldiers were engaged in a remorseless and depressing retreat, not only from an impossible war but also from an ideology that had collapsed. The circumstances were horrendous. Occasionally, he wrote about the corpses on all sides, body parts shot to pieces, the eyeless faces, the slit throats. He was constantly searching for a way out, but he couldn't find one.

In less than a year his naive enthusiasm had turned to terror. Nothing about the new Europe; now it was a question of survival.

It went on until the spring of 1945. Mattson-Herzén had returned to Germany. He was wounded. In the entry for October 19, 1944, Lindman saw the explanation for the bullet wounds found by the pathologists. It was not exactly clear what had happened, but at some point in August 1944 he had been shot. He survived by some kind of miracle. Lindman observed that what characterised the diary was no longer fear. Another emotion crept in. Hate. He expressed his anger at what was happening. Hitler may have let them down, but not as much as all those people who failed to understand that the war was a crusade against Bolshevism. These were the people Mattson-Herzén started to hate in 1944. This emerged clearly from one of the letters he wrote to Kalmar. It was dated January 1945.

Dear Mother and Father!

I'm sorry I haven't written for so long, but we have been constantly on the move. You have no need to worry. I've come through comparatively unscathed. I've seen a lot of my former comrades killed, but I have never lost heart. I do wonder, however, why more Swedes have not rallied to the German flag. Do people fail to see what is at stake? Have they not realised that the Russians are going to subjugate everyone who fails to resist? I am sure that you understand what I mean. You didn't prevent me from joining up. I often think about Kalmar in quiet moments, but there are not so many of them.

Your loving son, August Mattson-Herzén.

Lindman read on. The entries became less frequent and shorter. Mattson-Herzén stayed in Germany until the end of the war. He was in Berlin as the city fell, street by street. He noted that on several occasions he was close to 'falling into the clutches of the Russians'. The last wartime entry was dated April 30.

I'm fighting for my life now, fighting to escape alive from this living hell. All is lost. Swapped my uniform for clothes taken from a dead German civilian. That's more or less the same as deserting, but everything is crumbling on all sides now. I shall try to escape over a bridge tonight.

It was not clear what happened next, but Mattson-Herzén did manage to get back to Sweden. The diary entries became shorter and sparser still. He noted that he got married. That his wife gave birth to children. But he wrote nothing about changing his name. Nor was there any mention of the music shop in Stockholm.

Molin—he was now Molin—moved to Alingsås, and then to Borås. Ten days in Scotland produced an unexpected burst of writing. After Scotland he seldom took up his pen, and then merely noted individual events, with no personal comment.

One entry, however, aroused Lindman's curiosity: 'March 12, 1993. Greetings card from the old portrait painter Wetterstedt, congratulating me on my birthday.'

On May 2, 1999 he makes his last entry: 'May 2, 1999. +7 degrees. My master jigsaw-puzzle maker Castro in Barcelona has died.'

Lindman closed the book. It was almost pitch-dark outside. He packed the letters, photographs and the diary into the raincoat again. Taking them with him, he left the house and drove back to Sveg.

HE WENT DOWN to the dining room shortly after seven. The girl emerged from the swing doors and smiled as she produced the menu.

'We've changed today,' she said. 'I wouldn't recommend the veal.'

Lindman chose elk fillet with béarnaise sauce and boiled potatoes. He had just finished eating when the girl came through the swing doors and announced that he was wanted on the phone. He went up the steps to reception. It was Larsson.

'How's it going?' Lindman asked.

'Nothing tangible to go on. The dogs haven't found a thing. I'll be staying overnight, at the hotel. I expect to be there in an hour. Will you keep me company while I have supper?'

Lindman said he would. At least I've something I can give him, he thought when the call was finished.

LARSSON WAS EXHAUSTED by the time he arrived at the hotel. Even so, he laughed happily as he sat down at the dining-room table. There was only one other guest, a man at a table next to the wall. Lindman supposed he must be one of the test drivers.

'When I was younger, I often used to go out for meals,' Larsson said, by way of explanation for his laughter. 'Now it only happens when I'm forced to spend the night away from home. When there's some violent crime or something similarly unpleasant to sort out.'

As he ate, he told Lindman what had happened during the day.

'We're marking time,' he said. 'We can find no tracks. Nobody saw anything, although we've traced four or five people who drove past that evening. We're wondering if there really is a link between Andersson and Molin. And if there is, what could it be?'

When he had finished eating he ordered a pot of tea. Lindman ordered coffee. Then he told Larsson about his visit to Berggren's, how he had got into her house, and his discovery of the diary in Molin's shed. He moved his coffee cup to one side and set out the letters, the photographs and the diary for Larsson to see.

'You've really overstepped the mark,' Larsson said, clearly irritated. 'I thought we'd agreed that you wouldn't keep poking your nose in.'

'I can only say I'm sorry.'

'What if Berggren had caught you?'

Lindman had no answer to that.

'It mustn't happen again,' Larsson said after a while. 'And it's better if we don't say anything to Rundström. He tends to be a bit touchy about things like that.' He poured himself another cup of tea, and examined the photographs. 'So Molin belonged to the Nazi party and went to fight for Hitler.'

'That's why Molin changed his name,' Lindman said. 'He was covering his tracks.'

Larsson had asked for his bill, and paid it. He took out a pen and wrote *Molin* on the back of it. 'I think better when I write things down,' he said. 'August Mattson-Herzén becomes Herbert Molin. You've spoken of his fear. It could be that he was scared that his past would catch up with him. You talked to his daughter, I suppose?'

'She said nothing about her father having been a Nazi. But then, it's like having a criminal in the family. You'd rather not talk about them. Do you think Andersson was another one with a past?'

'Let's see what we find in his house,' Larsson said, writing down *Andersson*. He drew an arrow with two tips between the two names, Andersson and Molin. Then he drew a swastika followed by a question mark next to Andersson's name. 'We'll have a serious chat with Fröken Berggren first thing tomorrow morning,' he said, writing her name and drawing an arrow between it and the other two. Then he crumpled the bill up and put it in the ashtray.

'We?'

'We can say that you are in attendance as my private assistant, unauthorised.' Larsson laughed aloud, then turned serious again. 'We have two horrific murders to deal with,' he said. 'I don't care whether everything goes by the book. I want you to be there. Two people listen better than one.'

They left the dining room. The man was still sitting at his table. They parted in reception, agreeing to meet the next morning at 7.30.

THAT NIGHT, LINDMAN slept like a log. Larsson slept badly, however. By the time he wished Lindman good morning in reception, he had already been to Andersson's house. Nothing had changed. They still had no clues pointing to who had killed Andersson.

As they were about to leave the hotel, Larsson turned to the girl in reception and asked if she had seen his bill from the previous night's dinner. It was only when he had got to bed that he realised he needed it for his expenses claim. She said she hadn't seen it.

'Didn't I leave it on the table?' Larsson asked.

'You crumpled it up and put it in the ashtray,' Lindman said.

Larsson shrugged. They decided to walk to Elsa Berggren's house. There wasn't a breath of wind, and the clouds had melted away.

As they walked to the bridge, Larsson pointed to the white-painted district courthouse. 'There was a nasty incident here a few years ago that wasn't widely reported. A violent assault. Two of those found guilty boasted of being neo-Nazis. I can't remember what their organisation was called. Keep Sweden Swedish, something like that.'

'Now they call themselves White Aryan Resistance,' said Lindman.

Larsson grimaced. 'Very nasty stuff. We thought we'd buried Nazism once and for all, but apparently it's alive and kicking, even if most of 'em are shaven-headed urchins.'

They had reached Berggren's house.

'Did you warn her that we were coming?' Lindman asked.

'I thought we'd give her a surprise.'

They went through the gate. Larsson rang the bell. The door opened almost immediately, as if she had been expecting them.

'Giuseppe Larsson, Östersund CID. I think you've already met Lindman. We have quite a few questions to ask you. It's to do with the investigation into the death of Herbert Molin.'

They stepped into the hall.

'I suppose this must be important, since you've come so early?'

'It certainly is,' Larsson said.

Lindman noticed that Larsson was much more brusque than he had expected. They went into the living room. Larsson proved to be a man who didn't beat about the bush.

'You have a Nazi uniform in one of your wardrobes,' he said.

Berggren stiffened. Then she looked at Lindman. Her eyes were cold. Lindman could see that she had immediately suspected him.

'Can you fetch it for us?' Larsson said.

'How do you know that I have a uniform in my wardrobe?'

'That's a question I have no intention of answering, but it's of relevance to two current murder investigations.'

She looked at them in astonishment. It seemed to Lindman that her surprised expression was genuine. She can't have been watching television, he thought. Or listening to the radio.

'Who else has been killed—besides Herbert Molin?'

'Abraham Andersson. Does that name mean anything to you?'

'Yes, he lived not far from Herbert. What happened?'

'All I can tell you so far is that he's been murdered.'

She stood up and left the room.

'She obviously didn't know that Andersson was dead,' Larsson said, softly. 'I don't think she's faking it.'

She came back with the uniform and cap. She put them down on the sofa. Larsson leaned forward to examine them.

'Who do they belong to?'

'Me.'

'But I hardly think you were the one who wore them.'

She thought for a while before answering. 'They belonged to my father. Karl-Evert Berggren. He's been dead for many years now.'

'So he fought in the Second World War, in the German army?'

'He was a member of the volunteer corps known as the Swedish Company.'

'I take it you know that Molin also used to be a Nazi in his youth, and was a volunteer in the Waffen-SS during the war?'

She sat up straight. 'Not "used to be". Herbert was just as convinced a National Socialist the day he died as he was as a young man. He and my father fought side by side. They remained good friends all their lives.'

'And you? Were you of the same political views as Molin?'

Her reply came with no hesitation. 'Of course. My father was one of the founders of the National Socialist Workers' Party in 1933. I have been giving the Hitler salute since I was ten. My parents could see what was happening. Jews flocking into the country, degeneration, moral decay. And the threat of communism. Nothing has changed. Now Sweden is being undermined by indiscriminate immigration. The very thought of mosques being built on Swedish soil makes me feel sick. And nobody is doing anything about it.'

Her outburst had set her off trembling. Lindman was nauseated, and wondered where all this hatred could have come from.

'So Molin's moving up here was no coincidence?'

'Of course not. Those of us who maintain the old ideals have a responsibility to help one another.'

'You keep it all secret, though?'

She snorted with disgust as she answered. 'Being faithful to the land of our fathers seems to be a criminal offence nowadays. If we are to be left in peace, we have to keep quiet about our views.'

'Nevertheless, somebody tracked down Molin, and killed him.'

'What has that got to do with his patriotic views? There must have been some other reason for Herbert's death.'

'What, for instance?'

'I find it impossible to understand.'

'These last few months. Did anything unexpected happen? Did he behave in any way differently?'

'He was just the same as he always was. I used to visit him once a week. He didn't mention anything that was worrying him.'

'Did Abraham Andersson share your views?' Larsson asked.

'No. Herbert used to talk to him occasionally, but they never discussed politics.'

'Have you any idea who might have killed Abraham Andersson?'

'I didn't know the man.'

'Can you tell me who was closest to Molin?'

'I suppose that must have been me. And his children. His daughter at least. His relationship with his son had been broken off.'

'Anybody else? Have you ever heard of anybody by the name of Wetterstedt, from Kalmar?'

She hesitated before answering. Larsson and Lindman exchanged glances. She had been surprised to hear the name Wetterstedt.

'He sometimes referred to a person of that name. Herbert was born and grew up in Kalmar. Wetterstedt may have been a portrait painter, but I'm not sure.'

Larsson had taken out his notebook and written down what she said. Then he said: 'I have one more question. Did you and Molin used to dance together when you visited him?'

For the third time she looked startled. 'We did, as a matter of fact.'

'Tango?'

'Not only that. We also did some of the old-fashioned dances. Molin was a passionate dancer. Very skilled. When he was young, I believe he dreamed of becoming a professional dancer, but instead he did his duty and answered the call to arms.'

'How far back do you remember his interest in dancing went?'

'I think it was aroused during the war.'

'Did he often talk about the war?'

'No. But my father did. They once had a week's leave at the same time. They went to Berlin together. My father told me that Herbert wanted to go out dancing every evening.'

'That will be all for the time being. But you will be called for further talks.'

'Am I suspected of some crime?'

'No.'

'Will you tell me how you knew about my father's uniform?'

'Some other time,' Larsson said, getting up.

She closed the door behind them. Larsson couldn't get away from her house fast enough. 'That's what I call a really nasty person,' he said when they came to the gate.

'There are more people than you would imagine who share her views,' Lindman said.

They walked back to the hotel in silence.

'What are you going to do now?' Larsson asked.

Lindman shrugged. 'I have to get out of here.'

Larsson hesitated before asking, 'How are you?'

'I was in pain one day but I'm OK now.'

They were standing outside the hotel entrance.

'Before you leave, I'd like you to show me that place where the tent was pitched.'

'When?' Lindman asked.

'How about now?'

THEY GOT OUT of Larsson's car and Lindman led the way down to the lake and along the shore to the campsite. He saw straight away that somebody had been there. He stopped in his tracks.

'I think someone's been here since I was here last.'

Larsson stared at him in surprise. 'Has something changed?'

'I can't tell yet.'

Lindman studied the place where the tent had been pitched. Superficially, everything seemed the same. Even so, he was certain somebody had been there since. Something was different. He walked around the clearing, examining the site from different angles. Then the penny dropped. He had sat on the fallen tree trunk. As he looked round, he'd had a broken twig in his hand. He had left it on the ground in front of him when he had stood up to leave, but it wasn't there any more. It was lying by the side of the path down to the water.

'Somebody has been sitting on this log,' Lindman said. He pointed to the twig. 'Can you take fingerprints from a twig?'

'I wouldn't be surprised,' Larsson said, taking a plastic bag from his pocket. 'We can always try. Are you sure?'

Lindman was certain. He remembered where he had left the twig. It had definitely been moved.

'In that case we'll call in a dog team,' Larsson said, taking out his mobile.

Lindman turned to look into the forest. He had the feeling that there might be somebody there, very close. Somebody keeping an eye on them.

Chapter 4

Silberstein lay on top of a hill, aiming his binoculars at Abraham Andersson's house. He could see three police cars. From time to time, someone in overalls would come out of the forest. He gathered that it was there, among the trees, that Andersson had been killed.

A dog like the one he had killed at Molin's place was tied to a line running between the house and a tree at the edge of the forest. He put the binoculars down, lay on his back and breathed deeply.

I'm mad, he thought. I could have been in Buenos Aires, instead of here in the Swedish wilderness. If that damned television set hadn't shown the face of an old man who'd been murdered, I wouldn't have needed to abandon my plan.

At dawn he had taken a taxi to the airport, where a friendly woman had helped him buy a ticket to Östersund. A hire car was waiting for him. He drove into town and once again bought a tent, sleeping-bag, camping stove, map, and the other things he needed, as well as enough wine and brandy to last him a week. Then he drove to a petrol station, where he bought a local paper. The dead man was front-page news. Silberstein couldn't understand the words, but the names Dunkärret and Glöte were mentioned after a reference to Abraham Andersson. He spread the map over the bonnet of the car. Dunkärret wasn't on the map, but Glöte was. He set about making a plan.

He decided on a place called Idre. He judged it to be far enough from Andersson's house. When he arrived, he pitched his tent at the end of a forest track. Then he drove north towards Linsell, and had no difficulty in finding the road marked by a sign saying DUNKÄRRET 2. But he didn't take that road; instead he continued towards Sveg.

Just before the road leading to Molin's house, he drove into the trees along a familiar, overgrown track. He parked his car and walked along the track. He didn't think the place would be guarded, but he kept stopping and listening. Eventually, he glimpsed the house through the trees. He waited for twenty minutes. Then he walked up to the house and the spot where he had left Molin's dead body. The remains of red and white police tape hung from trees.

He took his usual path to the lake and walked along the undulating shore, keeping his ears pricked all the time. The only sound was the wind rustling the trees. When he came to the place where he had pitched his first tent, he decided that violence had not warped him, despite everything. He was basically a kind man. Violence to another human being would be unthinkable in any other circumstances. All the hatred that built up inside me over those years deadened my senses, he thought. I was the one who lashed Molin's skin into bloody strips, but at the same time it wasn't me.

He sat down on the fallen trunk and fiddled with a pine twig. Had the hatred left him now? Would he be in peace for the years he had left to live? He had no way of knowing, but that was his hope.

He walked back to his car through the gloaming and drove into Sveg. Something remarkable happened then: he had dinner in a hotel, and at another table were two men talking about Molin and Andersson. At first he thought he was imagining things. He couldn't understand Swedish, but the names cropped up over and over again. After a while he went out to reception and, as there was nobody around, he looked in the hotel ledger and found that two of the hotel guests were described as 'CID Inspectors'.

He returned to the dining room and picked up some other names, including 'Elsa Bergén' or something of the sort. Then he watched one of the policemen write on the back of his bill, then crumple it up and drop it in the ashtray. After they left, Silberstein waited until the waitress was in the kitchen, then picked up the crumpled bill and tried to decipher what was on the back. The most important thing was the third name, Elsa Berggren. Linking the three names—Molin, Andersson and Berggren—were arrows forming a triangle. Next to Andersson's name was a swastika and a question mark.

He had driven to Glöte, parked the car behind some log stacks and picked his way through the trees until he came to the vicinity of Andersson's house, then climbed up the hill where he was now lying. He kept asking himself: who killed Andersson? And was it indirectly his fault because he had killed Molin? He needed the answers to those questions before he could return to Buenos Aires, or he would be haunted by the anxiety for the rest of his life.

He watched the police officers coming and going. They would assume that it was the same person who had killed both Molin and Andersson. He realised now, he had come back to make clear, somehow or other, that he wasn't the one who had killed Andersson. A thought started to evolve in his mind. He put down the binoculars. I must tell them they are on the wrong track, he thought. My only chance is to put a spanner in their works, to make them stop and think. The dog. The dog can help me, he thought.

LARSSON FINISHED his phone call. 'Very odd,' he said.
'What is?' Lindman asked.
'Andersson's dog has disappeared.'
'What do you mean disappeared?'
'What I say. Vanished. There's no sign of it. And the place is crawling with police.' Larsson put his mobile back in his jacket pocket. 'Still, it might turn up again before long. Dogs usually do.'
He started walking towards Molin's house. Lindman drew his jacket tighter round him, and hurried after him.
Larsson drove fast. When they arrived at Dunkärret, he immediately started shouting at one of the police officers there. He was a man in his fifties, small and very thin, by the name of Näsblom. Larsson was furious when he couldn't get a straight answer to his question about precisely when the dog had disappeared.
'We gave it some food last night,' Näsblom said. 'At about seven. I keep dogs myself, so I brought some dog food from home. It must have been after then.'
'Even I can work that out.' Larsson looked at his watch. 'OK, it's now one thirty. Don't you feed dogs in the morning as well?'
'I wasn't here then. I went home early this morning, and didn't come back until this afternoon.'
'But you must have seen if the dog was still there when you left?'
'I'm afraid I didn't. I suppose I thought it was in its kennel.'
Larsson shook his head in resignation. 'And none of your colleagues saw it disappear, or heard anything?'
'Nobody noticed anything at all.'
They walked over to the running line, with no dog attached.
'How can you be certain that it didn't just break loose?'
'I looked at the lead and the way it was attached to the running line when I fed it. It was a very sophisticated system. It couldn't possibly have broken loose.'
'I don't like this,' Larsson said to Lindman. 'Who apart from the killer could have taken the dog away? If it wasn't a lunatic or a sick animal rights supporter or somebody who makes a living from selling dogs, it must have been the murderer. That means he stayed around after murdering Molin and Andersson.'
'He might have come back, of course,' Lindman said.
Larsson looked at him in surprise. 'Why should he come back? Because he'd forgotten the dog? It doesn't add up.'
'I suppose the bottom line is that we don't know for sure that the same person murdered Molin and Andersson,' Lindman said.

'It goes against common sense and all my experience to think that two incidents like this would take place at almost the same time and in the same place without there being a common murderer.'

'I agree. But even so, the unexpected does happen occasionally.'

'We'll find out sooner or later,' Larsson said. We'll dig deep into the lives of both these men, and eventually find a link between them.'

Larsson started discussing the house-to-house operation currently being undertaken in the district with Näsblom. Lindman listened at first, but then he moved away. He could see it was time for him to leave. Larsson and his team will solve the case eventually, he thought. He wondered if he would live long enough to learn the solution.

He was overwhelmed by fear. If only he could, he would run away.

'I'm leaving now,' Lindman said.

Larsson looked hard at him. 'You've been a big help,' he said, holding out his hand.

They shook hands. It seemed to Lindman that Giuseppe Larsson was a very likable man.

Then it dawned on him that his car was in Sveg.

'I ought to hang around here for a while,' Larsson said. 'I'll ask Persson to drive you to your hotel.'

Persson dropped him off outside the hotel. The girl in reception smiled when he walked in.

'I'm leaving now,' he said.

'It can get cold as evening draws in,' she said. 'And quite slippery.'

'I'll drive carefully.'

He packed his things, paid his bill and left the hotel. He put his case in the boot and was just about to get behind the wheel when Veronica Molin walked up to him.

'I heard you were leaving from Inspector Larsson. I spoke to him on the phone a few minutes ago. I wanted to hear how things were going. He said you might still be around.'

Lindman locked the car door and accompanied her back to the hotel. They sat down in the dining room, which was empty.

'Inspector Larsson said he'd found a diary. Is that right?'

'That's correct,' Lindman said. 'I've glanced through it. But it belongs to you and your brother, of course. Once they release it. At the moment it's an important piece of evidence.'

'I didn't know my father kept a diary.' She lit a cigarette, then looked him in the eye. 'Inspector Larsson said the police are still struggling to find any leads. They haven't found anything specific.'

It seemed to Lindman that he might as well not beat about the bush. He should ask her the questions he had already formulated.

'Did you know your father was a Nazi?'

He couldn't tell if the question had come as a surprise or not.

'What do you mean by that?'

'Can it mean so very many different things? I read in his diary that as a young man he left Kalmar in 1942 to enlist with the German army. He fought for Hitler until the end of the war in 1945.'

'Is that what he wrote in his diary?'

'There were letters, too. And photographs. Your father in uniform.'

She shook her head. 'This comes as a hideous shock.'

'He never spoke about the war?'

'Never.'

'Nor about his political views?'

'I didn't even know he had any. When I was a child he often said he wasn't interested in politics. I had no idea he held extremist views.'

'It's all crystal clear in his diary.'

'Is that all it's about? Didn't he write anything about his family?'

'Very little.'

'It doesn't really surprise me. I grew up with the impression that we children were nothing more than a nuisance as far as Father was concerned. He never really bothered about us; he just pretended to.'

'By the way, your father had a woman friend here in Sveg. I don't know if she was his mistress.'

'A woman here in Sveg?'

'Her name is Elsa Berggren. She was the one who found his house for him. She shares his political views, too.'

'Do you think my father's opinions might have had something to do with his death?'

'I don't think anything. But the police have to keep all options open.'

She gave a shudder. 'I want to get away from here,' she said. 'Even more than before. I must see to the funeral. Then I'll be off. And I'll have to get used to the idea that my father was a Nazi.'

Lindman looked at his watch. He ought to leave now, before it was too late.

She accompanied him out into reception. 'Thank you for making the effort,' she said.

HE DROVE SOUTH, over the river and into the forest. Occasionally he would ease back on the accelerator when he realised he was driving too fast. Shortly after midnight he stopped at a hot-dog stall in Mora that was just shutting up shop. When he had finished eating, he drove south for another few hours, till he felt too tired to go any further. Then he parked in a lay-by and curled up on the back seat.

When he woke up it was 9 a.m. He walked round and round the car to stretch his legs. He would be home in Borås by nightfall.

He started thinking back to his conversation with Veronica Molin the night before. She hadn't been telling the truth. There was that business about her father. She had only pretended to be surprised that he was a Nazi. She had known, but tried to hide the fact. He couldn't put his finger on how he knew she wasn't telling the truth. And had she really not known about Berggren?

He made up his mind to go to Kalmar. Where Molin had been born. There should be a man there by the name of Wetterstedt. A portrait painter. Who knew Molin.

He rummaged around in the boot and came up with a tattered map of Sweden. This is madness, he thought; I have my illness to worry about. But he knew he couldn't let go now. He wanted to know what had happened to Molin.

He reached Kalmar by evening. It was November 6. It had started raining a few miles north of Västervik. The water glistened in the beam from his headlights as he drove into the town and looked about for somewhere to stay.

EARLY THE FOLLOWING DAY, Lindman walked down to the sea. He could just make out the Öland bridge through the fog that had settled over the Kalmarsund. He went to the water's edge and stood contemplating the sea as it lapped against the shore.

He wandered back towards town. He found a café, went in, ordered a cup of coffee and borrowed a telephone directory.

There was only one Wetterstedt in the Kalmar district. Emil Wetterstedt, artist. He lived in Lagmansgatan. Lindman turned the pages until he found a map of the area: he located the street in the centre of town, only a couple of blocks away.

He drained his cup and left the café. All the shops were still closed, but he saw one that sold mobile phones.

The block of flats in Lagmansgatan was three storeys high, with a grey façade. The front door was unlocked. From the names next to the bells, he saw that Wetterstedt lived in a flat on the top floor. He climbed the three flights and knocked on the door of the flat. No reply. He hammered on it hard. The door behind him opened. In the doorway was an elderly man in a dressing gown.

'I'm looking for Herr Wetterstedt,' Lindman said.

'He spends the autumn at his summer place.'

'Where is his summer place?'

'Who are you? We like to keep an eye on people who come sauntering about this building. Are you going to commission a portrait?'

'I want to speak to him about an urgent matter.'

The man eyed Lindman up and down. 'Emil's summer place is on Öland. In the south of the island. When you've gone past Alvaret you see a sign that says Lavender. It's a private road. That's where he lives.'

'Thank you for your help.' Lindman started for the stairs, but stopped. 'Just one more thing. How old is Herr Wetterstedt?'

'He's eighty-eight, but he's pretty spry.'

Lindman went back the way he had come. The shop selling mobile phones was open. A young man produced a battery that fitted Lindman's mobile. He paid, and even as he did so the phone bleeped to indicate that he had messages. Before leaving Kalmar, he sat in his car and listened to them. Elena had called three times, sounding increasingly resigned and curt.

He drove out of the hotel car park and looked for a road to the bridge. The fog was thick as he drove over the water. He came to Öland, turned right and headed south. He drove slowly. He could see no countryside, only fog. He almost missed the sign for LAVENDER 2.

The dirt road he turned into was full of potholes and evidently little used. It was dead straight, and disappeared into the fog. Eventually he came to a closed gate. On the other side was an ancient Volvo 444 and a Harley-Davidson. Lindman switched off his engine and clambered out. He opened the gate and continued along the path. There was still no sign of a house. A figure emerged from the mist, walking towards him. A young man with close-cropped hair, nattily dressed in a leather jacket and a light blue open-necked shirt.

'What are you doing here?' The voice was shrill, almost a shriek.

'I'm looking for Emil Wetterstedt.'

'Why?'

Lindman bristled at the cross-examination. 'I want to talk to him about Herbert Molin. I'm a police officer.'

The boy stared at him. His jaws worked away at a wad of chewing gum. 'Wait here,' he said. 'Don't shift from this spot.'

He was swallowed up by the fog. Lindman followed him, slowly. After only a few metres a house came into view. The boy disappeared through the front door. It was a whitewashed house, long and narrow, with a wing jutting out from one of the gable ends. Lindman waited. The door opened again and the boy approached.

'I thought I told you to stay put!' he shrieked.

'Is he going to receive me, or isn't he?' Lindman said.

The boy gestured to Lindman that he should follow him. Lindman had to bow his head when he entered through the door. The boy showed him into a room at the back of the house.

Emil Wetterstedt was sitting in an armchair in a corner. He had a blanket over his knees, and on a table next to his chair was a pile of books and a pair of glasses. The boy positioned himself behind the armchair. The old man had thin white hair and a wrinkled face, but the eyes he directed at Lindman were bright.

'I don't like being disturbed when I'm on holiday,' he said softly.

'I shan't take much of your time.'

'I don't accept commissions for portraits any more. In any case, your face is too round to inspire me. I prefer longer, thinner faces.'

'I haven't come here to ask you to paint my portrait. My name's Stefan Lindman. I'm a police officer. I spent some years working alongside Herbert Molin in Borås.'

'I have been told that he's dead. Do you know who did it?'

'Not yet.'

Wetterstedt gestured towards a chair. Reluctantly, the boy moved it into place. Lindman wondered what was going on. Who was this boy, whose assignment seemed to be to keep guard over the old man?

'What do you want to know?' asked Wetterstedt.

Lindman decided to get straight to the point. 'We don't have any specific clues pointing either to a motive or to a killer,' he said. 'That means we have to dig deep. Who was Herbert Molin? Can we find a motive hidden in his past? Those are the sort of questions we're asking ourselves, and others. People who knew him.'

'It was actually Herbert's father I knew. I was younger than he was, but older than Herbert.'

'And Axel Mattson-Herzén was a captain in the cavalry?'

'An honourable rank that ran in the family. One of his ancestors fought in the battle of Narva. The Swedes won, but the forefather fell. That tragedy gave rise to a family tradition. Every year, they celebrated the victory at Narva. I remember the family had a big bust of King Karl XII on a table.'

'Was there any other bust on that table?'

'What do you mean? Who?'

'Hitler.'

The boy standing behind the chair came to life. It was a momentary reaction, but Lindman noticed. Wetterstedt remained calm.

'What are you trying to suggest?'

'Molin volunteered to fight in Hitler's army during the war. We've also discovered that his family were Nazis. Is that right?'

Wetterstedt responded without hesitation. 'Of course it's right. I, too, was a Nazi. We don't need to play games, Officer. During the war, everybody with a grain of common sense sided with Hitler. The choice was between watching the relentless advance of communism, or putting up some resistance. Everything was set up.'

'Set up for what?'

'For a German invasion.' It was the boy who answered. Lindman looked at him in astonishment.

'But the situation here in Sweden is worse than ever,' Wetterstedt said. 'No discipline. We don't have borders any more. Anybody can get in wherever they like. I fear the national character of Sweden has been lost for ever. Nevertheless, one has to keep plugging away.'

Wetterstedt paused and turned to Lindman with a smile. 'I've never attempted to conceal my opinions. Obviously, there have been folk who've preferred not to acknowledge me in the street, but there has never been a shortage of people who have respected me for standing up for my opinions. People with the same views as mine, but who have preferred not to make them public, for various reasons.'

'Did you meet Herbert Molin often?'

'We haven't met at all for the last thirty years. We kept in touch through letters. He wrote letters, and I replied with postcards.'

'Did he ever mention that he was scared? Was there anything he was frightened of?'

'What could that have been? He chose to conceal his political identity. I can understand that, but I don't think he was afraid of being exposed. He wasn't fearful of papers landing up in the wrong hands.'

The boy coughed and Wetterstedt shut up immediately. He's said too much, Lindman thought. The boy is his minder.

'What papers are you referring to?'

Wetterstedt shook his head in vexation. 'There are so many papers in the world nowadays.' He drummed his fingers on the armrest. 'I'm an old man. Conversations tire me. I'd like you to leave now.'

The boy behind the chair grinned cheekily. It was clear to Lindman that the audience granted him by Wetterstedt was at an end.

'Magnus will see you out,' Wetterstedt said.

The boy whose name was Magnus opened the front door. The thick layer of fog was still enveloping the landscape.

'How far is it to the sea?' Lindman asked as they walked to the car.

'That's not a question I'm required to answer, is it?'

Lindman stopped in his tracks. He could feel the anger rising inside him. 'I always thought that Swedish Nazis had shaven heads and Doc Marten boots. I now realise they can look exactly like normal people. You, for example.'

The boy smiled. 'Emil has taught me how to deal with provocation.'

'Just what are your fantasies? That there's a future for Nazism in Sweden? Are you going to hunt down every immigrant? That would mean kicking out several million Swedes. Nazism is dead; it died with Hitler. Just what do you think you're doing? Licking an old man's arse? What do you think he can teach you?'

They'd come to the car and the motorbike. Lindman was so angry, he had broken out into a sweat.

The boy smiled. 'Not to make the same mistake as they made. Not to lose faith. Now clear off.'

Lindman drove slowly back to the bridge, thinking over what Wetterstedt had said. He was about to cross the bridge when his mobile rang. He pulled in to the side and answered.

'Giuseppe here. Are you back in Borås yet?'

Lindman wondered if he ought to say something about his meeting with Wetterstedt, but decided to say nothing for the time being.

'I'm nearly there. The weather's been pretty awful.'

'I wanted to phone you to say that we've found the dog.'

'Where?'

'Somewhere we'd never have guessed. In Molin's dog pen.'

'Dead?'

'No, as lively as they come. A bit short of food, though.' Larsson laughed merrily at the other end of the line. 'What do you say to that?'

'That someone is trying to tell you something.'

'Quite right. The question is: what? The dog is a message. A sort of bottle thrown into the sea with a note inside it. But what? To whom? Think about that, and get back to me.'

HE DREAMED THAT he was walking through the forest to Molin's house. The wind was blowing so hard that he could scarcely keep his balance. He had an axe in his hand.

He gave a start and was jerked out of his dream. A woman was standing in front of him, tapping him on the shoulder.

'We don't like people to be asleep in here,' she said sternly. 'This is a library, not a sun lounge.'

'I'm very sorry.'

Lindman looked dozily round the reading room. An elderly man was glaring disapprovingly at him. Lindman checked his watch. How long had he been asleep? Ten minutes, perhaps, surely not more.

He had made up his mind coming back over the bridge. He would make a nocturnal visit to Wetterstedt's flat. Until then, all he could do was wait. He had parked his car and found an ironmonger's, where he bought a screwdriver and the smallest jemmy he could find. Then he had picked out a cheap pair of gloves at a gents' outfitters. He wandered around the town until he felt hungry, ate at a pizzeria and read the local newspaper. Then it occurred to him that he would do well to go to the local library. In the history section he had found what he was looking for. A book on the Hitler period in Sweden.

After less than an hour's reading he realised something that he hadn't grasped before. That in the 1930s, and up to around 1943 or 1944, Nazism had been much more widespread in Sweden than most people nowadays were aware of. There had been various branches of Nazi parties that squabbled between themselves, but behind the men and women in the parades there had been a grey mass of anonymous people who had admired Hitler and would have liked nothing more than a German invasion and the setting up of a Nazi regime in Sweden. He found astonishing information about the government's concessions to the Germans, and how exports of iron ore from Sweden had been crucial in enabling the German munitions industry to satisfy Hitler's constant demand for more tanks and other war materials. What he vaguely remembered from his history classes was a very different picture: a Sweden that had remained strictly neutral.

That was when he must have fallen asleep.

He picked up the book again and started reading the last chapter. It was about the various attempts after the war to set up a Swedish Nazi party. Behind all those small groups and local organisations that kept coming and going, he could still sense the grey mass assembling.

He wondered where the boy who kept watch over Wetterstedt fitted in. Was there some kind of organisation that nobody knew about, where the likes of Molin, Berggren and Wetterstedt could make propaganda for their views? He thought about what Wetterstedt had said, about 'papers landing up in the wrong hands'.

He returned the book to its place on the shelf. It was dark when he left the library. He went to his car and phoned Elena. He couldn't put it off any longer. She sounded pleased when she heard his voice, but also cautious.

'Where are you?' she asked.

'I'm on my way. I'll be back by tomorrow.'

'How are you feeling?'

'I haven't the strength to go into that now.'

'You must realise that I am worried.'

'I'll be in Borås tomorrow, I promise.'

'Don't drive too fast.'

'I never do.'

'You always do.'

The connection was cut off. Lindman sighed, but made no attempt to phone again. The clock on the dashboard showed it was 7.25 p.m. He wouldn't dare to break into Wetterstedt's flat before midnight. I ought to go home, he thought. What will happen if I'm caught? I'll be sacked and disgraced. He had cancer, and so he had nothing to lose. Was that the way it was? He didn't know. He drew his jacket closer around him, and closed his eyes.

THE LAST LIGHTS in the windows of the flats in Lagmansgatan went out. Lindman was standing in the shadows under a tree, watching. It had started raining. He hurried across the street and tried the front door. To his surprise, it was still open. He slipped into the dark entrance hall and listened. He switched on his torch and crept up the stairs to the top floor. He shone his torch onto the door of Wetterstedt's flat. There were two locks, but neither of them was a safety lock.

He pushed the letterbox open and listened. All was quiet in the flat. He took out the jemmy. The torch was small enough for him to hold in his teeth. In his police career he had learned the basic techniques used by burglars to force open a door. He crouched down, put the jemmy on the floor and pushed the screwdriver as far into the crack between the door and the frame as it would go. He moved it back and forth, and the crack widened. He pushed it further in, then pulled it up to the lower of the two locks. He picked up the jemmy and forced it in at a point between the locks. He was sweating from the effort.

He wiped his brow. Then he forced the jemmy with all his might, simultaneously pressing hard against the screwdriver with his knee. The door gave way. The only noise was a creaking and the thud of the screwdriver landing on his shoe. He switched off his torch and listened, ready to flee if necessary. Nothing happened. He opened the door carefully and pulled it to behind him. He switched on his torch again, careful not to point it at a window.

He walked slowly round the flat, not sure what he was looking for. It was just three rooms, plus kitchen and bathroom, overflowing with furniture. The living room evidently also served as a studio. There was an empty easel, and an escritoire against one wall. He opened a drawer. Old pairs of glasses and packs of playing cards. He searched through the other drawers, still not knowing what he was looking for.

He moved on to the study, and went to the desk. The curtains were drawn. He took off his jacket and hung it over the desk lamp before switching it on. He looked through a pile of paper on the desk. It was mainly bills, and crossword puzzles torn out of newspapers.

Then he went through the drawers, which were unlocked. In the bottom left-hand drawer was a brown leather box file. Lindman took it out and laid it on the desk. There was a swastika impressed on the leather. He opened it carefully. It contained a bundle of typewritten sheets—carbon copies, not originals. They seemed to be some kind of accounts. At the top of the first page was a handwritten heading: *Comrades who continue to fulfil their commitments*. Then followed long lists of names in alphabetical order. In front of each name was a number. On the next page was another long list of names.

Under the letter D, after Karl Danielsson, the same hand as had written on the first page had noted: *Now deceased. Pledged an annual subscription for thirty years*. Annual subscription to what? Lindman wondered. There was no reference to the title of an organisation. He could see that many had died. In some places there was a handwritten note that future subscriptions had been specified in a will, in others '*paid by the son or daughter, no name given*'. He turned back to the letter B. There she was, Berggren, Elsa. He turned to the letter M. Sure enough, there was Molin, Herbert. He returned to the beginning. The letter A. No Andersson, Abraham.

Lindman closed the file and replaced it in the drawer. Were these the papers Wetterstedt had referred to? A Nazi old comrades association, or a political organisation? He turned off the desk lamp and sat in the dark. The air was heavy with the disgust he was feeling. All these 1,430 individuals still adhering to a doctrine that ought to have been done away with once and for all.

He sat there in the dark, making up his mind that it was time for him to set off for home. But something held him back. He took out the file once more, opened it and turned to the letter L.

IT WAS LIKE BEING on the receiving end of a punch, he reflected afterwards, on his way to Borås, driving far too fast through the darkness. It was his father's name there at the top of the page: *Evert Lindman, deceased, subscriptions pledged for twenty-five years.* He recalled as clear as day sitting with one of his father's friends, a solicitor, going through the estate. His father had left 15,000 kronor to something calling itself the Strong Sweden foundation. Lindman had wondered what kind of a foundation it was. He had been devastated by the death of his father, and lacked the strength to think any more about it.

Now, in Wetterstedt's stuffy flat, that donation had caught up with him. He couldn't close his eyes to facts. His father had been a Nazi. One of the type that kept quiet about it, didn't speak openly about their political opinions. It was incomprehensible, but true.

He checked everything meticulously before leaving the room. Then he opened the flat door, and went out, shutting it after him.

At that very moment there came the sound of the front door opening or closing downstairs. He stood motionless in the darkness, holding his breath and keeping his ears pricked. No sound. He went down one floor, tentatively. The lunacy of the whole undertaking had now hit him like a freezing-cold shower. Not only had he committed a pointless break-in, he had also unearthed a secret he would infinitely rather not have known anything about.

He paused, listened, and then walked down the last two flights to the front door. He looked round when he emerged into the street. No one. When he reached his car he looked round again, but could see no sign of anybody having followed him. He switched on the engine and backed out of his parking place. He didn't see the man in the shadows writing down his registration number.

Chapter 5

Lindman stood in the window, looking down over Allégatan. He could hear Fru Håkansson playing the piano in the flat downstairs. This was a regular occurrence, every day except Sunday. She played the piano from 11.15 to 12.15. Always the same Chopin piece, over and over again. In my chaotic world, she's the only thing that is unchanging, he thought.

He finished his breakfast and collected the dirty washing he was going to take to Elena's. Then he fetched a photo album he kept in a bureau, and sat with it on the living-room sofa. It had always been his father taking the pictures, never his mother, although he had used the self-timer whenever possible. Lindman studied the pictures of his parents, his mother on the left and his father on the right. He leafed through the album. There were his sisters side by side, his mother staring straight at the lens. What do my sisters know about their father's political views? he wondered. Presumably nothing. What did my mother know? And could she have shared his opinions?

He worked his way slowly through the album, one picture at a time.

His first day at school—it was 1969; he was seven. He remembered how proud he was of his new, dark blue blazer.

Summer 1971, he was nine. They had gone to Varberg, and rented a little cottage on the island of Getterön. Bath towels among the rocks, a transistor radio. It was idyllic there among the rocks, his father, mother, himself and his two teenaged sisters.

Pictures only show the surface, he thought. Something quite different was going on underneath. I had a father who led a double life.

The pictures slowly brought memories to life. In between, other memories came to mind, ones that had not been photographed.

He must have been twelve years old. He had been hoping for a new bike for ages. In the end his father gave in, and they drove to Borås.

They had to wait their turn in the shop. Another man was buying a bike for his son. He spoke broken Swedish. It took some time to complete the deal, and the man and the boy went off with the new bicycle. The shop owner apologised for the delay.

'Those Yugoslavians. We're lumbered with more and more of 'em.'

'What are they doing here?' his father said. 'They should be sent back. Haven't we got enough problems with all the Finns? Not to mention the Gypsies. We should send the whole lot packing.'

Lindman could remember it well. The shop assistant hadn't said anything more. Then they had bought the bicycle, fixed it to the roof of the car and driven back to Kinna. The memory was crystal clear. He remembered the smell of the shop—rubber and oil. And he remembered something else he had felt at the time—the fact that his father had expressed a political opinion. That was so unusual.

When he was growing up, nothing had ever been discussed among the family apart from insignificant matters. What to have for dinner, whether the lawn needed mowing. There was one exception: music. That was something they could talk about.

All his father listened to was old-fashioned jazz. Lindman could still remember the names of some of the musicians his father had tried in vain to persuade him to listen to and admire: King Oliver, the cornet player who had inspired Louis Armstrong; a clarinetist called Johnny Dodds; and the outstanding Bix Beiderbecke. Stefan had preferred to listen to the same music as his sisters. Often the Beatles, but more usually the Rolling Stones. His father had accepted that as far as music was concerned his daughters were a lost cause, but he thought that his son might just be saved.

When they went to Borås to buy a bicycle, his father had expressed an opinion that went a long way beyond deploring the stupidity of listening to pathetic pop music. What he said had to do with people, and their right to exist.

Lindman went to the bathroom and looked at his face in the mirror. As a child, he had always looked like his mother. The older he became, the more he resembled his father. Somebody must know, he thought, about my father and his politics. I must get in touch with my sisters. But right now there was something else that needed doing. Something more important.

Shortly after 7 p.m. he parked outside the block of flats in Norrby where Elena lived. He looked up at her window. Without Elena, I am nothing at the moment, he thought. Nothing at all.

SILBERSTEIN WAS HEADING north. He drove through Funäsdalen before turning into a smaller road and driving into the darkness to see where it would take him. He was climbing steeply now; perhaps he was in the mountains already. He drew up, switched off the engine and sat back to wait for daylight.

When dawn began to break, he set off again, climbing all the time. He noticed several chalets tucked among the rocks and bushes. There were no lights anywhere. He kept on going until he came to a gate blocking the road. He got out of the car to open it, and continued along the track after closing the gate behind him.

Eventually the road came to an end and he could go no further. He got out of the car and filled his lungs with the chilly air. He looked round: mountaintops, in the distance a long valley, and beyond that more mountains. A path led into the trees. He followed it. After a few hundred metres he came to an old wooden chalet. Nobody had been along the path for ages, he could see that. He went up to the chalet and peered in through the windows. The front door was locked. He tried to imagine where he would have hidden a key if the chalet had been his. There was a broken plant pot in front of one of the flat stones forming part of the steps up to the front door. He bent down and lifted the pot. No key. Then he felt underneath the stone, and there it was. He unlocked the door.

The chalet comprised a big living room, a kitchen and two small bedrooms. He went into the kitchen. The chalet had mains electricity, and there was a telephone. He looked in the big freezer. It was full of food. What could that mean? Was the chalet only empty for a short time? He had no way of knowing. He took out some packets of deep-frozen hamburgers and put them in the sink.

He sat down by the telephone and dialled the long number to Maria in Buenos Aires. He had never quite managed to work out the time difference. He could hear it ringing at the other end. Maria answered.

'It's me,' he said. 'Can you hear me all right?'

She spoke loudly and quickly, as she always did when she was nervous. I've been away for too long, he thought.

'Where are you?' she asked.

'I'm still in Europe. I'm looking at furniture. I'll be home soon.'

'Don Batista's been asking for you. He's upset. He says you promised to renovate an antique sofa for him. He wanted to give it to his daughter as a wedding present in December.'

'Tell him it will be ready in time. Maria, I'll soon be back home. I miss you, but this journey has been very important. A man of my age ought only to make journeys by himself. To find out who he really is. I'll be a different person when I get back.'

'What do you mean, a different person?' She sounded worried.

He knew that Maria was always worrying in case something changed. He wished he hadn't said that.

'I'll be changed for the better. I shall have dinner at home in future. I'll very seldom dine at La Cabaña and leave you alone.'

'When are you coming home?' she said.

'Soon. I'll ring again later. I don't know when. Goodbye, Maria.'

He put the phone down, and it at once occurred to him that he ought to have told her he loved her, even if he didn't. After all, she was the one who was always around.

He stood up, and started searching for the name of the owner of the chalet. He found an invoice addressed to a man named Frostengren with a home address in Stockholm. That persuaded him that he need not fear being disturbed. The only thing he would have to avoid was being seen when he joined the main road. And he had better keep an eye on the other cottages whenever he left or returned, to make sure they were all shut up for the winter. He could make this little chalet his base while he tried to find out what had happened to Andersson.

He spent the rest of the day in Frostengren's chalet. He slept a lot, drank coffee, grilled a hamburger and occasionally went out to look at the mountains. At about 2 p.m. it started raining. He switched on the light over the table in the living room and sat by the window to work out what to do next.

A spring was wound up, it seemed to him. When Molin died, it triggered some mechanism that meant Andersson had to be killed as well. Why, and by whom? He spent the whole day analysing these questions from different points of view. Was there a secret between the two men? Was there a risk that Andersson might reveal it after Molin's death? Somebody had been put in danger, and therefore Andersson had to die as well, to prevent the secret coming out?

He had seen the woman who came to visit Molin three times. He had guessed that she must have been Elsa Berggren. That was the name on the back of the bill the police officer had dropped into the ashtray. He gazed over the hills and tried to work out what the implications were. A triangle of Molin, Berggren and Andersson.

There was no other explanation, it seemed to him, but that there was some kind of link, a secret, between the three of them. Molin was dead, so Andersson had to die as well. That left only the woman. She must be the one with the key to all this.

In the evening, he worked out his plan. By midnight he knew what he was going to do. Next to the telephone was a directory. He found Elsa Berggren's number and an address. He checked the map of Sveg in the phone book and saw that it was a street on the south side of the river. He wrote the address on a scrap of paper.

He stayed in Frostengren's chalet for three more days. On the morning of the fourth day he cleaned the place, and waited until the afternoon before locking up and replacing the key under the stone.

He drove into Sveg just as it was getting dark. He parked on the edge of the little town and found his way to Berggren's house. He took a good look around, then returned to his car.

He still had a lot of hours to fill. He went into a supermarket, found himself a woollen hat big enough to be pulled down over his face, then joined the longest of the check-out queues, where the girl seemed to be the one most under pressure. He was sure as he left the store that nobody would remember what he looked like. When he got back to the car he used a knife he had taken from Frostengren's chalet to make holes in the hat for him to see through.

He drove over the bridge and parked where his car was invisible from the road. He set off at midnight, carrying a small axe that he had taken from the chalet. He waited until a heavy lorry had gone past, then hurried over the road and along the path down by the river.

LINDMAN STORMED out of Elena's home in a fury at 2 a.m. Even before he reached the street his rage had subsided, but he couldn't bring himself to go back. He got into his car and drove into town. He didn't want to go home yet. He pulled up at the Gustav Adolf church and switched off the engine.

Elena had been pleased to see him. They had sat in the kitchen and shared a bottle of wine. He had told her about his journey and the sudden pains he'd had in Sveg. He had told her about Molin and Andersson and Wetterstedt. Her eyes betrayed her concern. They had sat up for a long time, but she shook her head when he asked if she was tired. No, she wanted to hear everything about what he had been up to. Even so, after a while they had started clearing away before going to bed. She had asked him in passing if he couldn't have phoned her a bit more often. Hadn't he realised how worried she had been?

'You know I don't like telephones.'

'There's nothing to stop you ringing, saying hello and hanging up.'

'Now you're annoying me. You're pressurising me.'

'All I'm asking is why you don't phone me more often.'

He had grabbed his jacket and stormed out. He regretted it by the time he reached the stairs. He knew he shouldn't drive. If he had been caught in a police check, he would have been drunk in charge.

I'm running away, he thought. All the time I'm running away from my appointment on November 19. I go wandering around the forests in Härjedalen, I break into a flat in Kalmar and now I drive when I've been drinking. My fear is dictating my actions, and it's so strong that I can't even be with the person I'm closest to in the whole world, a woman who is totally honest and showing that she loves me.

He took out his mobile and dialled her number.

'I'm sorry. I didn't mean to hurt you.'

'I know that. Are you coming back?'

'No. I'll sleep at home.'

He didn't know why he had said that. She didn't say anything.

'I'll phone you tomorrow,' he said, trying to sound cheerful.

'We'll see,' she said wearily, and hung up.

He switched off his mobile, then got out of the car and walked back to Allégatan.

HE SLEPT BADLY and got up at 6 a.m. No doubt Elena would be awake already. He ought to phone her, but he didn't feel up to it. He forced himself to eat a substantial breakfast, then went to fetch his car. There was a squally wind blowing. He got into the car and took out his mobile. There was a message from Larsson. He called his number.

'How are you?' Larsson asked.

'Not too bad.'

'I just wanted to tell you we've made a bit of progress on the weapons used. In Molin's case there was a whole arsenal. Shotgun, tear-gas canisters, God only knows what else. We've been chasing up reported cases of weapons thefts, but we still don't know where they came from. But it was a different gun that killed Andersson. It means we're now faced with something we weren't really expecting.'

'Two different murderers?'

'Exactly.'

'It could still be the same one.'

'It could. But we can't ignore the other possibility. And we might well ask ourselves if this is the beginning of something that's got some way to go yet before it's finished.'

'You think there could be more acts of violence in store?'

Larsson roared with laughter. 'Acts of violence. Police officers do have a roundabout way of expressing themselves. I'll tell you a bit more about the way we're thinking. The first thing, of course, is the dog. We haven't a clue why it was taken.'

'It might be a macabre joke.'

'Could be. But the folks up here aren't all that inclined to go in for what you call macabre jokes. People are most upset and indignant. That's obvious when we talk to people.'

'What about Berggren?'

'Rundström took her to Östersund. Spent a whole day questioning her. She stuck to the same story. She has no idea who might have killed Molin. She'd only met Andersson once, briefly. We've even given her house the once-over to see if she had any weapons. Nothing.'

'Have you found any link between Andersson and Molin?'

'We're ferreting away. According to Andersson's widow, he only ever mentioned Molin as a neighbour, one of several. We've no reason to suspect that isn't true. That's about as far as we've got.'

'What about the diary? His journey to Scotland. The person referred to as "M".'

'I can't see why we should give that priority.'

'I just wondered.' Lindman took a deep breath, then told Larsson about his experiences in Kalmar and on Öland. He said nothing about the break-in, but he stressed Wetterstedt's Nazi views.

'I'll suggest to Rundström that we should bring in the national CID,' Larsson said. 'They have a section that specialises in terrorists and neo-Nazis. I can't believe that what we're up against here can be traced back to a few skinheads, but you never know.'

Lindman said he thought it was a sensible move, and wound up the call. He headed back for Allégatan, and had just pulled up outside his flat when his phone rang. It was Veronica Molin.

'I hope I'm not disturbing you. Where are you?'

'In Borås. You're not disturbing me. Where are you?'

'In Sveg. I got your number from Inspector Larsson. The policeman who claims to be investigating the murder of my father.' She made no attempt to conceal her contempt. That angered him.

'Larsson is one of the best police officers I've ever come across. What do you want?'

'I want you to come here. I think I know what happened, but I don't want to discuss it over the phone.'

'Talk to Larsson. I've got nothing to do with the investigation.'

'Just at the moment you are the only person I know who can help me. I'll pay for your flight here, and all the rest of your costs.'

'Are you saying you know who killed your father?'

'I think so. But there's another reason why I want you to come. I'm frightened.'

'Why are you frightened?'

'I don't want to talk about that on the phone either. I want you to come here. I'll be in touch again in a couple of hours.'

LINDMAN LANDED at Östersund airport on the island of Frösön at 10.25 the following morning. When Veronica Molin phoned him the second time, he had been determined to say no. There was nothing he could do to help her. But when the call came, he had said yes.

He wondered what was making him act the way he did. The fear digging at him, the illness he was trying to keep at bay? Or was it Elena that he couldn't cope with? He didn't know. The day he heard he had cancer, everything had been put out of joint. On top of everything else, he couldn't stop thinking about his father.

He had phoned Elena, who was subdued and noncommittal. He went to her flat at 7.15 and stayed the night. They had made love, but it was as if he hadn't really been there. She hadn't said anything. Nor had she asked why he suddenly had to go back to Härjedalen. When they said goodbye in her hall, he could feel her trying to envelop him in her love. He had tried to suppress his worries, but as he drove back to Allégatan he didn't feel that he had succeeded. He was in a panic, afraid that he was losing Elena, forcing her to desert him for her own sake.

When he walked down the aeroplane steps at Frösön he felt the fierce cold. The ground was white with frost. He rented a car—Veronica Molin would pay for it. He had intended going straight to Sveg, but changed his mind when he drove onto the bridge from Frösön to Östersund. It was unacceptable not to tell Larsson that he had come back. What reason should he give? Veronica Molin had contacted him confidentially, but he didn't want to keep it from Larsson.

He parked outside the National Rural Agency, then walked round the back to the police station. At reception he asked for Larsson. The girl recognised him from his earlier visit, and said that Larsson was in a meeting but it would be over soon. Lindman took a seat.

Larsson appeared at 11.30 a.m. He was unshaven and looked tired and worried. 'I ought to say that I'm surprised to see you, but nothing surprises me at the moment.' He sounded resigned.

They went to his office, and Lindman said what he'd made up his mind to say, that he'd come back because he couldn't settle in Borås.

Larsson eyed him sternly. 'Do you go ten-pin bowling?' he asked.

'Do I go *bowling*?'

'I do, when I feel restless. I sometimes find it difficult to cope too. Don't underestimate bowling. It's best to play with a few friends. The skittles you knock over can either be your enemies, or problems you can't solve and which are getting you down.'

'I've never tried it.'

'Take it as a friendly suggestion. Nothing more.'

'How's it going?'

'We've just had a meeting of the investigative team. Wheels are turning, routines are being followed, but we're getting nowhere.'

'Are there two murderers?'

'Presumably. There was a sort of fury about both murders. In Molin's case an insane fury. Somebody drags him round in a blood-stained tango and lashes him to death. There was anger behind the death of Andersson as well. More controlled. It was an ice-cold execution. I wonder if these two crimes, displaying such different temperaments, can possibly have been hatched in the same brain.'

'If it's the same murderer,' Lindman said, 'I suppose we'd have to assume that something happened subsequently that made it necessary for him to kill Andersson. But I still think the most likely explanation is two different murderers.'

'It's strange that nobody's reported anything. I can't ever remember knocking on so many doors and making so many appeals without hearing so much as a squeak in response.'

'Not hearing anything is also significant, of course. You're dealing with people who know exactly what they're doing.'

Larsson stood up. 'I like talking to you,' he said. 'You listen, and you ask the questions I need to hear. I'd like to carry on a bit longer, but I have an appointment with the forensic boys that can't wait.'

Driving to Sveg, Lindman remembered what Larsson had said about ten-pin bowling. I'm giving way to self-pity, he thought. I'm locking myself up in doom and gloom, and it's not doing me a bit of good. Larsson is quite right when he goes on about bowling. I have to take seriously what he's trying to tell me. I'm trying to convince myself that I'm going to overcome this illness, but at the same time I'm doing my best to play the role of a man on death row, beyond hope.

THE GIRL IN RECEPTION seemed pleased to see him. 'I thought you wouldn't be able to drag yourself away,' she chuckled.

Lindman laughed. It sounded too shrill and loud, he thought.

'I've given you your old room,' she said. 'Number three. You've a message from Fröken Molin. She said she'd be back around two.'

He went up to his room. It was as if he had never left. He went into the bathroom, opened his mouth and stuck out his tongue. It will turn out all right, he thought. I'll take my course of radiation therapy, and I'll be right as rain. There'll come a time when I look back on this period of my life as a mere interlude, a sort of nightmare, nothing more.

He went out to the pizzeria for lunch. When he got back, Veronica Molin was waiting for him in reception. He noticed again what a good-looking woman she was.

'Thank you for coming,' she said.

'The alternative was ten-pin bowling.'

She looked at him in surprise, then laughed. 'I'm glad you didn't say golf. I've never understood men who play golf.'

She looked around reception. Some test drivers had just come in, declaring in loud voices that it was high time for a beer.

'I don't normally invite men to my room,' she said, 'but at least we can be left in peace there.'

Her room was on the ground floor, at the end of the corridor. There were two armchairs. She'd switched on the bedside lamp and directed it away from them, so that the room was dimly lit. He smelt her perfume. He wondered how she would react if he were to tell her that what he most wanted to do just now was to make love to her.

'I've been trying to understand,' she said. 'Who would have had any reason for killing my father? It was beyond all comprehension at first.' She looked at him. 'I read that diary,' she said. 'What was in it came as a shock. I was ashamed to discover that my father had been an active Nazi. I hated him.'

Lindman wondered if he was ashamed of his own father. He was in a very peculiar situation. He and the woman opposite him had made the same discovery about their fathers.

'Anyway, it dawned on me that there might be an explanation in that diary for why he was killed. How well do you remember what was in it?' she asked.

'Pretty well. Not all the detail and dates, of course.'

'He describes a journey to Scotland.'

Lindman remembered that clearly. The long walks with 'M'.

'It was a long time ago. I wasn't very old, but I do remember my father going to Scotland to see a woman. I think her name was Monica, but I'm not sure. He had met her in Borås and she was also a police officer. They fell in love. My mother knew nothing about it. Not then at least. Anyway, he went to meet her. And he cheated her.'

'How?'

'He borrowed large sums of money from her, and never paid it back. My father was a gambler. On horses. He lost all her money. She demanded it back. He refused. She came to Borås once, that's how I know about this. She appeared at the door one evening and forced her way into the house. She told my mother everything and yelled at my father, threatening to kill him if he didn't return the money. I'd learned enough English to be able to understand what they were saying. My mother collapsed and my father was wild with rage, or maybe it was fear. She promised she would kill him in the end, no matter how long it took. I remember distinctly what she said.'

'So you're suggesting that after all those years she came here to exact vengeance?' Lindman shook his head. In his diary, Molin had described the Scotland trip in a way that didn't fit with what he had just heard. 'You have to tell the police about your theory. They'll look into it. For myself, I can't believe it. It doesn't sound credible.'

'Aren't most violent crimes incredible?'

'Why don't you want to tell this to Inspector Larsson?'

'I want to, but I wanted your advice first. How can I prevent the truth about my father from coming out? That he was a Nazi?'

'If it has nothing to do with the murder, there's no reason for the police to make any such information public.'

She stood up. 'You made a long journey for my sake,' she said. 'And I am afraid it wasn't necessary. I could have asked you over the telephone. For once, I've lost a little of my usual presence of mind.'

Lindman stood up.

'When are you leaving?' she asked.

'Tomorrow.'

'Can't we have dinner together? That's the least I can do for you.'

'I only hope they've changed the menu.'

'Seven thirty?'

'That suits me fine.'

SHE WAS RESERVED and distant during dinner. Lindman could feel himself getting cross. Partly because she had persuaded him to make this absurdly unnecessary journey on account of her exaggerated anxiety, and partly because he couldn't avoid being attracted by her.

They said goodbye in reception with hardly a word exchanged. She said she would send a cheque to Borås to cover his costs, and went to her room. Lindman fetched his jacket and went out.

As he walked through the deserted town, he thought about what she had said. The story about the woman in Scotland could conceivably be true, but he refused to believe that after all those years she had come to Sweden to take her revenge. It didn't make sense.

Without realising it, he had reached the old railway bridge. He crossed the bridge and turned into Berggren's street. There was light in two of the ground-floor windows. He was about to walk past when he thought he noticed a shadowy figure disappearing rapidly round one of the gable walls. He frowned. Then he opened the gate and approached the house. He stopped to listen. Not a sound. He peered round the corner. Nobody there. He must have been imagining things. He crept round to the back of the house. Nobody there either.

He never heard the footsteps behind him. Something struck the back of his neck. He was on the ground and the last thing he felt was a pair of hands tightening round his throat. Then nothing. Only darkness.

Chapter 6

Lindman opened his eyes. He sat up slowly and felt the back of his neck. There was some blood, and it hurt when he swallowed. Still, he was alive. He raised himself up, clinging on to the drainpipe on the house wall. Nothing to be seen, nor was there a sound.

He took out his mobile and phoned Larsson's home number. His hand was shaking. 'Can I speak to Giuseppe, please?'

While he waited Lindman moved a few paces from the house and stood in the shadow of a tree. Then he heard Larsson's voice, and was able to explain briefly what had happened.

'Are you hurt?' Larsson asked.

'The back of my neck is bleeding and it hurts a lot when I swallow, otherwise it's OK.'

'I'll try to get hold of Erik Johansson. Where exactly are you?'

'At the back of the house. By one of the gables. Under a tree. Something may have happened to Berggren.'

'Let's keep the line open,' Larsson said. 'Ring her doorbell.'

Lindman walked round to the front of the house and rang the bell. The outside light was on. He held the phone to his ear all the time.

The door opened. It was Elsa Berggren. She was still dressed. Lindman could see from her face that she was scared.

'It's all right. She's opened,' Lindman said into the telephone.

'Ask her if anything's happened.'

Lindman asked.

'Yes,' she said. 'I've been attacked. I've just phoned Inspector Johansson. He said he'd come.'

'Who attacked you?'

'He was wearing a hood. When I dragged it off him I caught sight of his face. I've never seen him before.'

Lindman passed this on.

'Wait there with her until Erik comes,' Larsson said. 'I'll drive over. Ask Erik to phone me when he turns up.'

Lindman stumbled as he walked in through the door. He felt dizzy and was forced to sit down. A clock somewhere struck a quarter-hour. She wanted to tell him what had happened, but he told her to wait.

'Inspector Johansson's the one who should listen to what you've got to say. Not me.'

JOHANSSON ARRIVED just as the clock was striking the next quarter-hour. 'What's happened?' he asked. Then he turned to Lindman. 'I didn't even know you were still here.'

'I came back. But that's irrelevant.'

'That's as maybe,' Johansson said, 'but to make things easier, perhaps you can explain how you came to be involved.'

'I was out walking, and thought I saw somebody acting suspiciously in the garden. I went to investigate and was knocked down.'

Johansson leaned over Lindman. 'You've got bruises on your neck. Are you sure you don't need a doctor?'

'Quite sure. Let's hear what Fröken Berggren has to say.'

Berggren was sitting on the edge of the sofa. Her voice was different, she could no longer conceal her fear. 'I was just on my way up to bed when there was a knock on the door. When I opened it, I had the safety chain on—but he flung himself at it so violently that it gave way. He told me to be quiet. I couldn't see his face because he was wearing a sort of hood with holes in it for his eyes. He dragged me into the living room and threatened me with an axe, and started asking me who'd killed Abraham Andersson. I tried to keep calm. I could see that he was getting nervous. He raised his axe, and so I made a run at him. I pulled the hood off him, and he ran out of the house.'

'Did he speak Swedish?'

'Broken English. I think he might have been an Italian. Or a southern European, in any case.'

'Can you describe what he looked like? How old was he?'

'It all happened very quickly. But he was old, not what I had expected. Greying hair, going bald, brown eyes. Dark jacket, dark trousers, I didn't notice his shoes.' She stood up and walked to the door. 'I'd say he was about this height, neither fat nor thin.' She marked a place on the frame with her hand, then sat down again.

'He threatened you,' Johansson said. 'How exactly?'

'He said he wanted the truth. Otherwise there'd be trouble. Who killed Abraham? That's all. I told him I didn't know. Then I realised he was actually implying something different. That was when I got really scared. He thought that I had killed him.'

Lindman felt his dizziness coming and going in waves. He stood up. 'I'm going out. I need some air.'

Once outside, Lindman began searching his memory for something to do with what Berggren had said. It had something to do with Larsson. Dinner at the hotel. There'd been another person there that evening. A man on his own. Lindman hadn't noticed his face. But there was something else about him. It eventually dawned on him what it was. The man hadn't said a single word to the waitress, despite the fact that he had summoned her several times. That man had been still there when they left.

He racked his brains. Larsson had scribbled things on the back of the bill, then crumpled it up and dropped it in the ashtray. There was something about that bit of paper. He couldn't remember what. And the man answered the description Berggren had given.

It wasn't until about 5 a.m. that Lindman had an opportunity to ask Larsson what he had scribbled on that bit of paper. Larsson arrived at Berggren's house at 1.50. Once he had taken stock of the facts, he had gone with Johansson and Lindman to the police station. An officer had been posted to keep watch over Berggren's house. They would mount yet another house-to-house operation. Somebody must have seen something, was Larsson's conviction.

'Remember that dinner we had at the hotel?' Lindman said. 'There was one other man in the dining room. Do you remember him?'

'Vaguely. Why do you ask?'

'He said nothing. That could mean that he didn't want to let us know that he was a foreigner.'

'Why the hell shouldn't he want to do that?'

'He must have guessed we were police officers. We used the names Molin and Mattson-Herzén during dinner. What's more, I think he looked a bit like the description Berggren tried to give us.'

Larsson shook his head. 'It's too circumstantial, too far-fetched.'

'Possibly. But even so. You sat there doodling on a piece of paper when you'd finished eating.'

'It was the bill. I asked about it the next day but it had disappeared. The waitress said she hadn't seen it.'

'That's the point. Where did it go?'

Larsson stopped rocking back and forwards in his chair.

'Are you saying that man took the bill after we'd left?'

'I'm just thinking aloud. One question is: what did you write?'

Larsson tried to remember. 'Names, I think. We were talking about the three of them: Molin, Andersson and Berggren. We were trying to find a link. I wrote down their names, and I joined them with arrows. I think I drew a swastika at the side of Andersson's name . . . and a question mark. I'm starting to catch on to the way you're thinking.'

'If he takes the bill, he does so because he has an interest. And if he has an interest it can only be because he's involved.'

Larsson raised a hand. 'Involved? How?'

'If this is the man who came to see Berggren last night and tried to strangle me, we ought to ask ourselves one more important question.'

'Which is?'

'A question about the question he asked Berggren: "Who killed Andersson?"'

Larsson shook his head in annoyance. 'You've lost me.'

'I'm suggesting that this question leads us to another question, the crucial one, the one he didn't ask.'

The penny dropped. It was as if Larsson started breathing again. 'Who murdered Molin?'

'Exactly,' Lindman said. 'You could draw various conclusions. The most likely is that he didn't ask the question about Molin because he already knew the answer: he was the one who killed Molin. I think it's time you started thinking new thoughts.'

'Let's hear them!'

'Somebody makes his way here to the forest and kills Molin. It's carefully planned. A few days later Andersson is killed by somebody else. For some reason, the man who killed Molin wants to know what happened. He comes back. He picks up a scrap of paper left on a restaurant table by a police officer. What does he find there? Not two names, but three.'

'Berggren?' Larsson asked as he opened the window.

'It seems to him that she must know the answer, so he tries to put pressure on her.'

'Who is this man?'

'I don't know. And he's not going to put up his tent in the same place. So the question is, where's he living?'

A FEW MINUTES LATER they were in the hotel reception. The girl at the desk looked at them in surprise.

'Two early birds looking for breakfast?'

'Breakfast can wait,' Larsson said. 'When we had dinner here last week, quite late, you may remember there was another customer in the dining room. What language did he speak?'

'English. But he came from Argentina.'

'How do you know?'

'He paid by credit card. He showed me his passport.'

She went into a back room and eventually came back with a Visa counterfoil. They read the name. Fernando Hereira.

Larsson grunted with pleasure. 'We've got him,' he said. 'Did he say where he'd come from? Or where he was going to?'

'No. He didn't say much at all. He was friendly, though.'

'Could you describe him?'

The girl thought for a moment. 'I've got an awful memory for faces.'

'But you must have seen something. How old was he?'

'Sixty, perhaps. Grey hair.'

'Eye colour?'

'I wouldn't remember that.'

'Was he fat or thin?'

'I don't think he was fat.'

'What was he wearing?'

'A blue shirt, I think. And a blazer, I'm not sure.'

'Can you remember anything else?'

'No.'

Larsson shook his head and sat down on one of the sofas in the reception area. Lindman joined him. It was 6.25 a.m. on November 11. Eight days to go before he was due to report to the hospital in Borås. Larsson yawned and rubbed his eyes. Neither of them spoke.

A door leading to the bedrooms opened. Lindman looked up and saw Veronica Molin.

SILBERSTEIN WATCHED the dawn approaching. He had gone straight back to Frostengren's chalet after the botched visit to the Berggren woman. The man he had seen behind the house, and had no choice but to knock down and frighten, was one of the police officers he had seen at the hotel. What was the man doing there? Was the woman's house being guarded after all? He had kept a careful watch on it before knocking on the door and pushing his way in.

He had driven fast through the night. The moment he was inside, he opened a bottle of wine and downed half of it. Calm gradually settled in him. He sat at the table next to the window, and steadily drank.

The Berggren woman had seen his face when she pulled the hood off. He hadn't expected that, and he had panicked. He ought to have stayed there and forced her to tell him what he was certain she knew. Instead he had fled and run into the policeman.

He carried on drinking, but held his intoxication in check. He found it hard to accept that a woman in her seventies could have murdered Andersson. She had said that she didn't know who killed him. Silberstein was sure from the start that she wasn't telling the truth. What was between these people that he couldn't work out?

Thoughts buzzed around in his head all night. Occasionally he went outside and gazed at the starry sky. His face was known now. The police would start putting two and two together. Sooner or later they would find his name on the credit card receipt at the hotel. That had been the one thing that had scotched his careful planning: running out of ready cash. The police would come looking for him.

He ought to get as far away as possible, but he knew he wouldn't do that, not until he found out what had happened to Andersson.

Dawn broke. He was tired. From time to time he nodded off as he sat looking at the mountains. He couldn't stay here; he had to move on or they would soon find him. He made up his mind. He gathered his belongings, the wine, some food. He didn't bother about the car. That could stay where it was. Perhaps somebody would find it tomorrow, perhaps he'd get a start. He left the house at about 9 a.m. and headed straight up the mountain. He stopped after only 100 metres and off-loaded some of his luggage. Then he set off again. He was drunk, kept stumbling, falling over and grazing his face on the rough ground. Even so, he kept on until he could no longer see the chalet.

By noon he hadn't the strength to go any further. He pitched his tent in the lee of a large rock, took off his shoes, rolled out his sleeping-bag and lay down, with a bottle of wine in his hand.

He thought about Maria as he emptied the bottle, how much she meant to him. Then he snuggled down and fell asleep.

When he woke up, he knew he had one more decision to make.

AT 10 A.M. THERE was to be a meeting in Johansson's office. Lindman had slept for a couple of hours at the hotel, but Larsson woke him soon after 9 a.m., telling him that he must attend.

Lindman got out of bed, and felt the back of his neck. It was tender. As he was getting dressed, he thought about Veronica Molin. They'd had breakfast together. Lindman had told her what had happened during the night. She had paid close attention without asking any questions. They had agreed to meet later in the day.

He examined his face in the bathroom mirror and was overcome by a feeling of unreality that he had no defencc against. IIe burst into tears and staggered out of the bathroom. I'm dying, he thought. I've got cancer. It's incurable, and I'm going to die.

His mobile was ringing. Elena.

'I had the feeling I ought to phone you.'

'Everything's OK here. I miss you.'

'You know where I am. When are you coming home?'

'I'll be back some time before I have to report to the hospital.'

'I dreamt last night that we went to England. Can't we do that? I've always wanted to see London.'

'Do we have to fix it now?'

'I'm just telling you about a dream I had. I thought it might be good to have something we could both look forward to.'

'Of course we'll go to London. If I live that long.'

'What do you mean by that?'

'Nothing. I'm just tired. I have to go to a meeting now.'

'Phone me tonight.'

Lindman promised to call. He put the phone down. Where would I be without Elena? he thought. Nowhere.

LARSSON TAPPED THE TABLE with his pen and started the meeting. He made a clear summary of what had happened the night before.

'Berggren has asked us to wait until this evening before questioning her in any more detail,' he said. 'That seems reasonable.'

'We have some footprints,' Johansson said. 'From inside Elsa's house, and from the garden. We have footprints from the Molin and Andersson murders. That will be a priority for the forensic boys now, establishing whether there's a match.'

Larsson agreed. 'The dogs picked up a scent as far as the bridge. We can assume that his car was parked there.'

'I've just been talking to Östersund,' said Rundström. 'They've triggered a computer search and come up with a Fernando Hereira in Västerås. He was arrested for VAT evasion some years ago—but he's over seventy now, so he's probably not the man we're after.'

'I don't know any Spanish,' Larsson said, 'but I have an idea that Fernando Hereira would be quite a common name.'

'We don't know if it's his real name,' Larsson said.

'We can chase him up through Interpol,' Rundström said. 'As soon as we have some fingerprints, that is.'

Several phones started ringing at once. Larsson proposed a ten-minute break and indicated to Lindman that they should go out into the corridor. They sat down in the reception area by the stuffed bear.

'I've been thinking about our chat,' Larsson said. 'That stuff about having to think again. A lot of the evidence suggests you might be right. A man speaking broken English turns up here and kills Molin. That rubbish Molin's daughter goes on about: owing money to some woman in the UK—I don't believe that for a moment. What you suggest could be right: the motive might have at its source something that happened a long time ago, during the war. The brutality, the fury we've witnessed suggests revenge. So far so good. But then he hangs around. That's what I can't work out. He ought to be running away.'

'Have you uncovered any links at all with Andersson?'

'Nothing. They were worlds apart. One played classical music and wrote pop songs as a hobby. The other was a retired police officer. How's your head, by the way.'

'It's OK, thanks.'

They went back to the conference room where the rest of them were assembled, but the meeting never got going again. Rundström's mobile rang. He answered, then raised his hand.

'They've found a rental car in the Funäsdalen mountains,' he said. 'The car was abandoned.'

'Who found it?' It was Larsson who asked.

'A man called Elmberg, he has a summer place there. He'd gone to check that his cottage was OK. Somebody had been there, and he thought it was a bit odd at this time of year. Then he found the car. He suspects the chalet where the car's parked has been broken into too.'

'Did he see anybody?'

'No. He didn't hang around. But he did notice the car had a foreign newspaper on the back seat.'

'Let's go,' Larsson said, putting on his jacket.

Rundström turned to Lindman. 'You'd better come too. I mean, you more or less saw him. Assuming it was him.'

Larsson asked Lindman to drive him because he had calls to make.

They were about to drive through Linsell when Rundström phoned: a shop assistant in Sveg had told the police that she had sold a knitted woollen hat the previous day.

'Unfortunately the girl can't remember what he looked like, nor does she know if he said anything,' Larsson said, with a sigh.

Elmberg was waiting for them just north of Funäsdalen. They hung around until Rundström and another car arrived. Then they continued a couple of kilometres along the main road before turning off.

It was a red Toyota. The newspaper on the back seat, *El País*, was Spanish. They continued on foot. The mountain towered above them. There was a chalet where the final steep ascent started. Rundström and Larsson reconnoitred, and decided there was nobody there. Both were armed, however, when they approached the front door. Rundström shouted a warning. No reply. Larsson flung the door open. They ran in. A minute later Larsson emerged to say that the chalet was empty, but that somebody had been there. They would now wait for the helicopter with the dog team. The forensic unit was on its way.

The helicopter came in from the northeast and landed in a field above the chalet. The dogs and dog handlers disembarked. The handlers let the dogs sniff at an unwashed glass Larsson had found. Then they set off into the mountains.

LARSSON CALLED OFF the search at around 5 p.m. Mist had come rolling in from the west, and that together with the gathering darkness made it pointless to go on.

They had started walking towards the mountain at 1 p.m. All approach roads were being watched. The dogs kept losing the scent, then finding it again. They headed due north, then branched off along a ridge heading west before turning north again. They had set off in line, then spread out as they walked along the ridge. It had been easy going to start with, not too steep. Even so, Lindman soon noticed that he was out of condition, but he didn't want to give up.

There was something else about this walk up the mountain. At first it was just a vague, imprecise feeling, but eventually it turned into a memory. He had been up this mountain before.

It was late summer, when he was seven or eight. His mother was away—her sister had been unexpectedly widowed and his mother had gone to Kristianstad to help her. One day his father announced that they were going to go on holiday. They would head north and live in a tent. Lindman had only a vague recollection of the car journey. He had been squashed in the back seat with one of his sisters and all the luggage. He was also fighting against carsickness.

The next day they had arrived at a place that Lindman seemed to remember was Vemdalsskalet. They had pitched their tent behind an old wooden cabin not far away from the mountain hotel.

There was a woman somewhere in the memory of that holiday. She had appeared just after they had pitched the tent. His father had seen her and had gone to greet her. Stefan and his sisters watched as their father shook hands with the woman and started talking, out of earshot. Stefan remembered asking his sisters if they knew who she was, but they had hissed at him to be quiet.

His father came back to join them, the woman as well. She was older than he was, with stripes of grey in her hair; and she was wearing the black and white uniform of a waitress. He could remember that there was something else about her, something off-putting, a ruthless streak. They had stood next to the tent, and his father told them that her name was Vera, that she was from Germany, and then she had shaken hands with them all in turn.

Lindman stopped. The helicopter came clattering in at a low altitude and started circling the valley below. He started walking again. They had walked on the mountain all those years ago as well. Not really long treks, always within easy distance of the hotel.

An unusually hot August evening in the mountains. Vera and his father were in deck chairs next to the wooden cabin. They were laughing. Stefan didn't like what he saw, and went away, to the back of the cabin. There was a door there, and he opened it. He was inside Vera's house. Two cramped rooms and a low ceiling. Some photographs on a bureau. He strained his eyes to conjure up those pictures. A wedding photo. Vera dressed in white, smiling, a garland of flowers in her hair, and her husband wearing an army uniform. Next to the wedding photograph was another picture in a frame. A picture of Hitler. At that moment the door opened. Vera was there, with his father. She said something in German, or Swedish with a German accent, he couldn't remember. But she had been angry, he remembered that. His father had led him away and boxed his ears.

Lindman shook his head. Thirty years ago his father had taken the children and visited a German woman who worked at a hotel in the mountains. Just under the surface was the whole of the Hitler era. Nothing had completely gone away, it had simply taken on new means of expression. Was there anything else? He searched his memory, but there was nothing more.

The helicopter circled round once more then flew off. Soon after that the mist came down and they turned back. They came to the chalet at about 6 p.m. Rundström seemed to be forever talking into his walkie-talkie. Larsson listened to a report from one of the forensic officers who had searched the chalet, and made notes. Then he poured himself a cup of coffee and came over to Lindman.

'Well, we've found out a few things at least,' he said. He balanced his cup on a stone and flicked through his notebook. 'The owner is a Kurt Frostengren and lives in Stockholm. He usually comes here in the summer, over Christmas and New Year, and a week in March for some skiing. The house is empty for the rest of the year. Someone broke in, set up his HQ here, then went away. He's from Buenos Aires.'

Lindman looked at him in surprise. 'How do you know?'

Larsson took out of his pocket a torn piece of newspaper. Doodled in the margin was the number 541. 'Fifty-four is Argentina,' he said. 'And one is Buenos Aires. The paper is dated June the 12th, when Frostengren was last here. He saved newspapers for making fires. The numbers have been written by somebody else. It must be Fernando Hereira. The newspaper in the car is Spanish. It can't be easy to find newspapers from Argentina in Sweden, but it's comparatively easy to find Spanish ones.'

'Is there a full telephone number in Argentina?'

'No.'

'If he's made a call to Buenos Aires, can it be traced?'

'We're doing that now.' Larsson bent down to pick up his coffee. 'We're beginning to get an idea of Hereira, but what about the other one? The one who killed Abraham Andersson, who's he?'

The question remained unanswered in the mist.

Half an hour later Larsson and Lindman returned to Sveg. They drove in silence through the forest. This time Larsson did the driving. A few kilometres short of Sveg he pulled onto the verge and stopped.

'I can't work it out,' Larsson said. 'A man from Argentina disappears up a mountain when he ought to be getting away from here as fast as possible. He doesn't flee; he comes back again.'

'It's possible,' Lindman said, 'that the man we're calling Fernando Hereira knows something we don't.'

Larsson shook his head. 'In that case, he wouldn't have put on a hood and asked Berggren those questions.'

'Then maybe he knows, or thinks he knows, that it was Berggren who killed Andersson. And he wants to make her confess.'

Larsson drummed his fingers on the wheel. 'Perhaps Berggren isn't telling the truth. She says the man who forced his way into her house asked her who had killed Andersson. He might well have said, "I know it was you who killed Andersson." Larsson restarted the engine. 'We'll get tough with Berggren.'

They continued to Sveg. As they were driving into the hotel courtyard, Larsson's mobile rang.

'It was Rundström,' he said when the call was over. 'The car was rented in Östersund by Fernando Hereira, an Argentinian citizen. Now we're getting somewhere. I'll be in touch,' he said.

Lindman got out of the car and collected his keys from reception. He went up to his room and lay down on the bed.

WHEN HE WOKE UP he looked at his watch: 9.15. He'd better hurry if he were going to get some dinner. Besides, he had an appointment with Veronica Molin.

She was waiting for him in the dining room. 'I knocked on your door,' she said. 'When you didn't answer, I assumed you were asleep.'

'It was a strenuous night and a long day. Have you eaten?'

'I have.'

Lindman ordered a beef steak. Veronica Molin was drinking water. He wanted wine. She watched him with a smile.

'I've never met a policeman as close up as this.'

'What's it like?'

'I think everybody's a bit frightened of policemen, deep down.' She paused. 'My brother's on his way here from the Caribbean,' she said. 'He works on a cruise ship. Maybe I said that already? He's a steward.'

'When's the funeral?'

'On Tuesday, eleven o'clock. Then I'm leaving.'

'Where to?'

'First London, then Madrid.'

Lindman's meal arrived.

'I'm only a simple policeman, but I'm curious about what you do.'

'I'm what the English call a "deal-maker". Or "broker". I bring interested parties together and help them to produce a contract. So that a business deal can take place.' She turned up a wineglass and slid it towards him. 'I've changed my mind.'

Lindman filled her glass. He drank her health. She seemed to be looking at him in a different way now, not as warily as before.

'The police think that the man who attacked you is the person who murdered my father.'

'Yes.'

'Who is this man?'

'We think he's an Argentinian called Fernando Hereira.'

'I hardly think my father knew anybody from Argentina. What is the motive supposed to be?'

'Something that happened during the war.'

She lit a cigarette. 'So the police don't believe my theory? About the woman from Scotland?'

'Nothing is excluded. We follow up every lead.'

'I shouldn't smoke while you're eating.'

'It doesn't matter. I've already got cancer.'

She looked at him in surprise. 'Did I hear you right?'

'It was a joke. I'm fully fit.'

'A strange sort of joke.'

'I suppose I wanted to see how you reacted.'

She put her head on one side and looked hard at him.

'Are you making a pass at me?'

He emptied his glass. 'You must be aware that you're very attractive.'

She didn't say anything and moved her glass away when Lindman tried to give her more. He filled his own glass and asked for the bill.

'I can't work out what connection this Hereira had with my father.'

'Nor can we. It will become clear sooner or later, though. We'll catch up with both the murderers.'

'I hope so.'

When Lindman had signed his bill, they went out to reception.

'Will you let me offer you a brandy?' she said. 'In my room. But don't expect anything else.'

They walked down the corridor. She unlocked her door. Lindman was standing as close to her as possible without actually touching her. On her desk was a laptop computer with a glittering screen.

'I have the whole of my life in this,' she said. 'I can still keep working while I'm waiting for the funeral.'

She poured some brandy for him from a bottle on the table. She didn't take any herself, but kicked off her shoes and sat on the bed. Lindman wanted to touch her now, undress her. His train of thought was interrupted when his mobile rang in his jacket pocket.

He didn't answer. 'Nothing that can't wait,' he said.

'Don't you have a girlfriend?'

He shook his head. 'It didn't work.'

He put his glass down and reached out his hand. She stared at it for a long time before taking it.

'You can sleep here,' she said. 'But please expect no more than me lying beside you.'

'I don't expect anything.'

She slid along the edge of the bed until she was sitting close to him. 'It's a long time since I met anybody who expects as much as you do.'

WHEN LINDMAN WOKE UP the next morning Veronica Molin had already left. There was a message on the computer screen: 'I've gone out. Make sure you've left by the time I get back. I like men who don't snore. You are one.'

Lindman left. When he came to his room he crept into bed. I was drunk, he thought. He reached for his mobile. There was a message from Elena. He felt a shooting pain in his stomach. He lay down again and pulled the bedclothes over his head, just as he had done as a child. Veronica had firmly rejected all advances. He had been feeling extremely passionate, but he'd had enough sense to leave her in peace.

He decided to stay in bed until 9 a.m. Then he would phone Elena.

Nine o'clock arrived. She answered at once.

'I was asleep last night,' he said. 'I can't have heard the phone.'

'Something scared me. Something I'd dreamed. I don't know what.'

'Everything's OK here,' he said. 'But I'm worried. The days are racing past. It'll soon be the 19th.'

'It'll all be fine. When are you coming home?'

'Very soon. I'll let you know.'

He didn't like discovering how easy it was to tell lies. He got out of bed. Staying between the sheets would do nothing to dispel his remorse. He dressed and went downstairs to the dining room.

His hangover was making him feel sick. He drank a glass of milk then sat down with a cup of coffee. His mobile rang. It was Larsson.

'Awake?'

'Just about. I'm having coffee.

'Then I'll join you.'

Ten minutes later Larsson came bounding into the dining room, unshaven, hollow-eyed, but full of energy. He poured himself a cup of coffee and sat down. He put a plastic bag on the table.

'Do you remember the name Hanna Tunberg?' he asked.

Lindman thought, then shook his head.

'She was the one who found Molin. His cleaning lady.'

'I remember. From the file I read in your office.'

'She phoned and said that she had something else to tell us. I'm on my way there now. I thought you might like to come with me.'

'By all means.'

Larsson opened the plastic bag and produced a photograph behind glass in a frame. It was of a woman in her sixties.

'This is Katrin Andersson. Andersson's wife.'

'Why have you brought that with you?'

'Because Hanna Tunberg asked me to. She wanted to see what Abraham's wife looked like. I don't know why. But I sent one of the boys out to Dunkärret this morning to fetch the photograph.'

Larsson finished his coffee and stood up. 'Hanna lives in Ytterberg,' he said. 'It's not far.'

THE HOUSE WAS OLD and well looked after. It was beautifully situated with views of the wooded hills. A dog started barking when they parked. A woman was standing next to an old tractor, waiting for them.

'Hanna Tunberg,' Larsson said. 'She's one of the old school—people who put their best clothes on when they have an appointment with the police. What's the betting that she's been doing some baking?' He smiled and got out of the car.

Larsson introduced Hanna Tunberg to Lindman. He found it hard to say how old she was. Sixty, perhaps, or maybe only just over fifty.

'I've made some coffee. My husband's gone out.'

The house smelt of tobacco, dog and lingonberries. The living-room walls were decorated with elk antlers, tapestries and some paintings with woodland motifs. Hanna Tunberg lit a cigarette, inhaled deeply and started coughing. There was a rattling noise in her lungs. She had fetched the coffee and filled the cups. There was a plate of buns on the table.

'You said there was something you wanted to tell me,' Larsson said.

'It's to do with that woman who used to visit Herr Molin.'

'You mean Fröken Berggren?'

'She was sometimes there when I went to do the cleaning,' she said. 'She always left as soon as she clapped eyes on me. Anyway, it was last spring. Towards the end of April. I went to the house to do the cleaning, but he wasn't there. I thought it was odd, because we'd agreed on the time.'

Larsson raised his hand to interrupt her. 'Did you always fix a time in advance when you were going to arrive?'

'Always. Anyway, he wasn't there. I didn't know what to do. I was quite certain that I hadn't got the wrong time. I waited. But he didn't come. I stood on a sledge so that I could see in through the window. I thought he might be ill, you see. The house was empty. Then I thought about Abraham Andersson. I knew they were in touch with each other. I thought maybe I should drive to Abraham's place. I knew where he lived. So I went there and knocked on the door. There was a long pause before Abraham answered.'

She stubbed out her cigarette and immediately lit another.

'It was about three in the afternoon,' she said, 'and he wasn't dressed yet. He was wearing trousers, but no shirt. And barefoot. I asked him if he knew where Herr Molin was. He said he didn't. Then he shut the door. He didn't want to let me in. And I knew why, of course.'

'He wasn't alone?'

'Exactly.'

'How did you know? Did you see anybody?'

'Not then. But I realised even so. I went back to the car. I'd parked some way short of the drive. I was just about to leave when I noticed a car standing behind the garage. It wasn't Abraham's.'

'How did you know that?'

'I don't know. I just got a feeling. I was going to drive away when I glanced in the rearview mirror and saw somebody coming out of the house. It was a woman. When she realised that I was still there she went back inside.'

Larsson picked up the plastic bag with the photograph of Katrin Andersson. He handed it over. She spilled ash on it.

'No,' she said. 'That wasn't her.'

'Who do you think it was, then?'

She hesitated. 'Fröken Berggren. But I can't be sure.'

'Why not?'

'It all happened so quickly.'

'But you had seen her before, hadn't you? And yet you couldn't identify her for sure.'

'I'm telling you the truth. I only saw her for a few seconds. She came out, saw the car and went back inside.'

'So she didn't want anybody to see her?'

Hanna Tunberg looked at him in surprise. 'Is that so strange? If she'd come out of a house where there was a half-naked man who wasn't her husband?'

'Why are you only telling us this now?'

'I didn't remember until today. My memory's not very good. I thought it might be important. If it was Elsa Berggren. I mean, she had contact with both Herbert and Abraham.'

Hanna Tunberg started coughing again, that rattling, scraping cough. She stubbed out her cigarette in irritation. Then she gasped for breath, stood halfway up and slumped forward over the table. Larsson stood up as she fell. He turned her over, onto her back.

'She's not breathing,' he said. 'Phone for an ambulance.'

He started giving her the kiss of life as Lindman took out his mobile.

IT TOOK THE AMBULANCE half an hour to get there. Larsson had given up by then. Hanna Tunberg was dead. Lindman had seen a lot of dead people, but only now did he grasp how close death actually is. One moment she had answered a question, the next she was dead.

As the ambulance left, Larsson looked at Lindman. 'It's hard to believe that it can be all over so quickly.'

They went outside. It had started raining. The dog barked.

'What did she say? That her husband had gone out?'

Lindman looked around. There was no sign of a car. The garage doors were open. There was nothing inside.

'He seems to have gone for a drive.'

'We'd better wait. Let's go in.'

They sat without speaking. The dog barked again. Then it, too, fell silent. Lindman looked at the carpet where Hanna Tunberg had died.

Larsson's mobile rang. Both of them gave a start. Larsson answered. He finished the call without having said much.

'That was the ambulance crew. They'd met Hanna's husband. He went with them. We don't need to stay here any longer.'

Neither of them moved.

'The question is,' Larsson said, 'was she telling the truth?'

'Why shouldn't she have been?'

Larsson got up and walked to the window. He stared out at the rain.

'Erik told me she was a gossipmonger. I had that in mind all the time she was speaking. I think she wanted to tell us something that might be important, but she didn't want to tell us how she'd found out about it.' Larsson left the window and sat down. 'If she'd lived for another five minutes I'd have been able to ask her. Now that's not possible.'

'But you think the gist of what she said was right?'

'I suspect that she either spotted something behind Andersson when he answered the door, or that she peeped in through a window. We'll never know which.' He stood up. 'Shall we go?'

'Just one question,' Lindman said. 'Or two, rather. What are the implications if it really was Berggren, as Hanna suggested? And if it wasn't her, who was it? And what does it all mean?'

'I make that three questions,' Larsson said. 'And they're all important. We can't answer any of them, though. Not yet, at least.'

IT WAS 12.30 when they arrived at the hotel. Larsson said he was hungry. The rain was still pattering on the car roof. They hurried into reception with their jackets pulled up over their heads.

The girl in reception stood up. 'Can you phone Erik Johansson?' she said. 'It's urgent.'

Larsson took his mobile out of his jacket pocket and cursed. It was switched off. He switched it on and sat on the sofa. Lindman thumbed through a brochure lying on the reception desk. *Old Mountain Pastures in Härjedalen*. Hanna Tunberg was still dying before his eyes.

Larsson stood up. Lindman could see that the call had worried him.

'Is something wrong?'

Larsson beckoned him into the empty dining room. 'It looks as if the man on the mountain may have found a road through the fog that wasn't being watched, and then stolen another car,' he said. 'Erik had just gone home for a meal, and he discovered that he'd been burgled. A pistol and a rifle had been taken. Plus some ammunition. It must have happened today, early in the morning. It could have been somebody else, of course. But our man is still in the area.'

THEY GATHERED in Johansson's office at 2.15. Lindman had been hesitant about joining them but Larsson insisted. The rain had passed and the low sun shone in through the open window. Johansson was worried. He switched his mobile telephone to loudspeaker mode, and Rundström's voice could be heard, despite a poor connection. The mist in the mountains of northwest Härjedalen was still there.

'We're marking time here,' he said.

'And the roadblocks?' Johansson asked.

'They're still in place. A Norwegian drunk drove straight into the ditch from shock when he saw police standing in the road.'

The connection was lost, then it came back.

'About the burglary. What ammo was stolen?' Rundström asked.

'Two magazines for the pistol and twelve cartridges for the Mauser.'

'I don't like this at all,' Rundström said. 'Did he leave any clues?'

'The house was empty,' Johansson said. 'My wife is in Järvsö visiting our daughter. I don't have any neighbours. The gun cupboard had been broken into. No footprints. No sign of a car.'

'We're wondering what to do. If he's the one who stole the guns there's not much point in our staying here. It would mean he'd already passed through our cordon.'

Larsson leaned towards the telephone. 'Larsson here. I think it's too soon to withdraw from up there. It might not have been him who broke into Erik's house. But I have a question. Do we know anything about what this Hereira might have in the way of food?'

'Frostengren claimed he didn't have anything in his pantry. On the other hand, the freezer was full. It was worth leaving it on to store all the berries and elk meat he'd been given by friends.'

'It's hardly possible to prepare an elk steak on a camping gas stove. Sooner or later he'll have to find a shop and buy some food.'

'We've been checking the houses in the area. There's one old fellow who lives here all the year round. Hudin, he's called, in a place called Högvreten. Apart from him, there are only holiday cottages here.'

'Anything else?'

'Not at the moment.'

'OK, thanks. We'll talk again later.' Johansson switched the telephone off.

'Let's have a run-through now,' Larsson said.

There was a mass of detail and reports to sort out. Lindman tried to listen, but found that his head was full of images of women. Hanna Tunberg falling dead on the floor. Veronica Molin, her hand and her back as she lay asleep. And Elena. Especially Elena. He was ashamed of having told Veronica Molin that there was no one in his life.

He tried to concentrate on what was being said round the table. They talked about the weapons used when Molin was murdered. Larsson had a list of guns reported stolen in Sweden in recent months. He glanced through them, then put it on one side. No Swedish border control post had any information about a man called Fernando Hereira from Argentina passing through.

'Interpol are looking into that right now,' Larsson said.

There was a preliminary summary of Abraham Andersson's life, but it was far from complete. So far, they had found nothing at all to link him with Molin.

They turned their attention to Hanna Tunberg for a while. Johansson said that she had been one of the leading lights when the Sveg curling club was formed.

'I can remember her sweeping the ice clear as soon as it was cold enough in the autumn.'

'And now she's dead,' Larsson said. 'That was a horrific experience, believe you me. Anyway, the last thing she did was to tell us she thought she'd seen Berggren in Andersson's house some time last spring. If she was right, it could mean we've established a link between Andersson and Molin. A woman. And we must also bear in mind that, so far, Berggren has denied anything more than a fleeting acquaintance with Andersson.'

Larsson reached for a file and picked out a piece of paper. 'Katrin Andersson, Abraham's widow, told the Helsingborg police that she'd never heard the name Elsa Berggren. She claims that her husband never—I'm quoting here—"kept any secrets from me".' Larsson snapped the file shut. 'We've all heard that before.'

'Is there anything else that links them?' Johansson asked. 'We know that Elsa and Molin were Nazis. Was Andersson a Nazi?'

'He was a paid-up member of the Centre Party,' Larsson said. 'For a while he was even an elected member of the Helsingborg Town Council. We can assume that not only was Andersson a man with no links to neo-Nazism, but also that he took great exception to it. It would be interesting to know how he'd have reacted if he'd realised that he had a former Waffen-SS officer for a neighbour.'

'Maybe he did know,' Lindman heard himself saying.

Larsson looked at him. It was quiet in the room. 'Say that again.'

'If Andersson had discovered that his neighbour, Molin, was a Nazi, and perhaps Berggren as well, that could indicate that there was in fact a link.'

'And what would that be?'

'It could have been blackmail. Molin had done everything he could to disappear from view, to hide his past. He was scared of something. If Andersson discovered his secret, the whole of Molin's existence would be under threat. Berggren had bought the house on Molin's behalf. Suddenly he needed her help again.'

Larsson shook his head doubtfully. 'Does that really add up? If

Andersson had been killed before Molin, I could have understood it. But not afterwards. When Molin was already dead.'

'There's another possibility, of course. Berggren could have realised, or assumed, that Andersson was somehow responsible for what happened to Molin, and taken revenge.'

Johansson protested. 'Are you suggesting that Elsa, a woman in her seventies, dragged Andersson into the forest, tied him to a tree and shot him? That can't be right. Besides, she didn't have a gun.'

'Guns can be stolen, as we know,' Larsson said, icily.

'I can't see Elsa as a murderer.'

What Stefan says is worth bearing in mind, of course,' Larsson said. 'But let's not sit around here speculating. We should be gathering more facts. And we should concentrate on Berggren.'

Those present at the meeting went their various ways, leaving only Larsson and Lindman in the office. The sun had gone. Larsson sat at the desk. Lindman opened a bottle of mineral water.

'I'm thinking of spending this evening here in the office,' Larsson said. 'Going through some papers again. I think our discussion today has given us a few new leads. Berggren worries me. I can't fathom her out. If Hanna Tunberg really did see what she said she saw, what does it mean? But Erik is right. It's hard to imagine her dragging a man into the forest, tying him to a tree and then executing him.'

'Is there somebody else involved in all of this, somebody lurking in the shadows whom we haven't yet identified?'

'Someone who may share the political views of Berggren and Molin? Are you thinking of some kind of neo-Nazi network?'

'We know they exist.'

'So Berggren decides that Andersson has to be killed. She sends for somebody suitable from her brown-shirted brotherhood to take care of it. Is that what you're saying?'

'I can hear how crazy it sounds.'

'Not *that* crazy,' Larsson said. 'I'll keep it in mind as I chew my way through the files tonight.'

LINDMAN WALKED BACK to the hotel. There was no light in Veronica Molin's room.

'How long are you staying?' the girl in reception asked.

'Until Wednesday, if that's all right.'

'We shan't be full until the weekend. A group of orienteerers from Lithuania are coming to set up a training camp.'

Lindman collected his key. 'Is there a bowling alley in Sveg?'

'No,' she said, surprised.

When he got to his room he lay on the bed. It was something to do with Hanna Tunberg, he thought. Something to do with her death. He started remembering.

He was five or six years old. He was at home, with his father. It was evening. He was on the floor playing with a car, behind the red sofa in the living room. His eyes were concentrated on the invisible road he had mapped out on the carpet. He could hear the rustling of newspaper pages. A friendly noise, but not completely without menace. His father sometimes used to read things that annoyed him. Things that could result in the newspaper being ripped to shreds. 'These damned socialists,' he would say.

Stefan drove his car along a winding road. He knew his father was in the dark green armchair next to the fire. Then the rustling stopped, there was a groan followed by a thud.

He slowly stood up and peered over the back of the sofa. His father had fallen to the floor. He was groaning. Lindman approached him cautiously. His father looked at him with fear in his eyes. His lips were blue. They were moving, forming words. 'I don't want to die like this. I want to die upright, like a man.'

The images faded. What followed was like a kaleidoscope: his mother screaming; an ambulance; his father in a sickbed, his lips less blue. A few words that somebody must have repeated over and over again. A heart attack. Very slight.

What he remembered now with crystal clarity were the words, 'I want to die upright, like a man.' Like a soldier in Hitler's army, Lindman thought. Marching for a Fourth Reich that wouldn't be crushed like the Third.

He took his jacket and left the room. Somewhere among all those memories he had dozed off for a while. It was 9 p.m. already. He didn't want to eat in the hotel, so he made his way to a hot-dog stall he had noticed by the bridge. He ate some mashed potato and two half-grilled sausages. Then he returned to the hotel.

He walked down the street, to the front of the hotel. There was a light in Veronica Molin's room. The curtains were drawn, but there was a narrow gap in the middle. He stood on tiptoe to look through the window. She was sitting at her computer, with her back to him. He couldn't see what she was doing. He was about to move on when she got up and moved out of view. The computer screen was shimmering. There was some kind of pattern on it. At first he couldn't make out what it was. Then he recognised it. The screen was filled by a swastika.

Chapter 7

It was like receiving a powerful electric shock. He was almost knocked backwards. She had lied to him. Not only had she known that her father was a Nazi, but she was one herself.

He ducked into the courtyard of the building next door, and forced himself to remain calm, to act like a police officer. He ought to speak to Larsson without delay. There again, perhaps not just yet.

He walked back to the hotel. There was only one thing to do. Talk to her. Two men were playing cards in reception. They nodded to him but concentrated on their game. Lindman stopped at her door and knocked. She opened immediately. He could see over her shoulder that the computer screen was blank.

'I was about to go to bed,' she said.

'Not just yet. We need to talk.'

She let him in. 'I want to sleep alone tonight. Just so that you know.'

'That's not why I've come. Although I do wonder why you wanted me to sleep here. Without my being allowed to touch you.'

'I do admit that I can feel lonely at times.'

She sat down on the bed, and just like last night pulled up her legs beneath her. He was attracted by her, and his wounded anger only made the feeling stronger. He sat on the creaking chair.

'What do you want?' she asked. 'Has something happened?'

'I've come about a lie.'

'Whose?'

'Yours.'

She raised her eyebrows. 'I don't know what you're talking about.'

'Then I'll come straight to the point. A few minutes ago you were working at your computer. Your screen was filled with a swastika.'

It was a few seconds before the penny dropped. Then she glanced at the window and the curtains.

'Precisely,' he said. 'I looked in. You'd be right to complain about that. I shouldn't have. But it was just an impulse. And I saw the swastika.' He could see that she was perfectly calm.

'That's absolutely right. There was a swastika on my screen not long ago. Black against a red background. But what's the lie?'

'You said you were trying to protect your father's past, but in fact it was yourself you were trying to protect. You are a Nazi.'

'Is that what you think?' She stood up and lit a cigarette. 'What do you know about computers? About the Internet?'

'Not a lot,' he admitted.

She sat down at her computer and gestured him to pull his chair closer. She pressed a button on her keyboard. The screen came to life.

'This network embracing the whole globe has its underworld, just as the real world does. You can find anything at all there. There's endless amounts of information about where you can buy guns, drugs, pornographic pictures of little children. Everything.'

She pressed various keys. The swastika returned.

'This as well. Lots of Nazi organisations, including several Swedish ones, publicise their opinions. I was sitting here trying to understand. I was looking for the people who are members of Nazi organisations today. How many of them there are, how they think.'

She switched off. The screen went black.

'Now I'd like you to leave,' she said. 'You chose to jump to a conclusion on the basis of a picture you saw on my screen when you were snooping around. We've nothing more to say to each other.'

Lindman didn't know what to do. She was upset, convincingly so. She stood up and flung open the door. She ushered Lindman out into the corridor and closed the door behind him.

He went up to his room, wondering why he had reacted as he did. He was rescued from his self-reproach by a telephone call. It was Larsson. He thought he might as well tell him what had happened.

'It's a dangerous habit, peeping into little girls' bedrooms. You never know what you might see,' he said, laughing.

'I acted like an idiot.'

'We all do sometimes. Not all at the same time, with luck.'

'What did you want?'

'Somebody to talk to, I suppose.'

'Are you still in Johansson's office?'

'Yes, and I've got coffee.'

'I'll be there.'

As he passed the front of the hotel, he glanced at Veronica Molin's window. The light was still on, but the gap in the curtains had gone.

Larsson was waiting for him outside the community centre. They went inside. The building was deserted.

'Any news from the mountain?' Lindman asked.

They were in the office by now. There were two vacuum flasks on the desk, marked HÄRJEDALEN COUNTY COUNCIL. Lindman shook his head when Larsson offered him a cup.

'Rundström has been phoning on and off. They've moved their base down to Funäsdalen. No joy from the roadblocks as yet. Rundström's worried, though. If they don't find him tomorrow, it can only mean that he's broken through the cordon. And it probably was him who burgled Erik's place.' Larsson was looking at a map on the wall. He drew a circle with his finger round Funäsdalen.

'What bugs me is why he hasn't left the area ages ago,' he said. 'The only explanation I can think of is that he hasn't finished yet. That thought makes me more and more apprehensive.'

'There's a missing link,' Lindman said slowly. 'A person. The question is, though, is it a murderer or another victim?'

They sat in silence. Lindman found it difficult to concentrate. He wanted to help Larsson, but he was thinking about Veronica Molin all the time. And he ought to have phoned Elena by now. He looked at his watch. It was 11 p.m. already. She would be asleep. Too bad.

'I have to ring home,' he said, and went out.

He stood beside the stuffed bear, hoping it might protect him.

She wasn't asleep. 'I know you're ill,' she said, 'but do you really have the right to treat me like you are doing?'

'I've been pretty busy talking to Larsson.'

'And so you don't have time to phone me, is that it? We have to have a serious talk. Not now, though. Later.'

'I miss you. I don't know whether I'm coming or going at the moment. But I do miss you.'

'Are you sure you haven't met another woman up there?'

That shook him. Hard.

'Don't be silly,' he said. He could hear that she was depressed, unhappy, and that made him feel even guiltier. 'I'm standing next to a stuffed bear,' he said. 'He sends his greetings.'

She didn't answer.

'Are you still there?'

'I'm still here. But I'm going to sleep now. Phone me tomorrow.'

Lindman went back to the office. Larsson was poring over an open file. His hair was a mess, his eyes bloodshot.

'Berggren,' he said. 'I'll have another chat with her tomorrow.'

'What are you hoping to achieve?'

'Clarity. There's something she's not telling us.' Larsson stood up and stretched. 'We'll keep on trying to fit the old girl into the picture. With a bit of luck, we'll find a place for her in the end.'

The telephone rang. Larsson answered, sat down and listened. 'We're on our way,' he said, and hung up.

'That was Rundström. Twenty minutes ago a car drove straight through one of the roadblocks.'

He pointed to the spot on the map. It was a crossroads southeast of Funäsdalen, about twenty kilometres from Frostengren's chalet.

'A dark blue saloon car, possibly a Golf,' Larsson said. 'The driver was a man. His appearance could be in line with the descriptions we've had previously. The officers didn't have time to see much.' Larsson looked at his watch. 'If he really puts his foot down he could be here in two hours. All the blocks in Funäsdalen are being moved. They'll build a wall behind him. It's here that there is no check at the moment.' He picked up the telephone.

Lindman waited while Larsson spoke to Johansson about the roadblock they needed to set up. He put the phone down.

'It doesn't add up,' Lindman said. 'Why on earth would he break into Johansson's place and then go back to the mountain?'

'Nothing adds up. But whoever is in that car could be the one with the guns. And he might start using them. We're very short-staffed just now. Will you come with us?'

'Yes.'

'Erik's bringing a gun for you.'

'I thought they'd been stolen?'

Larsson pulled a face. 'He had an extra pistol, which he presumably hasn't registered either. Hidden away in the cellar. Plus his police-issue weapon. Erik will call out the two police officers in Sveg.'

Three-quarters of an hour later they had set up a roadblock three kilometres northwest of Sveg.

THE CAR THEY were waiting for never arrived. Five other cars passed through. Johansson knew two of the drivers. The other three were strangers: two women who lived to the west of Sveg, and a young man in a fur hat who had been staying with relatives in Hede and was now on his way south. All were allowed to continue.

They spread out a map on the bonnet of one of the police cars, and examined it by torchlight. Was there some other route that they had overlooked? They couldn't see any alternative. Larsson was acting as a sort of one-man call centre, keeping in touch with officers stationed at various points in the forest. Lindman heard him getting more annoyed every time he spoke. Then Johansson's telephone rang.

'You what?' he shouted.

He signalled for the wet map to be unfolded again as he listened.

'Shooting,' he said. 'Twenty-five minutes ago by the lake, Löten, three kilometres from the road to Hårdabyn. The call was from somebody called Rune Wallén. He lives near there. He said he was woken by something that sounded like a bang. He went outside, and there was another bang. He counted ten shots altogether.'

'Right, let's regroup,' Larsson said. 'The roadblock must stay, but Stefan and I and some of the men further north will head for the scene. Now we know that guns are being used. Caution is the watchword, no reckless intervention.'

'Shouldn't we call a national alert on this?' Johansson said.

'You bet we will,' Larsson said. 'You can arrange that. Phone Östersund. And take charge of the roadblock here.'

'Be careful,' Johansson said.

Larsson didn't seem to hear.

Lindman drove, while Larsson spoke to Rundström. He described what had happened. Then he put the telephone down.

'What's going on?' he said. 'What the bloody hell is going on?'

IT TOOK THEM thirty-five minutes to reach the place described by Rune Wallén. Lindman pulled up when Larsson shouted, pointing at a dark blue Golf at the side of the road, halfway into the ditch.

They crouched as they ran from the car, guns drawn. They peered into the darkness, listening intently. Eventually they heard the sound of a car approaching. The headlights drew nearer in the darkness and the police car came to a halt. It was Rundström and another officer.

'Have you seen anything?' Rundström shouted.

'The car seems to be empty,' Larsson said. 'We waited for you to get here before moving in to examine it.'

'You and I will approach the car,' Rundström said. 'You others stay where you are.'

Larsson and Rundström closed in on the Golf from each side.

'There's nothing here,' Larsson cried. 'Give us more light.'

Lindman moved the car up and directed the headlights at the Golf.

Wallén had not been mistaken. The Golf was riddled with bullet holes. There were three in the windscreen, the front left-hand tyre had been punctured and there were holes in the bonnet as well.

They shone their torches into the car.

Larsson pointed. 'That could be blood.'

The driver's door was open wide. They shone their torches on the ground, but could see no trace of blood on the road or the verge.

They formed a chain, shining their torches into trees. There was no sign of anybody, nor of any tracks. They continued into the trees for about 100 metres before Larsson gave the order to turn back. There was a distant sound of a siren approaching from the east.

The car's keys were in the ignition. Larsson opened the boot. There were some tins of food and a sleeping-bag. They exchanged looks.

'A dark blue sleeping-bag,' Rundström said. 'Labelled "Alpin".'

He searched the bank of numbers in his mobile telephone, then called one of them. 'Inspector Rundström here,' he said. 'I'm sorry to wake you. Didn't you say there was a sleeping-bag in your chalet? What brand was it?' He listened. 'Can you remember if you had any tins of Bullen's Party Sausages in your pantry?'

Frostengren's reply seemed to be comprehensive.

'That's all I wanted to know,' Rundström said. 'Many thanks.'

He broke the connection. 'So, Frostengren's sleeping-bag wasn't labelled "Alpin". That needn't be significant, of course. Hereira presumably had some stuff of his own. But the sausages were his.'

The police car came racing up, switched off its siren and pulled up. The forensic officer who got out had some police tape with him, and Lindman helped to cordon off the Golf. Larsson and Rundström stood back to let the forensic specialist get on with his work. They beckoned Lindman to join them.

'What do we do now?' Larsson asked. 'None of us understands what's happened, if we're honest.'

'Facts are facts,' Rundström said. 'The man we've been hunting in the mountains has broken through our cordon. He steals a car. Then someone steps into the road and takes a few pot shots at him. Shoots to kill, because he's aiming at the windscreen. Hereira must have been incredibly lucky, unless he's lying wounded or dead somewhere out there in the forest. The dog handler will be here any minute. But my sense is that Hereira has survived. The stain on the car seat doesn't suggest a serious wound. Assuming it is blood, of course.'

'Have we got a time scale?' Larsson said.

'It was four oh-three when you phoned me,' Rundström said.

'So this drama must have taken place between three thirty and three forty-five.'

The penny dropped for all three of them at the same time.

'The cars,' Larsson said slowly. 'Two passed through our roadblock shortly before Wallén phoned to tell us about the shooting.'

They all realised what that meant. The man who did the shooting could have passed through the cordon already.

Larsson looked at Lindman. 'Can you remember? The last two cars to pass through?'

'The first was a woman in a green Saab. Erik knew her. Then there was a red Ford Escort. A young man in a fur hat. Driving back south after visiting some relatives in Hede.'

'Registration number?'

Larsson phoned Johansson and explained what had happened. He waited, then put his mobile back in his pocket. 'ABB 003,' he said.

'Let's put a marker on that car straight away,' Rundström said. 'We want the owner now, no delays.'

He got out his mobile. A car drew up with the dog handler, two other officers and Dolly the German shepherd. The dog found a scent immediately. The officers headed into the forest.

Rundström exploded in anger when he had finished his call. 'The bloody computer's down. We can't trace the car,' he said.

IT WAS STILL DARK at 6 a.m when the police officers and the dog returned from the forest.

'She lost the scent,' the dog handler said. 'She's tired as well. We'll have to get some more dogs here.'

Lindman followed Larsson to the other side of the road. 'How could anybody know that Hereira was going to come down this very road tonight?' he asked.

'Whoever did the shooting must have been in contact with Hereira.'

'It's the only possibility I can see. Either directly with Hereira, or with a third party who was a link between the two of them.'

'And then he stakes out this road, intending to kill him.'

'I can't think of any other explanation. Unless there's a leak from the police. Somebody passing on information about where we were setting up roadblocks, and why.'

'That doesn't sound plausible,' Larsson said. 'One thing's certain in any case. We've got to identify the man driving that red Ford. Did you see his face?'

'No.' Lindman suddenly felt dizzy. It came out of nowhere. He was forced to grab hold of Larsson so as not to fall.

'Are you ill?'

'I don't know. Everything started spinning round.'

'You'd better go back to Sveg.'

Lindman could see that Larsson was genuinely concerned.

'Are you going to faint?'

Lindman shook his head. He didn't want to tell him the truth, which was that he felt as if he could keel over at any moment.

Larsson drove him back to Sveg himself.

IT WAS 1.30 P.M. when he woke up. He got out of bed. He didn't feel dizzy any more. He felt hungry. Even so, his curiosity got the better of him. He phoned Larsson, who answered with a bellowing 'Yes?' 'It's Lindman,' he said. 'How's it going?'

'We've established who the owner is. A man called Anders Harner. His address is a PO box in Albufeira in Portugal. But Harner's seventy-seven, and the man in that car was certainly not an old man.'

'Perhaps it was his son. Or some other relative.'

'Or the car had been stolen. We're chasing that one up. And the forensic lad reckons it could well have been Erik's gun that was used last night. How are you, by the way? Have you had some sleep?'

'I don't feel dizzy any more.'

'I had a bad conscience. I've roped you into this business, and I shouldn't have forgotten that you're ill.'

'I wanted to join in.'

Lindman went to the dining room. He felt better after a meal, but he was still tired when he went back to his room.

There was a knock on the door. It was Veronica Molin.

'Am I disturbing you?'

'Not at all.'

'I've come to apologise. I reacted too strongly last night.'

'It was my fault. I was stupid.'

He wanted to ask her in, but there was dirty laundry lying around.

'The room hasn't been cleaned,' he said.

She smiled. 'Mine has.' She looked at her watch. 'I'm meeting my brother at Östersund airport in four hours. There's time for us to talk.'

He took his jacket and followed her down the stairs. He was just behind her and had to force himself not to reach out and touch her.

Her computer was switched off.

'I still don't believe that my father died because of something he might have done when he was a German soldier,' she said. 'The war ended more than fifty years ago. I think his death is somehow connected with that woman in Scotland.'

Lindman decided on the spur of the moment to tell her about the discovery he had made in Wetterstedt's flat. He didn't know why. Perhaps to establish the fact that they had a secret to share. He told her without saying he had broken into the flat. He told her about the network, and the foundation called Strong Sweden.

'It's clear that Nazi ideas are alive and well. When all this is over I'll talk to my boss in Borås. There must be grounds for the security services to look into this in earnest.'

She listened intently to what he had to say. 'You're doing the right thing,' she said eventually.

'We've got to fight against this lunacy,' he said. 'These people are spreading the madness further into the world.'

She looked at her watch.

'I know you have to collect your brother,' Lindman said. 'I'll go now.' He turned and walked to the door.

He was about to open it when he felt her hand on his arm.

'You've got to fetch your brother,' he said.

His mobile rang in his jacket pocket.

'You'd better answer.'

It was Larsson. 'Something very odd has happened,' he said.

'What?'

'Berggren has phoned Erik. She says she wants to confess to the murder of Abraham Andersson.'

LARSSON WAS WAITING for him at the community centre. 'They're on the way to Östersund now,' he said. 'She's under arrest, and will be remanded in custody tomorrow. Erik is with her.'

'What did she say?'

Larsson pointed at a tape recorder on the desk. 'A tape of the interrogation is on its way to Östersund,' he said, 'but I had two tape recorders. I thought you might like to hear the copy. You'll be on your own here. I have to rest for a bit.'

'You can borrow my hotel room if you like.'

'There's a sofa in the other room. That'll do. Listen to the tape, then tell me what you think.' Larsson closed the door behind him.

Lindman switched on the tape recorder.

GL: We are commencing this interrogation, on November 13, 1999, at fifteen oh-seven. The interrogation is being conducted at the police station in Sveg by Detective Inspector Giuseppe Larsson. The witness is Inspector Erik Johansson. Would you please give us your name and personal details?

EB: Elsa Maria Berggren, born May 10, 1925, in Tranås.

GL: Thank you. Now, please tell us what happened.

EB: I want to confess to the murder of Abraham Andersson.

GL: Why did you kill him?

EB: He threatened to expose the man living nearby who was killed shortly beforehand, Herbert Molin, as a former National Socialist. I didn't want that. He also threatened to expose me

as a convinced National Socialist. And he also blackmailed Herbert. He demanded money from him every month.
GL: How long had that been going on?
EB: Since a year or so after Herbert moved here. Eight or nine years, I suppose.
GL: When did you decide to kill Andersson?
EB: I can't remember the exact date, but after Herbert was killed he contacted me and said he expected me to carry on with the payments. Otherwise he would expose me as well. That was no doubt when I made up my mind.
GL: Then what happened?
EB: I killed him a few days later.
GL: Can you tell us how it happened?
EB: I drove to his place in the evening. I took my shotgun with me. I threatened to kill him if he didn't stop trying to blackmail me. He didn't think I was serious, so I forced him to walk out into the trees not far from the house and shot him.
GL: Where is the shotgun now?
EB: At the bottom of the River Ljusnan.
GL: Can you say where you threw the gun into the river?
EB: From the old bridge here in Sveg.
GL: A few days ago you were attacked in your home by a masked man wanting to know who killed Abraham Andersson. Is there anything you said at that time that you wish to change now?
EB: No. It happened exactly as I said it did at the time.
GL: OK, let's go back to what happened at Andersson's place. You said that you 'forced him to walk out into the trees not far from the house and shot him'. You shot him from in front?
EB: Yes.
GL: Can you say roughly how far away from him you were?
EB: Three metres or so.
GL: Can you remember what time it was when this happened?
EB: Round about midnight.
GL: What happened after you'd shot him?
EB: I looked to make sure he was dead. He was. Then I tied him to a tree trunk. I had a washing line with me.
GL: So you tied him up after you'd shot him? Why did you do that?
EB: I wanted to make it look as if it was something different.
GL: Something different from what?
EB: A murder a woman could have done. I made it look more like an execution.

Larsson formally arrested Berggren and brought the interrogation to a close. Lindman stopped the tape and stood up to stretch his back. It was stuffy in the room. He opened a window and thought about what he had heard. He felt the need to stretch his legs. He wrote a note and put it on the desk. *Short walk. Stefan.*

He walked quickly as he was cold. The path by the river was well lit. He had the feeling that somebody was following him. He stopped and turned. Nobody in sight. Although, had there been a shadowy figure dodging out of the light? I'm imagining things, he told himself. He continued towards the bridge from which Berggren claimed to have dropped her shotgun into the river. Was she telling the truth? He had to assume so. Nobody confesses to a murder they haven't committed unless there's a very special reason to protect the real culprit. He came to the bridge, then turned back. There was one question that Larsson had overlooked. Why had she chosen just this day to confess? Why not yesterday? Why not tomorrow?

He came back to the community centre and passed behind it. The window was still ajar. Larsson was on the phone. Talking to Rundström, Lindman could hear. He went in to the police offices. Larsson was finishing his conversation.

Lindman looked at the window and said, 'I've just realised that from outside you can hear every word that's said in here, loud and clear, when the window's open.'

'You think that somebody's been listening to our phone calls?'

'It's a possibility.'

Larsson closed the window. 'For safety's sake,' he said with a smile. 'What do you think about her confession?'

'Did it say in the papers that he was tied to a tree trunk?'

'Yes, but not that a washing line was used. I also spoke to one of the forensic boys who examined the scene. He could see no flaw in what she described.'

'So she did it?'

'We have to assume so. If we find the shotgun in the river tomorrow, we can soon establish if the fatal shot came from that gun.'

'Why do you think she decided to confess today?'

'I don't know. Maybe I ought to have asked her that. I suppose she had only just made up her mind.'

There was a knock on the half-open door. A boy came in with a pizza box. Larsson paid the bill and put it in his pocket. The boy left.

'This is the most continental thing about Sveg,' he said. 'They have a pizzeria. Would you like some?'

Lindman nodded. Larsson cut the pizza in half with a ruler.

'Police officers soon put on weight,' he said. 'Stress and careless eating habits. A lot of us die from heart problems. Which is probably not all that surprising.'

'I've got cancer,' Lindman said. 'Perhaps I'm an exception.'

Larsson sat with a piece of pizza in his hand. 'Bowling,' he said. 'That would make you healthy again, no question.'

Lindman couldn't help laughing.

They ate in silence, then Larsson put the carton and the remains of his pizza on top of the wastepaper basket.

'We're getting the odd bit of information in,' he said, wiping his mouth. 'Interpol in Buenos Aires have sent a mysterious message telling us that there's somebody called Fernando Hereira in jail for life, for counterfeiting. Maybe if we have a bit of patience we'll get something more sensible from them. You never know.'

'The red Ford?'

'Disappeared into thin air. Like the driver. There's a nationwide alert for the car. Something will happen, given time. Rundström's a persistent bastard.'

Lindman tried to make a summary in his head. 'I take it that you'll be telling the media that you have the person responsible for the murder of Abraham Andersson?'

Larsson looked up in surprise. 'Why on earth should I do that? If what we think is right, it could mean that Hereira will clear off. Don't forget he put Berggren under pressure on that score. I think she was telling the truth about that, at least. Our first task tomorrow morning is to look for the shotgun in the river.'

It was now 9.15. Larsson phoned home. Lindman went out and stood next to the stuffed bear. Then he phoned Elena.

'Where are you?'

'Next to the bear,' he said. 'We've had a confession. One of the murders might have been solved. It was a woman. Killed a man who'd been blackmailing her. She shot him.'

'No woman would ever do that.'

'Why not?'

'Women defend themselves. They never attack.'

'I don't think it's quite as straightforward as that.' He hadn't the energy to try to explain.

'What are you doing just now?'

'Talking to Larsson.'

'Doesn't he have a family to go home to?'

'Right now he's talking to his wife on the telephone.'

'Does he know that I exist?'

'I think so. I've probably mentioned your name. Or he'll have heard me talking to you on the telephone.'

'Anyway, I'm glad you phoned. But don't ring again until tomorrow. I'm going to bed early tonight.'

Lindman went back to the office. Larsson had finished his call.

'That window standing ajar,' he said. 'It seems plausible that there could have been somebody there, listening to what was said. I've been trying to remember when it was open. Impossible, of course.'

'Maybe you should be thinking about what information came from this room, and nowhere else.'

Larsson contemplated his hands. 'We decided on the roadblocks here,' he said eventually. 'We talked about a man on his way from Funäsdalen towards the southwest.'

Lindman hesitated, then said, 'This last day or so I've had the feeling that somebody has been following me. A shadow somewhere behind me. Noises too. But I can't be sure.'

Larsson said nothing. He pushed aside two small plastic bags lying on top of a file. One of them fell on the floor. 'The forensic boys forgot a couple of plastic bags,' he said. 'Odds and ends they'd found on the road not far from the blue Golf.'

Lindman bent down to look. One of them contained a receipt from a petrol station. Shell. It was dirty, hardly legible. Lindman studied the text. The receipt was from a filling station near Söderköping. He looked at Larsson. Thoughts were whirring around in his brain.

'Berggren didn't kill Andersson,' he said slowly. 'We're into something much bigger than that, Larsson. Berggren didn't kill him.'

SNOW WAS FALLING. Larsson went to the window to check the thermometer. It was –1°C. He sat down and looked at Lindman. Lindman would remember that moment, a clear, unmistakable image of a turning point. It was made up of the falling snow, Larsson, and the story itself, what happened in Kalmar, the discovery he had made when he broke into Wetterstedt's flat. Larsson listened with great interest.

Lindman was trying to create an overall picture. That dirty filling station receipt from a Shell garage in Söderköping was a key that fitted all doors. At last it was possible to see things clearly.

Somebody had set off from Kalmar for Härjedalen in a red Ford Escort belonging to a man by the name of Harner who had a PO box in Portugal. On the way, in Söderköping, he stopped to fill up with petrol. He continued to a country road west of Sveg, then started shooting at a car coming from the mountains. He was trying to kill the man who most probably was responsible for the murder of Molin.

Neither Lindman nor Larsson were the type of police officer who believed in coincidences. Somewhere in the Nazi underworld, inhabited by the likes of Wetterstedt and the Strong Sweden foundation, Lindman's visit had stirred up unrest. They couldn't be certain that he was the one who'd broken into the flat. Or could they? Lindman remembered the front door shutting as he left the flat, the feeling that somebody was watching him. It could be that the shadow following him in Kalmar was the same as the one in Sveg.

Their thinking had been closer to the truth than they had dared to believe, Lindman was sure. It was all to do with the underworld where old Nazis had come across something new that enabled the old madness to join up with the new version. Somebody had broken into this shadow world and killed Molin. A shudder had run through the old Nazis. Who was their enemy? Was it the man who had killed Molin? Could it mean that Andersson had known about the whole organisation, and had threatened to expose it? They couldn't know that. But a Ford Escort had been filled up with petrol and driven to Härjedalen by a man intent on killing somebody. And Berggren had decided to take responsibility for a murder she almost certainly hadn't committed. There was an organisation, to which Lindman's own father was continuing to give support long after his death. Molin had been a member, as was Berggren. But not Andersson. Nevertheless, somehow or other he had discovered its existence.

It took Lindman half an hour to work it all out. 'How much did Andersson know?' he said. 'We can't tell. But whatever it was, it was too much.'

Snow was falling more densely now. Larsson had angled his desk lamp so that it shone out into the darkness.

'All you've told me makes me more than ever convinced that the Special Branch must be brought in,' Larsson said.

'What about the information you've had from me?' Lindman asked.

'We may have received an anonymous tip-off. Don't worry, I'm not going to report you for breaking down the door of that Nazi's flat.'

It was 10.15. They examined the situation from various angles. Shuffled the pieces around. A couple of hours ago Berggren had been playing a central role. Now she had been sidelined, at least for the time being. At the front of stage were Fernando Hereira and the man in the red Ford Escort.

THERE WAS A CLATTERING from the entrance of the community centre. Johansson trudged in, snow in his thinning hair.

'I very nearly came off the road,' he said, brushing the snow from his jacket. 'I got in a skid. I was close to catastrophe.'

'You drive too fast.'

'Very possibly.'

Larsson had vacated the desk chair, and Johansson sat down with a yawn. Larsson told him about the petrol receipt and the conclusions they had drawn. Johansson soon pricked up his ears.

'They've traced Anders Harner. He says the Escort is his all right, but it's in a garage in Stockholm. A place run by somebody called Mattias Sundelin. I've got his telephone number here.'

Johansson had opened his briefcase and was taking out some faxes. He called the number and switched his telephone to loudspeaker mode. A man answered.

'I'm trying to get in touch with Mattias Sundelin.'

'Mattias here,' said a gravelly voice.

'This is Inspector Johansson from the police in Sveg. It's about a red Ford Escort, registration number ABB 003. The owner is Anders Harner. He tells us it's in your garage. Is that correct?'

'Yes, that's correct. What's this all about?'

'We need to trace that car. Where is the garage?'

'In Kungsholmen.'

'Please drive there now and check that the car is still there.'

'I can't do that. I've been drinking wine.'

'Is there somebody else who could check?'

'You can try Pelle Niklasson. I've got his number here.'

Johansson wrote it down, thanked Sundelin and rang off. Then he called the new number. The man who answered said he was Pelle Niklasson. Johansson repeated the questions.

'How long will it take you to get there and check if the car's where it should be?'

'Forty minutes. Can't it wait until tomorrow?'

'No. Write down this number. Phone me as soon as you know.'

They waited. Thirty-seven minutes later, the phone rang.

'The car isn't here,' Pelle Niklasson said.

Larsson and Lindman sat up and leaned towards the loudspeaker.

'Has it been stolen?'

'It's supposed to be impossible to steal a car from here. This garage charges high fees in return for maximum security. No car can be driven away without our checking on the person collecting it.'

'So everything is recorded?'

'In the computer, yes. I don't know how to run that thing, though. It's the other lads who look after the computer side.'

'These other lads, have you got access to their personal details?'

He went to look, then returned to the telephone.

'I've found copies of their driving licences.'

'Have you got a fax there?'

'Yes.'

Johansson gave Niklasson the police fax number.

They waited again. There was a ring, and paper emerged from the machine. Four driving licences. Johansson read out the names: Klas Herrström, Simon Lukac, Magnus Holmström, Werner Mäkinen.

Lindman didn't even listen to the fourth name. He recognised the third one. He took the photocopy. The face was just an outline, with no features distinguishable. Even so, he was certain.

'I think we've got him,' he said slowly.

'Who?'

'Magnus Holmström. I met him on Öland when I visited Wetterstedt. He's a Nazi. He's our man. I'm sure.'

Nobody spoke.

'Let's bring Stockholm in now,' Larsson said. 'They'll have to go to the garage and get a decent picture of this lad. But where is he now?'

The telephone rang. It was Pelle Niklasson, wanting to know if the faxes had come through all right.

'Yes, thank you, we've got them,' said Johansson. 'One of your staff is called Magnus Holmström. How long has he worked there?'

'Just a couple of months.'

'What kind of an impression of him have you got?'

'He's pretty discreet. Doesn't say much. I don't really have much of an impression of him. And he's been off work since last Monday.'

'Good, thank you.'

By the time Johansson rang off, Larsson had already phoned the Stockholm police.

'Maybe they should go looking for him on Öland,' Lindman said. 'That's where I came across him, after all. And the car was filled up in Söderköping.'

Larsson slapped his forehead in irritation. 'I'm too tired,' he bellowed. 'We should have thought of that from the first, of course.'

He picked up the phone and started dialling. It took him ages to find the officer in Stockholm he had spoken to earlier. While he was waiting, Lindman gave him directions to Wetterstedt's house on Öland.

It was 1.30 a.m. by the time Larsson finished. He turned to Lindman. 'I don't think much more is going to happen tonight. The best thing we can do now is get some sleep.'

LINDMAN WALKED BACK to the hotel. The snow felt soft under his feet. The whole town was asleep. No light in Veronica Molin's window.

He undressed, showered and went to bed, thinking about Magnus Holmström all the time. Discreet, Niklasson had called him. But Lindman had also seen another side of him. Cold as ice. He had no doubt at all that it could have been Holmström who had tried to kill Hereira. The question was, did he also kill Andersson? It was possible that Berggren was guilty, but Lindman could not believe it. One could take it for granted that Holmström could have told her about anything that wasn't in the newspapers, such as the washing line.

He turned off the light.

He was brought back to consciousness by the sound of the telephone ringing. He fumbled for his mobile. It was Larsson.

'I thought you'd like to know. Molin's house is on fire. Erik and I are on our way there. The alarm was raised a quarter of an hour ago. A snowplough went past and the driver saw the glow among the trees.'

'Do you think the fire has any significance?' Lindman asked.

'The only thing I can think of is that somebody knew about Molin's diary but didn't know that you'd already found it.'

'So it has to be arson?'

'I wouldn't like to say. I'll be in touch.'

Lindman put the phone on the bedside table. The light coming in through the window was reflected by the snow. He couldn't get to sleep. He got up to pull down the blinds and shut out the light. Then he saw something that madc him start. There was a man in the street outside. A figure in the half-light. Staring up at his window. Lindman was wearing a white vest. Perhaps it was visible. Lindman held his breath. The man slowly raised his arms. It looked like a sign of submission. Then he turned on his heel and walked out of the light.

Lindman wondered if he had imagined it. Then he saw the footprints in the snow.

He flung on his clothes and hurried out of the room. Reception was deserted. He ran out into the darkness. He stood stock-still and looked around. Then he walked over to the place where the man had been standing. The footsteps were clear in the snow.

They formed a pattern he had seen before. The man had marked out the steps of the tango in the glittering, new-fallen snow.

Chapter 8

He checked to make sure he had his mobile in his pocket, then started following the tracks. Not many people were out in the streets. The only tracks visible were from the man he was following. Straight, confident strides. Heading north, towards the railway station. He looked round. Not a soul in sight, no shadowy figures now, just this one set of footprints in the snow.

Lindman paused when he came to the station. The tracks continued round the deserted, unlit building towards the rails and the platform. If his suspicions were correct, he was now following the man who had killed Molin, who had tortured him and whipped him to death. He turned, walked back until he was under a streetlight, and phoned Larsson. Busy. They'll be at the scene of the fire by now, he thought. He tried to decide what to do. Then he started walking south. He turned off when he came to a long warehouse and found himself among the railway lines. He could see the station some distance away. He kept walking across the tracks and into the shadows on the other side, then slowly approached the station again. He walked to the back of an old guard's van and peered round it.

The snow muffled all sounds, and so he didn't hear the man creeping up behind him and hitting him hard on the back of his head.

It was pitch-dark when he opened his eyes. There was a pounding in the back of his head. He was no longer outdoors. He was sitting on a chair. He couldn't move. He was tied to a chair, and there was a blindfold round his eyes. He was terrified. He had been captured. He had done exactly what he shouldn't have done: gone off on his own, without warning his colleagues.

Where was he? There was a smell in the room he recognised, but couldn't place. He had been in this room before, but where was it?

Then somebody started talking to him in English. A man's voice, coming from his left. The foreign accent was obvious.

'I'm sorry I had to knock you out, but this meeting was necessary.'

Lindman made no reply. Silence was the only protection he had at the moment.

'I'm tired,' the voice said. 'I want to go home, but I need the answers to some questions. Just one question. Who am I?'

Lindman tried to work out what it meant. Not the words, but what lay behind them. The man gave the impression of being perfectly calm.

'I'd like a reply,' the voice said. 'Who am I?'

Lindman realised he would have to respond.

'I saw you in the snow under my hotel window,' he said. 'You left some prints in the snow like those in Herbert Molin's house.'

'I killed him. It was necessary.'

Lindman was soaked in sweat. He wants to talk, he thought. What I need is time, time to work out where I am and what I can do.

'I realise it must have had something to do with the war,' he said.

'Herbert Molin killed my father.'

The words were spoken calmly and slowly. Lindman had no doubt that Hereira was speaking the truth.

'What happened?'

'They hanged Josef Lehmann,' the voice said. 'In late 1945. He deserved it. He had killed many people in the terror-stricken concentration camps he governed. But they should have hanged his brother as well. Waldemar Lehmann. He was worse. What he enjoyed most was setting up others to carry out the torture. He trained people to become monsters. He educated the henchmen of death.'

There was a sigh, or a sob. A creaking noise. Lindman had heard it before. A chair, or maybe a sofa that creaked in that way.

'I want to go home,' the voice said. 'Back to what remains of my life. But first I must know who killed Abraham Andersson. I must know if I have to bear some of the responsibility for what happened.'

'You came along in a blue Golf,' Lindman said. 'Somebody stepped into the road and shot at you. Whoever shot you could well have been the person who killed Abraham Andersson.'

'You know a lot,' the voice said. 'But then, you're a policeman. It's your job to know.' There was a clinking of a bottle, a top being unscrewed. Some swigs, but no glass, Lindman thought. He's drinking straight out of the bottle. There was a faint smell of alcohol.

Then the man described what had happened fifty-four years ago.

'Waldemar Lehmann was a master. A genius at torturing people. One day Herbert Molin entered his life.'

The bottle clinked again. This man is drinking himself silly, Lindman thought. Does that mean he will lose control of what he's doing? He could feel his fear growing.

'My father was a dancing master. A peaceful man who loved to teach people how to dance. One day, the man who would hide behind the name of Herbert Molin came to him as a pupil. He had been granted a week's leave, which he was spending in Berlin. I remember seeing that young soldier several times. I liked him. He never spoke, but he smiled. I can see his face now, and I recognised him when I eventually caught up with him. I was twelve at the time. My father gave his lessons at home. When the war started in 1939 he'd had his dance studio taken away from him. One day a Star of David had appeared on the door. We saw our friends disappear, but my father survived. Until August Mattson-Herzén became my father's pupil.'

The voice ground to a halt. Lindman was trying desperately to think where he could be. That was the first thing he needed to know if he were to find a way of escaping.

The man was talking again. 'The young soldier became one of Waldemar Lehmann's henchmen. Lehmann must have found out that Mattson-Herzén was having dancing lessons from one of those disgusting Jews that were still in Berlin. I don't know what he did to convince the young soldier, but he succeeded in changing Mattson-Herzén into a monster. He came for his dancing lesson one afternoon. I used to sit out in the hall, listening to what went on in the big room. I could hear my father's friendly voice, counting the bars and saying things like "left foot", "right foot". Then the gramophone stopped. There wasn't a sound. I thought at first they were having a rest. The door opened. The soldier hurried out of the flat. He generally came out and gave me a smile, but nothing of that today. I went to the living room. My father was dead.'

Lindman experienced the rest of what the man had to say as a long, drawn-out scream.

'Mattson-Herzén had strangled him with his own belt! Then shoved a shattered gramophone record into his mouth. The label was covered in blood, but I could see that it was a tango. I've spent the rest of my life looking for the man who did that to my father. It wasn't until I happened to bump into Höllner that I discovered that my father's murderer was a Swede, somebody who hadn't even been forced into serving Hitler. I found him in the end, an old man who'd hidden himself with a new name, away up here in the forest. I killed him. I gave him his final dancing lesson.'

Lindman waited for him to go on, but nothing was said for a while.

'Who was Höllner?'

'A man who happened to be in the same restaurant as me one night in Buenos Aires. He was a German emigrant, from Berlin. A man who hated Hitler, like me. That was one starting point. The other was Waldemar Lehmann, who had tortured and murdered prisoners in various concentration camps. He disappeared in the chaos at the end of the war and couldn't be traced. He was high on the list of war criminals that was headed by Bormann. One of those looking for him was an English major, called Stuckford. He'd also been present when Josef Lehmann was hanged. Stuckford's researches revealed that a Swedish soldier had been one of Waldemar Lehmann's henchmen towards the end of the war, and that, egged on by Lehmann, the Swede had murdered his dancing master. Long after the war, Höllner and Stuckford met at a conference for people trying to trace war criminals. Höllner learned about the murder of a dancing master in Berlin, and that the man responsible was a Swede called Mattson-Herzén. Another Nazi had passed the information to Stuckford while being interrogated. Höllner told me all this. He also said that Stuckford occasionally visited Buenos Aires.'

Lindman heard Hereira reach for the bottle again.

'The next time Stuckford was in Buenos Aires, I met him. I explained that I was the son of the dancing master. About a year after that meeting, Stuckford wrote that Mattson-Herzén had changed his name to Molin after the war and was still alive. Stuckford's contacts were eventually able to trace Mattson-Herzén to these forests.'

He paused. 'Have you any questions?'

'I would like to know why you took Andersson's dog.'

'I wanted to tell you that you were wrong. You thought I had killed the other man as well. I moved the dog to create confusion.'

Lindman heard Hereira stand up. The floor vibrated.

'I thought it would die away,' the voice said. 'All those terrible things that happened so many years ago. But the thoughts that were born in Hitler's twisted mind are still alive. They have other names now, but they are the same thoughts, the same disgusting conviction that a whole people can be killed off if another people or race ordains it. The new technology, computers, the international networks, they all help these groups to cooperate. They are still ruining lives.'

Lindman realised that Hereira was close to breaking point. He can't let me go, Lindman thought, because I'd arrest him. He knows that he's captured a police officer. That's the worst thing you can do, whether you're in Sweden or Argentina. As long as I haven't seen his face he can go away and leave me here. I must make sure he doesn't take off this blindfold.

'Who was the man in the road who tried to shoot me?'

'A young Swedish neo-Nazi. His name's Magnus Holmström.'

'Has he been arrested?'

'Not yet.'

'Was it her who asked him to come?'

Lindman realised that he meant Elsa Berggren.

'We don't know.'

'But there must have been a motive, surely?'

Be careful now, Lindman thought. Don't say too much. He wants to know if he's to blame. Which he is, of course. When he killed Molin, it was like turning over a stone: the woodlice scattered in all directions.

There were still a lot of things he didn't understand. He had the feeling that a link was missing, some thread holding everything together that he hadn't found yet. Nor had Larsson, nobody had.

'Was it you who set fire to Molin's house?'

That seemed a question it wasn't too dangerous to ask.

'I assumed the police would go there, but perhaps not you. I was right. You stayed in the hotel.'

'Why me? Why not one of the other officers?'

The man didn't answer. Lindman wondered if he had overstepped the mark. He waited. Everything was still. Had the man left the room? Lindman strained all his senses. Then a clock started striking. Lindman knew where he was. In Berggren's house.

The blindfold was suddenly ripped off. He was in Berggren's living room, on the very chair he had sat on when he first went there.

Fernando Hereira was very pale and thin. Unshaven and with dark shadows under his eyes. His hair was grey and unkempt and his clothes were dirty. So this was the man who'd killed Molin so brutally, then dragged him around in a bloodstained tango.

The clock had struck the half-hour, 5.30 a.m. Lindman had been unconscious for longer than he had thought. On the table in front of the man was a bottle of brandy. The man took a swig.

'What punishment will I get?'

'I can't tell you that. It's up to the court.'

Hereira shook his head sadly. 'Nobody will understand. I want to explain to Molin's daughter why I killed her father. Stuckford told me that Molin had a daughter. Veronica. She must be here.'

'Molin will be buried today. The funeral's at eleven.'

Hereira gave a start. 'Today?'

Lindman had been given the opportunity he'd been hoping for. 'Veronica didn't know her father was a Nazi. She's very upset now that she does know. I think she'll understand.'

'The question is, if I let you go and ask you to contact the girl on my behalf, will you allow me the time I need before you arrest me?'

'How do I know you won't treat Veronica as you treated her father?'

'You can't know that. But why should I? She didn't kill my father.'

'You attacked me.'

'It was necessary. I regret it, of course. I'll let you go. I'll stay here. You talk to the girl, tell her where I am. Once she's left me, the police can come and collect me.'

Was he telling the truth? Lindman knew that it wasn't something he could take for granted. 'Needless to say, I can't let Veronica come to you on her own,' he said.

'I want to see her on her own. I will not lay a finger on her.' Hereira slammed his fist down on the table.

Lindman could feel his misgivings rising. 'I can give you the time you need,' he said, 'and you can talk to her on the telephone.'

He could see the positive glint in Hereira's eye.

'I'm already committing myself to more than I should,' Lindman said. 'As a police officer, I shouldn't be doing this.'

'Can I trust you?'

'We have to trust each other. There's no other possibility.'

Hereira cut the tape tying Lindman to the chair.

Lindman felt dizzy as he walked to the door. His legs were stiff, and the back of his neck was extremely sore.

'I'll wait for her to phone,' Hereira said. 'I'll probably talk to her for about an hour. Then you can tell your colleagues where I am.'

It was 6.30 when he got back to the hotel. He knocked on her door. She opened it so quickly that he almost recoiled. She was already dressed. Her computer was shimmering in the background.

'I have to talk to you. I know it's early. I thought you might have stayed in Östersund for the night, because of the snow.'

'My brother never showed up.'

'Why not?'

'He'd changed his mind. He phoned. He didn't want to go to the funeral. I got back here late last night. What is so urgent?'

Lindman started back to reception. She followed him. They sat down and he told her what had happened.

'I'll talk to him,' she said after a while, 'but I want to be alone when I phone him. When the call is over, I'll knock on your door.'

Lindman gave her the paper with the telephone number. Then he went to his room. He looked at his watch. In twenty minutes he would contact Larsson and tell him where he could find Hereira.

He went to the bathroom, but found that there was no toilet paper left. He went back to reception. He saw her through the window. Veronica Molin, out in the street. In a hurry.

He stopped short. Tried to work it out. There was no doubt that Veronica Molin was on her way to Hereira. He ought to have foreseen that. It's something to do with her computer, he thought. Something she had said. Maybe something I'd thought without really understanding the implications. His alarm was growing apace.

He turned to the girl. 'Fröken Molin's key,' he said. 'I must have it.'

She stared at him in bewilderment. 'I can't give it to you.'

Lindman slammed his fist on the desk. 'I'm a police officer,' he roared. 'Give me the key.'

She took the key from beneath the desk. He grabbed it, raced along the corridor and opened her door. The computer was on. The screen was glowing. He stared at it in horror. Everything fell into place. Now he could see how it all hung together. Most of all he could see how catastrophically wrong he had been.

IT WAS 7.05 A.M. and still dark. Lindman ran. Several times he slipped and almost fell in the snow. I ought to have caught on long ago, when she asked me to come back, he thought. Why wasn't I suspicious? I'm only now asking the questions that cried out to be asked then.

He came to the bridge. He took out his mobile and tried Larsson's number. A female voice asking him to try again later. Then he saw somebody coming towards him. He could see from the light of the street lamps who it was. He'd had coffee with the man in his kitchen: Björn Wigren. The old man recognised Lindman.

'Are you still here?' he asked, in surprise.

Lindman searched through his pockets for paper and pencil but found nothing. 'I need your help. Have you anything to write with?'

'No. What's happening?'

Lindman looked around. 'Come over here,' he said.

They went to where the bridge joined the road. There was a drift of virgin snow there. Lindman squatted down and wrote in the snow with his finger.

ELSA'S HOUSE. VERONICA. DANGEROUS. STEFAN.

He stood up. 'Stand here and wait until some police officers turn up. Show them this message. Is that clear?'

'What does it mean?'

'Nothing that affects you for the moment, but it's very important. You'll be doing the police a great service if you make sure they see it.'

'I'll stay here. I was only going out for a morning stroll.'

Lindman left Wigren and ran over the bridge to Elsa Berggren's house. Tried to keep calm. I must give the impression that I don't know anything, he told himself. Veronica Molin must carry on believing that I'm still the idiot she's had every reason to think I am so far.

He thought about the night she'd let him sleep by her side. No doubt she'd got up while he was asleep and searched his room. That was why she'd let him sleep in her bed. He'd been vain and conceited, and he'd betrayed Elena. Veronica had made the most of his weakness.

He rang the bell. Fernando Hereira peeped out from behind the curtain covering the glass part of the front door. Lindman was relieved to see that nothing had happened to him yet. Everybody had the right to have their actions tried in a court of law.

Hereira opened the door. 'You've come too soon,' he said brusquely.

'I can wait.'

Lindman wondered if he ought to tell Hereira the truth straight away, but decided to wait. She might be listening. He knew now that Veronica was capable of anything at all. He must draw out this meeting for as long as possible, so that Larsson and the rest had time to get here. He went into the living room. Veronica looked at him.

He gave her a smile. 'I can wait outside,' he said in English. 'If you haven't finished, that is.'

'I'd like you to stay,' she said.

Hereira had nothing against that either.

Lindman sat on the chair that gave him a clear view of the front door, and of the windows behind the other two. Veronica was still looking hard at him. He returned her gaze, repeating over and over to himself: I know nothing, I know nothing.

Hereira started speaking, giving a detailed account of his meeting with the man called Höllner in a Buenos Aires restaurant. Lindman approved: the more Hereira spun out his story, the better.

Then he gave a start. A face had appeared in the window behind Veronica. Wigren. So he had left the bridge; he hadn't been able to control his inquisitiveness.

Lindman could hardly keep his anger in check. He couldn't imagine that Larsson or anybody else would see the message in the snow by the bridge. And now there was no one waiting for them.

The face disappeared again. Lindman said a silent prayer, hoping that Wigren would go back to the bridge. It might not be too late.

A mobile phone rang. Veronica picked up her handbag, took out the telephone and answered the call. Whoever it is phoning, it's giving me more time, Lindman thought.

Veronica listened to what the caller was saying without speaking herself. Then she switched off and returned the phone to her handbag. When she took her hand out, it was holding a pistol.

She stood up slowly and took two steps to one side. From there she could cover both Lindman and Hereira. Lindman held his breath.

'That was the receptionist at the hotel,' she said. 'She phoned to tell me that you had taken my key and gone into my room. And of course I know I didn't switch off the computer.'

He knew it was pointless trying to talk himself out of the situation. He glanced at the window. No sign of Wigren. He could only hope.

'I don't understand,' Hereira said. 'What's going on?'

'It's just that Veronica is not what she pretends to be. She might devote part of her time to business deals, but she spends the rest of her life spreading the cause of Nazism throughout the world.' On her computer screen he had seen a letter in which she discussed old Nazi ideals that would last for ever.

Hereira stared at him in astonishment. 'She is a Nazi?'

'Perhaps it's better if I explain it myself,' said Veronica.

She spoke slowly and in perfect English, a person with no doubt as to the justice of her cause. Molin had been his daughter's hero, a man in whose footsteps she had never hesitated to follow. She belonged to a new era that adopted the ideals championing the absolute right of the stronger, and the concepts of supermen and subhuman creatures, and adapted them to contemporary reality. She described raw, unlimited power, the right of the strong to rule over the weak, a world in which people in poor countries were doomed to extinction.

Lindman listened. Her conviction was ineradicable and she really had no inkling of how lunatic she sounded. It struck Lindman that the face he'd found so attractive now seemed sunken and ugly.

She stared at Hereira. 'You killed my father, and therefore I'm going to kill you. I know that you stayed here afterwards because you wanted to know what had happened to Abraham Andersson. He had somehow found out about my father's past. So he had to die.'

'Was it you who killed him?' Hereira understood now.

'There's an international network,' Veronica said. 'The Strong Sweden foundation is a part of it. I'm one of the leaders. Executing Andersson to be certain that he could never reveal what he knew was not a problem. There are plenty of people who are always ready to carry out an order, without hesitation.'

'How did Andersson discover that your father was a Nazi?'

'An unfortunate coincidence. Elsa has a sister who was for many years a member of the Helsingborg Symphony Orchestra. She mentioned to Andersson, when he decided to move up here, that Elsa lived in Sveg and was a National Socialist. He started spying on her, and eventually on my father as well.'

'Magnus Holmström,' Lindman said. 'Is he the man you ordered to kill Abraham Andersson? Was it you who forced Elsa Berggren to confess to the murder? Did you threaten to kill her as well?'

'You know quite a lot,' she said. 'But it won't help you.'

'What do you mean to do?'

'Kill you,' she said calmly. 'But first I shall put down the man who murdered my father.'

Lindman was certain he was dealing with a madwoman. Time, he thought. That's all I need, time. 'You'll never get away,' he said.

'Of course I shall,' she said. 'I'll arrange it to look as if you shot him and then killed yourself. Nobody will think it strange that a policeman with cancer should commit suicide, especially after he's just killed another human being. The weapon can't be traced to me. I shall go from here to the church. It will never occur to anybody that a daughter about to bury her father would that same morning be killing two other people.'

Lindman heard the faintest of noises in the hall. He knew at once it was the front door being opened. He shifted in his chair, and caught sight of Larsson. Their eyes met. Larsson had a gun in his hand. I must tell him what's happening, he thought.

'So you shoot us both, one then the other,' he said.

She was on her guard. 'Why do you raise your voice?'

She moved rapidly so that she could see into the hall. Larsson wasn't there, but Veronica stood motionless, listening.

Then everything happened very quickly. She started towards the doorway. Lindman knew she wouldn't hesitate to shoot. From that range she couldn't miss. He grabbed the lamp on the table and flung it at one of the windows. The pane shattered. At the same time he threw himself at Hereira in such a way that both he and the sofa tumbled over backwards. As they fell down at the side of Hereira, he saw her turn. She fired. Hereira's body jerked. Then another bang. When Lindman realised he hadn't been hit this time either, he looked up and saw Larsson lying on the floor. Veronica had disappeared.

Hereira was moaning, but the bullet had only grazed his temple. Lindman scrambled over the overturned sofa and rushed to Larsson.

'I don't think it's too bad,' Larsson said.

He was white in the face from pain and shock. Lindman fetched a towel and pressed it against Larsson's blood-covered shoulder.

Lindman called the emergency number. The operator in Östersund said that reinforcements and an ambulance would be dispatched without delay.

'I'll be all right,' Larsson said. 'Go and find her. Is she mad?'

'Completely off her head. She's a fanatical Nazi.'

'No doubt that explains everything,' Larsson said.

'Don't talk. Lie still.'

'I wasn't thinking straight,' Larsson said. 'You'd better stay here until the reinforcements arrive. You can't go after her by yourself.'

But Lindman had already picked up Larsson's gun. He had no intention of waiting. She had not only fooled him, she had tried to kill him. That made him furious. As Lindman left the house, the thought went through his head that he was a man with cancer who was determined not to miss the chance of undergoing treatment and being cured.

There was no sign of Veronica. He tried to make out her footprints in the snow, but there had been too much traffic, too many walkers. He tried to think. What would she have done? She would find herself a car, he decided. She's shot three people. She has to run away.

He ran to the new bridge, and crossed over. There were two petrol stations on the other side. Some drivers were filling their tanks. Lindman paused and looked around. If somebody had produced a gun and tried to steal a car, there would have been turmoil. Was he thinking along the wrong lines? Behind her cool, calm exterior he had seen a confused, fanatical person. Maybe she would react differently? He looked at the church to his left. Was it possible? He ran to the church. Slowly he opened one of the doors. There was a coffin at the far end, in front of the altar. Molin's coffin. He squatted down, aiming Larsson's gun with both hands. There was nobody there. He crept inside, ducking down behind the back pew. Everything was quiet. He peered cautiously over the back of the pew. There was no sign of her. He walked down the centre aisle, still crouching, his gun at the ready. When he reached the vestry he raised his gun and entered. She was standing next to the wall at the side of the door. Motionless, with her gun pointing straight at his chest.

'Drop the gun,' she said. Her voice was low, almost a whisper.

He bent down and put Larsson's pistol on the stone floor.

'You won't even leave me in peace inside a church,' she said. 'Not even on the day my father's going to be buried.'

'What are you going to do?'

'Kill you.'

It was the second time he'd heard her say it.

'How did you know I was here?' she asked in the same low voice.

Lindman could see that the gun was aimed now at his legs, not his chest. She's going to pieces, he thought.

'Why don't you give up?' he said.

She didn't answer, simply shook her head. Then came the moment he was waiting for. The hand holding the gun dropped down as she turned to look out of the window. He flung himself backwards into the main part of the church, then started running down the centre aisle.

All of a sudden he fell headlong. He hadn't seen a corner of the carpet sticking up. Then came the shot. It smashed into the pew beside him. Another shot. The echo sounded like a thunderclap. Silence. He heard a thud behind him. When he looked round, he could see her, just in front of her father's coffin. His heart was pounding. What had happened? Then he heard Johansson's voice from the organ loft.

'Lie still. Don't move. Veronica Molin, can you hear me? Lie still.'

'She's not moving,' Lindman shouted.

There was a clattering on the stairs and Johansson appeared in the centre aisle. Lindman scrambled to his feet. They approached the motionless body with trepidation, Johansson with his pistol held in both hands before him.

'She's dead.' Lindman pointed. 'You hit her in the eye.'

Johansson gulped. 'I aimed for her legs. I'm not that bad a shot.'

They walked up to her. Right next to her, on the lower edge of the stone underhang of the pulpit was an obvious bullet mark.

'A ricochet,' Lindman said. 'You missed her, but the bullet bounced off the pulpit and killed her.'

Johansson shook his head in bewilderment. Lindman understood. The man had never shot at a human being before. Now he had, and the woman he had tried to hit in the leg was dead.

'It couldn't be helped,' Lindman said. 'That's the way it goes sometimes. But it's over now. It's all over.'

HALF AN HOUR LATER, Lindman arrived at the Berggren house and found Rundström there. Larsson was on his way to hospital, but the ambulance man said that Hereira had melted into thin air.

'We'll get him,' Rundström said.

'I wouldn't bet on it,' Lindman said. 'We don't know his real name. He's been very good at hiding so far.'

A man in overalls appeared. He was carrying a dripping-wet shotgun that he put on the table. 'I found it straight away,' he said.

Rundström eyed the shotgun. 'I wonder if the prosecutor will be able to nail Berggren for all the lies she's told us,' he said. 'Even if it was this Holmström who killed Andersson and threw the shotgun into the river. He's obviously the arsonist as well. Molin's house has been well and truly torched.'

'Hereira told me he had started the fire,' Lindman said.

'So much has happened that's beyond me,' Rundström said. 'It seems to me that you, Stefan Lindman, the police officer from Borås, are the only person around who can bring me up to speed on what's been happening on my patch this morning.'

LINDMAN SPENT THE REST of the day in Johansson's office. At 1.45 Rundström received a call informing him that Holmström had been arrested in Arboga, still in the Ford Escort they had put a marker on. It was 5 p.m. by the time Rundström declared that he felt sufficiently in the picture. He accompanied Lindman to his hotel. They said their goodbyes in reception.

'It's all been very peculiar,' Rundström said, 'but I reckon that I've come round to understanding most of what's been going on. You never do understand everything. There are always gaps.'

THAT EVENING Lindman had dinner in the hotel, then phoned Elena and said he'd be coming home. He was on his way to bed when Rundström phoned to say that Larsson was doing pretty well in the circumstances. The wound was serious, but not life-threatening. Johansson was in a much worse state. He'd had a nervous collapse. And Hereira was still at large. Rundström ended by telling Lindman that Special Branch was now involved.

'We've turned over a very large stone,' he said. 'This Nazi network is far more extensive than anybody ever dreamed of.'

Lindman lay awake for ages after that. He wondered how the funeral had gone. Most of all, it was memories of his father flooding through his mind. I'll never understand him, he thought. I won't ever be able to forgive him either, even if he is dead and buried.

The following morning Lindman was taken to the airport in Frösön. Just before 11 a.m. his plane touched down at Landvetter. Elena was there to meet him, and he was extremely pleased to see her.

A FEW DAYS LATER, on November 19, sleet was falling in Borås as Lindman walked up the hill to the hospital. He felt calm, and was confident of coping with whatever was in store for him.

Epilogue

On Sunday, April 9, 2000, Stefan collected Elena early in the morning. On the way to the airport they talked about which of them was looking forward more to the trip. Elena, who had seldom been even a few kilometres from Borås, or Stefan, whose doctor had given him hope that he had overcome his cancer, thanks to the radiotherapy and the subsequent operation.

As they took off, Stefan experienced a feeling of liberation. For six months he had lived with a fear that hardly left him. Now it had gone. His doctor had told him he would have to have tests for five years, but he felt that he had taken that vital step back to normal life.

Elena looked at him. 'A penny for your thoughts.'

'What I haven't dared to think for half a year.'

She said nothing, but took hold of his hand.

They landed at Gatwick, and after passing through passport control they went their different ways. Elena was spending two days in London, visiting a distant relative in one of London's suburbs. Stefan would be continuing his journey on a domestic flight.

Giuseppe had phoned from Östersund a few days earlier and told him that the Swedish police and Interpol had drawn a blank. Presumably Fernando Hereira was back in South America by now, using a different name—his real one. Giuseppe didn't think they would ever find him. He said that Magnus Holmström's case would come to court the following week. There was enough evidence to convict him and earn him a long jail sentence.

It was over, but there was one connection that Stefan still wanted to look into—the mysterious person identified as 'M' in Molin's diary. Stefan had been helped by a clerical assistant called Evelyn, who had worked for the police in Borås for many years. Together they had searched for and eventually found the report on the visit to Borås by a party of British police officers in November 1971, with a list of names. They had even found a photograph on the wall of an archive room. The picture was taken outside the police station. Olausson was there, posing with four British police officers, two of them women. One of those was called Margaret Simmons.

Molin was not in the picture, but he had been there. The following year, he had gone to see Margaret, in Dornoch, a coastal town north of Inverness. Margaret Simmons no longer lived there; she had moved when she retired in 1980. Evelyn had helped Stefan to trace her. One day in February, just when he had started to believe he was going to live and eventually return to work, she phoned him in triumph and supplied him with an address and a telephone number in Inverness.

AND THAT WAS WHERE he now was, in room number 12 on the top floor of a small, friendly hotel. He had gone walking after dinner—quays, promenades, the town centre—and slept deeply that night.

He rose early the next morning. It was drizzling over Inverness. After breakfast he phoned the number Evelyn had given him.

A man answered. 'Simmons.'

'My name's Stefan Lindman. I'm from Sweden. I'd like to speak to Margaret Simmons.'

'My mother's not at home. She's at Culloden today.'

'Where's that?'

'Not far from Inverness. The site of the last battle to take place on British soil in 1746. Mum likes to wander around the battlefield. She says she likes to listen to the voices of the dead. She says it prepares her for her own death. Call tomorrow morning.'

Stefan decided not to wait until the next day. He went down to reception and asked for directions to Culloden.

The man smiled. 'Today's a good time to go there. The weather's the same as when the battle was fought. Mist, rain and a breeze.'

Stefan drove out of Inverness in his rented car. He followed the signs off the main road. There were two coaches and a few cars in the car park. Stefan gazed over the moor. He could see the sea and the mountains in the distance.

He went out into the gusting wind to the battlefield. The moor was deserted. He went back, and bought a ticket for the museum. He couldn't see anyone who might have been Margaret. Some schoolchildren were on their way into a lecture room. He followed them. Just as he got in, the lights went out and a film started. He groped his way to a seat in the front row. The film lasted half an hour. He stayed put when the lights came on again. The children jostled their way out.

Stefan looked round. He recognised her immediately from the photograph. She was in the back row, wearing a black raincoat. Stefan waited until she left the lecture room before following her.

It was raining, but Margaret Simmons hadn't raised her umbrella. The wind was too strong. She was heading for one of the paths that meandered through the battlefield.

Stefan followed her to the middle of the battlefield. She turned to look at him. He saw that she was heavily made up, short and thin.

'Are you following me? Who are you?'

'My name is Stefan Lindman, I'm from Sweden. I'm a police officer.'

'You must have spoken to my son. He's the only one who knows where I am.'

'He was most helpful.'

'What do you want?'

'You visited a town in Sweden called Borås in the autumn of 1971. You met a policeman by the name of Herbert Molin. The following year he came to see you in Dornoch.'

She eyed him up and down, saying nothing. 'I'd like to continue my walk, if you don't mind,' she said eventually.

She started walking again. Stefan walked beside her.

'Is Herbert dead?' she asked, out of the blue.

'Yes, he's dead. Herbert Molin was murdered.'

She stopped in her tracks. 'What happened?' she asked.

'His past caught up with him. He was killed by a man who wanted to avenge something he'd done during the war.'

'Have you caught the murderer?'

'No. He got away. He has an Argentinian passport in the name of Fernando Hereira, and we think he lives in Buenos Aires. But we assume that that's not his real name.'

'What had Herbert done?'

'He murdered a Jewish dancing master in Berlin.'

She looked around at the battlefield, then started walking again.

'Molin kept a diary,' Stefan said. 'He was a Nazi, and fought as a volunteer for Hitler. But maybe you knew about that?'

She didn't answer, but rapped her umbrella hard onto the ground.

'The only thing in his diary that he took the trouble to write up properly was the visit he made to Dornoch. It says that he went for long walks there with "M".'

She looked at him in surprise.

'I have wondered,' Stefan said. 'About what happened.'

'He'd fallen in love with me. Pure stupidity, of course. And I was married. I nearly died of shock when he phoned out of the blue and announced that he was in Scotland. He tried to talk me into going back to Sweden with him.'

They had come to the edge of the battlefield. She turned to look at Stefan. 'I usually have a cup of tea at this time. Then I go out again. Would you join me?'

'Yes, thank you.'

In the cafeteria, Margaret chose a window table from where she could see the battlefield, and beyond it Inverness and the sea.

'I didn't like him,' she said firmly. 'I couldn't shake him off, even though I'd made it clear that his journey was a waste of time. He told me he'd *been* a Nazi. He claimed to regret it all. He insisted it had been a youthful mistake.' She looked at him. 'But it wasn't true that he regretted it, is that it?'

'I believe that he was a Nazi until the day he died. He even handed his Nazi beliefs down to his daughter. She's dead too.'

'How come?'

'She was shot in an exchange of fire with the police. She damn nearly killed me.'

'I want to hear the whole story from the start. Herbert Molin is starting to interest me, and that's something new.'

WHEN HE CAME to the end, they sat there in silence for ages, staring out at the rain, which was easing off now.

'I'll stay here a bit longer. I haven't really finished with the dead yet. Your story was remarkable,' she said, and smiled. 'Good luck.'

'What with?'

'You might find him one day. Aron Silberstein. The one who murdered Herbert.'

'So he told you what had happened in Berlin?'

'He told me about his fear. The man who had been his dancing master was called Lukas Silberstein. He had a son called Aron. Herbert was afraid someone would take revenge, and he thought that is where it would come from. He remembered that little boy, Aron. I think Herbert dreamed about him every night. I have an instinct that he was the one who tracked Herbert down in the end.'

'Aron Silberstein?'

'I have a good memory. That was the name he told me. Anyway, it's time for us to say goodbye. I'm going back to my dead souls.'

He watched her marching resolutely back onto the battlefield. He went into the museum and bought a picture postcard. Then he sat down on a bench and wrote to Giuseppe.

Giuseppe, It's raining here in Scotland, but it's very beautiful. The man who killed Herbert Molin is called Aron Silberstein. Best wishes, Stefan.

HENNING MANKELL

Henning Mankell's books are something of a publishing phenomenon—they are spectacularly successful in his native Sweden and he has also sold more than twenty million copies worldwide. He is best known for his novels featuring detective Kurt Wallander, who is so well-loved and realistically drawn that the author regularly receives letters addressed to his fictional character.

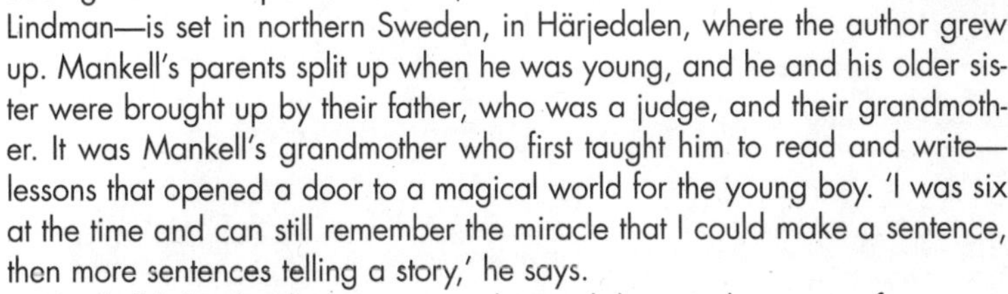

The Return of the Dancing Master—a departure from the Wallander series introducing a new police officer, Stefan Lindman—is set in northern Sweden, in Härjedalen, where the author grew up. Mankell's parents split up when he was young, and he and his older sister were brought up by their father, who was a judge, and their grandmother. It was Mankell's grandmother who first taught him to read and write—lessons that opened a door to a magical world for the young boy. 'I was six at the time and can still remember the miracle that I could make a sentence, then more sentences telling a story,' he says.

Mankell left school at sixteen and joined the merchant navy for a couple of years before returning to Sweden to start a career in the theatre, working as a stagehand in Stockholm. He wrote in his spare time, first a well-received play and then his debut novel, *The Stone-Blaster*, which was published in 1972 when he was twenty-four. His output since that time has been diverse—as well as crime novels he has continued to write for the theatre and has also written children's books and novels about Africa.

As a child growing up among the vast pine forests of Härjedalen, Mankell had always longed to travel to Africa. In 1972 he flew there for the first time, and an enduring love of the continent took root. 'I don't know why,' he says, 'but when I got off the plane in Africa I had a curious feeling of coming home.' He has lived in Africa on and off for thirty years, working as an actor, theatre director and manager in Mozambique, where he runs the Teatro Avanida in the capital Maputo. He is married to Eva Bergman, daughter of film director Ingmar Bergman, and divides his time between Mozambique and Sweden.

Jennifer Donnelly

A Gathering Light

Mattie Gokey can't forget the promise she made to her dying mother—a promise to stay on the family farm and help raise her three sisters.

The trouble is that keeping her word will mean an end to all her dreams . . .

When summer comes to the North Woods, time slows down. And some days it stops altogether. The sky, grey and lowering for much of the year, becomes an ocean of blue, so vast and brilliant you can't help but stop what you're doing—pinning wet sheets to the line maybe, or shucking a bushel of corn on the back steps—to stare up at it.

As I stand here on the porch of the Glenmore, the finest hotel on all of Big Moose Lake, I tell myself that today—Thursday, July 12, 1906—is such a day. Time has stopped, and the beauty and calm of this perfect afternoon will never end. The guests up from New York, all in their summer whites, will play croquet on the lawn for ever. The children of doctors and lawyers from Utica, Rome and Syracuse will always run through the woods, laughing and shrieking. I believe these things. With all my heart. For I am good at telling myself lies.

Until Ada Bouchard comes out of the doorway and slips her hand into mine. And Mrs Morrison, the manager's wife, walks right by us, pausing at the top of the steps. At any other time, she'd scorch our ears for standing idle. Her eyes fasten on the dock. And the steamer alongside it.

'That's the *Zilpha*, ain't it, Mattie?' Ada whispers. 'They've been dragging the lake, ain't they?'

I squeeze her hand. 'I don't think so. I think they were just looking along the shoreline. Cook says they probably got lost, that couple. Couldn't find their way back in the dark and spent the night under some pines, that's all.'

'I'm scared, Mattie. Ain't you?'

I don't answer her. I'm not scared, not exactly, but I can't explain how I feel. Words fail me sometimes. I have read most every one in the *Webster's International Dictionary of the English Language*, but I still have trouble making them come when I want them to.

Right now I want a word that describes the feeling you get—a cold, sick feeling deep down inside—when you know something is happening that will change you. What is the word for that feeling? For knowledge and fear and loss all mixed together? *Malbominance*? *Frisdom*? *Dreadnaciousness*?

Standing on that porch, under that flawless sky, I tell myself that nothing bad can happen at the Glenmore, not on such a day as this. And then I see Cook running up from the dock, ashen and breathless, her skirt in her hands, and I know that I am wrong.

'Mattie, open the parlour!' she shouts. 'Quick, girl!'

I barely hear her. My eyes are on Mr Crabb, the *Zilpha*'s engineer. He is coming up the path carrying a woman in his arms. Her head lolls against him like a broken flower. Water drips from her skirt.

'Oh, Mattie, look at her. Oh, jeezum, Mattie, look,' Ada says.

'*Sssh*, Ada. She got soaked, that's all. The boat tipped and they swam to shore and she . . . she must've fainted.'

'Dear Lord,' Mrs Morrison says, her hands coming up to her mouth.

'Mattie! Ada! Why are you standing there like a pair of jackasses?' Cook wheezes, heaving her bulky body up the steps. 'Open the spare room, Mattie. The one off the parlour. Pull the shades and lay an old blanket on the bed. Ada, go fix a pot of coffee and some sandwiches. Shift yourselves!'

There are children in the parlour playing hide-and-seek. I chase them out and unlock the door to a small bedroom. I realise I've forgotten the blanket and run back to the closet for it. I'm back in the room snapping it open over the ticking just as Mr Crabb comes in. He lays her down on the bed and puts a pillow under her head. The Morrisons come in. Mr Sperry, the Glenmore's owner, is right behind them. He stares at her, goes pale, and walks out again.

I force myself to look at her. Her eyes are dull and empty. There is an ugly gash on her forehead and her lips are bruised. Yesterday she'd sat by herself on the porch and I'd brought her lemonade. I hadn't charged her for it. She looked like she didn't have much money.

Behind me, Cook badgers Mr Crabb. 'What about the man she was with? Carl Grahm?'

'No sign of him,' he says. 'Not yet, leastways. We got the boat. They'd tipped it, all right. In South Bay.'

'I'll have to get hold of the family,' Mrs Morrison says. 'They're in Albany.'

'No, that was only the man, Grahm,' Cook says. 'The girl lived in South Otselic. I looked in the register.'

Mrs Morrison nods. 'I'll ring the operator. See if she can connect me with someone who can get a message to the family. Oh dear! Oh, her poor, poor mother!' She hurries from the room.

'She'll be making a second call before the day's out,' Cook says. 'Ask me, people who can't swim have no business on a lake.'

'Too confident, that fellow,' Mr Morrison says. 'I asked him could he handle a skiff and he told me yes. Only a darn fool from the city could tip a boat on a calm day . . .' He says more, but I don't hear him. It feels like there are iron bands around my chest. I close my eyes and try to breathe deeply. Behind my eyes I see a package of letters tied with a pale blue ribbon. Letters that are upstairs under my mattress. Letters that I promised to burn. I can see the address on the top one: *Chester Gillette, 17½ Main Street, Cortland, New York.*

Cook folds Grace Brown's hands over her chest and closes her eyes. 'There's coffee in the kitchen. And sandwiches,' she tells the men.

'We'll take something with us, if that's all right,' Mr Morrison says. 'We're going out again. Just in case Grahm made it to shore and got lost in the woods.'

'His name's not Carl Grahm. It's Chester. Chester Gillette.' The words burst out of me before I can stop them.

'How do you know that, Mattie?' Cook asks. They are all looking at me now—Cook, Mr Morrison and Mr Crabb.

'I . . . I heard her call him that, I guess,' I stammer, suddenly afraid.

Cook's eyes narrow. 'Did you see something, Mattie? Do you know something you should tell us?'

What had I seen? Too much. What did I know? Only that knowledge carries a damned high price.

frac • tious

My youngest sister, Beth, who is five, will surely grow up to be a riverman—standing upstream on the dam, calling out warnings to the men below that the logs are coming down. She has the lungs for it.

It was a spring morning. End of March. Not quite four months ago, though it seems much longer. We were late for school and there were still chores to do before we left, but Beth didn't care. She just sat there ignoring the cornmeal mush I'd made her, bellowing like some opera singer up from Utica to perform at one of the hotels.

'Beth, hush now and eat your mush,' I scolded, fumbling her hair into a braid. Most mornings I didn't mind her noise, but that morning I had to talk to Pa about something very important, and I was all nerves.

The kitchen door banged open and Lou, all of eleven, passed behind the table with a bucket of milk. She'd forgotten to take off her boots and was tracking manure across the floor.

'*A-hitching up our braces and a-binding up our feet.*'

'Beth, please!' I said. 'Lou, your boots! Mind your boots!'

'*A-grinding up our axes for our kind is hard to beat . . .*'

'What? I can't hardly hear you, Matt,' Lou said. 'Cripes' sake, shut up, will you?' she yelled, clapping a hand over Beth's mouth.

Beth squealed and threw herself back against the chair. The chair went over and hit Lou's bucket. The milk and Beth went all over the floor. Then Beth was bawling and Lou was shouting and I was wishing for my mother. As I do every day. A hundred times at least.

When Mamma was alive, she could make breakfast for seven people, hear our lessons, patch Pa's trousers and pack our dinner. All at the same time and without ever raising her voice.

Abby, fourteen, came in cradling four brown eggs in her apron. She put them in a bowl inside the pie safe, then stared at the scene before her. 'Pa's only got the pigs left to do. He'll be in shortly,' she said.

'Pa's going to tan your ass, Beth,' Lou said.

'He'll tan yours for saying *ass*,' Beth replied, still sniffling.

'That's enough! Both of you!' I shouted, dreading the thought of Pa getting his strap and heaving the whack of it against their legs. 'No one's getting a tanning. Go get Barney.'

Beth and Lou ran to the stove and dragged poor Barney out from behind it. Pa's old hunting dog is lame and blind. Uncle Vernon says Pa ought to shoot him. Pa says he'd rather shoot Uncle Vernon.

Lou stood Barney by the puddle. He couldn't see the milk, but he could smell it, and he lapped it up greedily. What little he left, Abby got with a rag. Barney hadn't tasted milk for ages. Neither had we. The cows are dry over the winter. One had just freshened, though, so there was a little bit of milk for the first time in months and Pa was no doubt expecting to see some of it on his mush. There was an inch or two left in the bucket. I added a bit of water to it and poured it into a jug that I set by his bowl.

'Pa'll know, Matt,' Lou said.

'How? Is Barney going to tell him?'

'When Barney drinks milk, he farts something wicked.'

'Lou, just because you walk like a boy and dress like a boy doesn't mean you have to talk like one. Mamma wouldn't like it,' I said.

'Well, Mamma's not here any more, so I'll talk as I please.'

Abby, rinsing her rag at the sink, whirled round. 'Be quiet, Lou!' she shouted, startling us, for Abby never shouts.

As the two of them continued to snipe, we heard footsteps in the shed off the back of the kitchen. The bickering stopped. We thought it was Pa. But then we heard a knock and a shuffle, and knew it was only Tommy Hubbard, the neighbour boy, hungry again.

'You itching, Tom?' I called.

'No, Matt.'

'Come get some breakfast, then. Wash your hands first.'

Last time I'd let him in to eat he gave us fleas. Tommy has six brothers and sisters. They live on the Uncas Road, same as us, but farther up, in a shabby plank house. Their land divides ours from the Loomises' land on one side, notching in from the road. They have no pa or they have lots of pas, depending on who you listen to. Emmie, Tommy's mother, does the best she can cleaning rooms at the hotels and selling the little paintings she makes to the tourists, but it isn't enough. Her kids are always hungry. Her house is cold. She can't pay her taxes.

Tommy came inside. He had one of his sisters by the hand. Pa hadn't eaten yet and there wasn't so much left in the pot. 'I just brung Jenny is all,' he said quickly. 'I ain't hungry myself.'

'It's all right, Tom. There's plenty,' I said.

'She can have mine. I'm sick to death of this damned slop,' Lou said. Her kindnesses often took a roundabout path.

Everyone was sick of cornmeal mush. Myself included. We'd been eating it with maple sugar for breakfast and dinner for weeks. And for supper, buckwheat pancakes with the last of fall's stewed apples. Most everything we'd put in the root cellar in September was gone. We'd eaten the last of the venison in January. The ham and bacon, too. We'd killed one of our roosters and four hens and we only had ten birds left. Pa didn't want to touch them as they provided us with a few eggs now and would make us more eggs—and chickens, too—come summer.

Jenny Hubbard waited patiently, her eyes large and solemn, as I sprinkled maple sugar on Lou's leavings and passed the bowl to her. I gave Tom as much as I could spare from the pot.

'Matt, you pick your word of the day yet?' Abby asked.

Abby, gentle and mild. More like our mother than any of the rest of us. Lou takes after Pa. Our brother Lawton, too. Coal-black hair, blue eyes. Lou acts like Pa, too. Angry all the time now. Since Mamma died. And Lawton went away.

'Can I pick it, Mattie? Can I?' Beth begged. She scrambled out of her chair and raced into the parlour. I kept my precious dictionary there, out of harm's way, along with the books I borrowed from Miss Wilcox, and my mother's Waverly Editions of Best Loved American Classics.

Beth returned to the kitchen table, carrying the dictionary as if it were made of gold. 'Pick the word,' I told her. She carefully flipped a few pages forwards, then a few back, then put her index finger on the left-hand page. '*Fff . . . fraaak . . . fraktee . . . frakteeus*?' she said.

'I don't think there's any such word. Spell it,' I said.

'F-r-a-c-t-i-o-u-s.'

'*Frakshus*,' I said. 'Tommy, what's the meaning?'

Tommy peered at the dictionary. '"Apt to break out into a passion . . . snappish, peevish, irritable, cross,"' he read. '"P-per-verse."'

'Isn't that just perfect?' I said. '*Fractious*,' I repeated, relishing the bite of the *f*, teeth against lip. A new word. Bright with possibilities. 'Your turn, Jenny. Can you make a sentence from the word?'

Jenny frowned, then said, 'Ma was fractious when she chucked the fry pan at me 'cause I knocked her whiskey bottle over.'

'She chucked a fry pan at you?' Beth asked. 'Why'd she do that?'

'Because she was out of sorts,' Abby said.

'Because she was drinking,' Jenny said, licking her spoon.

Jenny Hubbard is only six years old, but the growing season is short in the North Woods, and children, like the corn, have to come up fast if they are to come up at all.

'Your mamma drinks whiskey?' Beth asked. 'Mammas shouldn't drink whiskey—'

'Come on, Beth, let's go. We're going to be late,' Abby said, hurrying her up from the table.

Books were gathered. Dinner pails, too. Abby bossed Lou and Beth into their coats. Tommy and Jenny ate silently. I hadn't had more than a few bites of my mush. 'Finish mine, will you, Tom?' I said, sliding my bowl over to him. 'I'm not hungry.' I plugged the sink, poured hot water into it from the kettle, added a bit of cold from the pump and started washing. 'Where are the rest of you kids?'

'Susie and Billy went to Weaver's with the baby. Myrton and Clara went to try at the hotel.'

'Your ma's not good today?'

'She won't come out from under the bed. Says she's scared of the wind.' Tommy looked at his bowl, then at me. 'You think she's crazy, Mattie? You think the county'll take her?'

Emmie Hubbard certainly was crazy, and I was pretty sure the county would take her one day. But I couldn't say that to Tommy. He was only twelve years old. 'You know, Tom,' I finally said, 'there are times I want to hide under the bed myself.'

'When? I can't see you crawling under no bed, Matt.'

'End of February. We got four feet in two days, remember? All I wanted to do was crawl under something and never come out. Most of us feel like that from time to time. Your ma, she does what she feels. That's the only difference. I'll go over to her before school. See if I can find a jar of apples and some maple sugar to take. Think she'd like that?'

'She would. I know she would. Thank you, Mattie.'

I packed Tommy and Jenny off to school, hoping that by the time I got to the Hubbards', Weaver's mamma would already be there. She was better at getting Emmie out from under the bed than I was. I finished the washing, looking out of the window as I did, at the bare trees and the brown fields, searching for spots of yellow among the patches of snow. I was awful tired of the snow and the rain and the mud.

People call that time of year—when the root cellar is nearly empty and the garden not yet planted—the six weeks' want. Years past, we always had money come March to buy meat and flour and potatoes. Pa would go off logging at the end of November up at Indian or Raquette Lake. He'd stay there all winter. He drove teams of horses hitched to jumpers—low flat sledges with big runners. The loads were piled as high as a man standing on another man's shoulders. He took them down off the mountains over icy roads, relying on the weight of the logs and his own skill to keep the jumper from hurtling down the hills and killing the horses and anything else in its way.

Come March, the snow would melt and the roads would soften, and it became impossible to drag the heavy loads over them. As it got towards the end of the month, we would look for Pa every day. We never knew just when he would arrive. Or how. In the back of someone's wagon if he was lucky. On foot if he wasn't. We often heard him before we saw him, singing a new song he'd learned.

We girls would all run to him. Lawton would walk. Mamma would try her best to hang back and be proper, but she never could. He would smile at her, and then she was running down the path to him, crying because she was so glad he was home. He'd hold her face in his hands, keeping her at arm's length, and wipe her tears away with his dirty thumbs. We'd all want to hug him, but he wouldn't let us. 'Don't come near me. I'm crawling,' he'd say. He'd take his clothes off in the back of the house, douse them with kerosene, and burn them. He'd douse his head, too, and Lawton would comb the dead lice from his hair.

Mamma would be boiling water while he did all this, and filling our big tin tub. Then Pa would have a bath in the middle of the kitchen, his first one in months. When he was clean, we would have a feast. Ham steaks with gravy. Mashed potatoes with rivers of butter running down them. The last of the corn and the beans. And for dessert, a blueberry pie made with the last of the preserved berries. Then there were presents for each one of us. There might be a penknife for Lawton, and ribbons and candy for us girls. And for Mamma, a dozen glass buttons and a bolt of fabric for a new dress. We'd all sit in the parlour that night, in the glow of the cylinder stove, eating the caramels and chocolates Pa had brought, and listen to his tales. It was better than Christmas, those nights that Pa came out of the woods.

He hadn't gone into the woods this year. He didn't want us by ourselves. Without his logging money, things had been hard indeed. As I stood there drying the dishes, I hoped the fact that we were flat broke and would be for weeks yet, until Pa could sell his milk and butter again, would make him listen to what I had to say and tell me yes.

I finally heard him come into the shed, and then he was in the kitchen, a small snuffling bundle in his arms. 'That devil of a sow ate four of her piglets,' he said. 'Every one except the runt. I'm going to put him in with Barney. Lord, this dog stinks! What's he been eating?'

'Probably got into something in the yard. Here, Pa.' I put a bowl of mush on the table and stirred maple sugar into it. Then I poured the watery milk over it and hoped to God he didn't ask for more. Then I poured him a cup of hot tea. Black and sweet, just the way he liked it. I sat down across from him, practising my words in my head. I'd just about worked up the nerve to open my mouth when Pa spoke first.

'I'm sugaring tomorrow. Sap's flowing like a river. You're to stay home and help me boil tomorrow. Your sisters, too.'

'Pa, I can't. I'll fall behind if I miss a day, and my examinations are coming up.'

'Cows can't eat learning, Mattie. I need to buy hay. Beckers' Farm and Feed don't take credit, so I'll need to sell some syrup to get it.'

I started to argue, but Pa looked up from his bowl and I knew to stop. 'You're lucky you're going at all,' he said. 'And it's only because you getting your diploma meant something to your mother. You won't be going next year. I can't run this place by myself.'

I looked at the table. I was angry with my father for keeping me home, even for a day, but he was right; he couldn't run a sixty-acre farm alone. *Fractious*, I thought. *Cross*, *irritable*, *peevish.* Fits my father to a T. I took a deep breath and plunged ahead.

'Pa, I want to ask you something,' I said.

'Mmm?' He raised an eyebrow and kept on eating.

'Can I work at one of the camps this season? Maybe the Glenmore? Abby's old enough to get the meals and look after everyone. I asked her and she said she'd be fine and I thought that if I—'

'No.'

'But Pa—'

'You don't have to go looking for work. There's plenty right here.'

I knew he'd say no. Why had I even asked? I stared at my hands—red, cracked, old woman's hands—and saw what was in store for me: a whole summer of drudgery and no money for it. Doing everything that fell on the eldest in a family of four girls with a dead mother.

'Pa, they pay well,' I said. 'I thought I could keep back some of the money for myself and give the rest to you. I know you need it.'

'You can't be up at a hotel by yourself. It's not right.'

'But I won't be by myself! Ada Bouchard and Frances Hill and Weaver are all going to the Glenmore. And the Morrisons—the ones managing the place—are decent folk.'

'Weaver Smith is no recommendation.'

'Please, Pa,' I whispered.

'No, Mattie. And that's the end of it.'

I wanted to argue but his jaw was set firm, and I saw a little muscle jumping in his cheek. Lawton used to make that muscle jump. Last time he did, Pa swung a peavey at him and he ran off, and no one heard from him for months. Until a postcard came from Albany.

I finished the dishes without a word and left for the Hubbards'. I wanted to earn money. Desperately. I had a plan. Well, more a dream than a plan, and the Glenmore was only part of it. But I wasn't feeling hopeful about it just then. If Pa said no to the Glenmore, which was only a few miles up the road, what would he say to New York City?

abe • ce • dar • i • an

If spring has a taste, it tastes like fiddleheads. Green and crisp and new. I was supposed to be picking them, me and Weaver both. We were going to fill two buckets—split one for ourselves and sell one to the chef at the Eagle Bay Hotel—but I was too busy eating them. 'Choofe . . .' I tried to say, but my mouth was full. 'Weba . . . choofe a wurb. . .'

'My mamma's pig's got better manners. Why don't you swallow first?' Weaver said.

'Choose a word, Weaver,' I finally said. 'Winner reads, loser picks.'

'Are you two fooling again?' Minnie asked. She was sitting near us on a rock. She was in the family way and was very fat and grumpy.

'We're duelling, not fooling, Mrs Compeau,' Weaver replied. 'It's a serious business, and we would appreciate quiet from the seconds.'

Minnie grumbled and sighed. She lumbered off the rock and crouched down among the fiddleheads, snapping off one after another, shoving them into her mouth with the heel of her hand.

Weaver flipped open the book he was holding. His eyes lit on a word. '*Iniquitous*,' he said. We stood back-to-back, cocking the thumbs on our right hands and sticking out our pointer fingers to make guns.

'To the death, Miss Gokey,' he said solemnly.

'To the death, Mr Smith.'

'Minnie, you give the orders.'

'No. It's silly.'

'Come on. Just do it.'

'Count off,' Minnie sighed.

We walked away from each other, counting off paces. At ten, we turned.

'Draw.' Minnie yawned. 'Fire!'

'Evil!' Weaver yelled.

'Immoral!' I shouted.

'Sinful!'

'Unjust!'

'Nefarious!'

'"*Nefarious*"? Jeezum, Weaver! Um . . . hold on, I have one . . .'

'Too late, Matt. You're dead,' Minnie said.

Weaver smirked at me and blew on the tip of his finger. 'Start picking,' he said. He made a cushion out of his jacket and settled himself down with *The Count of Monte Cristo*. I should have known better than to challenge Weaver to a word duel. He always won.

Picking fiddleheads was only one of our money-making schemes. If it wasn't fiddleheads we were gathering, it was wild strawberries or blueberries. We'd end up with ten cents here, a quarter there. I needed money. Quite a bit. New York City, people said, was very expensive.

'"On the 24th of February, 1810, the lookout at Notre-Dame de la Garde signalled the three-master",' Weaver began. As he read, I poked around with a stick, searching for the tiny green furls coming up through the wet, rotted leaves, each one curled in on itself like the end of a fiddle. There are enough fiddleheads for two buckets today and another two tomorrow. We leave plenty alone to become ferns.

I got my first bucket filled maybe one-third of the way, and then I got taken outside myself like I always do by a good story.

'"We will leave Danglars struggling with the demon of hatred,"' Weaver read, '"and endeavouring to insinuate in the ear of the ship owner . . ." Hey! Get picking, Matt! Mattie, did you hear me?'

'All right,' I sighed.

Weaver closed the book. 'Forget it. I'll help. We'll never get done otherwise. Give me a hand.'

I reached for him and he pulled himself up, nearly pulling me over as he did. I have known Weaver Smith for over ten years now. He is my best friend. Him and Minnie both.

Weaver was the only black boy in Eagle Bay. Maybe in all of the North Woods. I had never seen another. Weaver's mamma moved herself and Weaver up here from Mississippi after Weaver's father was killed right in front of them by three white men for no other reason than not moving off the sidewalk when they passed. She decided the farther north they got, the better. 'Heat makes white people mean,' she told Weaver and, having heard about a place called the Great North Woods, a place that sounded cold and safe, decided she and her son would move there. They lived about a mile up the Uncas Road, just south of the Hubbards, in an old log house that someone abandoned years ago.

Weaver's mamma took in washing. She raised chickens, too. Scores of them. During the warmer months, she fried up four or five every evening, and baked biscuits and pies, too, and took it all down to the Eagle Bay railroad station the next day in her cart to meet the trains. Between the engineer and the conductors and all the hungry tourists, she sold everything she made. She put every penny she earned in an old cigar box that she kept under her bed so that she could send Weaver away to college. To the Columbia University in New York City. Miss Wilcox, our teacher, encouraged him to apply. He'd been granted a scholarship and planned to study history and politics and then go on to law school one day. He was the first freeborn boy in his family. His grandparents were slaves, and even his parents were born slaves, though Mr Lincoln freed them when they were tiny children.

'*The Count of Monte Cristo*'s a good book already, isn't it, Mattie? And we're only on the second chapter,' Weaver said.

'It sure is,' I replied, bending down by a big clutch of fiddleheads.

'You writing any more stories yourself?' Minnie asked me.

'I've no time. No paper, either. I used up every page in my composition book. But I'm reading a lot. And learning my word of the day.'

'You ought to use your words, not collect them. You ought to write with them. That's what they're for,' Weaver said.

'I told you I can't. Don't you listen? And anyway, there's nothing to write about in Eagle Bay. Maybe in Paris, where Mr Dumas lives—where they have kings and musketeers, but not here,' I said, sounding testier than I wanted to.

'The stories Miss Wilcox sent to New York weren't about kings or musketeers,' Weaver said. 'That one about the hermit Alvah Dunning and his Christmas all by himself, that was the best story I ever read.'

I shrugged, poking in the leaves.

'What about New York? You hear anything?' Weaver asked.

'No.'

'That letter will come, Matt,' Weaver said. 'I know it. And in the meantime nothing can stop you from writing if you really want to.'

'It's all right for you, Weaver,' I shot back angrily. 'Your mamma lets you alone. What if you had three sisters to look after and a father and a big damn farm that's nothing but endless damn work? What about that? You think you'd be writing stories then?' I felt my throat tightening and swallowed a few times to get the lump out.

Weaver's eyes locked on mine. 'It's not work that stops you, is it, Matt? Or time? It's that promise. She shouldn't have made you do it.'

'She was dying. You would've done the same for your mother,' I said, looking at the ground. I could feel my eyes filling with tears.

'God took her life and she took yours.'

'You shut up, Weaver! You don't know anything about it!' I shouted, the tears spilling.

'You sure have a big mouth, Weaver Smith,' Minnie scolded. 'Look what you did. You should say you're sorry.'

'I'm not sorry. It's true.'

'Lots of things are true. Doesn't mean you can go round saying them,' Minnie said.

A few months back, Weaver took my composition book—which I had tossed into the woods—and he gave it to Miss Wilcox.

This composition book was where I wrote my stories and poems. I'd only shown them to three people: my mamma, Minnie and Weaver. Mamma said they made her cry, and Minnie said they were awfully good. Weaver said they were better than good and told me I should show them to Miss Parrish, our teacher before Miss Wilcox came. He said she would know what to do with them.

I didn't want to, but he kept badgering, so I finally did. I don't know what I was hoping for. A bit of encouragement, I guess. I didn't get it. Miss Parrish took me aside one day after school let out. She said she'd read my stories and found them morbid and dispiriting.

I just took my composition book and left, tears of shame scalding my eyes. Weaver was waiting for me outside the schoolhouse. He asked me what Miss Parrish had said, but I wouldn't tell him. I waited until we were a mile out of town, then I pitched my composition book into the woods. He ran right after it. He said since I'd thrown it away it wasn't mine any more. It was his and he could do as he liked with it.

He kept hold of it and he waited. And then Miss Parrish's mother took ill and she left to go to nurse her, and the school trustees got Miss Wilcox, who was renting the old Foster house in Inlet, to take her place. And Weaver gave Miss Wilcox my composition book without even telling me. And she read my stories and told me I had a rare gift.

And ever since, because of the two of them, Weaver and Miss Wilcox both, I am wanting things I have no business wanting, and what they call a gift seems to me more like a burden.

'Mattie . . .' Weaver said, still dropping fiddleheads into his bucket.

I did not answer him. I did not bother to straighten or look at him. I tried not to think about what he'd said.

'Mattie, what's your word of the day?'

'*Abecedarian*,' I said quietly.

He walked up to me and took my bucket away. I had to look at him then. I saw that his eyes said he was sorry even if his mouth wouldn't.

'What's it mean?'

'As a noun, someone who's learning the alphabet. A beginner. A novice. As an adjective, rudimentary or primary.'

'Use it in a sentence.'

'Weaver Smith should abandon his abecedarian efforts at eloquence and admit that Mathilda Gokey is the superior word duelist.'

Weaver smiled. He put both pails down. 'Draw,' he said.

'Mattie, what in blazes are you doing?'

It's Cook. She startles me. 'Nothing, ma'am,' I stammer, slamming the cellar door shut. 'I . . . I . . . was just—'

'Don't let me see you out of that chair again until the ice cream's done.' Cook is snappish. More so than usual. We all are. Help and guests alike. Snappish and sad.

I walk back to the ice-cream churn and feel Grace Brown's letters hanging heavy in my skirt pocket. Why did Cook have to come back into the kitchen just then? Two more seconds and I would've been down the cellar stairs and in front of the huge coal furnace. The letters would have caught immediately, I could have been done with them.

And ever since Grace Brown handed the letters to me, I have sorely wanted to be done with them. She gave them to me yesterday afternoon on the porch, after I'd brought her a lemonade. I'd felt sorry for her; I could tell she'd been crying. I knew why, too. She'd had a fight with her beau at dinner. It was over a chapel. She wanted to go and find a chapel, but he wanted to go boating.

Just as I was turning to go back inside, she asked me to wait. She opened her gentleman friend's suitcase and pulled a bundle of letters from it. She took a few more from her bag, undid the ribbon around them, tied all the letters together, and asked me to burn them.

'Miss, I can't—' I'd started to say.

She took hold of my arm. 'Burn them. Please,' she whispered. 'Promise me you will. No one can ever see them. Please!'

And then she pressed them into my hands, and I nodded yes. 'Of course I will, miss. I'll do it right away.'

And then he—Carl or Chester or whatever he called himself—shouted to her from the lawn, 'Billy, you coming? I got a boat!'

I'd put the letters in my pocket and had forgotten all about them until I went upstairs later in the day to change into a fresh apron. I slipped them under my mattress, figuring I would wait to burn them, just in case Grace Brown changed her mind and asked for them back.

I'd run upstairs to get the letters right after Grace's body was brought in, and I'd been waiting ever since for Cook to turn her back.

The door from the dining room swings open and Fran Hill marches in, an empty tray on her shoulder. 'Lord! I don't see how sitting on your backside watching an illustrated lecture about castles in France can make people so hungry,' she says.

'Nerves,' Cook says. 'People eat too much when they're nervy.'

The door bangs open again. It's Ada. 'Man from the Boonville paper's here. Mrs Morrison says I should bring him coffee.'

Weaver is on her heels. 'Mr Morrison says to tell you he wants sandwiches for the searchers when they come in off the lake tonight.'

Cook puts water on to boil and opens a metal canister on the counter next to the stove. 'Weaver, I told you to bring up some coffee this morning. Go and get it now.'

The kitchen was busy enough with the hotel full, busier still in the hours since the body was recovered. Mrs Morrison had informed us that the sheriff was coming from Herkimer tomorrow. And the coroner. And there were bound to be men from the city papers, too. Cook was determined that the Glenmore not be found wanting. She'd baked enough bread and biscuits to feed every man, woman and child in the county.

Weaver disappears into the cellar, where the large sack of coffee beans is kept. As he does, I hear gunshots coming from the lake.

Ada and Fran draw near to me. 'If he was still alive, someone would have found him by now,' Fran says. 'Or he would have found his way back. Those gunshots carry.'

'I looked in the register,' Ada whispers. 'Their last names weren't the same. I don't think they were married.'

'I bet they were eloping,' I say. 'I served them at dinnertime. I heard them talk about a chapel.'

'Did you, Matt?' Ada asks.

'Yes, I did,' I say, telling myself that fighting is talking. Sort of. 'Maybe Grace Brown's father didn't like Carl Grahm,' I add. 'Maybe he didn't have any money. So they ran away to get married . . .'

'. . . and decided to take a romantic boat ride together first, to declare their love for each other on the lake . . .' Ada adds wistfully.

'. . . and the boat tipped and they fell out and he tried to save her, but he couldn't. She slipped from his grasp . . .' I say. 'And then he drowned, too. He gave up struggling, because he didn't want to live when he saw that she was gone. And now they'll be together for ever.'

'Together for ever,' Frannie echoes.

'At the bottom of Big Moose Lake. Just as dead as two doornails,' Cook says. 'You let that be a lesson to you, Frances Hill,' she adds. 'Girls who sneak off with boys end badly. You hear me?'

Fran blinks. 'Why, Mrs Hennessey, I'm sure I don't know what you mean,' she says. She is such a good actress, she should be on stage.

'And I'm sure you do. Where were you two nights ago at midnight?'

'Right here, of course. In bed asleep.'

'Not sneaking off to meet Ed Compeau, by any chance?'

Fran's caught. She turns as red as a cherry. Cook takes Fran's chin in her hand and says, 'A boy wants to go somewhere with you, you tell him to call on you proper or not at all. You hear?'

'Yes, ma'am,' Fran mumbles, and from the look on her face I know she is as unsettled as I am at seeing signs of softness from Cook.

I look at the thin gold ring with a chipped opal and two dull garnets on my left hand. I've never thought it pretty, but I'm suddenly glad, very glad, that Royal gave it to me. Glad, too, that he always calls for me at the Glenmore's kitchen door, where everyone can see him.

mis • no • mer

Nothing on our entire farm was as unyielding, as immovable and uncompromising as Pleasant the mule. I was in our cornfield trying to get him to pull the plough. 'Giddy-up, Pleasant! Giddy-up!' I shouted, snapping the reins against his haunches. He didn't move.

'Come on, Pleasant . . . come on, mule,' Beth wheedled, holding a lump of maple sugar out to him.

'Here boy, here mule,' Tommy Hubbard called, waving an old straw hat. Pleasant liked to eat them.

'Move your fat ass, you jackass,' Lou swore, tugging on his bridle. But Pleasant would not be budged.

It was dry and remarkably warm for the start of April, and I was tired and dirty and dripping with sweat. Pa had kept me home from school again, and I'd wanted to go so badly. I told him I was waiting on a letter, one that was going to come care of Miss Wilcox. I told him I had to go. Pa wanted to plant corn mid-May, at the latest. He was trying to build our dairy herd. He wanted to keep the calves if he could, rather than sell them, but we needed to grow enough corn to feed them. I was to have two acres turned over that day, and I'd only got a third of the way through before Pleasant had quit. Pa would've done it if he could, but he was with Daisy, who was calving. So it fell to me.

I bent down and picked up a stone. I was just winding up to throw it at Pleasant's behind when I heard a voice behind me say, 'Peg him with that and you'll scare him. He's like to run.'

I turned round. A tall blond boy was standing at the edge of the field, watching me. He was taller than I remembered. Broad-shouldered. And handsome. Handsomest one out of all the Loomis boys. He had the rim of a wagon wheel resting on his shoulder.

'Hey, Royal,' I said, trying to keep my eyes from roosting on him.

'Hey.'

The Loomis farm bordered ours. It was much bigger. Ninety acres. They had more bog than we did, but Mr Loomis and his boys had managed to clear forty acres. We'd only got about twenty-five cleared. Pa had hoped to clear another five acres over the summer. But he couldn't without Lawton.

Royal let the wagon wheel slide to the ground. 'Let me have him,' he said, taking the reins. 'Giddy-up, you!' he shouted, snapping them smartly against Pleasant's rump. Much harder than I had. Pleasant budged. Boy, did he. Tommy, Beth and Lou cheered, and I felt as dumb as a bag of hammers.

Royal was the second-eldest boy in his family. There were two younger ones. Daniel, the eldest, had just got engaged to Belinda Becker from the Farm and Feed Beckers in Old Forge.

Dan and Belinda's engagement was big news. It was a good match, what with Dan so capable and Belinda sure of a nice dowry. My aunt

Josie said there was supposed to have been a second engagement. She said Royal had been sweet on Martha Miller, whose father is the minister in Inlet, but he broke it off. Nobody knew why, but Aunt Josie said it was because Martha's people aren't worth a darn. Mr Miller has a nice pair of greys and Martha wears pretty dresses, but they don't pay their bills.

Dan and Royal were only a year apart, nineteen and eighteen, and they were for ever in competition. One was always trying to outdo the other. I hadn't seen much of them over the last year. They used to come and fetch Lawton for fishing trips, and we all used to walk to school together, but Dan and Royal left school early. Neither one was much for book learning.

I watched Royal as he ploughed a row, turned at the end of the field and came back. 'Thanks, Royal,' I mumbled. 'I'll take him now.'

'That's all right. I'll finish it. Whyn't you follow along behind and pull the stones?'

I traipsed after him, picking up stones and roots. He moved fast and it was hard to keep up with him.

'Soil's good. Dark and rich. Should get a good crop out of it. Why you call your mule Pleasant? He's anything but.'

'It's a misnomer,' I said, pleased to be able to use my word of the day.

'You call your mule Miss? Miss Pleasant? It's a boy mule!'

'No, not "Miss Pleasant", *misnomer.* It means a misapplied name. Like when you call a fat person Slim. Misnomer. It comes from *mesnommer*, which is French—old French—for "to misname". It's my word of the day. I pick a word out of the dictionary every morning and memorise it and try to use it. It helps build vocabulary.'

Royal gave me a look over his shoulder—a wincing, withering look—and I closed my mouth and wondered what it was girls like Belinda Becker had to say that made boys want to listen to them.

'Where's your pa, anyway?' Royal asked.

'With Daisy. Who's calving.'

There were more questions. What was Pa using for fertiliser? How many acres was he going to clear? Was he planting any potatoes this spring? And wasn't it hard for him to run the farm alone?

'He's not alone. He has me,' I said.

'But you're still in school, ain't you? Why aren't you out yet, anyway? School's for children and you're what . . . fifteen?'

'Sixteen.'

'Where's Lawton? Ain't he coming back?'

'You writing a column for the paper, Royal?' Lou asked.

Royal didn't laugh. I did, though. He was quiet after that. Two hours later, he'd finished the field entirely. We sat down for a rest, and I gave him a piece of the johnnycake I'd brought and poured him switchel from a jug. I gave pieces to Tommy and Lou and Beth as well.

Royal watched Tommy eating. 'Hubbards is always hungry, ain't they? Can't never seem to fill 'em up,' he said. 'Why you here, Tom?'

Tommy looked at his johnnycake, crumbly and yellow in his dirty hands. 'Like to help Mattie, I guess. Like to help her pa.'

Royal shrugged, then took a bite of his own cake. 'This is good,' he said. I was about to tell him that Abby made it, but then his honey-coloured eyes were on me, not the johnnycake, and I didn't.

I heard a shout and saw Pa waving from the barn. He walked up to us and sat down. I gave him my glass of switchel. 'Daisy had a bull calf,' he said wearily, and then he smiled.

My pa was so handsome when he smiled, with his eyes as blue as cornflowers and his beautiful white teeth. He hardly did any more, and it felt like a hard rain letting up.

Beth, Lou and Tommy chased off to see the new calf. Pa finished my switchel and I poured him some more. Switchel is easier to drink than plain water when you are hot and thirsty. Mixing a little vinegar, ginger and maple syrup into the water helps it to digest.

Pa looked at Royal, his shirt soaked with sweat, and my hands, dirty from the stones, and Pleasant unhitched, and put it all together. 'I'm obliged to you,' he said. 'It's a son's work, planting. Not a daughter's. Thought I had a son to do it.'

'Pa,' I said quietly.

'Don't understand why he left. Couldn't tear me away from land like this,' Royal said.

I bristled at that. I was angry at Lawton for leaving, too. But Royal was not family and therefore had no right to speak against him. Thing of it was, I didn't understand why my brother had left, either. I knew they'd had a fight, he and Pa. I saw them going at one another in the barn. First fists and then Pa had gone for his peavey. Then Lawton had run into the house, thrown his things into an old flour sack and marched out again. I'd run after him but Pa stopped me. Some days later I asked him what the fight was about. But he wouldn't tell me and, from the anger in his eyes, I knew better than to press.

Royal and Pa talked farming for a bit, then Royal picked up his wheel and said he had to get along to the forge. Pa walked Pleasant back to the barn, asking the mule if he had any idea why Frank Loomis had four good sons and he didn't have one.

som • nif • er • ous

'In the pantheon of great writers Milton stands second only to Shakespeare,' Miss Wilcox said, her boot heels making *pok pok* noises on the bare wood floor as she crossed and recrossed the room. 'Now, of course one may argue that Donne deserves . . .'

'*Pssst*, Mattie! Mattie, look!'

I slid my eyes off the book I was sharing with Weaver, towards the desk to my left. Jim and Will Loomis had a spider on a thread. They were letting it crawl back and forth on its leash, giggling like idiots.

I rolled my eyes. At sixteen I was too old to be attending the Inlet Common School. The leaving age is fourteen, and most don't make it that far. But our old teacher, Miss Parrish, told Miss Wilcox about Weaver and myself before she left. She said that we were smart enough to earn high school diplomas and that it was a shame that we couldn't. The only high school in the area was in Old Forge, a town ten miles south of Eagle Bay. It was too far to travel every day, especially in winter. Miss Wilcox said she would teach us the course work herself if we wanted to learn it, and she did. She had taught in a fancy girls' academy in New York City, and she knew plenty.

Weaver and I had spent most of the year preparing for our exit examinations. We were going to take the hardest ones—the Board of Regents—in English composition, literature, history, science and mathematics. The Columbia University is a serious and fearsome place, and a condition of Weaver's acceptance is that he earn B-pluses or better on all of his exams. He'd been studying hard, and so had I, but that day in the schoolhouse, I wasn't sure why I'd bothered. Weaver received his letter back in January, and though it was now the beginning of the second week of April, no letter had come for me.

I tried to put my mind back on *Paradise Lost*, but it was hard going. *Somniferous* was my word of the day. It means sleep inducing, and it was a good one to describe that dull and endless poem.

'And why do we read Shakespeare and Milton and Donne, Mr Bouchard?' Miss Wilcox asked.

Mike Bouchard turned scarlet. 'Because we have to, ma'am?'

'No, Mr Bouchard, because it is a classic. And we must have a good, working acquaintance with the classics if we are to understand the works that follow them and progress in our own literary endeavours. And where would Milton have been without Homer, Mr James Loomis? Why, without Milton, Victor Frankenstein's monster would never have been created . . .'

At the mere mention of that magic word *Frankenstein,* the Loomis boys straightened up. Miss Wilcox had promised since November that we'd read *Frankenstein* as our last book of the year, as long as everyone—meaning mainly Jim and Will—behaved.

'. . . We read the classics to be inspired by the great thoughts of great minds,' Miss Wilcox continued. She had curly auburn hair, and emerald-green eyes. She wore gold jewellery and the most beautiful clothes. She always looked so odd in our plain schoolroom, like some precious jewel put in a battered old gift box.

After torturing us with a few more pages of *Paradise Lost*, Miss Wilcox finally finished the lesson and dismissed the class. Jim and Will Loomis tore out of the schoolhouse, cuffing Tommy Hubbard on their way, shouting, 'Hubbard, Hubbard, nothing in your cupboard!' The Loomis boys were always agitating with the Hubbards, like a pack of hounds after possums.

Mary Higby and I gathered up the half-dozen copies of the book that our class of twelve shared. Abby cleaned the board and Lou collected the slates we'd used to do arithmetic earlier in the day.

I was ready to leave when Miss Wilcox said, 'Mattie, stay after, will you?' We were all 'Mr' and 'Miss' during class, but afterwards she called us by our first names. I told Weaver and my sisters that I'd catch up. When the others were gone, Miss Wilcox opened her desk, took out an envelope and held it out to me. It had a return address and as soon as I saw what it was, my mouth went as dry as salt.

'Here, Mattie. Take it.' Miss Wilcox was smiling.

I took it. Miss Wilcox drew an enamelled case from her bag, pulled a cigarette from it, and lit it. My aunt Josie had told me and my sisters that Miss Wilcox was fast. Beth thought she meant the way our teacher drove her automobile, but I knew it had more to do with her smoking and having bobbed hair.

I took a deep breath and ripped the envelope open. There was a sheet of paper inside clipped to my battered composition book. *Dear Miss Gokey*, it read. *It is with great pleasure that I write to inform you of your acceptance to Barnard College. Furthermore, I am pleased to award you a full Hayes scholarship sufficient to meet the cost of your first year's tuition, contingent upon the successful completion of your high school degree. This scholarship is renewable each year. With all best wishes, Dean Laura Drake Gill.*

'Mattie! What does it *say*?'

I looked at my teacher, barely able to breathe, much less speak. 'It says I'm accepted,' I finally said. 'And that I've got a scholarship. A full scholarship. As long as I pass my exams.'

Miss Wilcox let out a whoop and hugged me. Good and hard. She took me by my arms and kissed my cheek, and I saw that her eyes were shiny. I didn't know why it meant so much to her that I'd got myself into college, but I was glad that it did.

'I knew you'd do it, Mattie! I knew that Laura Gill would see your talent. Those stories you sent were excellent! Didn't I tell you they were?' She twirled round in a circle. 'Can you imagine?' she asked, laughing. 'You're going to be a college student. You and Weaver both! This fall! In New York City, no less!'

As soon as she said it, as soon as she talked about my dream like that and brought it out in the light and made it real, I saw only the impossibility of it all. I had a pa who would never let me go. I had no money and no prospect of getting any. And I had made a promise—one that would keep me here even if I had all the money in the world. My feelings must have been on my face, because Miss Wilcox's smile suddenly faded.

'You're working at the Glenmore this summer, aren't you?' she said.

I shook my head. 'My pa said no.'

'Well, not to worry. My sister Annabelle will give you room and board in exchange for a bit of housekeeping. She has a town house in Murray Hill and she's all alone in it, so there would be plenty of room for you. Between the scholarship and Annabelle, that's tuition, housing and meals taken care of. For book money and clothing and such, you could always get a job. Something part-time, perhaps.'

'I suppose I could,' I said weakly.

'What about your father? Can he help you at all?'

'No, ma'am.'

'Mattie . . . you've told him, haven't you?'

'No, ma'am, I haven't.'

Miss Wilcox nodded, curt and determined. 'I'll talk to him, Mattie. I'll tell him if you want me to,' she said.

I laughed at that—a flat, joyless laugh—then said, 'No, ma'am, I don't. Not unless you know how to duck a peavey.'

un • man

'Afternoon, Mattie!' Mr Eckler called from the bow of his boat. 'Got a new one. Just come in. By a Mrs Wharton. *House of Mirth,* it's called. I tucked it in behind the coffee beans, under "W". You'll see it.'

'Thank you, Mr Eckler!' I called back, excited at the prospect of a new book.

The Fulton Chain Floating Library is a tiny room, an over-eager closet, really, below decks in Charlie Eckler's pickle boat. It is nothing like the proper library they have in Old Forge, but it has its own element of surprise. Mr Eckler uses the room to store his wares, and when he finally gets round to moving a chest of tea or a sack of cornmeal, you never knew what you might find. And, once in a while, the main library in Herkimer sends up a new book or two.

The boat is a floating grocery store and serves all the camps and hotels along the Fulton Chain. Nothing on water—or land, for that matter—looks quite like it. There are milk cans on top of it, bins full of fruits and vegetables on the deck, and a huge pickle barrel in the back, from which it takes its name. Inside the cabin are sacks of flour, cornmeal, sugar, oats and salt; a basket of eggs; jars of candy; bottles of honey and maple syrup; a box of cigars; a box of venison jerky; and three lead-lined tea chests packed with ice—one for fresh meat, one for fish, and the third for cream and butter. Mr Eckler sells a few other items as well, like nails and hammers, needles and thread, postcards and pens, cough drops and fly dope.

I stepped onto the boat and went belowdecks. *The House of Mirth* was under 'W', like Mr Eckler said it would be. I signed it out in a ledger he kept on top of a molasses barrel. I remembered to get the ten-pound bag of cornmeal we needed.

Just as I was about to climb back upstairs, something caught my eye—a box of composition books. Real pretty ones with hard covers and a ribbon. I picked one up. Its pages were smooth and white.

When I got back on deck, I saw that Royal Loomis had come on board. He was paying for ten pounds of flour, a tin of tooth powder and a bag of nails. He frowned at the amount on the till and counted his change twice, chewing on a toothpick all the while.

'Hey, Royal,' I said.

'Hey.'

I handed Mr Eckler fifty cents of my father's money for the cornmeal. 'How much is this?' I asked, holding up one of the pretty composition books. I had sixty cents from all the fiddleheads Weaver and I had sold to the Eagle Bay Hotel. It was money I knew I should have given to my pa. I'd meant to, I just hadn't got round to it.

'Them notebooks? Them are expensive, Mattie. Eye-talians made 'em. Got to get forty-five cents apiece,' he said.

Forty-five cents was a good deal of money, but I had more ideas for stories and poems. I took the money from my pocket and gave it to Mr Eckler quickly, so the thing was done and I couldn't change my mind. Then I watched breathlessly as he wrapped my purchase in brown paper and tied it with string. I thanked him as he handed me the package, but he didn't hear me because Mr Pulling, the stationmaster, was asking him the price of his oranges.

I heard a thump on the dock behind me. 'You like a ride, Matt?' said a voice at my elbow. It was Royal.

'Who? Me?'

'Ain't nobody else here named Matt.'

'All right,' I said, grateful for the offer.

I put the cornmeal in the back of the buckboard, climbed up on the hard wooden seat and settled myself next to Royal. Buckboards are all anyone drives in the North Woods. They are plain—just a few planks with a pair of axles nailed on under them, a seat or two, and maybe a wagon box on the top. Plain is what works best on the bad roads.

'Giddy-up!' Royal told the horses. He coaxed them to turn the creaky rig round in the hotel's drive. The horses, a pair of bays, were new. Pa said Mr Loomis had bought them cheap from a man outside Old Forge who'd lost his farm to the bank.

Royal raised his hand in greeting to Mr Satterlee, the tax assessor, who passed us on his way to the hotel. 'Bet he's just come from the Hubbards',' Royal said. 'He's slapping a lien on their land. That good-for-nothing Emmie didn't pay her taxes again.'

I wondered at his harshness. 'Royal, what do you have against the Hubbards?' I asked. 'They're just poor folks. They don't hurt anyone.'

I got a snort for an answer. Royal didn't speak at all as we went up the hotel's long drive. We passed the railroad station and crossed the tracks and then the highway—a narrow dirt road that ran between Old Forge and Inlet. That was Eagle Bay, every bit of it—a bay on Fourth Lake, a hotel sitting on it, a railroad station, a set of railroad tracks and a dirt road. As he steered the team towards the Uncas Road, he suddenly said, 'You still playing that game? Fooling with words and such.'

'It's not fooling,' I said defensively. He made my word of the day sound childish and silly.

'What was the word today?'

'*Unman*.'

'What's it mean?'

'To break down the manly spirit. To deprive of courage.'

'Huh. Had that right on the tip of your tongue, didn't you?' He nodded at the book in my lap. 'What you got there?'

'A novel. *The House of Mirth*.'

He shook his head. 'Words and stories,' he said, turning onto the Uncas Road. 'Waste of time, if you ask me.'

'I didn't ask you.'

'A man's got to know how to read and write, of course, to get along in the world and all, but beyond that, words are just words. They're not very exciting. Not like fishing or hunting.'

'How would you know, Royal? You don't read. Nothing's more exciting than a book.'

'That so?' he said.

'Yes, that's so,' I said. Finishing it. Or so I thought.

'Huh,' he said. And then he snapped the reins. Hard. And barked, 'Giddy-up!' Loudly. I heard the horses snort as he gave them their head. The buckboard shuddered, then picked up speed.

I looked at the team, new and unpredictable, and then at the Uncas Road, which was nothing but rocks and holes. 'Are we in a hurry, Royal?' I asked.

He looked at me. His eyes sparked mischief. 'This is the first time I've had them out. Don't really know what they'll do. Sure like to see what they're made of, though . . . Hee-YAW!'

The horses lurched forward; their hoofs pounding. Mrs Wharton's novel slid off my lap and thudded to the floor, along with my new composition book. 'Royal, stop!' I shouted, clutching the dashboard. The buckboard was bouncing over the rutted road so hard I was sure one of us would fly out of it. But Royal stood up on the seat, cracked the reins and spurred the team on. 'Slow down! Right now!' I screamed. But he couldn't hear me. He was too busy whooping and laughing.

'Stop, Royal! Please!' I begged. And then we hit a deep hole and I was thrown across the seat. I banged my head on the seat back and only kept myself from falling out by grabbing his leg. We took a bend so hard, I felt the wheels on the right side come off the ground, then crash back down. I managed to right myself, one hand still clutching Royal, the other scrabbling at the dashboard. After what seemed like for ever, Royal finally slowed the team to a trot and then to a walk. He sat down. The horses pulled at the reins, snorting and shaking their heads. He talked to them, shushing them, calming them down.

'Hoo-wee!' he said to me. 'Thought we was in the ditch for a second there.' And then he touched me. He leaned across the seat and pressed his hand to my heart. Palm flat against my ribs. In the split second before I slapped it away, I felt my heart beat hard against it.

'Ticker's pounding fit to burst,' he said, laughing. 'Like to see a book do that.'

I picked my things up off the buckboard's floor with shaking hands. I wanted to answer Royal back with something clever and cutting. I wanted to defend my beloved books, to tell him there's a difference between excitement and terror, but I was too angry to speak. I tried to catch my breath, but every gulp of air brought the smell of him with it—warm skin, tilled earth, horses. I closed my eyes but only saw him standing on the buckboard seat, whooping. Tall and strong against the sky. Heedless. Fearless. Perfect and beautiful.

I thought of my word of the day. Can a girl be unmanned? I wondered. By a boy? Can she be unbrained?

Hamlet is drooling again. I toss him a buttermilk pancake from the plate I'm holding, and he swallows it in one gulp. Hamlet belongs to Mr Phillip Palmer—a lawyer from New Jersey. I met him two weeks ago, just after he arrived. He bounded into the dining room and backed me into a corner, trying to get at a platter of bacon I was carrying. Hamlet, that is. Not Mr Palmer.

'He won't hurt you, honey!' Mr Palmer yelled from the hall. 'His name is Hamlet. You know why I call him that?'

'No, sir, I have no idea,' I said, not wanting to spoil his fun.

'Because he's a Great Dane! Ha! Ha! Ha! Get it?'

I would have liked to tell Mr Palmer just how old and feeble that joke is, but instead I said, 'Oh, of course, sir! How clever of you!' And for my smiles and admiring words, I earned an extra dollar a week to feed Hamlet and walk him in the woods.

I did not normally look forward to Hamlet's after-supper walk, but tonight I am glad of it. I have figured out a new way to get rid of Grace Brown's letters, and Hamlet is going to help me.

I finish feeding the dog and bring the plate back into the kitchen. Supper ended over an hour ago. It's dusky now. The kitchen is empty except for Bill, the dishwasher, and Henry, the underchef, who is holding a carving knife in one hand.

'Hamlet sends his compliments, Henry,' I say. Henry is German and started at the Glenmore the same week that I did.

'Cooking pancake for dog,' he grumbles. 'For this I make journey to America? Mattie, haf you seen my vetstone?'

He means 'whetstone'. 'No, I'm sorry, Henry, I haven't,' I say, heading back out of the door. I have told him over and over again that sharpening a knife after dark brings bad luck. He doesn't believe me, though, so now I have hidden the whetstone.

'Come on, boy,' I say. Hamlet's ears prick up. 'Let's go.' He trots along. We cross the front lawn and head down to the lake. I look back over my shoulder. The Glenmore is all lit up. I can see people on the porch. The men's cigar tips glow like fireflies in the dark.

We get to the water's edge. 'Wait, Hamlet,' I say. He stands patiently as I scoop up a handful of stones. 'Come on, now,' I tell him, leading him onto the dock. He follows me happily.

All I have to do now is slip a few stones into one of the envelopes and throw the bundle into the water. It's not exactly what Grace Brown asked of me, but it will have to do. I'm just reaching into my pocket for the letters when out of the darkness a voice says, 'Going swimming, Matt?'

I'm so startled that I cry out and drop all my stones. I look to my right and there is Weaver, still in his waiter's jacket, his trousers rolled up to his knees, sitting on the edge of the dock.

'Very funny, Weaver! You frightened me to death!'

'Sorry.'

'What are you doing out here?' I ask, then realise I know the answer already. He comes here every night now to grieve. I should have remembered that.

'I was looking at the boat,' he replies. 'The one that couple took out. The *Zilpha* towed it back.'

'Where is it?'

'There.' He points to the far end of the dock. A skiff is tied there. Its cushions are gone and its oarlocks are empty. 'I went into the parlour after supper. To look at her.' He is staring out at the lake. He closes his eyes. When he opens them again, his cheeks are wet. His hand finds mine. 'I hate this place, Mattie,' he says. 'It kills everything.'

wan

A week had passed since my letter had arrived from Barnard College, but I was no closer to figuring out a way to get myself there.

A blue jay flew overhead, screeching at me, pulling me out of my thoughts. I looked up and realised I had walked past the drive to the Cliff House on Fourth Lake and was nearly at the turnoff that led to my friend Minnie Compeau's house. I neatened the bunch of violets in my hand. I'd picked them for Minnie. To cheer her up. The baby was only a month off and it was making her tired and weepy and *wan*.

Wan, my word of the day, means having a sickly hue or an unnatural pallor. Showing ill health, fatigue or unhappiness; lacking in forcefulness or competence.

Halfway down the dirt road Minnie's house came into view. It was a one-room log house, low and squat. Minnie's husband, Jim, had built it from trees he'd felled. Their land was on the north shore of Fourth Lake, and they were hoping to take in boarders one day when they had more acreage cleared and a better house built.

I turned onto Minnie's drive, feeling in my pocket for the letter from Barnard. I'd brought it to show her. I had so much I wanted to tell Minnie, but I didn't get to tell her anything that day, because as I was halfway up the plank path, I heard a terrible scream, full of fear and pain. It came from inside the house.

'Minnie!' I shouted, dropping my flowers. 'Minnie, what is it?'

All I got for an answer was a low moan. Someone was killing her, I was sure of it. I ran onto the porch, grabbed a log from the woodpile, and dashed inside, ready to bash that someone's head in.

'Put that down, you fool,' a woman's voice said from behind me.

But before I could even turn round to see who'd spoken, another scream pierced the air. I looked across the room and saw my friend. She was lying in her bed, heaving and arching and screaming.

'Minnie! Min, what is it? What's wrong?'

'Nothing's wrong. She's in labour,' the voice behind me said.

I whirled round and saw a hefty blonde woman stirring rags into a pot of boiling water. Mrs Crego. The midwife.

Labour. The baby. Minnie was having her baby. 'But, she . . . she's not due,' I stammered. 'She's only eight months gone.'

'Then Dr Wallace is a bigger fool than you are.'

'You building a fire, Matt?' a weak voice rasped.

I turned again. Minnie was looking at me and laughing, and I realised I was still holding the log aloft. Then, quick as it came, her laughter stopped and she groaned, and the fear came back into her face. I saw her twist herself against it, saw her hands clutch at the bed-sheets. 'Oh, Mattie, it's going to tear me apart,' she whimpered.

Mrs Crego pushed me towards Minnie. 'Since you're here, you might as well help,' she said. 'Baby won't make up his mind. First he wants to come early, now he don't want to come at all.' She went to dig in her basket and pulled out dried herbs, a knob of ginger and a jar of chicken fat. 'I was on my way up the road to visit Arlene Tanney—she's due in a week—and I thought I'd just stop in to check on Minnie,' Mrs Crego went on. 'Found her on the porch steps. Said she'd been having pains off and on for two days. Said she told the doctor, but he said she shouldn't worry about it. The jackass. She's lucky I came by. Luckier still you did. It's going to take two of us to get this baby out.'

'But . . . but Mrs Crego,' I stammered, 'I can't help . . . I . . . I don't know what to do.'

'You'll have to. There's no one else,' she said. 'You've helped your father bring calves, haven't you? It's the same thing. Pretty much.'

Oh no, it isn't, I thought. I loved our cows, but I loved Minnie so much more.

The next six hours were the longest of my life. Mrs Crego ran me ragged. I built a fire to warm up the house. I rubbed Minnie's back and her feet. Mrs Crego sat on the milking stool and rubbed Minnie's belly and pressed it and put her ear against it. Minnie's belly was so big it scared me. I wondered how whatever was in it would ever get out. I stroked her head and sang 'Won't You Come Home, Bill Bailey?', her favourite song, only I changed Bill Bailey to Jim Compeau, which made her laugh when she wasn't moaning.

Towards afternoon Mrs Crego took another herb out of her basket. Pennyroyal. She made a tea out of it and made Minnie drink a big cupful. The pains got worse. She was in agony. She suddenly wanted to push, but Mrs Crego wouldn't let her. *She* pushed Minnie's belly instead and rubbed and kneaded until she was panting and the sweat was streaming down her face. Minnie looked up at me, her eyes searching mine, and said, 'Mattie, will you tell Jim I love him?'

'I'm not telling him any such mush. Tell him yourself when the baby's out.'

'He's not coming out, Matt.'

'Hush. He is, too. He's just taking his time, that's all.'

Mrs Crego sat down on the milking stool again and placed her hands on Minnie's belly, moving them all around. It seemed to me that she was listening with her hands. She frowned as she listened.

'Is he coming out now?' I asked.

'They. She's got two babies.' Mrs Crego stood up and heated more water. She dunked her hands in it, then soaped them up, and her wrists and arms, up to her elbows. Then she rubbed her hands with chicken fat and shoved the milking stool back in place. 'One wants to come out feet first. I'm going to try and turn him. Hold her now, Mattie.'

I threaded my arms through Minnie's. 'What's going on, Matt?' she whispered. She sounded so scared.

'It's all right, Min, it's all right . . .' But it wasn't.

Mrs Crego put her left hand on Minnie's belly. Her right hand disappeared under Minnie's shift. Minnie screamed and I thought for sure Mrs Crego would kill her. I held her arms tightly and buried my face in her back and prayed for it to end. I'd never known it was like this for a woman. Never. We'd always been sent to Aunt Josie's when Mamma's time was near. We would stay there overnight, and when we came back, there was Mamma smiling with a new baby in her arms.

'He's turned!' Mrs Crego suddenly shouted.

I risked a glance at her. Her hands were on Minnie's knees; her right one was bloodied. Minnie's screams had become short, repeating keens, the kind an animal makes when it's badly hurt.

'Come on, girl, push!' Mrs Crego yelled.

I let go of Minnie's arms. She took my hands, squeezed them so I thought she would crush them, and pushed for all she was worth. I could feel her against me, arching and gripping, could feel her bones shifting and cracking. And then, finally, with a noise that was part scream, part groan, part grunt, and sounded like it came from deep inside the earth instead of deep inside Minnie, a baby came.

'Here he is! Go on, Minnie, push! Good girl! Good girl!' Mrs Crego cheered, guiding the baby out.

He was tiny and blue and covered in blood and what looked like lard, and he struck me as thoroughly unappealing. I started laughing, delighted to see him despite his appearance and, two seconds later, Mrs Crego handed him to me and I was sobbing, overwhelmed to be holding my oldest friend's brand-new child.

The second baby, a girl, came with far less ado. Mrs Crego tied off the thick grey cords attached to the babies' bellies and cut them, which made me feel woozy. We got Minnie cleaned up and the babies, too, and found fresh sheets for the bed. Then Mrs Crego told me to sit down and catch my breath, but I must have fallen asleep, because when I opened my eyes, I saw Minnie nursing one of the babies and smelt biscuits baking and soup simmering.

Mrs Crego handed me a cup of plain tea. 'You look worse than Minnie does,' she said, laughing. Minnie laughed, too.

I did not laugh. 'I am never going to marry,' I said. 'Never.'

'Well, we'll see about that,' Mrs Crego said. Her face softened. 'The pain stops, you know, Mattie. And the memory of it fades. Minnie will forget all about this one day.'

'Maybe she will, but I surely won't,' I said.

There were footsteps on the porch, and then Jim was inside, bellowing for his supper. He stopped his noise as soon as he saw me and Mrs Crego, and his wife in bed with two new babies beside her.

'You've got a son,' Mrs Crego said to him. 'And a daughter, too.'

'Min?' he whispered, looking at his wife.

Minnie tried to say something but couldn't. She just lifted one of the babies up for him to take. The emotion on his face, and then between him and Minnie, was so strong, so naked, that I had to look away.

I shifted in my chair, feeling awkward, and heard the letter crinkle in my pocket. I had been so excited to tell Minnie all about Barnard, but it didn't seem like so much now. I stared into my teacup, wondering what it was like to have what Minnie had. To have somebody love you like Jim loved her. To have two tiny new lives in your care.

I wondered if all those things were the best things to have or if it was better to have words and stories. Miss Wilcox had books but no family. Minnie had a family now, but those babies would keep her from reading for a good long time. Some people, like my aunt Josie, had neither love nor books. Nobody I knew had both.

plain • tive

'Is this how you spend the money I give you? Making up Mother Goose rhymes?'

I jerked awake at the sound of the angry voice, uncertain for a few seconds where I was. My eyes grew accustomed to the lamplight and I saw my new composition book under my hand and realised it was late at night and that I'd fallen asleep at the kitchen table.

'Answer me, Mattie!'

I sat up. 'What, Pa? What money?' I mumbled, blinking at him.

There was fury on his face and alcohol on his breath. Through the sleep fog in my head, I remembered that he'd gone to Old Forge earlier that afternoon to sell his syrup. It was his habit on these trips to go into one of the saloons there and allow himself a glass or two of whiskey and some male conversation. He usually didn't get back before midnight. I'd planned to be in bed well before then.

'The housekeeping money! The fifty cents I give you for a bag of cornmeal! Is this where it's gone?'

Before I could answer him, he grabbed my new composition book off the table and ripped out the poem I'd been writing.

'*. . . a loon repeats her plaintive cry, and in the pine boughs, breezes sigh . . .*' he read. Then he crumpled the page, opened the oven door, and threw it on the coals.

'Please, Pa, don't. I didn't spend the housekeeping money on it. I swear it. The cornmeal's in the cellar. You can look,' I pleaded, reaching for my composition book.

'Then where did you get the money for this?' he asked, holding it away from me.

I swallowed hard. 'From picking fiddleheads. Me and Weaver. We sold them. I made sixty cents.'

The muscle in Pa's cheek jumped. When he finally spoke, his voice was raspy. 'You mean to tell me we've been eating mush for days on end and you had sixty cents all this time?'

And then there was a loud, sharp crack and lights were going off in my head and I was on the floor, not at all sure how I'd got there. Until I tasted blood in my mouth and my eyes cleared and I saw Pa standing over me, his hand raised.

He blinked at me and lowered his hand. I got up. Slowly. My legs were shaky and weak. I steadied myself against the kitchen table and wiped the blood off my mouth. I couldn't look at my pa, so I looked at the table instead. There was a bill of sale on top of it, and money—a dirty, wrinkled bill. Ten dollars. For twelve gallons of maple syrup. I knew he'd been hoping for twenty.

I looked at him then. He looked tired. So tired. And worn and old.

'Mattie . . . Mattie, I'm sorry . . . I didn't mean to . . .' he said, reaching for me.

I shook him off. 'Never mind, Pa. Go to bed. We've got the upper field to plough tomorrow.'

Uri • ah, the Hit • tite, stink • pot, wart • hog

John the Baptist was looking dustier than a man should. Even a man who spent all his time wandering around in a desert.

'Mattie, be careful with that! You know those figurines mean the world to me.'

'Yes, Aunt Josie,' I said obediently. I did not want to anger my aunt. Not today. I wanted her in a good mood, for I had finally thought up a way to get myself to Barnard. My aunt Josie had money. Quite a bit of it. Her husband, my uncle Vernon, made a good living with his sawmills. Maybe, just maybe, she would loan a little bit of it to me.

I was cleaning house for my aunt as I did every Wednesday after school. And she was sitting in a chair by the window, watching me work. My uncle and aunt live in the nicest house in Inlet—a three-storey clapboard painted gold with dark green trim. They have no children, but my aunt has nearly two hundred figurines. She says her rheumatism keeps her from doing any real work because it makes her bones ache. Pa says his bones would ache, too, if they had as much lard hanging off them as hers do. She is a big woman.

Pa does not like my aunt Josie, and he did not want me to clean her house. I had started helping my aunt to please Mamma—Josie was unwell and Mamma had worried about her—and it wasn't right to stop just because Mamma died. I knew she wouldn't want me to.

Aunt Josie does not like my pa, either. She never thought he was good enough for my mother. Josie and my mamma grew up in a big house in Old Forge. Josie married a rich man, and she thought my mother ought to have married a rich man, too. She thought Mamma was too fine to live on a farm, and often told her so. But Aunt Josie and Uncle Vernon didn't sleep in the same room like my mother and father had, and Uncle Vernon never kissed her on the lips when he thought no one was looking, or sang her songs.

I put John the Baptist down and picked up Christ in the Garden of Gethsemane. As I polished him, I wondered why on earth someone would collect such junk. Words were so much better to collect. Although I had to admit I hadn't had much luck with my word of the day that morning. *Uriah, the Hittite* was the first word the dictionary had yielded, followed by *stinkpot*, then *warthog*. And then I'd slammed the book shut, disgusted.

I was just going to tell my aunt about Barnard and ask her for the money, when she spoke first.

'There's Alma on her way home,' she said, peering out of the window and craning her neck. Alma McIntyre was the postmistress and my aunt's good friend. 'Who's she talking to, Mattie?'

I looked out of the window. 'It's Mr Satterlee,' I said. 'She's giving him an envelope.'

'Is she? I wonder what's in it. Arn's been seen up at the Hubbard place twice this week, Mattie. You know anything about it?'

'No, ma'am,' I replied, trying to find an opening in the conversation so I could make my request, but my aunt didn't give me one.

'There goes Emily Wilcox,' she said, watching my teacher walk by. 'You know, Mattie, I'm certain that she is from the Iverson Wilcoxes of New York City, but it's odd because Iverson Wilcox has three daughters—two married, one a spinster. But Annabelle Wilcox is a Miss and Emily Wilcox is a Miss—Alma says the return address on her letters always say *Miss* Wilcox. And Emily teaches. She would have to be a Miss if she teaches. She gets letters from a Mrs Edward Mayhew—Alma's sure that's Charlotte, the third sister, and she's obviously married—but if only one is supposed to be a spinster, why are two of them Misses? She also gets letters from an Iverson Jr—that's her brother, of course. And from a Mr Theodore Baxter—I don't know who he is. And from a Mr John Van Eck of Scribner and Sons—a publishing concern. What's a young woman doing corresponding with publishers? They're a very shady bunch. You mark my words, Mattie, there's something fast about that woman.'

As soon as my teacher had turned a corner and Aunt Josie couldn't see her any more, she stopped disparaging Miss Wilcox and changed the topic. To me.

'I heard you were out gallivanting with Royal Loomis,' she said.

I groaned, wondering if the entire county knew. I still hadn't heard the end of it, especially from Weaver, who'd said, 'Gee, Matt, I always knew you liked dumb animals, but Royal Loomis?'

'I wasn't "gallivanting". Royal and I happened to be at the pickle boat at the same time and he gave me a ride home, that's all.'

But Aunt Josie was having none of it. 'Perhaps I can help you out with your trousseau, Mathilda. After you're engaged, that is.'

I turned round to face her, determined to nip her engagement talk in the bud. 'Don't you think you're rushing things a bit, Aunt Josie? It was just a ride home.'

'Now, Mattie, I understand you're probably thinking that attention from a boy like Royal Loomis is more than a plain girl like you should expect. But if he's showing interest, you'd do well to pursue it. You might not get another chance with a boy like Royal.'

I felt my face turn red. I know I have too many freckles and lank brown hair. I know that my hands are rough and my body is small and sturdy. I know I do not look like Belinda Becker or Martha Miller—all blond and pale and airy, with ribbons in their hair. I know all this and I do not need my aunt to remind me.

'Oh, Mattie, dear, I didn't mean to make you blush! I know this must all be very new to you, and I know it must be hard—having lost your dear mother. But please don't fret, dear. I understand a mother's duty towards her daughter, and since your own mamma is gone, I will fulfill it for her. Is there anything you need to ask me, dear?'

I clutched the figurine I was polishing. 'Yes, Aunt Josie, there is.'

'Go ahead, dear.'

My words came out of me in a big, desperate gush. 'Aunt Josie, I want to go to college. If you were going to give me money for china and silver, would you give it to me for books and train fare instead? I've been accepted. To Barnard College. In New York City. I applied over the winter and I got in. I want to study literature, but I haven't the money to go and I thought that maybe if you and Uncle Vernon . . .'

Everything changed as I spoke. Aunt Josie's smile slid off her face like ice off a tin roof.

My aunt didn't reply right away. 'You are just as bad as your no-account brother,' she said finally. 'Selfish and thoughtless. What on earth can you be thinking? Leaving your sisters when they need you?' She nodded at the figurine I was clutching. 'Pride. Very fitting. Pride goeth before a fall. You're on a very high horse, Mathilda. I don't know who put you there, but you'd best get down off it. And fast.'

The lecture would have gone on, but there was a sudden smell of smoke. It had my aunt up and out of her chair in no time, waddling off to the kitchen to check on the pie she had baking. For an invalid, she moves faster than a water snake when she has a mind to.

I remained on the ladder, looking at the figurine in my hand. You're wrong, Aunt Josie, I thought. It's not pride I'm feeling. It's another sin. Worse than all the other ones, which are immediate, violent and hot. This one sits inside you quietly and eats you from the inside out. It's the Eighth Deadly Sin. The one God left out. Hope.

xe • roph • i • lous

Mrs Loomis's kitchen was so orderly and clean that it scared me. Kind of like Mrs Loomis herself did. I was standing in her kitchen, along with Lou and Beth, apologising for Daisy, our cow. She and her calf had smashed through the fence that divides our land from Frank Loomis's. I could see them out of the kitchen window, wallowing in the cow pond.

'I'm sorry about the fence, Mrs Loomis,' I said. 'Pa's fixing it now.'

'That's the second time this month, Mattie.'

'I know it, ma'am. I don't know why she does it,' I said, twisting the rope noose I'd brought with me to fetch Daisy back.

'Must be she's headstrong, then. Tie her in her stall for a few days and cut her feed. That'll fix her.'

'Yes, ma'am,' I said, knowing I would do no such thing to Daisy. 'Well, I guess I'll go and get her now. Come on, Lou, Beth.'

Mrs Loomis had taken a tray of molasses cookies out of the oven just as we'd arrived and they were cooling on the counter. My sisters couldn't take their eyes off them. Mrs Loomis saw them looking. Her thin lips got even thinner. She gave the girls one to split. She didn't give one to me. I saw Mr Loomis take some eggs to Emmie Hubbard yesterday. I thought it was very kind of him and wondered how he put up with such a mean and stingy wife.

Xerophilous, my word of the day, means able to withstand drought. Standing in Mrs Loomis's spotless kitchen, I wondered if only plants could be xerophilous, or if people could be, too.

'Let me see if one of the boys is around to help you,' Mrs Loomis said. 'Will! Jim! Royal!' she shouted out of the window.

'It's all right, we can manage,' I said, heading for the back door.

I walked past the barn to the cow pond. Daisy was at the farthest end of the pond. She was bellowing like someone had cut off all four of her legs. Baldwin the calf was hollering, too.

'Come on, Daisy!' I shouted. 'Come on, girl!'

Lou and Beth finished their cookie and started calling to the cow, too. Between the three of us shouting and Daisy and Baldwin bawling, we were making quite a racket.

'Sounds like the Old Forge town band. Just about as loud and just about as bad.'

I turned round. It was Royal. His shirtsleeves were rolled up, showing his muscled arms, already brown from the sun. His hair, golden and too long, was curling over his ears. He saw me looking and I blushed. Furiously.

Royal stooped down and picked up a few stones. Then he walked round behind Daisy and aimed at her backside. The first one surprised her and the second one got her moving. She ran right towards us. Lou was able to grab her and I slipped the noose over her head. We didn't need to tie Baldwin. He would follow his mother.

I thanked Royal, though it killed me. 'I don't know why she comes here,' I said. 'She has a fine pond of her own.'

Royal laughed. 'She don't come 'cause she wants a swim. It's him she's after,' he said, pointing past the pond to the pasture behind it. Standing at the very edge of the field in the shadows of some pines stood a bull. He was huge and fearsome and as black as midnight, and he was watching us. I hoped that the fence around him was stronger than the one Daisy had ploughed through.

'Well, thanks again, Royal. We'd best be going,' I said, starting off towards the dirt drive that led back home.

'I'll walk you,' he said.

'You don't have to.'

He shrugged. ''T'ain't nothing.'

'I want to lead her, Matt,' Beth said. I let her. Lou walked next to her, her cropped hair swinging free.

Royal talked about farming as we walked. About the corn he and Dan were going to plant and how his father was thinking about buying some sheep. He talked steadily, never giving me a chance to speak. After a while, though, he took a breath, and I told him I was going to college. I told him that I had been accepted to Barnard and that if I could only come up with some money, I would go.

'What on earth you want to do that for?' he asked, frowning.

'To learn, Royal. To read books and see if maybe I can write one myself some day.'

'Don't know why you'd want to do that.'

'Because I do,' I said, annoyed by his reaction. 'And anyways, what do you care?'

He shrugged again. 'Guess I don't. Don't understand it, that's all. Your pa know you're planning this?'

'No, and don't you tell him, either,' I said.

We had fallen behind my sisters and the cows, and it was no surprise when, halfway to the Uncas Road, they disappeared over a hill.

What was a surprise, though, was when Royal stopped suddenly and kissed me. On my mouth. Quick and hard. I didn't protest, I couldn't—I was speechless. All I could think was that kisses from boys like Royal Loomis were for girls like Martha Miller, not me. He took a step back and looked at me. He had an odd expression on his face, the kind of look Lou gets when she's tasted something I've cooked and is trying to decide if she can stomach it.

And then he did it again, pulling me to him, pressing his body against mine. The feel of him, and smell of him, and taste of him, made me dizzy. His hands were on my back, pressing me tighter against him. And then on my waist. And then one moved higher and before I knew what was happening, he was kneading my breast.

'Stop it, Royal,' I said, breaking away, my face flaming.

'What's wrong?' he asked. 'You saving them?' And then he laughed and started back home.

mono • chro • mat • ic

'No, no, no, Mattie! *X* is the *unknown* quantity. If it were known, you wouldn't need the *X*, would you?

I was standing in the middle of the highway, on the verge of despair, staring at the equation he'd drawn in the dirt. We'd spent all week on polynomials. I still didn't understand them, and we had a test coming at the end of the week, a practice for our Regents exam. 'I'm going to fail, Weaver, I know I am.'

'No, you're not. Just calm down.'

'But I can't see how—'

'Hold on a minute, will you?' He chewed his lip and stared off down the road. He sighed and shook his head. Then, all of a sudden, he snapped his fingers and smiled. 'Remember your word of the day?' he asked me, writing *monochromatic* in the dirt.

'Yes,' I said. 'It means of one colour. Or it can describe a person who's colour-blind. But what does that have to do with algebra?'

'Say you didn't have a dictionary, but you knew prefixes, suffixes, and roots. Same way you know the value of numbers. How would you get at the meaning of a word?'

'Well, you'd look at the pieces. *Mono*, a prefix for 'single' from the Greek word *monos*. And *chroma*, for 'colour', also from the Greek. The *ic* at the end would tell you it's an adjective. Then you'd blend all the pieces into one to get the meaning.'

'Exactly! Algebra's the same, Matt. You blend all the pieces into one to get the meaning, which in this case is a number, not a word. You combine your knowns with your unknowns, your numbers with your *X*s and *Y*s, one by one, until you have all your values. Then you add them or subtract them or whatever the equation tells you to do, and then you have your final value, the *meaning*.'

He wrote out another equation, and I began to see what he was talking about. 'Solve it,' he said, handing me the stick. I stumbled a bit with the first one and he had to help me, but by the time he'd written out three more, I'd got the idea well enough.

'Just keep at it. You'll get it,' he told me. 'I know you will.'

I shook my head, thinking about Barnard and how badly I wanted to go there. 'I don't know why I should,' I said. 'There's no point.'

'Don't say that, Matt. Did your aunt give you anything?'

'A lecture.'

'Did you tell your pa yet?'

'No.'

'Why don't you tell him? Maybe he'd let you go.'

'Not a chance, Weaver,' I said.

We started walking again. We were halfway to Eagle Bay on our way home from school. As we rounded the last bend in the road before Eagle Bay, we saw the afternoon train pull into the station.

'There's Lincoln and my mamma,' Weaver said. 'Let's see if she's finished up, Matt. Maybe we can get a ride.'

We crossed the tracks and walked to the station. We threaded our way among the tourists and the conductors and Mr Pulling, the stationmaster, and some workmen bound for one of the hotels.

Weaver's mamma was selling chicken and biscuits and pie. Lincoln, her hinny, was hitched to the Smiths' cart, facing away from the train, so that Weaver's mamma could more easily get at her wares.

'Need some help, Mamma?' Weaver asked.

'Oh yes, honey!' she said. Her face lit up like a lamp at the sight of her son. It always did. Weaver's mamma has a first name, of course. It is Aleeta. And strangers call her Mrs Smith. But everyone around Eagle Bay calls her Weaver's mamma, for that's what she is.

'Hello, Mattie, darlin',' she said to me in her soft drawl.

I greeted her and she handed me a biscuit. She was handsome like her son. Her eyes were kind, but they didn't match her smooth, young face. They had an ancient look to them, as if she'd seen most everything there was to see in this world and would be surprised by nothing.

'See that lady waving from the window, Weaver? Take this to her,' she said, handing him a bundle wrapped in newspaper. She made another bundle. 'That's for the engineer, Mattie. Hand it up to him, honey.' I put my books down in her cart and took the bundle. I walked to the front of the train, not liking the *chumpf chumpf* noises it made.

'That you, Mattie Gokey?' a big voice boomed down at me.

'Yes, it is, Mr Myers. I brought your supper.'

Hank Myers, his face red and sweaty, leaned down and scooped up his bundle. He lived in Inlet. Everyone knew him. He threw candy out of the window for the children on the stretches between towns.

'Here's the money. Tell Weaver's mamma thank you.' He tossed me some coins and a bull's-eye which went in my pocket for Beth.

As I walked back to the Smiths' cart, I passed a couple from the city standing by their luggage. 'Gee whiz, Trudy, hold on, will you?' I heard the man say impatiently. 'I don't see a porter anywhere. Ah! There's a darky. You, boy! I need some help over here!'

Weaver was farther down the platform, but he heard the man. He turned round and I saw a bad look in his eyes. One I knew too well.

I skirted round the man, caught up with Weaver, and took his sleeve. 'Don't pay him any mind,' I said, pulling him along.

'You! Sam! I said I need help over here!'

Weaver shook me off. He turned round and smiled. A huge, horrible smile. 'Why, sure, Mistuh Boss, suh!' he hollered. 'I be right along, suh, right along! On de double!'

'Weaver!' his mother called. Her voice sounded frightened.

'Weaver, don't!' I hissed, not knowing what he was going to do but knowing from experience that it wouldn't be smart or good.

'Here I is, suh!' he said, bowing to the couple.

'Take my bags to that wagon,' the man said, pointing at a waiting buckboard.

'Right away, boss!'

Weaver picked up the largest one, a sleek leather suitcase with shiny brass clasps, lifted it over his head and threw it on the ground.

'Hey!' the man yelled.

'Lan' sakes! I sure is sorry, suh! I'se one clumsy darky, all right. Don't worry, Mistuh Suh, I'll fix it. Yessuh!' Weaver said. And then he hauled off and kicked the suitcase. So hard that it sprang open. Clothes flew everywhere. He kicked it again. 'Yes, suh! Right away, suh! I'se coming, suh! Sho nuff!' he shouted.

The man shouted, too. So did his wife. And Weaver's mamma. But still Weaver kicked the case. Over and over again. And then the conductors were hurrying out of the station, where they'd gone for a cup of coffee, and Mr Pulling, too, and Mr Myers was jumping down from the train, yelling and waving, and in my panic I thought about Weaver's father. And I imagined what Weaver must have seen. White hands on black skin. So many white hands. And I knew that the men running towards us would only make things worse. So I jumped between Weaver and the suitcase, just as he was winding up another kick.

'Please, Weaver,' I said, flinching. 'Stop.'

And he did. He turned away at the last possible second and kicked a mailbag instead of me. I took him by his wrists very gently and pushed him backwards, one step at a time. His arms were stiff and trembly. I could smell anger coming off him. And grief. I pushed him over to his mamma's cart, then I gathered the man's clothing and put it back in the suitcase. The case was badly dented, but the clasps still worked. I closed it and placed it with the rest of the man's luggage.

'Now, see here! He damaged my things!' the man sputtered.

'He's sorry, sir. He didn't mean to.'

'He certainly did mean to! Do you have a cop in this place?'

'No, please!' It was Weaver's mamma. Her eyes were frantic. She was clutching her chicken money. 'I'll pay you—'

But she didn't get to finish her sentence, because another voice cut in. 'No, mister, you surely don't want to make trouble. Best be on your way before his pa shows up. Or his brothers. He's got five. And each one of 'em's meaner than the next.'

It was Royal. He was standing on the platform, arms crossed over his chest. He stood tall. Jim and Will were right behind him. I didn't know where he'd come from. I saw his father's buckboard with milk cans in it. He must have been delivering.

The man looked Royal up and down. He looked at Mr Pulling and Mr Myers, whose faces betrayed nothing, and then he looked up the tracks as if expecting to see Weaver's father and his five brothers bearing down on him. He shot his cuffs. 'Well!' he said. 'Well.' Then he picked up his suitcase, took his wife by the elbow and stalked off to the waiting buckboard.

'That boy's going to bring a world of trouble on his head one day,' Mr Pulling said. 'Everything all right now?'

'Sure is,' Royal said. Then, after Mr Pulling left, he said, 'You like a ride home, Matt?'

'Thank you, Royal, but I'd better see to Weaver.'

He shrugged.

I ran back over to the Smiths' cart. Weaver's mamma had Weaver off to one side and was giving him the tongue-lashing of the century. She was furious. I couldn't hear it all, but I did hear that 'damn fools who get themselves locked up in jail can't go to college.' Weaver's eyes were on the ground, his head was hanging. He raised it for a few seconds, long enough to say something to her, and then in an instant all the rage left her and Weaver put his arms round her.

I didn't think I should intrude, so I dropped the money from Mr Myers into the change can and ran to catch up with Royal. He was about to cross the tracks in the buckboard. Jim and Will were in the back. 'Can I still have that ride?' I called to him.

'Sure.'

I ran round to the other side of the buckboard and climbed in. I was glad to sit down next to him. Glad to have his company on the way home. I was upset by what had happened and in need of someone to talk it over with. 'Thank you, Royal,' I said.

'For what? I'm on my way home anyway.'

'For getting Weaver out of trouble.'

'Looks like he's still got plenty,' he said, glancing back at Weaver and his mother.

'I think his mamma's upset because of what happened to his pa,' I said. Royal knew what had happened to Weaver's father; everyone did.

'Might well be,' Royal said, urging his team across the tracks.

'Maybe that started off just like this suitcase thing did,' I said, my emotions still churning. 'With just a few words. And then the words turned into insults and threats and worse, and then a man was dead. Just because of words.'

Royal was silent, chewing on all I'd said, I imagined.

'I know you told me words are just words, Royal, but words are powerful things—'

I felt a poke in my back. 'Hey, Mattie.'

I turned round. 'What, Jim? What do you want?' I asked, irritated.

'There goes Seymour! Ain't you going to wave?'

'Who?'

'Seymour, Mattie! Seymour Butts!'

Jim and Will howled with laughter. Royal didn't actually laugh, but he grinned. And I was silent the rest of the way home.

Dead. That's what I'll be if Cook catches me walking down the hotel's main staircase as if I were a paying guest. We are only supposed to use the back stairs, but I'd have to walk right by Cook's bedroom to get to them and she's a light sleeper.

It's midnight. I hear the huge grandfather clock in the hall strike the hour. It's dark, but I don't dare light a lamp. There's a big summer moon, though, and the Glenmore has lots of windows, so I can see well enough to not fall down the stairs.

The main house has four storeys plus an attic. Forty rooms in all. When the hotel is fully booked, as it is now, there are over a hundred people in the building. I get to the bottom of the staircase and listen. Now the only sound is the ticking of the clock. To my right is the dining room. It's dark and empty. I pray I don't run into anyone. I pass along the hallway that leads to the parlour and get a fright when I see light spilling out of the room onto the hall carpet, but then I remember: that's where Grace Brown is laid out.

I creep through the dining room towards the doors to the kitchen. Once inside the kitchen, it takes my eyes a few seconds to adjust to the heavier darkness. Then, slowly, Cook's worktable and her big, looming range come into focus. The cellar door is just to the left of them. I twist the knob, and . . . it's locked.

Now what? Grace Brown is gone and her letters should be, too. For a moment I consider sneaking out to the lake and pitching the letters off the dock as I'd planned to do earlier, but it's not decent to run around outside in your nightclothes. I'll have to wait until tomorrow.

I leave the kitchen and head back to the attic. I tell my feet to take me directly upstairs, but they have their own ideas. They take me to the parlour instead, and then to the little bedroom off it. The bruises on Grace Brown's lips look darker in the lamplight, and the cut on her forehead looks meaner.

She probably hit her head on the gunwale as the boat tipped, I tell myself. Yes, that would explain it. That *does* explain it. I do not want to ponder this question any longer, for it brings too many others with it. I neaten Grace's skirt instead.

Her clothes are still damp. Her hair is, too. She had left a small case in the hall. Someone has placed it on the floor next to the bed. Carl Grahm's things are not here. He took them with him. I'd wondered, as I saw him and Grace walk across the lawn to the boathouse, what kind of fool takes a suitcase and a tennis racket rowing?

I am very sorry for Grace Brown, here among strangers. She should be in her mother's house. I decide it's only proper that I keep her company for a spell and I sit down in a wicker chair, wincing as it creaks. I look at the cut, livid and ugly, on her forehead, and the questions I've kept penned up all day rush at me.

Why did Grace Brown give me her letters to burn? Why had she looked so sad? And Carl Grahm—was he Carl or was he Chester? Why did he write 'Carl Grahm, Albany' in the register if Grace called him Chester and addressed her letters to 'Chester Gillette'?

I pull the letters from my pocket. I shouldn't do this; I know it's wrong, but so is that wound on Grace Brown's forehead. I slide the top letter out from under the ribbon, open it, and start to read.

South Otselic, N.Y.

June 19, 1906,

My Dear Chester,

I have done nothing but cry since I got here. If you were only here I would not feel so badly . . . I can't help thinking you will never come for me . . . I am so frightened, dear . . . please write and tell me you will come for me before papa makes me tell the whole affair, or they will find it out for themselves. I can't just rest one single minute until I hear from you . . .

Why did Grace want him to come for her? And why was she so frightened that he wouldn't? He had, hadn't he? He'd brought her to the Glenmore. And why do I care? Why?

re • cou • ri • um • phor • a • tion

'Pa! Pa, come quick! There's a monster in the manure pile! I thought he was dead, but he's not! I poked him with a stick and he growled at me! You've got to come and kill him. Quick! So we can get his sack of gold. He's got a sack of gold with him!'

I heard all this from the milk house. I was pouring buckets of warm milk through a length of cheesecloth to strain out flies and bits of hay. I wiped my hands and went into the barn itself to see what the commotion was all about. Pa was walking towards the door. Abby was already outside. Lou was up in the hayloft, tossing down bales.

'What's going on?' I asked her.

'Beth's telling tales again,' she said. 'I hope she gets a licking.'

I followed my family outside and round to the back of the barn and saw, to my shock, that Beth was not telling tales at all. There was a man, a very dirty man with long, wild black hair, lying in our manure pile.

Beth still had her stick. She prodded him with it. 'Mr Monster?' she whispered. 'Mr Monster, are you dead?'

The monster turned over on his back, opened his bloodshot eyes, and winced at the light. 'Ba da holy jeez, yes. Yes, I tink so,' he said.

'Uncle Fifty!' Beth shouted.

'Damn it, Francis!' my father barked. 'Get up out of there!'

'*B'jour, mon frère. Tais-toi, eh? Ma tête, elle est très tendre . . .*'

'*C'est pas assez que tout que tu dis c'est de la merde, François? Tu veux coucher dans la merde, aussi?*'

Only my uncle Fifty, my father's younger brother, can make him angry enough to speak French.

'Mattie, go to my bedroom and get him some clothes,' Pa said. Don't let him in the house until he washes. Make him some coffee, too.' He looked at his brother one more time then returned to the cows.

'Come on, Uncle Fifty, let's get you cleaned up,' I said impatiently. By the time I got water boiled for a bath and got the nits and tangles out of my uncle's hair, I'd be good and late for school. And Miss Wilcox was giving the last of the Regents exams.

Lou came running out. 'Uncle Fifty!' she shouted. She looked at him and her smile changed to a frown. 'Uncle Fifty, why are you sitting in the manure?'

'Because da manure, she warm,' he said, getting to his feet. 'I come last night, very late, Louisa. I don't wake up da whole house, no? So I sleep out here.'

'You smell terrible!' Lou said, pinching her nose.

'What? I smell sweet as da rose! You give your uncle François a beeg keese!' He put out his arms and staggered towards her, and she ran away squealing and laughing.

'Uncle Fifty . . . what's in that bag?' Beth asked, eyeing his satchel.

'In dere? Oh, noting. Just dirty clothes,' he said. Beth's face fell.

'Uncle Fifty, you come on,' I said. 'I haven't got time for this. I've got important tests to take today.'

'Test? What kine of test?'

'For my high school diploma. The last exams are today.'

'Ba da holy jeez, Mathilde! You wan smart girl for to take dese test. You go on to school. Your mamma will help me wid da bath.'

'Oh, Uncle Fifty, you haven't heard, have you?'

'Heard what?'

I sighed. 'Come on. There's lots to tell you. And none of it good.'

I had Lou to help me, so I was able to get my uncle seen to quicker than I'd thought. I had to hold his hand, though, after I told him about my mother and brother. Uncle Fifty doesn't hold much back. When he's happy he laughs, and when he is heartbroken—as he was to hear my mamma had died—he cries like a child.

Miss Wilcox was standing outside the schoolhouse looking for me when I arrived. 'I thought you weren't coming, Mattie! What happened?' she asked. 'Weaver's on his second exam already.'

I explained everything, settled myself, and started my tests. Each one was two hours long. We'd taken two yesterday and were taking three more today. When we had finished, I felt pretty confident. They were my best subjects, though—composition, literature and history. Yesterday's—mathematics and science—had been harder. On the walk home, Weaver told me he thought he'd done quite well in mathematics and history and fairly well in literature and science, but he was worried about composition. It would be a week until we found out our grades.

By the time I got home, it was nearly six o'clock and I'd forgotten all about my uncle. Until I smelt cooking. And heard music from a harmonica, and laughter. And saw lights blazing in the kitchen. It didn't smell, or sound, or even look like my house. Not at all.

'Ba cripes!' my uncle bellowed when I came in the door. He was clean, his hair was shorter, and his beard had been trimmed. He was wearing a fresh shirt and trousers and my mother's apron. 'Where you been? Da supper, she ready since two weeks!'

'I'm sorry, Uncle Fifty,' I said. 'I had a lot of exams.'

'You pass all your test?'

'I don't know. I hope so. I think so.'

'Come on, Mattie, wash up, would you? We're starving!' Beth said.

Uncle Fifty had cooked a feast for us—a real lumberjack supper. He made us all sit down at the table, then he started pulling dishes out of the warming oven one after another. We could barely believe our eyes. There was fried pork and milk gravy, potatoes hashed with onions, baked beans flavoured with smoky bacon, hot biscuits, and a stack of pancakes stuck together with butter and maple sugar.

'Uncle Fifty, I didn't know you could cook,' Abby said.

'I learn dis weentair. Da cook on da St Regis job, he drop dead. Bad heart. All da lombairjock have to take turn cooking. I learn.'

I ate until I thought I would burst out of my dress. And when we were all so stuffed that we were groaning, Uncle Fifty took a rhubarb pie out of the oven and we ate that, too, doused with fresh cream.

When dinner was over, my father and uncle went to sit in the parlour. Uncle Fifty took his whiskey bottle, his satchel, his Croghan boots and a tin of mink oil with him. Beth's eyes never left his satchel as he walked out of the room. 'Do you really think he's got dirty clothes in there?' she whispered.

'I think the dishes need scraping,' I said. 'Get started.'

We washed the dishes just as fast as we could so that we could go sit with our uncle. His visits were rare. He mostly lived in Three Rivers, Quebec, where he and my father were born, and only showed up every two or three years, when logging jobs brought him near.

By the time we settled ourselves in the parlour, Pa had made a fire in the stove. He was mending Pleasant's bellyband and Uncle Fifty was oiling his boots. He drank his whiskey while he worked, and he told us stories—which is what we'd all been waiting for. He told us about the jams and the danger of breaking them up. He told us that he was the number one champion logroller on the St Lawrence, and that he could knock any jack off any log, any jack at all. Except for one—my pa.

It had been years since Pa worked a drive, but I could tell from the look on his face as my uncle talked that he missed it. I saw the pride in his eyes as Uncle Fifty said my pa was the most sure-footed riverman he'd ever seen.

They were whoppers, my uncle's stories, every one. We knew it and we didn't care. We just loved the telling. His full name is François Pierre, but Pa told us his initials really stand for Fifty Percent, because you can only believe half anything he says.

Pa and Fifty are four years apart in age. Pa is forty and my uncle thirty-six. They have the same rugged faces, the same blue eyes and black hair, but that is where the resemblance ends. Uncle Fifty is always smiling and my father is always grim. Fifty sounds like the Frenchman he is. My father sounds like he was born and bred in New York and has no more French in him than Barney the dog does.

I once asked my mother why Pa never spoke French, and she said, 'Because the scars run too deep.' I thought she must have meant the ones on his back. Pa's stepfather put them there with a belt. Pa's real father died when he was six. His mother had seven other children and married the first man who asked her, because she had to feed them. Pa never talked about his mother or his stepfather, but Uncle Fifty did. He told us that the man beat them and their mother for nothing. He did not speak French and wouldn't allow it to be spoken in the house, because he thought his stepchildren would use it to talk behind his back. My father forgot once and that's how he got the scars. I try my best to remember those scars whenever Pa is harsh. I try to remember that hard knocks leave dents.

Pa ran away from home when he was twelve and found work in a lumber camp. He worked his way south, into New York, and never went back to Quebec. His mother died some years back, and his brothers and sisters scattered. Uncle Fifty was the only one he ever saw.

Our uncle kept us entertained with his stories for hours. But around eleven o'clock, Beth got sleepy-eyed and Lou started yawning and Pa told us it was time for bed. Beth cast one last, hopeful glance at our uncle's satchel. Uncle Fifty saw her do it and smiled. He opened the bag and said, 'Well, I plaintee tired myself. I tink I get out my nightshirt now and . . . ba gosh! Wat is in here? Where you tink all dese present come from? I don't reemembair to buy no present!'

Beth jumped up and down. Lou squealed. Even Abby was excited. I was, too. Uncle Fifty always gave the nicest presents. That night he started with Beth and worked his way up, always pretending he'd forgotten to get something for the next one in line. It was agony waiting for your turn. Beth received her very own harmonica with an instruction book and loved it so much, she burst into tears. For Lou, there was a carved wooden box containing a dozen hand-tied fishing flies. Abby was given a gold-plated locket, which made her flush pink with pleasure. And then it was my turn.

'Oh no! I forget someting for Mathilde!' my uncle cried, looking at me. He dug in his bag. 'No, no, wait! I have someting . . .' He placed a narrow ivorine box in my hands, and when I opened it, I gasped. It was a fountain pen, with a metal nib and a silver-plated case and cap. I had never had a pen—only pencils—and I couldn't even imagine what it would feel like to put words onto paper in rich blue ink instead of smudgy lead. I could feel my eyes welling up as I thanked my uncle.

Pa was next—he got a new wool shirt—then Uncle Fifty pulled out a fearsome hunting knife and a pretty beaded bag. 'For Lawton. And your mamma,' he said. 'Maybe you geev heem da knife when he come home, eh?'

'But Uncle Fifty, he ain't never—' Beth started to say. A look from Abby silenced her.

'And maybe you girls can share da bag.'

We all nodded and said we would, but no one took the bag and no one touched the knife. We thanked our uncle again, and hugged him and kissed him, and then it really was time for bed. I picked up all the brown wrapping paper, smoothing it out for another use, as my sisters made their trips to the outhouse.

While I waited for my turn, I went to fetch more wood. On my way back, just as I was about to push the parlour door open, I heard my uncle say, 'Why you not come back and drive da logs, Michel?'

Pa laughed. 'And let four girls raise themselves? All that whiskey's addled your brain.'

'Your Ellen, she make you come off da reevair. Don't tink I don't know. But she gone now, and I tink da reevair be a better ting for you. You like dis farming?'

'I do.'

'Now who tell da tales, eh?' I heard my uncle snort. 'And someting else,' he continued, 'why your son leave, eh?'

There was no answer.

'I tink I know. I tink because you wan miserable sonbitch, dat's why.'

'You've had too much whiskey, Francis. As usual.'

Pa came out then, on his way to the outhouse, and I pretended only to be bringing the wood and not eavesdropping.

'I am proud of you, Mathilde, for all dese test you take. Very proud,' Fifty said, as I opened the door to the cylinder stove.

'Thank you, Uncle Fifty.' I was pleased that he said it, but I wished my father could have told me he was proud of me, too.

'What you do now wid all dese test? You be teechair?'

I shook my head. 'No, Uncle Fifty. You need more schooling for that.'

He thought about that, then said, 'Why you don't go for dis schooling? You plaintee smart girl. Dis schooling, it cost money?'

'The school doesn't. But the train ticket and clothes and books do.'

'How much? Twentee dollair? Thirtee? I give you da money.'

I smiled at him. His offer was so kind, but I knew he'd spent most of his stake, if not all of it, on the supper and our extravagant presents. 'Good night, Uncle Fifty,' I said, getting up to kiss his cheek. 'I'm glad you've come to see us. We missed you.'

'You tink I don't have it, but you see,' he said, winking at me. 'I don't just tell de tale. Not always.'

I waited till Pa came back in before I made a trip to the outhouse myself and then made my way upstairs to my bed.

Lawton was the one who had discovered that voices in the parlour carry right through the wall into the stairwell. I could hear my father and uncle still talking as I walked up the treads.

'Francis, you spent your entire stake, didn't you? On the supper and the presents and whiskey.'

'No, I deed not.'

'I don't believe you.'

'Well, den, look here, Meester Poleeseman . . . a bankair's draft for wan hondred dollair. What you say now, eh?'

'A banker's draft?' Pa said.

'A banker's draft?' I whispered. My goodness, he really does have the money, I thought. He has a hundred dollars and he's going to give me some of it and I am going to college after all.

'Dat's right. Da boss, he give us our money one-half in cash, one-half in dis paper.'

'I'd say he's looking out for you, Fran. You going to hold on to it for a change? Put it in a bank instead of pissing it all away?'

'You wait and see what I do. Dat's all I say. In five, six day, I go to Old Forge and cash dis paper. Den you be surprise, indeed. Now, Michel . . . where is dat whiskey? Where da hell she go?'

I nearly flew the rest of the way up the staircase. As I burrowed down under the covers in the bed I shared with Lou I pictured the look on Pa's face as I told him I was leaving. He'd be furious, but only because he was losing a pair of hands. He wouldn't miss me one bit, but that was all right. I wouldn't miss him, either.

It had been such a long, eventful day that I had completely forgotten to look up a word in my dictionary. It was too late now so I made up my own word. *Recouriumphoration. Re* for 'again', and *cour* for 'courage' and a bit of *triumph* tacked on, too, for good measure. Maybe it will get into the dictionary one day, I thought. And if it does, everyone will know its meaning: to have one's hope restored.

fur • tive

'How about wintergreen hearts, Mattie? Should I get those as well as lemon drops? Abby likes them, too. Lou likes the horehound candy.'

'Why don't you get a few of each?' I said. 'Just stand out of the way, Beth, so folks can get round you.'

The two of us were on the pickle boat with a dozen other people, tourists mainly. We'd just dropped off four cans of milk and three pounds of butter. We'd received no money for them. Pa had bartered with Mr Eckler for a side of bacon earlier in the week, and the delivery was payment against it.

When I had bought my composition book from Mr Eckler a few weeks before, I'd only spent forty-five of the sixty cents I'd made picking fiddleheads. I still had fifteen cents left, and I was using it that afternoon to buy candy for my sisters. It would be a *furtive* purchase, as I really should have given the money to Pa, but after he'd hit me, I'd decided I wouldn't. *Furtive,* my word of the day, means doing something in a stealthy way, being sly or surreptitious.

That fifteen cents was all the money I had in the world right then, but I felt I could afford to be generous with it. Uncle Fifty had left for Old Forge that morning. He planned to stay there overnight and return on the morning train. I'd have my thirty dollars the next day.

'I think I'm going to get some coconut drops, too, Mattie,' Beth said, still deliberating. 'Or maybe some King Leo sticks. Or Necco's.'

'All right, just don't be all day,' I told her.

I saw the Loomises' buckboard draw up to the dock. Royal was driving. I wondered how he managed to be so handsome no matter what he was doing—ploughing, walking, driving, whatever. I thought about the kiss he'd given me, and it made me feel warm and swoony.

Royal's mother was with him. They didn't see me. Beth and I were on the far side of the boat. Mrs Loomis got out, and Royal handed her down a basket of eggs and a large crock of butter. She boarded the pickle boat and gave them to Mr Eckler. He gave her a dollar bill in return. She thanked him and returned to the dock.

'All right, I'm ready,' Beth said.

'Go pay, then,' I said, giving her my money.

She trotted to the back of the boat. 'I'm going to the circus next week. The one in Boonville,' I heard her tell Charlie Eckler.

'Are you, dolly?'

'Yes, sir. My uncle promised to take me. He went to Old Forge this morning, but he's coming back tomorrow and then he's going to take me. Me and Lou both.'

'Well, you'll have a fine time, I'm sure. That'll be ten cents.'

I was watching Royal. He was talking to John Denio, a driver for the Glenmore. They were nodding and laughing. I couldn't take my eyes off him. Had someone that handsome really kissed me?

As I continued to moon, his mother climbed back into the buckboard. Mr Denio made small talk with them for a few more minutes, then headed towards the dock to pick up some guests. As soon as he left them, Mrs Loomis fished in her pocket for the money Mr Eckler had given her, then handed it to Royal. She said something to him, and he nodded and put the dollar bill in his pocket. And then she turned her head and looked all around herself and caught me watching. Her eyes narrowed, and if eyes could talk, hers would have said, 'Mind your own damn business, Mattie Gokey.' I thought it was very strange, as I did not care one hoot what Mrs Loomis did with her egg money.

I watched them head up the drive and then Beth handed me a nickel change and we jumped down off the boat onto the dock. We climbed into our buckboard and I told Pleasant to giddy-up, and of course he didn't budge until I snapped him a good one with the reins. The ride home was uneventful, but when I turned the buckboard into our drive, I got quite a surprise. There was an automobile in it. A Ford. I knew who it belonged to. I got the buckboard into the barn and Pleasant into the pasture, then went inside. When I opened the kitchen door, I saw Lou and Abby sitting on the staircase, leaning towards the wall.

'What's going on?' I asked.

'Miss Wilcox is in the parlour with Pa,' Abby whispered. 'She brought your exam results. You got an A-plus on your English literature and composition tests, an A in history, a B in science, and a B-minus in mathematics. Her and Pa are talking about you. She says you have genius in you and that Pa should let you go to college.'

My heart had sunk to some place down around my ankles. Miss Wilcox meant well, I knew she did, but I also knew Pa. I sat down next to Lou on the step below Abby. Beth sat below us and passed out candy as if we were all spectators at some theatre show. I strained my ears, trying to hear what was being said.

'. . . she's gifted, Mr Gokey. She has a unique voice. And she could make something more of herself, much more, if she were allowed—'

'She don't need to make something more. She's fine as she is.'

'She could be a writer, sir. A real one. A good one.'

'She's already a writer. She writes stories and poems in them notebooks of hers all the time.'

'But she needs to be around people who can nurture her talent and develop it.'

There was a silence. As I sat there on the stairs, I could picture my father's face. There would be anger on it as there so often is, but underneath it, there would be uncertainty and the painful shyness he has around educated people and their big words.

'She wants to go, Mr Gokey. Very badly,' Miss Wilcox said.

'Well, I blame you for that, ma'am. You went and put ideas in her head. I haven't got the money to send her. And even if I did, why would I send my girl where she don't know anyone? She's got a flighty streak in her. Got it from her mamma. She was flighty, too.'

'Surely not, Mr Gokey. I only visited with your wife on two or three occasions, but my reading of her was a woman who loved—'

'Your *reading* of her?'

Oh Lord, I thought. I nearly got to my feet, then realised he couldn't possibly have his peavey with him. Not in the parlour.

'People ain't books, Miss Wilcox. What's inside 'em ain't all type-writ on the page for you to read. Now, if you're about through, ma'am, I've got ploughing to do.'

There was silence again, then: 'I am. Goodbye, Mr Gokey. Thank you for your time.'

I heard her brisk step in the hallway, and then she was gone. Next thing I knew, Pa was in the kitchen. We all scrambled to our feet. 'I guess the four of you just happened to be coming down the stairs all at once,' he said. 'Wouldn't be you were listening in on conversations you had no business listening in on?' No one said a word. 'Abby, you salt the butter yet? Lou, you muck out the cow stalls? Beth, have the chickens been fed?' My sisters scattered.

Pa looked at me. 'You couldn't tell me yourself?' he asked.

His eyes were hard and his voice was, too.

'What for, Pa? So you could say no?'

He blinked at me and his eyes looked hurt, and I thought, just for a second, that he was going to say something tender to me, but no. 'Go, then, Mattie. I won't stop you. But don't come back if you do,' he said. Then he walked out of the kitchen, slamming the door behind him.

ses • qui • pe • da • lian

'*Sesquipedalian* is a funny word, Daisy,' I whispered to the cow. 'It means one and a half feet in length, but it also means given to using long words. It's such a long word itself, though, that it is what it accuses others of being. It is a hypocrite, Daisy, well and truly, but I still like it. And I plan on dropping it into a conversation or two when I'm in New York City.' Daisy chewed her cud as I milked her. It was near the end of April and twelve of our twenty cows had calved and we were drowning in milk.

'Mattie?'

I turned my head to see Beth behind me.

'Why isn't Uncle Fifty back? He said he'd be back from Old Forge by dinnertime today and it's already gone five. He told me he was going to take me to see the circus in Boonville. He said he was.'

'He'll be back. He probably just got talking with someone and took a later train. You know what he's like. He'll be back soon.'

'Are you sure, Matt?'

'I'm sure,' I said. I wasn't. I didn't want to admit it, but I was just as worried as Beth was. Our uncle should have been back hours before.

'Hallooo!' a man's voice shouted from the barn door.

'It's Mr Eckler,' Beth said, skipping off to see him.

'Well, hello there, my girl! Your pa around?'

'I'm right here, Charlie,' Pa called out.

'I brought you the bacon we traded for. It's a nice piece of meat.

And I wanted to ask if I can get five cans from you tomorrow instead of four, and any extra butter you've got.'

'I've got the milk. Cows are giving about fifteen pounds of milk a day each. Got plenty. Should have the butter, too.'

'Glad to hear it. Well, I've gotta get back, but say . . . I saw your brother this morning.'

'What was he doing? Taking the slow train home?'

'No, not quite. He was on a fast train, if you take my meaning. Bound for Utica.'

'Poleaxed?'

'Yup.'

I felt all the breath go out of me. I leaned my forehead against Daisy and squeezed my eyes closed.

My father spat a mouthful of tobacco juice. 'Bet he don't even make it to Utica. Bet he don't get past Remsen,' he said.

'All right then, Michael. I'll see you tomorrow.'

'Night, Charlie.'

'Pa?' Beth's voice was quavery. 'What's *poleaxed* mean? Where's Uncle Fifty? He said he'd take me to the circus, Pa.'

'You can't believe everything your uncle says.'

'But he said he'd take me!'

'Beth, he ain't going to and that's that, so hush.'

'But he promised! I hate him, Pa!' she sobbed. 'I hate him!'

I was sure Beth was going to get cracked for that, but Pa only said, 'No more than he's going to hate himself in a day or two.' Then he told her to stop her noise and take the bacon in to Abby.

I sat slumped on my milking stool, knowing that the last chance I had to go to Barnard was on its way into the till of some bartender. Knowing that my uncle was off on a three-day spree. Or four. Or five. Or however many days it took to spend a hundred dollars. It was a hard and hopeless thing.

'What is it?' a brusque voice suddenly said. It was Pa. He was standing next to Daisy, frowning down at me.

'Nothing,' I said, wiping my eyes. I grabbed my bucket, brushed past him, and went to work in the milk house. I heard his footsteps behind me as I poured the milk into a separating pan.

'Mattie, I don't know what Francis might've said to you, but when he promises things, it's the whiskey promising, not him. You know that, don't you? He don't mean bad; he can't help it.'

'I'm fine, Pa,' I said sharply. 'I'll be along.'

He stood where he was for a few seconds, then left. When I'd cried myself dry, I wiped my face, covered the milk pans with cheesecloth and left the barn for the kitchen. Abby had started the supper. There would be no apple fritters or *tarte au sucre* tonight. No songs. No music. No stories. But there would be fresh spinach, the first crop. And potatoes fried with the bacon Pa had traded for. There would be a big jug of milk, a loaf of bread, and a dish of butter to spread on it.

My father had put these things on the table.

I looked at him washing his hands at the sink, splashing water on his face. My mamma left us. My brother, too. And now my feckless, reckless uncle had as well. My pa stayed, though. My pa always stayed. I looked at him. And saw the sweat stains on his shirt. And his big, scarred hands. And his dirty, weary face. I remembered how, lying in my bed a few nights before, I had looked forward to showing him my uncle's money. To telling him I was leaving. And I was so ashamed.

You can't argue with the dead. No matter what you say, they get the last word. I try to have it out with Grace as I sit with her. I tell her that she was wrong to have given me her letters and that sneaking around on her behalf will cost me my job if I'm not careful.

I look at her and I wonder how she got her nickname, Billy. It was what Chester—no, *Carl*, his name is *Carl*—had called her. Did her pa give it to her? Maybe she had a brother who called her that.

I open another letter.

South Otselic

June 21, 1906
My Dear Chester,

I am just ready for bed, and am so ill I could not help writing to you. This p.m. my brother brought me a letter from one of the girls, and after I read it I fainted. Chester, I came home because I thought I could trust you. This girl wrote me that you seemed to be having an awfully good time and she guessed my coming home had done you good, as you had not seemed so cheerful in weeks . . . I should have known, Chester, that you didn't care for me, but somehow I trusted you more than anyone else . . .

Voices drift past the window. Men's voices. I freeze.

'. . . thinks his name is Gillette.' That's Mr Morrison, the manager.

'Who?' That's Mr Sperry, the owner.

'Mattie Gokey. She said that she heard the girl call him Gillette. Chester Gillette.'

'Well, hell, Andy, I called the police department in Albany and told them that a Carl Grahm had likely drowned and asked them to notify the family. That's what it said in the register, "Carl Grahm, Albany".'

The voices fade. I bolt out of the parlour, race down the hallway and up the main staircase. I make it to the first landing just as the front door opens, and duck down behind the railing, not daring to breathe.

'. . . and there's Gillettes down Cortland way, too,' Mr Sperry says. 'Well-heeled bunch. One of them owns a big skirt factory.'

'South Otselic, where the girl's from . . . that's near Cortland, isn't it?' Mr Morrison says.

'Thirty miles outside it. Mrs Morrison ever get hold of her folks?'

'Yes, she did. Farm family.'

Mr Sperry takes a deep breath and blows it out again. He is silent for a few seconds, then says, 'You fancy a nightcap, Andy?'

'I do.'

'I'll get the bottle. Let's have it on the porch, though. Wouldn't be right to drink in the parlour. Not tonight.'

Mr Sperry disappears down the hall and Mr Morrison busies himself at the reception desk, sorting telephone messages and checking the telegraph machine. I stay put on the landing.

A few minutes go by, then Mr Sperry re-emerges with a bottle in one hand and two glasses in the other.

'Dwight, look at this,' Mr Morrison says, coming out from behind the desk.

'What is it?'

'A wire from Albany. From the chief of police. About Carl Grahm.'

'What's it say?'

'It says there's no such person by that name living in the city.'

The two men look at each other, then they go out on the porch. And I run back to the attic and shove Grace Brown's letters back under my mattress and climb into bed and squeeze my eyes shut and press my hands over my ears and pray and pray and pray for sleep to come.

tott • lish

'Mattie, I'm having the Reverend Miller for tea tomorrow; you'll make sure those figurines are sparkling, won't you?'

'Yes, Aunt Josie.'

She wasn't concerned about her figurines. She just wanted to keep me up on my step-stool dusting, and away from the parlour door, so I couldn't hear what she was saying or see what she was doing. The door wouldn't close all the way and I could see my aunt and Alma

McIntyre through the gap. They were sitting at the kitchen table. My aunt was holding an envelope up to the light.

'This is *stealing*, Josie,' I heard Mrs McIntyre say. 'We're stealing Emmie Hubbard's mail.'

'It's not "stealing", Alma. It's "helping". We're trying to help a neighbour, that's all,' my aunt said.

'Arn Satterlee gave it to me right before I closed for lunch. I've got to put it into the outgoing mailbag by two o'clock or it won't get to Emmie today.'

'You will, Alma, you will; it'll only take a minute . . .'

My aunt said more, but her voice dropped and I couldn't hear it. I got down off the step-stool and moved it closer to the door.

'You all right in there, Mattie?' she hollered.

'Yes, Aunt Josie. I'm just moving the step-stool.'

'Don't come too close to the door with it. The floor's uneven right around there and the stool's tottlish. I wouldn't want you to fall, dear.'

'I won't, Aunt Josie.'

Tottlish means tippy, and is used mostly to describe boats. Miss Parrish never let us use words like tottlish in our essays, but Miss Wilcox did. She said words like those are *vernacular.* I decided tottlish would be my word of the day even though *rectitude* was what the dictionary had given me. I wasn't sure I'd find tottlish in the dictionary.

I heard the sound of water running and the kettle being filled, and I knew that the two of them weren't making a pot of tea. From their conversation I had figured out that Arn Satterlee was sending Emmie Hubbard a letter, and since it was Arn sending it, and Emmie getting it, it had to be about her taxes.

'Alma, look! Oh, my goodness! Arn Satterlee is auctioning Emmie Hubbard's land to recover the back taxes. She owes twelve dollars and seventy cents and hasn't paid a penny of it.'

'But why, Josie? Why now? Emmie never pays her taxes on time.'

'Because she's "habitually derelict" . . . It says so right here, see?'

'Oh, nonsense! This year's no different from any other. Arn gives her a warning or puts a lien on the property if the county makes him, but he never goes so far as to put the land up for sale.'

'Look here, Alma,' my aunt said, 'it says there's an interested party.'

'Who'd be interested? You think it's one of her neighbours?'

'Don't see how it could be. She's only got the three. There's Aleeta Smith, and she wouldn't do a thing like that. Michael Gokey wouldn't, either. And even if they would, they couldn't afford to. That only leaves Frank Loomis, and I doubt he has the money, either.'

There was a pause, then Mrs McIntyre said, 'He wouldn't want Emmie gone, anyway.'

Their voices dropped way down low then and I couldn't hear. Only '. . . disgraceful, Josie . . .' and '. . . I wouldn't tolerate it . . .' and '. . . fills her belly, all right . . .' I couldn't sense their meaning but thought they must be talking bad of Emmie like most everyone does.

They were silent for a minute or so, then my aunt clucked her tongue and said, 'Alma, I'm sure that no local person would do a thing like this. It's a city person from New York, I just know it.'

'Oh, Josie, this is terrible! What will happen to those children?'

'I imagine the county will take them.'

'Poor little things!'

I had heard enough. I got down off the step-stool again and dragged it all the way across the room to the fireplace. The mantelpiece was covered with figurines. I polished it viciously, for I was upset.

Where would Emmie get that kind of money? I wondered. I knew the answer: she wouldn't. Any one of her neighbours would've loaned it to her if they'd had it, but no one did. Aunt Josie did, though. And if she really cared about Emmie and her children, she could have given it to her. And if she'd really cared about me, she could have helped me get to New York City. But all she cared about was her damn figurines.

Emmie would lose her house and land, and the county would take her kids. I couldn't bear the thought of her children being taken and separated and farmed out to strangers. It was one more hard and hopeless thing, and I was tired of hard and hopeless things.

au • gur

'We could walk to Inlet and look in the window of O'Hara's,' Ada Bouchard said. 'They've got some pretty fabric just come in.'

'Or hike up to Moss Lake,' Abby said.

'Or Dart's Lake,' Jane Miley said.

'We could go visit Minnie and see the babies,' Fran Hill said.

'Or sit under the pines and read,' I said.

'*Read?* On a day like today? You need your head checked, Mattie,' Fran said. 'Let's draw straws. Short one decides what we do.'

We were all outside, clustered at the bottom of the Uncas Road. We were off on a jaunt, we just had to decide where. It was a warm and glorious spring afternoon, a Saturday.

Fran broke off some twigs from a bush and made one shorter than the rest. We were about to start drawing them when my choice was made for me. A buckboard pulled up, one drawn by two bay horses.

'Well, Royal Loomis! What brings you this way?' Fran asked.

Royal shrugged. 'Went out for a ride and ended up here,' he said.

'Come to gaze at the lake?' Fran teased.

'Something like that. Hey, Matt, you feel like taking a ride?'

I almost fell over. 'Me?' I said, shading my eyes to look up at him.

'Get in, will you?'

I looked at my friends, not sure what to do. Fran winked. 'Go on!' she whispered. Jane looked at me like she'd never seen me before.

'Well . . . yes, all right,' I said, climbing up.

Royal snapped the reins as soon as I was settled. Jane leaned over to Ada and whispered something in her ear. I realised I would be a topic of conversation among my friends for the rest of the day.

'Want to go to Higby's?' Royal asked. 'Man who works at the boathouse is a friend. They're getting the boats ready for the season. He'll let us take a skiff for free.'

'All right,' I said, thinking that this was all very odd. Then I had a new thought. 'Royal, don't you think you can kiss me again, or anything else. I won't have it,' I said.

He looked at me sideways. 'All right, Matt, I won't. Not unless you want me to.'

'I don't want you to. I mean it,' I said. I'm not your batting practice, I thought. Someone to get it right with before you go see Martha Miller.

'Hey, Matt? How about we just go boating, huh?'

'All right, then.'

'Good.'

When we arrived at Higby's, Royal unhitched his team and put them in the corral. His friend let us have our pick of boats and Royal rowed us out onto Big Moose. I sat facing him and let the perfection of a spring day in the North Woods take my breath away. Royal didn't talk much, but he did point out a family of mallards and a blue heron. I watched him as he watched the heron take flight, his eyes never leaving it, and wondered if maybe I'd been wrong about him. Maybe his quietness masked a great and boiling soul.

It was a quaint notion and one he soon dispelled.

'Skunk et all my chicks last night,' he said. 'Guts and feathers all over the yard. I'd planned to raise 'em and sell 'em come fall.'

'I'm sorry to hear that, Royal.'

He sighed. 'At least I've still got the hen. She oughta breed again, and if she don't, at least she'll fatten up nice. Make good eating.'

'I'm sure she will.'

'I'll miss that money, though. I'm saving up, trying to put some money aside for when I'm out on my own.'

'Are you? What do you want to do?'

'Farm. Land's getting dear up here. A man's got to have a few dollars behind him nowadays. I'd like to have a going dairy concern. Maybe even my own cheese factory some day.'

He was silent for a few seconds, then he said, 'You couldn't give me enough land, Matt. I'd want fifty acres just for my dairy herd. Fifty more for sheep. Twenty for corn, twenty for potatoes and twenty for fruit. Why, you could keep every camp on the lake swimming in berries all summer long.'

'Yes, you could,' I said, trailing my hand in the lake. I realised that I'd never heard Royal talk so much in all the years I'd known him. For the first time, I had seen what was in his heart. I wondered if he would ever want to look deep enough to see what was in mine.

When he finished talking about chickens and cheese and berries, I took a turn talking. I talked about Barnard. And how even though I knew I couldn't go, I still wished I could.

'Why would you want to do that?' he asked. 'Go all the way to New York City just to read books?'

'So maybe I can learn how to write them some day, Royal. I told you this already,' I said, suddenly wanting him to understand.

'Why can't you read books right here? School's a waste of money.'

'I wish I'd never told you,' I said crossly. 'You don't even listen.'

He moved forwards until his knees touched mine. 'I heard what you said, it just don't make sense. Why do you always want to read about other people's lives, Matt? Ain't your own good enough for you?'

I didn't reply to that because I knew my voice would quaver if I did. Turned out I didn't need to, because he kissed me. Even though I'd told him earlier that I didn't want him to. Plain old kisses at first and then a real deep one. And then he put his arms round me and held me to him as best he could in a rowing boat, and it felt so good. No one had so much as hugged me since my mamma died. I wished I had the words to describe how I felt. My word of the day, *augur*, which means to foretell things from omens, had nothing to do with it as far as I could see. I felt warm in his arms. He moved his hands to my breasts. He was more gentle than the time before, but I still pushed him away.

'Stop it, Royal. I'll jump out of the boat if you don't, I swear I will.'

'Let me, Mattie,' he whispered. 'It's all right for a boy and girl to do that . . . as long as they're sparking.'

'Sparking?' I said, shocked. 'That is news to me, Royal.'

'Why else would I have taken you boating? And why did I kiss you in the woods when your cow got out? Why did I plough your field for you? For someone who reads so many books, you're awfully stupid.'

'But, Royal . . . I thought that you and Martha Miller were an item.'

'People talk too much and so do you,' he said. And then he kissed me again, and I tried to tell myself that none of this made any sense. He'd never shown a bit of interest in me unless I counted that one kiss he'd given me when Daisy got out, and now we were sparking. But his lips were sweeter than anything I'd ever tasted. And so I closed my eyes and all I knew was his nearness. And all I wanted was my own story and no one else's. And so I said nothing. Nothing at all.

glean

'Lou, stop.'

'"*. . . then comes Junior in a baby carriage . . .*"'

'Lou!'

'You're blushing, Matt! You're sweet on Royal! I know you are!'

'Nobody's sweet on anybody. And stop saying so.'

Lou started singing her stupid song again, but then something appeared up ahead of us on the road that interested her far more than tormenting me did. An automobile.

The driver pulled up and cut the engine. It was Miss Wilcox. She removed her goggles. 'Hello, Mattie! Lou!' she called, her cheeks pink.

'Hello, Miss Wilcox,' we said together.

'Where are you two off to?'

'We're on our way home from Burnap's. Pleasant, our mule, cracked his bit. We had to get it repaired,' I explained.

'I see. I have been for a drive. Up to Beaver River and back. I'm famished now. Driving always gives me an appetite. Why don't you two hop in? We'll go back to my house and have some lunch.'

I was frightened of the automobile. 'I think we'd best get home, ma'am,' I said. 'Our pa will be looking for us. He needs the bit.'

'Oh, come on, Matt! Pa won't mind,' Lou pleaded.

'I'll tell you what . . . come for lunch and then I'll drive you home. It'll save some time.'

'Pleeeeeease, Matt?' Lou begged.

'I guess it's all right,' I said, more for Miss Wilcox's sake than Lou's. For all her excitement, she seemed a little bit lonely. And I was curious, too. I had never seen the inside of my teacher's house.

Miss Wilcox got out, crank in hand, and started the engine again. It coughed and sputtered, finally caught. When we were seated, she engaged the gears and we were off. 'It's wonderful here in the woods,' Miss Wilcox said, swerving to avoid a squirrel. 'Such freedom! You can do whatever you like and no one minds.'

No, but how they talk! I thought.

Glean, my word of the day that day, has a simple meaning—to gather after the reapers. It is a farming word, but it fits people other than farmers. Aunt Josie is a gleaner. She combs through other people's leavings, looking for enough bits to make a whole story.

Miss Wilcox drove us the mile and a half up the road to Inlet. The old Foster camp on Fourth Lake is a two-storey log house with a stone foundation. Dr Foster is dead now. His sister inherited the house and rents it out. My teacher had been living in it all year.

Miss Wilcox pulled into the driveway and we went inside. It was cool and dark indoors and smelt like oil soap. There were carpets everywhere and wainscoting halfway up the walls and velvet curtains thick and heavy enough to shut out the whole world.

Miss Wilcox led us to an enormous, spotless white kitchen, where she set about fixing us dainty little sandwiches with the crusts cut off, and tiny iced cakes, and tea. I tried to help, but she wouldn't let me. She put the lunch on a tray then led us out of the kitchen, down a different hallway and through a set of tall sliding doors.

What I saw next stopped me dead in my tracks. Books, hundreds of them. In crates. In piles on the floor. In bookcases that stretched from floor to ceiling and lined the entire room. I turned round and round in a slow circle, feeling as if I'd just stumbled into Ali Baba's cave. I was breathless, close to tears, and positively dizzy with greed.

'Won't you sit down and have lunch, Mattie?' Miss Wilcox asked.

But eating was the last thing on my mind. 'Are these all Dr Foster's books?' I whispered.

'No, they're mine. I had them sent up from the city. They're in a bit of a shambles. I never seem to get around to arranging them properly.'

'There are so many, Miss Wilcox.'

She laughed. 'Not really. I think you and Weaver have read half of them already.'

But I hadn't. There were dozens of names I didn't know. Eliot. Zola. Whitman. Wilde. Dickinson. Goethe. And all those were in just one stack! I reached out and touched the cover of one called *The Earth.* I could almost hear the characters inside, murmuring and jostling, impatient for me to open the cover and let them out.

'You can borrow anything you like, Mattie,' I heard Miss Wilcox say. 'Mattie?'

I realised I was being rude, so I made myself stop staring at the books and looked at the rest of the room. There was a large fireplace with two settees in front of it, facing each other across a low table. Lou sat on one of them, stuffing herself with sandwiches. There was a writing table under a window, with pens and pencils and a stack of good paper. I touched the top sheet. It felt like satin. A few more sheets, covered with handwriting all in lines like a poem, were spread haphazardly across the tabletop. Miss Wilcox shuffled them into a pile.

'I'm sorry,' I said, remembering myself. 'I didn't mean to pry.'

'That's all right. It's just a lot of scribbling. Won't you eat something?'

I sat down and took a sandwich and, to make conversation, Miss Wilcox said she had seen me riding with a handsome boy.

'That's Royal Loomis. Mattie's sweet on him,' Lou said.

'No, I'm not,' I said quickly. I was, of course. I was as dopey as a calf for him, but I didn't want my teacher to know.

Miss Wilcox raised an eyebrow.

'I'm not. I don't like any of the boys round here.'

'Why not?'

'I suppose it's hard to like anyone real after Captain Wentworth and Colonel Brandon,' I said, trying my best to sound worldly wise. 'Jane Austen ruins you for farm boys and loggers.'

Miss Wilcox laughed. 'Jane Austen ruins you for everything else, too,' she said. 'Do you like her books?'

'I like them some.'

'Just "some"? Why not a lot?'

'Well, ma'am, I think she lies.'

'Why do you think that, Mattie?'

I was not used to my elders asking me what I think—not even Miss Wilcox—and it made me nervous. I had to collect myself before I answered her. 'Well, it seems to me that there are books that tell stories, and then there are books that tell truths . . .' I began.

'Go on,' she said.

'The first kind, they show you life like you want it to be. With villains getting what they deserve and the hero seeing what a fool he's been and marrying the heroine and happy endings and all that. Like *Sense and Sensibility* or *Persuasion.* But the second kind, they show you life more like it is. Like in *Huckleberry Finn* where Huck's pa is a no-good drunk and Jim suffers so. The first kind makes you cheerful and contented, but the second kind shakes you up.'

'People like happy endings. They don't want to be shaken up.'

'I guess not, ma'am. It's just that there are no Captain Wentworths, are there? But there are plenty of Pap Finns.' My voice trembled as I spoke, as it did whenever I was angry. 'I feel let down sometimes. Why do writers make things sugary when life isn't that way?' I asked too loudly. 'Why don't they tell the truth? Why don't they tell how a pigpen looks after the sow's eaten her children? Or how it is for a girl when her baby won't come out? Or that cancer has a smell to it? All those books, Miss Wilcox,' I said, pointing at a pile of them, 'and I bet not one of them will tell you what cancer smells like. I can, though. It stinks. Like meat gone bad and dirty clothes and bog water all mixed together. Why doesn't anyone tell you that?'

No one spoke for a few seconds. Then Lou said quietly, 'Cripes, Mattie. You oughtn't to talk like that.'

'I'm sorry, Miss Wilcox,' I said, looking at the floor. 'I don't mean to be coarse. I just . . . I don't know why I should care what happens to people in a drawing room in London or Paris when no one in those places cares what happens to people in Eagle Bay.'

Miss Wilcox's eyes were fixed on me. 'Make them care, Mattie,' she said softly. 'And don't you ever be sorry.'

She glanced at Lou, set the whole plate of cakes before her, then rose and beckoned me to her writing table. She picked up a glass paperweight shaped like an apple and took two books from under it. '*Thérèse Raquin*,' she said solemnly, 'and *Tess of the D'Urbervilles*. Best not tell anyone you have them.' Then she took her writing paper out of its box, put the books in the box, covered them with a few sheets of paper, and handed the box to me.

I smiled, thinking that my teacher sure was dramatic. 'Cripes, Miss Wilcox, they're not guns,' I said.

'No, they're not, Mattie, they're books. And a hundred times more dangerous.' Then she asked me, 'Has there been any progress?'

'No, ma'am. And there's not likely to be.'

'Would you consider working for me, then? I need help with my library, as you can see. I'd like you to come and arrange my books. I'll pay you. A dollar each time.'

'I can't, Miss Wilcox,' I said. 'I can't get away.'

'Surely you can, Mattie. Just for an hour or two. I'll drive you home. Come this Saturday.'

I shook my head. 'I've got the chickens to do. The coop needs whitewashing and Pa said he wants it done by Sunday.'

'I'll do it, Matt,' Lou said. 'Me and Abby and Beth. Pa won't know. He'll be out ploughing. He won't raise Cain, long as it gets done.'

I looked at my sister and saw the crumbs round her mouth and her blue eyes big and hopeful, and I loved her so much I had to look away.

'If you come, you can borrow anything you like, Mattie. Anything at all,' Miss Wilcox said.

I imagined myself here on a Saturday afternoon, in this calm, quiet room, digging among all these books, gleaning my own treasures.

And then I smiled and said yes.

de • his • cence

It was seven o'clock on a May evening. It was after the supper was cooked and served, the dishes washed, the pots scrubbed and put away. Lou and Beth were polishing their boots. Abby was sitting in front of the fire with a heap of darning. Pa was mending Pleasant's bridle. And me? I was standing in the middle of the kitchen, looking at my family, my heart pounding so hard I thought it would burst.

I felt as if the very walls themselves were pressing in upon me. As if I would go crazy if I stayed in this prison of a kitchen for one second longer. I leaned against the sink and closed my eyes. I must have sighed or groaned or something, because Abby suddenly said, 'What's wrong, Mattie?'

I opened my eyes again and saw her looking up at me. Even Pa did. *Dehiscence* was my word of the day. It means when pods or fruits burst open so that their seeds can come out. How was it that I could learn a new word every day, yet never know the right ones to tell my family how I felt?

'Nothing's wrong. I'm fine. Just tired, that's all. I . . . I think I forgot to latch the barn door,' I lied, then ran to the shed, grabbed my shawl, and kept going until I got to the eastern edge of Pa's land, and the place where my mother is buried.

I walked around her grave, trying to get hold of myself. My head felt giddy and light, like the time Minnie and I filched brandy from her father's cupboard. Only this time it wasn't alcohol I'd had too much of. It was books. I should have stopped after Zola and Hardy, but I hadn't. I'd gone right on like a greedy pig to *Leaves of Grass* by Walt Whitman, *Songs of Innocence* by William Blake, and *A Distant Music* by Emily Baxter.

I'd borrowed the volumes of poetry on Saturday, when I'd gone back to Miss Wilcox's house to start organising her books. 'You can keep this one, Mattie,' she'd said about the Baxter, 'but keep it to yourself.' I didn't need telling. I'd read articles about *A Distant Music* in Aunt Josie's newspapers. They said that Emily Baxter was 'an affront to common decency', 'a blight on American womanhood'. It had been banned by the Catholic Church and publicly burned in Boston.

I thought there would be curse words in it for sure, but there weren't—only poems. One was about a young woman who gets an apartment in a city by herself and eats her first supper in it all alone. But it wasn't sad, not one bit. Another was about a mother with six children, who finds out she's got a seventh coming and gets so low spirited, she hangs herself. And one was about God being a woman instead of a man. That must've been the one that made the Pope boiling mad.

Emily Baxter's poems made my head hurt. They made me think of so many questions and possibilities. I was agitated something fierce. There was a whole other world beyond Eagle Bay, with people like Emily Baxter in it, thinking all the things you thought but weren't supposed to. Writing them, too. And when I read what they'd wrote, I wanted to be in that world. Even if it meant I had to leave this one. And my sisters. And my friends. And Royal.

I stopped pacing and hugged myself for warmth. My eyes fell on my mamma's headstone. ELLEN GOKEY. BELOVED WIFE AND MOTHER. BORN SEPTEMBER 14, 1868. DIED NOVEMBER 11, 1905. I missed her all the time, I missed her dreadfully just then. I wondered what she would make of Emily Baxter.

I traced the letters of my mother's name on the cold grey stone and conjured my favourite memories of her. I saw her reading to us at night from *Little Women* or *The Last of the Mohicans*. I saw her reading the poems I wrote her for her birthday. She used to tell me that I wrote real nice, as nice as Louisa May Alcott, even. I remembered her singing as she cooked. I remember how she made us fancy braided hairdos and how she trudged through the winter fields on snowshoes to bring Emmie Hubbard's kids a pot of stew.

I tried very hard to remember only the good things about my mamma. To remember her the way she was before she got sick. But I couldn't. No matter how hard I struggled to keep my last images of her at bay, they came anyway.

I saw her as she looked right before she died, her body wasted, her face hollowed out. I saw her as she wept and moaned with pain. I saw her as she kissed Lawton and me and my sisters over and over again, pressing our faces between her hands. I saw her as she begged me never to go away, as she made me promise to take care of her babies.

And I saw myself, tears in my eyes, promising her I would.

The memories faded. I opened my eyes. It was getting late. Pa would be wondering where I was. As I turned to go, I nearly trod on the body of a young robin half hidden in the grass. Its wings were twisted and bent. Its body stiff and bloodied. A hawk's work, I thought, wondering if the robin had seen the brilliant blue of the sky and felt the sun on its back before its wings were broken.

I mean to go to sleep, too. I try to, but I can't. Every time I shut my eyes, I see Grace's battered face.

I wait for a bit. Until I hear no bedsprings creaking, no sighs or groans as some girl tries to make herself comfortable in the heat. And then quietly, carefully, I unfold the letter. It's dark in the room now, but there's a window next to my bed and I can make out Grace's words if I hold her pages in the moonlight.

South Otselic

June 23, 1906
My Dear Chester,

I am just wild because I have been home nearly a week and have not had one line from you . . . I miss you, oh dear, you don't know how much I miss you. I am coming back next week unless you can come for me right away. I am so lonesome I can't stand it. Week ago tonight we were together . . .

There is no Carl Grahm, only a Chester, a 'Dear Chester'. He lived in Cortland, not Albany, because the letters are addressed to him there. And Grace lived there, too, at some point, even though the return address on her letters says South Otselic, because she mentions she left the place, and says she will come back if he doesn't come for her.

I open another letter. It has no greeting.

S. Otselic

Sunday Night

I was glad to hear from you and surprised as well . . . You tell me not to worry and think less about how I feel and have a good time. Don't you think if you were me you would worry? . . . I understand how you feel about the affair. You consider it as something troublesome that you are bothered with. You think if it wasn't for me you could do as you liked all summer and not be obliged to give up your position there. I don't suppose you have ever considered how it puts me out of all the good times for the summer and how I had to give up my position there . . .

Was Grace sick? I wonder. Is that why she had to give up her position? Did they work at the same place? Maybe at that place Mr Sperry was talking about—the skirt factory that the well-heeled Cortland Gillettes owned. But why would they both have to give up their positions? It didn't make any sense.

> *. . . Chester, I don't suppose you will ever know how I regret being all this trouble to you. My whole life is ruined and in a measure yours is, too. Of course it's worse for me than for you, but the world and you, too, may think I am the one to blame, but somehow I can't—just simply can't think I am, Chester. I said no so many times, dear. Of course the world will not know that but it's true all the same. . .*

My eyes latch on to one line again: *I said no so many times, dear* . . . and then I gasp out loud, because I have said no a few times myself, dear, and I finally understand why Grace was so upset. She was carrying a baby—Chester Gillette's baby—*that's* why she had to give up her position and go home. That's why she was so desperate for him to come and take her away. Before her belly got big and the whole world found out.

And then I think of something else . . . that I am the only person, the only person in the entire world, who knows this.

mal • e • dic • tion

It was a Saturday, my very favourite day of the week, for on Saturdays I got to work in Miss Wilcox's library. I was about to knock on her door, when I heard voices inside. Loud, angry voices.

'And what about your father? And Charlotte? And Iverson Junior? The shame of it all! They can't even go out in public! Have you never once thought of them, Emily?' That was a man's voice.

'They're not children. They'll manage.' That was Miss Wilcox.

I raised my hand to knock, then lowered it again. Miss Wilcox was expecting me but this was surely a private discussion and I thought maybe she'd prefer for me to come back later. I stood there dithering.

'Emily, just come home.'

'Under what conditions, Teddy?'

'There's to be no more scribbling, no more foolishness. You're to come home and take up your duties and responsibilities. If you do, I promise I will do my best to forget any of this ever happened.'

'I can't. You know I can't.'

There were a few seconds of silence and then the man spoke again. He wasn't shouting any more. His voice was calm and steady and all the more frightening for it.

'What you've done is not only embarrassing, Emily, it is immoral. *Threnody* should never have been written, never mind published. Anthony Comstock has involved himself. Do you know who he is?'

'The apple-sauce king?'

I did not know Miss Wilcox could be so flippant. I didn't think she should be. Not around an angry man.

'He's the secretary for the Society for the Suppression of Vice. He's ruined people, driven some to suicide. Never did I think I would see your name alongside the names of deviants and pornographers.'

'I am neither a deviant nor a pornographer, Teddy. You know this.'

'He says you are obscene. And when Comstock says something, the entire country listens. You are doing grievous injury to the names of Wilcox and Baxter, Emily. I will seek help for you if you refuse to seek it yourself.'

'Meaning what, Teddy?'

'You leave me no choice, Emily. If you do not come home—on my conditions—I will sign you over to a doctor's care.'

There was a terrible crash and the sound of glass breaking, and then I heard Miss Wilcox scream, 'Get out! Get out!'

'Miss Wilcox! Are you all right?' I shouted, banging on the door.

The door was wrenched open and a man stormed by me. He was tall and pale, with fine dark hair and a moustache, and he barely gave me a glance.

I ran inside, frightened for my teacher. 'Miss Wilcox!' I shouted. 'Miss Wilcox, where are you?'

'In here, Mattie.'

I hurried into the library. The writing table had been upended. Papers were all over the floor. The beautiful apple paperweight had been smashed to bits.

'Miss Wilcox, are you all right?'

She was standing in the middle of the room, but her eyes were red and she was trembling. 'I'm fine, Mattie,' she said, 'but I think I'm going to lie down for a bit. Just leave the mess. I'll see to it. Help yourself to whatever's in the kitchen. Your money's on the table.'

I heard her speaking, but my eyes were on the broken glass and the scattered pages. He'd done this. *Malediction* was my word of the day. It means bad speaking, like a curse. I felt a shiver run up my spine and left the library to lock the front and back doors. When I returned Miss Wilcox was on the staircase.

'I think you should call for the sheriff, Miss Wilcox.'

Miss Wilcox turned round at that and said, 'He wouldn't come. It's not illegal, not yet at least, for a man to destroy his wife's home.'

I didn't say anything, but my eyes must have been as big and as round as two fried eggs.

'Yes, Mattie, that was my husband. Theodore Baxter.'

'Baxter? Then you're not . . . then that . . . that makes you . . .'

'Emily Baxter, poet.'

ab• scis • sion

According to the article I'd read in *Peterson's Magazine*, if you wish to attract a man, you need to be 'attentive and receptive to his every word, put his interests before yours, and use the eloquent, unspoken language of the female body to let him know that he is the very center of your universe'.

The first two bits of advice were clear to me. I had trouble with the third one, though. I thought it meant I should bat my lashes, but when I tried it, Royal looked at me with a puzzled expression, and asked if I'd got some grit in my eye.

We were halfway down the Loomises' drive. Daisy had gone and smashed through their fence again. Pa was furious. Mrs Loomis was, too. I pretended to be, but really I was glad, for it meant I got to see Royal without looking like I wanted to. He'd helped me get Daisy and Baldwin out of the pond again and now he was walking me home.

'Look at that stretch of land right there, Matt,' he said, sweeping his hand out in front of him. 'Nice and flat with a good stream. Make good growing land. I'd farm it for corn in a second.'

The stretch of land he was talking about included Emmie Hubbard's property and a bit of my father's, as well as Loomis land.

'Well, I think Emmie might have something to say about that. And my pa, too.'

He shrugged. 'A man can dream, can't he?'

And before I could say anything in reply, he asked me if I'd like to go riding with him to Inlet and back that very night. I said I would. And as soon as I told him yes, he let go of Daisy's rope, pulled me in under some maple trees and kissed me. He pressed himself into me and kissed my neck, and it was as if everything strong and solid inside me, heart and bones and muscle, softened and melted from the heat of him. For the first time, I dared to touch him. I ran my hands over his arms and laid them upon his chest. His heart was beating slow and steady unlike my own, which was thumping like a thresher. I guessed it must be different for a boy than it was for a girl. I felt his hands circling my waist, and then one slipped down lower. To a place

Mamma told me no one should ever touch, only a husband.

'Royal, no.'

'Aw, Mattie, it's all right.'

He pulled away from me and frowned and his face darkened and I felt I had done something wrong. My word of the day was *abscission*. It means cutting off or sudden termination. I felt its meaning as I looked at Royal's face, all clouded. 'I ain't playing, Matt, if that's what you think. I seen a ring in Tuttle's.'

I blinked for a reply, because I didn't understand what he meant.

He sighed. 'If I was to buy it, would you want it?'

Good Lord, *that* kind of ring. 'Oh yes! Yes, I would,' I whispered. And then I threw my arms round his neck and kissed him and nearly sobbed with relief when I felt him kiss me back. All I wanted was Royal right then, and I didn't think how saying yes to him would mean saying no to all the other things I wanted.

'All right, then,' he said. 'I'll call for you after supper tonight.'

'All right.'

He handed me Daisy's rope, and I walked the rest of the way home by myself. And it was only much later, after we'd been up to Inlet and back and I was upstairs in my bed remembering every one of his kisses, that I wondered if he was supposed to have said he loved me when he told me about the ring. Or if maybe that came later.

his • pid • u • lous

'*Bill Mitchell you know he kept our shanty. As mean a damn man as you ever did see . . .*'

'Beth, don't curse.'

'I didn't, Matt, it was the words in the song.'

'Can't you sing a nicer song? How about the one Reverend Miller taught you? "Onward, Christian Soldiers"?'

She wrinkled her nose. 'I like "Township Nineteen" better. The lumberjacks are more fun than Jesus.'

I sighed and let Beth sing. The two of us were on our way to Emmie Hubbard's. We were walking close together under our mother's old black umbrella. A soft, pattering rain was coming down.

Beth finished her song. 'Is Emmie going away, Matt?' she asked me. 'And her kids? That's what Tommy said.'

'I don't know. Maybe she'll tell us.'

Tommy and Jenny had come for breakfast again that morning, and Tommy had been very upset. He'd told us about a letter that had come from Arn Satterlee. It was the second one Emmie had received from

Arn. The first one—the one I knew about thanks to my aunt Josie—said that her land would be auctioned. Tommy said the second one had set August 20 as the date of the auction. He said the letter had his mother broken down and crying, and would I please come.

I hadn't been able to go right away. There was too much work in the mornings then, with the cows giving so much milk. Right after dinner, though, I wrapped up the leftover biscuits and set off up the road. I'd made extra with the Hubbard kids in mind. We could afford to be more generous with food since we had milk money coming in.

'Mattie, what's your word of the day today?' Beth asked me.

'*Hispidulous*.'

'What's it mean?'

'Covered in short hairs. Bristly.'

'You got a sentence for it?'

'It's *have*, Beth, not *got*, and no, I don't. I can't think of anything that's hispidulous.'

She thought for a few seconds, then said, 'Pa's face is with his beard. So's the piglet.'

I laughed. 'You're right,' I said.

She smiled at me and took my hand. 'I'm glad you're not going to college, Matt. You won't go, will you? You'll stay and marry Royal Loomis, won't you? Abby says he's sweet on you.'

'I'm not going anywhere, Beth,' I said, forcing a smile. More and more, I was seeing my dreams of going to college as just that—dreams. I couldn't leave. I knew that. Even if I wasn't sparking with Royal. I had promised my mamma I would stay.

When we got to Emmie's, I was surprised to see that her kids were all outside. Tommy and Susie were standing under a pine tree with Lucius, the baby. Jenny, Billy, Myrton and Clara were standing out in the muddy yard with their clothing soaked. As soon as they saw Beth and me, they swarmed us like kittens around a milk pail.

'Why are you kids out in the rain?' I asked them.

'Ma sent us out. She's busy,' Myrton said.

'Busy with what?' I asked.

'Mr Loomis is here. He's helping her fix the stove. She said it's dangerous and she doesn't want us back in the house till he's finished,' Tommy said.

'That's silly. I'm sure it's fine to go in,' I said.

'Mattie, you can't go in. Don't.' There was a lick of anger in Tom's voice. 'They've got the stove apart; there's pieces all over the floor.'

'Cripes, Tom, it's just a stove. I'll be careful of it,' I said, irritated.

'I've come all this way in the rain because you asked me to, and I'm not going back again without seeing your ma.'

I trotted up the broken steps onto the porch. The house's one front window was right next to the door. I glanced in before I knocked and what I saw stopped me dead in my tracks.

Emmie was bent over the stove with her skirts up round her waist. Mr Loomis was behind her with his pants down around his ankles. And neither of them was fixing anything.

I turned round, grabbed Beth's arm, and yanked her off the porch, where she'd followed me. 'Ow, Mattie! Let go, will you?' she howled.

'Tommy . . . tell your ma . . . tell her I'll call on her a bit later, all right? All right, Tom? Here . . . here are some biscuits. Take them in to her when . . . when you can.'

Tommy didn't answer me. His thin shoulders sagged from the weight of knowing. He took the food, but he wouldn't look at me. I was glad of it, for I couldn't have met his eyes.

'Ain't we going inside, Matt? I thought you wanted to see Emmie.'

'Later, Beth. Emmie's busy. She's fixing the stove. It's dangerous.'

'But you said—'

'Never mind what I said! Just come on!'

Beth whined all the way home. And I tried to tell myself that I had not just seen what I had seen, for it had looked so ugly and rude. I wondered if that was how it would be between Royal and myself when we were married. If it was, I'd tell him to keep himself to himself, for I wanted no part of it.

Poor Tommy. His brothers and sisters hadn't seemed to know what was happening, but he did. I hoped Mrs Loomis would never find out. Or Royal or his brothers. It would hurt them terribly.

As we finally turned into our own drive, our shoes sodden and our skirts muddied, I realised I had figured out a way to use my word of the day after all. Mr Loomis's shirt-tails had not quite covered his bare behind, and I had seen, though I truly wished I hadn't, that it was pale, flabby, and horribly *hispidulous*.

Put the letters away, Mattie, I say to myself. Go to sleep. You know all you need to know. But I don't. I know that Grace was pregnant. And I know she got that way because of Chester Gillette. And I think that they came to the Glenmore to elope. But I don't know why Chester Gillette wrote *Carl Grahm* in the guest book, and until I find that out, I'm going to keep reading. I shuffle through the bundle until I find what I'm after—a few letters written by Chester. I open one of them.

July 2, 1906
Dear Kid—
I certainly felt good when I got your letter although I also felt mean as I hadn't written all week. Saturday I went up to the lake and am so burned tonight I cannot wear a collar or coat. We went out in the canoe and to two other lakes, and had a good time . . . As for my plans for the Fourth I have made none as the only two girls I could get to go with me have made other arrangements because I didn't ask them until Saturday . . .

Now I see why Grace sounded so worried in all her letters. There were other girls. She wasn't the only one. What a mess of trouble she was in. Chester had put her in the family way and she needed him to marry her, but he didn't seem to want to. Not if she had to plead with him to come for her, not if he barely wrote to her, and when he did, told her about other girls he was taking around.

I can't imagine how frightened Grace must have been, alone with her terrible secret, waiting and waiting for Chester to come. I shudder to think what would happen to me if I ever found myself a baby before I found myself a husband. But then I comfort myself with the knowledge that Chester *did* do right by her in the end. He came and got her and brought her to the North Woods to elope, didn't he? Why else would he have brought her here if it wasn't to elope?

I open another letter from Chester. Maybe it will tell me what I want to know.

June 25, 1906
Dear Grace—
. . . Three of us fellows went up to the lake and camped in a small house that one of the boys owns. We had a dandy time even though there were no girls. We went swimming in the afternoon, and the water was great. I went out in the canoe in the evening and wished you had been there . . .

I stop reading. All of Chester's good and dandy times, I realise, took place on a lake. In a canoe. Earlier that day, when the men had brought Grace's body in, we all thought that her companion, Carl Grahm, had drowned, too. But there was no Carl Grahm. I couldn't find him anywhere. There was only Chester Gillette. And Chester Gillette could handle a boat. Chester Gillette could swim.

You have your answer now, don't you? I say to myself. That's what you get for prying.

But myself is not listening. She refuses to listen. She's picking up another letter and another and another, frantically looking for a different answer. She feels sick. Because she thinks she knows why Chester brought Grace here. And it wasn't to elope.

ico • sa • he • dron

'And don't you ever go in a room by yourself with a strange man, no matter what the reason. Even if he says you're just to bring him a towel. Or a cup of tea.'

'I'll be all right, Pa. The Morrisons run a respectable place.'

'That may be, but any low-down jack with a few dollars in his pocket can take a room at a fancy hotel. Things ain't always what they seem, Mattie. You remember that.'

It was two weeks before Decoration Day and the official start of the summer season, and here I was, sitting next to my father in the buckboard on my way to the Glenmore. My mamma's old carpetbag, packed with books and clothes, was on the floor between us.

Two days before, I'd gone into the barn to fetch Pleasant out and found him stiff and cold in his stall. Pa said it was old age. He was upset when I told him. He couldn't be without a mule but a good one cost about twenty dollars and he didn't have it. Old Ezra Rombaugh in Inlet said he'd sell Pa his six-year-old for fourteen dollars and let him pay off the cost so much every week. That's when he decided I would go to the Glenmore. He had no choice.

Icosahedron, my word of the day, means twenty-sided. It is an almost entirely useless word, unless, of course, you want to describe something with twenty sides. Then, it is perfect. It was a fitting word for Pleasant, who mostly dug his heels in and bit and kicked, but who got me to the Glenmore when I couldn't get there myself.

After talking to Ezra Rombaugh, Pa had enquired at the hotel to see if they still had any positions vacant, and they did. I was sorry I couldn't work for Miss Wilcox any more, but the Glenmore paid more and she was happy for me to go. She said my wages would more than cover the price of a train ticket to New York City. I hadn't the heart to tell her that I'd written to Dean Gill to say I wasn't coming.

I was to receive four dollars a week. Pa said I could keep back a dollar for myself. I told him I would keep back two or I would not go. 'You know I'm keeping company with Royal Loomis,' I said. 'I'll have need of a few dollars myself soon.' Pa blinked at me, but I didn't blink back. I'd counted on him still feeling bad enough about hitting me to let me have my way on this, and I was right. There is an advantage to be found in most everything that happens to you, even if it is not immediately apparent.

Pa turned right off the Big Moose Road, and then right again, into the Glenmore's drive. I could see the hotel now, looming tall. A trio of beautifully dressed women strolled towards the dock, parasols over their slender shoulders. Suddenly I wanted to tell my father to turn round. I didn't know the first thing about fine people, or how to behave around them. Pa needed that new mule badly, though—I knew he did—so I didn't say a word.

'Abby know how to deal with that stove?' he asked me as Licorice, the new mule, pulled the buckboard up to the Glenmore.

'Yes, Pa. Better than I do.' Abby was going to be in charge of everyone, and she would get the meals, too.

'I talked with Mr Sperry. You're to serve in the dining room and help in the kitchen and clean the rooms, but I don't want you nowhere near the bar, you hear? You stay away from the dancing pavilion, too.'

'Yes, Pa.'

'Anything happens and you want to come home, you just send word. I'll come and get you. Or Royal. One of us will.'

'I'll be fine, Pa. Really I will.'

I got out. My father did, too. He lifted my bag down, walked me to the kitchen door, and peered inside. I waited for him to hand me the carpetbag, but he didn't. He held it hard against him. 'Well, you going in or not?' he asked me.

'I need my bag, Pa.'

As he handed it to me, I saw he'd gripped it so tightly his knuckles had turned white. We were not the kissing kind, me and Pa, but I wished that maybe he would at least hug me goodbye. He just toed the ground and spat, though, told me to mind myself, and took off in the buckboard without once looking back.

ob • strep • er • ous

I was cleaning the table when I saw it. A dime. Lying next to the sugar bowl. I picked it up and ran after the woman who'd left it.

'Ma'am? Pardon me, ma'am!' I called.

She stopped in the doorway.

'You left this, ma'am,' I said, holding the coin out to her.

She smiled and shook her head. 'Yes, I did. For you.' And then she turned and walked out of the dining room.

'Put it in your pocket,' a voice behind me said. It was Weaver. 'It's a tip. They leave it for good service. But if you don't get your table cleared and your rear end back in the kitchen, it'll be the only one you ever get.' He started walking away, then turned and said, 'Boisterous.'

'Unruly,' I replied, hurrying back to clear my table.

As I pushed open the kitchen door, struggling to balance the heavy tray on my shoulder, Cook bawled at me for being too slow. 'Table ten needs water, butter and rolls! Look alive, Mattie!' she yelled.

'I'm sorry,' I said.

I rushed past the other girls and slammed my tray down by the sink. 'Don't slam it!' Bill the dishwasher yelled.

'I'm sorry,' I mumbled.

I ran to the warming oven, skidded on a slice of tomato, and just managed to right myself before I smashed into Henry, the new under-chef, who had arrived at the Glenmore the day before, same as me, and was carrying a basket of lobsters.

'*Mein Gott!* Vatch out!' he yelled.

'I'm sorry,' I whispered.

'You sure are,' Weaver said, whizzing past me.

'Weaver, Ada, Fran, pick up! Pick up!' Cook hollered.

I grabbed a clean tray, a dish of butter and a jug of water.

'Uncontrollable,' Weaver shot at me, on his way to the dining room.

'Clamorous,' I shot back. We had a word duel going for my word of the day—*obstreperous.* I saw that it was going to be tough to play my word games here. I'd barely had time to wash my face and braid my hair that morning, never mind look in my dictionary.

I rushed to the warming oven, got a basket down off the top of it and lined it with a clean napkin. I burned my fingers getting the hot rolls. My eyes watered, but I didn't dare let on.

'Obnoxious,' Weaver said, scooping rolls into a basket. He stuffed a corn dodger into his mouth, then yowled as Cook, passing us on a return trip to the oven from the icebox, cuffed his head.

'Bumptious,' I said, giggling. 'To the death, Mr Smith.' I blew on my finger like it was a pistol stock, hoisted my tray, and headed for the dining room.

It was my first full day at the Glenmore, and though it was only about six miles from my house, it was a different world—the world of tourists. Mrs Morrison was bossy and Cook was a bear, but I didn't mind. It all seemed like a grand adventure to me.

I placed the rolls and butter down on table ten. A family was dining there. A father, mother and their three young children. They talked and laughed. The father rubbed noses with his little girl. I stared at them until the mother noticed me and I had to look away.

Table nine was a party of four burly sporting gentlemen up from New York City. They'd gone fishing with a guide in the morning and planned to go back out at dusk.

Table eight was a single woman. She was sitting quietly, sipping lemonade and reading. I couldn't take my eyes off her. 'I'd kill for a dress like that,' Fran said as she passed by me. But it wasn't her dress I wanted, it was her freedom. She could sit by a window and read, with nobody to say, 'Are the chickens fed? What's for supper?'

Table seven was two young married couples. They had maps with them and were planning a tour of the area. The men wore light wool suits and had smooth, clean hands. The women wore cycling skirts.

Table six was the worst. The very worst. It was a single man. A Mr Maxwell. He was small and slight. He held the menu on the table and bent his head towards it, squinting and mopping his brow with his handkerchief as he studied it.

'I'm afraid I've left my glasses in my room,' he finally said. 'Would you mind reading the entrées for me?' I thought his eyes must be very bad indeed, because he looked at my bosom as he spoke, not my face.

'I'd be happy to,' I said. I leaned over him and started reciting. 'Baked ham, broiled spring chicken, boiled tongue . . .'

Just as I got to the veal in aspic, he pulled his napkin off his lap. Under it was something that looked rather like a frankfurter. Only no frankfurter I'd ever seen stood at attention.

'I'll have the veal in aspic,' he said, covering himself again.

My face was flaming as I went back into the kitchen. It was so red that Cook noticed it immediately. 'What have you done?' she barked.

'Nothing ma'am, I . . . I just stumbled, that's all,' I lied. I couldn't bear to say what really happened. Not to anyone.

Fran, picking up an order, heard us. She came up to me. 'Table six?' she whispered.

I nodded, looking at the floor.

'The dirty dog! He did it to me yesterday. You should drop something, all right. A jug of iced water. Right in his lap! Don't go back there, Matt. I'll get Weaver to take the table.'

I remembered what Pa had told me: he'd come after me, or get Royal to, if I wanted to go home. Then Weaver came up to me and pressed a dollar bill into my hand.

'Your tip,' he said. 'From table six.'

I shook my head. 'I don't want it,' I said. 'Not from him.'

'Don't be stupid. It's the easiest money you'll make all summer. Hell, the old duffer can flash *me* for a dollar.'

Fran appeared with a bucket of dirty water. 'I'd give it another look for a quarter,' she said, giggling.

Both Fran and Weaver jollied me until we were all three laughing, until I took the dollar and put it in my pocket along with the dimes and nickels I'd collected from my other tables.

li • mic • o • lous

It was evening, about eight or so, and Cook had sent me down to the boathouse, where the guides were giving a fly-casting demonstration, with a tray of sugar cookies and a pitcher of lemonade. When I came back, there was Henry—sitting on the kitchen steps, sharpening a filleting knife. 'Henry, don't do that!' I scolded. 'It's bad luck!'

I could do that now—scold Henry and tease Bill and joke with Charlie, the bartender, and the guides—for I'd been at the Glenmore a whole week and had received my first wages, and I belonged now.

'Vat luck? No luck but luck vat you make,' Henry said stubbornly, keeping on with his task.

Well, he made some luck all right. Bad luck. And not for himself.

I thought of that knife, and of the sharpening stone, the second I saw Weaver's face. It was maybe half an hour later and Cook and I were hanging out dishcloths on a line near the back steps when John Denio brought him to the kitchen door. We gasped at the sight of him, then hustled him inside as fast as we could, hoping the Morrisons and Mr Sperry wouldn't find out. But they did.

'Weaver, why can't you ever stay out of trouble?' Mr Sperry shouted, storming in from the dining room. 'I send you to Big Moose Station on a simple errand—to help John pick up new arrivals—and look what happens. One of the guests said there was a fight. Were you in it?'

Weaver lifted his chin. 'Yes, sir, I was.'

'Damn it, Weaver, you know my policy on fighting,' Mr Sperry said. 'What happened?'

John Denio answered. All three of us—Cook, Mr Denio, and myself—knew better than to let Weaver do the talking.

'He was attacked,' John said. 'In front of the station. The train was late. I went to talk to the stationmaster and left Weaver in the wagon. Three men came out of the Summit Hotel. Trappers. They were drunk. They said some things. Weaver answered back. One of them hauled him out of the seat and all three of them beat him. I heard the noise, ran out, and broke it up.'

'Three to one, Weaver? For God's sake, why didn't you keep quiet?'

'They called me nigger.'

Mr Sperry took Weaver's chin in his hand and grimaced at the damage. A cut eye that was already blackening. A nose that might well be broken. A lip as fat and shiny as a garden slug. 'It's just a word, son. I've been called worse,' he said.

'Beg your pardon, Mr Sperry, but you haven't,' Weaver said. 'I'm going to the justice of the peace tomorrow,' he added. 'I'm telling him what happened. I'm pressing charges.'

Mr Sperry sighed. 'You're just bent on kicking skunks, aren't you? From tomorrow on, you're to stay in the kitchen until your face heals.'

'But why, Mr Sperry?' Weaver asked, upset. He wouldn't earn tips working in the kitchen.

'Because I can't have you serving guests with a face like that.'

'But it's not right, sir. I shouldn't be called names. Shouldn't catch a beating. Shouldn't have to stay in the kitchen, either.'

'How old are you, Weaver? Seventeen or seven? Don't you know that what should be and what is are two different things? You should be dead. Luckily, you aren't. You think on that the next time you decide to take on three grown men.' He stormed back out. Cook went after him to ask about a delivery, John returned to his horses, and the two of us were left alone.

Limicolous, my word of the day, means something that lives in the mud. I thought it was a good word to describe the men who beat Weaver, and told him so. Weaver had other words to describe them, though.

'Hush, Weaver, just let it go,' I said, wrapping up a chunk of ice in a towel. 'A few days in the kitchen won't kill you. It's better than losing your job. Here, hold this against your lip.'

'Don't have much of a choice, do I?' he grumbled. He pressed the ice to his lip, winced, then said, 'Three more months, Matt. Just three more months and I'm gone from here. Once I get through Columbia, once I'm a lawyer, ain't no one ever going to call me boy or nigger or Sam. Or hit me. And if they do, I'll make sure they go to jail.'

'I know you will,' I said.

'I'll find myself a new place. A better place than this one, that's for sure. We both will, won't we, Matt?' he said, his eyes searching mine.

'Yes, we will,' I said, avoiding his gaze.

I hear a loon calling from the lake. The tourists all say it's a beautiful sound. I think it's the loneliest sound I know. I am still reading. Still looking for a different answer. Another outcome. A happier ending. But I already know I'm not going to find it.

South Otselic

June 28, '06
My Dear Chester,
. . . I think I shall die of joy when I see you, dear. I will tell you I am going to try and do a whole lot better, dear, I will try not to worry so much and I won't believe horrid things the girls write. I presume they do stretch things, dear. I am awfully pleased you had such a jolly time at the lake, dear, and I wish I had been there, too. I am very fond of water, although I can't swim . . .

It is a long letter and there are many more lines to read, but my eyes keep straying back to one line: *I am very fond of water, although I can't swim.* A chill grips me. He knew she couldn't swim. He knew it.

I begin to weep then. I hold my hands over my face so that no noise gets out, and cry as though my heart is breaking. I think it is.

There are a few more letters, but I can't read them. I should never have read the first one, never mind nearly all of them. I stare into the darkness and I can see Grace's face as she handed me the letters. I hear her saying, 'Burn them. Please. Promise me you will.'

I burrow down into my pillow and close my eyes. I desperately want to sleep. But the darkness swirls behind my eyelids, and all I can think about is the black water of the lake closing around me, filling my eyes and ears and mouth, pulling me down as I struggle against it. *I am very fond of water, although I can't swim . . .*

grav • id

It was a Wednesday afternoon, and I had a half day off from the Glenmore. Royal was driving me to Minnie's house on his way into Inlet. He'd come to fetch me at the hotel.

Royal talked a mile a minute as we rode. He told me about the new hybrid corn they had at Beckers' Farm and Feed. I nodded and did my best to listen, but I was thinking how the last time I saw her, Miss Wilcox had said that 'A Country Burial' by Emily Dickinson was perfection in eight lines. She'd also said that Emily Dickinson had had a hard time of it. Her pa was overbearing and hadn't let her read any books that he didn't like. She became a recluse. She had no husband, no children, no one to give her heart to. And that was sad. I was glad that I had someone to give my heart to. Even if he didn't know a poem from a potato.

Why didn't Emily Dickinson marry? I wondered. Why hadn't Jane Austen married? Or Emily Brontë? Or Louisa May Alcott? Mary Shelley married and Edith Wharton, too, but Miss Wilcox said both marriages were disasters. And then, of course, there was Miss Wilcox herself, with her thin-lipped bully of a husband.

'. . . it's really too late to plant, but Pa said to buy half a pound anyway, plant it and see what we get. Whoa! Whoa, there!' Royal said, stopping the horses at the bottom of Minnie's road. 'Matt, I'm going to let you out right here. Jim's drive is a bit narrow for this old wagon. I'll be back in a couple of hours.'

'All right,' I said, jumping down.

The buckboard disappeared round the bend, and I turned and headed up the road towards Minnie's house. As I walked, I waved to the hired hands who were building fences. I saw Thistle, one of the cows, grazing nearby. She was huge and would calve any day now. *Gravid* was my word of the day. It means pregnant. It also means burdened or loaded down. Looking at Thistle, with her heavy belly and her tired eyes, it made perfect sense.

I smelt the flowers I'd picked. I hoped Minnie would like them. It had been weeks since I had seen her, and I had so much to tell her.

When I got to her porch, the front door banged open. Jim greeted me sullenly and trotted down the steps to join the hired hands.

'Minnie?' I called, stepping inside. A nasty smell hit me. A sour reek of old food and dirty diapers.

'Matt, is that you?' a tired voice asked. Minnie was sitting on her bed, nursing her twins. She looked so thin and drawn that I barely recognised her. Her blond hair was greasy. Her clothing was stained. The babies were sucking at her hungrily.

'Yes, it's me. I brought you these,' I said, holding out the flowers.

'They're so pretty. Thank you. Will you put them in something?'

I went to find a glass or a jar, and it was then I noticed how filthy the place was. Plates and glasses crusted with food littered the table and counters, cutlery filled the sink. Dirty pots covered the stove top.

'I apologise for the state of things,' Minnie said. 'Jim's had four men helping him all week. Seems I just get one meal cooked and it's time for the next one. The babies are always hungry, too. Here, take them for a minute, will you? I'll make us a cup of tea.'

She handed one of the babies to me, wincing as she pulled him off her swollen, blue-veined breast. Her skin, where the baby's mouth had been, was livid. She saw me staring and covered herself. She handed me the other baby, and in no time flat, they were both screaming. Their diapers were soggy. I was trying to settle them, so they'd stop screaming, when the next thing I knew Minnie was standing over me, her arms at her side, her hands clenched.

'Give them to me! Give them back! Don't look at them like that! Don't look at me! Just get out! Go! Get out of here!' she shouted.

'Min . . . I . . . I'm sorry! I wasn't . . . I didn't mean . . .'

Minnie was hysterical. She crushed the babies to her and started to cry. 'You hate them, don't you, Mattie? Don't you?'

'Minnie! What are you saying?'

'I know you do. I hate them, too. Sometimes. I do.' Her voice had dropped to a whisper. Her eyes were tormented.

'You hush right now! You don't mean that!'

'I do. I wish I'd never had them. I wish I'd never got married.' The babies howled against her. She sat down on the bed and grimaced as they latched on to her. She leaned back against the pillows and closed her eyes. Tears leaked out from under her pale lashes.

'You're just weary, Min,' I said, stroking her hand. 'That's all.'

She opened her eyes. 'I don't know, Matt. It all seemed so exciting when we were first married, but it isn't now. Jim's always at me . . .'

'He's probably just worn down, too. It's hard work clearing—'

'Oh, don't be dense, Mattie! I mean *at me.* But I'm so sore. And I just can't have another baby. Not right after the twins. Mrs Crego said that nursing will keep me from quickening, but I think I'll go crazy with the pain. I'm sorry, Matt . . . I'm sorry I shouted. I'm just so tired . . .'

'I know you are. You lie there and rest. Let me make the tea.'

Within minutes Minnie had fallen asleep and the babies with her. I got busy. I boiled water and washed all the pots and pans and dishes. I filled the big black washing kettle with water, threw in a pailful of dirty diapers I'd found in the kitchen, and started a fire under it in the back yard. Then I scrubbed the table and swept the floor. I set the table, too, thinking the men would be back in for supper before long, and put my flowers in the middle of it. When I'd finished, the house looked and smelt much better. Then I heard wagon wheels at the bottom of the drive. I looked out of the window and saw Royal. Already. I'd never even had the chance to tell Minnie about him.

As I quickly patted my hair back into place, it hit me: Emily Dickinson was a damned sneaky genius. Holing up in her father's house, never marrying, becoming a recluse—that had sounded like giving up to me, but the more I thought about it, the more it seemed she fought by not fighting. Oh, maybe she was lonely at times, and cowed by her pa, but I bet at midnight, when the lights were out and her father was asleep, she went sliding down the banister and swinging from the chandelier. I bet she was just dizzy with freedom.

I looked at my friend Minnie, sleeping still. A year ago she was a girl, like me, but I couldn't see that girl any more. She was gone. And I knew in my bones that Emily Dickinson wouldn't have written even one poem if she'd had two howling babies, a husband bent on jamming another one into her, a house to run, a garden to tend, three cows to milk, twenty chickens to feed and four hired hands to cook for.

I knew then why they didn't marry. Emily and Jane and Louisa. I knew and it scared me. I didn't want to be lonely my whole life but I didn't want to give up my words. I didn't want to choose one over the other. Mark Twain didn't have to. Charles Dickens didn't. And John Milton didn't, either, though he might have made life easier for untold generations of schoolkids if he had.

Then Royal hollered for me and I had to wake Minnie to tell her goodbye. When I got outside, the afternoon was bright and sunny, and Royal took my hand as we rode to his brother's land, and he told me we would have land, too. He said he had some money saved up, and I proudly told him I had ten dollars and sixty cents. He said that was almost enough to pay for a stove or a calf. He pleased himself so much just talking about these things that he smiled and put his arm round me. It was the nicest feeling. Lucky and safe. I nestled against him and imagined what it would feel like to lie next to him in a pine bed in the dark, and suddenly nothing else seemed to matter.

sal • tant

'Not another one, Weaver, damn it!' Cook shouted, slapping her spatula against the worktable.

'Sorry,' Weaver said, bending down to pick up the pieces of a plate. He was on dishwashing duty and that was the second plate he had broken that morning.

'No, you're not,' Cook said. 'But you will be. Next thing you break is coming out of your wages. I've had it with you. Go down cellar and bring up some new plates. And don't you dare drop them.'

Four whole days had elapsed since Mr Sperry had put Weaver on kitchen duty, long enough for most people to get their noses back in joint, but Weaver was still furious about it.

I'd made a special effort that morning. I'd told him about *saltant*, my word of the day. 'It means dancing, leaping or jumping, Weaver,' I'd said. 'Its root comes from the Latin word *sal*, for salt. You can see the connection, can't you? A bit of salt sprinkled over eggs can make them dance, too.' I thought my observation was fascinating, but Weaver did not. He continued to sulk, and I think he would have kept up his surly behaviour all week, if Mr Higby hadn't come by.

Mr Higby owned Higby's camp on the south shore of Big Moose Lake and was the local justice of the peace. He was also Mr Sperry's brother-in-law, and when he appeared in the kitchen towards the end of the breakfast service, we all thought that's who he was after.

'Hello, Jim, you eaten?' Cook asked him. 'Mattie, go get Mr Sperry.'

'No need, Mrs Hennessey,' Mr Higby said. 'I'll find him. I've got to see Weaver first, anyway.'

'Lord God, what did he do now?' Cook sighed, walking to the cellar door. 'Weaver!' she shouted. 'Get those plates and get back up here! Mr Higby wants a word with you!'

Weaver came up and put the new plates down on the draining board.

'Just thought you'd like to know that I found the men who gave you that licking, Weaver,' Mr Higby said. 'They were raising Cain up at the Summit Hotel. Broke a stool and a window. When the bartender told me they were the same men who attacked you, I arrested them. John Denio's had a look at them and says I've got the right ones. Now I need you to do the same, and then I'm going to give them a short vacation in Herkimer. They'll get a cosy little room and some new clothes, too. The kind with stripes on 'em.'

For the first time in days, Weaver smiled. 'Thank you, Mr Higby. I appreciate you taking the time over it.'

'Just doing my job. I've got to find Dwight and talk business for a bit. I'll call for you on my way out.'

Mr Higby went to find Mr Sperry and Weaver went back to the sink. His head was high. His eyes, so dark with anger for the last four days, were filled with a clear and righteous light.

aby

When Tommy Hubbard appeared at the Glenmore's kitchen door at seven in the morning, I felt in my bones that something was wrong.

'Hello! Is Mattie here? Is she here?' he yelled.

'Who is that? Stop shouting!' Cook shouted.

'It's me, Tommy Hubbard. I need to see Mattie.'

'Don't you set foot in my kitchen, Tom!'

'I'm not itching, I swear, I—'

'You stay out there! I'll find her for you.'

'I'm right here,' I said, opening the door. Tears had washed tracks through the dirt on Tom's face. He was panting like a horse played out.

'I ran fast as I could, Mattie . . . fast as I could . . .' he sobbed.

'From where? From *home*?' It was a mile from Tommy's house to the Big Moose Road, and five more up to the Glenmore.

'You've got to come home,' he said. 'It's your pa and your sisters, Matt. They're powerful sick . . .'

I dropped the knife I was holding.

'I went over early to see if Lou wanted to go fishing, and I knocked and knocked but no one came. The cows were bellowing, so I went in the barn. Daisy's real bad. She ain't been milked. Ain't none of them have. I went inside the house . . . They're all real bad.'

I didn't hear anything else for I was already running. Down the back steps to the Glenmore's drive and out to the Big Moose Road. Tommy was right behind me. I didn't get more than a hundred yards down the road when I saw a buckboard coming towards me.

I ran to it, shouting and waving my arms. The driver stopped. It was John Denio coming to work from his home in Big Moose Station.

'Please, Mr Denio, my pa's sick. My whole family . . . I've got to get home—'

'Get in,' he said, reaching down for my hand and lifting me clear across him. Tommy scrambled into the back. Mr Denio turned his horses around in the road, then cracked the reins. I was more scared than I have ever been in my life.

As we turned into my drive, I heard the sound of a second buckboard turn in behind us. It was Royal. 'I was delivering to the Waldheim,' he shouted. 'Saw Mrs Hennessey on my way back. She told me what happened. Go on inside. I'll see to the cows.'

I was out of Mr Denio's buckboard before it stopped. I could hear Royal yelling at Tommy to tie the horses. I could hear the cows bellowing in pain. They were in the barn, which meant Pa had done a milking . . . but when? Yesterday? Two days ago? It only takes a day before the milk collects and swells the udder and infection sets in.

'Pa!' I yelled. I ran through the kitchen towards the stairs and found a figure crumpled at the bottom of them. 'Lou! Oh, Lou!' I screamed.

She picked her head up and blinked at me. Her eyes were glassy and her lips were cracked. Her coverall bib was crusted with vomit. 'Mattie . . .' she rasped. '. . . thirsty, Mattie . . .'

'It's all right, Lou, I'm here.' I lifted her up, draped her arm round my neck and dragged her up the stairs to our bedroom. I opened the door and gagged on the stink. The room was dark, the curtains drawn.

'Beth? Abby?' I whispered. There was no answer. I laid Lou down on our bed, then crossed the room and pulled on the curtain. I saw Beth then. She was lying in her and Abby's bed, still and pale.

'Beth!' I cried, rushing to her. Her eyes fluttered open and I sobbed with relief. She closed them again and began to weep, and I realised her bowels had let go. I touched her forehead. She was on fire.

'Ssshh, Beth, it's all right. I'll get you fixed up, I promise . . .' I said. I went back to Lou. 'Where's Abby?' I asked her.

She licked her lips. 'With Pa.'

I ran down the hallway to Pa's bedroom. My father was lying rigid in his bed, mumbling and shivering. My sister was slumped over him.

'Abby!' I called to her. 'Abby, wake up!'

She raised her head. Her eyes were dark hollows. Her cheekbones were sharp beneath her skin. 'He's real bad, Mattie,' she said.

'Since how long?'

'Since two days. Fever got worse this morning.'

'Go to bed, Ab. I'll look after him now.'

She raised herself up and walked towards the door, her steps as slow and shuffling as an old woman's. I touched my father's face. His skin was dry and hot. 'Pa,' I called softly. 'Pa.'

He opened his eyes and looked right through me. His hands scrabbled at the bedding. 'Pa, can you hear me?' I said.

'. . . killed her, I killed her . . .' he jabbered, '. . . my fault . . .'

I put my hands over my eyes then and whimpered with fear. I didn't know what to do. They were all so sick.

'Yarrow, Mattie,' Abby rasped from the doorway. 'Get him to take some yarrow tea. He's got fever and a deep cough. Try onions . . .'

'. . . and goose grease and turpentine . . . ,' I said, suddenly remembering how Mamma had treated coughs. Abby's voice calmed me and helped me to think. 'And baths. I'll try a cool sponge bath,' I said.

Abby's legs shook then and she had to grab the doorjamb to keep from collapsing. I helped her into bed next to Lou. She squeezed my hand and her eyes closed, and I was alone. Utterly alone. I tried to think of my word of the day, *aby*, to take the fear from my mind. It meant to endure, to atone, and I found I didn't care.

I raced downstairs and put the kettle on the stove to boil. Then I pumped water into a large enamelled basin, ran back upstairs, and stripped Beth's clothes off. I pulled her out of the bed onto the bare floor and washed her. When she was clean, I put a fresh nightgown on her and tucked her in with Abby and Lou. Her own bed was rank, but it would have to wait. Then I took Lou's dirty coveralls off her and drew the quilt up over all three of them. Abby was sweating now. Her underclothes were damp and her hair was plastered to her head.

I ran downstairs, pumped clean water into a jug, snatched a glass, and ran back up again. I gave everyone a good, tall drink, holding their heads up so they could swallow. I bundled all the clothing and Beth's soiled bedding, and took it outside. While I was in the yard, I looked up towards the barn. Three calves had been put in the pasture. Another was heading for the drive. Two more were in the cornfield, trampling the fragile plants. My heart lurched. We needed every ear, every stalk, for winter feed. A movement caught my eye. It was Tommy. He was near the beehives, trying to push another calf—Baldwin—towards the pasture, but Baldwin didn't want to go. Manure gushed from his backside and splashed all over Tommy. Tommy cursed and punched the calf in the face. Again and again and again.

'Stop it, Tommy!' I screamed, running to them.

Tommy looked at me and shrank back, shame flushing his cheeks. His eyes were red and watery. A livid welt bloomed under one. 'I was afraid,' he sobbed. 'I didn't mean for them to all get out . . .'

'Tommy, who hit you . . .' I started to say, reaching for him. But he ducked me and took off after the calf in the drive. Baldwin's bleats were soft little moans now. 'Come on, Baldwin. Come on, now,' I said to him. I gave him my fingers to suck, which soothed him, then managed to lead him to the pasture one step at a time. Once he was in, I went after the two calves in the corn. They were standing together, their heads above the young stalks. 'Come on, Bertie. Come on, Allie,' I called. But as soon as they heard me, they split apart and trotted off.

I ran into the milk house, grabbed the pails that Pa mixed their feed in, and clattered them together. Bertie pricked his ears. He trotted towards me. Allie followed and I was able to lead them to the pasture.

I ran back into the kitchen. The kettle was boiling furiously. I grabbed a handful of yarrow from the tin where Mamma kept it, put it in a teapot and poured hot water over it. I put the pot, several cups, and a jug of cold water on a tray. Just get it down them, I told myself, walking up the stairs. Then they'd sleep and I could see to feeding the pigs and chickens and starting a fire under the wash kettle and finding out from Royal and Mr Denio how bad the cows were. Having a plan gave me some confidence.

Every scrap of it disappeared, however, as soon as I got upstairs. Pa was shivering so hard, his bed rattled. It was the fever.

I put the tray down on his dresser and poured a cup of tea. 'Pa?' I whispered, touching his cheek. 'Pa, you need to drink this.' He didn't hear me, didn't even know I was there. 'Pa?' I said, louder now. 'Pa!'

He opened his eyes. His hands shot up at me; his fingers closed on my blouse. I screamed as he jerked me to him. I felt hot tea burn my legs, heard the cup smash on the floor.

I shook free of him, stumbled to the dresser and poured another cup of tea. 'You drink this, Pa!' I shouted at him. 'Right now! You stop your nonsense and drink this tea!'

He blinked at me, his eyes suddenly mild. 'Where's Lawton, Mattie?' he asked me. 'Is he back yet? I hear the cows . . .'

'He's back, Pa. He's . . . he's in the barn, milking,' I lied.

'That's good. I'm glad he's back,' he said. And then I saw that tears were rolling down his cheeks, and I was terrified. My father never cried. 'He ran away, Mattie. Ran away because I killed her.'

'Hush, Pa, don't talk so. You didn't kill anyone.' He was only babbling, but the more he talked, the more upset he became.

'I didn't kill her, Mattie,' he said, his voice rising. 'I didn't!'

I thought it best to humour him. 'Of course you didn't, Pa. No one says you did.'

'Lawton does. Said that I killed her with hard work. Said I should have moved us all to Inlet and worked in the sawmill. Said I killed your mother and I wasn't going to kill him.' And then his face crumpled and he sobbed like a child. 'I didn't kill her; I loved her . . .'

I had to steady myself against the dresser. I felt like someone had taken my legs out from under me. That's why they'd fought, I thought. That's why Pa had swung the peavey at Lawton and why Lawton had run away. Why he looked at us but never saw us. Oh, Lawton, I thought, some things should never, ever be said. Words are just words, Royal would say. But words are more powerful than anything.

'Lawton didn't mean it, Pa. The cancer killed Mamma, not you.'

He nodded, but his eyes were elsewhere and I knew he believed my brother's words, not mine. He was exhausted from his agitation, though, and I took advantage of it to make him swallow some tea. I undressed him, laying the dresser cloth over all the things I wasn't supposed to see and then I bathed him with cold water. He shivered terribly as I sponged him, and he clenched his teeth. When I was done, I pulled the bedding back over him, piled two quilts on top, and made him drink another cup of hot tea. I knew he needed to sweat. Sweating would bring the sickness out of him.

When he had closed his eyes, I picked up the tea tray to take it in to my sisters. I put what Lawton had said out of my mind. I didn't want to think about it.

I went in our bedroom and saw that Lou had sicked up the water I'd given her and that Abby was out of bed and lurching about trying to clean Beth, who'd messed herself again.

'Mattie! Matt, where are you?' a voice called from downstairs.

'Up here!'

Feet pounded up the stairs and then Royal was in the doorway. He winced at the smell.

'What is it?' I asked, coming out into the hallway.

'One of the cows is real bad. The one with the star on her head—'

'That's Daisy. It's not a star; it's a flower,' I said stupidly.

'She's suffering, Matt. Real bad. John wants . . . he wants to know where your pa keeps his gun.'

'No, Mattie, no! Don't let him!' Lou yelled from her bed.

I shook my head.

He took me by the shoulders. 'Matt, she's bad off . . . it ain't kind.'

'In the shed. Above the door.'

He went back downstairs, and I heard the crack of a rifle, heard Lou shout my name, then curse. I heard the chamber pot go over in my father's room, heard him tell someone named Armand to shoot the damn bear already.

Then I heard the sound of choked, quiet tears, as I sat down on the top step and wept.

fu • ga • cious

'You still taking the cod-liver oil I left at your place?' Mrs Loomis asked me. She was sitting on her front porch, shelling peas into a blue enamelled basin. I was sitting across from her, on an old wicker settee. Royal was next to me, his legs stretched out in front of him.

'Yes, ma'am,' I said. Mrs Loomis had come to our house a week ago, as soon as Royal had got home and told her how it was with us. She said it was one of the worst cases of grippe she'd ever seen. She doctored us and cooked for us and pulled us all through it. Weaver's mamma helped her. I don't know what we would have done without them. Pa had the remains of a cough and Beth was still too weak to get out of bed, but they were out of danger.

'Still feeding Beth plenty of ginger tea?'

'Yes, ma'am. She's a lot better. My pa said to tell you he's much obliged. And that he'll be over to pay a call in a day or two.'

'I don't want his thanks, Mattie. Seeing a neighbour through is thanks enough. You'll be getting back to the Glenmore soon, I expect?'

'Yes, ma'am. Pa's taking me tomorrow morning.'

She raised her head, fixing me with her faded blue eyes. 'You learning a lot up there? Cooking and ironing and such?' she asked.

'A bit.'

'That's good. Eileen Hennessey makes a nice piecrust. A good Baltimore cake, too. You should see if she'll give you some of her recipes.' She straightened her back. 'Well, I reckon that's that,' she said. 'Royal, take the pods out to the pigs before you come in.'

'Yup.'

The screen door slammed and we were alone.

'You got a day off any time soon?' Royal asked me.

'I don't think so. Don't dare ask for one. Not after being home for a whole week.'

'Huh.'

There was a minute or two of silence. I stared at Mrs Loomis's peony bushes. Some of the flowers were already loosing their petals. I hadn't had the inclination to look up a word while my family was sick and, even if I had, my dictionary was up at the Glenmore. *Fugacious* was one of the last words I'd found, though. It means falling or fading early, fleeting. The dying peonies reminded me of that.

'Well, here then,' Royal said suddenly. He held out a small square of tissue paper. It was folded over several times. I opened it and saw a dull gold ring inside. It was set with three stones—a chipped opal flanked by two tiny garnets. It must've been pretty once.

I looked at him. 'Royal, do you . . . do you love me?' I asked.

'Aw, Matt. I bought you a ring, didn't I?'

I looked at the ring again and thought how we'd lost two cows and would've lost more if it hadn't been for Royal.

'I've got ten dollars of my own saved up, Mattie. And my ma, she's got some put aside, too. She'll help us. And you'll have some savings, too, won't you, by the end of the summer? It'll be enough to make a start, all of it together.'

I stared at the ring hard.

'Will you, Mattie?'

I slipped the ring on my finger. 'I will, Royal,' I said. 'You'd best come home with me now so we can tell my pa.'

South Otselic

July 2, '06

My Dear Chester,

I hope you will excuse me if I don't follow the lines for I am half lying down. Have worked awfully hard today . . . This morning I helped mamma with the dinner. This p.m. I have been after strawberries. It was fun, only I got so awfully tired. The fields here are red with berries. Tonight mamma is canning them and making bread and cookies. Mamma says I am getting to be a splendid cook. What do you think of that?

I stop reading Grace's letter and stare off into the darkness. I miss my own mamma so much right now that it hurts. She used to can strawberries, too, and she made the most delicious pink strawberry cake. It was as sweet as her kiss on my cheek. Sometimes she would pick a basketful of berries in the afternoon and set them, sun-warmed and fragrant, on the kitchen table, along with a dish of fresh cream and one of maple sugar. We would dip them first into the cream, then in the sugar, then bite into them greedily.

Once, Mamma made this treat just for me and her. It was after I'd started my monthlies. She'd sat me down at the kitchen table and told me that I was a grown woman now, not a girl any more, and that a woman's virtue was the greatest treasure she possessed and that I must never, ever give mine to any man but the one I married.

Then I asked, 'How do you know if a man loves you, Mamma?'

'You just do.'

'How did you know? Did Pa say "I love you" and give you a nice card or something and then you knew?'

Mamma laughed. 'Does that sound like your pa?'

'Then how did you *know,* Mamma?'

'I just did.'

'But *how*, Mamma, *how*?'

She never answered me. She just shook her head and said, 'Oh, Mattie, you ask too many questions!'

Grace must have loved Chester very much to give him her virtue before they were married. I wonder how Grace convinced herself that Chester loved her. And if she kept pretending it right to the end. Men rarely come right out and tell you. Minnie says you have to look for signs. Do they wash before they come to call on you? Do they let you climb up in the buckboard yourself, or get out to help you?

Royal washes. And he puts on a clean shirt, too. And if he says he will call for me at seven o'clock, he is there at seven o'clock. He does other things, too. I lie back against my pillow and spend a long time silently repeating them to myself, but it's no use. Mamma said I would know. And I do. I guess I have all along.

'Poor, sad, stupid Grace,' I whisper to the darkness. 'Poor, sad, stupid Matt.'

thren • o • dy

'Mattie, you get the package that came for you?' Mrs Morrison asked me. She was standing behind the front desk, sorting through the mail. It was three o'clock and the dining room was closed until supper.

'No, ma'am. What package?'

'A package from the teacher. She left it about an hour ago. I looked for you, but I couldn't find you. I had Ada bring it upstairs.'

I thanked her and ran to the attic as fast as I could. I was powerfully curious. When I got upstairs, I saw that it was a heavy parcel, wrapped in brown paper and tied with twine. There was an envelope tucked under the twine, too. I opened the package first. There were three books: *Sister Carrie* by Theodore Dreiser; *The Jungle* by Upton Sinclair; and *Threnody,* a volume of poetry by Emily Baxter. I didn't know the meaning of *threnody*, so I pulled my dictionary out from under my bed and looked it up. It was defined as a song of lamentation, a funeral dirge. I smiled at that, pleased to know that I was not the only one in these parts given to things morbid and dispiriting. Next I opened the envelope and caught my breath as a five-dollar bill fluttered out. I picked it up. There was a letter, too.

Dear Mattie,

I thought you might like these books. I hope, particularly, that you enjoy the volume of poetry, as I wish to leave you something by which to remember me. I am departing Eagle Bay tomorrow. I won't be teaching next year. I had hoped to tell you this in person, but Mrs Morrison was unable to locate you. I am including Annabelle's, my sister's, address in this note. I've told her all about you and she's very eager to have you as a boarder. The enclosed will help get you to her house . . .

There was more, but I didn't read it. 'You can't go!' I said aloud and ran out of the room and was downstairs in the kitchen in no time flat. Weaver was sitting at the table, eating ice cream. Cook and Mr Sperry had the top of the stove off and were frowning down into it.

'Can I please take the trap, Mr Sperry?' I asked, panting. 'I've got to go to Inlet. I've got to.'

'Have you lost your mind? Supper's only a few hours away. And besides, you can't handle Demon by yourself,' Cook said.

'I'll be back in time, I swear it,' I said. 'And I can manage Demon. I know I can. Please, ma'am . . .'

'No. And that's the end of it,' Cook said.

'Mattie, what's this about?' Mr Sperry asked.

'It's a friend of mine. She's in trouble and I've got to go to her.'

'You can't go alone. Mrs Hennessey's right, Demon's a handful. I'd take you but I've got to get this stove working before supper.'

'But I've got to,' I sobbed. 'I've got to.'

Mr Sperry, Cook, and Weaver all looked at me. Weaver put his spoon down. 'I'll go with her,' he said.

Mr Sperry shook his head. 'Go on, then. But be back here ready to serve supper by six sharp. Or else.'

I hitched up Demon, Mr Sperry's own horse, and drove hell-for-leather all the way down Big Moose Road to Inlet. I told Weaver about the package on the way and who Miss Wilcox really was.

When we arrived at Dr Foster's camp, Weaver told me to go in. 'I'll wait outside,' he said. 'I can't stand a lot of female drama.'

I knew that was just his way of giving me time alone with Miss Wilcox, and I appreciated it. I ran up the back steps, past the boxes and crates piled up on the porch, and banged on the door.

'Mattie!' Miss Wilcox said, opening the door. 'How did you get here?'

'Miss Wilcox, why are you leaving? Please don't go!' I said.

'Oh, Mattie!' she said, hugging me. 'Come in and sit down.'

She led me into the library. I sat down next to her on the settee and looked around. The books were gone. The desk was bare.

I heard a match flare, smelt the sulphur. Miss Wilcox was smoking.

'Why are you leaving, Miss Wilcox?' I asked, fighting back my tears. 'You can't go. You're all I have.'

I felt her hand on my arm. 'Oh, Mattie, that's not true. You have your family and Weaver and all your other friends.'

'They aren't what you are!' I shouted angrily. 'Why are you leaving? *Why?*'

'My husband made good on his threat. He's furious about the new book. He's cut off my funds. And he's written to the school trustees and told them who I am. I've had to step down.'

'But you're a good teacher! The best one we ever had!'

'Unfortunately, Mattie, the trustees don't agree with you. They say I am a pernicious influence on young minds.'

'Can't you stay, anyway?'

'My husband is on his way, Mattie. My sister wired that he's a day away at most. If I'm still here when he arrives, the next stop for me is a doctor's office. And then a sanatorium and so many drugs pushed down my throat, I won't be able to remember my name, much less write.'

'He can't do that.'

'He can. He's a powerful man with powerful friends.'

'Where will you go?' I asked, afraid for her.

She sat back against the settee. 'My grandmother left me a little bit of money. It's in a trust and my husband can't touch it. Plus I have my car and a few pieces of jewellery. I'm going to hock them and go to

Paris.' She took another drag on her cigarette, then stubbed it out on a plate on the table.

'I'm driving the car back to New York tomorrow. It's big enough to hold my clothes and a few boxes of books. That's all I need for now. I'm having the rest of my things sent to my sister's. I'm going to hide out at her house while I sell the car. And once I'm in France, I'm going to do my best to get a divorce.'

'I'm sorry,' I said.

'For what?'

'For shouting at you. I was selfish.'

She squeezed my hand and said, 'You are many, many things, Mathilda Gokey, but selfish isn't one of them.'

We sat together in silence for a few minutes, Miss Wilcox smoking and holding my hand. I didn't ever want to leave this room. Or my teacher. But I knew the longer I stayed, the longer I kept her from packing. And come morning, she had to be gone.

'I have to go,' I finally said. 'Weaver's waiting for me outside. We have to be back by six or we're going to be in trouble.'

'Well, we can't have that, Mattie. Maybe you can visit me in Paris some day. Or maybe, if all goes well, I can come home sooner rather than later. And then we can have lunch on the Barnard campus.'

'I don't think so, Miss Wilcox,' I said, my eyes on the floor.

'But why not?'

'I'm not going to Barnard. I'm staying here.'

'My God, Mattie, why?' she asked, releasing my hand.

I couldn't answer her for a few seconds. 'Royal Loomis asked me to marry him,' I finally said. 'And I told him yes.'

Miss Wilcox looked like someone had drained all the sap from her. 'I see,' she said. She was about to say more, but I cut her off.

'Here's your five dollars back,' I said. 'Thank you, Miss Wilcox, it was very generous, but I won't be needing it.'

'No, Mattie, you keep it,' she said. 'Money can be tight when you're first married. Keep that for yourself. Use it for paper and pens.'

'Thank you,' I said, knowing that was what she wanted me to say.

'You take care of yourself, Mattie,' she said, walking me to the door.

'You, too, Miss Wilcox.'

She said goodbye to Weaver as I climbed into the trap. She gave him a hug and told him to study hard at Columbia. She told him she was going to spend some time in Paris and that he should come and visit her there. I looked back as we drove off and saw her silhouetted in the doorway. She looked small to me. Small and fragile and defenceless.

'Giddy-up!' I told Demon, snapping the reins. He broke into a trot.

'You all right?' Weaver asked.

'I'm fine,' I said, driving down the middle of the street. As soon as I made it out of the village, I pulled up on the reins until Demon stopped, then leaned my head into my hands.

'Aw, Matt,' Weaver said. 'She didn't die; you'll see her again.'

'She may as well have. I won't see her again. I know I won't.'

'You will so. She won't stay in France for ever. She'll be back in New York one day.'

'But I won't be,' I said quietly.

'What?'

I didn't want to tell him, but I had to. I'd kept it from him for weeks. 'Weaver, I'm not going. I'm not going to New York City,' I said.

'Not going? *Why?*'

'Royal and I . . . we're sparking. I'm going to . . . he's . . . I'm staying here. We're going to be married.'

'To *Royal*? Royal Loomis?'

'You know another Royal?'

'Jeezum, Mattie! I don't believe this! I've seen him call for you, seen you out riding together, but I didn't think it was serious. Why don't you marry Demon? Or Barney? Or that big rock over there?'

'Weaver, stop it.'

'But he's nowhere near good enough for you! Does he write? Does he read? Does he even know how?'

I wouldn't answer.

'You ever show him your composition book? He ever read your stories? Just tell me that. Just answer that one thing.'

I didn't answer. There wasn't much point. I couldn't explain to him that I wanted books and words, but I wanted someone to hold me, too. Or that leaving my family—that breaking the promise I'd made to my mamma—would be like tearing my own heart out.

Weaver railed on and on as we drove. I let him. There was nothing else I could do. I wished I was as strong as Weaver was. I wished I was as fearless. But I was not.

con • fab • u • late

'Ada! Weaver! Mattie! Frances! Get those pies outside! And that ice cream, too!' Cook bellowed from the doorway.

'Yes, ma'am!' we hollered in unison.

'And stop shouting! This is a resort, not a lumber camp!'

'Yes, ma'am!' we shouted, laughing as we clambered out of the kitchen, through the dining room, out of the front door, across the porch and down the steps to the Glenmore's front lawn.

'Chat,' Weaver said, passing me.

'Converse,' I shot back.

It was the Fourth of July, the biggest night of the summer season, and no hotel on Big Moose Lake, or Fourth Lake, or any other lake in the whole state of New York threw a better party than the Glenmore. We had about a hundred of our own guests, plus some guests from the other hotels who'd rowed across the lake especially, plus just about every family from Big Moose Station, Eagle Bay, and Inlet, too. Anyone could come, and most did. People saved up all year to bring their families.

The hotel itself looked as pretty as a painting. Red, white and blue bunting had been hung round the porch and the balconies. Every window was lit, even the dock was aglow with lanterns. Tables sagged under the weight of all the food and drink.

The lawn itself was teeming. There were people everywhere. Scores of tourists in linen suits and fancy dresses, and local people in their faded and mended Sunday best. My pa was there. He stood talking with Frank Loomis and George Burnap and a few other men. Weaver's mamma was talking to Alma McIntyre. My aunt Josie was interrogating poor Arn Satterlee about Emmie Hubbard's land. Uncle Vernon was talking to the Reverend Miller and his wife. Mrs Loomis was filling her plate with macaroni salad. Emmie Hubbard was swatting her kids away from the pie table. She didn't have the money to bring them, but Mr Sperry always let them in for free. No one was supposed to know, for Mr Sperry didn't like people thinking he was soft.

Weaver zoomed by again. 'Discuss,' he said.

'Confer,' I replied.

Confabulate was my word of the day and Weaver and I were duelling with it. It means to chat or talk familiarly. I like it a lot because it is a word that winks at you. It has shades of the word *fable* in it, as if it wants you to know that that's what most conversation is—people telling each other tales.

'Matt? Where should I put these? Mrs Hennessey handed them to me on my way in.'

It was Royal. He had a pie in each hand. I was aware of people's eyes on us. It made me feel special and proud. I took them from him and placed them on the dessert table.

'I'm going to talk to Tom L'Esperance,' he said, squeezing my arm. 'I'll see you later,' and then he was gone.

I passed Belinda Becker on my way back to the kitchen. She was wearing a very pretty dress and was leaning on Dan Loomis's arm. Martha Miller was with them. She stared at me long and hard with a face sour enough to shame a lemon.

I saw Minnie and Jim standing down by the lake. Minnie's face was turned up to her husband's. She still looked tired to me, but she was smiling. He was, too, and before they headed back up to the lawn, he bent his head to hers and kissed her. I knew it was sweet, what they had. Despite their troubles. I hoped I would have something like it.

'I thought you hated him,' I said, as Minnie ran up to me.

'You'll understand when you're married,' she said.

'Smug little witch.'

'Who's smug? Why didn't you tell me about Royal Loomis? It's all anyone's talking about!'

'I tried! You had a crying fit and passed out on me. I have lots to tell you, Min. So much—'

'Minnie! What kind of pie do you want?'

'Coming, Jim!' Minnie yelled. She kissed me and ran to him.

'Mattie! More chicken, please, *ja*?' It was Henry. He was manning the barbecue grill.

'Right away, Henry,' I said. Before I could run back inside, Ada came up to me, grabbed my hand, and said, 'Royal and Martha Miller just had a fight!'

I blinked at her. 'Royal? That can't be. He was just here. Did you see them fighting?'

'No. It was my nosy brother Mike. He was pissing out back of the boathouse. They didn't know he was there. He heard Martha tell Royal that it looked like his broken heart had healed up mighty quick.'

My own heart felt like lead. 'He told me he was going to talk to Tom L'Esperance.'

'Tom L'Esperance? He's not even here. I'm going to find Mike and see if he knows more. Maybe I can find Royal, too.'

'Ada, don't . . .' I started to say. Then I heard my name shouted and felt arms round my waist. It was my littlest sister. 'For heaven's sake, Beth, what's all round your mouth?'

'Strawberry pie, Matt! It's so good!' And then she ran off, screeching and giggling with two other little girls. I was glad to see her recovered and lively again.

'Mattie, my chicken, *ja*?' Henry shouted.

'I'll be back,' I said, running inside. I got the chicken and made another trip for corn and biscuits and bean salad.

As soon as I'd made sure Henry had everything he needed, I ran over to Abby and Minnie's sisters who were looking after the babies. 'Where's Lou?' I asked them.

Abby pointed towards a large brown keg. There was a wiry boy with a bad haircut standing next to it, sneaking a glass of beer.

'What's he got to do with Lou?' I said.

'Mattie, that *is* Lou.'

'Lord, Abby! What's she done to her hair?'

'Cut it off. All of it.'

I came up behind her. 'What are you doing?' I hissed, snatching the glass away.

'Drinking beer.' She snatched it back, guzzled its contents in one go, then let out a burp so long and so loud it made her lips flap.

I grabbed her wrist. 'Louisa Anne Gokey, I'm ashamed of you!'

'I don't care.'

'Look at your hair! What did Pa do when he saw you?'

'Nothing. He didn't even notice. He never does. Let go, Matt, let go!' And then she yanked her skinny arm free and flew off.

'What's wrong with her? She got the mange?' It was Royal.

'She cut her hair. Again.'

'Why?'

'Because she's angry.' So angry that she made me afraid. She was growing wild. Why didn't Pa see that? Why didn't he do something?

'She don't like the colour or something?'

'No, Royal, it's nothing to do with the colour,' I said impatiently. 'It's to do with losing our mother and then Lawton . . .' I saw that he was looking at his bean salad, not me, and gave up. 'Where were you?' I asked.

'Getting something to eat. Talking to Tom.'

'Is he here?'

'Tom? He's right over there,' he said, pointing to the porch. And he was. He was having a parley with Charlie Eckler.

Ada must've been wrong, I thought. Maybe her brother had made a mistake. Maybe Martha had fought with someone else, not Royal.

'Your pa oughtn't to clear those northern acres of his,' Royal said, swallowing a bite of pie. 'He told me he was thinking of it.'

'No? Why not?' I asked absently, still looking for Martha despite myself.

'I was up there berrying the other day. Where our land touches yours and the Hubbards'. He's got good blueberry bushes up there. Should keep 'em. Camps want 'em for pies and pancakes and such.'

Minnie, who'd managed to sneak away from Jim, joined us. So did

Ada and Fran. Royal went to talk to his brother.

'Oh, he's so handsome, Mattie!' Ada sighed as soon as he was out of earshot. 'How did you get him?'

Ada didn't mean anything by the question, but hearing it made me uneasy nonetheless. I often wondered the same thing myself.

'She'll be Mattie Loomis before long,' Minnie said. 'Did you set a date yet? I bet you're married before the hay's in. I'm sure of it.'

'I wouldn't be.'

I turned round, startled by the new voice. It was Martha Miller. She and Belinda Becker had joined our group. Belinda looked like she'd smelt something bad. Martha's face was pale and pinched.

'I hope you have a dowry, Mattie Gokey. A good one,' Martha said.

'Unlike some, Mattie doesn't *need* a dowry,' Minnie retorted.

'Not when she has such nice big bosoms,' Fran said, giggling.

I turned crimson and they all giggled. Even Belinda. Not Martha, though. She just looked at me with eyes that were hard and mean. I saw that they were puffy, too. She'd been crying.

'Royal's the second eldest,' she said. 'Dan will get the bulk of the Loomis farm one day. But the Loomis land borders your father's, doesn't it, Mattie?'

'Martha, come on. Let's go,' Belinda said.

Martha paid her no mind. 'If Royal marries you, he might be able to get his father to give him a few acres, and your father, too. Maybe ten or fifteen altogether. Why, he might even get your father's whole farm one day. After all, Lawton left and he's not coming back, is he?'

'Martha!' Belinda chided, tugging on her arm.

Martha shrugged her off. 'And then there's Emmie Hubbard's land,' she said. 'Twelve acres. Nice the way it nestles in between the Loomises' land and your father's, isn't it? Funny, too, how it just happens to be up for auction next month.'

'Oh, who cares, Martha? Whyn't you go poison the punch or something?' Fran said.

My blood froze up inside me. 'What are you saying, Martha?'

'Emmie doesn't pay her taxes on time for four or five years running and nobody cares. Now, all of a sudden Arn's auctioning her land. You don't wonder about that?'

'Only because there's an interested party,' I said, remembering Aunt Josie and Alma McIntyre steaming Emmie's letter open. 'Someone enquired. Someone from the city looking for cheap land.'

Martha smiled. 'Oh, there's an interested party all right, but he's not from the city. He lives right here and his name is Royal Loomis.'

Fran burst into laughter. 'You sure are a horse's ass, Martha. Royal doesn't have that kind of money.'

'No, but his mother does. Iva's been saving for two years. Skimming a quarter here, fifty cents there off the egg money or the butter money. She's the one who pushed Arn to slap a lien on Emmie.'

'Why'd she do a thing like that?' Ada asked.

Martha shrugged. 'She's got her reasons. She's also got herself a nice little bundle and she's giving it to Royal so he can buy the Hubbard land and farm it. And like I said, a few acres as a wedding gift from your pa, Mattie, and Royal's pa, too, would round it out nicely, wouldn't it?'

I couldn't answer her. The words stuck in my throat like burrs.

'Thought you were so smart, didn't you, Mattie? You, with your head always shoved in a book. Royal says you know a lot of words, but you don't even know how to please—'

'Martha, you say one more word and I'll slap your mouth right off your face,' Fran said. 'I swear to God I will.'

'Come on, Martha, let's go. Dan's waving for me,' Belinda said. She pulled on her friend's arm again and they left.

'Don't you mind her nonsense, Matt. She made it all up. She's so jealous over Royal, she's pissing vinegar,' Minnie said.

All the pride I had felt earlier, over Royal carrying the pies to me and people seeing him do it, vanished like a spooked doe. I felt sick. My friends could stick up for me and say all the nice things they wanted; it didn't matter. All I could hear was Royal's voice telling me, *Your pa oughtn't to clear those northern acres of his . . . he's got good blueberry bushes up there . . .* I felt such a fool for thinking that he might try to see past plain brown hair and plain brown eyes to what was inside me. Or value what he saw.

'Hey, Matt, is Cook going to let you watch the fireworks?' It was Royal.

We all looked at him—myself, Minnie, Ada and Fran. Not one of us said a word.

'Jim'll wonder where on earth I've got to,' Minnie said, rushing off.

'Cook wants us, Ada. Come on,' Fran said, following her.

'Guess I must've stepped in manure,' Royal said, watching them go.

I looked at the ground but didn't see it. I saw something that had happened the day I'd rushed home to nurse my sick family. I saw Tommy Hubbard. He was crying and hitting the calf. Someone had hit him, too. He had an ugly red welt under his eye. Royal hated Tommy. And Emmie. And all the Hubbards.

'Royal . . .'

'What?'

'Martha Miller just . . . she just told me some things.'

He snorted. 'You believe what she says?'

I looked up at him. 'Royal, are you the one fixing to buy Emmie Hubbard's land?'

He looked away and spat and then he looked right back at me with his beautiful amber eyes. 'Yes, Matt,' he said. 'Yes, I am.'

ide • al

'Jeezum, Mattie, you're in for it now!' Fran said. 'Why'd you leave the broom out in the middle of the kitchen?'

'I didn't! I swept the floor and put it away!' I was folding napkins in the dining room, readying the tables for tomorrow's breakfast.

'Cook just tripped over it and dropped a whole pot of consommé. She said for you to get in there right away.'

'But I didn't . . .'

'Go *on*, before she comes out here after you!'

Fran disappeared back into the kitchen. I just stood where I was, a lump growing in my throat, thinking how an earful from Cook would make a perfectly awful end to a perfectly awful day. *Ideal* was my word of the day. A standard of perfection, or something existing only in the imagination, was its meaning. The dictionary must have been playing a joke on me. There had been nothing perfect or excellent about this day. It was the fifth of July, my birthday. Fran and Ada knew the date very well. So did Weaver. I'd turned seventeen and no one had remembered. I'd been blue about it all day. I'd been blue about other things, too. About the rotten things Martha Miller had said to me at the party the night before. And the fight I'd had with Royal. Right after I'd asked if he was the one buying Emmie's land.

'I don't want to talk about that,' he'd said.

'Well, I do,' I said. 'Why do you want to buy Emmie's land, Royal?'

'Because it'll make good growing land, good pasture, too.'

I said nothing for a minute, trying to work up my courage, then I asked him, 'Is that the only reason?' I was afraid of the answer.

'No, Mattie, there's another . . . I want Emmie Hubbard gone.'

I saw Frank Loomis's hairy behind in my mind's eye and Emmie bent over the stove. 'Royal, you . . . you know?'

'For God's sake, Mattie. Everyone in the whole county knows.'

'I didn't know.'

'That ain't hardly a surprise. You're too interested in what Blueberry

Finn and Oliver Dickens and all the rest of them made-up people are doing to see what's going on right around you.'

'That's not true!'

He rolled his eyes.

'Royal, are you buying that land for us? To live on?'

'Yes.'

'I don't want it, Royal. How can we start a life there knowing we took it away from a widow and seven children? It's all they've got. If you buy it and kick the Hubbards off, where will they go?'

'To hell, I hope.'

'But Lucius . . .' I didn't know how to say it, so I stopped. Then I started again. 'That baby . . . he's your half-brother, isn't he?'

'None of Emmie's brats is any kin to me.'

'He can't help how he got here; he's only a baby,' I said softly.

He looked at me like I was Judas. Then he said, 'What if it was your pa, Mattie? Taking the first milk of the year over to Emmie's when you and your sisters hadn't yet tasted any? Lying to your ma, leaving her standing in the barn crying? You think you'd give a damn what happened to the Hubbards then?' His voice had turned husky. I saw that it cost him to say these things. 'My ma . . . she can't leave the house some days, she's that ashamed. Them books of yours tell you how that feels? You keep reading, maybe you'll find out.' And then he walked off and left me standing by myself.

I was upset the rest of the night. I didn't even hear the fireworks going off, and when the party was over and everything cleaned up and it was finally time for bed, I couldn't sleep. I'd stayed awake, turning it all over and over in my mind like a puzzle box. I didn't want to see Emmie kicked off her land. She was a trial, but I liked her and I liked her kids. I loved Tommy. He was around so much he was almost like our brother. But I could also understand Royal's feelings. If I were him and it were my father paying visits where he shouldn't and my mother crying, I'd want Emmie gone, too.

The kitchen door banged open again, startling me. 'For Pete's sake, Mattie, Cook wants you! Come on!' Fran ordered.

The lump in my throat got bigger. It was unfair that I was in trouble for something I hadn't even done. I opened the kitchen door expecting the rough edge of Cook's tongue, and instead I got the shock of my life when twenty people yelled 'Surprise!' at the top of their lungs.

Then there was singing and Cook emerged from the pantry bearing a white sheet cake with a candle stuck into it and *happy birthday, Mattie* written on it. I grinned ear to ear and thanked everyone and made a wish, and then there was ice cream and lemonade to go along with the cake, and a bouquet of wild flowers that the girls had picked.

After the little party, Cook bawled at everyone to get back to work and Mrs Morrison handed me a sugar sack. 'Your father left it with the milk this morning,' she said.

Inside the sack was a tiny painting of my house. The note inside it read: *My ma made this for you. Happy Birthday. Tommy Hubbard.* There was a homemade card in the sack, too, decorated with pressed flowers and hand-drawn hearts. My sisters had all written nice messages on the card. There was a small tin of butterscotch candies from my aunt Josie and uncle Vernon. And under all that, wrapped up in brown paper, was a thin, flat package. I opened it. It was a brand-new composition book. There was no inscription, but I knew it was from my pa. It was a nice thing for him to do and it should've made me happy, but instead it made me want to cry.

'Oh, Mattie, you've got a visitor,' Fran said in a sing-song voice.

I looked up and saw Royal in the doorway, looking as awkward as a hog on stilts. I was partly glad to see him, partly worried. I wondered if he was still angry and had come to get his ring back.

'Why, Royal Loomis!' Cook said. 'You here to bring me more of those nice strawberries?'

'Uh, no, ma'am. I . . . uh, brought this'—he held up a package—'for Matt.'

'Sit down for a spell, Royal. Like some cake? There's a few slices left over from Mattie's party. Mattie, get your guest some cake.'

I fixed some refreshments for Royal and sat down next to him. He pushed his package across the tabletop. 'For you. It's a book,' he said.

I couldn't believe it. He might as well have said it was a diamond necklace. 'Is it really?' I whispered.

He shrugged, pleased by my reaction but trying not to show it. 'I know you like books.'

My heart lifted. It soared! Martha was wrong about Royal. I was wrong about Royal. He did care enough to look down inside of me. He didn't like me for my pa's land; he liked me for me. He did! My fingers trembled as I undid the string. What had he chosen for me? What could it be? An Austen or a Brontë? Maybe a Zola or a Hardy?

I opened the paper and saw that it was a Farmer. Fannie Farmer. A cookbook.

Royal leaned forwards. 'Thought you might be needing that soon.'

I opened it. Someone else's name was written on the title page. I flipped through the pages. A few were stained.

'It ain't new, only secondhand. Got it at Tuttle's. It's got different sections, see? Meats and poultry . . . baked things . . .'

I could see in his eyes he wanted me to like it. I could see that he'd tried and it only made it worse.

'Why, Mattie, isn't that a nice gift?' Cook said, poking me in the back. 'So thoughtful and practical. I hope you said thank you . . .'

'Thank you, Royal,' I said, smiling so hard my face hurt. 'Thank you so very much.'

'Mattie.'

'Mmmm.'

It's very late. Or very early. I'm not sure which. Either way, I'm asleep. Finally asleep. And I want to stay that way. But I hear the sound of boot heels on the floorboards. They're coming towards my bed. It's Ada or Fran, must be, come to get me up. I don't want to get up. I want to sleep.

'Mattie?'

'Go away,' I murmur.

I hear something strange then. Water. I hear the sound of water dripping.

'Mattie?'

I open my eyes. Grace Brown is standing by my bed. She's holding my dictionary. Her eyes are as black and bottomless as the lake.

'Tell me, Mattie,' she says. 'Why does *gravid* sound like *grave*?'

do • lor

It was at the end of the dinner service on a beautiful afternoon that my father came to tell us that Weaver's mamma's house had burned down. Weaver raced out of the hotel right then and there. Cook made the rest of us—myself, Ada, Fran and Mike—wait until dinner was over, and then John Denio drove us all down in his buckboard.

During the ride, I thought about my words and their meanings, as I do when I'm anxious or scared, as a way of taking my mind off things. I fixed on *dolor*. It means grief, distress, or anguish.

We'd talked among ourselves on the way down the hill, never doubting that the fire was an accident. But as soon as we saw Lincoln, the hinny, lying in the road with blood soaked into the dust all around him, and dead chickens everywhere, and the pigsty smashed apart, we knew different.

My father was standing by the smoking ruins with Mr Loomis and Mr Pulling. Mr Sperry, Mr Higby, and a handful of neighbours from Fourth Lake were there, too. 'Pa, what happened?' I asked.

'The trappers who attacked Weaver. They must've just got out of jail. Weaver's mamma says they're the ones did this. Killed the hinny and most of the chickens. Pig got away, at least. Ran off into the woods. Got the Loomis boys out after her.'

I couldn't believe what he was telling me. 'Pa, no,' I said.

'She says they were mad as blazes about the jail time. She says they set fire to the house, then took off into the woods, heading north. At least that's what I think she said. She ain't making much sense right now. She's bad, Mattie. She fought with them. One broke her arm.'

I pressed my palms to my cheeks and shook my head.

'You listen to me now, Matt. No one knows for sure where those men got to. I don't want you outside the hotel after dark. Not till they're found. You keep Weaver in, too. You hear?'

I nodded, then bolted off to Emmie's.

Cook was already inside, trying to find some coffee or tea and muttering about the state of the place. Mrs Crego was there. Dr Wallace, too. And Weaver. Most of the Hubbard kids were huddled wide-eyed on a worn settee or sitting on the floor in front of it.

'Come on, Mamma, you've got to let the doctor see to your arm,' Weaver said.

Weaver's mamma shook her head no. She was sitting on Emmie's bed, cradling her right arm with her left and rocking back and forth. Emmie was sitting next to her, her arm round her, shushing her, telling her everything would be all right. Weaver's mamma didn't seem to hear her, though. She didn't hear anyone. She kept saying, 'It's gone, it's all gone! Oh, Jesus, help me—it's gone!'

Weaver knelt down in front of her. 'Mamma, please,' he said.

'Mrs Smith, I need to take a look at that arm,' Dr. Wallace said.

Emmie shooed him away. 'Leave her rock for a bit, she'll come round,' she said. Weaver's mamma kept rocking and keening.

I walked over to Weaver and took his hand. 'What is it? Why is she doing that? Is it the house?'

'I don't know,' he said. 'Maybe it's the animals . . . or her things. She had photographs and such. Or maybe it is the house—'

'The devil take the house!' Mrs Smith suddenly cried. 'You think I give a damn about an old shack?' She lifted her face. 'They found your college money, Weaver,' she said. 'They took it all. Every last nickel. It's gone, it's gone. Lord Jesus, it's all gone.'

lep • o • rine

'Where's Weaver? Where is he?' Cook asked me. 'He's always trying to wheedle a slice of coconut cream pie out of me. Now I've got one for him and he's disappeared. Mattie, go find him, will you?'

It wasn't like Cook to save slices of pie for anyone, but she was concerned about Weaver. We all were. I had an idea where he might be and I soon found him. He was sitting on the dock. He had his trouser legs rolled up and his feet in the water.

'Why isn't real life like book life?' I asked, sitting down next to him. 'Why aren't people plain and uncomplicated? Why don't they do what you expect them to do, like characters in a novel?' I took my shoes and stockings off and dangled my feet in the water, too.

Weaver looked at me. 'This is about Emmie, isn't it? You don't know what to make of her now.'

'No, I don't.'

Emmie Hubbard had us all puzzled. She had taken Weaver's mamma in and she'd tucked her up in her own bed and tended to her. She'd even had the presence of mind, on the day the Smiths' house burned, to make her kids pluck and clean all the chickens the trappers had killed, right away. She made stew out of a few, fried a few more, and sold the rest to the Eagle Bay Hotel before they went bad.

'I can't figure it out, Weaver,' I said. 'I saw my pa this morning when he was delivering. He said the Hubbard kids haven't been over for breakfast since the fire.'

'Cook says she saw Emmie at the train station the other day. Selling pies and biscuits. She told Cook my mamma told her what to do, and she did it.'

'Maybe she likes being the strong one for a change. Maybe she never had a chance to be that,' I said, kicking at the water. 'Or maybe she just got tired of being the town fruitcake. Probably wears a body out after a while.'

Weaver laughed, but it wasn't a real laugh. I could tell.

His mamma had lost her house. And some had said it was his fault for going to the justice. They said none of it would have ever happened if he'd just stepped aside for those trappers in the first place.

Mr Austin Klock, the undersheriff, came up from Herkimer to investigate the fire. By the time he left, those three men had a whole new list of charges against them. No one really thought they'd ever be made to answer them. They hadn't been seen since the day Weaver's house burned. Mr Klock said they were probably halfway to Canada.

Weaver had hardly eaten since the fire. Or spoken. Or smiled.

'Cook's got a piece of pie for you. Coconut cream. Your favourite,' I told him.

He didn't say anything.

'Did I tell you my word of the day? It's *leporine.* It means like a rabbit. You could use it to describe someone with buckteeth, maybe. Or a twitchy nose. It's an interesting word, *leporine.*'

No reply.

'I guess it's not so interesting.'

'I'm staying on here, Matt,' he finally said. 'After Labor Day. I just talked to Mr Morrison. He said he'd have work for me.'

'How can you do that?' I asked. 'You have to be in New York well before Labor Day. Don't classes start the first week of September?'

'I'm not going.'

'What?' I wondered if I'd heard him right.

'I'm not going to Columbia. Not until my mamma's well. I can't leave her now. Not all by herself.'

'She's not all by herself. She has Emmie looking after her.'

'For how long? It's only another month or so before Emmie's land is auctioned. And besides, I don't have the money now for my room or train fare or books or any of it.'

'What about your wages? Haven't you been saving them?'

'I'll need them to pay for a room for Mamma and me. My house burned down, remember?'

'But, Weaver, what about your scholarship? Won't you lose it?'

'There's always next fall. I'm sure I could get them to hold it over for a year,' he said, but I could hear in his voice that even he didn't believe it.

I did not cry when Miss Wilcox left. Or when Martha Miller said such mean things to me. I did not cry when Pa knocked me out of my chair, and I don't cry in my bed at night when I think about Barnard. But I cried then. Like a baby. I cried as if someone died.

Someone had.

I could see him in my mind's eye—a tall, proud black man in a suit and tie. He was a man who could cut down a roomful of other men with only the brilliance of his words. I saw him walking down a city street, brisk and solemn, a briefcase under his arm. He glanced at me, walked up a flight of stone steps and disappeared.

'Oh!' I sobbed. 'Oh, Weaver, no!'

'Matt, what is it? What's wrong?' he asked.

I scrambled to my feet. I couldn't bear it. To think of him stuck here.

Working in a dining room or a tannery or up at a lumber camp. Day after day. Until he was old and used up and all his dreams were dead.

'Go, Weaver, just go!' I cried. 'I'll look out for your mamma. Me and Royal and Minnie and Jim and Pa and Mrs Loomis. All of us. We will. Just go! Before you're stuck here for ever.' Like me.

It must be after four o'clock now. I haven't been able to go back to sleep. Not since Grace came to visit me. I have read all Grace's letters, all but the last one.

July 5, 1906
My Dear Chester,

I am curled up by the kitchen fire and every one else is in bed. This is the last letter I can write, dear. I feel as though you were not coming. Perhaps this is not right, I can't help feeling that I am never going to see you again. How I wish this was Monday. I am going down to stay with Maude next Sunday night, dear, and then go to DeRuyter the next morning and will get there about 10 o'clock. I am sorry I could not go to Hamilton, dear. Papa and mamma did not want me to go. They think I am just going out there to DeRuyter for a visit.

I have been bidding goodbye to some places today. There are so many nooks, dear, and all of them so dear to me. I have lived here nearly all my life. . .

Oh, dear, you don't realise what all of this is to me. I know I shall never see any of them again, and mamma! great heavens how I love mamma! I don't know what I shall do without her. Sometimes I think if I could tell mamma, but I can't. She has trouble enough as it is, and I couldn't break her heart like that. If I come back dead, perhaps if she does know, she won't be angry with me. I will never be happy again, dear. I wish I could die. You will never know what you have made me suffer, dear. I miss you and I want to see you but I wish I could die. I am going to bed now, dear, please come and don't let me wait there. It is for both of us to be there . . .

She knew. Somehow Grace Brown knew that she wasn't ever coming back. She hoped that Chester would take her away and do the right thing by her but, deep down inside, a part of her knew. It's why she wrote about never seeing the things and places and people she loved again. And why she imagined coming back dead. And why she wanted her letters burned.

I slide the letter back into its envelope. I gather all the letters together, slip the ribbon round them, and carefully retie it. I can hear Grace's voice. I can hear the grief and desperation and sorrow. Not in my ears, in my heart. I sit perfectly still for a long time, just holding the letters and looking out the window. In another hour or so, the sun will rise and Cook will barge in and wake us.

I look down at the bundle in my hands. At the pale blue ribbon. At the loopy handwriting, so like my own. If I burn these letters, who will hear Grace Brown's voice? Who will read her story?

ter • gi • ver • sa • tion

'Would you like a cup of tea, Mattie? How about you, Weaver?' Emmie Hubbard asked. Her eyes were calm and smiling and not the least bit crazy-looking.

'Yes, all right. Thank you,' I said, putting the chocolate cream pie I was holding down on the table.

'Yes, please,' Weaver said.

As Emmie took a tin of tea and some cups and saucers down from a shelf, Weaver and I glanced at each other. I could tell from his expression that he couldn't believe what we were seeing, either.

Emmie's house was tidy. The floor had been swept and the bed made. Her kids were clean; their faces were scrubbed and their clothes had been washed.

'Mattie, please thank Mrs Hennessey for the pie,' Emmie said.

'I . . . I will,' I said, embarrassed to find myself gawking.

Weaver and I had asked Mr Sperry if we could take Demon to visit Weaver's mamma after the dinner service. He said we could, and Cook had given us a pie to take with us.

Weaver sat down on the bed next to his mother. 'How are you feeling, Mamma?' he asked.

'My arm pains me some, but I'm all right,' she said.

The kettle whistled. Emmie leaned over the stove to get it. I remembered seeing her bent over the stove another time, for another reason. I had a feeling Frank Loomis wouldn't be fixing her stove again any time soon. Not while Weaver's mamma was around.

Emmie served the tea and cut slices of pie for everyone. The children loved the taste of chocolate. Even Lucius. We chatted for a while, and Weaver's mamma told us how Emmie was making fruit pies according to her recipe and selling every one down at the train station and how she, Weaver's mamma, minded Emmie's kids while Emmie was gone, but that was all she did, because Emmie didn't let her lift a finger. Emmie smiled and flushed and said it wasn't true. Why, just the day before they'd both been over picking beans out of the Smiths' garden and at least the trappers hadn't managed to destroy that.

But then Weaver forgot himself and asked Emmie why she didn't plant a garden herself. It wasn't too late to get beans and greens out of one, he said. And then the whole room went quiet and I could see from the look on his face that he'd suddenly remembered about the auction. Nobody wanted to talk about it, though. Least of all me, knowing, as I did, who was going to buy it.

'But Mamma, we have to talk about it . . .' Weaver pressed.

'Hush,' she said, her eyes darting to Emmie. 'I know, son. We will.'

Emmie looked at us and bit her lip. She pulled at a tendril of hair.

'Where's Tommy?' I asked, anxious to change the subject.

'Over at your place. Helping your pa,' Weaver's mamma said. 'They've got an arrangement now. Tom's to help with the ploughing and clearing, and your pa will pay him for it in milk and butter.'

We stayed for a few more minutes, and then we had to get back to the Glenmore. Weaver was quiet on the drive. I was the one who spoke first. 'Your mamma's one tough nut,' I said.

'Don't I know it.'

'I didn't think anybody could ever shape Emmie Hubbard up. God only knows how she did it. And with one arm broken, to boot.'

Weaver smiled a sad smile. 'You know, Matt,' he said, 'sometimes I wish there really was such a thing as a happy ending.'

'Sometimes there is. Depends on who's writing the story.'

'I mean in real life. Not in stories.'

Tergiversation, my word of the day, means fickleness of conduct, inconstancy, turning renegade. I felt like a renegade myself just then. I didn't believe in happy endings. Not in stories or real life. I knew better. But then I thought about Emmie's shabby little house and how it was warm and welcoming now. I imagined my pa showing Tommy how to handle a plough, and Tommy all manly and important as he brought home the milk and butter he'd earned. I thought about Weaver's mamma being looked after for once in her life. And Emmie's pride in doing the looking after.

And then I thought of Mrs Loomis crying in the barn, and Jim and Will tormenting the Hubbards every chance they got, and the set of Royal's jaw when he talked about wanting them gone.

'Me, too, Weaver,' I sighed. 'Me, too.'

lu • cif • er • ous

It was evening, right in the middle of the supper service. The dining room was full to bursting and Cook was in one of her tempers. I ran one order out and came right back in with a new one.

'Mattie, pick up for table seven. Pick up!' Cook barked.

I carried four bowls of soup to my table, sloshing them as I walked. I craned my neck trying to see the boathouse from the dining-room windows. The boats were all in for the evening. The dock was empty.

'They must've got back,' I said under my breath. 'They must have. So where are they?'

We were supposed to have eighty-seven for supper but two guests hadn't showed—rooms forty-two and forty-four. Carl Grahm and Grace Brown. They had table nine. I'd set it for them, but it was already eight o'clock and they still hadn't come in off the lake.

I'd waited on them earlier at dinner. They'd ordered soup and sandwiches, and they'd argued throughout the meal. I'd overheard them as I brought their food.

'. . . and there was a church right by the hotel in Utica,' Grace Brown said. 'We could have gone in and done it there.'

'We can do it up here, Billy. We'll ask if there's a chapel,' Carl Grahm said.

'Today, Chester. Please. You said you would. You promised me. I can't wait any longer. You mustn't expect me to.'

'All right, don't get so upset. Let's take a boat ride first, why don't we? It's a beautiful day. We'll ask about a chapel right after.'

'Chester, no! I don't want to go boating!'

The man ate all his lunch, then the girl's untouched soup, and then he asked for dessert. He told me to charge the meal to his room. Later, I'd seen Grace on the porch and she'd given me her letters and I'd stuffed them under my mattress and forgotten about them, because Cook had kept me busy all afternoon peeling potatoes.

I hadn't thought about them until the supper service started and I'd seen their empty table. Then I couldn't stop thinking about them.

'Mattie! Water's boiling!' Cook shouted now. 'Get a tray ready for room twelve.'

I grabbed a teapot and spooned leaves into it. I took the kettle off the flame and poured water into the pot. Just then Mr Morrison came into the kitchen to get himself a cup of coffee.

'Didn't see you at supper tonight, Andy,' Cook said. 'You all right?'

'I missed it. Too busy waiting for a couple of darn fools to bring my boat back.'

Cook snorted. 'Which two fools? The Glenmore's full of 'em.'

'Grahm. Room forty-two. Had a woman with him. Took a boat out after dinner and never came back.'

I dropped the teapot. It shattered. Scalding water splashed all over.

'Look what you did!' Cook screeched. 'What on earth's got into you? Get that mess cleaned up!'

I thought of my word of the day, *luciferous*, as I picked up the broken pieces of the teapot. It means bringing light. It has the name *Lucifer* in it. Lucifer was a beautiful angel who God chucked out of heaven for being rebellious. He found himself banished to hell, but instead of being sorry for angering God, he set about agitating again. He went to the Garden of Eden, wheedled Eve into eating from the Tree of Knowledge and got the whole of mankind kicked out of paradise for ever.

It was a dreadful thing that he did but right then I felt I understood why he did it. I even felt a little sorry for him. He probably just wanted some company, for it is very lonely knowing things.

Quietly, I get out of bed, dress, put up my hair and gather my belongings. I'm not sure of the time, but I would guess about five o'clock. When I am ready, I count out my savings. Between the money I started out with, and my wages and tips, and the extra money I made walking Hamlet, and the five dollars Miss Wilcox gave me, I have thirty-one dollars and twenty-five cents.

I leave the attic, careful to make no noise, and walk down the main stairs. I am in Mr Morrison's office, my mamma's old carpetbag in my hand, just as the sky is starting to lighten. I place Grace's letters on his desk, then write him a note, explaining how I got them.

I write three more notes, address them, and put them in the mail basket. The first is to my father. It has two dollars in it, the balance of what he owes on Licorice, the mule, and a promise that I will write. The second is to Weaver's mamma. It has twelve dollars and seventy cents in it and a note telling her to use the money to pay off Emmie's taxes. The third one has a ring in it—a small, dull ring with an opal and two garnets. It is addressed to Royal Loomis and says to see if Tuttle's will take it back and that I'm sorry and that I hope he gets his cheese factory some day.

I pass the coat tree on my way out of the office. There's a woman's boater hanging on it. Grace Brown put it there when she and Chester arrived. I lift the shabby little hat off its hook. I carry it into the parlour and place it next to Grace's body.

I take her hand. It is smooth and cold. I know it is a bad thing to break a promise, but I think now that it is a worse thing to let a promise break you. 'I'm not going to do it, Grace,' I whisper to her. 'Haunt me if you want to, but I'm not going to do it.'

At the back of the Glenmore, a little way into the woods, is a cottage where the male help sleeps. It is quiet and dark. I pick up a handful of pebbles and toss one at a window on the first floor. Nothing happens; no one comes, so I toss a second and a third, and finally the window opens and Mike Bouchard sticks his sleepy face out.

'That you, Mattie? What's up?'

'Get Weaver, Mike. I need to see him.'

His head disappears and, a few seconds later, Weaver's pops out.

'What do you want?' he asks me, looking cross.

'I'm leaving, Weaver.'

He pulls his head in and then barely a minute later, the cottage door opens and he's outside.

'Where are you going?'

I reach into my skirt pocket and press seven dollars into his hand.

'What's this for?'

'For your train ticket to New York. Use the money you earn here to pay for a few months' room and board in the city. You'll have to get a job when it runs out, but it'll get you started.'

Weaver shakes his head. 'Mattie, it's not just train fare and rent. You know that. It's my mamma. You know I can't leave her.'

'She'll be fine.'

'She won't. She's got nowhere to go after Emmie's place is sold.'

'Emmie's taxes have been paid. The auction's off. Didn't you hear?'

Weaver gave me a long look. 'No, I didn't,' he said.

'You will.'

'Mattie—'

'Goodbye, Weaver. I've got to go. Now. Before Cook gets up.'

Weaver takes hold of me and hugs me so hard, I think he'll break me right in two. I hug him back, my arms tight around his neck, trying to draw some of his strength and fearlessness into me.

'Why, Matt? Why are you going *now*?' he asks me.

I look at the Glenmore. I can see a light glowing in a window in a little bedroom off the parlour. 'Because Grace Brown can't,' I tell him.

We let go of each other. His eyes are welling.

'Don't, Weaver. If you do, I'll never make it. I'll run right back inside and put my apron on and that will be the end of it.'

He nods and swallows hard. He makes a gun of his hand and points it at me. 'To the death, Mathilda Gokey,' he says.

I smile and aim right back at him. 'To the death, Weaver Smith.'

It is just past ten o'clock. The dawn came and the sun rose on a flawless summer morning. I am standing, frightened but resolved, on the platform at Old Forge. Is there a word for that? Feeling scared of what's to come but eager for it, too? *Terricipatation*? *Joybodenous*? *Feager*? If there is, I mean to find it.

My carpetbag weighs heavy in my hand. I have most everything I own inside it. I also have my train ticket in there, an address for Miss Annabelle Wilcox of New York City, and two dollars and twenty-five cents. It is all I have left from the money I saved. It isn't very much at all. I will have to find a job right away.

It had only just gone light when I left the Glenmore, but I was able to get a ride into Eagle Bay from Bill Jarvis, who owns the Jarvis Hotel in Big Moose Station.

The *Clearwater* was still in dock when we arrived, and I was able to get a seat on its return run to Old Forge. I looked back once, just before Eagle Bay disappeared from sight, and I felt more lonely and frightened than I have ever felt in my life. I thought about turning round when I got to Old Forge, but I didn't. There's no going back once you're already gone.

Now, as I wait for my train, Grace's words echo in my memory. *I have been bidding goodbye to some places today. There are so many nooks, dear, and all of them so dear to me. I have lived here nearly all my life . . . Oh, dear, you don't realise what all of this is to me. I know I shall never see any of them again . . .*

A northbound train pulls in. An express. There are only a few people on it. A handful of tourists and some workmen get off, followed by two men wearing jackets and ties.

'That's him. Austin Klock. He's the undersheriff,' a man standing next to me says to his companion. 'Told you this was more than a run-of-the-mill drowning.' They pull out notepads. Reporters, I imagine.

'Who's the man with him?'

'County coroner. Isaac Coffin.'

'*Coffin*? You're kidding me, right?'

'Brother, I am not. Come on. Let's see if we can get a statement.'

The undersheriff holds his hands up as they approach him. 'Gentlemen, I know as much about it as you do. A girl drowned at the Glenmore. Her body's been recovered. Her companion's has not . . .'

Soon you'll know more, I think. A lot more. Soon you'll know that the girl was called Grace. And that she spent her last weeks on this earth pregnant and afraid, begging the man who'd made her so to come and take her away. But he'd had other ideas.

I close my eyes and I can see Chester Gillette. He's signing the guest book at the Glenmore. And having his dinner, and going for a boat ride. I see him row all the way out to South Bay. Maybe he and Grace get out and sit on the bank for a while. He leaves his suitcase there. They row some more. He waits until he's sure there's no one else around, and then he hits Grace. He tips the boat and swims to shore. Grace can't swim. He knows that because she told him. She'd drown even if she wasn't unconscious, but it's quieter this way. She can't scream for help.

I see Chester now, today. He's eating breakfast somewhere. Maybe up at Seventh Lake. Maybe at the Neodak in Inlet. Smiling. He's sure as hell not dead. Not him. I'd bet my last dollar on that.

I see Grace Brown, too. Stiff and cold in a room in the Glenmore with a tiny life that will never be, inside her.

And then I hear a whistle, shrill and piercing. I open my eyes and see the southbound train pulling in. Screeching and steaming, it comes to a halt. I cannot move.

'All aboard!' the conductor yells. 'This is the ten-fifteen New York Central for Utica, Herkimer, and all points south! Tickets, please!'

People are boarding the train. Mothers and children. Businessmen. Holidaymakers on their way home. Couples. And still I cannot move.

I think of my family. Of Beth's songs. Of Lou's swagger. Of Abby's gentle voice. I can see Pa sitting by the fire. And Emmie and Weaver's mamma picking beans. I see Royal ploughing his father's fields, gazing across them to my father's land with a look of love and longing he'd never shown me. I see Barney's blind eyes turned up to mine. And the poor dead robin at my mother's grave.

The conductor climbs up the metal steps on the side of the car. 'Last call! All aboard!' he bellows. The engine exhales. A huge cloud of steam billows up from under it.

'Wait!' I cry, stumbling forwards.

The conductor sees me. 'Come on, missy!' he yells. 'Her bark's worse than her bite!' He reaches down for me. I look around myself wildly, my heart bursting with grief and fear and joy. I am leaving, but I will take this place and its stories with me wherever I go.

I reach for his hand and clasp it. He hoists me onto the 10.15 south-bound. To Utica and Herkimer. And all points south. To Amsterdam and Albany and beyond. To New York City. To my future. My life.

JENNIFER DONNELLY

'Big Moose Lake, where Grace Brown's body was found, is about twenty-five miles from where I grew up,' says Jennifer Donnelly, who now lives in Brooklyn. 'My family has always been connected with the Adirondacks and my grandmother worked in the grand hotels like Mattie.' It was Donnelly's grandmother who first told her about Grace Brown and how she is still supposed to haunt the lake where she was murdered. 'Her letters certainly haunt me, as does Grace herself,' says Donnelly. 'They are achingly sad and beautiful and from the first day I read them, I couldn't get her words out of my head. I wrote *A Gathering Light* because I wanted something good to come of her death, and that something good was Mattie Gokey. Grace's life ends on Big Moose Lake, but, because of her words and their effect, Mattie's life begins there.'

Grace's story, however, is just part of the book. At its heart is the fictional character of Mattie—a young girl struggling to make something of her life. 'People who know me say Mattie is very like me, though I did not consciously base her on myself. I think she is an amalgamation of several of my female ancestors; of friends I had growing up in the area; and, perhaps oddly, of my great-grandfather. He was a lumberjack, farmer, horse-trader and sometime bootlegger, who was taken out of school when he was ten and made to work driving mules on the Erie Canal. His entire life was one of hard, physical labour and it permitted him no time to read. At the end of his life he was laid up in bed for weeks and asked for book after book, devouring them all.'

Jennifer Donnelly has also written a novel for children called *Humble Pie,* and *The Tea Rose*, an adult novel set in the East End of London. She lived in London for a short time when she was a student. 'I fell hopelessly in love with the city,' she says, 'especially the East End.'

Asked where she gets her ideas from, she says, 'I really don't. They get me. I have little control over it. It's very intimate and personal. Like falling in love. People try to give me ideas sometimes. It just doesn't work.'

ACKNOWLEDGMENTS AND PICTURE CREDITS: *The Da Vinci Code*: pages 6–8: illustration: Curtis Phillips-Cozier; Leonardo da Vinci: Getty Images; *The Vitruvian Man*: Getty Images/Taxi; *The Last Supper*: Corbis; page 169 © 2000 Nordel. *Up and Down in the Dales*: pages 170–172: illustration: Warren Chadwick-Cadwell @ Eastwing; page 277 © Roderick Field. *The Return of the Dancing Master*: pages 278–280: illustration: Rick Lecoat @ Shark Attack; page 421 © Ulla Lemberg/MIRA. *A Gathering Light*: pages 422–423: lake and trees: Getty Images; page 539 © Jerry Bauer.

DUSTJACKET CREDITS: Spine from top: *The Vitruvian Man*: Getty Images/Taxi; Curtis Phillips-Cozier; Warren Chadwick-Cadwell @ Eastwing; Rick Lecoat @ Shark Attack; lake and trees: Getty Images.

Printed by Maury Imprimeur SA, Malesherbes, France
Bound by Reliures Brun SA, Malesherbes, France

229AZ